Cathy Kelly lives in D[...] film critic for the *Su[...] where she also writes the *Dear Cathy* agony column. Her first novel, *Woman to Woman*, became an instant bestseller, spending eight weeks at Number One on the *Irish Times* bestseller list and eight weeks in the *Sunday Times* Top Ten.

Praise for *Woman to Woman*:

'A compulsive read' *Woman's Weekly*

'An unprecedented success story for a debut novel' *Sun*

'All the ingredients of the blockbuster are here ... a page turner' *Sunday Independent*

'A *tour-de-force* of the Jilly Cooper genre' *Lifetimes*

'Funny and clever' *Sunday World*

'Move over Maeve Binchy – Ireland could have a new writing queen ...' *Star*

WOMAN TO WOMAN

SHE'S THE ONE

Cathy Kelly

HEADLINE

First published in this omnibus edition in 2001 by
HEADLINE BOOK PUBLISHING

10 9 8 7 6 5 4 3 2 1

ISBN 0 7472 6790 1

Printed and bound in Great Britain by
Mackays of Chatham plc, Chatham, Kent

HEADLINE BOOK PUBLISHING
A division of Hodder Headline
338 Euston Road
London NW1 3BH

www.headline.co.uk
www.headline.com

WOMAN TO WOMAN

To Mum, with all my love

ACKNOWLEDGEMENTS

Thanks.

To John, who told me to stop talking about writing a book and to just do it, and for encouraging me all the way when I actually did. To Lucy, who gave me so much support, made the coffee, poured the gin and brought Tamsin out to meet her boyfriends while I typed. To Mum, who's been saying I could do it ever since we started that ill-fated Mills & Boon, and who has helped me in so many ways, always. To Dad for minding the zuppies, to Francis and Anne for their endless encouragement, and to Laura, my godchild, for being so absolutely adorable and a complete bookworm at the age of two. And of course, to Tamsin, who was here for all of it.

Thanks to Sarah Hamilton for being a wonderful friend and for coming up with the title, thanks to Moira Hannon, Joanne McElgunn and Lisa McDonnell for reading bits and not telling me it was brutal. Thanks to the *Sunday World*'s editor, Colm MacGinty and deputy editor, J. P. Thompson for making this a fantastic time in my life career-wise. And thank you to all my friends and colleagues in the *Sunday World* who are too numerous to name and who encouraged me, asked how it was going, helped me with computer nightmares and never asked if I was writing a sequel to *War and Peace* because it was taking so long. You know who you are. Thanks also to my fellow movie critics for the same thing.

Thanks to Padraig O'Reilly for amazing poster shots and lots of advice for the next book, and to Siobhain McClafferty of Cover Shots and her team for the others.

Last, but by no means least, thanks to everyone at Poolbeg for their enthusiasm, hard work and sheer professionalism. To Kate Cruise O'Brien for being a marvellous editor, who was endlessly encouraging when I was down in the dumps with brain rot, who helped me learn the difference between writing a book and writing for a newspaper and who gave me lots of wine (thanks, Joe!) to cheer me up. I couldn't have done it without you, Kate. To Philip MacDermott, Paula, Kieran, Sarah, Nicole and everyone else at Poolbeg for their hard work. And thanks to Jilly Cooper whose wonderful novels kept me going through all the dreadful bits.

CHAPTER ONE

Aisling stared at the crumpled-up receipt in her hand and tried desperately not to cry. A credit card counterfoil with smudged writing, it lay forlornly on the palm of her hand with the words 'Lingerie de Paris' plainly printed on the left-hand side.

Her hand trembled slightly as she pulled out a chair and sat down by the kitchen table, blind to the fact that her sleeve was resting on an island of marmalade and toast crumbs left by the boys' usual breakfast commando raid. She closed her eyes and crunched the receipt into a ball, willing the words to have changed when she looked again.

Just moments before, Friday had stretched out in front of her in a comforting and familiar routine. A visit to the dry-cleaner's with Michael's suits, a quick detour to the hairdresser's to get her hair blow-dried for the party and coffee with Fiona in the Merrion Centre for a thoroughly enjoyable gossip over a slightly too-big slice of carrot cake smothered in cream.

No carrot cake, she admonished herself automatically. A brown scone with a tiny bit of Flora and a cup of black coffee with no sugar. Got to stick to the diet. The first week was always the hardest but you've got to stick to it, or so the diet gurus repeated endlessly.

Diet! What am I thinking about bloody diets for, she wailed out loud. What was the point of living on dry toast and two ounces of lean turkey with a mini-Kit Kat treat a day when your entire life had just disintegrated.

Suddenly her regular trip to the dry-cleaner's and the bitching session with Fiona seemed a million miles away.

Michael never remembered to leave his suits out for dry-cleaning and she'd stopped reminding him since it was easier to

1

bring them downstairs herself than listen to him stomp around the bedroom muttering about women with premenstrual tension and complaining about being late for work.

She had also given up telling the twins to put their dirty football jerseys in the laundry basket. They copied their father slavishly in everything and, if he managed to escape from all things domestic, they followed suit. Aisling was used to finding remnants of tissues and receipts glued to every wet item of clothing when she emptied the machine. She had finally realised that she was stuck with two ten-year-old fledgling domestic incompetents along with a card-carrying anti-housework husband. She simply cleaned out the pockets herself.

That morning had been no different.

'Don't forget to bring my navy suit, Aisling, and tell them about the red wine stain on my yellow silk tie, will you?' Michael had shouted downstairs.

'Yes, my lord and master,' she muttered from the depths of the downstairs coat cupboard where she was riffling through duffel coats, soccer boots and the bits of the vacuum cleaner that she never used. She was looking for the boys' tennis rackets. The three-week summer camp in UCD always seemed like a good idea at the time because it certainly kept the boys out of trouble during the too-long holidays. But it meant three times as much organisation as it took to get them off to primary school. The camp timetable was a bit erratic and the boys always forgot to mention that they wanted some vital bit of equipment until five minutes before they were due to go.

Yesterday, it had been swimming goggles. Today, tennis rackets. 'I know I left them there, Mum,' wailed Phillip, hopping from one leg to the other in agitation, his dark eyes huge with anxiety. 'Somebody must have moved them!'

Somebody was responsible for a lot of things in the Moran household, Aisling thought darkly as she rummaged through old papers and a battered plastic toy box she thought she'd thrown out.

Somebody regularly ate all the chocolate biscuits, broke dishes and lost school jumpers. She'd just love to shake somebody.

Michael's voice, even more agitated than Phillip's, broke into her reverie.

'Aisling, where did you put my linen jacket? I want to wear it tonight and I can't see it in the bloody wardrobe! I'm going to be late, for God's sake!'

Triumphantly dragging two battered rackets out of the cupboard, Aisling handed them to a delighted Phillip and shouted back up the stairs, 'I put it in the spare bedroom wardrobe because your wardrobe is so full it would end up totally creased before you'd put it on.'

Two minutes later, Michael rushed the boys out the door to drop them at UCD before driving to work. Peace reigned again. The nine o'clock news blared loudly in the background. She left the breakfast dishes on the table to go upstairs and collect the suits, trousers and ties she was bringing to the cleaner's, scooping up her handbag and keys at the same time. She draped the dry-cleaning pile on the back of a kitchen chair as she had dozens of times before and reached absently into every pocket.

Among the bits of pocket fluff and unused match books Michael always seemed to have stashed in his pockets, she found it. Tucked into the inside pocket of the fine wool navy suit that looked so good with his yellow Paisley tie, was an ordinary credit card receipt, the sort of thing she wouldn't usually look at. But today was different. Something made her smooth it out and look. Fifty pounds' worth of goods from one of Dublin's most exclusive lingerie shops had been purchased with their joint credit card but had somehow never made it into *her* underwear drawer.

Unbelievably, her loving husband had been lying through his capped teeth when he muttered that expensive lunches with his newspaper colleagues and important contacts had sent his Visa card bill sky-high.

The receipt in Aisling's hand made her think that the hefty

3

bill he'd complained about had nothing to do with lunch at Le Coq Hardi. Instead of buying bottles of pricey Rioja and the best smoked salmon to loosen his political friends' tongues, the deputy editor of the *Sunday News* appeared to have been splashing out on goodies of another kind. Luxurious silky goodies.

Fifty pounds! Aisling marvelled. And in Lingerie de Paris at that. She had never even stood inside the door of the plushest underwear shop on Grafton Street. She'd seen enough adverts for the shop's dainty silk knickers and bras to realise that they were ruinously expensive.

Aisling felt a sliver of anger pierce the gloom in her heart. She'd been brought up to believe that spending money on clothes was practically sinful and she'd never spent more than fifteen pounds on a bra in her life.

Apart from the lacy crimson teddy the girls at work had bought for her honeymoon twelve years ago, and a few frivolous satin bits and pieces which never felt comfortable under her jeans, Aisling's lingerie collection consisted of the type of plain cotton knickers and sensible bras that wouldn't look out of place on a Mother Superior.

If she was knocked down by a bus, nobody was ever going to think she was a sexpot once they'd ripped off her sensible navy cardigan and long, full skirt to reveal underwear about as erotic as suet pudding. It would all match, of course, saggy off-white knickers, saggy off-white bra and saggy off-white body.

No amount of lycra underwear could conceal her spare tyre and cellulite-covered bum. Why waste money looking for sexy lingerie? Anyway, the sort of bras that could contain a well-endowed 38C generally looked as if they could also accommodate a few basketballs at a push and were, therefore, passion-killers of the most effective kind.

Passion-killers, hah! She laughed out loud, a little rasping noise that turned into a sob at the thought of Michael walking into a lingerie shop to buy something for another woman. Had he given the salesgirl a blank look when she asked what size he wanted? Splaying out his hands as though cupping a couple of oranges for the bra measurements?

Men never managed to check their wives' existing underwear before these shopping expeditions, Aisling had read in a magazine once. Instead, they muttered about small waists, ordinary hips and blushed when they said 'About your size' to shop assistants who'd seen it all before.

Had he asked for the best lingerie money could buy, keen to impress *her*? Or was she with him, smiling as he coughed up for knickers she knew he'd rip off later? Aisling couldn't bear to think about it.

Michael wouldn't cheat on her. He wouldn't, she was sure of that. He barely had time to play with the kids these days, for God's sake. He spent every spare moment working on the newspaper supplement which would '. . . push the circulation figures of the paper to the top!' as he was so fond of saying.

She was sick to the teeth of hearing about the last-minute problems, about how he nearly fired the darkroom technician who somehow managed to botch printing an entire roll of film from the fashion spread, shot at great expense in Cannes.

The newspaper had taken over their lives during the past year. Endless meetings and brainstorming sessions resulted in cancelled evenings out and lots of lonely weekends where Michael only appeared for bed and breakfast like a hotel guest who didn't fancy his room that much. He'd even missed the twins' Easter play where they played St Peter and St Paul in matching beige striped robes. Aisling had spent hours sewing the night before.

'I'm afraid I can't leave for another two hours at least,' he said apologetically when he rang moments before Aisling left for the school. 'I'm sorry. Give them my love, though, won't you? Tell them I'll bring them to McDonald's at the weekend, OK?'

'Daddy had to work, darlings,' she comforted her two small apostles when the applause had died down and the cast were being hugged and kissed by proud parents.

5

Thinking about the boys, two mirror images of their dark-haired father, she began to feel better. Michael loved the boys with all his heart, he wouldn't cheat on them. He wouldn't cheat on her. She just knew it.

There had to be an explanation for the Visa receipt. Yes, of course there was. She felt better now, on firmer ground when she thought about their family and what it meant to him. There was no way he'd risk losing his family for a fling with some floozie. Hell, she couldn't even imagine Michael in a bloody underwear shop. He *hated* shopping.

He'd always urged her to spend money on herself, to splash out on lacy little camisoles and those French knickers she'd bought years ago when her flatmate, Jo, had dragged her into Clerys for a rummage around the bargain bins.

'You never wear anything like that any more, darling,' Michael used to say when he spotted a sexy underwear feature in a magazine or paper. But he'd never gone into a lingerie shop to buy her a present himself in their entire marriage.

'How am I supposed to know you want sexy underwear if you don't tell me?' he demanded one Christmas Day when Aisling laughed out loud as she ripped the wrapping paper off another Delia Smith cookbook. 'For heaven's sake, it takes *you* two hours to buy one bloody shirt! How am I supposed to pick out something you'd like? And *underwear* at that!'

Aisling never pointed out that she knew exactly what he'd like for Christmas because she listened to him and carefully planned her gifts in October. But then she had time to meander around Henry Street, slipping in and out of shop after shop. Michael was always too busy for that.

Instead of turning up with the wrong size blouse or the wrong colour jumper, he simply thrust money into her hand. 'Go on, spoil yourself, Ash, and buy some nice clothes, won't you? Bring Fiona with you; she has great taste.'

Accepting the implied criticism meekly, Aisling duly ventured off on those hateful shopping trips with her svelte and aerobically toned neighbour. She blindly rattled through rails

6

of lovely clothes looking for something that Michael would like and that would actually flatter her figure.

Just when she had steeled up the courage to try it on, a size ten salesgirl with a degree in arrogance would sidle over and ask did she need any help. Aisling was sure that these nasty nymphets waited until there were at least ten other people in the shop before loudly asking the girl at the cash register if they had the pink shirt or whatever in a size sixteen.

Crimson with embarrassment, Aisling would then stand there self-consciously as the assistant looked her up and down with an expression of superiority written all over a face free of crow's feet and laugh lines.

Sometimes Aisling felt like slapping those girls across their insolent little faces and yelling that she had been a sexy size ten herself once. Before two kids and ten years of day-long access to the fridge had changed her figure. But what was the point?

Instead, she kept silent while an enraged and loyal Fiona went into Bitch Shopper overdrive, demanding to see their good stock since she '. . . couldn't possibly wear this sale rubbish'. Fiona could find snagged threads and missing buttons on anything the increasingly harassed assistants produced for her supercilious gaze.

Thank God for Fiona, Aisling thought when the sight of buttons straining reproachfully on tailored trousers and elegant blouses plunged her into gloom and they had to abandon the shopping expedition for a consolatory doughnut in Bewley's.

'Belfast,' announced Fiona, after one depressing afternoon when everything Aisling tried on looked either tent-like or too tight. 'That's where we should go. I love the shops there, they have lots of marvellous shops in the Castle Court centre and you'd love it. We could drive up on Monday, what do you think?'

'Brilliant!' Aisling felt better already. 'I'll start a diet tomorrow,' she vowed with sugar on her top lip and a cup of frothy cappuccino in front of her. But when tomorrow came, and she was serving up Michael's favourite shepherd's pie, she couldn't resist having a bit along with the Weight Watchers baked beans she'd cooked for herself. And well, a bit of Black Forest gateau would hardly hurt.

She'd always loved Black Forest gateau. In fact, she'd insisted on having it as her wedding cake despite her grandmother's outraged disapproval. She could still hear that frail voice grimly prophesying disaster for the young couple who had ignored tradition in favour of modern ideas.

Aisling could have laughed at the irony of it all. Granny Maguire had no doubt been smirking at her granddaughter's predicament from whichever outpost of the dearly departed she'd been sent to. Straight to Hell, Michael always joked after listening to a few minutes of Granny's vicious gossip.

Aisling thought of Michael and the Paul Costelloe silk tie she'd proudly left on his side of the bed for their anniversary the week before. She put the Visa receipt carefully on the table, sank her head onto her hands, and closed her eyes.

Twelve years ago this month, on a glorious sunny morning, Aisling Maguire had carefully dressed in a white lace gown and placed a coronet of white roses on her hair for her marriage to Michael Moran, the ambitious young journalist she'd adored since the first time she set eyes on his handsome face.

It had been a wonderful wedding. Mam had held her tight, tears in her eyes as she whispered, 'I hope you'll be happy, darling.' She and her new husband had run out of the hotel to find Michael's rusty old Renault carefully decorated with toilet rolls and tin cans, courtesy of his pals on the paper's soccer team.

That had been the best day of her life, until the crisp November morning Phillip and Paul had been born after ten difficult hours of labour. Exhausted and drained, she lay back in the bed with her babies in her arms while Michael smiled down at her, an expression of amazement on his face.

When Phillip's tiny hand curled around his father's little finger, Michael had actually cried before sitting down on the

8

bed and putting strong arms around his family, his wet cheek against Aisling's. Babies grasped fingers instinctively. She knew that. She'd read reams of mother-and-child literature. But she didn't say a word and let her husband believe that Phillip was holding his father's hand.

Just a few days before, she had dusted the ornate silver frame holding a group picture of the wedding. Her parents stared stonily at the camera in contrast to Michael's father and mother who had both developed a fit of the giggles during the photographs. Who'd have guessed that the Morans would stick it out for only twelve years instead of ''til death us do part'. Yes, death, or another woman.

'I knew you'd make a mess of your marriage,' she could hear her father saying maliciously, his gaze contemptuous as he looked at the daughter who never quite managed to please him. 'You never could do anything right.'

Tears welled up in Aisling's eyes and spilled down her cheeks onto her faded blue sweatshirt. It had belonged to Michael and she could remember him wearing it the summer he laid the patio himself after getting expensive French windows installed. She could see him now, sweat dampening his dark hair, a look of concentration on his face as he lifted another slab into place, expertly tapping it in with a hammer.

Maybe this is all a mistake, she thought helplessly. She got up to clear the breakfast table as she did every morning. Mechanically she wiped the toast crumbs onto a plate and carefully pushed the expanded packet of Rice Krispies back into their box. No matter how hard she tried to convince the boys to eat porridge, they insisted on Coco Pops or Rice Krispies day in, day out. Don't forget to buy cereal, she reminded herself, her mind slipping into housekeeping mode.

Once, she knew more about motor insurance than breakfast cereals, more about the age loading on a ten-year-old Porsche than on the dietary requirements of ten-year-old boys. Thirteen years ago, in the bustling insurance company on O'Connell Street, she had practically run one section of the motor department for months. When the department supervisor left abruptly for a better job, Aisling was asked to take over and she didn't hesitate.

Now, she sometimes wondered how she'd done it all. How she'd run her division calmly and capably, responsible for twelve people and thousands of accounts. She'd actually enjoyed it into the bargain. It had been a challenge for Aisling Maguire, career girl, but a terrifying prospect for Aisling Moran, housewife. She had always planned to go back to work when the twins were old enough but somehow, the longer she stayed at home, the harder it was to think about entering the job market again.

Delighted with his well-run home, beautifully cooked meals and happy, well-turned-out boys clamouring for fatherly attention when he got home from work, Michael never gave Aisling the push she required to get her back at work. As the years went by and their money problems shrank, there was enough money to pay for a childminder should Ash want to get a job. But why bother?

'The boys need you, darling,' he'd said every time she mentioned getting a job. 'Just because they're at school doesn't mean they don't need their mother when they get home, does it? Anyway, my secretary never stops moaning about leaving her three to her mother and every second Monday she's in late because one of them has a temperature or a cold or something. Be grateful you don't *have* to work!' he'd invariably add, obviously not counting running a house as work.

He was probably right, Aisling would sigh, familiar with the problems of working mothers courtesy of the magazines she loved to read. Every second page had a different story about women stuck in the endless cycle of work, kids and housework, with Saturdays spent cooking giant lasagnes to jam into the freezer. Michael was right. She was lucky he earned enough so she didn't need to work.

They only argued about it once, when Aisling's sister Sorcha, unbearably smug thanks to a recent promotion in the

London bank where she worked, asked why Aisling was letting her brain rot by sitting at home every day.

'I can't believe she said that to me,' Aisling said angrily in the car on the way home. 'She treats me like a second-class citizen because I'm not managing a bank or something. How dare she say that! I'd like to see *her* running a home and looking after the boys. I was working when that little bitch was still in primary school!'

'Don't mind her,' Michael said evenly. 'She's just jealous because you've got a husband, two lovely sons and a nice home. She'd kill to be married, not that any man would be stupid enough to take her. Anyway,' he took a hand off the steering wheel to pat Aisling's knee, 'you'd hate to go out to work. Everything's changed since you worked. I mean, where would you start?'

Aisling was incensed. 'What do you mean "where would you start"?' she demanded.

'You couldn't expect to just walk into a good job after seven years of housekeeping,' he said bluntly. 'You haven't any office skills any more, have you? Being able to make a perfect quiche isn't much good when you need a degree to get *any* job these days.'

She didn't speak all the way home, silently fuming. Michael waited until she climbed into bed before attempting to make up.

'Darling, you know the twins would hate a childminder, don't you? Just because they're at school, doesn't mean they don't need their mum.' He nuzzled her neck, planting soft kisses on her collarbone before moving down to kiss the sensitive skin between her breasts. 'You don't *need* to work, darling,' he murmured. 'I'll look after you.'

Aisling resigned herself to being a full-time housewife. When the twins were older, she dedicated herself to a series of gourmet cooking courses until she could whip up salmon *en croûte* with the best of them and make strawberry *millefeuilles* with her eyes closed. When she'd had her fill of cookery, she turned her hand to needlework and, within a year, the

11

dining-room chairs boasted intricate tapestry seat covers of golden sunflowers glowing in a midsummer sun.

By the time she'd finished the decorating techniques course, the house was a riot of rag-rolled walls, sponged radiators and ivy-leaf stencilling. Michael liked to joke that she'd stencil him if he sat still for long enough. Short of doing a brain surgery course, there wasn't much else that the adult education syllabus could offer her.

And here she was, still stuck in the kitchen with a mountain of ironing, the breakfast dishes to do and the knowledge that her husband was cheating imprinted on her brain. Being a dab hand with hollandaise sauce didn't stop your man from straying.

Please let it be a mistake, God. Of course, it could be some silly misunderstanding. I mean, I'd know if he was seeing someone else, wouldn't I?

He could have bought the underwear for *her* as a late anniversary present. He could be planning a surprise and, maybe, he meant her to find the receipt as a teaser. Then she remembered the flowers and the large box of chocolates he'd given her.

Flowers from a garage shop. He'd thrust them into her hands with a quick kiss on the cheek. Those multicoloured bouquets with not enough chrysanthemums or carnations to make a decent arrangement were always stacked outside garages for last-minute gifts. And that's just what her annivers-ary present had been – a last-minute gift.

Well, she could certainly arrange even the most stingy bouquet beautifully with the help of her last Christmas present, a large book on flower arranging which had obviously been at the top of the Christmas-gift-for-Granny pile in Eason's when Michael had raced in to do his last-minute shopping.

'Flowers! They're lovely,' she said, not even vaguely sur-prised that her husband had only remembered it was their anniversary when he was filling the car with petrol on the way home from work. He'd never been much of a man for

12

carefully thought-out presents. So how had he overcome this particular blind spot so spectacularly in Dublin's most expensive underwear shop?

It was unbelievable. Aisling shook her head as she thought of Michael with another woman, his naked body in someone else's arms, his mouth kissing another woman's lips, his eyes dark with desire. Did he murmur her name in the same husky voice he used when it was Aisling in his arms?

Who was this other woman? What did she look like? Questions bubbled in her mind as she tried to picture her rival. She was probably slim, beautiful and clever, with a high-profile job and conversational abilities beyond the special offers on bananas in Crazy Prices that week.

How did this happen to them? Never in a million years would she have dreamed that Michael could sleep with another woman, could betray their marriage.

Passionate affairs happened to people in Fiona and Pat Finucane's world where getting divorced and finding another partner was as easy as ordering a bottle of champagne at the most expensive restaurant in town.

But she didn't want to look for another man, a younger version of Michael. She had fallen in love with him thirteen years before and didn't want to replace him. But what if he wanted to replace her?

She squirted washing-up liquid into the sink and let a jet of hot water create a froth of soft bubbles. Plunging her gloveless hands into the sudsy warmth, she rinsed cups, plates and bowls from the boys' breakfast. It was the same routine every weekday; she listened to the Gerry Ryan radio show as she dried the dishes and stacked them away. But today it made her heart sink to the pit of her stomach.

Every part of her life, every mundane task in the family home, was suddenly threatened by the existence of some other woman, someone Michael had gone to bed with.

Aisling stopped clearing up and tried to focus her muddled thoughts. No, this could not be happening. He loved her. They were married! He couldn't go off with someone else, wouldn't go off with someone else. For God's sake, he roared with laughter when she told him Fiona's latest gossip about her cheating acquaintances.

Michael wouldn't betray her. She was jumping to conclusions. That was it. There was probably some perfectly reasonable explanation. Suddenly hopeful again, Aisling realised that there was one way to find out what was going on. If Michael bought anything with his credit card, he filed away the statement. He kept several accordion folders in his wardrobe where he kept bills, bank statements, birth certs and, of course, credit card statements.

Aisling untied the ribbons at the top of the first folder with trembling hands and rifled through the alphabetical sections looking for credit card receipts. At first she found nothing but bank statements and paid gas and electricity bills, neatly filed with a red pen marking 'Paid' on every one.

She tackled the second file, searched quickly through the Cs for credit cards and then onto V for Visa. And there they were, wedged in between a sheaf of medical insurance forms.

Aisling carefully removed the familiar credit card statements and spread them onto the soft beige bedroom carpet. The bloody cat was shedding hair again, she thought absently.

It didn't take long to find the debit for Lingerie de Paris. Unfortunately, it was nestled in between other, equally damning expenses which brought a lump to Aisling's throat.

Silk knickers followed numerous debits for costly meals in Dublin's trendiest restaurants, places she'd never been to. And then she found a debit to Jurys Inns, the plush hotel built near Christ Church Cathedral. The date, two days before their anniversary.

She stared at it blankly. Michael was never any good at remembering dates, but the tenth of June stood out in Aisling's mind. Phillip had picked up some sort of stomach bug and came home from school with a temperature. She had spent most of the afternoon bringing him to the bathroom where he tried to be sick sitting on his mother's lap like a fractious four-year-old. Typically, Michael had been in London. He was meeting bosses of the newspaper group's sister paper for discussions on the supplement. He wasn't due home until the next evening.

By the time the doctor had arrived at the house, Paul had started being sick and Aisling wasn't feeling too good herself. Three Maxalon injections later, the boys were sleeping soundly under their matching Manchester United duvet covers. She was curled up on the settee feeling washed out, miserable and with a sore arm, courtesy of Dr Lynch and his syringe.

'Look on the bright side,' Fiona said encouragingly when she phoned after spotting the doctor's car parked outside the Morans'. 'A twenty-four-hour bug is better than a weekend in a health farm, you're bound to lose a few pounds!'

'Fiona, you're mad, do you know that?' laughed Aisling. 'Only you would think about losing weight when you're staring at the inside of the toilet bowl.'

'But I made you laugh, didn't I?' her friend demanded. 'Laughing is essential for helping people recover from all sorts of illnesses. That's why I always phone up Pat's bitch of a sister when I'm sick. She's a complete hypochondriac. Ten minutes of listening to her blather on about colonic irrigation or the latest disorder she *thinks* she has after reading one of those health magazines has me in stitches.

'It's a psychological thing, it's the thought of sounding like a hypochondriac that does it. I think, "Do I sound like that?" and I feel better immediately!'

'Maybe I should give her a ring,' Aisling remarked. 'The twins aren't terribly talkative tonight and even the cat has gone out scouting for boyfriends.'

'Where's Michael?'

'In London with the editor and the managing director. They're discussing the supplement with the UK paper's MD – in between eating in the sort of restaurants that sends Egon Ronay into spasms of delight. He rang me earlier to say he'd just stopped off in the hotel to change his clothes before they went out to eat.

'He said they were going to that really plus restaurant, San Lorenzo's,' she added.

'Lucky old Michael,' remarked Fiona. 'They're always AWOL for the messy bits of child-rearing, aren't they? Pat practically vanished when Nicole had that awful gastroenteritis a few years ago, in case he might be called upon to do something involving nappies.'

'I know,' Aisling muttered, her mind on Michael's brusque phone call. 'I just wish he'd sounded a bit more sympathetic, though. Here I am stuck at home with the kids sick and he's off having a whale of a time. He couldn't talk to me for more than two minutes on the phone.' She broke off abruptly, suddenly feeling that she was being childish.

'You poor old thing,' Fiona answered, in the soft tone she reserved for her adored six-year-old daughter, Nicole. 'I'm going to pop down to the video shop and get you a nice, slushy, romantic film so you can sit in comfortable misery, all right? And when you're talking to Michael later, tell him you expect a bit of pampering and a huge bottle of perfume from the duty-free to cheer you up!'

'Well, I don't think he'll be ringing because he said I should go to bed early and that he mightn't be in 'til late,' Aisling answered.

'Leave a message for him, Ash. Most of those business hotels have an answering machine for each room. You can tell him you're miserable, make him feel guilty, he'll ring you back.'

'I don't know where he's staying,' Aisling realised. 'I forgot to ask.' Immediately she regretted saying it. She didn't want Fiona to know that Michael could go away without telling her where he was staying. It made it sound as if she and Michael didn't talk. And of course they did.

'Never mind,' Fiona said a little too briskly. 'He'll probably be in so late that he'd just wake you up if he rang. I'll get that video for you. I won't be long.'

An hour later, Aisling was watching *Sleepless in Seattle*. Flossie sat Buddha-like on her lap and a hot whiskey, courtesy of Pat's twelve-year-old Scotch, was in her hand. She didn't sleep much that night, lonely in the big double bed.

She spent a feverish night, tossing and turning, dreaming of mad surgeons racing after her waving syringes the size of hockey sticks. She woke up with the feeling of unease her nightmares always brought. She lay exhausted in bed watching the red digits on the bedside clock-radio tick inexorably towards seven. Why hadn't Michael phoned her from London?

But he didn't phone and, when he returned home that evening, he was so moody and quiet that she simply assumed some calamity had befallen the supplement.

'Everything's fine,' he answered testily when she dared to ask. 'I'm just tired after a day of meetings and a long business dinner.'

The effortless way he had lied hit her now like a punch in the stomach. No stuttering or stumbling. He'd lied with the calm of an accomplished liar. He hadn't even told her what hotel he was staying in and she'd never even thought to ask. Of course, if she *had* asked, he would, no doubt, have pointed out that she shouldn't bother trying to ring him because he was out at a business dinner.

Some dinner, she thought, dropping the credit card statement and scanning the next one. Who had he snuggled up with in Jury's when she was holding their ten-year-old twins' heads over the downstairs toilet? A few entries further down she came across a bill from Interflora which was for enough flowers to fill a stadium if the price was anything to go by.

Then it hit her. Fiona knew. She had to. Why else would she have asked where Michael was staying that night? Why would she have tried to gloss over the whole incident so quickly?

And why else would she have started that strange conversation about a couple of friends who were splitting up, even though Aisling had never met them? It had been the previous week when they had been grocery shopping together after lunch in the Merrion Inn.

They were wheeling their shopping trolleys past the frozen

17

food department when Fiona started talking about the latest husband she knew who was straying from the marital path.

'I can always tell,' pronounced Fiona. 'That man never did a day's exercise in his life and suddenly he was jogging around the track in UCD three times a week. What does that tell you, Aisling?'

She didn't wait for an answer. 'And the clothes! God, you should have seen him at that party in the Ryans' place last Christmas. He was wearing jeans at a cocktail party, can you believe it? I asked him had he joined Bon Jovi, but he wasn't at all amused.'

Fiona had paused long enough to fling a brace of Lean Cuisines into her trolley before continuing. 'Wives never notice, you see. All that extra grooming, workouts and new bikini underpants go totally unnoticed at home and, before you can say "affair", that's another marriage down the tubes.'

She had given Aisling a long, meaningful look as she spoke, a can't-you-read-between-the-lines look, Aisling realised now.

'Pat would never dream of playing away,' Fiona said once in an unguarded moment. 'He knows which side his bread is buttered,' she added. Fiona knew her husband would never stray in case he risked his partnership in her father's lucrative law firm.

As she smoothed out another statement and searched for yet more proof of her husband's lies, Aisling numbly realised that Michael had always buttered his own bread.

Her father had worked for an accountancy firm for twenty years and retired with just enough money to keep himself and her mother. Even if he had been able to help her husband in his meteoric rise to the top, Michael would never have accepted that help. He was a brilliant young journalist with his eyes firmly set on the top of the ladder and he had never needed family links to give him an entrée into the corridors of power.

Now, at the age of forty, he was deputy editor of one of the most successful Sunday newspapers in the country and, if his star continued to rise, he could soon be editor of one of the paper's sister titles.

But she might not be the woman by his side when he did it. Who would?

She dropped the last of Michael's statements onto the floor and rose to her feet slowly. She picked up the telephone by his side of the bed, not really seeing the empty orange juice glass he'd brought upstairs that morning and left for her to clear away. Under normal circumstances, she would have made the bed by this time and would probably be busy hoovering out the twins' room, tidying the books, comics and toys they carelessly abandoned on the floor.

Right now she didn't care if the whole house fell apart. She simply had to know what was happening, who Michael was seeing. And, maybe, find out that it was all some horrible mistake.

CHAPTER TWO

Fiona answered on the second ring.

'I was just about to phone you,' she exclaimed, 'to see if you fancied a trip into Dun Laoghaire to check out the shops. There's this lovely John Rocha suit I noticed in a magazine at the weekend and I've decided to splash out. We could have our coffee there, couldn't we? Or are you on bread and water for tonight?'

'I can't go shopping now, Fiona.' Aisling's voice quivered. She'd planned to be stoical, but Fiona's warm and friendly voice made her want to sit down and sob.

'I don't know what to do . . . It's about Michael,' she managed to say hoarsely. 'You knew, didn't you?'

Aisling could hear her friend's sharp intake of breath down the phone and for a brief moment she held her breath, hoping there was some reasonable explanation for the hotel bill, the flowers and the underwear.

'Knew what?'

'That he's having an affair.'

'Oh God, Ash. I wish you'd never found out.'

As she looked out the window at Fiona's perfectly manicured garden across the road, Aisling was amazed to see everything looking exactly the way it had the day before. The grass neatly shorn like a barber's number one cut, the petunias spreading out greedily in between the tiny fragrant lavender bushes. How could everything look so damn normal when her life had just suffered a cataclysmic upheaval?

'I'm sorry, so sorry,' repeated Fiona. 'I just didn't know how to tell you, how to find the words. I hoped it would blow over before you found out. That's the best way, he gets it out of his system and you never find out,' she added prosaically. 'I thought it was better not to say anything. But I kept wishing

I'd never seen them, because I felt so disloyal to you.'

'Just tell me who it is,' Aisling interjected, her tone pleading. 'Just tell me . . .'

Fiona paused and then spoke again, her voice strong and calm, as though reassuring a small child. 'It doesn't mean anything, Ash, honestly. They all do it, and then they get over it. Remember that, OK?'

'They all do it,' repeated Aisling hysterically. 'Is that supposed to make me feel better?'

'No. It's just supposed to make you feel less alone,' Fiona answered. 'You don't know her,' she continued in the same calm vein. 'Her name is Jennifer Carroll and she works in an advertising agency. I only recognised her because she's at every bloody party we go to. You know the type, goes to the opening of an envelope if she thinks she'll get her picture in the social columns. Are you all right, Ash?'

'Yes. Go on.'

'I went out to dinner with the girls from the tennis club when Pat was away last autumn.'

Fiona hesitated for a moment before continuing. 'Michael was in Le Caprice with this dark-haired woman. I thought it was something to do with the paper. Well, he meets so many different people. I didn't think anything of it at first, really.'

'What happened?' Aisling's voice was remarkably steady as she spoke. Fiona couldn't see her digging her nails into the palm of her right hand, clenching her fist as though her life depended on it.

'They were sitting at an out-of-the-way table, but I could still see them,' explained Fiona. 'He kissed her and it just wasn't a platonic type of kiss, you know? When I thought about what she was wearing, I put two and two together. You don't go out for a business dinner wearing a dress with slits practically up to your navel. God, men are all the same, aren't they?'

She paused and Aisling knew she was lighting a cigarette, those long, dark menthol cigarettes that looked faintly ridiculous and smelled like burning Polos. Michael always laughed

21

at them, calling them poseurs' cigarettes and asked why she didn't smoke real ones, like the Marlboros he was trying to give up.

'Fiona, why didn't you say something?' Aisling asked.

'I didn't know how to tell you. What could I say?' her friend answered quietly. 'That your bastard of a husband was cheating on you as publicly as he could? That he didn't seem to care who saw him and his bloody girlfriend because he knew that you'd never find out, stuck in your little wifey world?'

Aisling sat with the receiver in one hand as she stared blankly outside.

'I'm coming over,' Fiona said quickly. 'We need a huge cup of tea and a good talk.'

The phone clicked in Aisling's ear and she put it down slowly before turning automatically towards the dressing table to put some lipstick on. As she twisted up the tube of pink lipstick she stopped and looked at herself in the mirror. A pale face with serious eyes stared back, the startling blue irises diminished by pupils enlarged with misery. Her eyes had always been her best feature, but lately she hadn't bothered with make-up. Without mascara to darken her fair lashes, her eyes were undefined and pale in her bare face.

As always nowadays, her unruly light brown, long hair was tied back with a red scrunchie. The combination of no make-up, starkly tied-back hair and a loose sweatshirt, which did nothing to flatter her generous curves, made her look tired and worn. She stared long and hard at herself in the mirror.

She remembered the summer she had first met Michael, when her hair was long and bleached with strands of gold from ten days on an idyllic Greek island and her skin glowed thanks to hours basking in the glorious Mediterranean sun.

He had called her beautiful then and never stopped wanting to touch her skin and kiss her lips, putting his arms possessively around her golden shoulders when they walked through the streets of Corfu town.

As she held her lank hair away from her face, Aisling

wished she could recapture that distant Greek summer and feel young and pretty again. Wouldn't it be wonderful not to feel thirty-five and boring, another frumpy housewife with no prospects, no waistline and a preoccupied husband. God knows, there were plenty of women like her out there. She saw them all the time in the supermarket, listlessly pushing trolleys full of fuel for teenagers and husbands who were never home.

She'd never wanted to become one of them, one of the women who sat on the edge of the sofa at parties trying hard to listen and blend in, trying to think of something funny to say while their more confident sisters fitted in perfectly.

'Hit me if I ever turn out like that, won't you?' she'd told Michael after their engagement party. His matronly cousin had bored her to tears with advice about the right washing machine.

'Don't worry, darling,' he'd laughed, 'you're never going to turn into an Elsie, I promise!'

But she had. Well, sort of. Maybe she didn't discuss the advantages of a Zanussi as opposed to a Whirlpool when they went out, but she certainly didn't fit in the way she used to. And Michael knew it.

That was the hardest thing about going out to parties or dinners these days; being aware of Michael looking at her distantly across the room as if she had failed some secret test. She hated sitting around a dinner table with two or three glamorous career women sparkling around Michael and vying for his attention, while she sat in isolation, too self-conscious to chat to the men placed beside her. No wonder he'd wanted another woman.

She wasn't beautiful, particularly clever or even good at some high-powered job. She was a housewife and, even though that's what he'd wanted her to be a few years ago, that's not what he wanted now.

Maybe if she'd stayed the woman he married, that enthusiastic girl who'd walked blindly through life, hoping for the best instead of settling into domestic bliss like Ma in Little

23

House on the Prairie, maybe then he would have still loved her.

She looked at least ten years older than she really was with her pale, slightly plump face and the beginnings of a double chin. But she had finally decided to do something about it. Without breathing a word to Michael, she had started a diet. Not one of her diet on Monday, stuff your face on Tuesday diets, but a proper diet. She had decided that this was the real diet, the one which would change her life. That, however, was last week.

Sadly, she dropped the lipstick onto the lace-covered dressing table. What was the point, she asked herself? Why bother trying to look better now? He had gone and found someone else anyway.

'Ash, let me in,' Fiona roared up at the open bedroom window. 'I've brought the Hobnobs, darling. What more does a woman need!'

An hour later, Aisling was sitting in the passenger seat of Fiona's sleek black Nissan NX as her friend expertly manoeuvred the car into a parking space in the Frascati Centre.

'Don't back out on me now,' warned Fiona, climbing out of the car and slamming the door with a careless bang. 'You're going to look stunning tonight if it kills both of us!'

It just might do that, thought Aisling to herself as her friend frogmarched her towards the expensive boutique she'd always avoided in the chic Blackrock shopping centre. She had been looking forward to the launch party for months now, eager to meet the team of journalists she had heard so much about from Michael in the past year but had never met.

Michael had been working late more and more. The odd newsroom parties seemed to have dried up along with any chitchat at the Morans' kitchen table. Working late my ass, Aisling growled to herself as she followed her friend into the shop.

'Shopping is the only cure for a broken heart,' Fiona continued gaily, slim brown arms outstretched to rifle through racks of expensive little black numbers.

24

In a daze thanks to a five-milligram Valium, Aisling moved sedately towards the party dresses, separating the hangers with totally steady fingers. She was beginning to feel quite good, happy almost. Something sexy, she smiled inwardly, fingering the rich brocade and crêpe outfits, looking for a dress to knock the spots off Michael's bloody fancy woman. Aisling knew that the Valium was giving her an unrealistic high, but she simply didn't care and sank into the numb happiness she felt flooding her head.

For a day that had started out in the worst possible way, it was certainly improving, Aisling thought with a giggle as she picked out a totally unsuitable black velvet sheath and waved it at Fiona.

'You should be on Valium more often,' Fiona remarked, putting the black velvet back on the rack and steering Aisling towards the back of the shop.

'The larger sizes, Modom,' Fiona said with a flourish, plucking a subtle grape-coloured jacket off the rack and holding it up against the other woman.

Generously cut on the hanger, the jacket and its matching flowing skirt seemed to have shrunk on Aisling. She peered out of the changing cubicle self-consciously, not wanting anyone but Fiona to see her.

'Maybe something with a better cut . . .' muttered Fiona, eyes narrowed as she stood back examining the outfit.

'Not better cut. Just bigger,' said Aisling flatly, the Valium giggle gone out of her voice. 'I seem to be getting bigger all the time. No wonder Michael went for, what did you say her name was?'

'Don't torture yourself thinking about her, Aisling,' Fiona answered impatiently.

'I can't help it. I can't stop thinking about her, whatever her name is. But I bet she's slim and glamorous. Am I right?'

'OK, she has a good figure and I suppose you'd call her glamorous. To my mind, she's a bit over the top. You know, all red talons, more make-up than Joan Collins and lots of expensive outfits with too much embroidery and huge gold buttons. Like this sort of thing, actually.' Fiona swiped a short denim jacket out from the rails and held it up against her torso with a grimace.

'I wouldn't be seen dead in this,' she announced. 'Denim and sequins, how passé.'

And I wouldn't fit into it even if I wanted to, thought Aisling despondently. She gazed around at the racks of clothes and wondered if they had a generous size sixteen in anything glamorous.

She hated shopping nowadays. But tonight was going to be different. Tonight she had planned to splash out on something which would make her feel good, make her feel a little like the confident woman Michael married.

She had actually managed to lose three pounds in the last week. One main meal a day, as much black tea or coffee as you liked, brown bread or scones for light meals and lots of fruit and vegetables. 'You won't be hungry on our four-week summer diet!' promised the magazine she'd ripped the diet out of. And she hadn't been hungry at all, apart from the sheer longing for a chocolate digestive with her lunchtime coffee.

Now she wondered if there was any point in trying to lose weight. She had planned to look her best tonight, to make Michael proud of her in front of all the new newspaper staff. The supplement was finally being produced after a year of talking about it. Aisling had decided to jump-start her own life to celebrate Michael's hard work.

She'd wasted far too much time while she wallowed in domestic misery, hidden under masses of laundry and dirty dishes.

Plenty of women worked and looked after a family, she knew that. There was no reason why she shouldn't. It could be just what she needed, Fiona had said encouragingly. Now that the boys were older and were walking to school on their own, there was no excuse for Aisling to stay at home. Surely it couldn't be too hard to get a job and climb out of the rut she'd fallen into?

Sometimes, she felt a pang of nostalgia for her old life. Those carefree days living with Jo in Rathmines, when the two single girls had spent every penny of their wages on clothes, make-up and cheap bottles of wine for parties, seemed idyllic. They worked hard all week and played hard at the weekends, always on the move and ready for the next party. Jo never wanted to climb out of her warm bed on Monday morning, but Aisling was up bright and early, raring to go. Plenty of people complained about working in the cramped insurance office in the city centre, but she had loved it.

Every night of the weekend was party night. During the week, they often went to the pictures if they fancied what was showing in the Stella cinema. Afterwards, they'd buy chips and onion rings to eat in the flat's tiny sitting room while discussing the merits of Robert Redford as opposed to hunky young Richard Gere.

Now Aisling went out only to shop or to bring the kids to school or to have a quick cup of coffee in Fiona's before her friend raced off for a game of tennis or an aerobics class. She often spent the entire day on her own, cooking, polishing and waiting for the twins and Michael to come home and liven up her life.

It was a lonely existence, she realised. Was that all she could expect from the rest of her life? She'd planned to hang up her apron and get a job. But what was the point now?

If she couldn't keep her husband, how could she ever keep a job? Who wanted thirty-five-year-old housewives in their office, anyway? And let's face it, her typing skills weren't amazing ten years ago, so how would she cope with a computer?

All she knew about the world of technology was limited to what she'd learned on a speedy tour of the *News* three years previously when they had finally upgraded their system.

Fifteen minutes watching somebody playing hangman on a computer was hardly what you'd call experience.

Thinking of the paper wrenched her mind back to Michael.

Maybe everyone in the bloody office knew. How could she face Michael's colleagues at the supplement launch party tonight knowing what she did, wondering if everyone there was in on the secret? She wouldn't even have the chance to confront Michael before the party either. He'd told her he wasn't coming home beforehand, adding that Aisling should make her own way there.

Charming, she thought, wondering whether he made his girlfriend get to parties on her own or did he sweep up to her house bearing flowers and offers of X-rated antics in the back of a taxi?

'Ash, try this on,' Fiona's voice broke into her daydream and she stared at the dress her friend was holding up in astonishment.

'Red is perfect for your colouring and with a bit of trollopy crimson lipstick and your hair done, you'll knock them all for six!' Fiona said encouragingly.

Aisling took the dress, a low-cut swirl of red crêpe, into the changing room and held it up to her face. Brighter than anything she'd worn for ages, the rich colour made her pale face seem paler than ever.

'Make-up, Ash, you need make-up,' advised Fiona before pulling the changing cubicle curtain over. 'Does Liz Hurley look like that *without* make-up? See what I mean? All you need is half an hour in front of the mirror and you'll look stunning in that dress.'

As she stared at her reflection in the large mirror, Aisling made a decision. Why not, she thought? If I'm going to face all the people who know what's been going on, I might as well do it in style.

CHAPTER THREE

Bending slightly sideways in her grey swivel chair, Jo reached down and slowly slid the chemist's paper bag out of her briefcase. She was trying to remove it with as little rustling as possible, hoping that Brenda, who was sitting at the opposite desk blowing kisses down the phone to her current boyfriend, wouldn't hear anything.

If only she'd stuck the package in her fake crocodile-skin handbag in the first place, she wouldn't have to smuggle it clandestinely out of her briefcase now. She'd been waiting all morning for the right moment to sneak the distinctive blue and white bag into the toilet without someone demanding to know what she'd been buying in the chemist when they had enough make-up around to cover Claudia Schiffer from head to toe.

That was one of the main problems of working in such a small office, and the office of a women's magazine into the bargain, she thought ruefully. Everyone knew everything about you and, being inveterate shoppers, they wanted to know what you'd bought when you came back from the shops at lunchtime.

Personal matters were totally public in the cramped offices of *Style*, where the only privacy to be had was when you locked the door of the tiny toilet and shower cubicle. Everyone who worked in what the interior designer described as a '. . . relaxing contemporary open-plan workspace . . .' could listen to your most intimate phone calls, could hear you talking to the bank about your overdraft, and knew when you'd forgotten your mother's birthday.

What's more, they were all endlessly curious about shopping, shopaholism being the main qualification necessary for working in a women's magazine. Entire lunch-breaks could be

29

spent oohing and aahing over a sale bargain hat for that wedding or a new babygro for baby Jessica.

Jo wanted to keep this latest purchase to herself. A pregnancy testing kit was not the sort of thing you could hold up and scream, 'Look what I got for a tenner in Marks and Spencer's this morning!' Absolutely not.

It was all so unexpected, such a surprise. Jo was still too stunned to know what she thought about it. She certainly didn't want the rest of the office to know anything about it until she knew whether she was pregnant or not. Or until she knew how she felt about being pregnant, which was more to the point. God, it was confusing.

She sighed, jammed the paper bag into her open handbag and closed her eyes briefly. It wasn't as if she'd had much time to think about being pregnant. She'd only worked out that her period was late when she opened the phone bill that morning.

Late for work as usual. She was trying to gulp down a cup of coffee while opening her post and sticking folders into her tattered old briefcase when she came upon the phone bill. Astronomical, what else? All that time ringing Sligo talking to her mother and the boys. She was about to jam it behind the coffee jar when she stopped herself.

Write it down, you moron, she muttered, remembering how very irritating it had been to have to pay the phone company a reconnection fee the last time she'd filed a bill behind the coffee and forgotten about it.

Three pens had to be thrown in the bin before she found one that worked and opened her diary to write, 'Pay phone bill' in the following week. And then she noticed it. Or rather didn't notice it.

The capital P which stood for period wasn't there. Details of her fluctuating bank balance were noted along with appointments for interviews and a green biro squiggle she couldn't read. But no mention of her period. She flicked through the pages rapidly.

'Omigod,' Jo muttered. 'Omigod!' Unless her contact lenses needed to be replaced, she hadn't had a period since the second week in April and it was now the beginning of June. She had either stopped menstruating because she was menopausal – unlikely at the age of thirty-four – or she was pregnant. But it couldn't be. They always used condoms *and* spermicide, so how could she be pregnant?

She'd bought the pregnancy testing kit at the chemist across the road from her apartment, but she was running too late to do the test at home.

Which was why she was waiting for the right moment to slip nonchalantly into the office loo without catching anyone's eye. Well, it wasn't the sort of news to broadcast to your colleagues when your brain was still reeling from the shock and your boyfriend was still blissfully unaware of impending fatherhood.

She thought of Richard: clever, witty, good-looking in a boyish way, a talented photographer and an inveterate charmer of women. Of all the words you could use to describe her boyfriend of the last two years, fatherly would have been last on her list. Well, maybe conventional would be last on the list but fatherly wouldn't be far behind.

Three years older than she was, he looked as if he was heading towards thirty, never mind forty, and thought that settling down was something other people did – when they were ten years older than he was.

The thought of being married with 2.5 kids, a semi with a conservatory and an estate car filled him with the dread most men reserved for having their mothers-in-law to stay. At the mention of the word commitment, his eyes glazed over and he would pick up the remote control and switch channels rapidly, searching for something which involved a muddy field, a football or a newscast with in-depth sports coverage.

Of course, when you were a sports photographer you *had* to keep up with current sporting events, but one tiny piece of Jo's mind was beginning to think that the manic channel-hopping which ensued the last time she talked about buying a place together was a ploy to avoid talking about settling down.

31

She'd known what he was like when she first met him, shortly after he'd given up his secure and pensionable job with one newspaper to set up a sports agency with a couple of other like-minded, risk-taking photographers.

'It was driving me out of my mind working for just one paper.' He told her about his low boredom threshold as they drank red wine and completely ignored the press-photographer awards ceremony going on around them. 'This way, we're our own bosses and we control what we do and what we don't do.'

'Absolutely,' breathed Jo, fascinated by his ambition and his Scandinavian blondness. She thanked God that she'd agreed to make up a party of ten people to cheer on *Style*'s fashion photographer as he accepted his award.

She'd nearly cried off and stayed in to watch *Coronation Street* instead. There is a God after all, she thought happily. She wondered whether she should risk going to the loo to reapply some Crimson Kiss lipstick and adjust her strapless dress in case someone else nabbed the most fascinating man she'd met in years. No, she decided firmly.

Who cared if her boobs were about to spill out of the figure-hugging hot red dress she'd borrowed from the fashion cupboard at work?

Her rippling tortoiseshell hair was piled on top of her head in a haphazard manner, designed to suggest she'd just got out of bed. Mascara emphasised her dark eyes beautifully and only the most observant onlooker would notice the wobbly dark line above her lashes where the hand holding her eyeliner pen had slipped. Jo knew she looked good and she wanted this fair-haired hunk to know it too.

'I can't stand people who just sit still and let life happen to them. I want to *make* it happen, I want that excitement and that energy,' Richard said passionately. 'It's what keeps me going.'

Gazing deeply into his eyes, Jo fell for him like a ton of bricks, low boredom threshold and all. She should have wondered what kind of man would dump a perfectly safe job to run a risky freelance agency. But she hadn't.

She was the sort of individual who woke in the morning with her guts spasming with nerves if she had a difficult interview ahead of her. She found Richard's adventurous spirit intriguing. And frankly, very sexy.

There was something macho about taking such a huge gamble and something equally attractive about realising that his dream had paid off tenfold.

That wasn't enough for Richard, though. Once the agency was making money, he was eager for the next challenge, longing for adventure, while Jo began to yearn for quiet domesticity. He wanted to take up parachuting. She was scared of heights. He signed up for a scuba diving course and gave her a course of diving lessons for her birthday, even though she hated getting water in her eyes. But how could she now complain about the very traits she'd found so exciting in him in the first place?

'Interest rates and conveyancing fees are probably responsible for more heart attacks than five pints of Guinness a day, darling,' he'd said only the week before when the most gorgeous cottage in the Wicklow mountains just jumped out of the property pages at her. The picture of the cottage bathed in sunlight made Jo long for the house with twelve-inch-thick stone walls and a box-tree herb garden.

'Darling, you know I love living in the city,' he said, throwing the property pages onto the floor and nuzzling her neck as he breathed in the scent of the vanilla perfume he loved her to wear.

'Anyway, setting up the agency has swallowed up most of my capital and I don't want to take on a mortgage when I can keep renting my flat in Merrion Square for well under the market rate. You'd be mad to sell your apartment so soon after buying it,' he added. 'Let's leave things the way they are.' And they went to bed.

Once Richard had his arms around her, making her feel more turned on and more desirable than any man had been able to do before, she wasn't able to think about anything, never mind buying a house together. All she wanted was his lean body wrapped around hers, his fingers tangled in her hair and his lips gently kissing her skin. When he murmured *exactly* what he was going to do just before he did it, she melted into a quiver of anticipation.

His voice did the most amazing things to her head, not to mention the effect he was having lower down. And when they finally came together in a surge of passion, the intensity of her orgasm made Jo shudder, and wonder how she'd ever thought she'd enjoyed lovemaking with anyone else.

'We're wonderful in bed together,' he said afterwards. It was amazing the way they were perfectly in tune in bed, even though they weren't so in tune out of it, Jo thought to herself.

As she was about to throw a bundle of old papers in the bin a few days later, she looked longingly at the property section and wondered was she mad to think about settling down. Richard was happy the way things were, so why wasn't she? His bachelor pad in the city centre was perfect for a man who liked nothing better than to sway the few short yards from Dublin's trendy hostelries to his front door on a Saturday night.

Trips to Anfield and Wembley where nightclubbing the night away was par for the course, this was Richard's idea of fun. Not getting up for the three a.m. feed.

Would he want their baby, she asked herself? You could go round and round in circles and never figure it out. What was the point in dreaming up problems for the future until she knew for sure?

Ten minutes in the loo would tell her for certain. She looked around at the empty desks abandoned in the lunch-time rush.

The only person in the editorial office was Brenda and she was thankfully otherwise engaged, telling Mark – or was it Kevin – about the lingerie catalogue she'd been perusing that morning, ostensibly for a feature on mail-order underwear.

'You'd really like the black bra with those teeny, weeny knickers,' Brenda purred down the phone, no doubt sending

34

poor Mark/Kevin into a frenzy with the seduction techniques she'd honed after three years of industriously filling in 'How Sexy Are You?' questionnaires in *Cosmopolitan*.

At least Brenda was too busy to listen, thought Jo, as she psyched herself up to do the test. She gave up pretending to study a feature article on the latest tanning creams and had just picked up the small elegant handbag which went with nothing she owned, when she was rudely interrupted. Dropping the bag like a shot, Jo straightened up and smiled broadly at the editor.

'Got a minute, Jo?' inquired Rhona McNamara. She perched one well-upholstered hip on the desk and rearranged the silken folds of her expensive Jaeger skirt.

'Of course. What is it?' With as much nonchalance as she could muster, Jo casually scooped up the magazines from her desk and dropped them on top of the paper bag which was sticking out the top of her handbag in a very noticeable manner. You couldn't do anything personal around here without someone landing on top of you, she cursed inwardly.

'What do you think about changing the format of the new beauty products section? I've been thinking that we should get readers to test certain things and give marks out of ten.'

Rhona's fingers flew about as she spoke, a habit which would make the casual observer think she was using sign language. In fact, she was just trying to keep her hands occupied until they got hold of her next cigarette.

'I think that's a great idea,' Jo answered. Obviously, she couldn't say that she didn't give a damn who tested the bloody make-up when she was faced with this momentous, no *huge* event in her life. When a pregnancy testing kit was burning a hole in her handbag just aching to be used.

'It's a fresh way of looking at products and, since we're all so blasé about lotions and potions, it would be marvellous to get readers to give their opinion about things,' Rhona said in a voice which required some sort of reaction.

'Er . . . I'll include an advert for guinea pigs on the beauty page, although I'll have to drop something to fit it in.' Jo started rooting through the piles of paper on her desk for the dummy or advance pages of the beauty section.

With only two days to go before printing, the July edition of *Style* was nearly totally finished and any changes had to be agreed and inserted within the next twenty-four hours.

Jo still had an entire piece to write about packing for your summer holidays and had managed to leave the ideas she'd jotted down for the article at home.

'D'you know, I haven't been talking to you all week,' Rhona commented, picking up the tanning article and scanning it for mistakes. 'You look a little bit pale, Jo. Are you feeling all right?'

'Fine,' answered Jo as brightly as she could. She raked her dark curls with her fingers and wished she'd bothered with proper make-up on this of all mornings.

'I've had a lot of late nights recently,' she lied, 'and I'm a little tired. Maybe that Elizabeth Arden magic stuff you keep in your desk could give my complexion a bit of a boost?'

Rhona looked at her shrewdly for a moment, taking in her deputy editor's pale, freckled skin, tired brown eyes and un-lipsticked mouth.

Jo took her job as fashion editor very seriously and was nearly always dressed to kill in on-the-knee skirts which showed off her long legs and fitted jewel-coloured jackets which were just perfect for her Monroe-esque curves. She was usually better made-up than Ivana Trump.

Today, she was wearing a fawn-coloured linen ensemble which would have cost an arm and a leg if Jo didn't have a fashion editor's discount at every top shop in Dublin. Chic in the extreme, the effect of the outfit was ruined by the fact that she wasn't wearing more make-up or jewellery and her normally wavy hair had flopped in the June heat. It was very unlike Jo, thought Rhona.

'Come on into my office and we'll have a bitch.' She smiled at Jo, slid off the desk and walked into her tiny office.

It was compact and untidy, with clothes hangers dangling off every nail and magazines, press releases and sticky layout pages covering every available surface. There wasn't enough room to swing a cat in its ten-by-twelve confines.

Rhona's office was, however, blissfully private and a haven for the nicotine-addicted who weren't allowed to smoke anywhere else in the Georgian three-storey house which was home to both *Style* and a tiny secretarial agency.

Jo followed the editor into the untidy room and pushed a clump of plastic-covered dresses to one side of the dusty cream settee which took up at least half of one wall. She plonked herself down tiredly and leaned back into the soft cushions. She levered off her shoes and wondered if this sudden exhaustion was pregnancy or shock.

'Is lover boy wearing you out at home?' Rhona teased, immediately lighting up a cigarette.

Despite herself, Jo blushed. She could feel her face redden and she could also see Rhona looking at her in amazement, cigarette suspended in mid-air as she stared at her deputy with a dumbfounded expression.

How was she going to get out of this one? Jo groaned silently. The woman with whom she'd shared kiss-by-kiss accounts of various lovers over numerous bottles of red wine was not going to believe that just *talking* about sex with Richard would send her blushing to her roots. No way.

Rhona knew her much better than that. Which meant that she was going to have to spill the beans. Only how could she spill anything until she knew for sure?

'Did I say the wrong thing?' Rhona sat down heavily and looked anxiously at her deputy. 'Are you having problems? You know you can always talk to me, Jo, don't you? I don't want to interfere, I just want to help.'

'I don't think you can help me this time,' Jo replied with a small laugh. Here goes, she thought. 'Unless you've been secretly training as an obstetrician and haven't told the rest of us!'

'You're not pregnant, are you?' Rhona squealed. 'Stupid question. Congratulations, Jo! I shouldn't be smoking, should I?' She hastily stubbed out her barely touched Dunhill as though a baby was going to pop out any minute and wail if there was so much as a hint of nicotine in the air.

'Slow down, Rhona. I don't know if I'm pregnant yet. I missed my period this month and it only really hit me this morning so I don't know for sure.' It sounded even stranger actually *saying* it out loud.

'You haven't done a test?' Rhona looked surprised. 'The new ones can tell you if you're pregnant just a day after your period is due.'

'I know, I know.' Jo looked mildly exasperated. 'I was going to do it here, I just didn't want Ms Nosey Parker out there to pick anything up with her radar ears.'

'Fair enough,' Rhona replied. 'I'll send her out for fags and you can pee in privacy . . .'

Rhona stopped mid-sentence and looked Jo straight in the face. 'It is Richard's, isn't it?'

'Of course it bloody is!' Jo said, affronted. 'How many men do you think I'm seeing? One a day and two on Sunday! Come on, Rhona.'

'Sorry, sorry. It's just that you don't seem pleased about it and I just thought, maybe it wasn't his and . . . Forget I said that, please, Jo. I thought you'd be happy if it was Richard's and you seem a little off, you know.'

She leaned over and put her arms around Jo's now tense body, hugging her tightly. 'You know I'm here for you, no matter what happens.'

'Thanks.' Jo stood up, running a ringless hand over her stomach as though she'd be able to tell what lay beneath her linen waistcoat just by touching her belly. What would it be like to feel a baby growing inside her?

Would she feel totally at one with her unborn child, sensitive to every kick and wriggle? If she played her favourite music on the car stereo, would the baby be born liking the same tunes?

Then it came to her with piercing clarity: she wanted this child. She wanted it more than anything she'd ever wanted before, even if Richard didn't. That was the nub of the problem. It was no use wasting time wondering whether he wanted their child, littering her brain with doubts when, all along, she knew what *she* wanted.

She wanted a baby, maybe she had wanted one for years. Trying to be the nineties career woman had meant keeping up the façade of a perfect life, complete with a handsome lover, total independence and a job most women would kill for.

Career women didn't long for babies and a man's pyjamas permanently under the pillows, but suddenly, that's just what Jo wanted.

For once she didn't care if the magazine's publisher demoted her to writing picture captions or gave her job to the horrible, sneaky Emma who was always angling to backstab her way up the career ladder. All she wanted was a beautiful, healthy baby.

'I'm pregnant,' she said aloud, suddenly grinning at Rhona with a smile which lit up her whole face. 'I'm pregnant! I just know it!'

'Well let's send Brenda out for champagne then,' Rhona suggested before hugging Jo to her considerable bosom. 'And for something from the deli. I'm starved.'

'When were you ever not starved?' Jo got up with renewed energy and manoeuvred her feet into her brown suede court shoes.

'I'm going to do the test, to be sure to be sure, if you know what I mean. But I know already. Is that normal?' She looked at Rhona, the mother of three under-tens, for confirmation.

'Absolutely,' answered Rhona. 'I knew I was pregnant the first time because I woke up one morning and couldn't eat a thing, which is not like me, as you know. The day Lynne was born was the happiest day of my life, I always say, mainly because I'd been so sick all the time I was carrying her.'

'I feel fine,' interrupted Jo. 'Hungry actually. I think I need something nutritious to eat, like a Twix.'

'Or a poppy-seed baguette filled with sun-dried tomatoes, Parma ham and chunks of Gruyère washed down with an icy Diet Coke,' said Rhona, who had not been a magazine restaurant reviewer for nothing. 'I'm supposed to be on a diet, but there are only so many things you can do with brown rice and green vegetables,' she added mournfully, thinking of the considerable difference between what she should be eating and what she wanted to eat.

Tall and big-boned, Rhona was always denying herself something in the hope that she'd miraculously turn into a carbon copy of her sleek, younger sister and, more importantly, fit into all the lovely clothes she'd bought for 'when I get thin'.

Sadly, her predilection for all the wrong food meant that she was never going to be anything smaller than a size fourteen. Her 'thin' clothes were getting closer to the second-hand shop every day.

'Brenda,' called Rhona loudly, winking at Jo, 'are you busy? I want you to do something for me.'

Hastily cutting off her steamy conversation, Brenda hurried over to the editor's office with the speed of one hoping to be promoted, while Jo grabbed her handbag and headed for the loo.

By the time she had peed into the tiny tester and put it back into its little plastic case, her heart was thumping along at advanced-aerobics-class level.

She rummaged around for some lipstick in her tiny make-up bag and thought about telling Richard.

She could bring him out to Fitzer's, his favourite restaurant, and tell him the wonderful news over the clam linguini. 'Darling, we're going to have a baby!'

She could see it all in her mind. She would wear the Jasper Conran jacket she'd bought in a discount store in Belfast.

'My darling, that's wonderful!' he'd cry before ordering champagne and toasting their baby. Then they'd go back to her place and plan their future together. A Georgian town house in Dalkey, she daydreamed, with plenty of room for Richard's darkroom and a desk where she could write the novel she was always talking about.

Or maybe an artisan's cottage in Enniskerry, a cross

between *Homes and Gardens* and the Habitat catalogue. Of course, they'd have to get a new bed because Richard's futon wouldn't be suitable for the baby and her ancient double bed was sprouting springs faster than a dodgy biro. There were so many things to buy! She'd better get to Mothercare quickly and get started.

'She's gone. Let me in,' shouted Rhona outside the door.

'Oh Rhona, it's so exciting.' Jo smiled, opened the door and carried the tester into the editor's office as if it was an unexploded bomb. 'I almost can't believe it. Me, a mother! Even saying it sounds strange. What if I'm no good at it,' she asked, suddenly anxious, 'no good at being a mother. Does it just come naturally? I mean, it's not as if I have any real experience of babies or anything. Oh, and what about work? Is it *really* that hard being a working mother?'

Rhona burst out laughing. 'Don't get me started, Jo. You'll learn. I mean, it's not exactly a doddle, I can tell you. First of all,' she started ticking imaginary points off on her fingers, 'you're exhausted and you wonder are you doing everything wrong from feeding to nappy-changing to winding them after their feed.'

'Then, you go to work and leave your precious baby with some woman you're convinced turns into an axe murderer every time you walk out the front door, and then, when your baby walks for the first time, you're not there.

'Ms Axe Murderer is there. You, on the other hand, are listening to some po-faced advertiser telling you that they don't want their anti-wrinkle cream on the opposite page to a feature on how to stop the ravages of time with plastic surgery.' She stopped with a sigh. 'Is there anything else you want to ask?'

'No, just give me a prescription for Prozac and I'll be fine,' said Jo with wide eyes. 'I suppose I never really thought about how difficult it was before. You know me, Rho, I can't walk out the front door without spending half an hour on my hair, throwing at least three outfits on the bed when I'm trying to figure out what look to go for that day and taking another fifteen minutes to do my make-up. It's that liquid eyeliner,' she added. 'It's impossible to get it right.'

'Liquid eyeliner will be the least of your problems, darling, let me tell you. You'll be lucky if you can actually brush your teeth in the morning if your little pet is anything like mine were. And as for leaving three outfits on the bed . . .! Forget it. Five-year-old girls love wearing Mummy's clothes and Mummy's make-up, usually at the same time.

'Believe me, Jo, you won't be long tidying everything you value away from sticky little fingers. It's better now that Susie is finally at school,' she reflected. 'Although she has this thing about Liga biscuits. I still get embarrassed when I think about that time in the Conrad Hotel when I opened my cheque book and it was all glued together with molten Liga.'

'Oh yes, that was a howl and I didn't have any money with me!' Jo started laughing at the memory, and, realising what was in front of her, laughed even harder. 'I can't wait to see Richard when we've got a terrible two-year-old toddling around playing with his Nikons.'

Rhona didn't smile. She'd known Richard from the two years he'd been going out with Jo. She had a rather different vision of his reaction and she didn't find the picture at all amusing.

Without a doubt, Richard would commit murder if he saw any child messing around with any of his possessions. If he stayed around long enough for the child in question to reach the grand old age of two, that was. 'Does he know?' she asked quietly.

'Not yet,' Jo confessed. 'I didn't want to tell him until I was sure. I just wanted it to be between us. But I'm so glad I told you.' She smiled fondly at the other woman.

'Give us a look at the tester then,' demanded Rhona.

Like a magician about to produce a rabbit from a hat, Jo whisked off the plastic lid and gave a whoop of joy.

'Yahoo! I'm pregnant: officially! Just think, Rhona. This is a new life inside me!' She beamed, looking down at her still-slender waist. 'A whole new life in every sense, really.

God, I can't wait to tell Richard.' She sighed. 'He's in Cork today and I know he has the mobile phone with him, but I just can't tell him over the phone.'

'Probably not. Let's go out to lunch, my treat. As you're eating for two officially, you'll need some help in choosing the right foods so you don't end up with a couple of difficult pounds to shift.' Rhona grinned at her slim deputy.

'It must be awful to have to diet,' commiserated Jo. 'I have such a fast metabolism. I mean, I've always been able to eat what I wanted and I never put on weight.'

'Don't remind me. It's not fair to have someone like you on the staff. Able to stuff herself with chocolate and still not have so much as one love handle.'

Rhona picked up her handbag, stuck a pair of sunglasses on her head and held out her hand to haul Jo off the settee. 'Come on, Mummy. Let's toast your wonderful news with some mineral water and something fattening, with cream and chocolate sauce and ooh, I don't know . . .'

'Did I hear you mention food?' Tony, the magazine's chief sub-editor, peered into the office. 'Does anybody ever do anything but talk about food around here any more?' he inquired. 'I was sort of hoping we might work on the magazine this afternoon . . . You know, that A4-sized thing that pays all our wages and currently has a couple of blank pages in it waiting to be filled with gems of wisdom from your pen, Madame Editor?'

'OK.' Rhona took her sunglasses off her head and looked at Jo wryly. 'Back to work, I'm afraid. You and I,' she whispered conspiratorially, 'will celebrate later.'

'Thanks.' Jo smiled as she walked to the door. 'But I just couldn't do any more work today. I'll get one of the girls to finish subbing that article and I'm going home, via the doctor's,' she added with a huge grin. 'Actually, I've got that party at the *News* this evening but I'd love not to go. I want Richard all to myself when I give him the news.'

Rhona couldn't help herself. 'Jo, have you thought about the fact that he mightn't want a baby?' she asked gently.

For a moment Jo's face was blank. Then a broad smile swept over her face, lighting up her eyes and curving her full mouth up in that warm and sexy smile which had been knocking men for six ever since she'd been fifteen. 'Of course he will,' she said confidently. 'He'll be delighted, I promise!'

As she sat in her temperamental Volkswagen trying to exit the Stephen's Green multi-storey car park, Jo was still thinking about what Rhona had said.

OK, so Richard had never been exactly wild about kids. Last Christmas he had refused point blank to go to the all-day party Rhona gave every year where the *Style* staff lounged around their editor's roomy Wicklow farmhouse with glasses of mulled wine, while their offspring watched videos and played on the tiny indoor bouncing castle. That didn't mean he hated children; he just wasn't mad about other people's, that was all.

He told Jo to make his excuses.

'Tell them I'm working, Jo, will you? There's no way I'm going to spend an entire day at a bloody kids' party. I know she's your boss and you have to go, but I don't. You don't really mind, do you, darling?' he wheedled.

Once Richard had decided not to do something, nothing on earth could make him change his mind. Jo went on her own.

The party had been a huge success although somebody had accidentally turned the cooker off and the coq au vin was icy and virtually raw when the guests arrived.

Rhona's husband Ted had returned from a booze-buying session at the local off-licence with five extra people and no diet tonic, but nothing could spoil the day.

After downing a super-strength cocktail Jo had mixed up for her with a bit of just about everything from the drinks cabinet, Rhona relaxed enough to serve beans and sausages. Sick of eating every type of turkey dish possible during Christmas, everyone wolfed down their food and had a whale of a time.

Jo really wished that Richard had come after all. But there

wasn't much time for introspection with *Style*'s receptionist, Annette, perched tipsily on the arm of Jo's chair and a hysterical conversation about the rumoured sexual tendencies of the most pious newscaster on the TV going on all around her.

He'd have loved it, Jo thought a little sadly as she gave a corner of cheesy Pringle to Mutt, Rhona's slavering black and white spaniel whose main preoccupation in life was food.

For some reason, that picture stuck in her mind. Her friends and colleagues had let their hair down and enjoyed themselves with their husbands, wives, partners and children.

She'd hated being the only person there on her own although she wouldn't have admitted it for the world. As she told Rhona, she'd enjoyed herself immensely and if the other woman suspected that Richard wasn't actually working, but just hadn't wanted to come, she didn't say so.

The only squabbles were 'You drank the last two times so it's my turn and you have to drive' arguments every time Ted came in with more booze. Everyone had a great time. Nobody complained about the noise coming from the converted garage as boisterous children did their level best to out-bounce each other.

Who'd have guessed that Frederick, the marvellously camp make-up artist who worked on most of *Style*'s fashion shoots, would turn out to be the children's favourite playmate.

'I like children, sweetie. I just don't know if I could eat a whole one!' had been Frederick's favourite phrase, borrowed from W. C. Fields. It never failed to raise a laugh. But after six vodkas and a lethal alcoholic concoction which included peach schnapps and Grand Marnier, Frederick was up on the bouncy castle with the five-year-olds, happily trying to demonstrate the double somersault he claimed to have been able to do in his youth.

How could you not like children, Jo wondered as the parking attendant handed her a fistful of coins and a receipt.

Richard didn't hate children. How could he? He'd been an only child who'd never had anyone to compete with at home.

His besotted mother looked after him as if he was the crown prince of Brunei.

That's it, she thought triumphantly. He's never had to compete with a brother or sister for affection and he never learned to deal with children. All he needs is a little time to get used to the idea. We must have at least seven months left for that.

She roared off around the Green, whizzing past taxi-drivers and lumbering buses like a rally-driver. You're not bad, Bessie, when you get going, she told her car. But I may have to trade you in for something more baby-friendly – or at least something with a bit of suspension.

The surgery was full when she got there. Two harassed mothers tried to quieten cross toddlers and an elderly man with a hacking cough occupied two seats. One sulky adolescent mutinously insisted he go in to see the doctor by himself. 'I'm not a child any more,' he hissed at his mother.

'Stop acting like one, then,' she hissed back.

He turned pinker than the outbreak of spots on his hairless face when he noticed Jo looking at him.

Jo grabbed a dog-eared magazine off the centre table and squeezed in between the teenager and one of the mothers. She was in for a long wait, she calculated, judging by the exhausted expressions on everyone's faces. Still, it was only just after three and she had just had the most wonderful news in the world, so she couldn't complain about waiting for the doctor. She couldn't complain about anything.

She wanted to tell Richard so badly it was killing her. She wanted to tell everyone in the waiting room. Instead, she turned her attention to a year-old copy of *Elle* and flicked through the pages with a professional eye.

Jo could no longer look at any publication aimed at women without wondering whether *Style* would look good with a wrap-around calorie counter, three more pages on travel or whatever.

She was just reading an in-depth report about cervical cancer – the sort of article which would have once had her

46

reaching for her edition of *Everywoman* in terror – when a woman walked into the waiting room with a baby cradled papoose-like on her chest.

Jo stared at them, taking in every detail. The baby girl, dressed in pink which matched her soft rounded cheeks, had obviously been sleeping until the noisy surgery waiting room woke her up.

She blinked long dark eyelashes and stared drowsily up at her mother with enormous eyes, smiling a toothless grin when Mum murmured comforting words.

Jo held her breath as she looked at the mother and baby. She had a million questions she wanted to ask, but she didn't say a word. This was what she wanted, thought Jo as the mother gently kissed her baby's downy head, this bond between a mother and her child, a love that was holier than anything she'd ever felt in a church. And now she was going to experience it.

Back to *Elle*. She discovered that shimmery pink was in, black was out and anyone wearing last year's opaque black tights would be arrested by the fashion police. She had just started reading an ancient edition of *Hello!* and was looking at pictures of Michael Jackson's wedding when the doctor called her name. Thank God for that. One more page about Cindy Crawford's workout wardrobe or her marvellous fashion sense, and she'd have gone mad.

The last time she'd been in the clinical-looking surgery, she was in the grip of a particularly virulent stomach bug and had nearly been sick all over the expensive cream floor tiles. Today's visit was definitely an improvement.

'I'm pregnant.' Saying that brought a gleam to her eyes, she just knew it. 'I thought I needed a professional opinion, although I've done a test and it was positive. Are those tests accurate, Dr Daly?' Jo asked in concern.

'Used properly, they're excellent. But I'd prefer to make sure.' Ten minutes and another positive pregnancy test later, the doctor was working out dates and talking about diet and folic acid supplements.

By the time Jo turned her key in her front door lock, it was nearly six. She couldn't wait to make herself a huge cup of sugary tea. She switched the kettle on and peered into the fridge.

Two weepy tomatoes, a soggy courgette, a jar with a scraping of crumb-filled honey at the bottom, a half-full tin of beans and a tub of spreadable cheese covered with green fluff stared back at her dismally.

Only the milk, butter and two yogurt pots looked healthy enough for human consumption. This won't do, she thought. Time to get your act together, Ms Ryan, she told herself as she closed the fridge door. At least she had those potato waffles in the freezer. They were carbohydrates, weren't they? She switched on the answering machine and listened to her messages while she poured boiling water over a tea bag.

Rhona had rung to see how she got on with the doctor. Her sister-in-law had been on to tell her about a surprise birthday party for Shane's fortieth. Could she ring back during the day when he was out? asked Mary against a background noise of a washing machine about to lift into orbit.

Jo was chuckling at the idea of her older brother's face when he realised he'd been duped when she heard Richard's voice: 'Hi, Jo. I'm in Naas on a job for the *Independent*. I'm going to drive straight to the party when I'm finished, OK? William is coming with me and he's bringing his sister along because she's home from Paris. He can't just leave her on her own in the flat. I'm covering the party for the *Herald* as a favour in case the Def Leppard guys or Dennis Hopper turn up. That's it. Sorry I missed you but I'll see you there. Bye.'

Oh no, Jo thought despondently. I wanted to go with you, Richard. Blast you. She plucked the tea bag from her cup and added the last dribble of milk and sugar. A few chocolate digestives, I think, she muttered miserably. She opened the junk cupboard where she kept a bag of mini-Mars bars, biscuits and several bottles of 7-Up for emergencies.

He said he was going to bring me to the bloody party, she muttered as she carried her tea and biscuits into the bedroom.

What the hell is he bringing Will and his stupid sister for? Are they more important to him than I am?

She took a bite of chocolate digestive and washed it down with hot, sweet tea. She turned on the radio and sat down heavily on the bed. How was she going to get the energy to change her clothes?

She looked at the pile of unironed clothes draped on her white cane chair. Last month's 'de-junk your life' feature flashed before her eyes and she thanked God that nobody in the office could see the chaos that was her bedroom.

She was reasonably tidy at work. Losing a vital piece of paper *there* could prove disastrous so she forced herself to dump all the press releases, old newspaper cuttings and scrawled phone messages before they swamped her desk.

At home, however, she flung linen jackets onto the chair only to find them crumpled and requiring half an hour of ironing a week later.

A tangle of tights lay on the flowered blue quilt, silky beige and black skeins abandoned during her frantic attempts that morning to find a ladderless pair of sheer tights to go with her linen outfit.

It was a pretty room, decorated in the blue-sprigged Laura Ashley wallpaper she'd instantly adored when she spotted it in the shop. The white cane dressing table, bookcase and bedside table looked just right with the wallpaper, and matched the long white muslin curtain which hung elegantly from a brass pole.

It all would have been property-supplement-perfect if it hadn't been for the piles of paperbacks and magazines stacked untidily on the bedside table, the sheaf of newspapers dropped casually onto the floor beside her bed and the heap of blouses, T-shirts and trousers on the chair.

The oval dressing table was like a chemist shop's display with bottles of perfume, body lotion and endless old lipsticks she just couldn't bear to throw out. A picture of her and Richard on their last holiday in New York had pride of place beside the walnut jewellery box he'd bought her last year.

What a bloody mess, she thought, remembering Rhona's words of wisdom on small children and their effect on untidy mothers. I'll tidy up tomorrow, she promised. Now what to wear for the party?

Jo glanced briefly at the mirror – could do with a dust, she rebuked herself – and was amazed by what she saw. She *felt* exhausted, but the face that stared back at her positively glowed. Her eyes shone and her skin was healthily flushed with a radiance no expensive face cream would ever be able to match.

Marvellous! I feel like I've been squashed under a cement mixer and I look great! The people who made Oil of Ulay had better learn how to bottle this.

All those articles she'd written about motherhood and the Blooming Pregnancy fashion features came to mind.

She laughed out loud at the thought of pregnant women reading her zero-experience-of-pregnancy claptrap. 'Your skin will bloom and your hair will be shinier than any salon treatment could ever make it . . .' she giggled. And I hadn't a clue what I was talking about.

Let's put that blooming beauty to good use, she decided, as she finished the last bit of biscuit. After a quick shower, an even quicker blast of the hairdryer and ten careful minutes spent applying make-up, she cast a critical eye over herself. The launch of Michael Moran's long-awaited glossy supplement would doubtless be a glitzy, high-profile affair.

Jo had no intention of turning up looking anything but her best, especially as the bosses of two model agencies had told her they were going to be there – with some of their most stunning girls, naturally. The threat of rock star involvement meant that the city's model population would be out in force, an army of perfectly groomed women who were paid to look stunning – and who instantly made other women green with jealousy.

With Richard prowling around, Nikon slung round his neck as he searched for photo opportunities, Jo didn't want to look any less gorgeous than these professional beauties.

Neither did she want to look tired and pale when she told him their wonderful news. Something sexy was definitely required.

She opened the wardrobe door and stood back as her black suede sandals, a fluffy pink slipper and a wire hanger fell out. She searched through jackets, dresses, skirts and trousers, rejecting outfit after outfit until she came upon the perfect one – an elegant midnight blue slip dress which looked deceptively simple unless you knew how much it had cost and realised that only brilliant – and expensive – designers made bias-cut gowns so flattering.

Jo twirled in front of the mirror, twisting and turning to see her figure from every angle. She looked beautiful. A string of glass beads, tiny pearl earrings and high-heeled shoes completed the outfit.

With her tortoiseshell hair cascading down her shoulders in the natural waves she'd never managed to tame, dark eyes shimmering with a faint dusting of Lancôme's silvery grey eyeshadow and the dress swirling around her, she felt like some Thirties movie star. Katharine Hepburn maybe, she thought, remembering rainy Saturday afternoons watching old movies on the TV.

She sprayed her neck and wrists lightly with perfume. Go get 'em, Jo.

CHAPTER FOUR

It was eight o'clock exactly according to the clock on the dashboard. It was time to go in, time to face her husband and the entire staff of the *News* who undoubtedly knew exactly what was going on in her marriage. Or her non-marriage as the case might be, Aisling thought glumly.

The launch party had been going on for at least an hour already, she reckoned. But she had been sitting quietly in the car since she'd arrived, nervously fiddling with her car keys and wondering how to slip in as unobtrusively as possible.

Jo would be there, she reminded herself. Thank God for that. Even though it was over twelve years since she'd shared a matchbox-sized flat in Rathmines with the lively trainee journalist, they'd still remained friends.

Aisling knew that it was largely thanks to Jo's determination that they'd seen each other regularly over the past ten years.

When their lives had diverged – one of them climbing up the career ladder and the other climbing the stairs with piles of laundry – Aisling had begun to wonder whether a high-flyer like Jo would be bothered to keep in touch.

The question became academic when the demands of Jo's job meant she had neither the time nor the energy to socialise outside work. Aisling found that two adorable baby boys required twice as much work as one. Consumed by love for her darlings, she retired from normal non-baby life until the boys reached school-going age and she began to pick up the pieces of her old life again.

Meeting Nuala, an old friend from work, Aisling realised that her world had changed utterly over the past few years while Nuala's was just the same. Nuala talked about flexitime, staffing cutbacks and brokers who irritated her on the phone.

Aisling felt instantly boring, another mother droning on about her lovely children.

She wasn't surprised when Nuala didn't ring back to arrange another lunchtime meeting. That was why Aisling had assumed Jo would be the same. Too busy to squeeze in a hurried sandwich with someone she'd been close to years before. People changed, moved on.

It was a pleasant surprise to find out that she was wrong. Jo was determined to keep in contact, always on the phone or arriving for lunch when she was in the vicinity.

No matter how long an interval between their meetings, they would always slip back into their familiar friendship, laughing at the same things and reminiscing about the days when they hadn't enough money for the gas meter and wrapped themselves up with blankets to keep warm while watching their tiny portable TV.

'I still have this recurring nightmare about not having the rent money and coming back to the flat to find our clothes on the road,' Aisling said, one freezing December morning when Jo had dropped by with Christmas presents for the boys and a beautiful enamelled brooch for Aisling. 'I wake up thinking the landlord is banging on the door and the *relief* to find it's all a nightmare.'

'I know the feeling,' Jo shuddered, even though they were sitting in front of the fire in Aisling's primrose yellow living room. 'God, it was awful not to have enough money, always scraping by.'

'I was buying this gorgeous red jacket the other day and I was just at the cash register with my cheque book when I realised that it cost *more than two months' rent* in Mount Pleasant Avenue! Isn't that unbelievable?' Jo took another sip of coffee. 'I nearly put it back. I mean, *two months' rent*! My mother would be horrified if she saw me spending that much money on clothes.'

'I think, by now, she's figured out that you've expensive tastes in clothes!' laughed Aisling, looking pointedly at the elegant cream crêpe trouser suit Jo was wearing. 'And nobody's likely to think that those shoes were in the £9.99 bargain bin in Penney's.'

'True.' Jo looked down at the cream-coloured soft leather pumps she was wearing. 'It's crazy, really, the money I spend on clothes. But all the fashion correspondents are the same,' she protested.

'If I turned up at a fashion show in my old grey leggings and a sloppy old T-shirt, they'd all wet themselves with glee. So I *have* to spend money on clothes!'

Aisling laughed. No matter what elevated circles Jo moved in, she was always the same – funny, kind and totally lacking in pretension. The same warm-hearted girl who'd lend her less glamorous flatmate anything, even her newest and best-loved dress.

Jo had always been a friend to rely on, the sort of person who'd be there with a box of tissues, a comforting hug and a buoyant speech no matter what happened, Aisling reflected. Unlike her sister, Sorcha, who was so tied up with her job in London that she barely had time to come home for Christmas, Jo genuinely enjoyed Aisling's company. So what if Sorcha thought her older sister has turned into a non-person just because Aisling didn't have a high-powered career by day, and didn't go to management courses at night.

Jo Ryan, deputy and fashion editor of fashionable *Style* magazine, was one of Aisling's best friends and not even Sorcha could call Jo boring. Lively, clever and a little bit wild, maybe. But boring, no.

Funny, warm, and a little too trusting when it came to men – or so Aisling had always thought – Jo had finally met the man of her dreams after years of meeting Mr Wrong after Mr Wrong.

'You'll love him, Ash,' Jo said happily down the phone, one romance-filled week after meeting Richard. 'He's perfect – better than Richard Gere!'

'*That* good?' Aisling chuckled. 'Are you sure he's real, or has he escaped from the pages of GQ?'

'He's real all right.' Jo's throaty laugh told Aisling everything. The gorgeous photographer had obviously made it to first base. Aisling thought Jo should have waited a bit longer before going to bed with her new boyfriend. Michael had been *her* first and only lover. But, things were different now.

She hoped Richard wasn't like some of the other men Jo had been involved with. Jo always seemed to make huge mistakes when it came to men. She fell for each one passionately and wholeheartedly, only waking up to their faults when it was too late. Maybe this time would be different.

Aisling hadn't seen much of her friend since Richard had come on the scene. She briefly wondered if Jo had heard any rumours about Michael's affair.

Surely not, she thought. Jo would have told her if she'd heard anything. Or would she? Aisling's head was spinning thinking about it all. And I'm the one who thinks *Jo* goes around with rose-tinted glasses. How ironic.

Please let Jo be here tonight, Aisling prayed fervently. She and Jo always ended up sitting together at journalistic parties. Aisling was grateful to her more extrovert friend for introducing her to the ever-changing pool of reporters, subs and photographers.

There were always loads of people she didn't know, Aisling reflected, thinking of the occasions she'd tagged along with Jo after Michael had hotfooted it in another direction.

'Come on and meet Lorraine,' Jo would say. 'She reviews books for *The Times* and you'll have loads to talk about.' Instantly, Aisling felt as if she belonged, as if she had something to talk about. Jo never made her feel colourless or uninteresting, the way Michael did.

When she was with Jo, Aisling felt more like her old self again, more like the girl who'd gone to the College of Commerce Christmas party as the blonde from Abba. Jo had been the red-haired one, in sequins and flares. Who cared that it wasn't even fancy dress?

God, she thought, did I ever do that? What did we look like? They hadn't cared what they'd looked like after half a bottle of Malibu drunk in the toilets. She'd never been able to so much as *look* at a bottle of Malibu after that evening. Vodka didn't give you such bad hangovers, Jo pointed out. Gin was even better.

I hope it isn't one of those parties with nothing but wine, Aisling thought. Tonight, of all nights, she needed the buzz from a proper drink, the gentle loosening of inhibitions which made her feel less awkward.

Michael would probably give her one of his reproving looks when he saw her drinking. Once he'd been a great man for a few beers while watching TV, but he'd recently become very anti-booze and patted his now flat stomach smugly as he refused his customary weekend Budweiser.

He wanted to stay lithe for his girlfriend, no doubt, she thought bitterly.

'I'm not drinking beer at home any more,' he'd informed her in January, when she'd just unpacked the shopping all on her own and was stowing two six-packs in the larder. 'It's so unhealthy. And a few glasses of red wine is much better, and more enjoyable. That's what the Italians drink every day and look at how healthy they are.' He looked pointedly at Aisling as she guiltily took a large tub of Bailey's ice cream out of a shopping bag. Ten billion calories at least.

'A friend told me that scientists actually recommend a couple of glasses of red wine a day along with a Mediterranean diet,' he continued. 'I must get one of my students to do a piece on it.'

Aisling wondered if the 'friend' he'd talked about then was the same femme fatale he'd taken to Le Caprice and if the bitch preferred wine connoisseurs to men who drank pints?

Probably. Maybe she was one of those women who delicately sipped two white wine spritzers before loudly proclaiming that she would only drink mineral water for the rest of the night.

How different from me, Aisling thought. Practically under the table after five gin and tonics, she often ended up giggling and silly at parties. Of course, enduring Michael's diatribe in the taxi home was part and parcel of these occasions.

'How could you tell that story tonight?' he thundered the night Aisling told the managing director's wife her hilarious story about the first time she had her diaphragm fitted.

'Jesus, I shouldn't bring you to parties if you're going to embarrass me like this. I don't know what they're going to think.'

There was no point, Aisling decided, in saying that the managing director's wife had obviously loved the story and had burst out laughing as soon as a shocked Michael was out of earshot. No point at all, really.

Who the hell was Michael to tell her she shouldn't have a few drinks at parties? He was screwing some damn woman, breaking his marriage vows as if they weren't worth the paper they were written on. He had no right to tell her what she could or couldn't do. She'd drink what she felt like, especially tonight.

Maybe she did drink too much when she was out. So what? If she felt inadequate in his friends' company, he was responsible. He always kept her at arm's length from his colleagues and made her feel stupid in contrast to the editor's wife, a physics lecturer no less.

Well, Michael certainly couldn't make her feel any worse than she did now. He'd already found another woman, what could top that for humiliation? Blast him! She was going to have the biggest drink she could lay her hands on and she didn't give a damn if Michael saw her do it.

It was time to go in. Aisling checked her make-up in the rear-view mirror and rubbed at a tiny smudge of mascara below her eye. You weren't supposed to rub the delicate skin around your eyes roughly, she knew from those endless magazine articles.

Once she'd hit thirty, she really meant to look after her skin properly. But the new make-up routine fell by the wayside. Before long, Aisling was back to soap and water with a little Oil of Ulay when she remembered it.

Would Michael have stayed in love with her if she had

pampered her skin and spent hours toning, plucking, waxing and beautifying herself? Probably not. If he'd wanted a glamorous career woman to show off to his friends, nothing short of a miracle could have made him stay with his un-careerist wife.

She obliterated the mascara smudge, rubbing away the heavy foundation she'd applied to hide her reddened eyes. Damn, she muttered, rummaging in her meagre make-up bag for a tiny tube of concealer to hide the damage.

Polyfilla was what she needed, Aisling thought miserably as she peered into the mirror. A passing couple looked into her dusty red Starlet as they walked hand in hand through the back gate to the newspaper premises.

Casually dressed in jeans, trendy Timberland boots and matching chunky cord jackets, they strode past quickly. The girl stared straight at Aisling before looking away, flicking long chestnut hair out of her eyes with the confidence of youthful beauty.

Aisling flushed under their scrutiny and imagined that they were thinking, 'Why bother?' Just a boring old housewife trying to tart herself up when all the powder and paint in the world couldn't cover up the beginnings of a double chin.

A drink would be nice, she thought again. Just one large one to give her courage and help her smile at the strange faces. If she could still manage a smile when she'd confronted Michael, of course. Aisling took a deep breath and opened the car door.

She couldn't see anyone else in the corner of the car park where she'd parked. Near the door, a leather-clad figure was parking a motorcycle.

She hadn't been on a motorbike in years and the idea of a spin down the motorway, with the wind in her face and no time to think about her life, was suddenly very appealing.

She'd rented one of those scooters on that brilliant holiday in Greece. Her father had grimly warned her about broken limbs and permanent scars. That did it. Wearing her old denim shorts and T-shirt, she'd sped along the rocky roads with Jo

58

racing along beside her on an equally battered scooter, laughing into the wind with the sheer joy of it all.

'Last one home has to go out with Spiros,' screeched Jo, pumping her foot up and down on the gas pedal. She wasn't going to be the one accompanying the over-hairy owner of their apartment block to dinner in the taverna.

They were probably only going at fifteen miles an hour but it felt like flying as they passed tiny white villas gleaming in the hot Aegean sun, smiling at the local women huddled in their all-encompassing black dresses.

She wouldn't dream of riding on a scooter any more. Scooters and motorbikes were for the slim young girls you saw in tampon adverts, girls with bum-length hair, minuscule white shorts and lots of attitude. They were most definitely not for women who couldn't do up their jeans any more.

The newsroom was probably full of them, she reflected, cute model types drafted in to pose for snaps with the managing director. Maybe she could ask them for hints. She could drag a few of them up to Michael and ask them was he worth fighting for?

For a moment, she savoured a picture of Michael's face, red with anger at his wife calmly telling a group of gorgeous young women that he was a lying, cheating bastard. She'd never be able to do it, though. Fiona would, she'd *love* to do it, if Pat was ever dumb enough to betray her.

Aisling knew she'd only ever dream about slapping Michael. Like she'd dreamed of slapping her father's face every time he made her feel worthless and stupid. Was that all men ever did?

She leaned against the car and closed her eyes for a moment. She was dreading tonight, smiling hello to all Michael's colleagues, wondering what they'd think when they saw her – Michael Moran's once-slim wife transformed into a busty hausfrau with no conversation and zero style. No wonder he'd got himself a mistress when that was what he had to go home to at night, she could almost hear them saying. Damn him!

She slammed the car door shut and smoothed down her dress. No chickening out now.

Aisling was slightly out of breath when she made it to the imposing front doors where a security guard with a clipboard and a self-important expression on his face gazed down at her.

'I'm . . . er . . . expected at the party,' she stammered. 'The supplement . . . My husband works here . . .'

'Name?' queried the guard loftily, pen poised over his list.

'Aisling Moran,' she answered and, as if by magic, the man's stony face lit up.

'Mrs Moran! Grand to meet you at last. Come on in before those news hounds drink the place dry!'

She found herself being bustled over to the stairs where the guard yelled up for Mick '. . . to escort Mrs Moran to the party.'

Aisling had barely put a foot on the bottom step before another, much younger man in a similar navy uniform and a very short haircut materialised and walked with her up the stairs.

Aisling muttered something about not having been escorted anywhere for years.

'Not at all, Ma'am,' the muscular young man smiled cheerily. 'These stairs are a bit steep if you're not used to them and God knows you'd never find your way around the warren upstairs if you didn't know where you were going!'

He couldn't have been more than nine or ten years younger than she was but, from the way he was walking beside her at a snail's pace and the way he called her 'Ma'am', she was obviously a dead ringer for his mother. Marvellous.

'Bye now.' He gave her a good luck sort of grin and walked briskly back the way they had come, leaving her standing outside the newsroom, her heart thumping at the thought of making her entrance alone.

What are you doing here, she asked herself wretchedly? Why aren't you sitting at home with your head buried firmly in the sand as usual?

Because you have to find out what's going on, the voice in

her head pointed out calmly. And if you don't find out now, you never will. It's up to you whether you try and ignore his infidelity or whether you demand that it ends. Get a grip on yourself, Aisling, she said out loud. Go on!

She put one hand tentatively on the door before it swung back on her violently as two men in suits with ties askew pushed their way out of the office giggling hysterically.

'Aisling Moran! How are you?' Suddenly, she was grabbed by one of the revellers and enveloped in a bear hug.

'Tom,' she said with pleasure as she recognised the paper's chief sub-editor, one of Michael's best friends.

'I haven't seen you in an age,' he said warmly. A huge smile lit up his grey-bearded face. A tall man with hunched shoulders, Tom had always been in shape, but now sported a little pot belly under his straining shirt.

Aisling noticed the heavy sprinkling of grey in his hair and beard and realised, with a shock, that she hadn't seen him for well over two years.

But then, I haven't exactly turned the clock backwards myself, she thought wryly.

'How are you?' he roared merrily, sending strong whiskey fumes in her direction.

'This is your husband's big night, eh? You must be so proud. We all are.'

I'm bloody delirious, she thought, grinning back with a saccharine smile.

Tom pushed the swing doors open and led Aisling into a room which buzzed with activity. MTV, RTE, Super and Sky Sports belted out at top volume from the bank of TV screens on one wall. Nobody seemed to notice the cacophony made by Pearl Jam's latest hit, a droning Formula One race and the news in two languages. Instead, they screeched with laughter, talked rapidly and gestured for more drink as two harassed-looking girls wearing black skirts and white shirts circled the room balancing glasses on large trays.

People stood around in little groups of two or three, laughing and shouting at each other, sharing the jokes of colleagues who worked long hours together and knew each other better than their families.

'Are you saying I got that story from another paper?' she heard someone say indignantly.

'You'd swallow a brick, Pat!' said another voice. 'He's only winding you up for a bet. That's another drink you owe me, by the way, Shay.'

'They're all on form tonight,' chuckled Tom.

Aisling thought they all looked glamorous and dynamic. She'd always been in awe of her husband's colleagues, especially the women.

'Here we are,' she heard Tom say, as they pushed their way to the centre of the room where a group of people stood, listening to a tall, dark man.

Michael was holding court, as usual. He had this incredibly irritating habit of pontificating on all sorts of subjects, although politics was his favourite.

At home, he generally started giving Aisling his views on the most recent political crisis when she was ready to turn out her bedside light, or when she was just settling down to watch *ER*. He never realised that she was doing something else and wasn't necessarily interested in what he thought about the Labour Party's conference, or Bill Clinton's speech. But then he never noticed the way her eyes glazed over when he really got going.

Tonight he was on form, preaching about the changing role of newspapers in a world of instant TV news updates. It gave Aisling a glimmer of satisfaction to see one of the not-so-eager listeners raise her eyebrows at a colleague, tacit understanding of the boss's irritating idiosyncracies. Not everyone was as awestruck in his presence as Michael liked to imagine. For a brief moment, that was a very satisfying thought.

She watched silently, trying to look at him like a stranger seeing him for the first time. Tall, dark-eyed and with the type of bone structure the Marlboro man would have died for, he was, as most of his male colleagues complained, almost too bloody good-looking to have any brains at all.

Unfortunately for all the begrudgers, he was a brilliant writer and an even better editor. He had an ego to match. When the yearly influx of journalism students brought eager young women into the office, keen to learn every nuance of the job, they invariably developed crushes on the good-looking deputy editor.

Michael always made this sound funny, telling Aisling how they blushed when they offered to get him a sandwich at lunchtime or asked his advice on their stories instead of talking to the news editor. Despite the way he made these stories amusing, Aisling knew he was flattered by the attention. With Michael, flattery got you everywhere.

Not a quality to make a wife feel secure, Aisling reflected. She watched two of the younger female onlookers gaze longingly at her husband as though he were fillet steak and they'd been starved for a month.

Aisling could have told his admirers that he stared in that intense, Robert Redford sort of manner purely to focus his eyes when he wasn't wearing the stylish designer wire-rimmed glasses he'd bought a couple of years previously.

Of course, she never got the chance to tell anyone and she suspected that they wouldn't believe her anyway. She could imagine these particular admirers privately thinking that the deputy editor's piercing gaze was deeply sexy, something intended for them alone. Big mistake, girls.

'Michael, look who's arrived!' Tom announced cheerily. The entire group turned towards the newcomers. Aisling felt her face flush pinkly as everyone looked at her and hated herself for it. Michael leaned over and took her hand. He led her gently into the centre of the group, almost as if he was pleased to see her. What an actor.

'Aisling, these are most of my team for the supplement. Everyone else, this is Aisling, my wife.' Who was writing his lines, she wondered? Was this his 'caring editor' performance, designed to beguile the gazing students?

Aisling could see the amazement in the women's eyes as they took in her flushed face and less than perfect figure

63

hidden under a loud crimson dress. Gorgeous, clever Michael, one of the most talented journalists in Dublin, married to that! She was used to it now, that look of pity when her husband's admirers realised that their hero was stuck with the least attractive woman in the room.

At least she'd always been sure that *thinking* about her husband was as far as any of his female fans had ever got. She now had devastating proof that one woman had got a lot further than thinking.

As they muttered 'Hello' with varying degrees of enthusiasm, Aisling wondered if *she* was one of them. Maybe that was why Michael hadn't introduced anyone individually.

Perhaps she was standing there as cool as a cucumber, the blonde with the pancake make-up and the Kim Basinger lips, or the tall brunette with tortoiseshell glasses emphasising almond-shaped blue eyes and a thin silk blouse which left nobody in any doubt that she had bypassed the bra drawer when she was getting dressed.

Aisling watched her for a moment and turned her attention to the other women in the group. Would she recognise the other woman from Fiona's description, would she intuitively know who she was?

'Are you all right?' Her husband's voice broke into her thoughts. She raised cool blue eyes to meet his. Strange, she had expected him to look different now that she knew his secret, but he didn't.

He looked exactly the same as ever, a five o'clock shadow darkening his jaw, eyebrows raised in a quizzical expression.

Until today she'd have staked her life that Michael wouldn't dream of doing anything more than talking to another woman. She gazed at her husband, noticing the dark smudges under his eyes from the long nights he'd been working late to put the finishing touches to the supplement. That was what he'd said anyhow.

It was more likely he was exhausted from spending hours with *her*, sharing meals in their favourite restaurant before steaming up the windows of his car; the same car she drove to the supermarket at weekends with the boys squabbling in the back.

God, the betrayal. It hurt so much and it made her so angry. Twelve years of marriage had meant *nothing* to him if he could just forget about her and their sons for a few hot nights with some floozie.

'Are you all right?' he asked again. She turned away. Tom returned with the drink he'd offered to get for her: a large tumbler full of gin and tonic, strong and cool with plenty of ice clinking around the glass.

She smiled thanks at Tom and took a deep reviving slug, feeling the gin hit her system like an injection of adrenaline.

Michael had already moved his attention to the next subject, his personal interpretation of the latest political crisis in Washington.

'We have to talk.' Aisling surprised herself with the calmness of her voice as she reached out and tapped him on the shoulder. Ignoring the look of surprise on his companions' faces, she walked away from the group with him grudgingly following until they were out of earshot.

'What is it?' he asked impatiently. 'Why couldn't you tell me in the first place? Tell me, what's the big fuss?'

She looked steadily up at him. Would he lie or tell the truth? Probably lie.

'The big fuss is about Jennifer Carroll. Does that name sound a bit familiar to you?' She gazed at him expectantly. 'I know you're having an affair, Michael. So I think we need a private talk, don't you? Or do you want everyone on the premises to hear about your sordid secret, if they don't already know, that is,' she spat.

His eyes darkened. He stared at her with the same blank look she'd seen when he was stuck talking to someone he didn't like: cold and indifferent, his face impassive, his eyes saying nothing.

'How did you find out?' he asked, as casually as though she'd mentioned that the car was out of petrol.

'You should be more careful with your credit card receipts,' she answered. 'Didn't you know I'd find out if you left a receipt for Lingerie de bloody Paris in your navy suit pocket? Or did you want me to find out?'

'No.' He stared down at some spot on the grey speckled office carpet, seemingly miles away as though contemplating whether eighty per cent wool was more serviceable than pure wool carpet. 'I didn't want you to find out because it would hurt you and I never meant to do that.'

'Yeah, right.' Aisling laughed harshly, feeling red spots of colour burning on her cheeks. 'You just wanted everyone else to find out that you were cheating on your stupid wife. Let her find out from the neighbours! Was that the way you wanted it? Is there anything else I should know or are you taking out an advert in next week's paper?'

He had stopped looking at the carpet and was looking at her sadly, almost pityingly. Shrewd, dark eyes took in the new dress and the garish bright lipstick.

'Maybe I should have asked Fiona if you have a few other women stashed away somewhere? Or was one enough? Did you have a bet on with that bloody bitch to see how long you could keep me fooled?'

She paused for breath and took a huge drink from her glass. Her hands shook so much that the ice rattled noisily.

'It wasn't like that, Aisling,' he answered slowly. 'I didn't tell anyone and I thought we were discreet, although obviously I was wrong. I never wanted to hurt you.'

'Don't tell me,' she interrupted, 'it didn't mean a thing and you can't even remember her name. Is that your next line? Because *I* know her name, even if you pretend to have forgotten it. Jennifer Carroll, isn't it?'

She looked at him triumphantly, as though they were playing Trivial Pursuit and she'd just won a piece of pie.

'Just tell me one thing, Michael, why? Why did you do it? Don't you love me any more, don't you care about our marriage and the boys?'

Michael's eyes were still cold.

'I've loved you for thirteen years, Aisling,' he said. 'But I'm

66

not *in love* with you any more.' The emphasis on 'in love' hit her like a bullet. Was he really saying what she thought he was saying?

Michael shrugged and splayed his hands out in a gesture of apology.

'I'm sorry, but it's not as if you wanted to make our marriage work, is it? You just wanted to crawl into your shell and hide from the world.' She stared at him, disbelieving what she was hearing.

'You, the boys and your damned house, that's all that mattered to you. Not me.'

'You never wanted to be a part of my life, you never asked me anything about *my* day, what *I* did. It was always the boys. Did you ever remember that *we* got married, not you, me and two kids, but *us*?' As he warmed to what was obviously a familiar theme, his voice sounded harsher than she'd ever heard it before.

'No, you don't remember, do you?' he snarled. 'You cut me out of your cosy little life and I couldn't deal with that.'

He stopped, but his words hung in the air like icicles, cold and deadly. He could have stabbed her with them and it wouldn't have hurt as much as the look on his face hurt her.

She didn't want the marriage to work? For God's sake, she desperately wanted it to work but he hadn't given her any choice in the matter. He'd just run after some woman and now he wanted to make it all her fault!

'You've made it pretty clear that you don't want to be part of my life,' he continued, 'so I wanted someone who did want to be with me.'

His voice was calm. Maddeningly calm. She'd just confronted him with the biggest crisis a marriage could face and he was looking at her with calm indifference. He spoke about their marriage as if it was already dead as a dodo.

'Don't give me that rubbish!' she screamed. 'Lingerie de Paris and nights in Jurys isn't about our marriage not working. It's about sex – you and some other woman having sex.

'You just couldn't stop yourself, could you? Everything we

had just wasn't enough for you. So don't try and blame me. Don't tell me it's my fault!'

She stopped abruptly, aware that people nearby had stopped talking.

Normally, she'd have been embarrassed, but tonight she didn't give a damn who heard her. 'How dare you . . .'

'I'm not trying to blame you,' Michael interrupted. 'It's just that . . .' He sighed heavily. 'Look, we can't talk about this here with everyone watching and listening. Let's wait 'til we get home, OK?'

'Home! Let's wait 'til we get home!' she repeated shrilly. 'You conveniently forgot about home when you were shacked up with that bitch in a Dublin hotel, lying that you were in London! So you can forget about coming home with me! Your home is with your bloody girlfriend and I don't want to see you until you've dumped her!'

'Aisling.' He tried to grab her but she managed to shrug his arm off. The door. Where was the door? She couldn't see through her tears. She just pushed past the double doors before he caught up with her.

'Stop,' he commanded. And she did. Turning her round to face him, Michael looked her in the eyes, his pupils boring into hers intently.

'I never wanted to hurt you, Aisling,' he repeated. 'You have to believe that. But you've changed. I don't know what's happened to you, but you're different. It's as if you shut yourself off from me and I can't live like that. I'm sorry.

'You're right about me not coming home,' he added. 'It wouldn't work. It's better if I don't come home tonight. I wanted to tell you everything a long time ago, but I could never find the right time. I didn't want to hurt the kids but there's no time that's right for kids in the middle of a marriage break-up.'

She could feel the blood pumping through her body, keeping her alive when all she wanted to do was die.

She'd given him the chance, the chance to say he loved her and that it had all been an awful mistake. But he hadn't used

68

it. He had turned her own words against her.

God, if only she hadn't said he shouldn't come home, if only she'd kept her mouth shut and let him explain, let him beg forgiveness, surely everything would have been all right?

She'd given him a cast-iron excuse to leave. Aisling had never quite understood the expression 'time stood still', until that moment.

He was standing just a few feet away from her wearing a pale blue shirt with the top buttons open to reveal a few inches of tanned neck, a neck she had snuggled into when they sat on the couch watching TV late at night. His after-shave permeated the air and, if she reached out, she could touch him, hold him in her arms and be safe for ever.

Perhaps if she wished hard enough, she could turn back the clock and keep her mouth shut. Then he'd stay with her. Then he wouldn't need anyone else.

But it was too late. He didn't want her. He wanted another woman in his arms and in his life. Blindly, she took another huge gulp of her drink, wanting to blot out what had just happened.

'I'll stay in Tom's tonight and I'll be over to pick up some stuff in the morning.' Michael looked at her coolly, his eyes raking in the new dress and her flushed face, red from downing too much gin too rapidly.

'I better go back in. The MD is going to launch the supplement in a few minutes.'

Aisling looked at him mutely.

'Don't have any more to drink, Aisling,' he added coldly. 'I'm not going to drive you home if you get drunk, so you're on your own.'

With that he was gone, back to his besotted students and the whispering of colleagues who had seen everything.

Aisling slowly drained her glass and turned towards the stairs. So this is what heartache feels like, she thought numbly, walking slowly down the stairs, her beautiful new dress billowing out behind her.

The security guard at the door saw her walking towards him like a sleepwalker, her expression vacant and her eyes dull. He wanted to ask if she was all right, but he wasn't sure how to do it.

CHAPTER FIVE

Jo parked the car and got out quickly, noticing Aisling's car parked several spaces away. Great, she thought. She slammed the door shut and slipped her keys into her bag. We'll be able to catch up on all the gossip.

Jo hadn't walked more than five steps before she saw Aisling emerge from the front entrance. Even from a distance, Jo could see that her friend's complexion was ashen, an expression of sheer pain on her face.

Jesus, Jo thought, shocked. What could have happened? She ran towards Aisling, feeling the silk of her dress shimmer loosely around her body as she moved and realising that dainty heels and no bra were not ideal for running on gravel.

'What's wrong, Aisling? What's wrong?' Catching Aisling's hand in hers, Jo looked at her friend anxiously, her eyes seeking some reason for this terrible pallor, this frightening look of despair. 'Talk to me, Ash, please,' she pleaded.

'He's left me. He's in love with someone else,' Aisling said flatly, gazing into the middle distance with grief-stricken eyes.

Jo couldn't believe what she was hearing; Michael had left her? How ridiculous! Michael adored Aisling, worshipped the ground she walked on, didn't he?

Surely Aisling had got it wrong . . . or had she? Jo was dumbstruck. She simply didn't know what to say. Aisling stood there silently, the lines around her eyes and mouth set in hard, unyielding creases.

'He's not in love with me, you see,' said Aisling, like a child reciting a poem learned by rote. 'He's in love with her and it's all my fault.' She started to cry properly, great big heaving sobs which shook her body, as if she was coughing her last breath.

'Oh Ash.'

71

'I found out today,' Aisling wept. 'Fiona told me, she'd known for ages but she couldn't tell me. I know she couldn't tell me. And I was going to confront him, get him to say he was sorry and it would be all right. Everything would stay the same. But he won't, he won't . . .'

Aisling buried her head in Jo's shoulder, sobbing onto the silver knitted wrap Jo had worn to cover her slip dress in case she felt chilly.

What could Jo do but hold Aisling, trying to ease the hurt with a friend's arms when all Aisling wanted was her husband's arms, and his voice telling her it was over, that he loved her and no one else. But Jo suspected that Michael wouldn't be saying that. Not ever again, maybe. Who could have guessed, who'd have known, that this seemingly devoted couple were on their way to splitting up? Maybe she'd have seen it coming if she hadn't buried herself in Richard's life, neglecting her old friends for him.

'Come and sit in my car,' she cajoled. 'Please, Aisling, please.'

'Can't. I have to go home to the boys. I told the baby-sitter I wouldn't be long.'

Aisling sniffled and found a scrunched-up piece of tissue in her bag among the shopping lists and Saturday morning under-elevens' soccer timetables. She took a deep breath and looked at Jo.

'Don't be silly, Ash. Just sit with me for a few moments and stop crying. You can't drive home like this.'

She steered Aisling over to her car, opened the passenger door and helped her in as if she was an invalid.

'I'm so sorry, so sorry,' sobbed Aisling. 'I just don't know what to do. How could this happen, I just don't know?'

'Oh, you poor thing.' Jo leaned over the handbrake and hugged Aisling warmly, wishing she knew what to say. She tried to remember the sort of advice the magazine's agony aunt would give, but found herself remembering the medical advice for first-time mothers over the age of thirty.

Aisling hiccuped. 'I knew things were different lately, but I

72

thought it was me. I thought I'd got into a rut and that I had to sort myself out. But I never even thought of this. How could I?

'Was I the only person who didn't know or should I have realised something was wrong? I don't know.' She broke off suddenly, staring out the windscreen at nothing in particular.

'Look Ash, there's no point torturing yourself now. Maybe it was just a short-term thing, maybe he's sorry but he's not able to admit it.'

'No, it's not just a fling. It's serious. He said our marriage was over.'

Jo stared silently at her friend, knowing that there was no quick solution to this problem. She opened the glove compartment, found a pack of travel tissues and handed Aisling one to replace the soggy, twisted one which was crumbling in her hands.

Just moments ago, she had felt like someone living a glorious dream life of motherhood, with a fairytale wedding and contented family life just waiting in the wings. Now she felt about a hundred years old and very weary. Aisling and Michael had always epitomised the perfect couple to her: what hope was there if *they* couldn't make it?

It wasn't as if Jo hadn't witnessed enough relationship and marriage break-ups already. She knew plenty of people who'd fought tooth and nail over every stick of furniture in their soon-to-be-sold house and automatically hissed 'that *bitch*' or 'what a *bastard*' when anyone mentioned their ex-partners' names.

She'd learned to be careful when she bumped into people she hadn't seen for a while – you just never knew what a simple question like 'How's Gerry?' could provoke.

'Burning in Hell, I hope!' snarled one bitter friend the previous Christmas, when Jo had innocently inquired after the other woman's once-adored husband.

She knew it was silly, but she'd always had this rose-coloured view of the Morans' marriage. Maybe it was because she'd been so close to Aisling all those years ago and so

73

thrilled when she'd fallen in love with Michael, but Jo really believed that they were perfect for one another. How blind had she been? A perfect house, two lovely children, a wife delighted to play housekeeper-cum-nanny and a handsome husband didn't necessarily make an ideal marriage.

'I have to go home, Jo.' Aisling straightened up. 'The boys are with the baby-sitter and I must go home to them, honestly.' She smiled briefly, the professional-mother smile dusted off and brought down from the attic for an emergency. 'You go on, I'll be fine.'

'I can't leave you like this.' Jo was horrified. 'Don't be ridiculous, Ash . . .'

'You're here to go to the party. They expect you.' Aisling shrugged, checking her blotchy face in the mirror. 'I'll talk to you tomorrow.' She managed a grim smile.

'I'm sorry, Jo. I shouldn't have told you this, it's not your problem.'

'Of course, it's . . . well, OK, it's not my problem,' Jo stammered, 'but you're my friend, Ash, and you shouldn't be on your own tonight. I just have to see Richard for a moment . . .' She broke off, desperate to tell Richard her news and knowing that Aisling wouldn't want to wait there a moment longer. 'There's something I *have* to tell him.'

'Don't worry,' replied Aisling brusquely. 'I'll ring Fiona when I get home. She'll come in.' Aisling opened the car door and got out with Jo following her.

God, this was awful, Jo thought in distress. What was she going to do? Damn Richard for not picking her up earlier. She'd have told him about the baby by now and she could've driven Aisling home, instead of having to leave her in this condition. What the hell was she to do?

Aisling made the decision for her.

'Thank you, Jo.' Aisling reached over and took Jo's hand. 'I'll phone you tomorrow. You go on in.'

'Don't go . . . Ash,' begged Jo. 'Hang on for a couple of minutes, please. I can't let you drive home on your own in this state.'

74

'I'm fine,' Aisling insisted. 'Fiona will be at home this evening. She wants me to ring her as soon as I get in.'

'You can't drive like this,' protested Jo.

'I'm fine, really. I'll be home in half an hour.'

'You promise you'll ring Fiona?' Jo demanded, feeling torn.

'Yes. I promise, I promise on my granny's life.' The corner of Aisling's mouth lifted into a slight smile at the words, an old joke shared by two flatmates many years ago. Aisling had always hated her grandmother with a vengeance.

But how was the landlord supposed to know that when the demure insurance clerk from the basement flat innocently promised not to have any parties, 'On my granny's life.'

Then Aisling was gone, hurrying towards her car before Jo had a chance to stop her. She watched Aisling drive slowly out the front gate with misgivings, praying that she'd get home safely, hoping she would have the sense to ring her neighbour for help. Mind you, what could anyone do?

Suddenly she didn't feel like going to a party after all. Poor Aisling, she thought, and what about Phillip and Paul? They were too young to deal with their parents splitting up. How could a couple of ten-year-olds understand the notion of separation or divorce? Jo's hand slipped to rest on her stomach. I'll never let anyone hurt you, my darling, she murmured. Nobody will hurt you.

She walked slowly towards the entrance, the jaunty spring in her step gone. When she pushed open the heavy newsroom doors, she was greeted with cries of hello as her ex-colleagues waved celebratory bottles of beer and glasses. The usual suspects were out in force, she noticed, making her way expertly through the throng, waving hello here, shaking hands there, without stopping at all. It was a trick she'd learned early in her journalistic career and was very useful for avoiding people you couldn't stand or people who'd talk all night once they'd started.

Jo skirted the groups of merrymakers, smiling and waving to all comers. She needed a party like she needed a hole in the head but there was no escaping this one. Half an hour with

Janice would undoubtedly cheer her up.

Janice O'Brien was talking nineteen to the dozen as per usual at a makeshift bar at the back of the newsroom. Janice and her companions *appeared* to be testing different types of lager and seeing who could tell the difference between Smirnoff, Stolichnaya and Absolut.

Jo knew better. With someone else paying the bar bill, the *News* team could pile up empty bottles faster than women queuing to see the Chippendales. Ridiculously large numbers of bottles were already empty, lined up against the wall awaiting disposal.

'Where have you been, sexy?' Nick Cullen slid an arm around her and planted a hot, beery kiss on her cheek. Tall, muscular and able to hold his beer better than any barrel, Nick was a brilliant reporter and a dreadful flirt, always keen to bring the female reporters off to the pub.

'You can't be pissed already,' Jo asked as she pushed him away.

'In an act of selflessness,' Brian Reddin interrupted, 'we started earlier on our own so we wouldn't drink this bar dry.'

'Thank God you've come!' said Janice gratefully, pulling her friend over to lean against a photocopier. 'This pair of lushes have been keeping me prisoner here, making me get them drinks all evening.'

'All that exercise must be great training for the marathon, then,' Jo commented. 'I still can't believe you're drunk already,' she added, poking Nick in the chest.

'Is Richard coming tonight?' Janice inquired, reaching back to the bar as she poured a stiff gin and tonic for her friend.

'Yes. I thought he'd be here already but I couldn't see his car,' said Jo, scanning the room for a sight of her boyfriend's short blond hair.

'He's supposed to be working tonight and didn't have time to pick me up before he got here, so where in the hell could he be? Unless he was in earlier and decided to wait until the party was really going. Did he?' she looked at the others.

'We haven't seen your Viking at all this evening,' interjected Nick, using the nickname which irritated the hell out of Richard, 'so you're mine for the night, gorgeous. Love the dress.' His bleary eyes lit up appreciatively as he took in Jo's curves accentuated by her clinging silken dress.

'Thanks, Nick, I wore it specially for you, of course.'

'Oh really . . . D'you fancy you and I taking a stroll to the photocopier to see if you really *can* photocopy your bum and bonk at the same time?'

'Since I don't fancy seeing my derrière in full blown-up glory all over the newsroom next time I come here, I think I'll pass, if it's all the same to you,' she replied tartly.

Jo took the drink Janice had poured for her, knowing that refusing alcohol would automatically start Janice's mind ticking furiously. She waited until Janice was mixing up a drink for herself, then she reached back and swopped her gin and tonic for a glass of mineral water.

Then she hoisted herself onto one of the desks and sat back as Janice filled her in on the latest gossip. Everyone was asking who would get the fashion editor's job when Anita Brady left the following month to edit a new woman's magazine.

'They'll never get anyone as good,' remarked Janice, reaching out to spear a cocktail sausage from a passing waitress. 'Oh, these are lovely,' she squealed as she bit into the succulent flesh. 'Come back here immediately!'

'Anita's hell to work for,' she added, taking four more sausages from the waitress. 'But she's good at her job, so you have to learn to live with the temper tantrums. It's the husband I feel sorry for. You can't blame him for seeking solace in the arms of another woman when he's married to the sort of cow who could put Mike Tyson in hospital.'

Jo looked up sharply, searching Janice's face for a hint of ambiguity. Did she know about Michael and Aisling? But Janice had moved on from infidelity to incompetence.

'That nauseous Denise Keogh from features. She obviously thinks she's a dead cert for the job even though she has as much fashion sense as a lobotomised gorilla.'

77

'Don't mock, Janice,' interrupted Brian. 'The odds are two to one that she gets the job and you've a tenner on her to win!'

'Only because her uncle owns shares in the bloody paper,' said Janice caustically, 'and because I like to bet on dead certs. If she *does* get the job, I'll bet you twenty quid that her first fashion spread is on leg warmers, tank tops and frizzy hair. Oh yeah, and blue eyeliner.'

She broke off as they spotted Richard pushing his way through the partygoers. A tall willowy blonde in a slinky black mini-dress followed close behind like a puppy on a lead.

'Nice dress she's nearly wearing,' remarked the columnist with a flash of the bitchiness for which she was renowned. 'I've got scarves bigger than that.'

'Miaow, miaow.' Nick wagged a finger in Janice's direction. 'I think it's a lovely dress.'

'You would,' she replied smartly. 'That's because when you think at all, you think from below the belt.'

Nick sniggered into his beer again and nearly lost his balance as a result, but Jo didn't notice even when he grabbed her to steady himself. She watched her boyfriend, the father of her unborn baby, talking animatedly with his beautiful companion as he strolled round the room sizing up photographic opportunities.

The blonde simpered and giggled every few steps, licking her lips in what she obviously thought was a very sexy manner.

'Hello, darling.' Richard smiled at Jo when he and the blonde reached her corner of the room. 'This is Sascha, Will's sister. She's just started freelancing in Paris with *Now* magazine and she's doing a piece on Dublin social life.'

'I thought she was working undercover on a prostitution story,' Janice muttered under her breath.

Nobody heard. They were all staring at the blonde apparition in front of them. Sascha smiled at the group from sleepy green eyes, seemingly unconcerned that she'd forgotten either a reporter's notebook or tape recorder and had been gazing only at the handsome photographer instead of keeping her eyes peeled for material.

'I'm sure I know you from somewhere, don't I?' asked Janice, eyes narrowed as she tried to remember where she'd seen the other woman before.

'Didn't you do some modelling for one of the British catalogues?' she asked. 'Next, was it?'

'Yeah,' Sascha smiled again, displaying perfect white teeth and the self-confidence of a woman who knows she'd look fabulous wearing a bin-liner.

'I was with the Première agency for a couple of years and I did a lot of work in Japan.' She paused, giving the three men the benefit of another practised hundred-watt smile.

'I've left modelling. I'm just getting into writing now. I feel I'm a natural writer, y'know, it comes from in here.' She touched her tanned cleavage. Richard's gaze slid down to the spot in question as if mesmerised by her model-girl 32A chest. 'So I'm going to try reporting and then go home and get on with a book or something.'

The two female journalists stared silently at her beautiful blank face, wondering what besotted commissioning editor had given Sascha the job of writing about one of the world's literary capitals, when it was clear that any word longer than two syllables would involve a lengthy consultation with the dictionary.

'When did you start writing?' Jo asked kindly.

'Last month,' said Sascha happily. 'I've just done an article on modelling and some of the girls said I wouldn't be able to do it, but I think writing comes from the heart, doesn't it? I know I can do it.'

Sascha smiled at everyone broadly. 'I've been doing this personal development course and when I focus my energy on something, I can make it happen. That's what my counsellor says anyway. You're all writers, huh?'

'You could say that,' Janice answered, sarcasm dripping from every syllable. 'We just dabble, you understand. I'm still not sure whether I should stick with writing or focus on brain surgery, perhaps. Decisions, decisions.'

Jo smiled nervously up at Richard, hoping that he'd read her mind and leave Sascha to her life story so they could talk quietly together. 'Would you like a drink, darling?' she murmured. But he had other ideas.

'No, duty first. I better take a few pictures.'

Jo moved closer to him, breathing in the lemony smell of Eau Sauvage and the faint fragrance of fabric conditioner from his pristine cotton shirt. God, she loved the way he smelled, the way his skin tasted, the way he always looked.

Tonight, dressed in a plain charcoal grey suit which she knew had cost about a month's salary, he oozed style and elegance. Compared to Brian and Nick in their casual chain-store chic, *he* looked like a model from the Next catalogue.

And he was all hers. She couldn't help feeling a little self-satisfied as she pulled his head down and whispered into his ear. 'I've something really, really special to tell you. Follow me.'

With an apologetic glance at Sascha, Richard followed Jo into one of the glass-fronted offices which opened onto the newsroom. He leaned up against a steel grey filing cabinet and Jo wrapped her arms around his waist, leaning her head against the comforting bulk of his chest.

'You know you said that you never expected to settle down with anyone in the way you have with me,' she began. 'Well, I think we're going to become really settled soon. In about seven months,' she added with a little laugh.

'We're going to have a baby!' Looking up excitedly, Jo waited to see Richard's reaction. He was going to be thrilled, she was sure.

'Well,' she whispered, 'what do you think? You're pleased, aren't you?' He was speechless.

Of course, it was a shock, a *huge* shock, she knew that. And it would take a moment to sink in. But he'd be so pleased, wouldn't he?'

'Say something,' she said nervously.

'Oh, I just don't know what . . .' He stopped mid-sentence,

an expression of mounting shock on his face.

'How could it happen?' he stuttered. 'This is unbelievable, I don't believe it.'

'I know it's a shock, darling,' she said swiftly, wanting him to take her in his arms. 'I'm having our baby, Richard,' she said softly. 'Aren't you pleased?'

She stared up at him, willing him to smile and kiss her. She wanted to feel strong arms around her and his voice telling her it would be all right. But he stared at her with the sort of expression she had only ever seen on his face when Ireland was thrashed at Landsdowne Road or when an entire roll of film had been overexposed.

Jo felt nausea quiver in the pit of her stomach. She couldn't believe this was happening. This was the moment when Richard should kiss her and hug her as if she was Belleek china. If she was china, he obviously didn't like the pattern. What the hell was going on?

'B-b-but how?' he asked incredulously.

Jo's temper suddenly snapped. 'Jesus, Richard, what do you want, a biology lesson? How the bloody hell do you think it happened?'

She knew she sounded shrewish and she didn't care. Richard was supposed to love her and she had just told him the most wonderful news in the world. And all he could do was stammer and stutter and ask how it happened!

'This is our baby!' she cried. 'Don't you care? Aren't you happy? We're going to be parents in seven months, Richard!'

'I don't believe this,' he said hoarsely, 'how could you be pregnant?'

'Well I suppose it must have something to do with making love, which we do all the time, and the fact that condoms aren't one hundred per cent safe. Look, I only found out this morning,' she said, suddenly weary.

'I know we didn't plan it . . .'

'You can say that again,' he snapped.

'Look, it just happened, right? I'm as surprised as you are, Richard.' Jo rubbed one hand over her left temple, feeling the familiar throbbing migraine build up.

'What was I supposed to do? Shut up and pray it would go away, like a terrified sixteen-year-old girl? I thought you'd be happy and that you wanted to settle down finally,' she hesitated for a moment. 'The baby's due in January.'

'What do you mean it's due in January?' he asked. 'Jesus, we're not ready for a baby, I mean, why didn't you tell me?' he said incredulously.

'I *am* telling you,' she answered.

'I do not believe this is happening, I just don't believe it,' he repeated, running a hand jerkily through his hair. 'OK, let's think about this. Who else have you told? Not that bloody Janice I hope, otherwise it'll be all over the place like a rash. You know what she's like,' he spat.

'I didn't want to tell anyone until I told you,' she faltered.

'Look Jo, this is an awful mess, can't you see? I don't want children, not now anyway. I'm not ready for all that stuff yet, you know that. What made you think differently?'

Jo stepped away from him. For the second time that day, her pulse was racing and she could feel the blood racing in her veins.

All she wanted to do was sink into her bed at home and close her eyes, or start reading her latest book, curled up under the duvet. And not think, not think about anything.

'Let me get this straight. You don't want this child,' Jo said quietly, 'and you don't want to settle down with me. Have I got that right?'

Her face was pale as she looked at him, wanting the truth, hoping that his answering smile would abruptly banish any doubts. She could hear sounds of merriment coming from the newsroom. Corks were popping. Jo guessed that the paper's managing director was about to launch the supplement with a champagne toast.

At the sound, Richard unconsciously reached for the camera slung around his neck on a fraying Canon strap and looked longingly in the direction of the party.

Jo was close to tears but she had to get an answer from him.

'Talk to me, Richard. What do you want to do?'

'Oh God, Jo, why did you get pregnant, now of all times?' He ran a hand through his hair and for a brief moment she remembered lying in the Egyptian cotton sheets on his bed, running her fingers through his hair while he lay sexually sated in her arms. They were so close, that was why she could never have imagined this.

'Why now, of all times? In a few years, yes, but not now.' He looked at her beseechingly, like a naughty boy who's just sent his football through the neighbour's kitchen window.

'Will can look after the agency for a few years and I planned to go to London to work with one of the sports papers there. It's a brilliant opportunity, darling. I was going to ask you to come with me.' He was pleading now.

'It'll be marvellous. Just a few more years and then we can settle down and maybe have kids if you really want them . . .'

His voice rose excitedly as he looked eagerly at Jo, waiting for her to agree, waiting for her to smile and say what she'd always said, 'Whatever you want.'

Memories came flooding back to her, memories of the times she'd asked him about his previous relationships. Among the litany of model girlfriends, there had been one long-lasting relationship with a German girl who had left Dublin when she and Richard broke up.

'Beate wanted to settle down and I just wasn't ready for that.' Richard shrugged. 'We were too young.' She'd believed his simple explanation, grateful that he hadn't wanted to marry any of her predecessors, and that he'd been too young to settle down with the only one who sounded like a true love.

Richard Fitzgerald had once been the Don Juan of the photographic world, but she had tamed him. He'd given up a lifetime of bimbos to be with her, or so she'd thought.

He wasn't too young to settle down any more: he was thirty-seven to her thirty-four. Surely it was time for him to stop running away from responsibility and start a family? Obviously not.

83

Commitment-phobic, Janice had called him the first time she had seen him. Perhaps her friend had been right.

Richard gently stroked her palm, tracing delicate circles and kneading the fleshy base of her thumb. People with lots of soft flesh in that precise spot were supposed to be very sensual he had always said, joking that she must be the sexiest woman in the world because of her soft, caressing hands.

Before, when he'd murmured endearments into her ear and stroked her skin, her heart leapt with love for this funny and talented man. Not tonight.

'Darling, don't be upset, please.' He was all charm again. He'd always been able to charm his way out of any trouble. He just smiled that boyish smile and wheedled until she gave in and forgave him.

Like that time he'd promised to pick her up from the office Christmas party and simply never showed up. It had taken two hours to get a taxi that night because the streets were black with ice and half the city had left the car at home so they could get drunk.

He'd been so contrite, so full of remorse at having forgotten all about the party, that she'd forgiven him by lunchtime the next day. It was funny the way he never forgot any professional commitments, only personal ones.

'We can have children later, my darling,' he said pleadingly. 'We're not ready for this yet, are we?' he murmured, reaching out to stroke her cheek, waiting for her to give in. She always gave in, Jo realised suddenly. For all his relaxed charm and boyishness, Richard always got his own way. In everything. It didn't matter whether they'd argued over where to go for dinner or what film to see, somehow Richard always got what he wanted. For once, he was out of luck.

'What are you suggesting?' she asked, her voice dangerously low.

'Well,' he looked around as if to check that nobody could hear them, 'you know, get rid of it.'

She snatched her hand away as though his fingers were burning her, staring him in the face angrily.

'And if I don't "get rid of it" as you so euphemistically call it, what then?'

'Jo, you're being unreasonable. All I'm saying is that this is the wrong time in my life for a baby.' Richard's face was fast losing its engaging smile. 'I'm not ready for it. *We're* not ready for it.'

'No, *you're* not ready. You're so bloody selfish,' she hissed. 'You just couldn't bear to have to think about someone else besides yourself. We can't have a defenceless baby interrupting your plans, or getting in the way of your life, can we?'

'There's no need to be insulting.' Richard gave her one of his superior looks and tried another tack. 'We should talk about this tomorrow when you're less hysterical.'

'Hysterical!' Jo hadn't felt so close to hitting anyone in years. 'That's typical! Just because I'm pregnant, I've suddenly turned into a neurotic, moody brood mare with no brain whatsoever,' she shouted.

'Shush, someone will hear,' Richard hissed.

'Oh, we can't have that, can we?' she snarled. 'Listen, I don't care who hears me. In fact, I want everyone to hear me so I can find out what they think about the wonderful photographer everyone adores begging his girlfriend to have an abortion because it's ". . . not the right time in my life". When will it be the right time, Richard? Because you're running out of time, you're nearly forty, don't forget.

'It's not as if we were two scared teenagers or didn't have any money either,' she glared at him. 'We can certainly afford another mouth to feed and let's face it, the world will hardly be scandalised by us having a baby and not being married, Richard. So what's wrong with me having our baby?'

If someone had told her that her feelings for him could be reversed in a matter of moments, she'd have laughed at the idea. Nothing could wipe out the love she felt for Richard, the bond which tied them to each other, she would have said. But that was before he had looked her in the eye and suggested that she abort the child she wanted with all her soul.

'I'm no good with children,' Richard said helplessly. His

85

fingers played nervously with the frayed camera strap in a way that she found suddenly irritating.

'If you want it, it's your decision. I'll give you the money if you change your mind.'

'Keep your money. I don't want it or any part of you,' Jo said coldly. 'I'm having this baby, Richard, and that's final. You can go off with Sascha and play at being adults. She's just about the right IQ level for you and she's unlikely to ask you to do anything more taxing than teach her to read!'

Furious, Richard turned and stormed back into the newsroom while Jo walked slowly over to an open window and breathed in deeply. Gradually her pulse slowed down and she opened her eyes to stare out at the city silhouetted in the dusk.

In the middle of the towering spires and office blocks, she could see the minty-green-domed roof of Rathmines church, the one she and Aisling had gone to when they lived a stone's throw around the corner. Well, the one Aisling had gone to.

She remembered the thrill of Sunday mornings in the flat when there was nobody there to tell you to get up and get ready for Mass. Luxuriating in her comfy single bed, Jo always snuggled in deeper, resisting Aisling's attempts to get her to come to eleven Mass.

Aisling had loved sitting in the huge dark church. She said that Sunday Mass in the huge church was the only time that the various people of Dublin's flatland came together, until Jo remarked that not everyone in Rathmines was Catholic.

'You know what I mean,' Aisling said in exasperation. 'It doesn't matter to me what religion people are, it's just that sense of being together for a while. It would feel the same in any church or mosque or whatever,' she added passionately.

Sometimes she managed to drag Jo out of bed and hurried her along with the other, more eager churchgoers. And Jo had enjoyed Mass. The anonymity of this church made a change from Mass in her small home town where you knew everyone's great-granny's uncle, what they did for a living and why young P. J. had turned out bad.

In Innisbhail, she'd explained to Aisling, all you had to do was ask the chemist for some throat lozenges and half an hour later every second person on the street would ask you how you were feeling.

She'd had so many plans when she left her home town in Sligo to go to journalism college. Journalistically, she was going to change the world and if she didn't win a Pulitzer prize for her ruthless exposés of injustice, she was damn well going to win the Booker for her novels.

So much for literature, she thought wryly, when you can't even find yourself a decent man who'll stand by you. Her hands involuntarily slid down towards her stomach, caressing the tiny bulge which was probably more Twix bars than baby.

That other girl, the one with all those crazy dreams, was long gone. In her place was a strong woman who was determined to be the best mother she could for her baby, her fatherless baby.

She'd certainly written enough articles about single parents, now she was going to find out what it really felt like. When she'd interviewed women who'd been left holding the baby, she'd wondered how they got by on their own. Now that her own selfish boyfriend had run for the hills, she was going to find out about single motherhood the hard way.

CHAPTER SIX

Warm breath fanned her cheek. Aisling stretched her limbs
under the duvet. She knew she had to get up. But . . . Just
another few minutes on the warm, soft sheets, just a bit
longer . . .

Hold on a moment. Her brain switched on weakly. It's
Saturday. Why was Michael trying to wake her early on a
Saturday morning, she wondered sleepily? And why did she
have this leaden feeling in her head?

A waft of hot, fishy breath made her open gluey eyelids to
gaze up at Flossie who was standing on Michael's pillow. Push
off, Aisling groaned, wishing Flossie would go away and let her
have just a few more hours in bed. Why hadn't Michael let
the cat out? Couldn't he do anything around the house?

She moved into a more comfortable position and pretended
to be asleep, hoping the cat would be fooled and leave. Flossie
didn't budge and started up her secret weapon, a peculiar
bad-tempered miaow which was simply impossible to ignore.

'All right, all right! I swear I'm getting you a cat-flap today!'

Aisling struggled up on the pillow. It felt as if an army band
was rehearsing some horrible marching song, using her skull
for drums. She squinted at the clock-radio – 8.17 a.m. and
Saturday. Where the hell was Michael? He couldn't have gone
to the office already, could he?

Then her brain made the unwelcome connection.

Michael hadn't let the cat out because Michael wasn't
there. He had left her. Their marriage was over and she had a
hangover roughly the size of France. She'd only just woken up
and immediately she wanted to go right back to sleep, maybe
for a hundred years.

Rolling over onto her stomach and abruptly dislodging
Flossie, Aisling laid her head heavily on the pillow and felt

miserable. Sober and sick, she began to remember the day before with horrible clarity.

Underwear, expensive underwear. Oh God, she remembered. She could dimly remember shopping with Fiona, her mind befuddled with Valium. And of course that slice of banoffi in the coffee shop which must have been at least 400 calories. Forget the bloody banoffi.

She could even recall arriving at Michael's office, even though the picture in her head was Technicolor high drama, very *Gone with the Wind* and utterly removed from reality. But after that . . . It was all hazy, like she had been utterly drunk and had blacked out.

Only she hadn't got drunk until much later. She hadn't got drunk until she arrived home and proceeded to drink everything in the house with an anguished Jo begging her to stop.

'You don't know what he's done,' she remembered saying as she sat at the kitchen table with the brandy bottle in one hand and a tissue in the other.

Of course Jo knew damn well what had happened. Aisling had explained everything in lurid detail, over and over again as she sank deeper into depression. And deeper into the brandy bottle. They'd discussed the whole sordid thing endlessly, from the 'men stray, so what?' theory put forward by Jo when she still thought it would all blow over, to the 'OK, he's a bastard – *all* men are bastards' conclusion.

She remembered Jo telling her about the baby, and about Richard's reaction.

'I couldn't believe it, Ash,' Jo had said, staring into the depths of the mug of tea she was cradling in her hands. 'I just never thought he'd react like that.'

'The funny thing is,' Jo continued, 'I wasn't really sure what I wanted myself at first. I kept wondering was I ready for motherhood and stuff like that. And then I did the test and I just knew, I knew I wanted the baby so badly.'

She paused and looked at Aisling, dark eyes brimming with unshed tears. 'You know what I mean, you felt that way about the twins, I remember. When you got pregnant, I really envied you. You were so happy, so content. Look at me,' she gave a sad little laugh, 'I'm a bloody wreck.'

Swept up in her own misery and with three large brandies inside her to numb the pain, Aisling hadn't really registered the awful state Jo was in.

'He'll change his mind,' she'd declared confidently. What a stupid thing to say. Poor Jo, alone except for a drunken friend wallowing in self-pity. She must have been so drunk. She couldn't even remember Jo leaving and she had no idea how she got into bed. Did she get into bed herself or did Jo help her? How horrible. And what sort of a mother did that make her?

Too damn drunk to notice if the poor twins had been sick or needed her in the middle of the night. Who knew what terrible thing could have happened and she wouldn't have been able to pull herself out of the bed to help them. She was just a useless, fat cow. No wonder Michael hadn't wanted her.

Staring at the sulky lump which Flossie had curled herself into on the end of the bed, Aisling remembered the confrontation with the man she loved and she wanted to curl up catlike herself and die.

What had she done? Why had she given him the chance to leave? She should have said nothing and maybe everything would have been all right. As each moment passed, another agonising moment of the night before came back to her, little spiteful daggers shooting into her heart.

She remembered confronting Michael in front of everyone, screaming like a fishwife in her eye-catching red dress, baring her soul and her dirty laundry in public. And she remembered hearing his cold response.

He didn't love her, he couldn't bear to be in the same house as her, for God's sake. She had been discarded like an old pair of shoes, used and dumped when they started letting rain in and were no longer fashionable. His horrible cutting words came flooding back into her mind and she finally stopped fighting the misery. Hot, hopeless tears soaked into the pillow as her predicament became clear: she was alone, alone for always.

The thought made her cry harder, so she didn't hear Paul run into the bedroom, shouting: 'Mum, Mum. Look what Phillip did! Mum? Mum?'

Despite her misery, Aisling's mummy autopilot cranked into action and she buried her swollen eyes in the pillow so that he wouldn't see how wretched she looked.

'I'm sick, darling. I think I've got that awful cold Aunt Fiona had and my eyes hurt. But you can help, Paul. Would you let Flossie out and . . . get me some milk?'

It was a calculated move. Phillip would have demanded to know why. *Why* was she sick, why wasn't Daddy there, why did he have to get the milk, why couldn't he have the money for rollerblades? Luckily, Paul was less cerebral. Not as clever at school as his twin, he was much easier to handle and could be told what to do, as long as Phillip wasn't with him.

Getting milk was a mission from Mum and he was a special agent, ready to spring into action. Full of delighted self-importance and with his brother's misdemeanour forgotten, Paul was already swinging down the banisters, eager to prove himself manly enough to look after his mother.

God, the lies adultery generated, Aisling thought morosely. Well, I can't tell two ten-year-olds that their father has run off with another woman and that their mother is on the verge of a nervous breakdown. Hah! There was a film about that: *Women on the Edge of a Nervous Breakdown.*

She'd seen it in the video shop although she'd never got it out. Perhaps now was the time to watch it. Maybe it had hints on how to get a life. Like 'lose two stone, get a great job, get yourself a toy boy and murder your cheating husband'. Easier said than done, of course.

Grimacing at the dull ache in her head, Aisling hauled herself out of bed and stood in front of the mirror, not exactly delighted with what she saw. Her eyelids were swollen and pink like pigs' trotters, her face was an unbecoming shade of beige with grey highlights and her hair was greasy after a night of sweating out more gin and brandy than was good for your liver.

91

Even the cute Honey Bunny picture on her nightie was faded and misshapen after years in the sixty-degree hot wash. Just like me, she mouthed silently. Wonderful. How come Danielle Steel's heroines never looked like they'd spent the night under a bush in the park when their lovers walked out on them, she thought miserably, picking up her brush.

They always looked even more fragile and doll-like than ever, with every bit of Estée Lauder still in its rightful place and not a hair escaping from the artful chignon they'd been taught to do in their Swiss finishing school.

They didn't let themselves go, reach for the gin and scrub their skin raw from using kitchen roll to wipe away the tears. Deep in dreamland, she nearly jumped out of her skin when the phone rang, its blistering peal assaulting her already painful head. She let out a deep breath, wondering whether she'd be able to face answering it. What would she say if it was her mother ringing up for a chat?

Hi, Mum. Yes, I'm fine. I've had a pretty normal week, y'know. The twins love summer camp, I've finished redecorating the downstairs toilet and Michael has left me, that's all really. How about you?

The phone continued to ring. Go on, do it, she muttered. You can't hide for ever. Her hands were shaking as she picked up the receiver and she didn't know whether she was shaking with delayed shock or hangover.

'I was nearly going to hang up,' exclaimed Jo, sounding worried. 'How do you feel?'

'Delirious. Except for the fact that my head is about to explode with a hangover and my life is in pieces.'

'Join the club,' Jo said mournfully. 'I've been going over everything in my head and wondering what I've done wrong.' She sniffled. 'Sorry. I didn't mean to moan at you. It's not your fault that my bloody lover has abandoned me and my bump.'

'It's not your fault either, Jo. I've been thinking about you and how useless I was last night. I'm sorry. All I could do was cry about my problems. You must be in bits, you poor thing.' Back in her familiar role as comforter, Aisling began to feel

92

marginally better all of a sudden. Someone else's troubles made her momentarily forget her own and she could wallow in Jo's misery instead.

After all, she was married to Michael and nobody could take that away from her, whereas Jo was left with nothing but an extra toothbrush in her bathroom and an unborn child whose feckless father had disowned him/her. What could be worse than having one of the most wonderful times of your life ruined when you were left to go through it all on your own. Then again, what help had being married been to her? Damn all. Married or unmarried, no commitment was worth the paper it was written on unless the other person meant it.

'I was awake half the night thinking just that: that it was *all* my fault,' Jo was saying. 'My fault for getting pregnant and my fault for blithely assuming that Richard would want to be a father, as opposed to being just a sperm donor, of course.' Her voice was bitter and harsh.

'Not that he minded being a sperm donor from the fun point of view . . .'

'None of them do,' interrupted Aisling drily.

'Too bloody true. But at least most men can accept their responsibilities. Richard certainly doesn't want to. Oh damn. There's my doorbell.' Jo sounded flustered. 'Hold on a minute, will you.'

Poor, poor Jo, Aisling reflected, automatically starting to pull up the duvet and plump the pillows with the phone wedged in the crook of her neck.

Remembering her own pregnancy made her smile to herself as she worked: that magic moment when she told Michael they were having a baby – that was before she knew she was carrying twins, of course. Buying the cots and the double buggy, reading Penelope Leach as they sat together in front of the fire, stroking her rounded belly proudly and waiting for baby kicks.

Whatever happened, she'd had that togetherness. But Jo didn't. From believing that she was one half of an expectant couple, Jo had abruptly become a one-parent family. That's what I am too, she realised.

A deserted wife with two kids, no career prospects and a washing machine on the verge of packing it in. Another bloody statistic. Add one to the deserted wives' register, one to the single mothers' register and one to the womanising bastard list, she thought bitterly.

Tears stung her eyes. Don't be such a wimp. You don't know that for sure. You don't know what'll happen, so don't think about it. He'll change his mind, you know he will, he has to. He can't give up on us after all we've been through and he won't give up the twins, will he?

Would another woman give him enough to make him forget everything he'd once treasured? She thought of the woman Fiona had described to her, a glamorous career woman who was doubtless much more interesting to talk to than a harassed housewife.

Was it her fault for making that seduction too easy? Should she have abandoned the ironing, hoovering and cooking to read the Karma Sutra, picking up hints to spice up their sex life and waxing, painting and oiling herself in an effort to turn into a siren who could keep any man glued to the bedroom?

What was it model Jerry Hall had said about keeping Mick Jagger by her side: be a cook in the kitchen, a maid in the dining room and a whore in the bedroom.

Why wasn't it enough to be an ordinary wife and mother? Oh God, it all seemed so hopeless.

She swallowed hard and ran a harsh hand over her eyes, trying to obliterate the tears and the misery which was about to creep up on her again. Reaching into her bedside drawer, her fingers found the small plastic jar of pills Fiona had given her the day before. Years of dosing herself on vitamin pills meant she could just put two of the tiny tablets in her mouth and swallow without water. Screwing up her face at the acrid taste, she covered the mouthpiece with one hand, and yelled.

'Paul, love, are you coming with that milk?'

Her answer was the sound of feet pounding up the stairs as

her black-haired first-born – Phillip arrived ten minutes later – raced upstairs, across the landing and into her room bearing a plastic tumbler of milk. It was one of the green plastic tumblers the twins drank out of when they were small. Paul had always loved his one and the way it gave everything a special, plastic taste.

'I spilled a bit,' he said unnecessarily, handing her the tumbler with two inches of milk sloshing around in the bottom and milk splashes clinging to the side. 'But I cleaned it up.'

'Thank you,' Aisling said gravely, wondering what item of clothing her untidy son had ripped off the radiator to clean up with. Still, cleaning up at all was a start.

'Have you got a headache, Mum?' he asked, spotting the tablets with eagle-eyed ten-year-old's eyes. 'Why were you crying?'

'I didn't sleep, darling, and I've got a dreadful headache. But the milk will help.' She rumpled his hair affectionately and he grinned at her, his eyes crinkling up just like his father's. Other mothers had talked about their sons hitting twelve and suddenly shrugging off each affectionate gesture, furious if their mothers hugged them the way they'd been doing for years. Thank God she still had a few years of night-time cuddles before the twins became too grown-up for hair-rumpling and tickling sessions.

'Mum, can we have money for McDonald's today?' Paul asked. 'Mr Breslin is bringing us all to Stillorgan after the match and we can go into McDonald's if you let us.'

'Yes. But no milkshakes. You know how sick they make you.'

'I promise.'

He was out the door and yelling for his brother in a flash and Aisling felt the tension leave her body as another normal day in the Moran family home began to unfold. Everything was going to be fine, she just knew it. Last night was just a glitch, a bad patch that had to come out into the open. They shared so much: the boys, their life, their home. How could

Michael give all that up? The man who had cried in her arms when the boys were born wouldn't be able to leave them for some floozie. He'd come back. It was just a matter of time.

'Sorry about that,' Jo said. 'My next-door neighbour's alarm went off and she couldn't remember the code, so we had to ring her son and . . . oh, it took ages.'

'What are you doing today?' Aisling asked briskly, her new-found optimism giving her strength.

'I don't know.' Jo sounded forlorn. 'I had planned to hit Mothercare and look at baby clothes before buying some books on pregnancy . . . But I don't know if I'd be able to face it now.'

'Well, that's just what we're going to do,' Aisling said firmly. 'Lounging around crying won't solve anything. I've got to get the boys ready for soccer and then I'll meet you in the Ilac Centre outside Dunnes at . . .' she glanced at her watch, 'half ten and we can start shopping. Oh, and I'll bring some of my pregnancy books – it's not as if Michael and I are going to decide to have another child right now.'

Jo said nothing, mainly because she didn't know what to say to such a bizarrely blinkered idea.

'That's settled,' Aisling declared. 'I'll see you then.'

Hanging up, Jo sat for a moment on the couch in her small living room, thinking about her friend's sudden change of mood. Last night she had been scared that Aisling would drink herself into unconsciousness; now it seemed as if the previous day's events had never happened.

Was Aisling blotting everything out or was she really as well as she sounded? Leaning back against a cushion, Jo contemplated the whole messy situation. Which of us is worse off, she asked herself.

Gratefully sitting down on a bench in the centre of the busy shopping centre at twenty-five minutes past ten, Jo was still thinking about Aisling's predicament. Leaning back against the wooden bench, she looped her handbag strap around her wrist and tried to relax. Casually dressed in jeans and a cream cotton cricket sweater with her hair curling around her shoulders and a smattering of freckles on her face, Jo was the picture of health and casual chic. That was on the outside, of course.

On the inside, her stomach was gurgling away volcanically, considering whether to send her second breakfast up the way it came or not. Nausea came over her in waves and she wondered how long she could last without having to race for the loo which was, naturally, at the other end of the centre.

Please don't let me be sick, she prayed silently. I promise never to eat muesli ever again. She closed her eyes and willed her stomach away from the notion of morning sickness. Just let me be OK long enough to meet Aisling and then you can be as sick as you want, right?

Amazingly, her stomach obeyed and the nausea subsided. It must be all those stomach-toning classes, she thought proudly, opening her eyes with relief. Now I can even control the insides as well as the outsides!

Six minutes later, she watched Aisling emerge from the car-park exit, her well-rounded figure hidden in a long navy and cream striped shirt worn over navy ski pants.

'Sorry I'm late,' she gasped, sitting down on a corner of the bench, her face flushed from rushing down six flights of stairs. 'Everyone and their granny were ahead of me looking for parking spaces so I had to keep going up and up. You look lovely,' she finished.

'Make-up is a wonderful thing,' Jo remarked. 'You should have seen me an hour ago. This morning sickness thing is not funny, not bloody funny at all.'

'You poor thing,' Aisling said comfortingly. 'It is horrible. But you're looking all right now, aren't you?'

'I think so,' Jo stood up gingerly, took a deep breath and found that she didn't feel sick any more. 'Right. Let's shop.'

Twenty pounds' worth of pregnancy books and a pair of elastic-waisted trousers later, both women were tired of shopping. They'd been in what felt like every shop in Dublin and the Eason's bag was growing heavier with every step.

Deciding that she was now ravenously hungry, Jo suggested an early pub lunch.

'They make the most amazing toasted sandwiches in here,' she said, leading the way into a small pub on Mary Street. Like an oasis in the middle of one of the city's busiest shopping districts, the inside of the quaint, atmospheric pub was cool and welcoming. The pub's trademark dark wooden chairs and stools were already occupied by regulars who knew better than to saunter into Keating's during the lunchtime rush if they wanted a seat.

Aromatic smells of barbequed chicken, toasted cheese and garlicky potatoes filled the air and, by the time she led Aisling upstairs to sit in two huge armchairs in the tiny gallery, Jo was hungry enough to eat for three, never mind two.

'Listen to this,' she murmured, scouring the handwritten menu hungrily. 'Toasted BLTs on garlic bread or cajun chicken with sautéed mushrooms . . . mmm. The food is just amazing here. I could eat two of everything right now! But I'll have . . . the chicken. Yes, chicken.'

'The cheese salad sandwich sounds nice,' said Aisling, wondering why she didn't feel hungrier. 'Cheese salad on brown,' she smiled at the casually dressed young waiter who'd appeared pen in hand beside them.

'And a little bottle of white wine, if you have icy-cold ones, thanks.' She smiled at him again, but he was already gazing warmly at Jo, eager to please the attractive brunette who was biting her full lips tentatively as she considered what to have.

Wouldn't it be nice to have that effect on men, Aisling mused, watching the waiter watching Jo. She was used to being ignored when she was out with Jo, although she had never been jealous of her friend's ability to attract men effortlessly. Aisling had simply never considered herself attractive enough to compete with Jo's potent sex appeal.

It had been exactly the same when they shared the flat. No matter how long Aisling had spent curling her eyelashes with the horrible metal curler or applying judicious amounts of blusher to where her cheekbones *should* have been, she always felt a little dowdy beside Jo.

Even in those awful second-hand dungarees of hers with her hair tumbling around her shoulders like she'd just been standing in a wind tunnel, Jo still looked good. Men flocked to her as though hypnotised or, as Jo liked to joke, 'like slugs drawn to begonias'.

'Chicken with garlic potatoes,' Jo said firmly. 'And a cup of coffee. Do you have decaffeinated?'

'Of course,' murmured the waiter. 'Do you want anything else?'

'No.'

'I'm surprised he didn't offer you a full massage and champagne,' Aisling remarked when he'd gone, full of twenty-something unfulfilled lust.

'Young guys are all the same,' Jo said dismissively, settling back into her armchair. 'Give them one smile and they're already imagining you with your clothes off.'

'Not in my experience, they aren't. The last time I smiled at a young man he was packing my shopping in Dunnes and he looked at me like I was on day release from John of God's.' Aisling sighed heavily.

'But how can I expect strangers to fancy me if my husband doesn't.' Now the Valium was wearing off, she felt miserable again, miserable and hopeless.

'Come on, Ash,' soothed Jo, patting her on the knee. 'There's no point torturing yourself. It's not your fault.'

'But it is,' she wailed. 'It is. It's all my fault. I pushed him away. No wonder he wanted someone else.' She started to cry silently, her body shaking as the tears started rolling down her face.

Jo could do nothing except clasp Aisling's hand between her own. That bastard, thought Jo vehemently.

'Salad sandwich and wine,' announced the waiter, planting a small plate, a wine glass and a small green bottle on the table in front of Aisling without looking at her, 'and chicken.' The timbre of his voice changed as he gently placed a large heaped dinner plate before Jo. 'Your coffee is coming,' he added, gazing at her hopefully.

Jo ignored him. 'Ash, you can't go to pieces, you can't,' she said gently. 'He's gone, but the boys aren't. They need you now and you can't let them down.'

She grabbed the paper napkin the waiter had laid reverently in front of her and handed it to Aisling. 'Blow,' she commanded. Aisling blew.

'Listen, I wish it was different, but it isn't. We've both been dumped, nothing's going to change that, Ash. So we've got two choices: we could both go to pieces, cry all day, beg them to come back and bawl in front of anyone who'll listen.' Jo took a deep breath.

'We could decide to be victims. My baby would be born totally screwed up because I'd be totally screwed up having her, and the twins would turn into little brats from being dragged back and forth between you and Michael.

'We can't do that to them, can we, Ash?'

Aisling shook her head silently.

'Or we can fight back, survive on our own,' Jo emphasised the words heavily, determined to get her message past the wall of misery Aisling was erecting around herself.

'Maybe Michael *will* come running back to you, but you can't rely on that. You have to be strong on your own and so do I. Who knows,' she added wryly, 'Richard could be frantically speaking to my answering machine as we speak, begging forgiveness . . .' She broke off with a sarcastic chuckle.

She could just picture his face the night before, furious that he wasn't getting his own way for once. The chances of him changing his mind about the baby were slimmer than her chances of fitting into her jeans in about six months' time.

'You're right, you're absolutely right.' Aisling opened her eyes abruptly and rubbed the napkin over her cheeks. Then she sat up in her chair and picked up the wine bottle. She poured most of the contents into her glass and took a deep draught.

'I know he's not coming back, you know.' Her voice shook

as she said it. 'I just don't want to think about it. I don't want to believe it. I want to exist in the happy place in my head where everything's all right, where he's just at work and where he'll be home tonight.'

'I know.' Jo stared back at Aisling. Picking up her fork, Jo stuck it into a steaming pile of slivered golden potatoes oozing with garlic.

'Despite everything, despite what Richard said about the baby, I'd still take him back,' she said quietly. 'But he's not coming back though, is he? So it's up to me now. It's up to us. We have to get on with it, Ash,' she urged. 'You've got to get some sort of a life for yourself, get a job and . . .'

'Get a job *now*! I can barely think straight, never mind actually do something I've been terrified of for years!' Almost crying again, Aisling stared at her friend in horror.

Jo went on eating.

'You can't be serious?' Aisling demanded.

'Of course I am,' the other woman answered with her mouth full. 'Realistically, you're now a one-parent family and, even if Michael is so wracked with guilt that he pays you huge amounts of maintenance for the boys for the next couple of months, it will inevitably change.' She knew she was being brutal, but Aisling had to face facts. 'You don't know what he's going to do now, and he could, well *they* could, have a family and . . .' she paused to fork up more chicken, spearing a delicious-looking bit of potato as well.

Aisling stared dully at her untouched sandwich, her eyes red-rimmed and sad. God this was difficult, Jo thought. 'I'm sorry, Ash. I'm trying to help, but I'm not making a very good job of it, am I?'

Aisling took another large slug of wine and prodded her sandwich listlessly. She wasn't even vaguely hungry now, although Jo's chicken was disappearing faster than 99p knickers in a sale.

She knew Jo was speaking the truth. Hideous to imagine Michael setting up another home with that woman and having more children.

'I suppose you're right,' she said slowly, twisting her wine glass around by its thin stem. 'There's one slight problem. What am I going to do?'

'Work in an office, of course. What you did before.'

'That was eleven years ago. Everything's computerised now and I haven't a clue how to work a computer. Anyway, who's going to employ me?' Aisling asked. 'There are three hundred thousand unemployed people in this country, so who the hell is going to take on a housewife with two kids, no experience, no skills and no confidence?'

Jo stirred three packets of sugar into her coffee, poured in milk and took a sip. 'When Michael met you, you were virtually running the entire motor department, not to mention studying for your Insurance Institute exams at night. You did all that when you were just twenty-two and you're trying to tell me that you couldn't do it now, when you're older and more experienced?'

'It's *because* I'm older that it seems impossible,' said Aisling weakly. 'We thought we could do anything when we were twenty-two, for God's sake. It's all totally different now, Jo. You don't understand!'

'Understand what?'

'Just because you've a brilliant job at the magazine and buckets of confidence, doesn't mean that everyone else is the same. Look at you,' Aisling cried. 'You're a successful journalist, you've got your own car, your own apartment, your own bank account and independence.

'Maybe you think that's nothing because most of your friends are journalists. But not everyone is talented and clever and able to walk into any job anywhere. I'm not afraid to work, Jo, but I'm afraid of looking for work and being told I'm too old or unskilled or useless.' She stopped miserably.

'Ash, when we met, what is it . . . fourteen, no, fifteen years ago, you were the one who was going to make something of her life,' said Jo passionately.

'I was absolutely terrified of being in Dublin, of going to college, of having no one to go home to at night and talk about what went wrong that day. It was awful, you know what I was like.' She gulped down some more coffee. 'You gave me the confidence to stick it out in college when I really wanted to run home to my mother, and you kept me from falling for every asshole who asked me out. You were so strong,' Jo added gently. 'You still are. It's just that you've forgotten.'

Had she forgotten, or was Jo just being kind, Aisling wondered? Had she ever been sure of herself, ready to stick her neck out because she knew she could do anything?

For a moment she remembered sitting in the kitchen at home, all dressed up in clothes from her first proper pay-packet and telling a fascinated Sorcha what the department head had said to her that evening. Mum had been cooking dinner, eyes on the soup she was stirring on the spotless cooker but listening to every word about the motor department and how Margaret Synnott thought Aisling should start studying for the Insurance Institute exams as soon as possible.

'She said loads of people *say* they're going to do them, but most of them don't actually bother. But you get a bonus for each part of the exams you pass and she said if I want to get on, it would be worth it,' Aisling said, basking in Sorcha's admiration of her new black leather boots.

'I know I said I was never going to study again in my whole life after the Leaving, but I don't mind this. What do you think, Mum?'

Her mother stopped stirring and turned around, a warm smile on her face. Eithne Maguire had never been to a beauty parlour in her life, she got her hair inexpertly cut at the tiny hairdressing salon over the butcher's shop and never spent money on her wardrobe when she could buy something for her children. But when she smiled, her whole face lit up and her blue eyes shone.

'I'm so proud of you, Aisling. I've always known you could do anything you put your mind to. Where did I get such a bright daughter,' she said fondly, hugging her first-born. 'We're all so proud of you.'

103

This wasn't strictly true and they both knew it. Nothing Aisling could do would ever be enough for her father but, for a few hours, that didn't matter. Her mother, the one who'd always protected her from her strict and puritanical father and from his mother's constant sniping, was proud of her daughter. That was enough.

There were tears in Aisling's eyes as she leaned over and hugged Jo, but they weren't sad tears.

'Thank you. Nobody but Mum has said anything like that to me in years.'

'Well they should have,' replied Jo, forking up another mouthful of food. 'Since your bloody control freak of a father ripped every shred of confidence out of you when you were a kid, I'm not surprised that you still feel that way. Michael ought to have given you a pep talk every day to make sure you didn't sink back into the mire of insecurity, but,' she shrugged expressively, 'he's a man, so why would he bother? Ash, you can do it without him, I know you can.'

'I'm still hungry,' she added, scooping up the last bits of chicken off her plate.

'Here.' Aisling pushed her untouched sandwich over to her friend and waved to the waiter.

'Another coffee and another bottle of wine,' she said sharply. She wasn't going to waste her time smiling at him this time. Career women didn't have time to worry about rude waiters.

It was nearly half one by the time they'd walked back to the Ilac Centre and said goodbye beside the lifts to the car park. Jo wanted to go home via the office and pick up some work she had to finish before Monday, Aisling needed to get some groceries before the boys got home from football at three. She only needed bread and milk and she could get that at the newsagent's.

She'd spent her last tenner on lunch so she walked back towards the Ilac's cash dispenser and slid her card in. She was just punching in her PIN number when a thought struck her – how much money did they have in the cashsave account?

Michael topped up their current account with his salary, but he put anything left over in the cashsave account.

'If we put everything in the current account, we'll just keep writing cheques,' he said. 'We've got to save something. You never know when you're going to need a lump sum, Aisling.'

Aisling never pointed out that she was anything but reckless when it came to money. Years of listening to her grandmother drone on about wasting money had instilled in her a sense of economy. When they were first married, she bought her fruit and vegetables from a tiny greengrocer, bought meat cheaply from a small, family-run butcher and wouldn't have dreamed of buying bread when she could bake it herself.

Now that Michael was earning a good salary, she'd stopped the time-consuming trekking around buying cheap fruit and vegetables and bought everything in the supermarket. But she still carefully cut out money-off coupons, turned her old T-shirts into dusters and made her own soup, bread and marmalade. Nobody could accuse *her* of frittering away the family's money.

She pressed the 'account inquiry' button, chose the cashsave account and waited. There'd been at least three thousand pounds in there the last time she'd looked. Michael kept saying he was going to transfer it into the building society account, their 'holiday' fund.

But when she'd asked him about taking a holiday the previous month, Michael had been very vague about when he could take time off. The supplement had changed everything, he muttered, he couldn't just leave the country a month after getting it off the ground.

No wonder he hadn't been keen to look at the brochures she'd picked up from the travel agency, Aisling thought grimly. Three weeks camping in France with the family obviously paled beside the thought of a scorching week in the sun rubbing Ambre Solaire into that bitch!

She scowled as she looked at the small green numbers on the cash dispenser screen. Jesus! What was wrong? Three hundred and thirty pounds was all that was left in the cashsave account. Aisling stared at the figures intently. That couldn't be right.

She was sure he hadn't moved the money, or maybe he had and just hadn't told her? Flustered, she pushed the button to check the current account. They were nearly two hundred pounds overdrawn. Aisling looked at the little 'dr' beside the total and felt weak. What the hell was going on? Why were they overdrawn? She hadn't spent very much lately, apart from the dress she'd bought yesterday.

'Do you want more time?' demanded the little green letters on the screen. Just more money, thought Aisling, feeling the faint stirrings of temper. She quickly withdrew two hundred pounds, as much as she could take out in one day. Snatching her money from the machine, she stuffed it into her purse and turned round rapidly, cannoning into a young man waiting behind her.

'Watch out, missus!' he said to her departing back. Aisling didn't even hear him. She was already halfway to the lifts, her growing rage giving her a fierce, angry energy. All the lifts were on the upper floors and a small crowd of shoppers waited for them, idling away the time examining their shopping bags and chatting.

Normally, Aisling would have waited for the lift, not keen on panting up endless flights of stairs. Today, she ran up the stairs, her heart pumping and her temper boiling. How *dare* he take everything out of the account! How dare he!

What sort of a bastard was he to leave her and the boys, and then take all their bloody money into the bargain! What the hell were she and the twins supposed to live on? How were they going to pay the mortgage or buy food without any money? What a bastard! She could kill him, *would* kill him.

Wait until I get my hands on you, Michael Moran, she growled under her breath as she marched towards her car. You'll be sorry you ever heard of bloody Jennifer Carroll, I'll see to that! Aisling dragged open the car door and threw her handbag in. I never thought he'd stoop so low as to take

106

money from his kids' mouths, she thought, grinding the gearshift into first.

She'd never driven out of the city centre so fast. Barely noticing amber lights, she wove in and out of different lanes, gritting her teeth and swearing at other drivers.

No matter how terrible the previous day had been, no matter how devastated she'd felt when Michael told her he didn't love her, she'd had one consolation. The boys. If Michael wanted some high-flying career woman with legs up to her armpits and a wardrobe full of basques and suspender belts, then he could have her.

But Aisling would always have the boys, their beloved boys. And if Michael ever got bored with Ms Carroll, he could always come home for Phillip and Paul's sakes. And for hers. She wouldn't turn him away, couldn't turn him away. She loved him, despite everything.

That thought had consoled her, knowing that Michael would find it hard to be apart from his children and that he'd *have* to come home. Eventually.

Or so she'd thought. Obviously, she'd been wrong. If he could callously strip their bank account, knowing that Aisling had no other means to support the twins, then he'd gone too far. He could discard her, but not Phillip and Paul. Damn him, but she'd fight him tooth and nail for every penny the boys needed!

What sort of man would get up early the morning after leaving his wife, and drain their bank account? Suddenly it all made sense. Aisling, you fool! If you could only withdraw two hundred pounds with your bank card in one day, that's all he could take out too. Which meant that he hadn't just grabbed the money this morning, he'd been siphoning it out for a few weeks! What a pig!

She'd never forgive him. If he thought she was going to be a pushover, crying every time she saw him and begging him to come back, he was wrong. She was going to be as hard as nails and every bit as cunning as he had been to protect her children. Watch out you bastard, she hissed.

When she opened the front door, she immediately knew he'd been there. Flyers for a pizza company were thrown casually on the hall table, the way only Michael left them. That always drove her mad. Why couldn't he bring them into the kitchen and either stick them in the basket where she put the bills or put them in the bin? Because tidying up was *her* job, of course.

She didn't even bother to pick up the flyers, but ran upstairs to their bedroom. His side of the wardrobe was open, a couple of metal hangers lay on the bottom shelf where Michael usually kept his shoes.

He'd taken everything, suits, trousers, and the shirts she ironed so carefully, leaving nothing but a forgotten belt hanging forlornly from the tie rack inside the door. She checked the drawers and their en suite bathroom. Everything of Michael's was gone. Only a damp ring remained beside the sink as proof that his aftershave had stood there, the big bottle of Eternity for Men she'd bought him for Christmas, thinking that forty quid a bottle was a bit pricey.

He'd even remembered to take his shower gel, the tangy lemon-scented one he preferred to her coconut version.

He'd remembered everything, she thought bitterly. He'd never managed to do that during their twelve years of marriage. Packing for holidays had always been a nightmare, as she had to remember everything Michael and the boys needed. If she didn't stick his shaving kit in the suitcase, he was quite likely to forget it. Not so today. This time Michael wasn't coming back after two weeks.

Good. She didn't want him back. But she damn well wanted to know where their money was. In the bedroom, she picked up the phone and dialled the *News*.

'The deputy editor's office,' she snapped.

'Hello.' His voice sounded the same as it had the night before. Calm and relaxed. She was going to knock that out of him, that was for sure.

'What the hell have you done with the money from the cashsave account?' she demanded.

'Aisling?'

'No, it's Cindy-bloody-Crawford. Of course it's me, your poor bewildered wife, the one who never noticed you taking all our money from our joint account. How did you do it, huh? Take out two hundred with your card every day in anticipation of dumping me?'

'Stop screaming down the phone, Aisling,' he said coldly. 'And stop making wild accusations. I didn't *steal* anything.'

'Where's the money then?'

'In a separate account, your account.'

'What account?' she demanded.

'Didn't you read my note?'

'No, I didn't.'

'It's on the bed, on your side.'

It was all her side now.

'Listen,' Michael said wearily, 'I opened an account for you last month. I knew this would all come to a head and I wanted to sort out things financially. I'm not going to let the kids starve just because we've split up, so I talked to a solicitor about the best way to handle things, and he advised me to open an account for you.'

Aisling was dumbstruck. He'd talked to a solicitor over a month ago. He must have been planning this for months. What a bastard.

'Are you listening, Aisling?' His voice interrupted her thoughts. 'There's one thousand five hundred in the account. I left the details on the dressing table. I'm going to close the current and cashsave accounts. We don't need joint accounts any more.'

She sat down on the bed, only half listening. He'd consulted a solicitor over a month ago, that was how sure he was that their marriage was over.

'I can't believe you've been cold-bloodedly planning this without telling me,' she said slowly.

'I haven't time to discuss it,' he said harshly. 'I'll look after the boys financially, but I'm not keeping you in luxury for the rest of your life. I'm not a bottomless pit, Aisling. You'll have to get a job. You've always said you wanted one, anyway.'

'And you never wanted me to get one,' she screamed. 'You absolute bastard! I'd like to kill you!'

'I don't have time to listen to your insults,' Michael said coldly. 'I've a job to do. Unlike you.' With that, he hung up, leaving Aisling mouthing furiously at the dialling tone.

The note was on her pillow, a page ripped from a notebook and covered with Michael's distinctive scrawl. A small, blue lodgement receipt was under it.

'Aisling, I'm sorry you aren't here. I wanted to talk to you about money and about the boys. I've opened an account for you and put half of the holiday money in it. I'd like to talk to the boys myself, it's important that they hear it from both of us. I'll ring you later about coming over this evening.'

That was it. No 'love, Michael'. Well, he didn't, did he? Damn him. He even expected her to wait patiently for him to turn up in the evening so they could tell the boys together. He could bloody well stuff his idea of dropping in when he wanted. He'd have to consult her before he set foot in the house. If Michael wanted to fight, she'd fight back!

CHAPTER SEVEN

Fiona thought it was a brilliant idea.

'Of course Pat can help you get a job! He's always moaning about hiring twenty-year-old office juniors and having them leave as soon as they're trained to work the computers properly.'

Fiona sat down on one of the Morans' pine kitchen chairs, scarred from endless Dinky toy games, and crossed long, sleek legs encased in black lycra sports leggings. 'He'd jump at the chance to hire someone like you.'

'Do you really think so?' Fiona was as generous as she was eccentric. Aisling didn't want her to badger poor Pat into hiring their suddenly single neighbour as a huge favour. If she was going back to work, she certainly needed a leg up, but not charity.

'I'm very rusty, Fiona, and I'd be eager to learn, but only if Pat thinks it would work,' she said earnestly.

'Don't be ridiculous, Aisling. If you can whip up a four course meal in two hours without becoming hysterical when the freezer packs in and defrosts your home-made ice cream into slop, then you'll have no trouble answering a few phones.'

'And Daddy adores you, you know,' Fiona added with a smile. 'He always wants to sit beside you at dinner parties and you'll probably have to fight him off once he sees you sitting all secretarial behind the reception desk!'

Despite herself, Aisling burst out laughing, thinking of Fiona's imposing and steely-eyed barrister father trying to inveigle her into his office for a passionate session on an antique desk strewn with legal tomes and writs.

'I just can't see that happening.' She grinned.

'Well I certainly can,' replied Fiona. 'Since Mother left him,

111

he's like a fourteen-year-old who's just discovered what sex is all about and is anxious to try it out as often as possible. I told you that he almost ended up in bed with one of the bridesmaids at my cousin's wedding?'

'Really?'

'You have no idea what he's like. Mad as a March hare and twice as randy. The thing is, women just love him, they always have,' Fiona paused to light up a cigarette.

'I know,' she muttered, 'I don't know why I keep smoking these things if I'm so keen on being fit. Pat gives me the same bloody lecture every day, but a girl's got to have some vices.'

'I wasn't going to say anything,' protested Aisling. 'I can hardly talk about being fit under the circumstances. My thighs haven't seen the inside of a pair of lycra leggings for years and if my stomach gets any bigger, I'll need those horrible roll-on things Granny wore.'

'Over my dead body,' Fiona said firmly. 'The only roll-on product modern girls use is deodorant, my dear. Aisling Moran, career woman, is going to be sleek, healthy and devastatingly sexy, even if I have to personally drag you to the gym three times a week.'

She got up and stuck her cigarette under the tap for a moment. 'I'll talk to Pat when I get back from my step class and find out what's the story workwise. There's always someone away and hiring temps from the agencies costs a fortune. He'll be thrilled to get his hands on you. Well, Daddy certainly would.'

Aisling giggled again. No matter what disaster hung over life like a dark cloud, a few moments in Fiona's company listening to her spiky and bitchy comments on life in general could raise anyone's spirits.

Through Fiona's eyes, Aisling was changing her life for the better, going back to work as a confident and mature woman. Not for a moment would Fiona see Aisling as a terrified and lonely wife, suddenly single and unsure of what life held for her and her two sons.

That was part of her charm, Aisling realised. Fiona viewed

life through tinted glasses and if they weren't always rose-tinted, they certainly made everything in life look more interesting.

If her husband of ten years decided to leave his fun-loving, tennis-mad wife, Aisling knew that Fiona would take a deep breath and start again, searching for a better life and a faithful mate without being destroyed by the break-up.

She watched her friend pull on a pink sweatshirt over the tiny hot pink lycra leotard which Aisling reckoned wouldn't fit one of her thighs. Tanned from frequent trips to the Finucanes' villa in Spain and a perfect size ten thanks to aerobics every second day, Fiona looked fantastic.

When she was dressed in the exquisite clothes she adored shopping for, with her long nails beautifully manicured, her gold Cartier watch catching the light and her rich chestnut hair shimmering from endless salon treatments, she looked every inch a rich bitch. Thank God she wasn't.

Aisling remember the day the Finucanes had moved into the huge red-brick house across the road, a fleet of removal vans lined up outside full of expensive-looking pieces of furniture. At least ten harassed men in overalls spent the afternoon carrying furniture into the house, struggling with huge pine wardrobes, enormous squashy sofas and a gleaming dining-room table which looked big enough for at least twenty people.

Aisling couldn't help peering out of her bedroom window, fascinated to see what sort of furniture the new neighbours had. A tall, immaculately dressed brunette roared up in her sporty black car and marched into the house with a small fluffy dog in tow. Aisling decided that her new neighbour was obviously some high-powered career woman and wasn't the sort who'd be interested in coming over for morning coffee.

So she got quite a shock when Fiona arrived on the doorstep two days later, introduced herself and asked were the people two doors away totally mad or just mildly insane?

'All I said was that my husband and I had moved in across the road and that we wanted to say hello to everyone when the poor dear turned white as a sheet, told me she didn't want to buy anything and slammed the door in my face,' Fiona complained.

'She's deaf,' explained Aisling, 'and probably a little bit mad into the bargain. If you think she's bad you should meet her brother. He stills thinks it's 1944 and he's working undercover as a spy in France.'

'Isn't there anyone normal living around here?' demanded Fiona.

'We're pretty normal,' Aisling replied. 'Most of the time, anyway. Do you want to come in for coffee?'

'I'd love to. If I don't get at least four doses of caffeine into my system before eleven in the morning, it goes into shock. I could go home and bring some disgustingly sweet biscuits if you want any?' she offered.

Aisling laughed. 'Believe me, I've got loads of disgustingly sweet things here. Too many in fact.'

They'd been friends ever since. Sometimes they did their shopping together, chatting volubly while they waited impatiently in the supermarket queue or wandering through clothes shops while Fiona shopped and Aisling vowed to diet.

She'd always urged Aisling to join her in the gym or come playing tennis with her friends. Now she gave Aisling a determined look as she picked up her keys.

'You've got to get out and you've got to start looking after yourself, darling. I've seen enough girls fall to pieces when their marriages go sour and I don't want to see it happen to you. Tomorrow you and I are going shopping for trainers and I don't want any arguments, right?' She grinned and poked Aisling in the arm.

When Fiona had gone, Aisling went into the sitting room where Phillip was sitting cross-legged on the floor, eating Rice Krispies and watching some spiky-haired DJ counting down the Top Ten hits. There were comics and football cards strewn all over the carpet, along with two empty crisp packets and Phillip's discarded socks.

'Phillip, this place is a mess! Tidy it up.'

'Why? Who's coming?' he answered back smartly. 'Dad?'

Aisling felt that knot in her stomach again, the one which sprang into action when she thought of the effect Michael's departure would have on the twins.

The night before, she'd told them their father was going to be away for a week. She didn't know what to say and decided that she'd break the news to them gently.

Paul had simply looked surprised. 'I thought Dad was coming to watch us play soccer on Saturday,' he said slowly. 'Will he be back in time?'

'I don't know, darling.' Feeling guilty for lying and even guiltier for stopping Michael coming home to tell them himself, Aisling gave Paul a kiss on the cheek and turned to say goodnight to Phillip. Dressed in his favourite Manchester United pyjamas with a comic propped up in front of him, he gazed at her steadily but didn't say anything.

Aisling kissed him and gently stroked the purple bruise on his left arm he insisted he'd got from banging into the goalposts at school.

'Goodnight, Giggs, or is it Cantona tonight?' she asked.

'None of them,' he answered dully.

She forced herself to smile and left the door ajar on her way out so the boys would have the glow of the landing light for comfort. She switched off their light and headed downstairs. She went straight for the drinks cabinet and a stiff gin and tonic.

Phillip knew something was wrong. Of course he did. Children detected every nuance of their parents' relationship, she'd read in a magazine once. Phillip certainly did. Michael always said that Phillip was a budding investigative reporter – inquisitive, pushy and as unstoppable as a freight train. 'Why?' was his favourite word.

This time, Phillip, I don't know *why*, Aisling thought morosely. She stared blankly at the comics and crisp wrappers scattered on the rug. The place needed hoovering as usual. She had to tell the boys. She should have told them last night. There was no point pretending everything was OK. They'd find out sometime. Phillip looked up at her, the TV forgotten and anxiety in his big, sad eyes.

'Is Dad coming home today?'

Phillip's question didn't surprise her. She looked at his earnest, questioning face, those dark eyes reminding her so painfully of his father. Decision time. Don't be a coward, Aisling. Tell them now, you have to.

'Where's Paul?' she asked resolutely.

'Upstairs,' he answered.

Aisling went to the bottom of the stairs.

'Paul,' she called. 'Come downstairs. I want to talk to you.'

He ran down the stairs noisily, jumped the bottom two steps and landed heavily on both feet. Sockless of course. If Phillip wasn't wearing his socks, Paul wasn't either.

Running into the sitting room, he skidded to a halt and thumped down on the floor beside his twin. He picked up one of the crisp wrappers and looked inside.

'You've eaten mine!' he said accusingly, glaring at Phillip.

'I didn't!'

'You did . . .'

'Quiet!' shouted Aisling. Damn, she hadn't meant to shout. 'Boys, there's something I've got to tell you,' she began in a softer tone. 'It's about your father and I . . .'

She stopped, aware of the enormity of what she was about to tell them. What words could you use to say 'your father's left me', she asked herself? They were still looking at her, mini versions of Michael, the same features, the same colouring.

For a brief moment, she remembered the day she'd told him she was pregnant. Wrapped up in their own private world as they walked through Bushy Park on a freezing March day, they'd gone through names they liked and tried to imagine what their baby would look like.

'Like you, I hope,' she'd smiled, wanting their child to have Michael's dark looks instead of her own pale skin and mousey hair.

'No, you,' he'd murmured, pushing aside her parka hood to kiss the soft curve of her neck.

Phillip and Paul were still staring at her, waiting much too patiently. Poor kids, she thought, they knew something was wrong. All she could do was soften the blow, make it as friendly as possible.

Even though her heart was full of rage at what Michael had done, she couldn't use the boys like Exocet missiles, turning them against their father as ammunition in a marital war. She shouldn't have told Michael to get stuffed when he'd rung the night before.

She tried again. 'Dad and I have been fighting lately, and . . .'

Jesus, what could she say? He's gone, he doesn't live here any more? It all sounded so horrible, so final. If they were only a few years older they could understand. But at ten, how could they be expected to?

'Dad has moved out for a while, boys. He hasn't been happy . . .'

'Why, why wasn't he happy?' asked Phillip anxiously. 'Was it my fault? I didn't mean to keep asking for rollerblades.'

'No, no, darling. It's nothing to do with you. Dad loves both of you, he's just . . . he needs to be on his own for a while. He wants you to be strong and understand that he loves you very much.'

'But why's he gone then?' Paul was looking at her with so much confusion in his eyes, that she didn't know whether to hug him or cry herself.

'Dad and I don't always get on,' she said slowly. 'Sometimes adults fight and need some time on their own, and that's what Dad wants. Time on his own. You'll still see him,' she added, trying to sound reassuring.

'Why, Mum?'

For once, Paul was asking all the questions. Phillip just stood there, head bent, his thick, dark hair falling over his forehead. Aisling reached out to stroke it, but he wrenched away from her hand.

'I'll tell you what, let's go to McDonald's for lunch. Does that sound like a good idea?'

'OK.' Paul looked as if he might cry.

'We went to McDonald's yesterday. I thought we weren't supposed to eat burgers all the time?' said Phillip sullenly.

'Not all the time, no,' answered Aisling. 'Sometimes we can break the rules, can't we? Where are your socks, boys? I'll give you five minutes to be ready to go, OK?'

Paul sprinted up the stairs in search of his missing socks, while Phillip stared at the floor. Aisling put her arms around him and hugged him tightly, feeling the tension and misery in his body.

'Darling, I'm so sorry about this. It's not your fault, it had nothing to do with you or rollerblades, or anything like that. This is between Dad and me . . .'

'It doesn't matter,' he said suddenly. He pulled away from her and picked his socks up off the floor. 'I'm not hungry.'

Aisling sat on the edge of the bed, talking quietly on the phone so the boys wouldn't hear her and wake up. It was nearly half nine but it was still bright outside. A man and woman were walking a dog on the other side of the road, holding hands as their brown and white terrier ran eagerly in and out of gardens.

'It's so unfair. The boys are so upset. I feel as if it's my fault, as if *I'm* ruining their childhood.'

'Don't be silly, you're doing all you can,' Fiona answered. 'What else can you do?'

'Oh, I don't know.' Aisling sighed heavily, thinking about the day's events. Lunch had been a disaster. Phillip refused to eat anything. Paul had followed suit, leaving a half-eaten quarter-pounder and most of his chips to Aisling. Normally, she'd have wolfed them down. But today she didn't feel remotely hungry.

'What do you think about the temping job Pat suggested?' Fiona asked.

'Bloody terrified, that's what I think. I don't know what scares me most, actually going back to work or finding out that I can't remember anything after twelve years. I'd hate to

118

let Pat down when he's been so good giving me this chance.'

'Rubbish, of course you'll be fine. It's nothing demanding, honestly. You've got a week to think about it, anyway,' Fiona pointed out. 'Elizabeth isn't going on maternity leave for another three weeks, so you've lots of time to get used to the job. It'll be a doddle for you.'

'Thank you, Fiona. Thanks for everything, cheering me up, getting me a job and oh . . . just for being there,' Aisling said gratefully. 'I don't know what I'd have done without you or Jo.'

'How is she?'

'Actually, she's doing pretty well. I was talking to her earlier and she'd just come in from a long walk in Portmarnock. Said she wanted to tire herself out so she'd sleep tonight. Poor thing.'

'What was the boyfriend like?' Fiona asked.

'I don't really know, I only met him a couple of times and we didn't exactly talk. Michael wasn't too keen on him, but then,' Aisling gave a little hollow laugh, 'Michael's judgement has been a little faulty lately. Or maybe it's *my* judgement that's been faulty.'

She paused for a moment.

'Stop moping,' ordered Fiona, 'and give me the low-down on this horrible man. Is he gorgeous or a complete scumbag?'

'He's very handsome, all blond hair, blue eyes and white teeth. He could advertise toothpaste.'

'But still a scumbag?'

'I think so. Actually, most of Jo's boyfriends have had some fatal flaw or another, like not wanting to settle down. Which is odd, really,' Aisling said reflectively. 'I've read that women who've been abused or hurt as children automatically go for the type of men who'll abuse their kids, it's a vicious circle.'

'She wasn't abused, was she?' Fiona asked in amazement.

'Lord no. But her father died when she was young and I often think she unconsciously picks men who are going to leave eventually, sort of like her father left,' added Aisling. 'Strangers meeting Jo would probably think she has everything, a great

119

career and great looks. In reality, she has as many problems as anyone else, more maybe.'

'I know what that's like,' remarked Fiona. 'Before my mother and father split up, they were always fighting, at each other's throats like pit bulls. But because we had the big house, the Jag, the housekeeper, etc., everyone assumed we had the life of Riley. Everything looked so different from the inside,' she added.

'We all pretended everything was perfect, but I never brought girls home from school in case they witnessed one of Mummy's rages. Daddy had given her these china figurines over the years and when she got really vexed she'd fling them at him. By the time she left, there wasn't a china ornament in the house, she'd smashed them all.' Fiona gave a little laugh. 'So I know all about covering up, I'm an expert at it.'

'I'm sorry, Fiona,' said Aisling sympathetically. 'I never knew.'

'Oh, I just don't talk about it any more. It took me ages to get it out of my system, but I'm fine now. The point is,' Fiona said emphatically, 'that things would have been a lot better if they'd just split up, instead of carrying on a bloody charade for years.'

'What went wrong?' asked Aisling, unable to conceal her curiosity. She'd never heard Fiona talk about her mother before, except to say that they rarely met up because her mother lived in Arizona.

'Drink,' Fiona said abruptly. 'She drank like a fish, all her family did. That's why you'll never see me drinking too much, I'm too bloody terrified to. It runs in families and I don't want it to run in mine any more.'

Christ, thought Aisling, remembering the nearly empty bottle of gin in the drinks cupboard. She'd been drinking far too much all weekend.

'I'd better be going, Ash,' Fiona said. 'Pat was off playing snooker all afternoon and wants to have a cosy family night in to make up for it. I'll be over tomorrow to discuss your working wardrobe,' she added. 'We'll have to find something drop-dead gorgeous to give you confidence on the first day.'

'Something drop-dead gorgeous from *my* wardrobe?' exclaimed Aisling.

'If we can't find something, we'll just have to go shopping,' continued Fiona gleefully. 'Fun, fun, fun!'

'Goodbye, you irrepressible shopper,' laughed Aisling, hanging up.

Right, she decided. No gin tonight. Just think of Fiona's mother.

The next morning she brought the boys to school and waved them in like she did every other Monday morning.

It just didn't feel like every other Monday. Last week, she'd been a reasonably contented, well, not totally *dis*contented woman. Now she was separated and broke.

With her finances very much in mind, she headed for Roches Stores in the Frascati Centre and took a basket instead of a trolley. Walking around aisles scented with the delicious smell of freshly baked bread, Aisling shopped carefully, adding up the prices in her head.

Twenty pounds seemed so much to pay for such a small amount of shopping. That expensive conditioner would have to go back, there was a much cheaper generic one. And one-fifty for those little pots of fromage frais? Ridiculous.

At home, she put everything away and sat down with a cup of coffee and a pen and paper. She listed the various household bills, working out how much money she needed every week. The total seemed huge, especially compared to the money she had in the bank. One and a half thousand wouldn't go very far. What would Michael pay for the boys' keep, she wondered?

The phone rang as she was hanging out the washing. Damn. She raced in, nearly tripping over a raised slab on the patio in the process.

'Hello,' she said breathlessly.

'Hello, Aisling,' said her mother. 'I've been wondering if you were all sick or something since I haven't heard from you all weekend. Are the boys OK?'

121

Only a mother knew how to ask questions that were loaded with meaning, thought Aisling, wondering where to start. She had been expecting the call. Or rather, dreading it.

It was a rare weekend when Aisling didn't ring her mother at some point or another. She usually waited until Sunday afternoon to ring because her father was invariably having a little nap over the newspapers and wouldn't answer the phone.

There was always something for Seán Maguire to complain about. These days, twenty-two-year-old Nicola was the bane of his life, constantly on the phone talking to 'that boyfriend of hers' or going out in unsuitable clothes. Enduring one of his five-minute moans was a waste of her time, Aisling thought. It didn't surprise her that Nicola's twin brother, Nicholas, was never in trouble with his father. Seán had always wanted a son, something he'd never let Aisling forget.

'I was worried, Aisling,' her mother was saying.

'The boys are fine, Mum.' It was time to bite the bullet. 'I'm afraid the problem is Michael . . .'

'Oh Lord, what's wrong with him? I just *knew* there was something wrong!'

'There's nothing wrong with him, Mum,' Aisling said. Nothing a slap on the face wouldn't cure, anyway. 'He's . . . er, we've split up.'

'What! I can't believe it, Aisling, that's terrible, just terrible.'

Aisling had never heard her mother so shocked. This was so difficult. Please God don't let Mum figure out everything. I couldn't face discussing the whole bloody thing again.

Aisling could hear her mother pulling up a kitchen chair to sit down on. The phone in the Maguire home was in the kitchen, making it impossible to have any sort of private conversation at all, Nicola constantly complained to her older sister. Eithne Maguire's voice quavered as she spoke again.

'But why, Aisling? What happened? Have you been having problems and why didn't you tell me? And what about the boys, poor lambs?'

Aisling felt a lump in her throat. Why did all this have to be so hard? Why didn't stationary companies print separation cards, like the change of address ones. It would be so much easier. 'Mrs and Mrs Moran have split up and henceforth Mr Moran will be residing at Number 10 Primrose Avenue with a Cindy Crawford lookalike while Mrs soon-to-be-ex Moran will be remaining in the family pad fielding telephone calls from curious relatives.'

'The boys are doing all right, Mum. Michael and I haven't been getting on and we had a fight. He's moved out for a while, that's all.'

'*That's all?*' demanded her mother. 'What do you mean, "that's all"? Is this serious? Is he gone for good, Aisling? Tell me.'

Aisling gave up. There was no point trying to pretend that she and Michael were in the middle of an amicable separation. She might as well tell the truth even though it hurt like hell.

'Listen Mum, I'll tell you the truth, but I don't want Father to know, right?' she said fiercely. 'You can tell him that we've grown apart and are perfectly happy with the situation, I just don't want him knowing.'

'All right, love,' Mum said softly. 'Just tell me everything.'

Everything took three-quarters of an hour and two cups of tea. Father would undoubtedly have a seizure when he got the itemised phone bill – itemised so that Nicola '. . . couldn't ruin me ringing that lout . . .'

While her mother was making the second cup of tea, Aisling idly mused that Telecom Eireann should have a special 'disaster' phone-call rate, a once-a-month reduction so that people with problems could ring their relatives and receive family counselling. They'd make a fortune.

'Are you not having a cup yourself, love?' Her mother asked in concern when she picked up the receiver again.

'No. I've gone off tea and coffee. Weird, isn't it? And I haven't so much as looked at a chocolate biscuit all weekend!'

'Well, that's good, darling,' answered her mother, sounding

123

unsure as to the benefits of a chocolate biscuit aversion in the middle of a crisis.

'It's just that I've always tried so hard to stop myself eating biscuits,' explained Aisling. 'I wanted to be slim and a size ten, like the woman Michael married. But I couldn't help myself, I kept eating and kept hating myself for eating. It was a vicious circle I couldn't escape. And now I'm not hungry at all and he isn't here to see it . . .' Her voice broke for the first time since they'd started talking. 'Oh Mum, what's going to happen? What went wrong?'

'I don't know, love,' her mother answered. 'I don't think it's that simple or that black and white. When your father and I were married, we knew it was for keeps, no matter what happened. And Lord knows, I've felt like getting a divorce myself more often than I'd care to admit. Your father hasn't been easy, you know that,' she added. 'But it's different now. Everyone expects more from life, everyone wants to be happy. They demand it. Nobody wants to try any more.'

'I wanted to try,' sobbed Aisling. 'He didn't. He's a bastard, isn't he?'

Her mother said nothing.

'Well he is, isn't he? Don't you think so? Or is it all my fault?'

'It's not your fault, Aisling. I just don't want to start criticising Michael. I made that mistake once with your father when he and your grandmother had a big row. By the time they were great pals again, he'd remembered the things I'd said about her and I don't think he ever forgave me for it.'

'You mean that Michael and I might get back together,' whispered Aisling hopefully.

'Nobody knows what's going to happen,' her mother said diplomatically. 'I just can't see the two of you split up for very long. Michael isn't stupid. He'll miss the boys and his life with you. He won't be able to forget all about the last twelve years just like that.'

'You think so?'

Aisling was ten once again, with a big tear in her new green striped dress from climbing over the fence at the back of the park and getting stuck on the barbed wire. She was waiting for her mother to fix it, to fix everything. Mam always knew the right thing to say. Her gentle and kind voice softened the harshest blow. She could mend any rip with her tiny, almost invisible stitches, dry the bitterest tears with the right words, and straighten out Aisling's world when everything seemed awry.

Now Aisling wanted her to fix something that had been battered radically out of shape. It wasn't fair, was it?

'I'm sorry, Mam,' she said quickly. 'I shouldn't have asked that. Jesus, if I don't know what's going to happen or how he's going to think, I can hardly ask you.'

'Aisling, I'd love to tell you it'll all work out between you and Michael, but I can't. It may not work out the way you want. And you'll have to face that. I do wish things were different, though,' sighed her mother. 'I know you're putting on a brave face, darling, but it's not going to be easy. I'd love if there was something I could say to make you feel better, but I don't know what to say.'

'As long as you don't tell Dad what's really happened,' begged Aisling, 'that's the best thing you could do.'

'Your father isn't that bad . . .' began Eithne loyally.

'Mam,' interrupted Aisling, 'he'd be disgusted we're splitting up and it would be all my fault. You know what he'd say. I can just do without that sort of disapproval right now. I mean, I have to psych myself up to get a job for a start. That's going to take about ten times more self-confidence than I've got as it is. I mean,' she said tiredly, 'I've been waking up in the middle of the night just *thinking* about it all in terror. What if I'm useless?'

'Don't be daft, Aisling.' Her mother's voice was firm. 'You've been running that house like clockwork for ten years, and you've never been afraid to get your hands dirty. Don't tell me you're afraid of working in an office, because you shouldn't be.'

There it was again. *Another* person who believed she was superwoman. Had she been incredibly successful at deceiving people into thinking she could do anything? Or, and this had to be wrong, did they actually believe that she *could* do anything? What a pity Michael hadn't felt the same.

CHAPTER EIGHT

Jo leaned weakly against the bath, ignoring the freezing tiles hard against her knees. She felt cold in just a T-shirt and knickers, but when the nausea hit her, she hadn't time to grab her dressing-gown. She barely had time to reach the bathroom before she retched.

She knelt by the toilet in exhaustion as the spasms in her stomach ceased. Maybe if she breathed deeply, she could calm the nausea with relaxing breaths. But even deep breathing felt too strenuous.

Instead, she just stayed where she was, closed her eyes and wished she could crawl back to bed until she felt better. Bed always seemed more appealing when you couldn't sleep late. This morning, the soft sky-blue sheets and cosy duvet were positively irresistible, simply because she had to leave them.

Rhona was already halfway to France, complete with the car, kids and enough books to last for three glorious weeks travelling around the Loire Valley. Jo had to edit the August edition of *Style* on her own. Usually, she loved the challenge of doing two jobs at once, planning the magazine and setting up fashion shoots in between chasing up articles and dealing with endless phone calls. Inevitably someone forgot to get a photo of this new designer or that TV chat show host at home, and the entire office would collapse into panic before Jo took charge and sorted whatever mini-disaster out.

Today she felt incapable of organising her underwear drawer, never mind Ireland's biggest-selling glossy magazine. It was ten past eight, she realised tiredly. Time to have breakfast. The very thought of eating made her feel ill.

She closed her eyes for a couple of blissful minutes, and steeled herself to get up and face the day.

Why did something so utterly wonderful as having a baby include one of the most horrible side effects imaginable? And why did she have to be one of the fifty per cent of expectant mothers who suffered from it? She hated the other fifty per cent.

Jo had read all about hormonal surges and gastric juices ganging up on you to make you sick as a pig. But the paragraph about overcoming morning sickness in her ancient edition of *Everywoman* had been the last straw.

Reading that having a small carbohydrate-rich breakfast '. . . brought to the wife by the husband as soon as possible after waking . . .' had made her feel even sicker, if that was possible. What she wouldn't have given to have Richard hovering over her in the morning, bringing sweet tea and sympathy along with toast and marmalade. Stop moping, Ryan, and get on with it.

She got up off the bathroom floor and washed her teeth. Her face was still deathly pale and she looked tired and drawn. Who cares, she said aloud. Nobody's going to be looking at me today. They'll just have to put up with a pale and interesting fashion editor for once.

It was only when Jo was gingerly sipping a cup of coffee that she remembered the lunchtime fashion show, a preview of the Autumn and Winter range from one of the country's most famous – and expensive – designers.

Jo had been invited weeks ago and would have to turn up, nausea or no nausea. It was going to be a glamorous, high-profile affair with every fashion editor in the country on full make-up alert, wearing the most expensive outfits from their wardrobes. An A-list fashion show, definitely. Designer Maxine was showing her collection in Stark's, a chic and over-priced restaurant where the price of one bottle of good wine would feed a family of five for a week.

Not that any of the fashion pack would actually *eat* very much. Eating and being a fashion journalist were mutually exclusive – you couldn't do both. Everyone would just pick at their food.

Jo nibbled the corner of a piece of cream cracker wearily. Why did the show have to be today? Instead of slopping into the office in a sweatshirt and comfortable jeans, she'd have to dress up and, for once, she just didn't have the energy for it. Damn, damn, damn, she muttered. She opened the wardrobe and stared at the crammed rails of clothes. She plucked a fitted red jacket from the middle of the rail and held it up to herself. Too bright, she decided, jamming it back into the wardrobe.

She mulled over a clinging navy shift dress with a matching short jacket. With the right sunglasses and pearls, it looked very Jackie O. But Jo wasn't in a Jackie O mood. She looked more like Jack Charlton.

It would have to be the hand-painted silk dress she'd got in the Design Centre. Pale gold with rich, burnt umber brush-strokes, the clinging dress always made her look like something from a medieval tapestry with her hair falling in curls around her bare shoulders. Perfect.

But it wasn't. Instead of highlighting her curves, the dress simply highlighted her belly. Flat just the week before, it had turned into a little mound overnight and the gold dress stretched across it unbecomingly.

The grey pinstripe trouser suit was just as bad. The ultra-expensive black lycra dress, which was guaranteed to vacuum-pack even the flabbiest tummy, was even worse. She wasn't in the mood to wear the navy crêpe trousers and matching mandarin shirt, even if it was loose enough to look good.

Baby, what am I going to do with you? Jo asked her bump. Poor Mummy can't go to Maxine's fashion show looking like a bag lady. What am I going to wear? You're going to have to get used to being asked this question, you know.

She stroked her belly softly, sure that the baby was listening to every word. You're going to be the most fashion-conscious baby the world has ever known, all right, darling?

If only Rhona wasn't on holidays. Jo could have rung up and asked if she could take the day off. And just blobbed around all day, watching the afternoon soaps and drinking tea.

Instead, she had to find some bloody thing which would fit her *and* look nice.

An hour later, she strode into the office looking as if she'd just spent the morning having the works done at the beauty parlour. Her glossy dark hair was coiled into an elegant knot held in place with tortoiseshell pins. She wore a slim-fitting navy jacket unbuttoned over a biscuit-coloured silk dress. Sheer tights and beige high-heeled mules completed the effect. Jo looked marvellous. Nobody would notice that her open jacket hid a softly rounded stomach.

'Thank God you're here,' gushed Emma Lynch, who rushed into Rhona's office just moments after Jo had arrived and put her briefcase down on the editor's desk.

'Why? What's happened?' Jo didn't look up as she opened the briefcase, and took out her diary and a computer disk. She couldn't stand Emma but she had to keep it to herself.

A twenty-six-year-old rich girl with delusions of brilliance and a penchant for tantrums, Emma was one of the most irritating people Jo had ever met. Unfortunately, she was also the publisher's niece and had recently been appointed to the position of junior features writer, despite her inability to write an entire paragraph without a grammatical error.

No talent and good connections make a winning combination, Rhona said drily. She had agreed to take Emma on for two years when she'd finished her one-year public relations course. Everyone else had regretted it ever since.

Emma's job was to rewrite press releases, get quotes from celebrities about their beauty hints and do general dogsbody work. Naturally, this wasn't good enough for Emma.

She moaned about not getting anything enjoyable to write and had started wheedling her uncle for promotion. She wanted to do 'proper' interviews, she'd been telling anyone who'd listen. Not just rewrite boring press releases or answer the phones. But something juicy. Today she'd found just what she was looking for.

'You won't *believe* what's happened!' Emma said dramatically. She said everything dramatically. It drove Jo mad.

130

'Poor Mary has got the most awful flu and can't go to London to do that interview with Helen Mirren. She rang in earlier and, because you weren't here, I took the liberty of ringing Uncle Mark and asking him what he thought . . .' Emma smiled a self-satisfied little smile. 'Well, to see if he thought I should go, actually. Because we couldn't keep them waiting just because you weren't in . . .'

'Hold on a minute, Emma,' Jo interrupted coolly. 'When did Mary ring in?'

'At ten past nine, and . . .'

Jo interrupted again. 'And what time was Mary's interview scheduled?'

'Half six in the Mayfair.'

'This evening?'

'Yes, but the flight was booked and everything . . .'

'Emma, why did you decide to ring Mark with something like this when you knew I was going to be in this morning, and when you also knew we had plenty of time to get someone else to interview Helen Mirren? Can you tell me that?' Jo's tone was sharp.

Normally she was able to ignore Emma's manipulative behaviour and constant running to 'Uncle Mark', but not today.

'Well, I just thought it would be . . .' stuttered Emma, going an ugly shade of pink.

'Better if *you* went, Emma? Or better to organise something without consulting me?'

Jo sat down in Rhona's big swivel chair and steepled her hands in front of her. She knew exactly what Emma had been up to. She'd made Jo look bad in front of Mark Denton, *Style*'s publisher, and netted a major interview for herself into the bargain.

Denton was a man famous for his lack of patience and his business skills, in that order. He was also unaccountably fond of his niece.

'I thought it would be helpful if I went.' Emma sniffed. Jo eyed her warily, realising that the younger woman was ready

131

to go into tantrum overdrive. Big mistake, Emma, she thought.

'Shut the door, Emma, and sit down,' Jo commanded.

Startled, Emma obeyed.

'Now you listen to me. Don't you dare go over my head ever again, do you understand? I'm the deputy editor and when Rhona is away, I'm acting editor. I will not stand for some little madam trying to tell me how to run this magazine, do you understand?' Jo hissed.

'If you want to learn *anything*, you've got to work *with* me, not against me, Emma. You got this job because of who you are, but if you ever want to get *any* job on merit,' she yelled, 'you'd better stop playing games and learn. And that means taking orders. You're not going to London for that interview.'

Emma was open-mouthed with shock, but Jo didn't stop.

'I'm rescheduling the interview so Mary can do it. You haven't the experience for this type of interview. Now cancel those plane tickets.'

With that, Jo picked up the phone and dialled Mary's number.

'You can't do that, I've got it all arranged!' shrieked Emma.

'I can and I will,' answered Jo icily. 'I presume you have some work to do, so do it!'

Emma flounced out of the room, slamming the door childishly. Straight off to ring Uncle Mark, no doubt, Jo thought wearily. With a great start to the morning.

She'd just finished talking to Helen Mirren's publicity consultant when Annette, the receptionist, came in with a cup of tea and a message from Mark Denton.

'He's in the car and wants you to ring him back pronto,' said Annette. 'I'm sure you can guess what it's about. I heard that little bitch phoning him as soon as she left your office.'

'That girl will be the death of me,' Jo said.

'Pity she couldn't be the death of herself,' Annette said.

Jo waited until she'd drunk most of her tea before phoning the boss. She'd need every spare ounce of self-control not to scream back at him once he got started.

Mark was one of those people capable of sending her into a frenzy of temper, something he regularly managed at the weekly editorial meetings. He remained calm, no matter what, while she was left open-mouthed with temper. How Rhona managed to get on with him so well was a complete mystery to Jo.

'What the hell is going on over there?' Mark demanded. 'I've just had Emma crying at me over the phone about some stupid bloody interview and wasting money on plane tickets. Jesus, don't tell me you can't run the place when bloody Rhona's away!'

Jo could feel her blood pressure rise along with her temper. Relax, she said to herself, don't lose your cool.

'There's no problem, Mark,' she replied calmly. 'Unfortunately, Mary is sick and can't fly to London for an interview she'd set up with Helen Mirren. Emma seems to have got the idea that *she* should go and had it all arranged until I got here.' She paused before the lie.

'It would be marvellous if Emma could have gone, but I happen to know that Helen is, er . . . very particular about interviewers, she prefers more experienced journalists.' She crossed her fingers at the lie. 'Emma just doesn't fit the bill. If she's that keen to interview someone, I can set up something less challenging for her, but she's not ready for big interviews yet.'

'What the hell's the problem, then?' Denton's voice was a fraction less aggressive. 'Why's she ringing me in floods? Rhona doesn't have this effect on her.'

Suddenly Jo snapped. If he wanted to know what the problem was, she was damn well going to tell him!

'The problem is that Emma finds it very difficult to take orders or to be told what to do, Mark,' Jo said candidly. 'She doesn't want to be a team player, she wants to be out on her own.

'We've had some great journalism students in the office and they've been eager to learn, willing to do any job to gain experience.' Her voice was raised and she just didn't care.

'Emma has never been like that. She thinks she knows it all

133

and she never wants to do what she's asked. She just doesn't understand that there's a lot more to journalism than interviewing someone famous. Emma thinks she's too good for the day-to-day jobs in a magazine. And to make matters worse,' Jo paused for breath, 'she does everything she can to create friction in the office. Ringing you this morning before I got in is a prime example of what I mean. That's Emma trying to make trouble and abusing her relationship with you,' she spat. 'I won't stand for it.

'If you want her to be the editor of *Style*, Mark, then make her editor. But until you do, don't expect me to kowtow to her just because she's your niece, right!'

There was a silence at the other end of the phone. Jo was wondering whether she'd gone too far when he spoke.

'At least I can rely on you for straight-talking, Jo,' Denton said flatly. 'And that certainly was straight-talking. I didn't know Emma was such a problem, Rhona never mentioned it before.'

'Emma is in awe of Rhona, so she never puts a foot out of place when she's around. She doesn't feel the same about *me*,' Jo admitted. 'That's the problem. She thinks she can use you to sideline me. I don't dislike Emma,' she lied. 'But I won't have some twenty-six-year-old with zero experience trying to tell me how to run this magazine.'

'Point taken,' he said coolly. 'I'll tell Emma not to run to me when something disagrees with her, but I want you to work with her, Jo. She's got her heart set on journalism and I promised her parents I'd give her a good start.' His voice softened. 'She's a sweet kid at heart, you just don't know her. That tough exterior is all a front.'

Yeah, thought Jo. She's just a cuddly little thing, like a bloody piranha. Still, you've got enough opinions off your chest for one day, Ryan. Keep your mouth shut if you want to keep working.

'I know what you mean,' she answered warmly. What an Oscar-winning performance.

'She's probably insecure. I never spotted it until now. I was

134

quite taken in by that tough act. Don't worry, Mark, I'll work with her. But she's got to learn to work under me, she'll never get on in this business if she automatically puts up her fists to the boss.'

'Yeah, you're right, Jo. Help her out, she's a good kid,' Mark said earnestly.

'Of course. I'll bring her in later and get this sorted out.'

'That's great, Jo. Talk to you tomorrow.'

With that, he was gone. Jo hung up with relief and leaned back in her chair. It was still only eleven o'clock, but she felt as if she'd been in the office all day. This isn't good for you, my darling, she addressed her bump.

By the time Jo had discussed the beauty pages and the lucrative suncream advertisement supplement with the beauty writer, Nikki, chief sub Tony and Aidan from advertising, it was nearly time to leave for the lunch. After redoing her lipstick and anchoring a few stray hairs back into the knot at the nape of her neck, she grabbed her handbag and marched out of Rhona's office.

Nikki was standing up beside the reception desk, talking rapidly on the phone and attempting to open her mascara at the same time.

Annette was unwrapping a sandwich covered in clingfilm and talking to Brenda, who was eating a rice cake and eyeing the mayonnaise squelching out of Annette's tuna sandwich hungrily.

Emma was nowhere to be seen.

'She went off to lunch half an hour ago,' Annette informed Jo. 'She said she wouldn't be back.'

'OK,' said Jo. 'Brenda, will you talk to Nikki about writing the suncream supplement. I was hoping to get Emma working on it, but if she's not back today, I want you to take over. How's the diet going?' she added, as Brenda spread a meagre amount of diet cottage cheese on another rice cake.

'Fine,' answered Brenda glumly. 'I've lost nearly a stone. I've only another ten pounds to go.'

'When's the wedding, anyway?' Jo asked.

'The end of July. My sister's lost all her weight and she's bought a size twelve wedding dress. I'm not going if I can't get into a size twelve.'

'Don't be daft, Brenda,' interjected Nikki, sliding tanned skinny arms into a slinky little pale gold cardigan. 'You'll look marvellous whatever size you are. I'll give you some of that wonderful Lancôme face tanner and you'll look sexy and sunkissed.'

'Nikki, you're starting to *sound* like a cosmetics press release,' laughed Jo.

'I sleep with make-up brochures under my pillow and *absorb* it all.' Nikki took a brush out of her handbag and ran it through her straight blonde bob. 'I don't put milk under my cornflakes any more, I replenish their lost moisture with a vital enriching fluid!'

'Don't mock it,' Jo said. 'Think how handy all that "replenishing moisture" jargon comes in when you're writing ad features!'

'That's this afternoon's work,' Nikki smiled on her way out the door. 'Now, I'm going to stuff my face in Bewley's with my beloved husband and he'll kill me if I'm late. Bye.'

'I'm going to be late myself,' Jo said, looking at her watch. 'Annette, I'm going to Stark's for Maxine's fashion show. God only knows when I'll be back. These damn things always start late. When Emma comes in, tell her she's not to leave this evening until she's seen me, right?'

'No problem,' said Annette.

The four o'clock news was blasting out of Annette's radio when Jo finally walked into the office, clutching a hand-painted silk scarf from Maxine's beautiful, albeit overpriced, new collection.

'Emma's gone home, Nikki had to leave early but left the beauty feature on your desk and you're to ring Anna from Models Inc. about who you're going to pick for the wedding dress feature.' Efficient as ever, Annette handed over a sheaf of pale yellow phone messages along with some post.

'I thought Emma was to stay until I'd talked to her,' said Jo crossly.

'Wouldn't listen, just marched off about five minutes after she got back from lunch,' Annette explained.

Jo sighed and walked into Rhona's office, wishing she'd had the chance to tackle Emma before the little bitch went home to Mummy with tales of woe about the horrible deputy editor. Would Denton sack her *before* or *after* her maternity leave?

'Oh, Jo,' called Annette. 'I nearly forgot. Richard rang and said he'd see you tonight at your place.'

Jo felt her heart quicken. Richard wanted to see her, he'd changed his mind, he *must* have! Oh, thank you, God, thank you, she whispered fervently. He wants me to give him another chance, I just know it.

Emma instantly forgotten, Jo rushed to the loo to see how she looked. Her carefully applied foundation had almost vanished in the summer heat and there were little smudges of mascara under her eyes. No problem. She whisked out her make-up bag and started the repair job.

How like Richard not to say *when* he was coming, she thought happily, blotting up excess lipstick with a tissue. But who cared what time he arrived? He was coming to see her, that was enough.

She was squirting another blast of Trésor onto her wrists when the doorbell rang.

Richard looked better than ever, blond hair gleaming against faintly tanned skin. A broad smile showed off the perfectly white teeth he brushed religiously.

'Jo, my darling,' he murmured, sliding one arm around her waist as he pulled her close for a slow, sensuous kiss.

'Oh, Richard,' she said softly. 'I've missed you so much.'

'I know, my darling, I know. These,' he produced a huge bouquet of pink roses from behind his back, 'are for you.'

Jo felt tears prickle behind her eyes. Pink roses. 'They're so beautiful,' she said tearfully. 'Thank you.'

137

'Don't cry,' Richard said quickly. 'Let's put these on ice.'

He bent down and picked up two bottles of white wine from the doorstep.

'It's your favourite, darling, German Riesling. Now, have you got anything to eat? I'm starved.'

'Er, no.' She'd spent the whole weekend planning to shop properly and had still only made it to the corner shop for milk, bread, cheese and ice cream. Chocolate-chip Häagen Dazs. Sinful but glorious.

Anyway, why didn't he bring something to eat if he was hungry? In fact, why had he brought wine when he *knew* she couldn't drink any? Oh well, he was just being Richard – thoughtful and thoughtless at the same time.

At least he was making an effort. He never remembered practical things, but he was trying. She'd just have to get used to his foibles when they were living together. So what if he always drank the last of the milk and then expected more to materialise magically, that was Richard for you. She could live with it. Thank God he was back. She loved him so much, she couldn't let her damn hormones screw their reunion up.

In the kitchen he'd found the corkscrew and was expertly opening the first bottle. She stared lovingly at the back of his neck, admiring the way the denim blue shirt clung to his strong shoulders.

'Glasses, darling?' he inquired. Jo opened a cupboard and handed him a wine glass.

'I can't drink, Richard, because of the baby.'

'Have a sip,' he said persuasively. 'Half a glass won't kill you.'

They sat on the big three-seater settee, the way they always had. He lounged at one end, the glass of wine beside him on a small table. Jo sat curled up beside him.

Sky Sports blared out of the TV, but Jo didn't mind. He paid the subscription so he never missed an important match and usually she sat and read while he watched, bored with the endless discussions of players and tactics.

138

Now, she sat peacefully, watching him watching TV, content just to be close to him.

Maybe it was the weekend without him, a weekend without his touch, that made her so needy. She'd missed him, missed his touch, missed his arms around her.

After two years with Richard, she'd almost forgotten all those times when she'd felt desperate for a man's touch, felt alone and unloved when her current man wrote himself out of her life. She certainly should have remembered what it felt like, it had happened often enough. But that was all in the past. Thankfully.

Her fingers spread out on Richard's chest as he watched the TV, luxuriating in the feeling of soft denim warmed by his skin. He didn't respond, totally absorbed in the game. Nothing changes, she thought happily, delighted at his presence and determined not to freak about the things which had always irritated her before. The poor man needed time to get used to pregnancy mood swings.

She felt perfectly happy. Serene, almost. This was bliss. He'd changed his mind, he'd come back to her and the baby. They had a future again. They were going to be parents. She was going to have the most beautiful, most adored baby in the whole world. It was all so perfect.

When the match was over, Richard was still hungry. 'Let's get pizza,' he said, stroking her cheek gently before kissing her on the forehead. 'A twelve-inch pepperoni with garlic bread. My wallet's in my jacket.' Jo felt hungry herself, despite the large lunch she'd wolfed down in Stark's.

He was opening the second bottle of wine when the pizza arrived. The quarter of a glass of wine that Jo had drunk was rattling acidly around her stomach, but she was still starving. They ate enthusiastically straight from the box, strings of mozzarella dripping juicily from the slices of pizza they pulled apart with their hands.

'Delicious,' Jo mumbled, her mouth full.

'Like you,' Richard grinned back.

They never got to see the Liverpool match. Instead, they

ended up on the carpet, kissing garlic butter off each other's mouths and pulling at clothes with greasy fingers.

When they finally made it into the bedroom, Richard finished undressing her, carefully unclasped her bra and buried his face between her breasts, fuller now than they'd ever been before. He licked each nipple eagerly before sucking them, making Jo arch her back with pleasure.

'Oh, darling,' she moaned, 'that's wonderful.' She ran her fingers through his hair as he kissed her breasts, sending quivering bolts of desire through her body.

'How's this?' he asked, sliding his hand down her belly until he was stroking the soft skin of her thighs, making her purr with pleasure. His fingers stroked the soft silk of her skin, gently roaming under the elastic of her silk panties to touch her softly, fingers tantalising and questing.

God she wanted him, she was ready for him, so ready. Who needed foreplay after a weekend apart?

'I've missed you, Richard,' she said, moving out from under him, straddling him and leaning down to kiss his lips gently. She nuzzled his neck while one hand fumbled with his belt, trying to open it without looking.

When she turned to look, her breasts, heavy and ripe, swung low and his lips moved to catch a nipple in his mouth. It was amazing, simply amazing what he could do to her. She felt sexier than ever before, as though being pregnant made everything make sense. Pregnant, she was utterly womanly and feminine, ripe and blooming, thanks to this man who was burning her skin with his touch.

'And I've missed you,' he groaned, his hands pulling her hips down hard onto his, grinding his hard body under hers. 'I want you now, Jo.'

Quickly, he slid her panties off and ripped off his boxer shorts. Pulling her on top of him again, he slid inside her, feeling her soft, welcoming and wet.

'Oh, Jo,' he moaned, burying himself in her as deep as he could. 'That's so good.'

It was, it was wonderful. She clung to him, sweat beading

140

on her upper lip as he thrust into her, again and again. She wanted him so much, she was so excited. She was nearly there, nearly coming.

'Oh, Jo,' he shouted, 'oh God!'

His body spasmed, as he thrust deep inside her before he collapsed on top of her body, breathing shallowly and quickly in post-orgasmic exhaustion.

Her own excitement dipped instantly, needing his friction to bring her to orgasm. Damn. As he lay on her heavily, she breathed more evenly and wrapped her arms around his body.

She wouldn't come now, the moment had passed.

'That was amazing, Jo,' he murmured.

Gently stroking his cheek, she felt a rush of emotions well up inside her. She loved him, but he was so selfish. Just because he was as horny as hell after a sex-free weekend didn't mean he had to completely forget about her satisfaction and make love like a chauvinist pig. She'd been so turned on and she'd missed him so much, she'd been crazy for him. And he hadn't cared that she hadn't come.

Damn him! Richard never changed, did he?

He shifted beside her, reached one hand up and caressed her face.

'I love you, Jo, you know that?'

Of course, she melted. He'd always had the power to do that to her, to make her forget his behaviour with just a few words. It didn't matter that she hadn't come. They were together, together with their baby. That was all that mattered.

Her fingers smoothed his hair, moved down to massage his shoulders. His skin was damp with sweat.

Together they'd made a baby, a precious life. Yes, they'd had their fights and they'd argued bitterly a few days ago, but that was natural. People fought and argued. Now Richard had accepted their baby and he wanted to be with her. OK, so he hadn't said it in so many words. But he meant it. He didn't have to *say* it. She knew.

'Darling, I'm so tired,' Richard said sleepily. He slid one arm under his head like a pillow. 'That was great, I'm just so tired. 'Night,' he muttered.

She watched him, sexy, handsome and thoughtless. But he was her man, the father of her unborn baby. Maybe fatherhood would knock some of the thoughtlessness out of him.

Moving gently so she wouldn't wake him, Jo untangled her limbs from his and climbed out of the bed, padding silently into the bathroom to wash her teeth. Almost too tired to take off her make-up, she forced herself to go through her usual beauty routine.

She splashed cleanser on her face, wiped away the grime of make-up and pollution with cotton wool, and brushed her teeth carefully. She quickly applied a film of moisturiser, then rubbed body lotion into her breasts, to keep pregnancy stretch marks at bay. That'd do.

She switched off the bathroom light and wandered into the sitting room and turned off the TV. Richard's jacket and jeans were flung on the settee and the huge pizza box sat opened on the glass coffee table. Grease-marked kitchen paper and two crumpled sections of tinfoil lay on the ground. The smell of garlic bread permeated the air. She'd tidy it up in the morning.

The sun didn't wake her, even when it shone in through a crack in the curtains at dawn, a shaft of light cutting through the dark of the bedroom like a floodlight. It was the morning sickness that did it, waking her up just after seven with bile rising in her throat. She knew she was going to be sick right now.

She got to the loo just in time, retching painfully as her sleepy body tried to come to terms with another bout of pregnancy nausea.

'Baby, how can you be *doing* this to me?' Jo groaned wretchedly, hanging over the toilet bowl for the nth morning in a row. 'Why can't I be one of those lucky cows who don't suffer from morning sickness?'

After ten minutes waiting to get worse, she began to feel

marginally better. Thank God. Jo got up shakily and reached for the Bathroom Duck. What a stupid bloody name, she thought, squirting a blast of lemon goo around the rim of the toilet. Doesn't look anything like a bloody duck.

Her mouth felt like the inside of a binman's wellie, she thought. That's daft too. Who the hell knows what a binman's wellie tastes like?

She couldn't face brushing her teeth so she stumbled into the kitchen and turned on the kettle. A cup of sweet tea would be the business. She was absolutely exhausted, but there was nothing like a session of puking to make you totally and undeniably awake.

One empty wine bottle stood on the counter and she jammed it head-first into the bin. Bloody ironic to feel like she was incredibly hung-over every day when she hadn't drunk more than half a glass of wine since getting pregnant.

The other bottle stood on the coffee table. By rights, Richard should have the most appalling hangover since he'd drunk most of the two bottles. But he'd probably be fine, all that training to be a sports photographer had made him immune to hangovers.

Sky News was chirpy and irritating. Jo watched it for half an hour and then decided to tidy up. What was the point in spending all morning groaning about being sick? Since she was up that early and since Richard would lie in bed for hours, she might as well take advantage of the fact and clean the flat.

It didn't take long to bin the remains of the pizza, but it would take a bit longer to get rid of the smell of garlic bread left hardening overnight on the coffee table. When she'd dumped everything and put down carpet freshener for when she could hoover, she picked up Richard's discarded clothes and folded them neatly.

His wallet lay on the hall table with the change from the pizza beside it. Jo smiled at the wallet, remembering buying it for him in Bloomingdale's in New York.

It had been made by Gucci and was miles cheaper than it

143

would have been in Dublin. 'So you'll think of me whenever you open your wallet,' she'd joked at the time. It was an old Dublin gag they'd both known and laughed at – how did you find your girlfriend? I opened my wallet and there she was.

Jo put the change into the wallet and tried to slide it into the inside pocket of his jacket. It wouldn't fit. Something bulky was blocking it. Puzzled, Jo pulled an envelope out of the pocket, smoothing it out to reveal a Ryanair travel folder. Something clicked inside her head and she opened it quickly. It couldn't be, no way. It just *couldn't* be.

The ticket was open-ended, executive class to London the following Monday morning. Jo stared at it for a moment. London. He was still going to London.

Her mind sped back over the previous night's events. Richard had never said anything to make her think he'd changed his mind. She'd just *assumed* that he had, assumed that his very presence was proof that he'd acquiesced. That he wanted her and their baby. The flowers, the wine, *everything*.

But he hadn't. What had he come for, a quick fuck? she thought bitterly. Why hadn't he *said* anything? Because that would be too difficult, too confrontational, of course.

'I hate rows,' he claimed from time to time, usually when they were in the middle of one. He preferred to walk away from the argument, get into his car and drive off for the day. Then he'd ring her the next day, say sorry and arrange dinner. By then, Jo's temper would have cooled and the fight would be shelved, if not forgotten.

Damn him, she wasn't going to let him run away this time. He wasn't going to breeze back into her life for a few hours and just breeze out again. This was serious. She was pregnant and he was going to run away again? No way.

'Richard,' she said loudly, shaking his shoulder. 'Wakey, wakey.'

He blinked tiredly, screwing up his eyes at the harsh sunlight streaming into the bedroom. 'What time is it?' he mumbled hoarsely.

'Ten past eight,' she snapped.

'Jesus, Jo, why did you wake me?' he groaned. 'I'm shat-tered.'

'*You're* shattered?' she screeched. 'What about me? When were you going to tell me about London, Richard? When? Were you going to ring from the airport? Or from your hotel in London?'

'Oh for God's sake,' he muttered, turning away from her in the bed. 'It's no big deal. I'm just going for a couple of weeks to see what it would be like working there. I'm not emigrat-ing.'

'Not yet, maybe, but you will. Ireland's too bloody boring for you, isn't it, Richard?' she demanded. 'You want *excite-ment*, don't you? The world would end if Richard Kennedy actually had to settle down for more than five minutes! All I want to know is where I fit into all of this? Or have you forgotten that I'm carrying our baby?'

'Don't be ridiculous, Jo!' He sat up in the bed, raked his hair out of his eyes and looked at her warily. 'I haven't forgotten. I just thought you might have given the subject some more thought. You know, what it'll mean to your career or whatever, and maybe even changed your mind. We don't have to do this now.'

Jo stared at him angrily. She couldn't believe what he was saying. If she hadn't wanted an abortion on Friday, she damn well wasn't going to want one now.

Richard pushed the duvet back abruptly and got out of bed. He strode into the bathroom and slammed the door behind him.

'I'm afraid we *do* have to do this now,' she shouted through the door. 'The baby isn't going to go away, Richard, I'm still having it.'

The toilet flushed. Richard marched out of the bathroom, wiping his face on a towel. He didn't speak.

'When you turned up last night, I thought *you'd* changed your mind,' Jo said fiercely. 'How can you do this to me? Is this your party piece, running away from women when you get them pregnant?'

145

It was as if she'd flicked a switch. His face changed in an instant, becoming dark like thunder. Jo had never seen him like this and she was stunned, afraid almost.

'I didn't do anything,' he snarled. 'You wanted to trap me, didn't you? Well it's not going to work.'

Almost absently, Jo took her old pink fluffy dressing-gown off the hook on the bedroom door and wrapped it around her. It was sunny outside. The weather forecast on Sky had promised balmy weather, but Jo still felt cold. She stood beside the bed and stared blankly at the dressing-table mirror, not seeing her reflection at all.

He picked up his watch from the dressing table and strapped it onto his wrist. She followed him into the sitting room where he picked up his clothes and dressed silently, barely contained rage in every movement.

'Richard,' she said tentatively. 'We have to talk . . .'

'No, we don't. You've made your bed, you lie on it,' he spat.

That did it. 'Don't talk to me like that, you arrogant pig!' she yelled. 'We both did it, do you think I got pregnant on my own?' She faced him angrily.

'Yeah, well I don't want it,' Richard said, venom in every syllable. 'I'm leaving.'

'You can't,' Jo said. 'How dare you talk to me like that, you're all the same, bloody men terrified of commitment!'

'And *you're* all the bloody same,' he answered harshly, 'getting pregnant at the drop of a hat because it's the only way to get a ring on your finger. Well it's been tried before, sweetie, and I didn't bite the bullet that time either!'

'What do you mean?' asked Jo, stunned.

He said nothing, just continued buttoning his jeans calmly.

Jesus, he couldn't be saying what she thought he was saying. 'Beate. She got pregnant, didn't she?'

'So?'

'Why did you never tell me?'

'There was nothing to tell,' he said flatly.

'Did she have the baby?' Jo asked.

'What is this?' he demanded. 'Twenty fucking questions?'

146

She hesitated at the anger in his voice. 'I just wanted to know.'

'Yes, all right? She had the baby and I have never seen it and she probably wouldn't let me, even if I wanted to, which I don't!' he slid his feet into his Italian suede slip-ons and picked up his jacket.

'Oh, Richard, why?'

'Look, just because you've always played happy families doesn't mean that everyone else does, right? You don't know what it's like to have a father who couldn't give a shit whether you lived or died, a father who'd kick you rather than say a kind word. I do,' he hissed. 'I know *just* what that's like and I'll tell you something, it turns you off the idea of having kids. I don't want any fucking kids. I decided that a long time ago. That's my choice. If you're so fired up about a woman's right to choose, why don't you ever think about a man's right to choose, eh?'

Jo said nothing, silent in the face of Richard's fury and anger, an anger which had lived inside him for thirty-seven long years.

'All that feminist stuff about a woman's body being her own, that all sounds great when it's about women,' he continued angrily, 'but let a man say what *he* really wants, and that's different! I don't want kids. Simple as that. That's my decision,' he hissed. 'I gave you the chance and you didn't take it. So you do what you want. You will anyway.'

With that, he picked up his jacket and car keys and walked to the door.

'Call me a bastard or whatever you want, I'm sorry. It's over.'

The front door slammed. She was alone.

CHAPTER NINE

Her shoes pinched. Why was she wearing those bloody shoes in the first place? Aisling realised they looked wrong about fifteen minutes after she left the house. By then, it was too late to turn back. They were too high, shoes bought for a wedding outfit that had languished in the wardrobe for three years after that one July day when the sun had thwarted the bridal party and stayed firmly behind the clouds.

They'd been too high then, sinking heavily into the grass outside the church. And they were still too high. Aisling did her best to walk quickly along Leeson Street, feeling totally self-conscious in her navy blazer, long cream skirt and cream court shoes.

The people sitting in motionless cars were probably office veterans, no doubt. Seasoned workers who knew what to wear to work and how to do more than switch on a computer. Could they see pure ignorance written all over her face? And pure fear, come to that?

Streams of people passed her by, walking quickly along the pavement, listening to Walkmans and staring straight ahead as they bypassed slow walkers and parking meters.

From open car windows, she could hear snippets of radio talk shows and the thumping bass of loud music. Aisling sneaked the odd sideways glance into the cars beside her. One attractive woman was peering into her rear-view mirror, mascara wand held aloft as she finished her morning make-up. Another driver was reading, a newspaper spread out on the steering wheel. Others just gazed vacantly out of their windscreens, probably praying for the car ahead to move.

It was all so hectic, Aisling thought in surprise. She hadn't seen Leeson Street this busy for years, nearly twelve years to be exact. Since she'd given up work, she was never there during the early morning rush. If she brought the boys into the city centre during the school holidays, she waited until the traffic jams were gone.

Now, in common with all the people walking purposefully towards offices, banks and shops, it was where she worked. Work. She had a job. Oh God. Those words hadn't seemed petrifying when she was twenty-two, confident in her ability to deal with any problems in the motor department. Had she really run that place or had she imagined it all? Right now, Aisling wasn't sure her former career hadn't been a dream. If she'd been as good as Mum and Jo were trying to convince her she was, why the hell was she scared out of her mind at the prospect of starting a much easier job when she was older?

Dodging the cars, like everyone else did, she crossed Leeson Street and turned right onto Pembroke Street Upper. She was sweating from the hasty walk and panicked that she hadn't put enough perfume on.

A subtle squirt of Chloé had seemed like the right idea at ten past seven. But after the long walk from Haddington Road where she'd decided to leave the car, she was hot and sticky, and wished she'd splashed on more perfume.

She hadn't wanted to overdo it. She wanted to appear like a working woman, someone who left the house at seven-fifty every morning like clockwork, with the kids fed, the kitchen tidy and a casserole defrosting for the evening. Not like a terrified ex-housewife overdoing it with gallons of perfume, high heels and an outfit which looked perfect in Quinnsworth and totally wrong behind a desk. Now she wished she'd had the presence of mind to put some deodorant in her bag.

Number seventeen. There it was, a rich dark green door with brass fittings and a gleaming brass plate beside it proclaiming that this was the office of Richardson, Reid and Finucane, Solicitors. A magnificent Georgian house in a line of magnificent houses, like something out of *Homes and Gardens*.

What she wouldn't give to be sitting at home right now, with a copy of the magazine spread on the kitchen table as

149

she contemplated another spurt of decorating. Anything, even stripping the wallpaper off the back bedroom, would be preferable to this sheer terror. Calm down, Aisling, she told herself. It's your first day, nobody is going to expect too much from you. Hopefully.

She walked carefully up the pristine stone steps and admired the two elegant bay trees in wooden tubs on either side of the door. To the right was an intercom and she pushed it slowly.

'Good morning,' said a clear voice. 'Can I help you?'

'Aisling Moran to see Ms Hogan,' Aisling answered, more calmly than she felt.

The voice said nothing, but a buzzing sound emanated from the side of the door. Feeling like a truant about to face the head nun, Aisling pushed and found herself in a formal, pale green lobby where a red-headed girl sat behind a low desk.

'Hello,' smiled the girl. 'Go up the stairs to the first landing and take the first door on your left.'

She could have been speaking in Swahili. With a fixed grin on her face, Aisling moved mechanically up the stairs, her brain trying to figure out the words 'first door on your left'.

Left, which was left? Was this it? She tentatively pushed open a green panelled door and walked into an airy, high-ceilinged room.

A petite woman in a grey skirt suit with a sweep of ash blonde hair to her shoulders stood before Aisling, a china cup and saucer in one hand and a beige folder in the other. Beautifully made-up grey eyes stared at Aisling for a moment before the woman smiled glacially.

'I'm Aisling Moran,' said Aisling nervously. This blonde vision looked at her as if she had just walked dog mess into the carpet.

'I know,' said the blonde coolly. 'I'm Vivienne Hogan, personal assistant to Mr Richardson and the personnel director. Welcome to Richardson, Reid and Finucane.'

Her expression was about as welcoming as a blizzard, but Aisling smiled back anyway.

'I'm afraid something's come up and I won't be able to bring you around the office and introduce you. Caroline Dennis will look after you. She'll be here in a moment,' Vivienne said, walking gracefully to the door. 'Sit down and make yourself comfortable.' She gestured towards a grey office chair.

'Thanks.'

The door shut silently. Aisling felt as if she could breathe again. Was she imagining it or had the other woman really been cold? And if so, what in the hell had she done to deserve such a frosty welcome? She tried to remember what she'd been like to newcomers to the motor department. Had she ever looked at them the way Vivienne had at her? God, she hoped not.

She sank into the chair and tried to take a few deep breaths. It didn't help. Focus on the room, Aisling. Relax.

The room looked like the drawing room it probably had been. It was papered with subtle embossed cream paper. A gilt-framed oil painting of a weary-looking horse hung on one wall.

Under normal circumstances, she'd have been fascinated by the ceiling mouldings which had vine leaves beautifully picked out in gold paint. Today she was too preoccupied to do much more than notice them.

As offices go, she thought, it was very nice.

Several metal filing cabinets filled one wall and there were two desks positioned opposite each other, both with computer keyboards and VDUs. A wire basket and a large pile of beige folders covered one desk, along with a very healthy plant and a large silver frame with a photo of a smiling little girl in a school uniform.

A tiny brown Koala bear clung to a pen in the red plastic pen holder and a rainbow-coloured mug proclaiming 'World's Greatest Mum' sat beside what looked like a very high-tech phone.

By contrast, the other desk was like something from an office manual, 'the perfect desk'. Not one stray piece of paper

151

spoiled the highly polished wood. White metal baskets were half empty and only a pen and a yellow Post-It pad beside the phone gave the impression that anyone had been using the desk at all. Obviously Ms Snotty Hogan's desk, Aisling decided bitchily.

A coffee percolator bubbled away in one corner of the room and the rich scent of freshly brewed coffee made her long for a cup. Should she help herself, Aisling wondered? Why not? She was an employee after all, even if not a very welcomed one.

She chose a bright red mug and was just starting to pour when the door opened again. Jumping guiltily, Aisling nearly spilled the coffee onto the pale carpet.

'Did I give you a fright?' inquired the intruder, a plump woman with a cluster of dark curls and a voluminous, bright floral dress.

'Sorry. Viv told me you were here and asked me to show you around. I'm Caroline, Pat's secretary.' She proffered a hand and Aisling shook it, grateful to meet at least one person who seemed pleased to see her.

'I'm Aisling and I hope it's OK to get some coffee but it just smelled so nice . . .'

'Oh, Viv should have offered you one but she'd madly busy this morning and obviously forgot. Your office is on the next floor but you'll have to come down here for coffee anyhow because Elizabeth's percolator has gone kaput.'

Caroline dropped a bulging brown handbag onto the chair beside the perfect desk and slung a white cotton cardigan over the armrests. Aisling was amazed. In her long, flowing dress and hippie-ish bead necklace, Caroline looked as if she'd be more at home behind the other desk.

So where did Vivienne sit? Not at the messy desk, that was for sure. And why was poor Caroline making excuses for Viv's rudeness? Aisling doubted that 'Viv would have offered' her a cup of coffee. Unless Aisling's throat was on fire, she reckoned.

'Elizabeth isn't going to be in today, she's feeling a bit

under the weather.' Caroline poured herself a mug of coffee and stirred in three sugars. Opening a square tin of assorted biscuits, she selected two chocolate biscuits and a pink wafer one.

'Want one?' she offered before taking a large bite of chocolate-covered digestive.

'No thanks,' answered Aisling, who hadn't even managed to finish her Special K.

'You'll *love* Elizabeth's office,' mumbled Caroline with her mouth full of biscuit. 'Well, *your* office! It's quite the nicest of all the assistants' ones. Of course, it's a bit isolated up there at the top,' she added. She took her coffee and led Aisling out onto the landing and up the stairs. 'But the view is wonderful! You're above Leo's office, Leo Murphy, that is. He's your boss. He's in court this morning according to Elizabeth, but he'll be back at one.'

Caroline stopped talking, breathless after the first flight of stairs. They climbed another two flights, past panelled green doors and sedately framed prints of Georgian Dublin in feathery ink and watercolours.

'This,' Caroline opened a door and showed Aisling another bright high-ceilinged room, 'is Leo's office.'

'Very nice,' said Aisling.

'You want to see Mr Richardson's office,' Caroline continued. 'It's beautiful. He collects antiques, you know. His office is like Sotheby's and his house is the same. Although I expect you know that.'

'Er, yes,' answered Aisling, although she didn't.

Why would she know that Edward Richardson collected antiques? She'd only met him a few times at Fiona's house and even then they'd talked about Fiona more than anything else. And about Nicole, of course, the apple of her grandfather's eye.

Obviously Caroline thought she was on intimate terms with Pat Finucane and, therefore, with his father-in-law. She followed Caroline up another flight of stairs to a small landing at the top of the building.

153

'I know it's small,' said Caroline, ushering Aisling into a tiny office dominated by a large window, 'but just look at the view.'

Aisling looked, and was impressed. Five huge filing cabinets took up a lot of the office space and there wasn't enough room to swing a cat, but the spectacular view the window afforded over Dublin's rooftops more than made up for the lack of space.

'It's wonderful,' breathed Aisling, squeezing between the desk and the cabinets to look out the window.

'I knew you'd like it,' smiled Caroline smugly, as though she'd designed the entire place herself. 'You may as well make yourself at home since Elizabeth isn't going to be in today. I'll get her calls transferred to my phone until you've got the hang of everything. You could start doing some typing, though, couldn't you? I'll give you some letters to look at so you can see the format.'

Aisling felt herself blanch. How the hell was she going to be able to type letters when she didn't know how to use the computer?

She gazed at the complicated-looking keyboard and knew she'd have to confess. Sort of.

'I don't know how to use this type of computer,' she said nervously.

'Oh,' said Caroline in surprise. 'This is an Apple Performa, it's a doddle, really. What have you worked on before?'

Aisling racked her brains for the name of the computer system the motor department had been buying before she'd left.

ICBM. That was it. 'An ICBM,' she lied confidently. 'No, an IBM. Sorry.' Moron, she told herself. You've just said you can use an inter-continental ballistic missile.

'I'd really prefer to be thoroughly acquainted with this system before I start typing,' she added quickly, hoping Caroline hadn't noticed her gaffe. 'Perhaps I can do something else until Elizabeth can brief me properly.' That sounded great, she thought. Very professional.

Caroline's eyebrows were furrowed as she considered this.

'You could do some filing,' she ventured. 'I know Elizabeth has been letting the filing slide a little because she hates going up and down the stairs all the time. There's a file room downstairs, two cabinets in Leo's office and the ones here. It's quite a trip up and down those stairs.'

'Of course I'll file,' Aisling said, relieved. 'Just show me where to start.'

She was leaning over a cabinet in the file room looking for Ms Sandra Burke's file when Vivienne walked in at a quarter past one.

'You're not at lunch?'

Aisling looked flustered. 'I didn't know when lunch was,' she said. 'There's so much filing to do, I just thought I'd keep working.'

'You'll be working through lunch often enough without starting on your first day,' Vivienne commented. 'Caroline was supposed to bring you to the canteen but she obviously forgot, I'm sorry.'

Amazing, thought Aisling, Ms Ice Queen is actually apologising for something. She was even more amazed when Vivienne told her to take a break and get a cup of coffee from the percolator in her office.

'Leave this until after lunch,' she added. 'The canteen is in the basement, although it's not precisely a canteen, more a badly equipped kitchen. There's a kettle, a fridge and a microwave in case you want to have something hot. Go down the corridor and take the second left, OK?'

'Fine,' said Aisling.

'I'm going to Baggot Street. Do you want anything from the shops?'

'No thanks, really. I'll just get a cup of coffee and I've brought a sandwich.'

'Well, get some proper coffee from my office, won't you,' Vivienne added. 'And I'll see you later this afternoon to see how you're getting on.' She smiled briefly, then opened a filing cabinet near the door, selected a file and left as quietly as she'd come in.

155

Marginally cheered up, Aisling left the file room and thought briefly about going down to the canteen for lunch.

If Caroline had accompanied her, she would have been delighted to meet the rest of the staff. But she just didn't feel up to marching in on her own, explaining who she was and what she was doing here to a bunch of curious strangers. Instead, she knocked gently on Vivienne and Caroline's office door and, when nobody answered, went in for some coffee.

She took a biscuit as well and looked at the desks with renewed interest. So *Vivienne* was the World's Greatest Mum, she thought. Presumably, she wasn't such a tough career woman at home. Maybe they'd just got off on the wrong foot. Some people were naturally prickly and needed time to get comfortable with others, she decided charitably.

At her desk, she ate her tuna fish sandwich hungrily and drank a Diet Coke. She'd found a recent copy of *Style* in one of Elizabeth's wire baskets and she flicked through the pages, only half concentrating on an article about summer camps as she wondered how the boys were getting on at theirs.

She hadn't planned on sending them to the day camp for the whole summer, but she'd no option now that she was working. Thank God that Fiona had offered to pick them up at three the first week.

'Only until I get sorted out,' Aisling said firmly when Fiona offered to help. 'You can't spend your whole summer minding them.'

Brave words. She was finding it hard enough to cope with her first day at work without feeling like an idiot.

She'd just taken another bite of her sandwich when her door opened suddenly and a very tall and very dark man walked in. He was heavily built, with the sort of tan which spoke of lots of outdoor pursuits. He had a shock of jet black hair and a suit to match.

'Aisling, isn't it?' he said in a deep voice.

'Yes,' she answered. 'Hello.'

'I'm Leo Murphy.'

He advanced with one large hand held out and leaned over

the desk. The way his eyes roamed over her made Aisling feel uneasy.

She didn't know whether it was his intense gaze or the way he was smiling like an alligator who had spotted his lunch, but she felt, well . . . uncomfortable.

Since he was still holding out his hand, she reached out her left hand, the one without tuna stuck to it, and awkwardly shook hands. He held her fingers for much longer than was necessary and, when he released it, he smiled, a very self-satisfied smile.

'Aisling, I'm delighted you're going to be with me when Liz is away.'

Nobody else had called the other woman Liz, but Aisling instinctively knew that Leo Murphy would enjoy shortening his secretary's name, turning the elegant Elizabeth into the snappy Liz.

'Liz, bring your notebook in here now.' She could just imagine him saying it. She hoped he wouldn't start calling her Ash, only her closest friends and family called her that.

'I hope you've been made to feel at home.' He pushed aside a pile of files and sat on the side of her desk, his big body dwarfing Aisling as he leaned over her.

'Tuna, mmm. Health-conscious, are we?' he didn't wait for her to reply. 'I'm pretty health-conscious myself. Rugby, you know.' He patted his bulky chest proudly. 'A man's got to work out, don't you agree?'

'Absolutely,' she answered.

'I can see we're going to get on very well,' he continued. 'Come on down to my office when you've finished lunch. I'll go over what I want from you.'

'Yes, Mr Murphy.'

He slid off the desk and headed for the door.

'And Aisling,' he turned to give her the benefit of another feral grin. 'It's Leo, not Mr Murphy. We don't stand on ceremony here.'

She rinsed her hands in the tiny bathroom on the third floor and knocked on Leo's door.

157

'Come in, Aisling. Have a seat.'

He sat behind the desk and stared at her. God, there was something about him she didn't like. She didn't know what it was, but there was definitely *something* odd about him.

'You haven't worked for some time, I believe. Pat's been very good to take you on, I'm sure you appreciate that.'

Aisling felt sick. The way he made it sound, Pat had given her the job for services rendered, the sort of services you wore a French maid's outfit and stockings for.

'Of course, I understand that you're going through a rough time,' Leo added. 'It can't be easy. We'll make this as pleasurable as possible, of course. We run a tight ship here and I need to know you're behind me one hundred per cent. Liz will fill you in on the day-to-day details of the job.'

He paused and Aisling wondered if she was supposed to say something.

'That's great, Mr . . . er, Leo,' she said. 'I want to work. I know I'm a bit rusty but I'm a hard worker. Elizabeth will be here for the next two weeks, won't she?'

'Yes. But when she's gone, don't hesitate to ask me anything. Anything,' he repeated in a syrupy voice. 'That's all for now.'

He picked up his phone and started dialling a number. Aisling got up to leave, anxious to get back to the solitude of her little office.

'Can you get me the Law Directory?' he asked suddenly. 'It's on top of the cabinet over there.'

He held the phone to his ear but his eyes were on her again.

She turned around and was suddenly struck by the thought that her cream skirt really needed a slip underneath it. Was he watching her, eyes taking in her VPL, she thought, horrified. She blushed furiously.

'Thanks.' He took the book and she left the room rapidly. Outside, she took a long, deep breath and wondered what was wrong with her. He hadn't said anything awful, had he? So why was she so spooked?

158

When Caroline popped her head around the door at five to two, Aisling was delighted to see her.

'Sorry I didn't get to see you for lunch. I had to race up to Grafton Street to look for a present for my husband. It's his birthday on Wednesday and they have shirts in Arnott's that he'd love. Did you find the canteen?'

'Vivienne told me where it was,' answered Aisling, 'but I had a sandwich here. I didn't know anyone and I thought I'd wait until I met everyone, you know,' she finished lamely.

'That's awful!' declared Caroline. 'I'll kill the girls for not coming and getting you. We've got two juniors who are so scatty that they'd forget their heads if they weren't screwed on. And I bet you never had any coffee, either, did you?'

'Yes, I did. Vivienne told me to get some from your office,' Aisling said.

'Come on down and get another one now and I'll send the motorbike courier off with your percolator this minute. Leo will go mad if he doesn't get his coffee in the morning, you know!'

She laughed at this and Aisling decided not to ask about Leo's decidedly odd behaviour. She could have picked him up the wrong way. It was only her first day after all. No doubt things would look different the next day with Elizabeth to guide her through the maze of office politics.

'I don't want mash. I want chips!' declared Paul crossly, pushing his plate away from him.

'You can't have chips,' snapped Aisling. 'You're not leaving this table without eating your dinner, mash and all.'

She scraped the last bit of mashed potato out of the saucepan onto her plate and dumped the saucepan noisily in the sink. Granted, the dinner wasn't one of her better efforts. But mashed potato, fish fingers and beans were all she'd felt up to cooking after her first day at work.

They *should* have been eating a delicious lasagne she'd made on Saturday. But she'd forgotten to time the oven to cook the damn thing.

159

Phillip said nothing. He stuck his fork in the small hillock of mash he'd made in the centre of his plate and slowly mixed the beans into it until he'd made a pale orange mess. Since the boys had come over from Fiona's at half six, just ten minutes after Aisling had got home, Phillip had been stonily silent.

Feeling guilty at being away all day and for snapping at Paul, Aisling tried again.

'Please eat your dinner, boys,' she begged. 'There's ice cream for dessert and we can go to the video shop afterwards for a treat, all right?'

'Do I have to eat this, Mum?' wailed Paul. 'I'm not hungry.'

Count to ten, Aisling. She tried the honest approach.

'Paul, I'm very tired because I've been working all day. I'm sorry that dinner isn't very nice but it's the best I can do. Please eat it.'

For once, it worked. Taken aback by such candour, Paul stuck his fork into a fish finger and ate a bit. And another bit. Seeing his twin eating, Phillip stopped making fork tracks across his mash and actually ate some.

Thank you God, Aisling said silently. She didn't care what she'd promised the previous night, she just *had* to have a drink tonight.

Back from the video shop, she left the boys watching *Flipper* for the millionth time and went upstairs to have a bath.

She stripped off her work clothes with relief and put on the peach-coloured satin dressing-gown she'd treated herself to the Christmas before. Soft and silky to the touch, it had always made her feel faintly glamorous. But not tonight. Only a two-week stay in a health farm and four hours under a beautician's expert care would make her feel anything other than a harassed working mother with smudged mascara, aching feet and limp hair from her hurried walk to the car after work.

Aisling added a liberal dose of Body Shop Neroli essential oil to the steaming, foamy bath. Five drops were enough to relax you, the instructions said. Five wouldn't have a chance, she thought, counting out ten. With a glass of icy white wine

160

– the last bottle from Michael's precious wine rack – by her side, she lay back into the bubbles and let the day wash away from her.

The sensation of warm water gently taking the aches and pains away was pure bliss. She took a big sip of wine and wriggled her toes with relief. High-heeled shoes were definitely the wrong thing for work.

What she needed was a pair of low-heeled ones like Vivienne had worn. She had a black pair which would fit the bill perfectly, even if they were a bit old. They'd look fine if she polished them up. There just wasn't enough money in the kitty for a new pair.

As the water cooled, she reached up with her left foot and twisted the hot tap on again. Heaven.

For the first time since Michael had left her, she wasn't thinking about him or crying over him. Worrying about how she was going to cope when Elizabeth was on maternity leave, not to mention dreading working for the distinctly seedy Leo Murphy, was occupying too much of her mind to think about her absent husband. He'd got her into this mess, she thought venomously, but she had to get herself out of it. And she would, damn him.

'Fine, it was fine,' she said airily, when Fiona rang full of inquiries about her first day at Richardson, Reid and Finucane. After all Pat had done about getting her the job, Aisling couldn't very well say she felt like she'd just run a marathon and was dreading the next day, could she?

'Pat was in court all day or he'd have been in to see how you were getting on,' Fiona explained. 'But he said Vivienne and Caroline were going to explain everything to you. How did you get on with them? Caroline's very nice but Vivienne always sounds like a bit of a workaholic to me.'

'Caroline's lovely,' Aisling was able to say truthfully. 'I didn't see much of Vivienne, really. Elizabeth, the girl I'm replacing, was out so I did the filing all day. It was simple enough, but pretty tiring. You see, I didn't want to admit that I couldn't use the word processor so that's why I volunteered to file. And I met Leo Murphy. He's a bit different,' she ventured.

'Yeah, Pat says he's an acquired taste,' Fiona answered. 'He's only been there a year or so, but he's great at conveyancing apparently. I've never met him. What's he look like?'

Picture Jack Nicholson in *The Shining*, Aisling thought.

'Very dark haired and well built,' was what she said. 'He prides himself on being muscular,' she couldn't resist throwing that in. 'He plays rugby and believes men should work out.'

'Gosh, you sound very well acquainted already!' chuckled Fiona. 'Is he a bit of a hunk?'

'Not really, no.' If only she knew.

'Do you think you'll enjoy working there?' Fiona asked seriously. 'I was on edge all day wondering how you were getting on.'

You and me both, Aisling said to herself.

'I really want it to work out for you,' Fiona added.

'Oh Fee, it's wonderful,' Aisling said warmly. She had to lie so she hoped she was doing it convincingly. 'It was a bit tough at first, but the girls are so nice, I know it'll work out fine.'

'That's great,' said Fiona in relieved tones. 'You need something to keep your mind off Michael. I was so worried about you last week, you know.'

'I do feel a lot better now,' Aisling admitted. 'Maybe it's just coping with all the practical things, feeding the boys, paying the bills, that kind of thing. I haven't let myself descend into total misery. And work will certainly help,' she said with a laugh. 'I didn't have much time to think about Michael today! Which is all thanks to you and Pat for getting me this job. You've both been wonderful.'

'What are friends for?' demanded Fiona.

'Not all friends are as good as you,' Aisling pointed out. 'I've had a few calls from friends of ours and they just don't know what to say. Poor Angela Dunn just stuttered and stammered and finally said she'd ring me in a few months, like I was going into mourning! Nobody from Michael's office has rung, although I suppose it must be awkward for them.'

She didn't say that this had hurt her deeply. All she'd wanted was a friendly voice on the phone, telling her that even though she and Michael weren't together, the friends they had known for the past ten years were still there. Break-ups certainly made you realise the value of true friends, like Fiona and Jo.

'Mum has been great,' Aisling added. 'She arrived on Tuesday with a freezer full of pies and stews for us. I said Michael had left, he hadn't died! Luckily, she saw the funny side of it.'

'Ash! You're dreadful!' laughed Fiona. 'What must your poor mother have thought? You're dreadful for joking about serious things. Anyway, your mum's generation aren't used to the idea of people splitting up and the poor woman must be in shock.'

'Oh, Mum knows my sense of humour by now. I think living with Dad has knocked her own sense of humour out of her, though. He wouldn't recognise a joke if it bit him on the bum. Mum put him on the phone the other night and it was like talking to the sideboard. He was on the verge of doing his "I'd hoped for more from you, Aisling" routine but he stopped. I think Mum must have grabbed the phone off him.'

'Don't mind him,' Fiona said indignantly. 'You've done so well with your life. What did he want, Einstein for a daughter?'

'Someone smarter than Einstein, I think,' Aisling said drily. 'Luckily Sorcha's achievements have made up for the shame of me being a mere housewife. I swear that his chest swells when he tells people she's working in a bank in London. Mind you,' she added, 'if Sorcha lived here, he wouldn't be so delighted with her because they fight like cats and dogs. Distance is a wonderful thing.'

'Has she heard?' Fiona inquired.

'She rang on Saturday and told me I was a fool to have stayed at home cleaning the toilet. She has a great way with words, that one. I did point out that there was more to my life than sticking my head under the rim to see what germs were

163

lurking, but I stopped myself. It was easier to say nothing.'

'Wait until *she* has a family and a home,' said Fiona sounding vexed. 'She'll find out it isn't so easy to be mother and chief bottle-washer after all.'

'Sorcha isn't going to have any children, my dear,' pointed out Aisling. 'She wants to have her tubes tied.'

'Around her neck, I hope,' muttered the other woman.

'She has that effect on me too, Fee. She completely ruined my ideas of what a little sister was supposed to be like. Thank God Nicola came along or I'd have always thought that little sisters were like some sort of biblical curse. You know, "And the Lord said, a little sister will be born, to ravage your bedroom, destroy your toys and keep you in eternal trouble until you leave home." '

'Was she really that bad?'

'Worse. And talking of kids, thanks for picking up the boys this afternoon, although Phillip has been like a briar since he came home.'

'He was a bit moody,' Fiona agreed. 'I thought he'd cheer up when he saw you . . .'

'No chance!' said Aisling. 'I think I've just crossed the line from Good Stay at Home Mummy to Bad Working Mummy. You should have seen the look on his face when he got beans, mash and fish fingers for dinner!'

'You've ruined all three of them with your gourmet cooking,' started Fiona, stopping abruptly when she realised what she'd said. 'Sorry.'

'You're right,' Aisling replied matter-of-factly. 'I did spoil them, Michael particularly. Home-made bread for breakfast, smoked salmon pâté at the weekends because he loved it, chicken *en croûte* or fresh pasta for his dinner and he never had to so much as wash up a cup or throw a towel in the laundry basket. I wonder is he allowed to get away with that type of behaviour with *her*? I don't think career women have much time for very old-fashioned men,' she added sarcastically.

★ ★ ★

Lying on her own in their big double bed later, she thought about what Fiona had said. She was right. Aisling had totally spoiled the three men in her life. She'd become obsessed with being the best housewife possible.

The house could have won prizes for cleanliness, her interior decoration was the same. She'd prided herself on her cooking, as though being a wizard with a food processor made up for her lack of abilities outside the home. And somewhere along the way, Aisling Moran had disappeared. That's what Michael had said. Had he been right?

He'd married her because he loved her, her vitality and her sense of humour. When she'd slowly lost her self-assurance, her belief in herself, she'd panicked. And thought that becoming the perfect homemaker was the answer. Only it hadn't been.

Michael had wanted Aisling, the woman he married. But she'd turned into Super Housewife, handy in the kitchen, but out of water anywhere else. Would a job have changed all that, she asked herself? A day in Richardson, Reid and Finucane had certainly given her lots to talk about.

She'd have enjoyed telling Michael about the different characters in the office and with his support behind her she probably wouldn't have been so uncomfortable in Leo Murphy's presence. But if Michael had still been with her, Leo would never have been so lecherous, she was sure of that. Being separated suddenly made her fair game for the likes of Leo. How the hell was she going to face him on her own?

Aisling sat up in bed and switched on her bedside light. It was ten past twelve, she had to be up in six and three-quarter hours and she didn't feel even vaguely like sleeping.

She plumped up her two pale yellow pillows behind her, then suddenly reached over and grabbed Michael's. For the past week, she'd made the bed every morning as if he was coming home that night, arranged his pillows just the way he liked them. She still slept on her side of the bed.

Why the hell was she doing that, she asked herself crossly? He wasn't coming back. In fact, even if he wanted to, he wasn't coming back. So there! He could stuff his pillows! She laughed at her own joke. Now, what to read? Something fluffy and romantic or something wonderfully scary?

Leaning down to her bedside table, Aisling found the book she wanted. It was funny how she'd got out of the habit of reading when she couldn't sleep at night, she thought. Michael always slept soundly and solidly, seven or eight hours no matter what. She'd never been so lucky but had rarely turned on her light to read at night in case it woke him. Not any more. She could read until dawn, steal all the duvet and all the pillows, and paint the entire bedroom whorehouse pink if she felt like it! So what if it was after twelve, she'd go to bed early tomorrow night. Satisfied with herself, Aisling settled back against her comfortable back rest. Perfect.

Tuesday was a good day. Elizabeth turned out to be a funny and warm woman in her early thirties who was delighted to be pregnant after four years of trying for a baby. Under her relaxed and expert tutelage, Aisling quickly learned how to use the word processor once she'd admitted that she had never used one before.

'I can't believe it's so easy,' Aisling exclaimed, after she'd managed to open files, save documents, print letters and keep file copies on floppy disks.

'Technology is the Emperor's New Clothes of the nineties,' said Elizabeth. 'Everyone's so scared of it that lots of people are terrified to touch a keyboard and the people who are good with computers try and lord it over everyone who isn't. Look how easily you've picked it up.'

'As long as I can do it when you're gone,' Aisling answered.

'I'm not going far,' laughed Elizabeth, patting her enormous bump. 'I'll probably spend the next few weeks stretched out on the couch at home watching reruns of *Knots Landing*, so just pick up the phone if you've got a problem.'

'Thanks. It's great to know that,' Aisling replied. 'I just hope I can handle Leo as easily,' she added guardedly. She was desperate to know what Elizabeth thought of her boss, but wasn't sure how to broach the subject. Perhaps Leo and Elizabeth got on like a house on fire. It might be a terrible blunder to ask if he made *her* feel as uncomfortable as he made Aisling.

'Oh, don't mind Leo,' the other woman said dismissively. 'His bark is much worse than his bite. He's moodier than any premenstrual woman *I've* ever known! Just ignore his moods. As long as you keep the office running efficiently and don't overbook him, he's a lamb, really.'

A lamb, huh? More like a wolf in sheep's clothing, Aisling reckoned. However, he'd been pretty harmless all day, acting the part of the busy boss. Aisling wished he'd always be like that. Unfortunately, she suspected that Elizabeth's presence had a lot to do with it. Who knew what he'd be like when she was gone and he could stare insolently at Aisling again?

Pat Finucane dropped into her office at lunchtime and apologised for not welcoming her in person the day before.

'How are you getting on?' he asked kindly.

'Brilliant,' said Elizabeth. 'She'll be running the whole place in a month. I just hope there's a job for me when I'm finished my maternity leave!'

Buoyed by Elizabeth's confidence in her, and by her improved relationship with Vivienne, Aisling left for home a much happier woman than she'd been the day before.

Her good mood wasn't to last.

'Hi, Aisling.' Michael's cold and distant voice on the phone hit her like a punch in the stomach.

'How are the boys?'

'Fine,' she replied, just as tersely.

'Now that I'm settled, I'd like to see them at the weekends. They can stay with me on Saturday and go home on Sunday evening, what do you think?'

She didn't know what to say. They were talking like a divorced couple already.

'I suppose that's all right,' she answered grudgingly. 'Where will they be staying?'

He hesitated for a moment. Could he be trying not to hurt her, she wondered?

'I'm living with Jennifer.'

God, it was like an ice pick in her guts. How could she have thought she was all right, she wondered blankly. Don't cry, don't let him see how upset you are.

'Where is that?' she asked in what she hoped was a nonchalant voice.

'Sandymount. It's just off Sandymount village.'

'How nice,' she replied. They were like two strangers talking, discussing property. They'd be talking about auctioneers' fees and stamp duty next.

'I don't want the boys to think that they don't have a father any more,' Michael said, suddenly intense. 'I want them to have *two* homes. That's so important.'

'It might be a bit of a shock to them to find you're living with someone else, Michael,' she interrupted caustically. 'This has all been rather sudden.'

'I know, I know,' he said worriedly. From the tone of his voice, she knew exactly what he was doing, running his fingers through his dark hair until it stood up in glossy peaks. She'd always smoothed it down, well, she *used* to smooth it down, a long, long time ago.

Neither of them spoke for a moment. The silence was almost worse than the stilted conversation.

'We have to talk about money,' she said finally.

'I hear you've got a job,' he put in.

'How did you know?'

'I rang Pat to find out how you were. I knew Fiona would have been talking to you.'

'Oh, give me a break, Michael,' she said angrily. 'If you wanted to know how I was, why couldn't you ring *me*! I was wondering why you were so silent, couldn't face talking to me, was that it?'

He sighed tiredly. 'I didn't ring up to fight, Aisling.'

'We're not fighting, Michael,' she snapped. 'I just want you to be up front with me. I'm not going to fall on my knees every time you ring and beg you to come back, OK! I've got over the begging wife stage.'

Damn him! He made her so angry. Why was he still playing games, weren't they over that?

'Don't be afraid to ring me, Michael. I want to talk about money, about the house, about all the practical things. And I want to know where you are so that if there's a problem with the boys, I can reach you.'

'That's fair enough,' he answered. 'I'm sorry, I should have rung. I don't know what to say to the boys.'

She was amazed. What an admission from Mr Know It All! At least she'd faced up to the realities of the situation and told the boys what was happening. He was scared to. Suddenly, Aisling felt a lot better. *She* was the strong one, she was the one who'd taken it on the chin. *She* was fighting back! What a nice feeling that was.

'You could try the truth,' she said smartly.

'You think so?'

'Well, they're ten years old, Michael, not ten *months*. I think they're going to put two and two together if they spend the night with you and *her*.' Aisling couldn't bear to say "Jennifer".

'You're right.'

Wow, it was a long time since she'd heard *that*. A slight smile lifted the corners of her mouth.

'Pick them up at one on Saturday,' she said decisively. 'They'll just be back from soccer and they'll be ravenous. You could always bring them to McDonald's, give them lunch and then tell them.'

This was hilarious. *She* was advising him on the best way to tell the boys that he now lived with another woman. Ironic wasn't the word for it.

'That's a great idea, Aisling,' he said sounding grateful. 'Thank you for making this easier.'

'I'm only doing this because I'm up for the Nobel Peace Prize,' she answered sarcastically. 'And because I want to protect the twins as much as possible. It won't do them any good to have us screaming at each other.'

'You're great,' Michael said. 'Thanks. I'll see you on Saturday, then?'

He hung up and Aisling did the same with relief. At least they'd talked. They had actually conversed like two adults. That had to be good, surely? She'd been dreading hearing from Michael and yearning for it in equal amounts. One part of her wanted to scream abuse at him, the other wanted him to come back, to hear him beg forgiveness and tell her he adored her still.

But there was no point harbouring secret hopes of a reunion when it was obvious Michael wanted her back like he wanted a hole in the head. This way, she was forced to meet reality face on.

'Mum, can we go out to play with Greg?' demanded Phillip, appearing in the kitchen with a football in his hands.

'All right, but stay in his garden if you're playing football. Don't play on the road, OK?'

'Yeah.'

Phillip was gone in a flash.

'Be back by eight,' Aisling shouted after him.

The front door slammed loudly. It was nearly seven, time for *Emmerdale*. The dinner dishes were still on the kitchen table but she didn't feel like tidying up. She quickly put the milk, butter and the cheese back in the fridge and left everything else. Time enough to do it later. Two weeks ago she wouldn't have been able to leave the mess without tidying up. Every dish would have been washed, dried and put away in fifteen minutes and she'd have then swept the kitchen floor and hoovered up the crumbs.

Not any more, she thought. There were no prizes for faultless housekeeping in the real world.

By Thursday evening, she was exhausted. Too exhausted to join Fiona at aerobics.

'Come on, you'll love it!' wheedled Fiona on the phone. 'Nicole's got her friends in and if you send the boys over, Pat will look after them all. You can do the beginners' class.'

170

'Oh, Fee, I really don't feel up to prancing around in my awful old leggings and spare tyre. It's so long since I did anything like that, I'd be *hopeless*,' Aisling answered. 'I'd really prefer it if you lent me one of your library of exercise tapes. I can start at home and that way I won't feel so flabby and unfit when I finally go with you.'

'OK. But you're definitely coming with me next week, aren't you?'

Aisling laughed. 'You never give up, do you? Let me get semi-fit before I go to the gym, Fee. I don't know if my self-confidence could face jumping up and down like an elephant in the middle of a group of Cindy Crawford look-alikes.'

'There won't be anyone like that in the beginners' class,' Fiona pointed out. 'The Cindy Crawford types all go to the advanced step class and make me feel like a heifer.'

'I'm *never* going near that place if there are women who can make *you* look fat!' Aisling was horrified at the thought. 'I'll come over and pick up Mr Motivator or Jane Fonda now and go for the burn later.'

'Nobody "goes for the burn" any more,' Fiona rebuked her. 'Even Jane admits she was wrong about the "no pain, no gain" motto. Anyway, she's had plastic surgery so I've lost my faith in her. She's too old-fashioned and I hate Mr Motivator. I've got a couple of step videos that are easier when you don't have a step; you could try them. You should also try Callanet-ics. It's not fat-burning but it's great for streamlining your shape.'

'That sounds painful,' said Aisling. 'Does it hurt?'

'Not a bit,' Fiona answered cheerfully.

Callan Pinckney's soothing American voice was telling Aisling how to stand with feet hip-distance apart, with one hand on her hip and the other reaching upwards. Painfully upwards. The video had only been on five minutes and Aisling already felt tired.

She didn't think she could reach a little bit more than she thought she could, as Callan kept saying encouragingly to a

171

class of very flexible-looking people.

Her arm was going to wrench itself out of her shoulder if she reached over any further. Thank God. She'd done it.

'Do one hundred,' Callan said crushingly.

'One hundred!' shrieked Aisling out loud, already wondering if she had ruptured something vital. You must be mad. But Callan wasn't listening. She was leaning over like a gymnast, gently moving her body back and forth, seemingly without excruciating pain.

I'll be in agony tomorrow, Aisling muttered to herself as she leaned, watching the counter on the screen clock up every little movement. She had to give up at 54 but Callan and her class stuck it out to 100. Masochists. Then it was time for the other side.

CHAPTER TEN

'It must be good for you if it hurts that much, mustn't it?' Aisling eased herself gingerly onto a bar stool in Larry Murphy's on Baggot Street.

'Current exercising wisdom doesn't recommend pain,' Jo said, as she picked up the bar food menu. 'I've never done Callanetics myself, but I've heard it's brilliant for toning you up. I suppose it's hard at first because your muscles aren't used to the movements. What do you want to eat?'

'A cheese sandwich on brown bread and a cup of tea,' Aisling answered.

'That sounds good,' Jo replied, and proceeded to order a sandwich for Aisling and fisherman's pie and chips for herself.

Aisling was going to say something about how that eating for two stuff was all old hat and just made you chubby as well as pregnant, but she thought better of it.

'You look good, anyway, even if your muscles are in agony,' Jo commented, taking in Aisling's definitely less bulky shape. In a long navy skirt and slim-fitting pink silk blouse, Aisling was looking better than she had for years, the long-hidden fine bone structure beginning to show on her face.

After years of wearing only the barest hint of make-up, she had started putting foundation, eyeliner and mascara on in the mornings as well as the usual eyeshadow and lipstick. Seeing Vivienne so smartly dressed and perfectly made-up every day made Aisling realise that the bare-faced look she'd worn for trips to the supermarket wasn't suitable for the office.

Her indigo-blue eyes were fringed by darkened lashes, a careful smudge of eyeliner highlighting what had always been her best feature. The coral lipstick she'd always favoured had been thrown in the bin by a disgusted Fiona who'd produced a pinkish-mauve one instead and insisted on painting it on with a brush.

'Fiona, I'll never get to work in the morning if I have to use a brush to put my lipstick on,' protested Aisling during the mini make-up session on Wednesday night.

'You don't *have* to paint it, but it does stay on longer that way,' Fiona said firmly, as she rooted through Aisling's top drawer. 'I can't believe you have silver eyeliner, Ash!'

'Jo and I bought loads of it in a discount shop when we were going through our Abba phase,' Aisling attempted to explain. 'It was supposed to make your eyes look bigger if you put it on the inside lower rim . . .'

'Give me strength! You'd look like a reject from a Seventies Top of the Pops Special if you wore that,' said Fiona. 'Why are you keeping it?'

'I can't bear to throw anything out.'

Fiona held up a bottle of congealed bronze nail polish. 'Darling, I think this has to go. In fact, let me throw all of this out.' She poked around in the drawer with flawless oyster-coloured nails, dislodging two Mary Quant eyeshadows in what looked suspiciously like glittering purple and sky blue.

'Very Charlie's Angels, but not so good for anyone over seventeen, despite what they've been wearing on the catwalk lately. Dump this junk, Aisling, and I'll bring over some decent stuff for you. I do tend to overspend at the cosmetics counter and you may as well get some use out of my binges.'

Aisling laughed. '*Tend to overspend!*' she said. 'Famous last words, Mrs Finucane!'

She was glad of Fiona's expert advice though. Her own attempts to look made-up hadn't been precisely successful. Pumping the brush in and out of her elderly mascara tube had left her with lashes like tarantula legs. With the right materials, however – what she reckoned was around thirty pounds' worth of Fiona's expensive Lancôme stuff – she was getting much better at applying subtle amounts of cosmetics and with excellent results.

'Fiona gave me this self-tanning stuff and I put some on last night,' Aisling revealed, as she poured a few drops of milk into her tea. 'It really does perk your complexion up.'

'Whatever it is, you look great,' complimented Jo. 'Maybe you should market the Dump Your Husband Diet.'

Aisling giggled into her tea. You could never stay maudlin for long around the irrepressible Jo.

'I think it's too much of a *crash* diet,' Aisling pointed out. 'A bit too shocking to the system.'

'I'm on the Seafood Diet,' announced Jo, taking a bite out of a fat-glistening chip. 'I see food and I eat it.'

She ate another chip, put her head to one side and stared at her friend with narrowed eyes.

'Your hair,' she announced after a moment. 'You should do something with your hair.'

'Like what?' asked Aisling self-consciously, smoothing back the escaping tendrils from her pony tail. Her wavy curtain of light brown hair reached to about four inches below her shoulders and was too long and unruly to leave it loose when she typed. She never coloured it and rarely used the hairdryer, but Aisling knew her hair would have been nicer in something more elegant than a pony tail.

'James, my hairdresser, could do wonders with your hair,' Jo said enthusiastically. 'You need a little lift, a better shape or *something*. But it needs to be cut.'

'I've had it this length for years,' Aisling said defensively. 'It's handy. I can tie it back.'

'Ash, you need something career-womanish now, not handy. Anyway, tying it back is the only thing you can really do with it at that length. It would take years off you if you cut it. You don't need to do anything radical, you know.'

Aisling still wasn't convinced. 'Like what?' she asked.

'Softer, shorter, more feathery.' Jo was getting into her stride now. 'With highlights!'

'I'm a bit old for highlights,' said Aisling morosely, remembering the Greek summer when she'd first met Michael. Her hair was longer then, longer and bleached gold in the sun. She was never going to look like that again.

'Do you want some more tea?' asked Jo. 'I'm so thirsty, I just have to have another pot. I'm off coffee for the baby's sake.'

'No thanks.' Aisling could feel the tears coming. Damn, she'd been doing so well. She hadn't cried since Wednesday when she'd opened her bedside drawer and found the snapshot of the family outside Kilkenny Castle two summers before.

Michael had been shading his eyes from the sun and an eager eight-year-old Phillip had moved away to talk to the friendly American woman who'd offered to take the picture for them. They'd looked such a family then, a unit. Staring at her own smiling round face as she held Michael's hand and tried to hold onto Paul's T-shirt, Aisling wondered if they really *had* been a happy family at all. Or if she had believed in the perfect family, while Michael had been planning his affair? She'd cried. Bawled her eyes out in fact, and woke up with red, puffy eyes which didn't go terribly well with the red blouse she'd carefully ironed the night before.

'I haven't cried since Wednesday,' she said wetly, searching in her handbag for a tissue.

'Sometimes I feel so strong and determined to succeed, and sometimes I just cry.'

'That's allowed,' Jo sighed. 'I feel like sobbing my eyes out half the time, in between those moments when I dream of strangling Richard with his camera strap.'

'I'm sorry,' sniffled Aisling. 'I didn't mean to whinge. Has Richard not got in touch with you yet?'

'Yes and no,' answered Jo flatly. 'Yes, he got in touch and no, I won't be seeing him again. Ever. Unless I'm called up to identify him on a slab in the morgue, that is. A girl can dream.'

Shocked out of her tears, Aisling stared anxiously at her friend. Had pregnancy scrambled her mind?

'Richard is a little shit,' announced Jo after a moment. 'Correction, he's a *big* shit. Another pot of tea, please.'

'He did come and see me,' she explained to Aisling. 'Bearing gifts and begging forgiveness. Or so I thought. That big shit let me take him to bed. He let me think everything was wonderful, fine, hunky dory until I found out that he's *still* going to London. With Sascha, the rocket scientist, I have no doubt,' she added. 'I have my suspicions about that bitch and my ex-beloved.'

'The pig!' Aisling was outraged.

'Oh I did better than "pig", I can tell you that,' said Jo with satisfaction. 'That bastard had better keep away from me for the rest of his life or he'll be getting dentures fitted!'

'Jo, you're priceless! Tell me, what really happened?'

'You wouldn't believe it if I told you. Do you know, my life is turning into one of those mini-series things from the States. You know the sort of thing – *She loved him, but he had a deep, dark secret that rocked her to the very core of her being* – in a deeper voice than I can do, of course. I quite fancy Jaclyn Smyth in my part or should that be Jane Seymour? It needs one of those dark, sultry and depressed heroines anyway. I can't imagine who should play scumbag himself.'

Jo took the tea from the barman. 'It's nearly half one,' she said. 'When do you have to be back?'

'Two. But it'll only take me five minutes from here.'

'OK. Here goes. The story of my life: part twenty-six.'

Aisling only made it back to the office in time by the skin of her teeth. She'd thought things were bad for *her*. Poor, poor Jo. Imagine having the father of your baby dump you like a Christmas kitten that had grown bigger and less chocolate-box-cute in January? Then, to add insult to injury, imagine finding out that he'd done it all before, that he'd already dumped another unwanted Christmas cat *plus* an unborn kitten. What a complete asshole.

'Thank God you're back,' said Elizabeth gratefully when Aisling walked into their tiny top-floor office. 'I feel awful. I've just got to go home and lie down or I swear I'll pass out!'

'Of course you've got to go,' Aisling said automatically. 'Are you able to drive? Should I ring Pete and get him to collect you?' Pete was Elizabeth's husband, an accountant who sounded as though he cherished the ground she walked on.

'No, I'll be fine. It's only to Stoneybatter. I'm just sorry for you, Aisling.' Elizabeth raised apologetic brown eyes to Aisling's. 'I think I'm going to have to take my maternity leave from today. I don't know if I could manage another week. I know there's still loads I haven't shown you . . .'

'Don't be silly,' chided Aisling, trying not to think of what it would be like to have the horrible Leo all to herself from this moment on. 'You need to get home and look after yourself. Richardson, Reid and Finucane will keep going even if I do forget to bring Leo his morning coffee and lose half his letters! Don't worry.'

By the time she'd walked Elizabeth slowly to her red Panda parked on Fitzwilliam Square and made sure that she was in a fit state to drive home, Aisling's mind was in overdrive.

Not only was she terrified of losing vital documents on the bloody Apple, but she didn't know if she'd be able to cope with Leo's abrupt and demanding requests.

'Where's the bloody Reilly file?' he'd screamed only that morning, forgetting that he hadn't actually asked for it.

That wasn't even *mentioning* his ability to make her stomach turn inside out when he got her alone in either office and asked her how she was getting on.

'Any problems?' he'd breathed the day before when she'd brought him his mid-afternoon coffee. ('Black and no sugar. I'm sweet enough!')

'Fine, Leo,' she'd said breezily. 'Elizabeth is being great and I hope I make as good a secretary when she's gone.'

Secretary, you big sleazeball, she thought to herself. Not a piece of meat in a skirt.

It did occur to her that she'd envied Jo for her ability to make men stare at her, dumbstruck by her sexy, totally natural charm. But there was a big difference between ogling and admiring. If any man ever dared to give Jo the same sort of insolent and undressing stare that Leo Murphy gave *her*, Jo would have cut him down to size in a moment.

No, Leo didn't look – he slavered and made her feel more

uncomfortable than she'd ever have imagined possible. But what could she do?

This was the only job she was likely to get. She couldn't leave just because of Leo. Women with two kids, an absent husband and no skills, bar the ability to make a perfect cheese soufflé, couldn't afford to be picky jobwise. She'd have to get used to Leo, his slimy looks, little grins and vaguely suggestive comments.

He was in subdued form all afternoon.

He barely registered the fact that Elizabeth had decided to go on maternity leave early, muttering 'Hmm' indifferently when Aisling told him. So much for loyalty.

'Get me the Wilkinson files,' he said finally. 'There must be at least three of them. And get Tom Wilkinson on the phone afterwards. By the way, I won't be in on Monday, so cancel my appointments and leave my diary free on Tuesday afternoon. That's all.'

He wasn't even looking at her, Aisling realised delightedly. Yahoo. She hurried down to the file room with a light heart. Maybe she'd been imagining him as a big bad wolf when he was just a bored boss who amused himself between cases by eyeing up the office temps.

When she went back into Leo's office with the bulky Wilkinson files, he was on the phone. Obviously a private call, since he made her or Elizabeth call everyone for him, even his dentist.

'Don't give me that!'

His strong fingers, covered with coarse black hair, played fiercely with one of the red office pencils, twisting it around and around rapidly, nearly breaking it. Snap! It broke.

Aisling dropped the files on his desk and almost ran to the door. If he was ringing Mrs Murphy, God help her. For a brief moment, Aisling relished the fact that *she* didn't have to endure any more of those cross phone calls from a husband irritated by work and determined to take it out on *someone*.

Safe in her office again, Aisling wished she could lock the door for the rest of the afternoon. She decided to start working on the letters Elizabeth had been doing before lunch and prayed that he wouldn't want her again. No such luck.

'Aisling, come down here.'

His voice on the intercom at a quarter to four made her heart sink. She'd been kept busy getting Elizabeth's unfinished work in order and cancelling Leo's appointments for Monday.

He hadn't even told her where he was going to be so she'd tried to sound both firm and mysterious on the phone.

'Mr Murphy has been called away on urgent business and won't be able to keep your appointment,' she'd said several times in her best posh voice.

Aisling didn't know why, but she firmly suspected that she was lying for Leo. Instinct told her that his sudden change of plans had nothing to do with a crucial conveyancing case.

Leo's face was still like thunder.

'Have you finished my dictation?' he snapped.

'Er, yes. Well, nearly.'

'How nearly?' he asked sarcastically.

Aisling could feel herself getting red in the face and wished she was anywhere except in this office right now. Cleaning out the garden shed in the company of several spiders and a few wasps would be nice by comparison.

'I've done six letters and I've got two left,' she stammered.

'Is that all?' Leo's heavy eyebrows were raised at least an inch as he stared contemptuously at her.

Aisling thought that doing six letters in an hour and a half as well as cancelling loads of appointments was pretty good for a novice. But she kept her mouth shut.

'You're not going to be much use to me if you can't keep up,' he said nastily.

'I'm sorry, Leo. I'll get faster, honestly.' She was begging and she knew it. She couldn't afford to lose this job. Please don't let him sack me, she prayed.

'Mmm. I hope so. Can you do shorthand? I've a letter to go out this evening.'

'Yes.' She'd have said yes if he'd asked could she parachute out the top window. Shorthand had never been a requirement in the motor department, but dealing with lengthy phone calls from irate customers had taught her how to scribble at high speed.

This particular skill had not deserted her and after two attempts to decipher what turned out to be 'contemporaneous' – which Aisling would have dearly loved to have changed to the more sensible and more suitable 'at the same time' – she finished Leo's letter in fifteen minutes.

He was long-winded, but maybe that was simply his legal training. If he could say something in ten words instead of two, Leo went for the ten words every time. Nobody in Leo's world just *did* anything – they gave it due consideration, previous problems notwithstanding, deliberated at length and finally reached conclusions, without prejudice, of course.

Once the letter was signed and in the post, Leo was a different man, charming, chatty. All glinting, admiring eyes. After sprinting noisily up the stairs, he casually dropped a few files onto Aisling's desk and settled himself comfortably against its side.

'So, what have you planned for the weekend?' he asked cosily, as though he hadn't been bawling her out just half an hour previously. Aisling smiled nervously as she opened another document on her computer just to give her something to do other than look at him.

Had he been snorting some sort of recreational pharmaceutical down in his office? Or was his type of two-facedness just part and parcel of office life? She was damned if she knew.

'Nothing much,' she said cheerily, hoping the conversation would stop there.

'You've two boys, haven't you?' Leo loosened his red spotted tie and opened the top button of his cream shirt.

'Yes,' she said, surprised that he knew.

'So you're rushing home to them, right?'

Jesus, she could see where this conversation was going. Leo was onto the second shirt button.

'Yes, they get so upset when I don't get home on time,' she

181

lied with as much sincerity as she could muster, thinking of the previous evening when Phillip and Paul had been so glued to a Power Rangers video in Fiona's that they hadn't wanted to come home at all.

'Pity.' Leo got up abruptly. 'We must have a drink some evening. I can't have a new member of staff without bringing her out for a drink, now can I?' He smiled, baring a set of wolfish canines.

She kept typing, wishing she could pull on her cinnamon-coloured cotton cardigan and do up all the buttons. The pale pink silk blouse she'd had for years had been washed to that comfortable softness she loved but, precisely because it *had* been washed to death, it was a bit on the see-through side.

She had that uncomfortable feeling that her white bra was visible through the pink silk. Guess who'd be looking.

She concentrated fiercely on her typing. Her fingers were clumsy.

'Gotta go,' he said after what seemed like an eternity. 'Be good.'

'Bye, Leo.' She smiled at him as he left. Please let him be gone for good. Please.

As she walked out the front door, Aisling felt like those military cadets she'd seen in movies, the ones who threw their caps into the sky with delight once they'd graduated despite the despotic sergeant who'd made their lives a misery.

The week was over. Finally. Thank you God! Suddenly fearful that Leo was lurking near the front door waiting to drag her off for a drink somewhere, she hurried to her car.

She was dog-tired, had a ladder creeping up her tights, knew she had to stop and get milk, and had promised the boys she'd pick up a video for them. But she didn't care. It was Friday. She could crash out in front of the TV because the week was over.

Aisling felt tired but good as she sat in her car on More-hampton Road. Five days ago, she'd been an outsider, the housewife masquerading as a career woman. Now she was

182

one of them, bunions, paper cuts and all. The week had been hell but she'd got through it.

She picked up a bottle of wine for herself in Superquinn and crisps for the boys along with two litres of milk. Hell, she needed a treat. In an ideal world, they'd never eat crisps, she wouldn't drink wine and cellulite would only affect supermodels. But it wasn't an ideal world. If the boys were happy watching TV and stuffing their faces with crisps while she crashed out with a book and a bottle of £4.99 plonk from somewhere unpronounceable in Spain, then the evening would be going pretty well.

Phillip and Paul were like two athletes on performance-enhancing drugs on Saturday morning.

'You're only going for one night,' exclaimed Aisling, taking Paul's swimming togs and three squashed-up T-shirts out of his bag.

'I might need them.' He tried to stuff it all back in along with his Independence Day alien spaceship and the dog-eared Paddington book he'd loved since he was four.

'You won't, darling,' Aisling said again. 'Let me do it. Daddy will forget to pack all this stuff back again tomorrow morning and you'll go mad if you leave anything behind.'

'I can go back and get it the next day,' Paul pointed out.

'I suppose you can.'

Aisling wondered how Ms Carroll would cope with two energetic ten-year-olds spreading muck through pale carpets and squabbling over the remote control.

For a few gleeful minutes, she thought how thoroughly enjoyable it would be to sabotage the trip. She could almost hear herself telling the boys that Daddy would want them to make themselves at home in his new house, that they should behave exactly the way they did here.

'Daddy would be upset if he thought you weren't having fun, boys, and I'm sure Jennifer wouldn't mind you bringing your soccer ball, your Oasis tapes and your Power Rangers videos.'

Stop it, she warned herself. The only damage you'd do

would be to the twins. Don't turn into one of those bitter women who use the children as ammunition.

'Behave yourselves, won't you?' she said as she packed their toothbrushes and the peppermint toothpaste they liked into a small spongebag.

'Yeah,' muttered Paul from the depths of the bottom of the wardrobe. He was rooting around among the books, toys and plastic cars he insisted on keeping.

'I'll miss you, you know,' she said quietly. He didn't hear.

It was five past one when she drove up to the house after picking the boys up from their soccer match. Michael had parked his car on the road, not in the driveway. It was at once both frighteningly familiar and terribly strange to see the silver gleaming Saab outside the house again.

'Dad's home!' yelled the twins in unison from the back seat.

Aisling felt a prickle behind her eyes at the sight of the car, a painful memory of those days when it had belonged there.

He climbed out of the driver's side when she drove in, tall and rangy in chinos and a cream and blue striped casual shirt she didn't recognise.

'Paul, Phillip, come here!' he yelled unnecessarily as the boys launched themselves at him.

'Dad, Dad, we missed you!'

'We won at soccer!'

'I got a medal in judo in summer camp!'

Michael picked Paul up and swung him around rapidly, releasing him suddenly into a giggling heap on the drive before grabbing Phillip in the same way.

They tussled for a few moments and then Michael picked up the soccer ball Phillip had dropped and ran onto the grass with it.

Whooping with joy at playing with Dad again, they followed him happily, tackling clumsily, tripping up and shouting at each other.

Aisling left them to it. They didn't need her. It wasn't right to think of the boys as her private property, but that's what she'd been doing. She had to face the fact that they didn't belong to either her or Michael. They were their children, not their possessions.

She walked into the kitchen, flicked on the kettle automatically and opened the washing-machine door.

Might as well get the clothes dry.

'How are you?'

Michael leaned against the jamb of the kitchen door, hands in his pockets, a relaxed look on his dark face. He stared at her, dark eyes blank. Blast him! Here she was hyped up and nervous about seeing him for the first time since that horrible Friday and he was looking at her as if he hadn't a care in the world. The shirt was definitely new. Obviously expensive. *He* hadn't been sitting home trawling through his wardrobe looking for suitable things to wear. He'd been shopping with Bitch.

'Fine,' she answered curtly.

'You're looking well, anyway. Have you lost some weight?'

She allowed herself to smile at him.

'I don't know. I've just been so busy. Maybe I have.'

'It suits you.'

His voice was admiring. What was he up to? Flattery wasn't going to get him anywhere.

'I hope you've figured out what to tell the boys,' she said, determined to burst his bubble.

'I have.' A wary look appeared on his face. 'I'm sorry you've had to deal with everything. I didn't want it to work out this way, you must understand that, Aisling.'

Oh God, she was going to cry. She'd been fine until he started this.

'I don't want to talk about it, Michael,' she said, turning away and bending down to drag the washing out of the machine. 'Make sure nobody gives them Coke before they go to bed, all right?' She couldn't bring herself to say *Jennifer*. 'When will you bring them back?'

'Is six OK?' he asked.

'Fine.'

185

She didn't turn around, she couldn't. She just wished he'd go out to the car and let her say goodbye to the boys on her own.

'We have to talk sometime, Aisling.'

'I know, I know. Just not now.'

'See you tomorrow then. I'll leave my phone number on the pad in case you need to contact me.'

She heard him searching through the jamjar where she kept odds and ends, looking for a pen that worked. 'I'll wait outside, Aisling. Bye.'

She slammed the door of the washing machine viciously and straightened up. The boys waved at her from the back seat, not a shred of sadness on their happy, laughing faces. She waved just as happily, a grin superglued onto her face.

When they were gone, she felt her entire body sag miserably. Whatever would she do until Sunday at six?

'Have dinner with us,' begged Fiona on the phone five minutes later.

'I'd love to,' said Aisling tearfully, glad that Fiona hadn't dropped over to witness her sobbing into a tea towel. She couldn't imagine being even vaguely hungry and the last time she'd had dinner with the Finucanes, Michael had been by her side. But anything was better than an evening on her own, an evening of remembering.

Dinner turned out to be Fiona's favourite menu, the simplest and quickest thing she could cook – or reheat. Smoked salmon and brown bread – 'No cooking,' she said triumphantly – followed by chicken Kiev straight from Marks and Spencer's with a few wilting bits of broccoli and baked potatoes cooked by herself.

'That was lovely, darling,' Pat told his wife afterwards, before sinking into an armchair, exhausted after an energetic round of golf.

The two women sat at the dining-room table picking at the chocolate mousse which had turned out miles lumpier than it had looked on the packet.

'I wish you'd teach me how to cook.' Fiona lit up a cigarette and inhaled deeply.

186

'You *can* cook, Fee,' Aisling pointed out. 'You know you can follow a recipe book as well as anyone else can, you just get bored in the middle and forget about it all until it's too late. Anyway, there's just no point killing yourself cooking gourmet dinners to the exclusion of all else. I can vouch for that,' she added somewhat bitterly. 'Sorry, I didn't mean to moan.'

'You're allowed,' the other woman answered.

'Shirley Conran said something about life being too short to stuff a mushroom. I wish I'd realised that long ago,' Aisling sighed.

'She also said that she'd prefer to lie on a bed than hoover under it,' laughed Fiona. 'I like that one!'

'After this last week, I'm a convert to that way of thinking,' Aisling said with a smile. 'Life is certainly too short to stuff mushrooms when you're working and looking after two kids. I finally tidied up the twins' room this afternoon and you'd swear it hadn't been done for a month. I've no idea how they can make the place that messy in such a short length of time.'

They chatted, drank coffee and retired to Fiona's Scandinavian white kitchen to stow the dinner dishes in the dishwasher.

By eleven, Pat was snoring in front of the TV and Aisling said her goodbyes.

'Thanks, Fee,' she said sincerely. 'I'm not sure I could have faced an evening of unadulterated aloneness.'

'Well, you got an evening of unadulterated excitement!' laughed Fiona. 'Plus an haute cuisine microwave-in-three-minutes dinner and a sleeping host. What more could you ask for?'

That night Aisling slept fitfully. She awoke in a cold sweat at five past seven and knew she'd never get back to sleep. Punching the pillows didn't help.

Tomorrow, she'd doubtless sleep through the alarm. Today, when she *could* stay in bed for hours, she was wide awake.

Plenty of time to clean, polish and hoover meant that the house was spotless when the doorbell rang a little after six that evening. You *could* have licked your dinner off the floor, Aisling decided, if you felt that way inclined, that was.

She opened the door gratefully and the boys exploded into the house, dragging their luggage after them like dead bodies.

Michael hadn't come in, he just waved at her from the car. 'Darlings, I missed you so much,' she said tearfully, hugging them both tightly.

Paul shrugged her off and headed for the kitchen. At least Phillip gave her another hug before he followed his twin.

'How did you get on?' she asked as brightly as she could. Please say she was a hideous old cow and the house was like a pit, she prayed unfairly.

'Jennifer is really nice,' announced Paul with all the tact of a traffic warden. 'She's got this great car, a Nissan 100X T-bar,' he added. 'Black. And she's brilliant at Quasar.'

Aisling felt about two feet tall. Two feet tall and stupid. And ugly. Not content with taking her husband, this bloody woman had managed to charm her boys as well. What a pity she hadn't taught them to hate the cow!

'She can't cook, Mum,' said Phillip loyally.

'Yeah, we're hungry.' Paul threw open the fridge door and peered inside anxiously.

Bread and water for you, Aisling wanted to say angrily, but she couldn't. It wasn't their fault.

'I'll make you something,' she said. 'Tell me . . .' she hesitated, 'what was she like? What's the house like?'

The How to Split Up Nicely books probably didn't recommend pumping your ten-year-old sons for information on their father's new girlfriend but she just had to find out something.

'She's got this great garage door that opens when you press this thing in the car,' Paul said enthusiastically.

Yeah, it's called somebody else's husband, thought Aisling sourly.

'But is the house nice?'

'It's OK. She's got a big telly.'

Great. What do you expect from kids who wouldn't notice dry rot if they saw it. Aisling wanted hard facts, modernist or romantic, all muslin curtains and brass headboards or Philippe

Starck lemon juicers and icy white sofas?

'She's got a conservatory,' volunteered Phillip. 'And lights in the back garden.'

For candlelit dinner parties, no doubt. Aisling ripped the plastic off a frozen pizza and jammed it under the grill.

'You can't have chips. Will you eat baked beans?'

'Yeah,' they chorused.

God, the food must have been awful. Beans were not high on the dinner excitement-ometer. Aisling cursed the rusty tin opener for the millionth time and reminded herself to get a new one. She slopped the entire can into a saucepan and stirred it angrily with a wooden spoon. She should have shares in Heinz by now.

'How's Daddy?'

'He brought us to McDonald's and got us a new video. I said I missed him, but he won't come home.' Phillip carefully poured orange juice into a glass and drank the contents in one gulp.

Aisling's spoon stopped stirring.

'What did you ask him?'

'I said we wanted him back and he said you and he had rowed and decided to be away from each other for a time,' Phillip said quickly, obviously repeating what he'd been told verbatim. 'He said you didn't love each other any more.'

He looked up at her, big dark eyes welling up with tears. Aisling cursed Michael and his truthfulness. How the hell did he expect two ten-year-olds to understand what she couldn't?

Beans forgotten, she pulled Phillip to her and held him tightly. His green sweatshirt smelled of Michael's aftershave and another scent she couldn't identify. Something heavy and cloying. *Her* perfume.

'Why can't he come home, Mum?' Phillip asked.

There was no answer to that one.

'Daddy needs to be away for a while. Not away from you boys,' she added hastily. 'Away from me. Mums and dads who've been married a long time sometimes need to have a break, you know. Lots of people do it. It can be good for everyone.' She faltered. 'People get very bored stuck together for ever. You wouldn't want to be friends with just Greg and no one else, now would you?'

'No.' Paul had stopped poking around in the fridge and was looking mutinous. 'But that's different!'

'Why?'

'We're boys. Boys don't stay with boys. They're just friends. Not like girls and boys.'

Oh well, thought Aisling. She wondered how to explain that boys sometimes ended up with boys, and girls with girls. But that particular version of the birds and the bees would have to wait until they'd got a grasp on the whole concept of mummies and daddies breaking up.

'It's not that simple, boys,' she said.

Phillip gave her a hard, inquisitive stare so like Michael's that she felt her jaw drop.

'Why not?'

Ask your bloody father, she wanted to yell. The beans began to bubble.

'Get plates, Phillip,' she commanded in a voice that left no room for arguments. 'Paul, lay the table.'

For once, they just did what they were told. She waited until they'd washed their hands and were sitting quietly at the table, cutlery at the ready, before she said anything.

'Boys, it's not easy for any of us. But your dad and I have split up for a while. It's very difficult for me, I miss Dad too. But he's gone for a while and we're just going to have to live with that. It's not your fault. He loves you both just as much as ever. So do I,' she added.

'This is a grown-up thing and we've got to get on with life. I don't want you getting miserable thinking he's never coming back or that he doesn't want to see you. Of course he does. That's why he brought you to see Jennifer today.' Even saying her name hurt.

'For the moment, you've got *two* homes. Isn't that great?' she added brightly.

'Yeah,' said Paul, 'and three cars. I want Jennifer to pick me up from camp in her car!'

'Great idea,' said Aisling from behind gritted teeth. Little turncoat. 'Here's your beans.'

She slopped a puddle of beans onto his plate and wondered was it too late to stick her head in the oven. The prospect of Leo Murphy, two irritable children and a glamorous rival turning up with a size eight bum and a sports car to pick up the kids was just too much for one woman to bear.

CHAPTER ELEVEN

Jo climbed out of the car slowly, grateful for the chance to stretch her legs after so long in the driving seat. Her back ached and her shoulders were stiff from continually crunching gears as she passed trundling juggernauts and carloads of tourists meandering along the road west. It had taken two weary hours to reach Longford, the half way point between Dublin and Jo's home town in the West. Holidaymakers enjoying the June sunshine had dawdled along the road all the way from the Naas Road, admiring cows, lamb-filled fields and the lush green countryside.

Fifteen years of travelling from Dublin to Sligo had made Jo immune to the charms of the N4. She didn't want to gaze at cows, so once she left the outskirts of the city, she just put her foot down and drove, eager to get the four-hour journey to Innisbhail over with.

By lunchtime, the rumbling in her stomach meant she just had to stop somewhere for something to eat and a break.

How do you expect to grow if you won't let Mummy eat properly? she addressed her tiny bump as she walked into the Longford Arms from the car park, massaging her aching neck with one hand. Proper lunch or just a sandwich? she wondered when she reached the reception area.

A handsome man standing at the desk followed her with his eyes, openly admiring the tall, leggy brunette in the flowing saffron-coloured dress.

Out of the corner of her eye, Jo saw him look and couldn't resist giving him a come-hitherish little smile. Then she casually flicked back her curls with one hand and walked into the dining room, her dress swirling around slender tanned ankles. She couldn't be bothered with men right now, but it was still nice to know that she hadn't lost her touch.

192

Fortified by a huge chicken salad, cheesecake and a Lucoz-ade for energy, she was back in the car by two and overtaking tourists' cars at five past.

As she drove past the villages and hamlets which had signposted every journey home since she'd been nineteen, Jo felt a growing sense of excitement.

She couldn't count the number of times she'd travelled down this road, dying to see her mother, Shane and Tom, full of news and eager to hear theirs. She certainly had some amazing news for them this time. But Jo had decided not to tell anyone until after Shane's birthday party. You're only forty once, she thought and it wouldn't be fair to disrupt the surprise party her sister-in-law, Mary, had been painstakingly planning for weeks by announcing the existence of another addition to the Ryan family.

She'd tell her mother, Jo decided. She'd have to. Her mother could detect something out of the ordinary in about two seconds, which was why Jo had only made a few hurried phone calls from the office since she'd found out she was pregnant. It wasn't that Laura Ryan would pass out at the news that her only daughter was pregnant *before* they'd gone through the big church wedding shenanigans. Her mother had never been one of those people who gossiped disapprovingly at the back of the church before Mass, the ones who tut-tutted over any poor girl who was pregnant and unmarried.

But Jo knew what her mother had gone through. It had been a huge struggle to raise three kids on her own when their father died. She had been both parent and sole breadwinner for four-year-old Jo, seven-year-old Tom and ten-year-old Shane. While Laura was able to run the small dairy farm her husband had left her, she was determined that her children never wanted for anything.

When times were lean she sold eggs from her Rhode Island Reds and the rich yellow butter she churned every week. Jo loved her job of collecting the eggs in the morning and evening, leaving one in each nest to confuse the hens into laying there again the next day. By the time they were

193

teenagers, the three Ryan kids could drive the tractor with ease, knew how to help a cow give birth and could milk in their sleep. When Tom decided to study to be a vet, Laura knitted Aran jumpers for sale in Innisbhail's craft shop to help pay his fees. Now that Shane ran the farm and had turned it into a much larger business, the bad times were over. Laura still kept her hens and made her own butter, but she'd handed over the farm to her elder son and was finally able to relax after twenty years of difficult single parenthood.

So much had changed since Jo had first talked to her mother about settling down and having a family. She'd been seventeen then, in the first flush of what she thought was the love of her life, dreaming of a fairytale wedding, exquisite children, a bungalow beside the sea with a tennis court out the back and a garden big enough for ten kids.

Seventeen years later, she could laugh at her teenage dreams. At least she could afford a baby now. Then, her entire fortune had consisted of a collection of much loved second-hand books, four David Bowie albums and thirty pounds in her post office account. Not exactly enough to keep a small child in nappies, never mind puréed vegetables.

She'd planned to rely on Steve, of course, her well-off, clever boyfriend. Would he have been a better father than Richard, she wondered?

She passed a bus bound for Dublin, ready to pick up scores of weary office workers and students and bring them back home for the weekend.

That particular journey was burned into her head like a cattle brand, hours of endlessly winding wet roads interspersed with mind-numbingly boring stops in rush-hour traffic and only one longed-for break in Mullingar for steaming tea. Four hours in a rackety bus had never been her ideal way to spend Friday evenings.

She remembered that freezing January night the bus had broken down outside Foxford and she and the other passengers had been stranded there for two hours before another bus arrived. Three squares of chocolate and a sip of tea from someone else's flask were not enough to keep hypothermia at bay when the wind whistled wickedly outside and the heating didn't work inside.

Her mother had been quite frantic when Jo finally reached home, convinced that there'd been some dreadful accident. Jo could understand how she'd felt. Just a few miles down the road from where the bus had broken down, the tiny white cross was still there, tucked neatly into the ditch at a deceptively gentle-looking bend. A few plastic flowers were jammed up close to the cross, just under the letters 'RIP'.

She'd thought those little grottoes were pretty when she'd been a child, always full of flowers, the small Virgin Marys in their sky-blue cloaks brightening the roadsides.

The road widened just before she reached Ballina. Jo remembered driving out that way with Steve, going to a party in his mother's precious Mercedes. Banana yellow with cream leather seats and an opulent interior smell Jo would never forget. It was Mrs Kavanagh's pride and joy.

Being Steve, he'd taken the corner badly and the car had nearly ended up in the ditch. Jo didn't know which thought had terrified him most – being injured or facing Mummy's wrath if he dented her car.

That had been Steve all over, but she hadn't seen it at the time. Of course, she hadn't seen it this time either. She'd screwed up exactly the same way seventeen years down the line. Awful though it was to face it, Richard and Steve seemed to share some awful genetic code, Bastards' DNA, which helped them forget responsibilities and promises as soon as something or someone more interesting appeared on the horizon.

You'd think I'd have copped on by now, Jo thought all of a sudden. What if I have a baby boy and he turns out to be a mini-Richard?

Don't be ridiculous. She patted her belly and turned up the volume. Mariah Carey's clear, piercing voice filled the car singing 'Always Be My Baby'. Mariah's man wanted to leave her but she knew he'd be back. Lucky girl. Jo was beginning to wonder if she could keep any man.

The car crested the hill and Innisbhail lay before her, a small town nestling in a shallow valley, facing a remarkably sedate Atlantic on the fourth side. On bad days, the sea was a murky grey, surf crashing violently against the rocky shore. Today it was calm and the couple of small fishing boats far out to sea bobbed serenely on the water.

In the distance, she could see the remains of the old abbey beside her mother's home and the small wood where she'd played as a child.

The view always brought a lump to Jo's throat. Today was no different. This is where your mummy comes from, she told the baby tremulously, wishing she didn't feel so emotionally precarious all the time.

Just last week, she'd cried when the owner of a health farm had rung up to say thanks for the lovely piece they'd written in the June issue. And on Wednesday, when she'd stupidly pulled out of a parking space in front of another driver on Capel Street and he'd responded with angry gestures and lots of honking, she'd felt like dissolving into tears.

Cop on, Jo, she commanded. Don't wimp out now.

She drove down the familiar winding road and into the town, past the convent where she'd gone to school and along the main street where she and Marie Brennan had spent five years walking their bikes wearily up the hill before the long cycle home. Everything looked exactly the same, apart from the bright orange plastic burger bar sign hanging over the old post office, jarring with the sedate black and white shop fronts on the left side of the road.

The seats outside O'Reilly's Bar had been repainted and someone had finally replaced the tired-looking hanging baskets with new wire ones from which rampant nasturtiums hung in wild clumps.

The Birkenstock twins were walking along past Dillon's, the butchers, their once-auburn hair tied back into greying sensible plaits as they marched steadily up the hill, nattering non-stop in German, no doubt. They'd tried to teach Jo once but she'd never got beyond the 'How are you? I'm fine' stage. She was sorry now that she hadn't made the effort to learn German. Then again, she was sorry she'd never learned how to play the piano, how to knit Aran and how to change her own spark plugs.

Well, there'd be plenty of time for that when she was the size of a house and could spend hours reclining on the settee, reading educational books and waiting for baby to make an appearance.

A man on the footpath was waving energetically at her. She jerked back to reality and stopped the car, opening the window all the way down.

'Hello!' roared Billy Gallagher enthusiastically, dragging two small cross-looking boys over to Jo's car.

'How are you?' His sunburned face was warm with greeting, as friendly as it had been when they'd been in high infants together and she'd stuck up for him when the big boys bullied him because he was the teacher's son.

'I'm fine, Billy. How are you? God, the boys are getting so big now, I can't believe the size of them!'

'Say hello to your auntie Jo, Connell and Michael,' he demanded, pulling the boys closer to the car.

No joy.

'Ah sure, they take after me.' He grinned. 'Shy.'

'You were never shy, Billy, don't give me that!' Jo laughed.

'A slow developer, then . . .'

'How's Marie?'

'Bringing her granny into Ballina to get her glasses changed. She'd have been here if she knew you were coming today,' he said, mildly reproachful. Jo knew that Marie would be vexed if she found her old friend was coming home for Shane's fortieth birthday party a day early and hadn't told her.

'It's so busy in the office now that I didn't know if I'd be able to get away a day early,' she said, not quite truthfully. It was difficult to pacify everyone when you lived a long way from home. Everyone thought they should be first on your visiting list.

197

She didn't want to upset Marie, but once she'd told her exactly what was going on, the other woman would definitely understand why she had come home early without mentioning it.

'Will I get her to ring you when she gets home?' asked Billy, as three-year-old Connell started to pull in the direction of an ice cream van.

'Do that. Bye boys, bye Billy.'

After that, she waved at people but didn't stop. You could be stopping all day, saying hello to this one and that, giving potted histories on what you'd done or where you'd been. Jo loved the friendliness of Innisbhail, the sensation of being enveloped in a warm, welcoming blanket. But it could be a bit overwhelming, especially when you were in a rush.

Two miles out of town, she took a left turn at the abbey and drove a quarter of a mile before turning left again, past the old green gates and over the cattle grid to park beside her mother's Mini.

The Albertine climbing rose was out in force, covering the front of the small, whitewashed cottage in a wreath of baby-pink flowers. She could smell its rich, heady scent on the afternoon air as Prince, the old sheepdog, stumbled sleepily out into the sunshine and started wagging his tail as soon as he saw her.

'Hello, old boy,' she said delightedly, rumpling his fur. Prince panted and wagged, gazing up with rheumy eyes, happy to have someone new to pet him.

'Darling, how wonderful to see you!' Laura Ryan stood at the porch, her hands covered in flour and more than a bit of it on her dark curly hair.

'Mum.' Jo ran up and hugged her mother, breathing in the smell of lemon soap she always used along with the scent of Charlie Red she'd worn ever since her seven-year-old grandson, Ben, had bought it for her for Christmas.

'You look good,' her mother said slowly, standing back and taking in her daughter's ever-so-slightly fuller figure which was admittedly well hidden by her flowing dress.

'Have you been baking or bathing in flour?' Jo demanded, laughing as she brushed flour from her mother's hair.

'Baking until Flo Doyle rang me to say she'd seen your car in the town. It's impossible to answer the phone when your hands are covered in flour.'

'Good to see the old bush telegraph is still working as reliably as ever!' Jo said.

'That woman has nothing better to do but look out her front window and use the phone all day long,' her mother answered, heading back into the kitchen to put the pastry lid on her apple tart. 'She rang "so I'd be prepared for you" to put it in her words. What does she think I'd be doing that I wouldn't want you to see? Having it off with the postman?'

Jo laughed and automatically went to the black iron range to move the heavy metal kettle onto the hottest plate. Prince followed her, his nose snuffling her dress in the hope that she had a couple of Mixed Ovals hidden somewhere. The kettle hissed satisfactorily, already nearly boiled.

'Just give me a moment to finish this one and I'm all yours,' her mother said, putting the finishing touches to the tart. 'There's coffee in the cupboard if you want it,' she added.

'No, I've given up coffee.' It had been nearly two weeks since Jo had tasted a drop of coffee.

'You've what?' Tart forgotten, Laura turned around and stared at her daughter. Dark brown eyes met dark brown eyes as her mother's quizzical gaze bored into Jo's head.

'Given up coffee, that's all,' Jo answered. Then she laughed out loud. She should have known better than to try and hide the news from her mother for even one millisecond. She should have just announced it as soon as she'd got out of the car.

'It's not good for babies, is it?' she said simply.

'Oh Jo!' Her mother's face crumpled into tears and she threw her arms around Jo, clinging to her as if for dear life.

'Oh my darling, that's wonderful news. I'm so happy for you, so happy. Now sit down,' she said, leading Jo to the old faded green armchair which had been in the kitchen as long as

199

Jo could remember. 'Sit down and tell me everything.'

Jo sank gratefully into the chair, feeling immeasurably comforted by her mother's love and affection. The small kitchen, with its flowery wallpaper, lace curtains and gallery of Seánie, Dan and Ben's finger paintings, was so familiar. So what if Richard had left her. She still had her family. Her mother pulled up a small stool and sat down beside Jo.

'When did you find out? And why are you only telling me now?' she demanded. 'If you told Richard's ratbag of a mother before me, I'll murder the pair of you!' She was only half joking. Although Laura Ryan had never actually met Richard's mother, she'd heard enough about her from Jo to loathe the other woman.

'That's the problem,' said Jo, wondering how best to broach the subject. Head on, she decided. 'Richard doesn't want to know. He's baby-phobic or commitment-phobic or something like that . . .'

Her mother's freckled face paled visibly. 'What do you mean, he doesn't want to know? It's his baby, what is there to know?'

'I mean that he didn't want me to have it, Mum. It was an accident, we didn't plan it or anything. But I thought he'd be happy, it's my fault really.' She sighed.

'Don't be ridiculous!' Laura said angrily. 'It's not just your fault. It takes two people to make a baby and he's old enough to know the consequences of sex. What did he expect?'

Jo barely registered that her mother was talking about sex in such a nonchalant manner.

'He expected me to be the sort of career woman who wouldn't want a baby messing up her perfect life,' said Jo in a wobbly voice. 'He wanted me to have an abortion, but I wouldn't.'

She broke down finally and sobbed. Her mother wrapped her arms around Jo, holding her close and whispering the same soft nothings she'd whispered thirty years before to comfort a little girl frightened of shadows in the bedroom after her father's funeral.

'There, there my love. Don't worry, Jo. We're all here for you, I promise. Anyway, I've always wanted to be there for the birth of a grandchild and this is the perfect opportunity.'

They sat like that for a while. Prince lay on the floor beside them, knowing something was up and waiting with his nose between his paws in an expectant manner.

'I'm OK, Mum, honestly.' Jo felt around for her handbag and got a tissue. 'I'm used to the idea, thinking about the baby is giving me some kind of strength.'

'Are you eating properly?' demanded her mother, getting up to make tea.

'Yes, Mum.' Jo laughed. 'Like a horse, in fact. I'm going to end up like the Michelin Man if I'm not careful. I've had the most dreadful morning sickness and I can't keep anything down before twelve. After that,' she said, 'I eat everything I can get my hands on!'

'You'll have some fruit cake, then, won't you?'

'Definitely.'

Jo laid out the china cups and saucers her mother always insisted on using and settled herself at the kitchen table. Hot sweet tea and mouthfuls of soft, crumbling cake gave her an energy boost and she started her story.

The scent of perfectly cooked apple tart filled the kitchen by the time she was finished.

'What's the plan for Shane's birthday anyway?' she asked.

'For a start, he'd better not see you or he'll know something's up,' her mother said, carefully laying four perfectly golden tarts on the table. 'He's gone to Killalla to look at some cows and he won't be back until late. Mary's coming over here with the boys and we're going to finish the cooking. We've got a hundred coming so that's a lot of sausage rolls.'

'Don't tell her, will you?' begged Jo. 'I don't want to ruin Shane's night. It's *his* party.'

'It's more Mary's, the amount of work she's done,' Laura said. 'She's made enough cakes and quiches to feed the five thousand, so if nobody's hungry we'll all have full freezers for the next month. I've said I'm going into Ballina shopping tomorrow so I won't be over to them for lunch,' her mother added, carrying the tarts away to the tiny pantry.

'It was the only excuse I could come up with. Mary's telling him she's going with me, but we plan to make up the salads here and bring everything down to O'Reilly's. She bought banners and balloons and everything, God bless her.'

'Shane is going to get quite a shock,' commented Jo.

'Shock isn't the word for it. Mary's been telling him he shouldn't let being forty bother him and that she's not going to make a fuss. I told him I'd get him a nice pullover and some socks and bring the pair of them out to the pub tomorrow evening before I go to bingo. Poor Shane. He hasn't a clue.'

They laughed together.

'He hates the thought of being forty, but I think he's a little upset that Mary and he aren't doing anything special tomorrow night. I can't wait to see his face when he realises he's been had,' Laura said with a grin.

'How are Tom and Karen?' asked Jo.

'It's been hard for them now Karen's back at work,' said Laura. 'Oisín is some handful and Anna, the girl who runs the crèche, is driven demented with him. Karen hates leaving him in the morning and I wouldn't be at all surprised if she gives up work to mind him herself.'

Lord, thought Jo to herself when her mother had gone outside to make up the hens' feed. If Karen couldn't cope with six-month-old Oisín despite having the back-up of a husband, two unmarried sisters living round the corner and a helpful mother-in-law, how the hell was *she* going to manage totally on her own? She knew that her extrovert sister-in-law loved her job as a beautician. The idea that *Karen*, of all people, wasn't able to combine motherhood and career gave Jo a headache thinking about it.

'I'm not giving up my job for any baby,' Karen had said defiantly when she was pregnant and an elderly neighbour commented that she'd better stop working before she began looking pregnant.

Mary had coped with two small children and her job as a

nurse, Jo reminded herself. Mary had worked four days a week in the local hospital even when Ben was going through the terrible twos and made valiant efforts to demolish any room he was left alone in for more than three minutes.

When Mary arrived at half seven, honking her horn excitedly and sprinting into the house to see her sister-in-law, Jo was desperate to ask her how she coped with both a new baby and a job. But she couldn't. She'd never really been interested in Karen and Mary's pregnancies, but now she was fairly bursting to ask questions.

Instead, she rolled out layer after layer of flaky pastry, leaving her mother and the nimble-fingered Mary to handle the lumps of sticky sausage meat. Prince sat glued to Mary's side, knowing she was soft-hearted enough to slip him the odd bit of sausage meat, something his mistress, who was watching his weight, never did.

'How's that gorgeous man of yours?' asked Mary with the smile she hadn't been able to take off her face all evening.

It would have been cruel to ruin Mary's evening by telling her the truth. She was so excited at the thought of the surprise birthday party that she was running on pure adrenalin.

'He's fine.' Jo didn't dare look at her mother.

'How's his back?' Mary inquired, her professional interest sparked by Richard's constant lower-disc problem.

'Fine,' Jo answered tautly, wondering whether he was getting a soothing massage from that Sascha bitch. A nice kick in the backside, that's the sort of treatment she'd like to give him now. She thought of all those evenings when she'd worn herself out gently rubbing massage oil into his aching muscles.

'He'd really want to watch his back, you know. He could have a lot of problems later in life,' Mary continued seriously, blithely unaware of the looks being passed between Laura and Jo.

'Tell us, love, what should we be wearing for autumn?' asked Laura, as though she actually gave a hoot for fashion.

'Oh yes!' said Mary eagerly. 'I was going to wear my velvet

dress tomorrow night, but if you think I should try something else, Jo?'

'What else have you got?' Jo asked, delighted to change the subject. 'I love that amber two-piece you wore for Oisín's christening. What about that?'

'Do you think that would be nice? I've gone off it because my tummy's sticking out,' sighed Mary.

'Get out of here! What tummy?' demanded Jo, thinking of her own expanding belly.

'Do I look all right?' begged Mary, adjusting her bra strap in the toilet mirror in O'Reilly's the following evening. 'Shane hasn't said I look nice at all.'

'He's shell-shocked, Mary,' Jo pointed out practically. 'The poor man still hasn't got over how you managed to set up this entire party without him hearing a whisper. He certainly hasn't got his brain sorted out enough to tell you that you look beautiful. And you do,' she added.

'Oh, I don't know,' said Mary tearfully, fiddling with her lustrous red curls.

'You look lovely,' Jo said firmly. 'Now come on out and get the dancing started. It's like a wedding out there, everyone's waiting for you two to start dancing!'

After several duty dances with old family friends, Jo was about to head outside for a breath of fresh air when a hand on her shoulder made her whirl around.

'Hello, Jo.' She'd have known that husky voice anywhere. Steve Kavanagh hadn't changed a bit.

He was still good-looking although he certainly hadn't got any younger. The gleaming blue eyes that used to dazzle her now had a generous scattering of tiny lines around them.

'How are you?'

For a moment, Jo couldn't think of anything to say. Her social smile deserted her and she just looked at him blankly. What did you say to the first man who'd ever broken your heart?

Get a grip, Jo, she told herself sharply. What have you been doing for the last seventeen years, if it wasn't learning how to get one up on this sneaky, two-timing pig?

'Wonderful, Steve, I'm wonderful,' she breathed in her best sexy voice.

'And how are you?'

Was it her imagination, or did his eyes light up at the tone of her voice?

'Fine. But you look fantastic,' he said, a hint of awe in his voice. Thank God she'd worn the Lainey Keogh dress that moulded her figure like a second skin.

'Thank you, Steve.' She smiled like a cat who'd just found a cat-flap in the cream bun factory door. 'Isn't Miriam with you tonight?'

'Yes, she's over by the bar. We were on our way back after dinner and thought we'd drop in.'

Thought you'd crash the party because you can't bear to miss anything, Jo thought nastily. There's no way you and your horrible wife were invited to this party.

'It's been a long time, Jo,' he said.

'Gosh, I suppose it has,' she replied. 'Ten years at least,' she added, knowing well it was fifteen.

'I think about you, about us, sometimes.' Steve stared at her, giving her the benefit of the lethal Kavanagh smile she'd never been able to resist when she was a teenager.

'Do you?' Jo smiled at him indulgently. 'Weren't we the mad things, convinced we were in love at seventeen?' She laughed, as though she hadn't spent months crying when she heard he was going to marry Miriam Timmons.

'Sometimes I see your picture in the magazine and wonder what it would have been like if we'd stayed together . . .'

'Goodness, Steve, you old romantic. We'd have killed each other if we'd stayed together. I couldn't imagine it!' it gave her a dart of pleasure to see him flinch as the barb struck home. Serves you right, you bastard, she thought. He wasn't ageing well.

Funny, thought Jo, eyeing him up surreptitiously. She used to think he dressed so well. Now she was a fashion editor and

Steve Kavanagh was standing before her wearing a red polo shirt which didn't go with his red cheeks and a pair of cream jeans which did nothing for his beer belly.

'Joanne, nice to see you.' Jo swivelled around to face her old-time enemy, the only person who'd ever called her by her full name since she'd insisted on being called Jo at the tomboyish age of ten.

'Miriam, what a surprise!' The chubby Miriam Timmons she'd known had grown up into a very thin woman, with a short helmet of frosted blonde hair and the sort of mahogany tan which would have cancer specialists shaking their heads in disbelief.

She was dressed beautifully, in a coffee-coloured suede skirt and a silk blouse, but the clothes hung on her bony frame like laundry on a clothes-horse. A cluster of gold bangles and gold necklaces rattled as she moved and she made sure that her ostentatious engagement diamond, in a setting as big as a knuckleduster, caught the light as she waved her hand.

'Well, Joanne, you're looking well. Are you here on your own?' Miriam looked around the room pointedly as though trying to seek out Jo's boyfriend. Jo would have bet a year's salary that Miriam knew damn well she was here on her own and wanted to rub it in. Boyfriend couldn't be bothered to come with you, huh? Jo could almost hear the words.

Miriam's heavily made-up eyes dropped to Jo's bare ring-finger. Two can play at that game, thought Jo.

'I didn't expect to see you two here,' she said. 'Mary didn't mention inviting you.' Take that, you gatecrashing cow, she thought venomously.

Miriam blinked nervously. She'd done that in French class when she tried to pretend she'd mislaid her grammar copy-book.

'We, we were . . . just passing and thought we'd drop in!' she faltered.

Score one to me. Jo smiled to herself.

'Steve was telling me you buy *Style*,' she added. 'It's lovely to know that the people at home follow your career. Although

I should point out, Steve,' she said, 'that the photo they've been using on my bylines recently is at least a year old. It was taken when I was at the Paris fashion shows last spring and it's ancient!'

Miriam was simmering.

'Duty calls,' sighed Jo regretfully. She slipped an arm around Steve's waist and gave him a peck on the cheek. 'So nice to see you, Steve,' she added warmly. 'Bye, Miriam.'

Jo turned and walked away, aware that two pairs of eyes were glued to her back. A little sexy sway wouldn't go amiss, she decided. What wouldn't she give to hear the conversation between Steve and Miriam now.

Maybe it had been plain old bitchy to vamp it up so much and kiss Steve goodbye, but she didn't care. Miriam deserved it. And the wonderful thing was, she hadn't felt a thing when she'd kissed Steve. Not a smidgen of regret at what might have been. She'd shed quite enough tears over him. Thank God she was cured. All she needed to do now was cure herself of Richard.

'It's so wonderful to be back!' Rhona stood at the office door, a huge smile on her tanned face and bags hanging off her arms. 'Did you miss me, darlings?' she trilled, dropping the bags to hug Jo warmly.

'Sorry I didn't ring last night, pet,' she whispered. 'We didn't get in until after eleven and I didn't want to interrupt your and baby's beauty sleep. And how has this place been while I've been away?' she added more loudly for the benefit of the rest of the staff.

'Great,' said Jo. 'We had a ball and it looks as if you did too.'

'I want to make loads of money and retire to France.' Rhona retrieved her bag and dragged out a batch of tiny tissue-paper-wrapped packages. 'Now these,' she said, doling them out to everyone, 'are only small pressies, but don't say I ever forget you.'

'Oooh lovely,' squealed Brenda, who'd found a pair of shell earrings in her package.

On the phone as ever, Nikki waved a hand-painted pottery candle-holder at Rhona and mouthed 'thank you'.

'I didn't know what to get you, Tony,' said Rhona, as the chief sub-editor emerged from the advertising office with a pile of papers in his hands. 'I knew you wouldn't like anything but booze, darling, but this lot would complain if I gave you any and not them, so I got you this.'

She produced a tiny bottle. Tony took it and peered through his glasses to see what the label said.

'Aphrodisiac oil!' he exclaimed.

'I just thought you might need some,' Rhona said innocently, batting eyelids sooty with mascara.

'You didn't complain the last time we went to bed, Rho Rho,' he countered. 'She said I was a tiger,' he told everyone with a dramatic sigh. 'Women . . .'

'What about them?' A deep voice behind them made everyone hop guiltily.

Standing outside Rhona's office, holding a heavy black briefcase, was Mark Denton. He did not look terribly amused. But then, Jo decided, he rarely did these days.

If Jo had been asked to describe Mark Denton, she would never have said that he was handsome. Some women said he was attractive, sexy even, although she could never see it. She had to admit that he was well built with rugby player's shoulders topping a lean, tall frame. But his Roman nose was crooked, his jaw could have broken rocks and the only sign that his chin had ever yielded against anything was the off-centre dent in it. Short, greying dark hair was raked back over a lined forehead. And his shrewd and piercing eyes looked as if they'd never shone with delight over anything – apart from a successful deal. Everything about Mark screamed money, power and taste. If you liked that sort of thing.

Today, he was dressed in a beautifully cut grey suit with a subtle yellow silk tie and polished shoes.

'I'm here for the sales meeting,' he announced.

Jo could have hit herself. She'd completely forgotten about the meeting and she should have reminded Rhona the moment the other woman came in. Mark Denton was invariably early, 'to catch people out' Rhona always said cheerfully and correctly.

He wouldn't be pleased to see the entire office having a whale of a time at half ten on a Monday morning when the publication of the August issue was only a week away.

He strode into his large office and slammed the briefcase onto the highly polished conference table.

'Coffee, Brenda,' hissed Jo. Brenda scurried off like a rat let out of the lab to make the rich Colombian coffee the boss preferred to instant.

Presents completely forgotten, the staff dropped everything and rooted around their desks for folders, sheets of ideas, notebooks and pens. Mark Denton had that effect on people.

Jo knew she had those papers about the advertisement feature on safe tanning, but she was damned if she could find them. Even the usually unflappable Nikki was frantically trawling through her briefcase, muttering curses as she went.

Only Rhona remained calm and cool. She picked up her bags, sailed into her office, sat back in her chair and lit a cigarette with relish.

'God, I miss this place when I'm away for longer than two weeks,' she shouted out the door.

'Maybe I wouldn't be happy in a French château after all. I really do get itchy feet after too long simply lolling around in the sun, drinking wine and reading novels.'

'Don't torture me,' moaned Jo, who was longing to lie down in the sun and read novels even if she couldn't have kept more than a teaspoon of wine down. 'That sounds like sheer bliss. I'd kill to be doing that right now, to be *anywhere* rather than here,' she added in a quieter tone so Mark wouldn't hear. 'I don't know how you deal with him, Rhona, he's so difficult.'

'That's because you spark off each other, darling.' Rhona put out her cigarette and picked up a fresh notepad from her desk. 'You two are like bullfrogs in a pond, each one determined to be in the right and boss of the pond.'

'I am not!' Jo was shocked. 'You never said that to me before. You said *he* was difficult!'

'Don't mind me.' The editor got up and slipped her arm around Jo. 'I'm still woozy from the journey and probably saying things I'll regret when I calm down. You're just the sweetest creature imaginable when Mark is on the premises, honestly.'

Jo sat back in her chair at the conference table while Nikki and Tony discussed ideas for the Autumn beauty supplement and mulled over what Rhona had said. There was no way she sparked off Mark, she decided crossly. It was all his fault. He irritated her beyond belief. Look at that meeting two weeks ago when he'd deliberately annoyed her by mentioning the poster campaign. All right, she should have noticed that the designers had spelt three words wrong on the mock-up, but at least she'd caught it in time. Lord knows what it would have cost to reprint two hundred posters because of a few careless spelling mistakes. But they didn't have to reprint so why did he have to bring it up at all?

'What do you think, Jo?'

Startled, she looked up to find them all looking at her expectantly, a distinctly quizzical look on Mark's face. Damn. She hated to be caught out by him of all people. There was no way she could brazen it out and pretend she knew what they'd been talking about.

'Sorry, I was miles away.'

'Obviously.'

Was she imagining it or was there a slight smile on his face? Probably a smirk, the pig.

'I've a lot of things on my mind,' she started hotly but got no further.

'I know the feeling,' Mark interrupted gently. 'Are you OK, you look a little pale? Would you like someone to get you some water?'

'No, no thanks,' answered Jo weakly. What was going on? Was Mark Denton, tough guy *extraordinaire* getting soft in his old age – or did she look absolutely dreadful, so dreadful that even he'd noticed?

'Mark's got a great idea for the September issue, but we've really got to get working on it immediately,' said Rhona briskly. She poured some Ballygowan into a glass and sent it down the conference table to Jo. 'He wants us to do a big fashion feature from New York, linked with an advertising supplement centred around the Mademoiselle chain of shops. It's pretty hush-hush right now, but they're opening two shops here, and four in the UK in November.

'Linking up with them would be a brilliant chance for us to push the readership figures up, especially if we could do some sort of competition with them,' Rhona continued. 'It would mean a higher profile for *Style* and lots of ads.'

'And lots of money,' said Aidan, the advertising manager, excitedly.

'I've made tentative inquiries and what we need to do next is to go to New York and try and put things in motion.' Mark paused for a moment and slowly took a sip of coffee from his cup. 'The thing is,' he began, 'I'd like you to get involved right now, Jo. I need you to come to New York with me. You'll know the right way to talk to these people and it'll be useful for setting up fashion shoots later, when we send a model and photographer out.'

'Oh.' Now she *was* stunned. Mark wanted her help in setting the deal up? Amazing. Jo's mind turned somersaults thinking about it all. A month ago she'd have hated the idea because it would have meant being separated from Richard. Not a problem she had now.

And it meant she could spend hours in Bloomingdale's, wandering through miles of beautiful designer clothes with her credit card at the ready. Of course, travelling with Mark would hardly be a thrill, but at least it would be a break.

'Do you think you could manage it?' Mark was looking at her very strangely now, heavy eyebrows knitted together in consternation. Was he actually *asking* her and not ordering? What was happening to him?

'I'd love to, of course,' she replied in a businesslike manner. 'When do we go?'

'Saturday?'

Saturday! She'd hardly be packed by Saturday. It took her at least a month of planning and thinking about her wardrobe to go away for a weekend, never mind a business trip to New York. She just nodded her head and said 'Right.'

'I'll set up meetings for Tuesday and Wednesday, which gives us Monday to recover from jet-lag,' Mark was saying. 'We should be finished by Thursday, Friday at the latest.'

'Lucky old you,' said Nikki enviously. 'I love New York and I adore the Village. Weren't you there only last year with Richard?'

Jo felt her stomach lurch at the mention of his name. She hadn't told the other girls in the office that she and Richard had broken up. She hadn't heard a word from the bastard since that horrible morning in her flat so it was pretty obvious that he was out of her life for good. She knew she had to tell people, but she kept putting it off. How could she tell them she was single again and pregnant all in the one fell swoop? It was so embarrassing, so humiliating.

'Nikki, do you have the pictures for the perfume ad feature?' said Rhona loudly. She knew that Jo was on the verge of tears and guessed the reason why.

For the next half an hour, the conversation around the conference table ranged from advertisement features to production problems. Jo sat quietly, answering questions and trying to join in. But she didn't feel up to it. Damn Richard.

Under the table, her hands caressed her tiny bump, gaining solace from the thought of the life inside her. Baby, baby, you make me strong, she said to herself.

When the meeting was over, Mark dismissed everybody curtly but asked Jo to stay. Instead of remaining at his seat at the top of the table, he moved into the chair beside her.

'I got the feeling that you're not keen on going to New York,' he began, splaying his hands onto the table as he spoke. He had strong fingers, more suited to a builder than a man who made deals on his mobile phone and drove a Porsche. There was no wedding ring on his left hand, something which never ceased to amaze the entire office.

Why wasn't Mark Denton married? There were always plenty of women hanging around him, Jo knew that. Quite a few of Jo's journalistic pals had expressed an interest in him and told Jo she was a lucky bitch to work for such an attractive man. She couldn't see it herself.

Rhona knew more about him than she let on, Jo knew that for sure. Whenever there were rumours about Mark and a mystery companion, Rhona pretended to know nothing. That was why she was such a good person to confide in. No secret would ever pass Rhona's lips once she'd sworn to keep it. He certainly wasn't gay. Definitely not.

'If there are personal reasons why you can't be away, I'll understand,' Mark said slowly. 'But I'd really like to have you with me. I know you'd make an excellent impression on these people, you talk their language and understand their ideas. I'm good on the business end but hopeless in that respect.' He laughed. 'I don't know the difference between one designer and another, but I know you do.'

Charmed by his frankness and complimentary manner, Jo relaxed.

'I'd love to go,' she replied. 'It was a surprise, that's all.'

'I've been thinking about it for a few days,' Mark said. 'I'd hate one of the other magazines to steal a march on us which is why I want to get this sorted out immediately. I hope this isn't disrupting your calendar too much, I hope you've nothing planned with Richard or anything . . .' His voice trailed off.

Was he pumping her for information about Richard? Jo wondered for a second. No, he couldn't be. How could he know?

'I've nothing planned,' she said brightly. 'Where are we going to stay?'

'The Manhattan Fitzpatrick. It's a beautiful hotel and it really is a home away from home. Sitting in the bar you'd think you were in Dublin because the place is packed with Irish people.'

'Lovely,' said Jo, meaning it. When she and Richard had gone to New York the previous summer, they'd stayed with one of his friends in a small apartment in Queens, an apartment with dodgy air-conditioning at that.

'By the way, thanks for putting me wise to Emma,' Mark added. 'I really had no idea what she was up to. I suppose I'm the doting uncle who sees her through rose-coloured glasses. She was always a handful as a child, so I don't know why I thought she'd change that much when she grew up. But she really is a good kid. She just needs to mature a bit, that's all.'

'I understand,' answered Jo automatically.

'Do you have any plans for lunch?' he asked. 'I'll be away all week so I won't have a chance to talk to you about the trip. If you're not doing anything, we could go to Dobbin's.'

'I'd love to have lunch,' she said truthfully. Might as well be hung for a sheep as for a lamb and anyway, she was starved. Dobbin's was a fantastic place for lunch even if it was too expensive for her purse. Mark Denton could certainly afford it.

She stood up and smiled at him.

'I've just got to finish an article and make a few phone calls,' she said. She didn't want him to think she'd drop her responsibilities like a shot at the mention of a free lunch.

'Fine. We'll go at half twelve.'

Back at her desk, Jo returned to the article she was writing on autumn's essential fashion buys and the ten wardrobe staples every woman needed. She flicked through an album of pictures from the top designers' autumn/winter collections and chewed the top of her pen. She hated following fashion blindly, telling ordinary women with ordinary curves that over-the-top Seventies stripes or snakeskin jeans were going to look as good on them as they did on skinny little Kate Moss.

Jo's idea of fashion was the sort of outfit which suited each individual wearer. 'Tailored black trousers are a must-have,' she wrote, as she had for the past three years.

'I'm glad to know I'm in fashion,' said Rhona, peering over Jo's shoulder at her VDU. 'Are elasticated waists allowed?' she asked, smoothing down her black tailored trousers.

'Of course,' replied Jo. 'Where did you get those trousers?' she demanded. 'The way my waist is going, I need elasticated ones myself.'

'Welcome to the club,' said Rhona. 'All you need is a belt to hide the elastic bit and you can breathe in comfort. Tell me,' she asked innocently, 'what did Mark want to talk to you about all on your ownio?'

Jo looked up suspiciously but Rhona's expression was serious.

'We're going to lunch to discuss the trip,' she said, knowing she sounded defensive and wondering why.

'Oh,' Rhona said. 'That's nice. Don't forget to come back to the office afterwards, will you? No sloping off for indiscreet drinkies in O'Dwyer's and ending up in Joy's nightclub at four in the morning.'

'Rhona!' Jo was scandalised and shocked. 'Are you mad?' Realising she was almost shouting, she whispered, 'Just because we manage to talk for the first time without coming to blows, doesn't mean we're engaged you know. For God's sake Rhona, I know I'm single, I'm not desperate!'

'You don't have to be desperate to fancy Mark,' Rhona answered mildly. 'Just because you're blind to his charms doesn't mean that lots of other women wouldn't rip out your contact lenses to be in your place, Jo.'

'Well, I'm not one of them,' hissed Jo. 'For a start, I won't be drinking and there's as much chance of him fancying me as there is of you winning the 3.30 at Leopardstown!'

'Fine,' grinned Rhona. 'I'll expect you back at two with a doggy bag and a bottle containing the two glasses of wine you couldn't drink.' She waggled one finger at Jo. 'Don't have fun, whatever else you do!'

At half twelve on the dot, Mark appeared beside Jo's desk, briefcase in hand.

'Are you ready?' he asked.

'Yes,' replied Jo nonchalantly. 'See you later,' she called in to Rhona's office on the way out.

Rhona's response was a wicked wink.

Knowing that Mark was behind her and couldn't see, Jo stuck her tongue out at Rhona. Fun with Mark Denton? Honestly, all that Chardonnay and the French sun must have scrambled Rhona's brain.

'Nice car,' she said as she settled herself into the low-slung passenger seat of the Porsche. 'It must cost a bomb to insure.'

'It does,' Mark answered wryly. 'But she's worth it,' he added, patting the steering wheel lovingly.

Here we go, thought Jo, another man in love with his car. She waited for the spiel – 'it goes from nought to sixty miles an hour in half a second and has triple cylinders and buckets of horse power . . .' Boring, boring, boring.

But he didn't say anything like that.

'I always dreamed of having a car like this,' he said instead. 'My father loved cars but he never had the money to buy anything but old wrecks. I remember him bringing me to a car show once, and we spent hours looking at all these beautiful sports cars. He said he'd love to drive one of them, just once before he died.' He paused, concentrating on turning right down Fitzwilliam Place.

Jo sneaked a sideways glance at him, amazed at this sudden softening of the hard-as-nails image. For once, his jaw wasn't as firmly set and he looked younger than his forty-three years, more approachable somehow.

'He died before I got my first business off the ground,' Mark explained, 'so he never got the chance to ride in a sports car. When I bought my first BMW, I drove to the graveyard in it. It was as if I was showing him that I'd done what he'd always dreamed of doing. I suppose that sounds very senti-mental to you, does it?' He turned to look at Jo.

She shook her head, still seeing a younger version of Mark standing beside his father's grave with tears in his eyes.

'I understand completely,' she said finally. 'I never really knew my father. He died when I was four and I can't

216

remember him at all. But I like to think he looks down on me sometimes. I'd like to think that he could see me and be glad that I'm doing well,' she said quietly.

'He has a lot to be proud of,' Mark said. 'You *have* done well.'

Jo flushed and then laughed to hide her embarrassment.

'I wouldn't say that,' she started.

'Why wouldn't you say that?' demanded Mark, braking at traffic lights and turning to look her straight in the face.

'Things aren't always what they seem, Mark,' she explained hesitantly. 'We all look at other people, see that they have X, Y and Z and think, "They're happy, they've got everything." But we don't see the other side of things at all, the problems people hide.' She shrugged. 'If you put up a good enough façade, you can fool everyone. Even yourself.' Yeah, she'd managed to fool herself all right, fool herself that Richard cared for her.

The car purred to a halt outside Dobbin's and Mark switched off the ignition.

'Do you want to talk about it?' he asked.

'Not really,' Jo replied, amazed that this man could be intuitive enough to know that she was talking about her own problems. 'Let's have lunch and talk about business.'

'That's fine by me,' he answered.

Seated in a booth up beside the wall, they stared at the menu silently. Everything sounded so beautiful, thought Jo hungrily. Tarragon vinaigrette, deep-fried brie on a redcurrant sauce . . .

'I love the way they describe food,' she said to break the silence. 'You couldn't imagine how it could taste any better than it sounds!'

He chuckled. 'That reminds me of an awful joke,' he said.

'Tell me,' she commanded.

'OK. This American guy goes into a restaurant in Ireland and says to the waitress that he wants a chicken smothered in gravy and she says, 'If you want it killed in that cruel way, sir, you better do it yourself!' I know, it's a dreadful joke.'

Jo broke out laughing and crumbs of the bread roll she'd just bitten into spewed out onto the table.

'Sorry,' she mumbled, her mouth still full. She swallowed and grinned over at him. 'That's daft but it's still funny. I used to love silly jokes like that, especially the elephant ones.'

'Elephant jokes?' he asked.

'Oh, they're totally silly but I love them,' she said. 'Here's one. Why do elephants paint the soles of their feet yellow? So they can hide upside down in bowls of custard.'

He laughed and said, 'You're right, that's silly.'

Just then the waiter appeared.

'We better pick something to eat,' Mark said, serious again, 'or we'll never get back to the office.'

'I'll have the avocado salad,' Jo said straight-faced, 'and chicken smothered in gravy!'

Mark burst out laughing while the waiter stood there with a bemused expression on his face.

'Sorry,' Jo grinned up at the waiter. 'I'll have the avocado salad, the monkfish and some water, not the sparkling stuff.'

She looked at Mark as he scanned the menu. He was a strange man and no mistake. He'd never been anything other than abrupt and businesslike with her during the three years she'd worked for him.

Today was startlingly different. He was still the boss, no doubt about that. If his dinner arrived with a single flaw, it would be dispatched back to the kitchen like a shot, she knew. Yet it was as if he'd suddenly decided to open up to her, to let the tough businessman façade drop a little. Wait until she told Rhona.

'I'll have the brie and the monkfish,' Mark announced, 'and a bottle of number 33.'

He hadn't even looked at the wine list, Jo realised. He obviously visited Dobbin's so often that he knew exactly what he wanted.

'I'm not drinking anything,' she said quickly before the waiter left.

'I'm sorry. I should have asked. Make that a glass of red

wine, will you?' he asked the waiter.

Jo was waiting for him to ask why she didn't want wine, but he didn't. He leaned back in the wooden bench seat and smiled at her over the small vase of carnations, a warm smile that lit up his face. He was almost handsome when he smiled. Maybe that was what made other women fancy him, his smile, something he rarely produced when he was in the office.

'So tell me, Ms Ryan, what spurred you on to become a journalist and a fashion journalist at that?'

She looked at him curiously. 'What's brought this on?' she asked bluntly.

'I suppose I don't know that much about you, other than what you've done for *Style* over the past three years, which has been excellent,' he added. 'And seeing as we're going to be travelling together, I thought it would be nice to know each other a bit better.'

His face was serious as he spoke and she found herself noticing that his eyes were a beautiful cool grey colour. Jo was suddenly glad she had washed her hair that morning and worn her navy silk dress even though she'd felt so weak when she woke up that she'd felt like wearing her dressing-gown into the office. And was it her imagination, or was he gazing at her in a distinctly un-bosslike way? Stop that, Jo, she reprimanded herself. He hasn't been interested in you in three years, he's hardly going to start now. There's got to be some ulterior motive for this 'tell me about yourself' stuff.

'Don't you have my CV in your files?' she asked smartly.

'Yes,' he admitted. 'But CVs are limited. They tell you when and where a person is born, what they got in Leaving Cert English and whether they like hang-gliding or knitting, all useless when it comes to getting to know someone.'

Amazing. He wanted to know about her. Maybe he was interested in her after all! How weird. Was she interested in him, she wondered? No, she couldn't be. She was pregnant with another man's child, a man who'd dumped her. She couldn't possibly fancy any man.

219

'Fair enough, I'll spill the beans, on one condition,' she said firmly.

'What's that?' he grinned.

'You tell me the same about you.'

'I'm afraid I'm very boring, Jo.'

'That doesn't matter. You don't talk, I don't talk!' She smiled triumphantly at him.

'You drive a hard bargain.'

'I thought that's why you were bringing me to New York with you,' she said cheekily.

'Of course, of course. For that, and because you understand the world of clothes. I've never been able to understand how they can make two yards of fabric into a dress and charge two grand for it,' he said. 'It's a complete rip-off.'

'I'd keep that particular sentiment to yourself when we're in New York,' Jo laughed, 'or we'll be going home empty-handed. The secret of understanding the fashion world is to tell all designers that they're either the new Coco Chanel or the most innovative designer you've ever seen, not that they're rip-off merchants!'

Their first courses arrived and Jo attacked her salad with gusto.

'No breakfast,' she explained between mouthfuls of avocado.

'Want some brie?' he said, holding out a piece on his fork, the sort of intimate gesture lovers make. She felt that ache in her chest again.

'No thanks,' she said, remembering all she'd read about avoiding soft cheeses during pregnancy for fear of listeria. She stared down into her plate, shuffling pieces of radicchio around in the oily dressing, terrified that the tears would start. What the hell was she doing wondering whether Mark Denton fancied her or not when the man she'd loved had walked out on her?

If Mark noticed her sudden change of face, he didn't mention it. 'Were you always interested in fashion?' he asked blandly.

Fashion, yes, she could talk about that for hours. Grabbing the lifebelt he'd thrown her, Jo started talking. She was still at it by the time Mark had paid the bill.

'That was lovely, I really enjoyed it,' she said truthfully as they left the restaurant.

'I'm glad,' Mark said, opening the passenger door for her. 'Actually, I brought you out because I wanted to talk to you about something.'

'Of course,' Jo replied. What would she do if he asked her out to dinner? Say yes? She'd have to say yes. Anyway, it would be fun. He was a very entertaining companion when he wanted to be.

He opened his door and slid into the driver's seat.

'It's Emma. After what you said to me when Rhona was away, I've been worrying about her. She really needs a firm hand and some guidance. I'd love it if you could take her under your wing, Jo.'

Jo felt herself deflate like a burst balloon. So that was what it was all about. He wasn't even vaguely interested in her. He'd simply been softening her up before asking her to look after his bloody niece. What a fool she'd been to even imagine that Mark Denton would be interested in someone like her. You're a complete moron, Jo Ryan.

'What would you like me to do?' she asked tersely.

'Take her on like a student. Train her how to write, how to interview people, you know the sort of thing. If you agree, I'd be delighted and so would Emma.'

It wouldn't kill me to be nice to the scheming little bitch, Jo decided. But she wasn't going to take any cheek from her.

'I'll take her on, Mark,' Jo said coolly. 'However, I want her to understand what I'm doing for her. She better be prepared to work hard and not whinge or run to you every five minutes if she wants my help.'

'I'll talk to her,' he said quickly. 'Thanks, Jo, this means a lot to me.'

She sat in stony silence until the car stopped outside the office.

'I'll see you at the airport at ten on Saturday morning, OK?' he said.

'Right. Thanks for lunch,' she said quickly before slamming the car door.

'How did you get on?' Rhona asked eagerly when Jo stalked into her office.

'Bloody awful,' Jo snapped. 'That man drives me insane.'

'Oh.' Rhona looked pensive. 'Maybe he'll grow on you when you're away.'

'I doubt it.'

CHAPTER TWELVE

Jo's fingers tightened their grip on the seat's armrests and she swallowed deeply. For the tenth time in five minutes she wished she'd never watched that bloody movie about the plane crash in the Andes.

She hated take-off, hated flying full stop. But taking off was the worst. At least when you were flying, you had no idea what was going on. The air-stewardesses smiled and passed out booze and the clouds were usually so thick that you hadn't a clue how far away the ground was. Taking off, however, was so immediate and fraught with danger. You could see *everything*.

If she looked out the window, Jo knew, she'd see the runway and Dublin airport and lots of housing estates growing smaller by the minute. She couldn't help herself, she had to see. Big mistake. The sprawling airport had turned into a matchbox-sized arrangement and the fields were beginning to develop that patchwork look.

The plane banked slightly and Jo wondered if you were allowed to leave your seat and sprint to the toilet when the seat belt sign was still on. Her old friend, nausea, was back. She'd have to climb over Mark Denton and the person in the aisle seat to get out, but she could do it. Or could she? Maybe she'd just breathe deeply and pray.

'Are you all right?' asked Mark, putting one large hand on her clenched left one.

'No.' She was too scared to lie. 'I hate flying,' she muttered. 'And I hate the window seat.'

'Let's talk about something to take your mind off it, then,' he said comfortingly.

'Did I ever tell you how Rhona and I met?' he asked, settling himself sideways in his seat, and keeping her hand firmly gripped in his large one.

'No.' Jo didn't feel like being humoured. She wanted to behave like a spoiled child and ignore him, make him suffer for bringing her out to lunch purely to talk about his horrible niece. She'd practically ignored him since they'd met in the airport. She'd given him a cool little smile when he'd brought her into the Aer Lingus business-class lounge where there was free tea, coffee, booze and newspapers – and lots of comfy armchairs to sink into.

Mark had managed to ignore the fact that she was ignoring *him* and had been consistently pleasant to her, as though he was humouring a spoiled child. She *hated* that.

'After that, I had to give her the job,' he was saying. 'You know Rhona.'

Yes, she did. She remembered Rhona's parting words to her which had been along the lines of, 'If you fall desperately in love with Mark when you're living the high life in New York, don't forget that I want to know all about it when you come home.'

Some bloody hope. A – why would anyone fall in love with a man when they were nearly three months pregnant with the child of another man who'd done a runner?

B – how could anyone feel even vaguely romantic squashed into a jumbo on a never-ending flight to New York?

And C – why would anyone be stupid enough to fall in love with Mark Denton? Rhona was mad sometimes, Jo decided.

Mark had stopped talking and was patting her hand.

'Better now?' he asked.

'Fine,' she muttered.

He ignored her cross expression and started talking again, obviously under the misapprehension that he was somehow being helpful. He kept the conversation going through the meal – roast chicken and rice, with a brown-bread scone, some sort of cheesecake thing and a foil-wrapped mint chocolate which he handed to Jo – only stopping while they watched the in-flight movie.

'I hate Julia Roberts,' grumbled Jo sleepily, wondering how

in the hell she could be tired when it was only lunchtime. True to form, she'd slept badly the night before, waking up in a cold sweat at three a.m. after dreaming that she'd arrived at Dublin airport for the eleven a.m. flight minus her passport, suitcase and, worst of all, her handbag.

A few minutes dozing would make her feel better. She wriggled around in the small seat, rolled up her sloppy grey sweatshirt into a makeshift pillow and closed her eyes. She woke two hours later, shocked to find that she was leaning comfortably against Mark's shoulder, snuggled up to him cosily.

'Sorry,' she said abruptly, sitting bolt upright. She hoped she hadn't snored or something equally awful. Richard used to say she snored in her sleep; it would be too embarrassing to snore on the boss's shoulder.

'You missed the coffee,' Mark said, stretching his arms and massaging the shoulder she'd been leaning against. Oh no, she groaned inwardly. He obviously hadn't been able to move for hours because she'd been glued to his side. He probably thought she'd done it on purpose, that she fancied him. How awful.

'I didn't wake you because I thought you needed the rest,' he said. 'You look very pale. Anyway, the coffee wasn't very nice. Nothing like the stuff in the office. Are you all right, Jo?'

Mark looked at her with concern in his eyes. Nice eyes, she decided. Kind eyes. It was time she stopped ignoring him and started behaving like an adult again.

'I'm fine,' she answered. As fine as you could be when you felt like a complete moron. 'Sorry about squashing your arm for so long.'

He grinned. 'That's OK. Would you like some water or orange juice?'

'Water would be lovely.' She was desperately thirsty all of a sudden. Since she always wrote that drinking lots of water on the plane and keeping your moisturiser handy were vital for flying, she might as well practise what she preached.

Mark waved in the direction of the air-stewardess. An

attractive redhead appeared at their seats a moment later.

'Can I help you?' she asked, giving Mark what Jo considered a very warm, come-hitherish smile. The stewardess's eyes took in Mark's cream polo shirt with the Ralph Lauren designer logo, his expensive Tiffany watch and the absence of a wedding ring on his strong left hand. Her smile deepened.

Mark certainly had his own quiet charm, Jo realised with a jolt. It was just as well he wasn't her type.

She'd always gone for handsome men, the sort of smooth, chiselled-featured boys who could model Armani suits. Mark was tall, well built and there wasn't an ounce of fat on him, but he was a million miles away from Richard Kennedy. Richard was movie-star gorgeous while Mark was rugged, a hard-working self-made man to Richard's model-boy look.

'Could we have some water?' Mark asked the stewardess before turning to Jo. 'Or do you want juice, Jo?'

'Water, thank you,' Jo said, watching the stewardess's smile shift from admiring to professional once she realised that Mark wasn't on his own.

You're welcome to him, Jo felt like saying. He's not mine. Of course, she didn't say anything of the sort. She sipped her water and eyed Mark surreptitiously. He was attractive really, very attractive in fact. Would it look bad if she got out her powder compact and put on some lipstick?

Kennedy airport was hot, sticky and crowded. Exhausted from the flight, Jo was glad when Mark took charge of the luggage, especially since her suitcase was crammed with at least a quarter of her wardrobe. He lifted her case and his leather suit-carrier effortlessly onto a trolley – without demanding to know why hers was so heavy and what had she brought, the way Richard always did – and led the way through the crowds out to the noisy arrivals hall. It was bedlam.

People of every skin colour imaginable pushed up against the barriers like a human rainbow, anxiously watching passengers emerge and shrieking loudly in different languages when they spotted their visitors. It was like being in Marks and

Spencer's on the first day of the January sales.

Jo was poked in the back by a child with a tennis racket and had her ankles bashed by someone else's trolley as she followed Mark through the throng. The blissful air-conditioned cool of the plane seemed miles away from the humid New York air.

Her white cotton T-shirt and jeans were pasted to her body. What she wanted most in the world was to lie down in a cool room and rest, then stand under a cool shower.

She was considering flinging herself on the trolley and letting Mark push her to the hotel, when she spotted him – a uniformed man in his twenties holding a sign that read, 'Fitzpatrick Manhattan Hotel, Mr Mark Denton'. Mark waved at the driver who immediately hurried over and took control of the trolley.

'Welcome to New York,' he said in a strong Cork accent. 'I'm Seán. Nice to meet you.' Jo could have kissed him. Seán loaded the cases in the back of the stretch Cadillac limo the hotel had provided while Jo slid onto the cool leather seats and sighed with relief.

She didn't care if her luggage ended up in Hong Kong, as long as she didn't have to look after it – or anything else for that matter.

As Seán wove through the heavy airport traffic, Jo stretched out her legs and wondered why she'd never travelled in a limo before. Was this what movie stars felt like when they eased from airport to airport in the comfort of a luxury car, distanced from the world behind darkened windows?

There was what looked like a tiny drinks cabinet fixed into the back of the driver's seat and she'd have loved to open it, just to see what was in it. But that would probably be as gauche as hell and she didn't want Mark to think she was overawed by sitting in a limo. She adopted her best 'I do this all the time' expression and stared out the window. Huge American cars raced past, gleaming Cadillacs and Buicks which would dwarf her own Golf.

Mark and Seán talked, discussing the quickest route into

227

Manhattan with many of the city's roads under repair. Half listening to them talk about parkways, expressways and toll roads, Jo stared at a skyline dominated by shining skyscrapers. It was like looking at the opening credits of *Dallas*.

This was her third trip to New York, but she knew that no matter how many times she visited, she'd still feel that special buzz from visiting the city she'd dreamed about when she was a kid. She loved it. The sprawling city buzzed with vitality, it was alive like nowhere else she'd ever been.

She was also amazed by how much Mark appeared to know about New York judging from his conversation with Seán. He'd never mentioned living there, but he seemed to know it so well. He talked about watching a Yankees game in Yankee Stadium – was that football or baseball, she wondered? Then again, she hardly knew anything about him other than what he did for a living, how he met Rhona, why he liked fast cars and that he had an unbelievably soft spot for his niece. Oh yeah, that he could talk the hind legs off a donkey to comfort someone with air-sickness.

When the limo pulled up at the hotel on Lexington Avenue, Jo clambered out of the back gratefully. Inside, the Fitzpatrick Manhattan was an oasis of calm, away from the buzz of traffic, screaming police sirens and the ever-present blaring taxi-drivers' horns. More European than American, the hotel was quiet and elegant, with Irish accents of all varieties mingling with American ones. From the bar to the right, the sound of Christy Moore's gentle singing drifted out on the air along with the sound of laughter.

'Do you like it?' asked Mark, who'd been watching her reaction from the moment they'd stepped inside.

'It's wonderful, a brilliant choice.' Jo's smile was genuine. The idea of staying in a glorious and sophisticated slice of Ireland in the middle of New York was just perfect.

Registration was speedy and, within minutes, Jo was being shown her suite, an airy sitting room furnished with beautiful reproduction furniture, two large settees, a writing desk and a massive TV concealed in a huge armoire.

The bedroom was nearly as big, with another TV and enough drawers to hold four times the contents of her suitcase. Even more importantly, it was perfectly cool, thanks to the magic of air-conditioning.

'You need a rest,' advised Mark, looking at her pale face and tired eyes. He stood awkwardly in the sitting room while she admired the bedroom and peeked into the bathroom. 'I'll go. If you want to have dinner with me, I'll ring you about eight and we can go out to eat. But you might have friends you want to meet,' he added hesitantly.

'No, I'd love dinner,' she answered. 'Just let me crash out first.'

'We're only here five minutes and you're already talking American!' he grinned down at her. She'd never noticed how tall he was before, he must be six foot, nearly as tall as Tom, her brother. 'I'll call you at eight,' he said and was gone.

Ten minutes later she lay up to her neck in bubbles in the black and white tiled bathroom. The bath, an old-fashioned deep enamelled one, had just cried out to be used and since every muscle in Jo's body ached, she'd given in and filled it.

So what if she was lying in a warm bubble bath in the middle of a sweltering July afternoon? Outside, New York buzzed in the heat. But inside, it was calm, serene and, since she'd turned the air-conditioning up, almost chilly. *The Four Seasons* rippled through the air from the New York classical radio station Jo had found on the radio after much knob-twiddling. She had turned the music up loud but she was amused by the idea that she'd still hear the phone if it rang because there was one in the bathroom. What a howl, she thought, picking it up with soapy fingers. Who would you ring from a bathroom phone? Hi, Mom, I'm having a pee, how are you? She just loved hotels.

When the phone rang at eight, Jo had dozed for an hour, ordered a pot of decaff from room service and dressed in her navy crêpe Mandarin shirt and trousers.

'I'll meet you downstairs,' said Mark.

He was waiting for her when she arrived, lounging in a wing

armchair, dressed in an expensive-looking charcoal-grey jacket, pale grey polo shirt and jeans. Jo nearly did a double take. Mark Denton in *jeans*!

'I even wear T-shirts sometimes,' he said drily, noticing her amazement. 'I expect that *you* sometimes wear a tracksuit, no make-up and stick your hair in a pony tail,' he added with a grin. 'Nothing like the elegant Ms Ryan we're used to in *Style*.'

'Touché,' she replied. 'And yes, I do sometimes forget to apply my make-up with a trowel. But a *tracksuit*?' she asked in mock horror. 'Never. I have jogging pants though, have occasionally worn odd socks because they've got separated in the wash, and I've got a pair of rather tattered leggings. Does that count?'

'Of course.' He slid an arm under her elbow and they walked to the door. It felt nice to be accompanied, to have a man escorting her out, even if it was only for show. Richard's absence made her feel so alone most of the time, as if she'd never have someone to hug and kiss again.

They walked slowly south along Lexington Avenue and Jo tried to forget her troubles and savour the sense of being somewhere totally different from home. The traffic jams of the afternoon were a thing of the past and now the streets were almost quiet by comparison, large sedans cruising along sedately with only the bright yellow cabs roaring up and down the streets at high speed.

The Fitzpatrick Manhattan was in an affluent area of Manhattan. Park Avenue was just one block over while Fifth Avenue was only another two blocks away. Well-dressed people walked along the streets, rushing the way all New Yorkers did. But they avoided eye contact as they walked. That was the big difference between many American big cities and Dublin, Jo felt.

On Jo's last visit, Rhona had filled her so full of warnings on being mugged or staring people in the eye in case they turned out to be complete weirdos, that Jo had been in a constant state of anxiety. She'd even carried the ubiquitous 'mugger's wallet', a purse containing a few dollars to give to any prospective muggers until she'd relaxed and stopped worrying. Now, walking at a leisurely pace with Mark – she'd swear he was walking particularly slow for her, as if he *knew* she didn't have the energy to walk quickly – she wasn't even slightly nervous. He knew New York, she felt safe with him.

'Here we are,' Mark announced, stopping at a brightly coloured café on a street corner. The Starlite Xpress Diner. He peered in the window at the board behind the chrome bar and read out the menu: 'Arnold Schwarzenegger Burger, Dolly Parton Sandwich . . . Oh look, Jo. You can have a Cindy Crawford hot dog!'

'Probably lettuce and a minuscule bun.' Jo laughed, taking in the customers sitting at small tables with paper cups, cans of Coke and styrofoam burger boxes.

'I just thought you'd like to experience dinner in a genuine New York diner,' Mark said with a deadpan expression. 'And it's only six dollars each.'

Jo eyed him speculatively. Was he kidding? Or was he serious? She didn't know. If he wasn't joking, he could have told her they were going casual and she'd have dressed accordingly. She certainly wouldn't have wasted her lovely – and very comfortable – navy outfit on the Starlite Xpress Diner.

'Right,' she said, with a firmness she didn't feel. Men. She'd never understand them. Mind you, Mark was so well off it was probably a thrill for him to eat in a diner instead of a ten-pounds-a-starter restaurant. 'Let's eat.'

He took pity on her.

'Jo, you are so gullible. I'm joking.'

'Pig!' she declared, giving him a light slap on the arm.

He laughed and grabbed the hand that had slapped him. Jo felt a shock of electricity shoot through her at the touch of his hand. She would have pulled her hand away, but his grip was so firm, firm and warm.

'I'm sorry. Forgive me.' His grey eyes glittered and the corners of his mouth turned up into a disarming smile. Silhouetted against the lights of the diner, he looked like a

231

great big bear of a man. Jo had the strangest desire to feel those big arms wrapped around her. Get a grip, Ryan!

'You looked so lovely and dressed up, I just couldn't resist teasing you,' explained Mark with a grin. 'I've actually had the Bill Clinton Burger here, and it was lovely but, like all his meals are reputed to be, absolutely huge. I couldn't finish it. We're going somewhere much nicer than this.'

'What could be nicer than this?' demanded Jo in mock amazement. 'I'm mad for a Dolly Parton Sandwich but I hope they've got curried chips on the menu.'

'Curried chips! You can't be serious!'

Jo tried to look offended. 'I love them, especially with onion rings and battered sausages. Oh yeah, and mushy peas.'

'There was me thinking you were one of those types who live off crispbreads,' remarked Mark.

'I've never had to diet,' explained Jo. 'Never used to, anyway,' she added ruefully, thinking of how she'd been eating for three, never mind two, most afternoons when the morning sickness wore off.

'Come on, then,' said Mark. 'I'm starving.'

He tucked her arm under his and they walked on.

Jo felt a spark of excitement ripple through her body at his touch. She didn't know why, but she wanted to slip one arm around his waist and feel him pull her in close as they walked.

This could not be happening, she thought. She was three months pregnant with one man's child, an absent man at that, and here she was getting all lovestruck over another one. Her boss into the bargain. Had jet-lag completely scrambled her brain?

'You'll love the restaurant we're going to,' Mark promised. 'It's like stepping into a scene from *Wall Street*. The whole place is full of business types in button-down shirts and braces and women with those hard-looking hairdos. All they do is talk about shares, stocks and deals.'

'You're kidding?'

'No, the men really do wear braces. And bow ties some-times. If you were into stock-market espionage, you could learn something here. Well, probably not,' he conceded. 'The tables are so close together that all the business types know that what you say in Smith and Wollensky's at half nine at night will be around the city by the time the Dow Jones opens the next morning. So they probably talk in code.'

'It sounds marvellously high-powered,' said Jo in delight.

'It is.'

Smith and Wollensky's was jam-packed by the time they walked in the door, but an advance call from the Fitzpatrick's concierge meant that they'd skipped the queue. A table would be ready by nine, the maître d' assured them. Jo and Mark squeezed through the people crowded up against the long bar, managed to grab one bar stool for Jo, and ordered drinks.

'I always forget that they don't measure spirits in this place,' said Mark with regret, looking at the massive vodka the barman was pouring into a solid glass tumbler.

'It's like Spain,' Jo said. 'They don't seem to have measures there, they just keep pouring until you say stop. If you don't know the rules and don't say stop,' she continued, 'every drink is a hangover waiting to happen. I remember the first time I went to Spain, it was a press trip when I worked with the *Sunday News*,' she explained, 'and the entire party spent four days fumbling for aspirin in the morning after the previous night's party.'

'There's a real drinking culture to journalism, isn't there?' asked Mark in a slightly tense tone. 'Is getting drunk all the time part of the scene?'

Jo took a sip of her orange juice and stared at him. He looked stiff, anxious, worried somehow.

'Well, it used to be, years ago. We spent a lot of time in the pub when I started in journalism. *Everyone* drank a lot more than they do now.' Why was she justifying it? She'd had every right to be drunk and silly if she wanted to. She was only twenty-one at the time, for God's sake!

'Why do you want to know?'

'No reason,' Mark said quickly, staring at her bottle of orange juice as if he was memorising the ingredients. He picked up his drink and drained it. 'I think you're right. I'll stick to orange juice too. Do you want another one?' he asked.

The penny dropped. Mark thought she was off the booze because she'd been an alcoholic. What a howl! She'd certainly been to enough press receptions where people got pie-eyed, but she'd never been stupid about drinking. It had been years since she'd been plastered. In fact, she could remember precisely the last time it had happened.

'Mark,' she said hesitantly. 'I'm not an alcoholic, I'm not on the wagon, you know. When I started off in journalism, the only people I hung around with were journalists and they all drank like fishes. But not any more. I think we all got sense,' she said, thinking of how the office booze-ups had changed nine years previously. Cirrhosis of the liver had finished off one of the paper's most talented reporters, a man famous both for his addiction to Scotch and his brilliant investigative journalism.

His death had shocked them all and they drank his health in one five-hour binge at the funeral. Jo said goodbye to the days of non-stop partying at that moment.

'I like wine and an Irish coffee now and again, and that's it,' she said firmly. 'Well, good champagne is nice, but only if it's good stuff, not the champagne cider they try and palm you off with at some press receptions.'

Mark stared at her intently. Jo considered the options for a moment – should she tell him the reason why she wasn't drinking? Or should she keep it to herself and have him constantly wondering why she wasn't joining him for a glass of wine?

No, she decided. She'd keep her pregnancy to herself. Even though Rhona was an excellent editor who'd juggled pregnancies, Caesareans, teething and first days at school along with an incredibly demanding job, Mark mightn't have the same faith in *her* doing it like that.

'I have this stomach problem, too much acid,' she improvised quickly. 'I can't drink when it flares up because alcohol makes everything worse. But I'll be fine in a few weeks.'

'I'm sorry to hear that you're sick,' Mark said, sounding concerned and relieved at the same time. 'You should have told me you weren't well, I would have got someone else to come to New York.'

'And there was me thinking that *I* was the only one who could help make the deal,' Jo said in mock misery. 'I think I'll go home now that I find I'm expendable . . .'

'No you won't,' said Mark quickly. 'I'm sorry. You *are* vital to the deal. I just didn't want to think that you came because you had to, because I'd ordered it,' he finished slowly. He turned away from her and raised his glass at the barman. 'Another screwdriver and an orange juice,' he commanded. He didn't turn back, he kept facing the bar as though he was fascinated by the bottles lined up against the back of the bar. The change in the atmosphere was palpable. It was as if he'd decided to close himself off, to put up the cool and aloof Denton façade again.

He thought she'd come because he was her boss and his word was law. Maybe it had been like that at first, she reflected. Of course it had. But now, everything was different. She liked him, liked the warm and funny man who'd been kind enough to keep her mind off her fear of flying, the man who'd noticed her pale face when they were pushing through the airport and had taken care of her luggage. None of these things were the actions of a boss. They were the actions of a friend. She'd worked for him for three years and it was only in the last week that she'd got a glimpse of the sort of person he really was. It was suddenly vitally important that he understood that.

'Mark.' Jo reached out and touched his shoulder, feeling the soft fabric of his jacket under her fingers. Cashmere, she realised, her fashion editor's instincts coming to the fore.

He turned and his grey eyes stared into her dark ones. 'Nobody made me come,' she said softly. 'I wanted to, and I'm glad I did because I'm really enjoying myself.'

He smiled, the tiny lines around his eyes crinkling up again in a way that Jo was finding unsettlingly sexy.

235

'Good.' Was it her imagination or was his voice deeper than usual?

The moment was charged with emotions. Jo didn't know what to say. He held her gaze, then his focus shifted and he stared intently at her face, eyes moving over her flushed cheeks, full lips painted in a burnished bronze colour, eyes fringed with chocolate-coloured lashes.

'Your table is ready, sir.' The slight, Italian waiter broke the spell and they both came to their senses again. 'This way.'

Mark gestured for Jo to go first and she followed the waiter, weaving through a maze of small tables, turning sideways to pass between the gaps where diners had pushed their chairs out from the tables.

She was thinking so hard about the tall man walking behind her, and hoping she looked all right from the back, that she nearly cannoned into another waiter with a tray of shellfish held high above the crowded tables.

'Sorry,' she apologised, stepping aside clumsily. In an instant, Mark's hand was on her waist, steadying her. It was like being touched by a burning poker, her flesh felt scorched by his touch.

'Madam,' said the waiter as he reached a table for two at the back of the restaurant. He held out Jo's seat and she sank into the chair. Across the table Mark smiled at her, but said nothing as the waiter handed them menus and a wine list.

The waiter reeled off a list of specials, but Jo heard none of it. Although her eyes were fixed on the waiter's face, her mind was racing back over the last few minutes, wondering exactly what had happened, what unspoken tension existed between them. She gazed down at the menu blankly.

'What do you think looks good?' asked Mark.

Choose something quickly, she thought. Scallops, yes, she'd have scallops. And melon and Parma ham for a starter.

'The melon and scallops,' she said quickly.

'The scallops are off the menu, or so the waiter said,' Mark pointed out gently. Jo felt herself blush, a warm flush of colour rising up her cheeks. It was like being fifteen again.

236

'Did he? I mustn't have been paying attention,' she answered. 'Maybe I'll have the grilled sole.'

'That sounds great,' Mark said. He flicked his wrist and the waiter appeared. Jo marvelled at his ability to summon people instantly. It was his presence, she decided, that made people jump to attention.

When the waiter had been dispatched with their orders, Mark leaned forward with his elbows on the table.

'We haven't talked business all day,' he remarked. 'I know we should just enjoy ourselves, but we better discuss our strategy for talking to these people on Tuesday.'

Jo felt herself shrink in her chair. So that was it. The moment was over. Obviously the spark of electricity she'd felt between them had been one-sided. Or else he wasn't interested and had decided to talk business to make sure she didn't get the wrong idea. The boss didn't mingle with the staff. She could take a hint.

'What sort of strategy did you have in mind?' she said coolly, determined to prove that she could be just as businesslike as he. If Mark Denton wanted to give her a message, she'd show him what a fast learner she was.

After dinner, they walked back to the hotel in silence. Unaccountably tired, Jo could think of nothing more to say. They'd discussed business tactics for over two hours and she was tired of talking about the importance of readership surveys and ABC market share.

She just wanted to close the door of her suite and slap herself for being stupid enough to think there could be *anything* between her and Mark.

This time he didn't take her arm. They walked several feet apart. When they reached the hotel, he stopped on the footpath.

'I think I'll go for a walk,' he said abruptly. 'I don't think I can sleep yet.'

'Fine,' she answered, not even looking at him, but gazing at the leather shop across the road as though something amazing in the window had suddenly caught her eye.

'Do you want me to call you for breakfast?' he asked.

'No,' she said sharply. 'I think I'll have a lie-in and then wander down to the Village and Chinatown to the markets. I'm sure you've lots of things to do, you don't want me tagging along with you.' Her voice was harder than she'd intended it to be. But she couldn't help herself. She felt hurt, bruised by his sudden indifference and the way he'd turned the evening around. He'd changed it from a magical, electric moment into a cold business meeting.

If he thought she was going to follow him like a puppy, desperate for attention, he'd another think coming.

'Fine,' he said crisply.

Jo marched into the hotel without looking back. In her suite, she threw her handbag onto the desk and picked up the TV remove control She flopped onto the huge settee, kicked off her shoes and put her feet up with relief. Damn Mark Denton. Damn him to hell. Who did he think he was giving her all sorts of enigmatic looks and then treating her as if she were his bloody secretary, someone who'd come along to do his bidding? He was a pig, just like all men. Just like Richard.

She flicked through the shopping channels, CNN, a late-night chat show, the bizarre Manhattan Cable TV and some rubbish with a Barbie doll-style nurse taking the pulse of a patient transfixed by her bosom. Jo watched the show for a moment, waiting for the requisite handsome doctor to come in and tell the nurse he loved her, despite the fact that he'd married her half-sister, slept with her mother, whatever. She hated American soaps with a passion. Nobody in them ever looked like normal people, all the women had plastic smiles, plastic boobs and twenty-inch waists.

She felt her own waist, remembering when she had been just as slender as the women on the TV. At nearly three months pregnant, her body had changed only a little but the extra inches on her waist felt so noticeable to Jo. With careful dressing, she didn't look pregnant at all. Only someone with hawk eyes – like her mother or Rhona – would guess her secret. But she was hungry so often that she knew she'd start putting on too much weight if she wasn't careful.

She still swam twice a week and had been doing step aerobics at the gym. But all those chocolate biscuits, Twixes and ice cream had to go somewhere.

She changed channels again. Goldie Hawn was standing on a yacht screaming at Kurt Russell. *Overboard*, Jo realised happily. She loved that film. There was just one thing missing. She picked up the phone.

'Could you send up a pot of tea and, er . . . do you have any chocolate biscuits?' she asked. 'Chocolate chip would be lovely, thank you. You have shortbread ones made in the hotel? They sound great too.'

Jo awoke in a cold sweat at half eight. Even the soft cotton sheets felt damp and she sat up in the bed, dazed by her dream. What had she been dreaming about? Mark, that was it. She'd been in a hotel bedroom with Mark Denton, a room decorated with crimson wall hangings and with a four-poster bed in the middle, scarlet and gold muslin curtains hiding the bed from prying eyes. She could just about make out lots of people trying to look behind the curtains, men in striped shirts with braces and bow ties.

And she and Mark lay on the bed, half wrapped up in silk sheets, his naked body curled around hers. He'd been kissing her, stroking her belly and telling her he couldn't wait for the baby to be born. She was naked too, she had been able to feel his skin burning into hers, his hands roaming all over her body . . . Oh my God, what a dream!

She pushed back the covers and went into the bathroom, her puffy-eyed and tired face showing the after-effects of a troubled night's sleep.

She wet a white face cloth under the tap and gently wiped her hot face. You look awful, she told her reflection. Her lustrous dark hair was greasy at the roots, her skin was flushed and wrinkled from the way she'd been sleeping on creased sheets and her eyes were puffy from a mixture of jet-lag and dehydration.

Tea, that's what she wanted. It mightn't improve her face, but it would make her insides feel better. She wrapped the hotel's fluffy white bathrobe around herself and phoned room service. She could get used to this type of thing.

Fifteen minutes later, she had showered and washed her hair. A gentle knock at the door signalled that breakfast was ready. A freckle-faced young man with a broad smile and a broader Belfast accent carried a heavily laden tray into the room and left it on the coffee table. Jo, who was never quite sure how much to tip, gave him three dollars. She hoped that was enough. 'Thanks. Enjoy your breakfast,' he said with another smile.

Sitting comfortably on the settee, Jo turned on the TV and listened to the news as she lifted the silver lid from a huge Irish fried breakfast. It smelled beautiful and she hadn't had to cook it herself. Perfect. She poured herself a cup of decaff, buttered some hot brown toast and tucked in. Why were you always ravenous the morning after a big meal? she wondered, munching toast. Well, she hadn't been eating breakfast much lately. Jo stopped mid-munch. She wasn't sick, didn't feel even vaguely nauseous, for the first time in nearly three months. She was thrilled. Of course she'd read that morning sickness could disappear as quickly as it had arrived, but she had begun to think that she'd *always* feel sick. Yahoo!

After breakfast she dressed quickly in jeans, a white T-shirt and a periwinkle-blue cotton sweater, put some money into a small leather bum bag and hung her sunglasses on the neck of her sweater. New York on a clear, sunny Sunday morning was quiet and relaxed. Only a few bright yellow cabs drove down Lexington Avenue, mingling with the light traffic speeding up to Central Park or down to the bookshops and coffee houses in the Village.

Jo walked for a few blocks, savouring the sun on her face and the feeling of warmth on her skin. Two well-dressed New Yorkers strode past her, arms full of newspapers and brown delicatessen bags. Everyone rushed on the east coast, thought

Jo, watching a young man glide past silently on rollerblades, overtaking a cruising taxi.

'Taxi,' yelled Jo, waving her hand in the air. The car stopped and she sidestepped a fat pigeon who'd been scurrying around on the pavement ahead of her.

'The Metropolitan Museum of Art,' she said to the driver, a pale-skinned man with dark hair and a skinny moustache. 'Fifth Avenue and 82nd.'

He looked at her uncomprehendingly. She tried it again, slower and more clearly.

'Sure. I know!' said the driver in a heavy foreign accent. 'Fifth Avenue. I get you there!'

The cab lurched off and immediately picked up speed, dodging traffic recklessly. Now that he knew where he was going, he was going to get her there in double-quick time. Hopefully, alive. Just my luck to get one of New York's novice taxi-drivers, thought Jo, sitting well back in the tattered seat and wondering if a quick novena would save her from death by automobile accident.

Somebody was watching over her, definitely. She emerged from the cab outside the Met feeling decidedly shaky. The driver grinned manically when she handed him a ten-dollar bill and drove off rapidly.

Once inside the gallery, Jo headed for the European galleries where the early Flemish paintings she loved hung. She'd never been in the gallery before, even though she and Richard had planned to spend two days there the last time they'd been in Manhattan. Somehow they'd ended up spending all their time with Richard's friends listening to jazz in smoky clubs in the Village and had never got around to doing any of the things she'd wanted to do. But she knew exactly where to go now thanks to her guidebook. So did lots of other tourists. Even early on a Sunday morning, a large group of Japanese tourists walked along staring blankly at the museum signs before consulting their guidebooks. The Met was so big there was no way to see everything in a few hours. People did what Jo was doing and just picked one or two things they had to see, hoping to absorb as much as they could before everything began to blur.

After two hours staring at Van Eycks and Brueghels, Jo was weary and her stomach was rumbling.

She bought some postcards of her favourite paintings on the way out and dithered about buying two pretty Manet prints she wanted to frame. It would be too difficult to lug them around all day, she decided finally. They'd either get bent or she'd leave them behind somewhere. She could always come back and get them during the week.

The cab ride to Greenwich Village was uneventful, mainly because the driver knew where he was going and wasn't trying to break some sort of land-speed record.

It was nearly lunchtime and the small pavement cafés on Bleecker Street were full of people enjoying Sunday brunch and reading newspapers. Jo bought a *New York Sunday Times* and wondered how she'd ever read it all in one day. It weighed nearly as much as her handbag and that was saying something. As a couple left a table outside a chic coffee shop, boasting every sort of coffee under the sun, Jo quickly dumped her paper on the white metal table and sank into a seat.

Within fifteen minutes she was tucking into a soft bagel spread with velvety cream cheese laced with morsels of smoked salmon. It was wonderful to sit in the sun, sipping her fragrant coffee and watching the world walk by. But Jo couldn't help but feel a little sad, sitting on her own while everyone and their granny seemed to be in pairs. There were couples everywhere, couples laughing and talking with their arms draped around each other or couples simply holding hands.

She found a tissue in her bum bag and blew her nose, remembering the last time she'd been in New York. It had been Richard's birthday, the day before they flew home, and they'd had a marvellous lunch in the Oyster Bar in Grand Central Station. Then they wandered around the shops, stopping off to spend an hour in Bloomingdale's where Richard dragged her, giggling, into the lingerie department. He'd whispered all the erotic things he was going to do to her as she picked out a selection of sexy, lacy bras and knickers.

Typically, he'd got bored quickly. By the time she'd actually decided what to buy, Richard had vanished into the camera department and she ended up paying for the underwear herself. When he took off the coffee-coloured silky bra set later, she'd forgotten that he hadn't actually bought it himself. They'd done every crazy, romantic thing you could do in New York and even visited the Empire State Building. They stared down at the city from the windy eighty-sixth floor and held hands. Richard laughed that they were recreating *Sleepless in Seattle*. 'No, it's *An Affair to Remember*,' she'd argued.

That had been over a year ago. Everything had changed so much since then. Jo gently laid a hand on her belly, as though she could feel the baby's heartbeat with her fingers. She wouldn't have turned back the clock for anything. Maybe she had Richard then, but now she had something much more precious. Her baby.

She was sitting cross-legged on the bed writing her post-cards in the late afternoon sun when the phone rang. It was Mark.

'Hello,' she said coolly.

'Did you have a good day?' he asked.

'Marvellous,' she replied. 'I went to the Metropolitan Museum of Art for a few hours this morning. I wanted to try out Robert De Niro's restaurant in TriBeCa so I could write a funny piece about it,' she said airily, 'but I didn't get that far. I might go down later. Then I read the *New York Sunday Times*, well, read a bit of it, in a coffee house in the Village.' Stick that in your pipe and smoke it, she thought defiantly. Your employee wasn't moping in her room, dying for you to bring her out. She was enjoying New York and its rich cultural life. So there.

'That sounds great.' He sounded unmoved by the bite in her voice. 'I'm going to dinner with some friends of mine on the Upper East Side this evening. I wonder if you'd like to come? It's OK if you've something else organised. I just didn't want to leave you going to dinner on your own.'

Jo didn't know what to say. She'd been thinking he didn't want anything more to do with her and now he was asking her out to dinner with some friends. She would never understand this man. For a moment, she considered saying no. Then she thought of the alternative.

Dinner on her own in a strange city was something she'd never enjoyed, although she'd tried it often enough when she was a news reporter for the *Sunday News*. She'd found that a single woman invariably got the worst table in any restaurant. Returning to the hotel to have a drink in the bar afterwards was out of the question unless you *liked* strange men chatting you up.

She'd spent enough of the day on her own, Jo decided firmly. She needed to get out. Who knows, she told herself, an evening out with Mark could even be mildly enjoyable.

When the taxi drew up outside a tall, elegant apartment building off Madison Avenue, Jo was very glad she'd decided to dress up and wear the hand-painted chocolate brown Mary Gregory dress. The whole place reeked of wealth and opulence. She stared at a vast marble entrance hall, not one but *two* doormen in green uniforms with gold frogging and what looked like an antique table between the two lifts in the hall.

Even the lift smelled of old money, Jo thought, as she stood beside Mark, checking her reflection in the darkened mirrors on either side of the lift.

'You'll like Rex and Suzanne,' said Mark. 'They're very warm friendly people.'

And very bloody rich, thought Jo, when the lift stopped at the top floor and opened onto a small hall with just one door off it. They even had their own *landing*! Mark pushed the bell and the door was opened by a plump dark-skinned woman in the maid's outfit of black dress and frilly white apron that Jo thought only existed in black and white Forties movies.

'Manuela,' said Mark warmly to the woman, who managed

to blush and grin at him at the same time.

'Signor Denton,' she grinned. 'You have not been here for a long time. We have missed you. Madam is in the drawing room.'

Jo looked around the huge entrance hall, a white oval room with three pieces of modern sculpture and an utterly stunning art deco chandelier hanging over what must be a Persian carpet. If this was the *hall*, Lord only knew what the rest of the place was like.

Mark took her arm and they followed Manuela, heels tip-tapping on the marble floor, into a huge, airy room filled with paintings, enormous glass vases of exotic lilies and the sound of Mozart.

'Mark, darling.' A stunning blonde woman got to her feet and hurried over to hug him warmly.

'Suzanne, it's lovely to see you,' he said affectionately.

'And this must be Jo.' Suzanne turned towards Jo and took both Jo's hands in hers. 'We're delighted to meet you,' she said earnestly.

Nonplussed by her friendly welcome, Jo smiled back brightly, immediately liking the tall, graceful woman whose hair fell in soft curls to her shoulders. She was wearing a chic caramel-coloured wrap dress and what looked like a real pearl choker around her neck. Suzanne could have walked off the couture fashion pages in *Elle*.

Only a faint crêping around her throat and small lines around the beautiful blue eyes indicated that she would never see forty again. She looked the way Jo hoped *she'd* look when she was older.

'Now come and say hello to everyone. We're all dying to meet you,' Suzanne said in a soft Southern accent, still holding one of Jo's hands.

'This is Rex.' The tall, grey-haired man, who'd risen when Jo and Mark entered the room, took her hand firmly in his.

'So nice to meet you, Jo. We're delighted you could join our little dinner party tonight. I hope you like New York.'

'How could you not like New York,' interrupted a man with the faint accent and olive skin of an Italian.

'I'm Carlo and I'm pleased to meet you.' He kissed her on both cheeks and then smiled at her, lustrous dark eyes openly admiring. 'I can see why you've been keeping this lady a secret, Mark,' Carlo said.

'I haven't kept anything a secret, Carlo,' Mark said sharply, bending down to shake hands with a woman who was dressed in a navy linen dress and was sitting back on one of the settees. 'Hello, Margaret, how are you? I was so sorry to hear about your accident.'

'I'm fine,' said Margaret. 'I've just got to take care of my ankle.' She gestured at the cast on her right ankle. 'It's just so irritating, not being able to ride, you know.'

Suzanne introduced Jo to the other members of the party, each one more charming and elegant than the last. Gold cuff links and diamond earrings glittered in the light from the Thirties uplighters on the walls. Jo knew that the clothes the women were wearing were genuine Gucci, Jil Sander and Dior.

Even their handbags had labels, Jo realised, as she caught sight of a brown leather bag peeking out from the side of Margaret's chair. Definitely a Kelly bag from Hermès, she realised with a jolt. About four grand's worth of handbag. It was like stepping onto the set of *Dynasty*. These people had serious money.

They had serious jobs too. Carlo was a publisher, Margaret and her husband were in banking – not behind the bureau de change counter, either – Rex was in property, the red-headed woman in black velvet worked in Sotheby's, the short grey-haired man did something to do with computers and the plump woman who chain-smoked was an artist.

'I used to be involved with an interior design firm,' Suzanne explained. 'I'm so busy with my charity work these days, I've rather let my design skills go. The last thing I did was this room.' She waved one graceful, manicured hand at the pale mint walls with their museum-load of paintings.

'It's truly beautiful,' Jo replied. 'The paintings are fabulous, and I love the sculptures in the hall.'

'That's my husband's hobby,' explained Suzanne, 'he loves collecting things. Every time we go to Europe, he drags something back, usually something huge that takes a month to ship.'

'Champagne, madam?' inquired Manuela, who had appeared at Jo's side with a champagne flute and a bottle of Cristal.

'Just a little,' Jo said. Three-quarters of a glass wouldn't kill her. She needed it to stop her staring around open-mouthed. Her entire *apartment* would fit into this room.

The guests talked about stocks, shares and the shocking price of duplexes on Fifth Avenue, while Jo simply sat and listened.

'Tell us about your work,' Suzanne said, turning to include Jo in the conversation. 'I've always imagined that being a fashion editor must be very glamorous. Is it?'

Since it was difficult to imagine anything more glamorous than these sophisticated New Yorkers, Jo laughed out loud. 'Not really,' she said. 'There's a certain amount of glamour about fashion shows. But the real work often involves crawling around on your knees in a photographic studio, trying to pin up the legs of a pair of trousers on a model who's five foot eight instead of the six-foot girl you booked!'

She kept Suzanne entertained talking all about *Style* with Carlo listening intently from his position across the fireplace. Jo didn't think he was even vaguely interested in what she was saying but, from the way his eyes were glued to her chest, he obviously fancied women with curves, even if the curves in question were pregnancy ones. She'd have loved to be able to tell him that she used to be a 34B pre-pregnancy.

At exactly half eight, Rex got up and helped Margaret to her feet.

'Dinner should be ready now, people,' he announced. 'I believe it's lobster tonight.'

Everybody made appreciative noises.

'I hope you eat lobster,' Suzanne asked Jo suddenly.

247

'Of course,' Jo said with a straight face. I eat it all the time, especially with baked beans and chips.

She stood up as Carlo approached, one tanned hand held out to take her in to her dinner but, before he reached her, Jo felt Mark's strong arm link hers.

'Won't you let me escort you into dinner, Madame Jo?' he asked with a grin.

'Only if we're eating lobster,' she whispered back, glad that he'd got there before Carlo.

She was put sitting opposite Mark at the highly polished round dining table, with a delighted Carlo on one side and Rex on the other.

'We're not standing on ceremony tonight,' Rex said, handing around a latticed silver basket filled with warm bread rolls. 'Carlo, pour the wine.'

'Will you have some?' Carlo murmured, holding a bottle of red over her glass and smiling at her with hot, Latin eyes.

'No thanks,' said Jo, hoping he'd take the hint. No to wine and no to you, Carlo. The just-baked scent of the rolls filled Jo's nostrils and made her all too aware of her empty stomach. She ate hungrily, enjoying the Caesar salad, lobster and summer pudding, swollen with ripe berries.

It was going to be a culture shock to her stomach when she returned to Dublin and had to put up with frozen pizzas, eggs scrambled rock-solid in the microwave and lasagne from a packet.

Carlo tried to monopolise Jo during dinner, asking her to tell him about Ireland before launching into his life history, ending with the story of a particularly bitter divorce.

At that point, his eyes stopped being lascivious and looked merely sad, but Jo had enough trouble dealing with her own problems without counselling anyone else. Feeling a little heartless, she patted his arm in a sisterly manner and turned towards Rex.

The discussion ranged from the price Amanda hoped a Degas statue of a dancer would fetch, to the difficulties faced by parents of bored English literature students.

'She says she's bored,' shrugged Ned, 'wants to give up college and go abroad for a year. I just don't know what to do.'

'We've tried everything,' added Margaret. 'I even promised to buy her a new BMW if she stuck it out for another year, but she says no.'

'Do you have children, Jo?' inquired Rex.

'No.' She grinned to herself. 'Not yet, anyway.' And when I do, they won't be getting BMWs in return for going to college, either.

'Don't rush into it,' shuddered the grey-haired man. 'My boys have cost me thousands of dollars, always changing what they want to major in. I tell them I never had any choice when I was their age. My family didn't have two dimes to rub together and I had to work *my* way through college. I think that's their problem, they've had everything handed to them on a plate.'

Jo couldn't resist glancing at Mark. He was looking at her intently, fingers locked over his empty plate, the grey eyes locked onto hers with a frightening concentration. He was definitely thinking of Emma. Good. It would do the little cow good not to have everything handed to her on a plate for once. If Mark got the message, that was.

'Maybe that's the secret,' Mark commented, 'having to work for everything. I had to, so had you, Rex. It made us fighters, it made us determined to succeed. And when we have youngsters to spoil,' he paused and grinned at Jo, 'we spoil them. We give them all the chances we never had and more. And then we wonder why they haven't our fire, our drive to succeed.'

Suzanne clapped. 'You said it!' she said. 'Bryony never did anything we wanted her to until the day I stopped her allowance. "Go mad in Donna Karan, travel to Morocco and hang out on the beach," I said. "Just do it on your own money".' She smiled triumphantly.

'Bryony soon found out she couldn't afford to pay for her own dry-cleaning. By Fall, she'd got over wanting to travel to Morocco like a hippie. Hippies can't buy nice clothes, eat in good restaurants and put gas in the Jeep. In fact, they can't even insure their Jeeps!'

Everyone laughed, even Jo, who remembered what it was like to put three pounds' worth of petrol in the car when she was broke.

'So what does Bryony do now?' asked Jo.

'She's working in Sotheby's with Amanda, as an assistant.' Amanda must be the redhead, Jo thought. 'The pay is dreadful, but she's being trained in the china department. One day,' Suzanne paused and winked at Rex, 'she may even earn half as much as Amanda.'

Amanda, a tall and stately woman in what was either a knock-off peach bouclé Chanel suit or the real thing, peered over her glasses at Suzanne and shook one bejewelled finger slowly. An emerald the size of a Malteser winked in the light. 'My dears, I earn peanuts. Or at least, that's what I tell the IRS.'

They chattered over the cheese and then strolled back into the living room where Manuela had a huge tray of coffee and tiny forest-green china cups ready.

'Are you happy you came?' Mark asked Jo slyly.

She looked him in the eye. 'I'm having a lovely time and I'm sorry for being so childish earlier. You do bring out the worst in me.'

'I'm sorry,' he murmured, leaning close to her so she could feel his breath soft against her neck. 'I'd hoped to bring out the best in you.'

There was no chance to say anything in return. They had caught up with the others and everyone was sinking back into the comfortable brocade sofas.

Jo and Mark sat beside each other on a sofa made for two. When he leaned forward to take a cup of coffee from Suzanne, his thigh touched Jo's. It was like the other night, she thought. His very nearness unnerved her, made her heart beat faster. The hand holding her coffee cup shook slightly.

When she'd finished her coffee, Suzanne asked Jo if she'd like to see the view from the balcony and the study.

'The study is my favourite room,' the other woman confided, walking like a model down the hall. 'I decorated it like
my grandfather's study in Mississippi. He was a judge and he
had hundreds of leather-bound law books. They lined the
walls and gave the place such character, I always thought.'

'I'd love to have a room like this,' said Jo. Huge dark
bookcases stood from floor to ceiling, while an old mahogany
desk and a worn leather chair sat in one corner. 'I have a small
apartment and there's no room for any sort of office or study,'
explained Jo, moving around the room, touching the gold-
leafed spines of the books, 'but I have a dream of buying a
little stone cottage in Wicklow and having lots of bookcases.
And lots of books, of course!'

'I'm sure Mark would love that,' Suzanne said earnestly. 'He
certainly loves books, never stopped reading that one time he
stayed with us in Colorado.'

Jo didn't know quite how to respond, so she picked a
leather-bound volume off a shelf and examined it carefully.
Washington Square by Henry James. She'd been in the real
Washington Square that afternoon.

Did Suzanne think that she and Mark were an item?
Whatever had given her *that* idea? Jo couldn't very well blurt
out that she and Mark had shared nothing more than one
dinner, one lunch and a very long, boring transatlantic flight.

She turned the pages slowly, wondering if Suzanne and Rex
were the sort of people who bought books they'd never read
just because they looked good.

'Maybe I shouldn't say this,' said Suzanne suddenly. 'But
when he asked could he bring you this evening, Rex and I
were so thrilled. He hasn't even so much as mentioned
another woman since, well, you know . . .'

Jo didn't know and she really wished she did. But she didn't
want to let the side down by asking. So she nodded sagely.

'Rex and I were very worried about him. He's never missed
visiting us for Thanksgiving since we met him in Boston all
those years ago. And last year he just called the day before and
said he couldn't come. We really missed his company. He's

251

such a fascinating man, but then, what am I telling *you* that for, Jo. You already know! Anyway,' Suzanne patted Jo's hand, 'we're so glad he's got over it all, and so glad that he's got someone as wonderful as you. And I can tell he loves you, just from the way he looks at you.'

'You can?' asked Jo faintly.

'You bet. Just remember to ask us to the wedding!'

It was nearly half four on Wednesday afternoon when Mark and Jo finally left Mademoiselle Inc. The heavy white door, with MI emblazoned on it in gold, slammed behind them as they walked onto 39th Street after two hours of negotiating.

The director of the Mademoiselle chain of shops was eager to work with *Style* and their in-house designer was even keener, thanks to Jo's praise for his beautiful designs.

The New York traffic was building up into rush-hour proportions and Jo sighed with exhaustion as she realised they hadn't a hope in hell of getting a taxi. But she hadn't reckoned on Mark's ability to whistle up a cab as well as any New York doorman.

'I think that went pretty well,' commented Mark, slamming the taxi door and dropping his briefcase onto the seat beside him. 'You were brilliant, Jo. You really impressed them and telling Marco that his designs were, what was it, ". . . a breath of fresh air into the jaded world of fashion", clinched the deal!'

'I'd have told him he was the new Karl Lagerfeld to get everything signed and get out of there. Thank God it's all over,' Jo said fervently. 'All this wheeling and dealing is exhausting. And I don't think I could have managed another cup of herb tea, no matter how many fashion supplements they were going to advertise in.'

'I thought you *liked* that stuff,' Mark said, astonished. 'You certainly drank enough of it.'

Jo looked at him incredulously. 'I was trying to be polite. Have you ever seen me drink anything that smelled like boiled socks before?'

Mark burst out laughing. 'You never cease to amaze me, Ms Ryan.' His eyes gleamed with amusement. 'I'm beginning to wonder what else you'd do to clinch a deal . . .? Marco certainly liked you and I'm sure Tony wouldn't have turned down an intimate dinner date if you'd asked him nicely.'

It was Jo's turn to laugh. 'I might stand a chance with Marco, but I think you'd be more Tony's type.'

'Damn,' said Mark quickly. 'You mean I missed the chance of a date? You could have told me. He was just my type.' He flicked his head in a camp manner and did his best to pout. He never stopped surprising her.

'I'll tell you what,' she said, 'make a detour to Bloomingdale's to drop me off and I'll ring Tony and tell him you're *wild* to meet him but only if he brings you to a gay biker club, all right?'

'Maybe not,' grinned Mark, patting her knee. 'I've gone off gay biker clubs since PVC became fashionable. *Everyone*'s doing it and I prefer leather. Anyway,' he said, leaning forward towards the driver, and adopting his normal voice, 'I want to do some shopping myself. Bloomingdale's,' he told the cab driver. 'I want to buy a present for my sister. It's her birthday next month and I'd love to get her something really nice. Will you help? I hate shopping,' he admitted.

'Of course. What were you thinking of getting?'

'If I knew *that* I wouldn't be asking you,' he pointed out.

Silk scarves were out because Denise already had loads of scarves. 'That's what I usually buy her,' admitted Mark sheepishly. 'I never know what she'd like.'

He might not know what Denise would like, but he certainly had very fixed ideas about what she *wouldn't* like, thought Jo after half an hour trailing around Bloomie's, where he vetoed every suggestion she made.

Perfume, jewellery, handbags and a glorious chenille jumper in a mulberry shade had all been rejected and even Jo, steadfast shopper that she was, was getting tired.

'I'll tell you what, Mark, I want to have a look around myself, so why don't you potter around and think about what

253

you want to buy Denise and meet me back here in three-quarters of an hour, right?' Before I kill you, she added silently.

Jo spent a blissful half an hour riffling through racks of Donna Karan, Prada and Emporio Armani. She hadn't enough time to try anything on and, since she didn't know how strapped she was going to be for money with the baby, she decided to keep her credit card firmly in her handbag. It wasn't easy. Being a cashless fashion editor in Bloomingdale's was like being a chocoholic with wired-up jaws in Cadbury's.

Next time, she promised herself, taking one last look at a beautiful jersey dress that would look perfect on her. She was passing the children's department when she stopped abruptly. They probably had the most divine baby clothes in the world: just a quick look wouldn't delay her too much.

Everything was so pretty, she thought, stroking the soft fabric of a tiny denim pinafore. There were even socks to match, tiny soft blue ones with miniature denim bows on one side. They'd look so beautiful on the baby, if it was a girl . . .

'I thought it was you.' Mark was beside her, leaning over to see what she'd picked up. 'I came looking for you because I assumed I'd have to drag you out of the premises once you'd got into a clothes-buying frenzy. You buying presents as well?'

The little socks felt so soft, so lovely. For some bizarre reason, Jo suddenly felt sad, felt like sitting down on the floor of the baby department and sobbing for herself and her baby, a baby with no daddy.

'No,' she mumbled, shoving the socks blindly at the rack they'd been on. 'Not presents.'

He caught up with her by the perfume counters. One large hand on her arm stopped her from rushing out the door.

'What's wrong, Jo? Did I say something wrong?'

'It's not you,' she sobbed. 'It's me.'

'Do you want to try some Poême?' interrupted a heavily made-up saleslady armed with a huge yellow bottle of perfume and a fixed smile.

'No thanks,' said Mark, putting an arm around Jo.

'Not you, sir. The lady.'

'No,' he snarled. 'Come on Jo, let's go.'

'I'm sorry,' Jo sniffled. 'I'm so sorry. It's just the baby, the baby's making me all mixed up and sad.'

'Baby. The baby?' repeated Mark in amazement.

'I'm having a baby and Richard has left me,' she mumbled. Then she leaned against his jacket and cried as if her heart would break.

CHAPTER THIRTEEN

Aisling zipped up her skirt and turned to look at herself in the mirror. Three months ago, she wouldn't have been able to get the grey herringbone skirt over her hips. Now she could slide into it with ease. Two months of Callanetics, lots of brisk walks and no chocolate digestives had worn her once-plump thighs and hips down a dress size.

She couldn't help feeling smug. When Michael came to pick up the boys tomorrow, she'd go outside and talk to him – something she'd avoided doing for ages – just to show him how well she looked. Nowadays when he picked up the boys at lunchtime on Saturdays, they ran out the front door with their overnight bags and Aisling never ventured out to say hello. When he brought them home on Sunday evenings before seven, she sat in the sitting room keeping an eye out for his car in order to have the front door open for the twins. She hadn't actually seen Michael for at least six weeks.

They'd talked on the phone of course, cool conversations with lots of silences and plenty of 'anyways'.

Two weeks ago he'd rung on a Thursday night to say he'd have to change his day to see the boys, thus ruining Aisling's plans to help Jo house-hunt.

'I can't pick up Phillip and Paul on Saturday because I'm going to London,' he announced. 'I'll pick them up on Sunday morning instead and bring them out to lunch.'

Aisling was furious, both at the cool way he'd told her the news and the fact that he'd given her only one day's notice of his change of plan. How dare he assume she wouldn't have any plans of her own!

'Thank you *so* much,' she hissed, 'for giving me plenty of notice. Do you have any idea of how this is going to affect the twins, do you, Michael? No, I suppose you don't. It's bad enough that you've left us,' she said, determined to put the boot in, 'but letting them down like this is appalling. How do you expect two ten-year-olds to understand that you can't see them as usual? They'll think you've dumped them too.'

Aisling knew she was being vicious, full of the bitterness she thought she'd managed to conceal for so long. But she couldn't help herself. She wanted to hurt Michael and she'd used the twins to do it. In reality, they appeared to be coping with the break-up quite well, something which amazed her. They seemed confident of Michael's love and loved visiting him at the weekends, excited at the idea of calling another place home. And since she'd started to get on with her life and no longer broke down crying at the drop of a hat, the happier atmosphere had cheered them all up.

'I'm sorry, Aisling,' Michael said, his voice suddenly hollow and exhausted. 'I've only just found out I have to go away. Letting the boys down is the last thing I want to do.'

Hearing the desolation in his voice, she immediately regretted the way she'd tried to hurt him. It wasn't as if she couldn't bring Phillip and Paul out with her and Jo. They'd love the chance to spend time with their auntie Jo, who always brought sweets, told them jokes and let them fiddle around with the windscreen wipers in the front seat of the car the way their mother wouldn't.

Anyway, Aisling missed them so much when they were gone at the weekend that she knew it would be lovely to have them with her on Saturday for a change. Guilt at her bitchiness overwhelmed her. She'd been a nasty, manipulative bitch on the phone, everything she hated in other people and Michael hadn't deserved it.

He hadn't phoned her since then. At least he'd had two weeks to forget what she'd said, she reflected. She wasn't proud of shrieking that he'd left her feeling less than useless. Damn him, she'd never meant to let herself down so much.

Now she had the chance to show him how much she'd changed, what she'd achieved. He'd get a bit of a shock to see that his wife wasn't the same old drudge.

257

CATHY KELLY

The sight of Aisling Moran, career woman, would certainly take him by surprise. Not that she was exactly that – a career woman, she thought wryly.

Keeping her nose to the grindstone in the employ of Richardson, Reid and Finucane did not exactly qualify her for any Businesswoman of the Year awards. Nor did ignoring barbed and often salacious comments from Leo Murphy, in between doing his typing and answering the phone. But she wasn't about to tell Michael that. No way.

Let him admire her new figure, her increased self-confidence and her air of calm. Aisling sighed at herself in the mirror. Who was she kidding? She certainly felt more confident about lots of things, but unfortunately, her confidence wavered when she needed it most. With Leo. Losing nearly three-quarters of a stone had given her more energy and a smidgen of her old self-assurance.

Dealing with all manner of problems with clients and other lawyers' secretaries had given her a sense of job satisfaction that cleaning the oven never had.

But everything fell to pieces when it came to Leo. Aisling loved the days he was out of the office. She typed up letters, filed documents, made appointments and dealt with clients effortlessly.

She was good at the job, she realised happily, great at organising things and coolly competent when it came to the finer details of office work.

Then she'd hear him bounding up the stairs to her tiny office and she'd feel a queasiness in the pit of her stomach.

'How's my lovely Mrs Moran today?' he said sometimes, when he was in a good mood.

'Gimme my appointment book,' he'd snarl when he wasn't. If a woman had behaved the way Leo Murphy did, with mood swings verging on the psychiatric, she'd have been called a premenstrual nuisance or a menopausal old cow.

Leo was just moody, Caroline said the day Aisling had ventured to ask if he'd always been so 'difficult'.

Moody! He should have been locked up, she decided. In

258

fact, he was so nasty when he was in his bad moods, that she had almost preferred him when he was playful, patting her on the shoulder in an overfamiliar way or calling her 'Honey' or 'Sweetheart.' Almost.

Wednesday had been the last straw. He'd come back from what was obviously a boozy lunch – not for the first time – in rare good humour.

'How are you, Aisling?' he said sauntering into her office. He placed both hands on her desk and leaned over, as though trying to see what was on her computer screen. He was too close for comfort. The smell of brandy on his breath was enough to make Aisling recoil.

'Mr R . . . R . . . Reid was looking for you,' she stuttered, the hairs standing up on her arms.

'He can wait,' Leo said in the precise tones of someone who was drunk but determined not to show it.

'So,' he clumsily pushed her wire in-tray to one side and sat down on the edge of her desk, less than two feet away from her. Aisling slid her chair back furtively, but she was jammed up against the window.

'So,' he repeated, 'how's your husband, Aisling? Still gone?'

Had anyone else said something so blatantly rude to her, Aisling would have been furious, maybe even walked out of the room and slammed the door. But Leo Murphy wasn't anyone. He was her boss.

The phone on her desk leaped to life, its shrill ring breaking Leo's spell. Aisling grabbed it.

'Leo Murphy's office,' she said quickly, wondering how she could still speak with her mouth so dry. 'Of course, Caroline. He's here now. I'll tell him Mr Reid's waiting for him.'

She didn't have to say another word. Leo left as quickly as he'd come, leaving her wondering whether she'd just imagined the whole scary scene.

He'd been so normal and businesslike the next day that she'd been able to relax a little, able to think she'd over-reacted.

'What would I do without you, Aisling?' He smiled when

she brought him a sandwich at lunchtime. She smiled briefly, glad that everything was back to normal.

But the incident still simmered in her mind, looming large in her head when the lights were out and she lay on her own in the big double bed. Should she say something to someone? To Vivienne? Two months ago, she wouldn't have dreamed of asking the other woman what time it was, never mind what she should do about Leo.

Yet she'd come to really like Vivienne, to admire her courage and determination. Once Vivienne had realised that Aisling wasn't some bored housewife toying with the idea of a job and using her contacts to get it, she'd dropped her frosty demeanour. In fact, she'd become a good friend. A single mother to eight-year-old Christine, Vivienne was a veteran of the childminder search and had given Aisling lots of advice on finding the right person to look after the twins.

Maybe she should tell Vivienne about Leo, Aisling mused. She really wanted to. But she hated to admit to anyone that she didn't know what to do, that he'd beaten her.

Aisling unzipped her small make-up bag, found her mascara and applied some to her upper eyelashes. She quickly ran her new lipstick over her lips and she was ready. She couldn't resist turning sideways again to see her reflection in the mirror. Yes, she could feel her hipbones, she thought happily, smoothing her hands over the soft wool of the skirt.

Vivienne caught up with Aisling as she hurried along Fitzwilliam Square. It was ten past nine and they were both late.

'Bloody Leeson Street Bridge,' fumed Vivienne, walking as rapidly as a long, sleek red skirt and spindly high heels would allow.

'Some moron stalled his car and I was stuck for three changes of the lights. That made me so late, I'm parked practically at Baggot Street and today's the day of the director's lunch, so I really needed to be in early.'

'I got stuck on the bridge too,' said Aisling. 'I hope Leo isn't in yet, he'll go mad if I'm late. But I know he's going out about eleven, so if you need any help with the lunch today, call me.'

'You're a star,' Vivienne said gratefully. 'I could do with some help because Caroline is on holiday this week and she usually gives me a hand. *And* we're using new caterers today, so I need to double check to make sure everything is perfect.'

'Just ring me, I'd love to help.'

Aisling felt slightly comforted by the fact that Vivienne was late. It could happen to anyone. If Leo was already in the office, she'd tell him Vivienne had been stuck in the same traffic jam. Then he'd know she hadn't simply overslept and was lying about what had delayed her. That was it, she'd tell him about Vivienne and the traffic on Leeson Street Bridge.

Leo was already there when she arrived at twelve minutes past nine, hair flying as she bounded up the stairs. He always locked his office at night and it was now open, proof that he was at his desk and listening for her.

'Aisling,' he called out, as she put a foot on the staircase to her tiny office. 'Come here.'

Breathing heavily from her sprint from the car to the office and aware that she looked hot and flushed, she went into his office.

'I'm sorry, Leo,' she apologised, 'the traffic was dreadful and I got stuck on Leeson Street Bridge for five minutes behind . . .'

'I don't want excuses,' he snapped, obviously irritated. 'I want you here before me in the morning. I want coffee on my desk when I arrive and,' he stared at her with distaste, 'I want a secretary who looks respectable and not like she's just run the mini marathon!'

Shocked, Aisling blinked rapidly, feeling her eyes prickle with tears. If he said one more thing, she'd cry. As if she hadn't cried enough recently.

But Leo had obviously said all he wanted to say and had started reading his newspaper.

Aisling turned on her heel and fled. Once inside her own sanctum, she shut the door and dropped her handbag.

He's a pig, a pig and I hate him, she howled. I hate him. How dare he speak to me like I'm some sort of slave. How dare he think he can ask me personal questions, leer at me and then treat me like this! I hate him!

After ten minutes, she felt calm enough to get him a cup of coffee. He was still reading the paper and didn't even look up when she entered the office. She placed the cup on his desk and left as silently as she'd come in.

Then she took the mug of strong, sweet coffee she'd poured for herself and went to the women's toilet. She fixed her hair back into a neat pony tail, washed her face and reapplied her make-up. She added a squirt of perfume from the tiny Allure sample she'd got in the chemist's.

Finished, she took a draught of coffee and looked at herself in the mirror. She stared at her reflection as if she was a stranger seeing her own face for the first time. Dispassionately, impartially.

An attractive woman stared back at her, a woman with recently discovered cheekbones, an oval-shaped face, a strong chin and large, expressive eyes the colour of just-washed denim. It was a strong face, a womanly face. The face of a woman who was a working mother, a survivor, someone who refused to let life knock her down.

She'd done a lot in the past three months, coped with her marriage breaking up, coped with going back to work, even coped with looking after two boisterous boys. She wasn't going to let some jumped-up bully ruin everything she'd achieved so far, was she? No way, Aisling said aloud. No way. Watch out Leo Murphy. Don't try your bullying tactics any more.

She remained in her office all morning, talking several times to Leo on the intercom as she transferred phone calls. He didn't ask to see her. She was grateful to be left alone.

'I'm going out now. I'll be back for the lunch at one,' he said in clipped tones on the intercom at five to eleven. Hope you crash, pig, Aisling said to herself.

He had just left when Vivienne rang.

262

'Can you come down and help, Aisling? I saw Leo go out, so I hoped you'd be free.'

'Sure. I'll be down in five minutes.'

Vivienne was wrestling with a sash window when Aisling walked into the boardroom.

'Damn thing's stuck,' wheezed Vivienne, pink-faced with exertion. 'That painter we had last month glued everything together with paint. I'll kill him. I just can't open this window and it's like an oven in here if you don't.'

It took both of them to free the window from the painted frame, but once they did the window slid up easily. A welcome cool breeze drifted in along with the noise of cars and motorbike couriers racing over to Leeson Street.

'It's a lovely room,' said Aisling, admiring the gilt-framed hunting prints and an imposing mahogany table in the centre of the room, surrounded by twenty high-backed chairs.

Aisling had peered in the door a few times but she'd never been at one of the monthly directors' meetings where Vivienne took minutes in her perfect Pitman shorthand.

She knew that Caroline usually brought in coffee, tea and biscuits midway through the meetings, and that sometimes the senior partner, Edward Richardson, opened a bottle of vintage port if the company had enjoyed an especially profitable month.

Not that anybody ever got drunk, Vivienne explained. 'Except that time when Tom Reid was taking this flu remedy and he had two glasses of port at the meeting and practically fell asleep!'

Today was going to be different. Richardson, Reid and Finucane were welcoming two new partners to the firm and celebrating the most successful year of business in their thirty-two-year history. So Edward decided to celebrate in style.

They could have taken a room in Le Coq Hardi or any one of Dublin's posh restaurants, but he preferred to host a private luncheon in the boardroom, a tradition dating back to the early days of the business.

263

'There are eight clients coming,' Vivienne said, looking at a notepad where she'd drawn up a list of things to do. 'That makes sixteen place settings and I hope they all fit. We've never had so many people at a lunch before. I just hope the caterers are up to scratch,' she added fervently.

She'd been responsible for organising these annual lunches for seven years and had used the same caterers every year. Until this year.

'I can't believe they've gone out of business,' she told Aisling two weeks previously. 'They were so reliable and the food was always beautiful. I just left it completely up to them. Lord knows where I'll get anyone as good.'

Exclusive Dining, picked out of the phone book, sounded perfect. Vivienne had been crossing her fingers for ten days now, praying that everything would go according to plan.

'Is this the right room?' asked a masculine voice. A sulky-looking young man in jeans and a fluorescent yellow T-shirt stood at the door with a big cardboard box in his arms.

'Yes,' said Vivienne. 'Put it over there, thank you,' she added, gesturing at a long table which stood at the far end of the room covered with a white tablecloth. He put the box down with an ominous clatter. I hope that's not the china, thought Aisling with a twinge of unease, or they'll be eating off cracked plates. Miraculously, nothing appeared to be broken. He took white plates out of the box one by one, banging each one noisily as he stacked them on the table.

'Sabrina is supposed to be coming at half eleven with the food, isn't she?' Vivienne asked him.

'Sabrina's sick. Debbie's doing the food,' he muttered, shoving the empty packing case out of the way under the table. 'I'll get the rest of the stuff out of the van. There are two more boxes, if you come with me to help.'

'What do you mean, "Sabrina's sick"?' asked Vivienne anxiously. 'She was fine yesterday. And who's Debbie, is she a partner or what? I've never met her.'

'She works for Sabrina sometimes,' he answered disinterestedly. Vivienne caught Aisling's eye and grimaced.

'I'll get the rest of the stuff and you ring Sabrina,' advised Aisling. 'I'm Aisling,' she said to the packer. 'What's your name?'

'Bob.'

'Right Bob,' she said resolutely. 'Show me the way to the van.'

She and Bob had unpacked all the china, cutlery, wine glasses and napkins when Vivienne returned, her face as white as her blouse.

'Sabrina has a twenty-four-hour bug and she can't work. But she says Debbie will be here on the dot of half eleven and she's very reliable although she hasn't done many lunches on her own . . . I have a bad feeling about this,' she whispered to Aisling. You and me both, thought Aisling.

It was nearly a quarter to twelve before Debbie arrived with lunch. Vivienne had carefully arranged place settings and adjusted the four baskets of flowers with uncharacteristic nervousness.

'I hate doing this,' revealed Vivienne. 'Leave me a mountain of documents to organise or get me to type hundred-page contracts, and I'm fine. But organising catering is a complete nightmare. I've never been much of a cook. *Christine* makes better toast than I do and I certainly can't come up with menus at the drop of a hat. Oh, here she is! Thank God.'

Debbie was energetic, fresh-faced and about nineteen.

'Hello all,' she said brightly, as she walked into the room carrying a large aluminium cold-food container. 'I'm Debbie, Sabrina's stand-in. Oh, everything look so pretty. The carnations are nice, I love carnations. Grab this for me, Bob?' she asked.

She and Bob blithely carried in the cold and hot food containers, while she chatted away volubly, discussing the traffic, the weather and how she was dying for a coffee.

'Can I smoke in here?' she asked, producing a pack of cigarettes when Vivienne handed her a mug of coffee.

'I'm afraid not,' replied Vivienne.

Debbie shrugged good-humouredly and sat down to drink her coffee. The fact that she was late wasn't even mentioned.

Aisling wondered whether Debbie had ever catered professionally before.

For all she knew, Debbie could have been a junior Masterchef winner who simply wasn't into the formalities of catering as a business. Maybe cooking was her forte and she wasn't interested in making the clients feel relaxed and confident about the meal.

But when she got a look at the dressed salmon, Aisling knew they were in trouble. The fish was the see-through rose colour of undercooked salmon. Food poisoning time, she thought.

It was perfectly arranged, dressed with beautifully cut pieces of lemon and cucumber, and almost definitely half-raw. She ran an experienced eye over the dressed crab with Dublin Bay prawns. The crab looked cooked but, if the salmon was undercooked, God only knew what condition the prawns were in. Shellfish food poisoning registered about eight on the food poisoning Richter scale, bested only by botulism. They really were in trouble.

Aisling might be nervous about her typing and scared of dealing with her difficult boss, but if there was one thing she was perfectly sure about, it was food.

'Vivienne,' she said. 'We've got a problem.'

'What is it?' asked Vivienne, busy positioning the white and red wine goblets in exactly the right places.

There was no point in beating around the bush. 'The salmon is practically raw, Vivienne,' Aisling said as gently as she could. 'Debbie hasn't cooked the fish properly. It's definitely still raw. And I don't like the look of the prawns either. We'll give everyone food poisoning.'

'Oh my God,' said the other woman in horror. 'You're not serious. What can we do, it's twelve now, they'll be here in forty-five minutes. Debbie!' she shrieked.

'Yes?'

'The food is raw!'

'Don't be silly, it couldn't be. I mean, I did my best,' began Debbie defensively.

Aisling bent down and tasted the coleslaw. It was faintly bitter, definitely off.

'We're in big trouble, girls. This is off too. When did you do all this, Debbie? Coleslaw wouldn't go off that quickly.'

Debbie's face was shocked, but Vivienne's was worse. They both looked as if they were going to cry.

'I swear I did the salmon the way the book said,' wailed Debbie. 'I let the water boil and turned it off . . . honestly.'

'Did you leave the fish in the fish kettle until it cooled?' asked Aisling.

'No. Was I supposed to?'

'That's part of the cooking, Debbie. What happened to the coleslaw?'

'I don't know. I'm a pastry chef really. I've never taken on this big a job myself. I'm so sorry.' She looked horrified. But then so did Vivienne. For once, the cool and calm senior secretary was totally at a loss.

'Look,' Aisling took a quick glance at Vivienne's face and decided to take charge, 'what cooking equipment have you got here?'

'We've got a microwave in the van . . . I'm so sorry,' Debbie repeated miserably. 'I did my best . . .'

Aisling calmed her down. 'Look, Debbie, we don't have time to start blaming anyone. We've got to come up with something else fairly rapidly. Bring the microwave into the canteen. That way, we've got two microwaves which we can use to heat the salmon up. It's the only way we can use it. We don't have enough time to recook it and cool it and we better have a proper first course if we don't have the buffet any more. OK, let me think.' Aisling stood back and looked at the food Debbie and Bob had brought up. There were plenty of salads, along with a cooked ham, a huge bowl of mixed lettuce and a cheese board.

Vivienne sat down on a chair and rubbed her temples shakily.

'I can't believe this is happening,' she said. 'I just can't believe it. Today is so important to Edward and I can't let him down.'

The difference between the two secretaries' relationships with their bosses was amazing, thought Aisling briefly. Vivienne didn't want things to go wrong because she'd be letting Edward down. If Aisling had arranged a lunch for Leo and it had gone wrong, she'd have been terrified that he'd kill her, never mind not wanting to upset him.

'Don't worry, Vivienne,' she said calmly. 'I've an idea. Bob, get the microwave and any pots you have from the van. Vivienne, you go with Bob to Quinnsworth in Baggot Street – he can double-park while you shop. I want you to get a pound of beef tomatoes,' she instructed. 'Debbie, do you have any herbs with you?'

'Er, yes,' answered Debbie.

'I need oregano, basil, thyme, parsley and olive oil. Oh yes, we need to make a vinaigrette. Have you got the ingredients for that?'

'Yes. I'll get everything I have.'

'Put it in the canteen, it's downstairs, Vivienne will show you. Right Vivienne, get the tomatoes, three or four French sticks, potatoes and, let's see, courgettes. Debbie and I will divide the cooked ham into starters with salad and when you get back we'll cook the potatoes and salmon. We better forget about the prawns.' She reached out and patted Vivienne's arm. 'It'll be fine, don't worry.'

Vivienne ran to her office to get money from petty cash.

Aisling carefully transferred the food to the basement canteen. A tiny white-tiled room with a table and four plastic chairs, a microwave, a kettle, a fridge and a grill that looked about twenty years old, it was totally unsuitable for cooking and serving a meal for sixteen people. It would have to do.

She slipped one of Debbie's white aprons over her clothes and washed her hands carefully, her mind on the best way to turn a disastrous buffet into a top-class lunch. It was seven minutes past twelve and lunch was supposed to be ready at one. But she felt remarkably calm and focused.

She cut the salmon into large chunks which she put into one of the large serving dishes Bob had just carried in.

Debbie arrived panting, with a box of herbs, oil, butter and cooking equipment.

'We'll use the ham, the potato and the pasta salads and make individual starters,' Aisling explained, breaking open a garlic bulb and expertly peeling and crushing several cloves with an old bread knife she'd found in a drawer.

Debbie handed her a sharp Sabatier knife from her box.

'Thanks,' said Aisling, never taking her eyes off what she was doing. 'Keep it very simple, all right,' she added, assembling a speedy vinaigrette as she talked. 'Just drizzle a little vinaigrette on each plate, place the radicchio in the centre, a little of the cooked salads on the left and the ham on the right.'

'Yes.'

Delighted that someone else had taken charge, Debbie started arranging the plates immediately. They were nearly finished ten minutes later when Vivienne and Bob arrived back with the shopping.

'You were quick,' said Aisling astonished.

'Necessity is the mother of invention,' answered Vivienne. 'I skipped the queue by begging everyone in front of me on the express checkout to let me go first. I said I was going to be fired if I didn't get back to the office on time and it worked!'

Debbie blanched at the mention of the word 'fired'.

'OK, Bob and Vivienne, you peel the potatoes,' ordered Aisling. 'Then wash them and cube them into very small cubes. We need them to cook very rapidly. Debbie, you prepare the courgettes. We'll just cook them in the microwave and serve them with a little butter and black pepper.'

'What are we making?' asked Vivienne as she carefully rolled up the sleeves of her blouse.

'Salmon with tomato and fresh herb salsa and courgettes and mashed potatoes. Because men love mashed potatoes and it's the quickest way to cook them with two microwaves.'

By one o'clock, all the guests had arrived and the board-room was full. The salmon and mashed potatoes were being kept hot in Debbie's portable ovens.

269

Vivienne dispensed drinks while Debbie carried the starters up from the canteen and left them on the long white-covered table.

'Make up a couple of starters with just salad, Debbie,' instructed Aisling when the other girl returned to the canteen. 'Just in case there's someone who doesn't want to eat the cold ham.'

'What will we do if there is someone who doesn't eat fish?' asked Debbie. 'They won't be able to eat the main course.'

'Oh no, I never thought,' Aisling paled. 'I'll do the salad. Get Vivienne to check if everyone will eat the fish. We'll have to give them a cold plate or maybe I can make them an omelette. You do have eggs, don't you?'

'They're all eating the ham,' said Vivienne with a relieved sigh when she walked into the canteen ten minutes later, 'and everyone wants the salmon. I managed to tell Edward what had happened and he says well done to you. And sent down this.' She produced a bottle of red wine and two glasses.

'I need this,' she added, filling one glass for Aisling and another for herself. 'I don't believe in drinking at lunchtime but today is definitely an exception.'

When the last of the main courses had gone upstairs, Aisling relaxed.

'They love it,' Vivienne said, when she came back down from the boardroom. 'What a relief. I never want to go through that ever again. I'm wrecked.' She slipped off her impossibly high shoes and sank down into a chair.

'You were amazing, Aisling. You really saved the day. And you were so unflappable.'

'Cooking calms me,' Aisling replied, putting Debbie's olive oil back in the box along with the herbs and butter. 'It's one of my favourite occupations and one of the things I'm best at. Unfortunately,' she added drily, 'I spent more time over the last five years worrying about making a perfect soufflé than worrying about the state of my marriage. And I spent much too much time *eating* the products of my cookery classes. My answer to everything was to bury myself at home and learn how to make flaky pastry and cream horns – and then eat them!' She laughed.

'Well, you're certainly not eating them now,' commented Vivienne. 'You look great. You've lost so much weight.'

Aisling flushed with pleasure at the compliment. Both Jo and Fiona had said the same thing yet she still didn't know how to take flattery. In her mind she was still an overweight, dull housewife waiting for twelve o'clock to chime and her carriage to turn into a pumpkin.

'Have you been dieting?' asked Vivienne.

'Not really. I don't have the time to cook stuff like I used to any more but I have been making a big effort to eat properly. Working certainly helps,' she added. 'It's easier to keep off the biscuits when you're not staring at the fridge all day long. Breaking up with Michael has done wonders for my figure. Maybe if I'd copped on earlier that he was bored with me and changed somehow, he wouldn't have left.'

Vivienne leaned over and poured Aisling another glass of wine.

'Well, I don't think it's ever that simple,' she said gently. 'I've never been married, but my relationship with Christine's father was a long-term thing, so I know all about letting relationships go stale. You can't say it was your fault things didn't work out any more than you can say it's the man's fault. It doesn't work like that. People change so much, that's what happens. Nobody ever tells you that in romantic novels, do they?

'Christine's father didn't want the same things I wanted,' she revealed. 'He wanted to remain single and fancy-free, which was OK by me before I got pregnant. But afterwards, I wanted to settle down, I wanted security. He didn't.'

She shrugged. 'We drifted apart and it wasn't really my fault or his fault. Was that what happened with you?'

'I suppose so,' admitted Aisling. 'We both changed. I couldn't see that in the beginning. I blamed Michael for everything from global warming to cellulite, but I can see what happened now, thank God. I went one way and Michael went another. I'd stopped thinking of him in the same way, I suppose,' she said. 'He wasn't so much my husband as the father of the twins, and breadwinner. I cut myself off from his world and he did the same to me. I notice it now because his being there isn't much different to his not being there.

'Apart from late-night conversations about what the boys did and what type of dinner was overheated to a crisp in the oven because he was late home, we didn't talk at all. Wow,' said Aisling, 'this is a very intense conversation. Are you sure you didn't put something in this wine, a bit of truth serum?'

Vivienne laughed. 'Trauma makes you want to unburden yourself – or at least that's what it says in Caroline's latest psychology book.'

'*Caroline* likes psychology books?' said Aisling. 'I can't imagine it.'

'She loves them. She's been doing a night-time accountancy course for the last two years and she says she'd never have dreamed of doing it without her books. She says they've given her the encouragement her upbringing never gave her.'

They finished off the bottle of wine, leaving a flustered Debbie to serve dessert, a raspberry roulade with cream.

'If there's any left over, bring it back,' ordered Vivienne, buttering a piece of French bread. 'It looks yummy and we're ravenous.'

Aisling was beginning to feel distinctly tipsy. She hadn't actually eaten any lunch and the wine, a particularly potent Rioja, had gone straight to her head.

'Eat,' advised Vivienne, making an enormous French bread sandwich with some ham and potato salad, 'or we'll be plastered.'

She cut the sandwich in half without too much of the filling squelching out and handed one piece to Aisling.

'Was it very difficult bringing up Christine on your own?' ventured Aisling. 'It's just that I've a friend who is pregnant and her boyfriend has left her. I wonder how hard it will be for her.'

'God help her! It's very hard,' said Vivienne through a

mouthful of crumbs, 'if it's anything like my experience. I mean, I adore Christine, she's everything in the world to me, but there have been some difficult times. It's hard being alone, but you know that. You're responsible for *everything*, nobody else. And it can be lonely, too.'

'I know. You miss adult conversations,' said Aisling reflectively.

'It's not even that,' Vivienne added. 'Your social life just disintegrates when you're a single parent, that's what I've found, anyway. Nobody invites a single woman to parties because the women are all terrified you're going to run off with their husbands.' She chuckled as though remembering something. 'And the husbands all think you're dying for it and chat you up madly!'

Aisling said nothing. Did Leo think she was dying for it? Probably.

'You lose all the friends who are couples,' Vivienne continued, 'and end up hanging out with your single friends. Most of whom don't have kids and can't understand why you can't stay out all night or have to stay sober to drive the baby-sitter home. Am I making this single parenthood thing sound too attractive for you?' she inquired with a large grin.

'Fantastic. How do you ever get time to work with such a hectic social life?' Aisling asked.

'Oh, you know, I fit a few hours in every week between visiting Leeson Street, picking up bored married men and trawling through singles pubs looking for Mr Might-Possibly-be-Mr-Right.' Vivienne took a big slug of wine. 'That probably sounds very bitter,' she said quietly.

'Has it been that tough?' Aisling asked gently.

'Yes and no. I'd love to have someone in my life but it's so hard to meet someone who wants a single mother. It's so hard to meet someone full stop. I'm thirty-four and the men my age are all married. Or have no intention of settling down,' she added.

'Sorry, this isn't what you need to hear, Aisling. I've been having a miserable week because Christine has the flu. I've got the most dreadful PMT and the video conked out on Wednesday evening when we were watching *101 Dalmatians*. Lord knows how much it will cost to fix, or if it's even worth fixing.'

'Ladies, you've been asked to join the party upstairs seeing as how you saved the day,' said a loud voice.

Pat Finucane stood at the door of the canteen.

'I've been telling everyone about your amazing culinary skills, Aisling, and how you managed to transform a disaster into a wonderful meal. They nearly licked their plates, you know. Those mashed potatoes were delicious.'

Aisling and Vivienne laughed at the same time.

'What did I say?' asked Pat.

'Aisling maintains that men love mashed potatoes and she's obviously right,' explained Vivienne. She slid her shoes back on and winked at Aisling.

'You must come over to my house for dinner some night next week and we'll continue our moan, right?'

'I'd love to,' said Aisling warmly. Maybe that would be just the right occasion to talk to Vivienne about Leo.

'It'll be spaghetti or something equally simple,' added Vivienne quickly. 'Or I could always ask Debbie to rustle up some fish . . .!'

'Well done.' Edward Richardson stood up and clapped when Aisling arrived at the boardroom door. The guests looked totally relaxed, with pink faces and loosened ties evidence that the wine was going down a treat. 'Gentlemen, I give you the estimable Aisling Moran.' He smiled, his pale blue tie still knotted in a perfect Windsor knot.

'When you open your own restaurant, my dear, I want to eat there every night. And you could teach my darling daughter to cook while you're at it!'

'Do you do dinner parties?' asked one man, as Pat offered Aisling a glass of wine.

'Well,' Aisling said slowly, 'I've never cooked for anyone but myself and my family . . .'

'It's just that my wife hates cooking and she'd jump at the

chance to have someone like you come in and rustle up a dinner party,' the man insisted.

'It's a great idea, Jim,' said Pat seriously. 'You'd be wonderful at it, Aisling.'

'Absolutely,' agreed Vivienne, accepting a glass of champagne. 'You never panicked once.'

'You could certainly cook for my parties,' added Tom Reid, Caroline's boss.

'It really would be a marvellous business venture,' said Edward encouragingly. 'Your talent and my tasting skills. You'd cook and I'd test everything!'

They all laughed.

'A toast,' said Edward, raising his glass, 'to Richardson, Reid and Finucane, to our new partners,' he smiled at the two new lawyers, 'to our continued business success and, to Aisling, who made our lunch wonderful! Cheers!'

'I'm serious about that,' said Jim. He grabbed Aisling's arm as she and Vivienne left. 'I'm Jim Coughlan and I'd love you to cook for us. My wife, Rachel, has just set up a small public relations business and she plans to do a lot of entertaining in the future. Can I tell her she can call you?'

Startled and flattered, Aisling thought for a moment. 'Sure,' she said finally. 'But I could only cook after office hours. I couldn't compromise working here.'

'No problem. Here's my number.' He handed her a cream and black embossed business card. 'I'll get Rachel to ring you here and you can call back when it's convenient.'

The men were still chatting around the boardroom table at half four, all notions of work abandoned.

'I just want to go home and lie down,' sighed Vivienne, pouring a mug of coffee for herself and Aisling in her office.

'Me too. But I've got to send out two letters by courier this evening. All they need is Leo's signature, but I doubt if I'll be able to get him out of the boardroom.'

'I've got to ask Edward something,' Vivienne said, 'so I'll mention the letters to Leo.'

Aisling brought her coffee upstairs, wishing it was half five and she could go home. She was tired and the idea of a hot bath was very appealing. Yet she felt elated by the way she'd coped today, flattered by what everyone had said.

She printed out the letters Leo was to sign. She'd love to cater for dinner parties. But it would be a big thing to take on. Where would she start? And how could she do it all on her own?

'Very tasty, Mrs Moran,' said Leo's deep voice behind her.

Aisling whirled around in surprise. He was standing in the doorway grinning at her. Leering, actually.

'The food was tasty as well,' he chuckled, delighted with his little joke. Aisling could feel the anger she'd been hiding simmer up inside her. Steady, don't do anything, she cautioned herself. He's just drunk, he's harmless. Don't say anything you'd regret, Aisling, just because you've had a few glasses of wine. You need this job, remember.

'I wanted you to sign these,' she said as calmly as she could, holding out the letters. He didn't move. She walked towards him and handed him the two sheets of paper.

'Thanks, Aisling.' He took the letters, keeping his eyes on her. She leaned over her desk and picked up a pen from the other side. As she did so, he slid one arm around her waist and let it move quickly down to brush her behind.

Enraged, she swung around and screamed at him.

'How dare you touch me, you pig! How dare you!'

'Don't give me that rubbish,' he snarled. 'You know you want it. Don't be all coy.'

He stepped towards her again, a half-grin on his face. He was going to grab her, to touch her, she just knew it. And she knew that she'd had enough.

When her right hand connected with his jaw it made a satisfying noise.

'Listen, you pervert, you can stick your job,' Aisling yelled. 'I've had enough of your comments, your salacious remarks and your appalling behaviour. You're an asshole, Leo Murphy, and I'm leaving!'

With that, she grabbed her handbag from behind her desk and ran out the door.

★ ★ ★

'I can't believe I did that!' Aisling said at half eight that night when Jo called round. 'I was totally furious at the time, a mixture of red wine and release at having stopped that chauvinistic pig. But now . . .' She broke off, rubbing the bridge of her nose to relieve the throbbing headache which was threatening to explode in her head.

'Aisling!' said Jo angrily. 'Don't you dare feel sorry for what you did. I can't believe that bastard. I only wish you'd said something to me and I would have told you exactly what to do a lot sooner. Who the hell does he think he is? That's sexual harassment and it's illegal. He can't get away with this, he can't! The Employment Equality Agency will tell us exactly what to do and believe you me, he'll rue the day he ever abused his position!'

'That's all very well, Jo,' sighed Aisling, 'but I still need a job right now. Anyway, who the hell is going to believe my side of the story?' she demanded. 'Leo is a lawyer, after all. He spends his life dealing with the law. By the time he's finished with me, my name will be mud. I'll have been "asking for it" or something.'

'Don't be ridiculous,' snapped Jo. 'Sorry. I didn't mean it that way. I'm just so angry that you never told me about it. I could have told you what he was doing was wrong, that you don't have to suffer that sort of crap.'

'I know,' Aisling said miserably, 'I know I should have done something sooner. It was all so strange and difficult. Getting a job in the first place seemed such a huge thing, I just didn't know how to handle myself, or him,' she added despondently. 'I was so pleased with myself when I hit him, but that wore off. All I've been thinking about since is why I *did* do it.'

'You should have done it weeks ago,' Jo pointed out. 'Look, Ash, ring Pat Finucane and tell him what happened. Ask him what he thinks. I could be wrong, but I doubt if he'll let this end here.'

'I can't drag Pat into this,' exclaimed Aisling.

'He's in it. He is a senior partner in a firm where one of his

277

colleagues is accused of sexually harassing someone else. He's hardly likely to brush the whole incident under the carpet.'

'Who's going to believe me though, Jo? I didn't tell anyone and it's his word against mine,' Aisling said dully. 'What have I done?'

CHAPTER FOURTEEN

Swathed in an ancient towelling dressing-gown with her hair in a wet pony tail, Jo lay on the settee and shuffled through a sheaf of estate agents' prospectuses. A can of Coke and a half-eaten Danish pastry lay on the coffee table beside her, on top of two property supplements.

She found the prospectus for the town house in Killiney and gazed at a photo of an elegant red-brick house with an off-white clematis flowering palely around a sage-green door. Number four had two bedrooms, one with an en suite bathroom, a kitchen/dining room, small sitting room and a tiny conservatory looking onto a pocket-handkerchief lawn surrounded by a rockery stuffed with alpine plants. Lovely. So, you couldn't swing a cat in any of the rooms, but she didn't want a mansion. Just solid walls so that the neighbours didn't come hammering on the door in the morning after a sleepless night listening to baby.

Jo leaned over to grab the can of Coke, careful not to overstretch because her lower back had been giving her mild twinges of pain all day. She turned her attention back to the serious business of house-hunting. The Killiney place was a definite possibility. It *was* expensive, but she had to move *somewhere* before the baby was born. The walls in her apartment were so thin that she could hear Mrs Roche's clock-radio go off every morning at half seven precisely. And, when the two girls who'd just moved into the apartment above had a dinner party, sleep was out of the question.

Jo wanted a garden for her child, somewhere to sit and mess around with toys, sand pits and Wendy houses. She had seen a lovely one in the Argos catalogue and had nearly rushed off and bought it until she reminded herself that it would be quite some time before her baby would be into

Wendy houses. She looked at the next prospectus, a small, whitewashed cottage in Dalkey which looked beautiful in the estate agent's photo. But she hadn't actually *seen* it yet and the descriptions, written in eloquent estate agent language, did not always match up with the actual premises once you got there.

On Monday, she'd seen one 'bijou des res with one rec, three beds, one bthrm, ofch and lge grdn. Nds sm modernisation,' and found a poky little house with zero charm, damp walls, three mouldy bedrooms that could have been used for a drug den and a wasteland out the back that looked suitable for botanic experiments into rampant weed growth.

'It needs some work,' admitted the weary-looking estate agent when he noticed Jo pulling her skirt close around her legs so it wouldn't brush against anything particularly virulent in the kitchen.

'If I was married to the person who ran Rentokil, and owned a builders' providers, I might consider it,' she replied. Then, sorry she'd sounded so sharp, she added, 'I need something that doesn't need too much work because I'm having a baby.'

After a lengthy conversation about first babies – Colm, the estate agent, had two and the second was only nine months and had never slept longer than four hours in his life – Jo drove off to see a ten-year-old mews house which didn't mention anything about modernisation in the prospectus.

As beautiful as the last place had been awful, Jo fell utterly in love with it and was disappointed to find out that someone had put in a successful bid for it that morning. Too depressed to even complain to the estate agent who could have rung up and told her not to bother coming, Jo flounced out to her car and drove home crossly. Two Twix bars sort of comforted her at home that evening while she watched *The Bill*.

After Monday's disasters, she decided to give house-hunting a miss on Tuesday evening. Instead, she'd gone to a reception for the launch of a new variety of eyeshadow and had eaten far too many vol-au-vents while watching four stick-thin models covered in body paint sashay elegantly around the room, leaving the waiters slack-jawed with amazement.

'They must be anorexic,' muttered Rhona, lighting another cigarette so she wouldn't break her diet and succumb to the lure of the Chinese sesame prawn toasts displayed invitingly on a nearby table.

'You'd be amazed at how many models eat like horses,' remarked Yvonne, the equally stick-thin fashion editor of a rival magazine.

Rhona raised one eyebrow sceptically. 'Yvonne, I've been on two press trips with you and I know that you think having more than half a grapefruit and one slice of toast for breakfast is sheer gluttony. You can hardly talk.'

Jo took a sneaky look at Yvonne's pert little behind encased in body-skimming lycra and swiped another two vol-au-vents from a passing waiter.

'I do love vol-au-vents,' added Rhona, inhaling deeply, 'but they're so fattening.'

Jo swallowed quickly and took a deep draught of orange juice.

'Goodies, girls.' Nikki appeared in front of the three of them waving elegant gold carrier bags.

Driving home, Jo examined the eyeshadow quartet, lipstick and nail varnish that the make-up company had given everyone who'd attended the launch. The lipstick would make her look like Morticia out of *The Addams Family*. She should have gone house-hunting, she reminded herself, but she'd needed cheering up and an evening with Rhona was the perfect antidote for misery.

The next day she skipped lunch – well, eating a McDonald's in the car was practically skipping lunch – and went to see a Sixties bungalow in Dun Laoghaire. Jo had felt suddenly tearful when she was elbowed painfully in the back by a tall blonde on the way to the tiny avocado-green bathroom. She hated bloody avocado green anyway. It was so Seventies.

She'd been too busy at work on Thursday and Friday to do any house-hunting but today she planned to spend the afternoon viewing properties.

She'd got a list of three houses to visit and that would probably take most of the afternoon. And she needed to go grocery shopping because she was nearly out of tuna. Her current pregnancy fetish was for tuna and peanut butter sandwiches.

Shuffling through the property supplements, Jo came across one advert that fascinated her. It wasn't so much the description of the house in the Dublin mountains that did it.

In fact, Number two Redwood Lane definitely sounded the worst out of all the properties she'd considered, especially when you read between the lines and realised that solid fuel heating probably meant dragging in turf for the fire. More worrying was the fact that there was no mention of a bathroom at all.

The words 'in need of enthusiastic restoration' would have put off all but the most dimwitted DIY fanatic and, since Jo's entire tool collection consisted of an oddly shaped 99p screwdriver with three different ends for different types of screw, it didn't make any sense for her to even *look* at the house.

But she didn't feel very sensible just then. Jo didn't know why, but the house fascinated her, more for the description of the view than for anything else.

'Set in a scenic spot in the Dublin mountains, the property is bordered by sycamore and beech trees and overlooks farmland. With a superb view of Dublin Bay, it has to be seen.'

Don't be silly, she told herself as she pulled on the red brushed-cotton tracksuit bottoms she seemed to live in these days. What in the hell would you want with a dilapidated old house halfway up the mountains when you don't have a clue how to do any of the renovation work yourself, probably couldn't afford it anyway, and are expecting a baby in four months?

It was no use. She put on the matching red baggy sweatshirt and brushed her still damp hair, a picture of a lovely cottage bathed in golden evening sun in her mind.

A cosy kitchen, its window seat filled with plump gingham cushions, where you could sit to look out at Dublin spread below in a vast valley. A pretty cottage garden with lavender and rosemary growing fragrantly outside the kitchen door . . . And a brass bed in a bedroom decorated with a pretty Victorian wallpaper, a pine wardrobe – well, maybe *two* pine wardrobes – and a dressing table with a bowl of coral pink roses on top, roses from her own garden . . . She could see it all.

Jo parked the Golf neatly outside the office, wondering what Mark's Porsche was doing there on a Saturday morning at half twelve. She'd dropped by the *Style* offices to pick up some papers she'd forgotten to bring home the previous evening. On Monday morning at ten, she was interviewing a TV fashion stylist about how to pick clothes for people to wear in various programmes and series. The RTE press office had faxed in a list of programmes the stylist had worked on and, while Jo knew she'd be able to talk to the stylist without this background information, she still preferred to have a person's accomplishments fresh in her mind before interviewing them. She'd never forgotten one of her first interviews when she'd been so badly prepared that she'd innocently asked an actress what it was like working with a theatre director rumoured to be very bad-tempered.

'It's not so bad working with him since he's my *husband*!' snapped the actress before storming off.

Jo unlocked the front door of the Georgian building that the magazine shared with another business and went up the two flights of stairs to the *Style* office.

The cream panelled door was open and Jo went in, expecting to see Mark in the conference room on the phone.

He was, however, sitting at Brenda's desk, flicking through the dummy for the October edition of the magazine, one shoulder jamming Brenda's phone up against his ear.

'Hello, Jo, I didn't think I'd see anyone in here today,' he said warmly.

'I forgot some papers for an interview on Monday,' she replied, hurrying over to her desk and cursing herself for being found wearing a tracksuit and ancient runners. She hadn't a scrap of make-up on except a bit of pale lipstick and her face was probably shiny with moisturiser.

'Who are you interviewing?' he asked. Jo was about to tell him when he spoke into the phone.

'Hello, Tim. No, that's OK. I wasn't holding for long.'

While he talked, Jo rooted around among the various press releases, magazines and colour transparencies on her desk and found the shiny, coiled-up fax paper.

Sliding the pages into her handbag, she walked past Mark, waving silently as she made for the door.

'Hold on, Tim,' he said suddenly. 'Don't go yet, Jo, will you? I'll only be on the phone for a few minutes.'

There was nothing she could do but wait. Well, she may as well take the weight off her feet. She returned to her desk and decided to phone Aisling again. Nobody had answered when she rang earlier that morning and Jo was worried about her after her horrific experience at the hands of that bastard of a lawyer. Jo could think of a few things she'd like to do to Mr Murphy and none of them would be legal. What a pig. The phone kept ringing in the Morans'. Nobody answered. Of course, the boys have Saturday morning soccer and Aisling is probably picking them up, Jo remembered. She'd try again later.

Mark was still on the phone.

She didn't want to sit there waiting for him to come off the phone, so she tried to look engrossed in her diary and wondered what he wanted. It was nearly two months since they'd returned from New York and in the intervening time he'd been courteous, charming and kind to her.

He'd taken her outburst about being pregnant in his stride, hugging her in a brotherly fashion when she'd broken down in Bloomingdale's. He'd brought her to a nearby coffee shop, ordered steaming hot chocolate for her and held her hand until she stopped crying.

At no point had he pushed her for information. He listened calmly and intently while she mumbled about the baby and how Richard had left her.

'I'm glad you told me, Jo,' he said later that evening, when she met him in the hotel lobby feeling mortally embarrassed for her earlier behaviour. 'If you need any help, you can count on me. We're like a big family in *Style* and I want you to know that I'll do anything I can to help,' he emphasised.

They had dinner in the hotel that night and Jo wondered if she'd imagined the charged atmosphere between them during the previous days. Now, he treated her like a favourite sister who'd just been ill, asked her was she too hot, too cold, did she want more water or would she like some orange juice. For all his bachelorhood, Mark obviously knew a lot about pregnancy because he scanned the menu like an experienced dad, vetoing anything with soft cheeses, pâté or alcohol in it.

'You can't be too careful,' he said, ordering mineral water for them both because he said it would do him good to abstain from wine during dinner.

Jo found this brotherly concern comforting and unflattering at the same time. It was lovely to be pampered and she felt sure that, had Mark been the baby's dad, he'd have ordered her to lie down and put her feet up as soon as he heard she was pregnant.

But it was a little disconcerting to be transformed from sexy colleague into sexless mum-to-be.

Just because I'm having a baby doesn't mean I'm not a sexual human being, she wanted to say. I'm not a one-dimensional creature who's desirable until she gets pregnant and then becomes every man's mother – sexless. Of course, she didn't say any such thing. Mark might be disgusted to find that she was even *thinking* about fancying him when she was pregnant with Richard's child.

For the past two months, every time he rang the office, he asked to be put through to Jo and asked her how she was feeling, how the baby was doing, and to tell her that if she needed time off, to take it.

'You've got to look after yourself,' he said, almost paternally.

She didn't know if he did this because he thought nobody else in the office knew she was pregnant and boyfriend-less, and therefore wanted to be discreet. Or if he thought he should ask about her health because she was an employee and he was merely following some sort of management protocol. But she was getting used to those conversations and found him much easier to talk to on the phone than she did in real life.

He made her chuckle – and displayed a surprising knowledge of what *really* went on in the office – by asking whether Brenda was actually working or ringing her current *amour*, when Brenda was sitting opposite Jo at the time and obviously listening in on the conversation with interest.

In person, however, Jo found herself avoiding Mark. She felt embarrassed by the way she'd flirted with him in New York. At least she hadn't thrown herself at him, that was her one consolation.

She was still lost in contemplating their changed relationship when he put down the phone.

'How are you today, Jo?' he asked. 'Is the baby still trying to kick his way out?'

She laughed, because that was exactly what it had felt like over the past few weeks. At first, she'd felt tiny movements inside her, something that left her thrilled and utterly amazed. Now, the baby was getting quite energetic and was kicking around like an embryonic Cantona.

'*She* is very active,' she corrected him with a grin. Although she didn't want to know what sex the baby was, Jo felt it in her bones that she was carrying a little girl.

'A female soccer player, then,' he grinned, coming over to stand beside her with his hands in the pockets of the jeans he wore with a casual navy cotton shirt. 'Does she kick all the time?'

'No. But she moves around a lot except when she's sleeping.' Jo stroked her bump lovingly and was disconcerted to look up and find Mark looking at her intently, his grey eyes tender and affectionate.

286

'I'd love to feel her kick,' he said hesitantly. 'Would you mind . . .'

'No,' replied Jo, astonished.

He placed one large hand gently on her bump, strong fingers spread sensitively as he tried to feel the baby's movements. They stayed like that for a few minutes and Jo wondered what this curious tableau would look like if any other member of staff happened to arrive unexpectedly.

She could smell Mark's aftershave, a spicy lemon scent she always associated with him. She could recognise most perfumes and aftershaves if she'd smelled them before, but she wasn't sure what type of aftershave Mark used. Maybe it was because the scent mingled with his own particular smell, a mix of just-washed hair, shaving gel, fabric conditioner from his shirt and the warm smell of healthy male.

She felt a sudden dart in her belly as the baby moved to the left, sending gentle ripples around her womb.

'I felt it! Did you feel it?' Mark said in awe. 'Stupid of me, of course *you* felt it. Wasn't it wonderful?'

As if delighted with this new audience, the baby wriggled again. Mark's face was a picture, Jo thought. His eyes were alight with amazement at feeling the baby move inside her.

'It's wonderful, a miracle,' he said finally, slowly moving his hand away from her.

Jo smiled back at him, embarrassment and uncomfortable scenes forgotten.

'You really are blooming,' Mark said, eyes taking in her flushed cheeks, glossy hair and the sparkle in her dark eyes. 'Tell me, Mum-to-Be, do you fancy a spot of lunch or are you doing something this afternoon?'

'Actually, I'm going house-hunting today,' she said, 'but I can't call around anywhere until at least half two. I was going to go swimming in Stillorgan and then head out to Killiney to see the first place.'

'Why don't you go swimming and then let me bring you for a quick lunch. I'll drive you around for the afternoon,' he offered. 'Go on, it'll be fun. I love looking at houses.'

287

'OK. You're on.'

Tired after her swim, Jo decided it was a great idea to let Mark drive her around for the afternoon, especially since she'd decided to visit the house in the Dublin mountains and her knowledge of anything further out than Sandyford was decidedly sketchy.

After soup and a sandwich in a pub in Stillorgan, they set off in Mark's Porsche. Jo relaxed back into the low leather seat.

The first house was crammed with viewers. Cars were parked for three hundred yards each side of the house and a stream of people stood trying to get in the front door.

'They can't all be thinking of buying this place, surely?' demanded Mark, trying to make a space for Jo to squeeze into the sitting room.

'It's the latest hobby,' she explained, 'and it's more fun than wandering up and down Woodie's. People just turn up to see what other people's houses are like.'

It was hard to get any idea of what the house *was* like, it was so full. They left soon after arriving. Next stop was an elegant two-storey Victorian residence in Greystones which was slightly beyond Jo's budget, but she'd decided to view it anyway. Obviously fewer people were prepared to trek out to Greystones from the city to indulge in their Sunday hobby. There were only five cars parked outside the house.

'This looks more like it,' said Mark, unfolding long limbs from the driver's seat. They gazed at the grey façade, large sash windows and fantastic harbour view.

Inside, the house was beautifully decorated and perfectly kept, yet it was so austere and cold that Jo disliked it immediately. She hated the formal sitting room with the black fireplace and the ornate cornices and she liked the long, narrow kitchen even less.

'I don't know what it is,' she leaned against Mark to whisper, 'but I don't like this place. It's just so . . . cold.'

'It is, isn't it,' he agreed. 'Let's go.'

The sun was shining as they drove towards Stepaside, the

Porsche's engine growling like a big cat with a hoarse throat.

'I wish my car sounded like this,' Jo said, thinking of the strange wheezing noise the Golf had been making recently whenever it went beyond thirty miles an hour.

'How old is it?' Mark asked, as he made a right turn up a steep hill surrounded by high hedges.

'Too old,' she replied. 'I need to get a new car, but I need a new house more.'

'Actually, I did wonder why you were house-hunting,' he remarked. 'I thought you'd only bought your apartment a couple of years ago and it was new, if I recall correctly.'

'It was,' she admitted. 'It's just that the walls are so thin, I don't know how it's going to work out when I have the baby. My next-door neighbour is a little old lady who gets up at half seven and goes to bed after the news at nine, so I don't know if she's going to be too happy listening to a crying baby half the night. She's terribly sweet,' Jo added, 'but she won't be able for all-night crying, I just know it.' Jo sighed. 'Mind you, I'm not sure I'm ready for that either.'

Mark chuckled. 'Some place up the mountains is perfect then,' he said with a grin. 'You can throw rock-'n'-roll parties, let the baby cry all night and nobody can complain!'

'I'd been thinking more of having extra space for the baby and starting a herb garden,' sniffed Jo, mildly insulted.

'I'm teasing you,' Mark said gently. 'Now, where is this place? Give me the brochure.'

Fifteen minutes later, after driving down several winding roads which they were sure were dead-ends, they arrived at Redwood Lane. It was a small tree-lined country lane with very few gateways. There were no cars parked outside number two, which wasn't surprising Jo thought, when they finally saw the place. A low granite cottage with a jungle for a front garden, dirty grey paint flaking off the woodwork around the leaded windows and a roof with more slates off than on, it was not your average estate agent's dream. It wasn't anybody's dream, thought Jo, wondering why she liked it so much. Was she out of her head to even *consider* buying it?

She gingerly picked her way along a path overgrown with nettles and dandelions with Mark following.

'Did the brochure mention that this place needs a total rehaul?' he asked incredulously.

'Er, yes,' Jo replied. She knocked on the front door, ignoring the peeling grey paint.

'Come in, come in,' said a loud voice. 'I thought you'd be late because it's so hard to find.'

Jo pushed the door open and went inside.

A tiny hall opened out onto a large kitchen on the left side and a sitting room on the right. The kitchen stretched right to the back of the house. A large leaded window gave a somewhat grimy view of the countryside beyond.

'I'm Margaret Middleton,' announced the large auburn-haired lady, getting up off a slightly dusty chair to greet them.

'Jo Ryan. We talked on the phone,' Jo replied.

'Do you want me to show you the house or would you prefer to look around on your own?' inquired Mrs Middleton.

'We'll look on our own,' Jo said firmly.

'Off you go, then. But watch those stairs, they're very steep,' the estate agent warned.

The wooden staircase at the far left side of the room did look very steep and led up to what had to be some sort of loft conversion. A huge old cream range took up most of one wall. A motley selection of cupboards and a battered dresser made up the rest of the kitchen fittings.

Dark beams criss-crossed the ceiling, giving the place an old-fashioned air, and Jo could immediately picture hanging dried flowers, strings of garlic and copper pots from the beams.

Nothing in the room had seen a paintbrush for a very long time and the scent of old cooking oil permeated the air. But even drab wallpaper and dirt couldn't hide its charm.

'Isn't it gorgeous?' said Jo, delighted with the place.

'It's got character,' Mark said slowly.

She turned around to grin at him before leaving the kitchen for a look at the sitting room. It had the same dark beams and leaded windows as the kitchen.

The large granite fireplace surrounded by black slate would have dominated the room had it not been for the lurid brown and orange carpet which clashed with the pale blue walls.

'I *love* the decor,' Mark said, feigning delight. 'I think we should get the person who did this place to redo the office, don't you?'

'Could we afford them?' Jo countered. 'Getting this hasn't-been-touched-since-1972 look can be very expensive.'

She got a tissue out of her handbag and went over to the window at the back of the room. As big as the window in the kitchen, it looked out on the same view. There was a window seat so you could sit and gaze out at the same time.

Jo perched on the edge of the dusty seat and rubbed the window with the tissue until she'd made a clean patch big enough to see out. There were several sycamores and a beech tree on the edge of the back garden and a wild hedge bordering it, but there were gaps in the greenery and you could look down at the fields below.

A couple of Friesians swished their tails contentedly in the field, enjoying the last rays of the early September sun. They obviously belonged to the farm she could see about half a mile away.

'As long as it's not a pig farm, we're flying,' she said.

'Why do I get the impression that you've already made your mind up about this house, Jo?' asked Mark.

Jo looked up at him. She really liked the house and was already thinking of all the possibilities it had with the right renovations and redecoration. But she wanted him to like it too, God knows why, she thought to herself.

'Do you hate it?' she asked.

'Jo.' He put a hand on her shoulder and smiled at her, grey eyes shining with amusement. 'I think it's got great character, but it's not what I like that's important. It's going to be your house, so it's up to you. But it's going to take some work,' he warned, looking around the room. 'It'll definitely need rewiring, which isn't cheap, and there are bound to be lots of other jobs to be done as well. I doubt if it's been occupied for a long

291

time, so who knows what's broken down or jammed since then.'

Jo looked crestfallen for a moment, then her face brightened. 'If it's such a dump, it's probably been on the market for years and I should be able to knock a few thousand off the asking price. That's it! That way I'll save enough money on actual cost to renovate it. Come on, let's see what's upstairs.'

She took Mark's hand and led him out of the room. She was on the second stair when she realised what she'd done. She was *holding his hand*! It had seemed such a natural thing to do at the time, as though they were looking at the house together, like a couple.

His hand felt warm and strong, fingers clasping hers firmly. She couldn't very well let go, now could she?

The upstairs was an attic conversion. The low sloping roof was covered in honey-coloured tongue-and-groove pine which gave both bedrooms an unusual, cosy look. A large fitted wardrobe, also made from pine, covered one wall in the big bedroom.

'Now that's what I need,' Jo said. She slid her hand awkwardly out of Mark's and opened the wardrobe.

Like everything else in the house, it was grimy inside. But it was spacious and well designed with enough shelves and hanging space to accommodate even Jo's vast wardrobe.

'The bathroom is very nice,' said Mark, who'd left Jo to investigate the rest of the upper storey. 'There's no shower, though.'

'It's lovely,' Jo said in surprise, appearing at the bathroom door. 'There was no mention of a bathroom in the advert and I'd begun to think there was an outside loo. It's a relief to find this.'

'Thankfully the artist who decorated downstairs wasn't allowed to have anything to do with the upstairs,' Mark added.

Plain white tiles, a plain white bathroom suite and cork floor tiles meant that the bathroom was by far the most subtly decorated room in the house.

292

'Apart from getting a shower put in, this doesn't need any work,' Jo said.

They were standing in the back garden discussing how the hell you'd clear the wilderness of weeds and thistles without a JCB, when the estate agent appeared.

'What do you think?'

Jo felt Mark jab her in the ribs. 'It has possibilities,' Jo said, trying to sound utterly unimpressed. 'But it would cost a bomb to make it habitable and the price is way too high.'

The estate agent's mouth opened. Obviously, Jo was the first person in a long time to do anything other than leave very rapidly after catching sight of the house. The fact that she was even *discussing* the house price made it a red-letter day.

'You're interested, then?' the estate agent asked hopefully.

'I don't know, darling,' Mark said, sliding an arm around Jo's shoulders. 'I know you like it but it's out of the question at that price. You'd want six grand knocked off the price before you could even consider it.'

Trying not to smile, Jo played along with him.

'I know, sweetheart.' She just hoped he wouldn't convulse with laughter at her calling him sweetheart. 'You're right. He's always right,' she deadpanned to the estate agent who now had a resigned look on her face.

'I'll tell you what, Mrs er . . .' Mark said.

'Mrs Middleton,' supplied the other woman.

'I'll phone you during the week to have a chat about the house. Come on, darling. Let's go.'

He kept his arm around Jo's shoulders and tightened his grip when he felt her shake with suppressed laughter. She finally let it out when he slammed the driver's door.

'That was priceless! I never knew you were so good at lying, Mark.'

'That wasn't lying, *darling*,' he joked, switching on the engine. 'That was business. It's playing your cards close to your chest. If we string her along for a while – assuming nobody else is interested in the place because she looked so thrilled that we were thinking about buying it – we could get a much lower price.'

'Just as well you were here, then,' Jo said, 'because I've never been able to play anything close to my chest in my life. I'd have said I loved the house and she'd have *added* a few quid to the price by the time we were finished.'

'Anyway,' she said, shifting in her seat so she was looking at Mark, 'what do you think about it?'

They were on a very narrow road and he was concentrating on the road ahead, giving Jo a chance to observe him as he drove. His profile was harsh, eyes narrowed as he stared at the winding road. He looked so serious and intense most of the time that it was such a surprise when he let his guard down to kid around with her.

He really was a very different man once you got to know him, she thought. Behind the cool business exterior lay a funny, affectionate person. It was odd to think she'd ever imagined him to be an arrogant boss who expected people to jump when he clicked his fingers.

He glanced over at her.

'Sorry, Jo. What did you say?'

'I wondered what you thought of the house. Do you think it's totally mad to even think about buying it?'

'Totally mad, I'd say. Oh, you mean the *house*.'

She swatted his arm with the rolled-up prospectus. 'Don't take advantage just because I called you sweetheart. I could call you lots of other names and they wouldn't all be as flattering, all right?' He shot her a grin.

'Yes Ma'am. Or is it Your Highness?'

'Your Highness will do fine,' she replied. 'Now, what do you think of the house?'

'First of all, you need a surveyor to go over it with a fine-tooth comb to see if there are any major problems, structural ones, subsidence or whatever. Then, we need to get a contractor to have a look and give us an estimate on what all the work will cost. Don't even think about how you'll redecorate the kitchen until you've got some idea about how

294

much you'll have to pay to make it habitable,' he advised.

'Then, if we can knock enough money off the list price to complete the repairs, it might be worth it. But it's probably going to take a couple of months to do. Are you ready for that?'

Jo didn't even take a moment to think about it. 'Of course,' she said impulsively. 'I love the house, it has so much character, so much . . . I don't know, warmth.' She searched for the right word, for once not able to find it.

'It feels like a home, despite all the dreadful carpets and everything,' she said finally. 'I've looked at loads of places over the past three weeks and I've only seen one I liked as much. Well, only one I liked as much and could afford,' she amended.

'You've convinced me,' Mark said. 'I've got a friend who's a contractor and I'll get him to look at the house during the week, if that's OK with you?'

'Wonderful.'

'It was very nice of Mark to drive you up to see the house,' said Rhona, putting a Canderel sweetener in her coffee and stirring it thoughtfully. 'I've always told you he was a nice man and you just couldn't see it. I'm so glad you're getting to know him now, personally,' she added, emphasis on the last word.

Jo looked at her suspiciously but Rhona's face was innocent. You never knew when Rhona was teasing or not, she was such a good actress. Jo put her cup of tea down on Rhona's desk and picked up a set of colour transparencies from an underwear company.

It was Monday afternoon and she and Rhona were going over all the articles they still needed for the October edition. Friday was printing day which meant everything had to be ready by Thursday, making this the busiest week for the *Style* team.

As usual, most of the big features were in, subbed and laid out. It was the niggly little details that still had to be sorted out.

CATHY KELLY

Jo still had to chase up the illustrator who was supposed to have already sent in his watercolour illustration of the restaurant reviewed in the issue. Nikki had developed bronchitis and was unlikely to be in all week, which meant that Jo had to find someone else to rewrite all the beauty product press releases for the *Top Ten Beauty Products We Love* page.

And Emma, who had begged to be allowed to interview three top Irish models for their beauty hints, had rung Annette that morning to say she couldn't make it and could someone else go because she didn't want to stand the girls up?

'I'll kill her,' raged Jo, when she heard this latest piece of news. 'How dare she do that! I don't care if her bloody leg is hanging off, she shouldn't drop her mess into our lap and expect us to deal with it. If she couldn't go, she should ring the models up herself and cancel.'

In the end, Rhona rang a freelance journalist who sometimes wrote features for the magazine and begged her to do the interviews. Crisis solved, the editor and deputy editor still had a lot of work to do, which was why they were poring over colour trannies of clothes, shoes, handbags and glamorous celebrities.

'I thought we could use this one on the *Fifty Ideas* pages,' Jo said, showing Rhona a picture of a silky cream body with a built-in push-up bra and lovely lace detail on the front. 'It's the most versatile piece of underwear, it's very flattering and it's pretty good value.'

Rhona took the transparencies and held them up to the window. 'I do like the basque and the hold-up stockings. I bet Mark would just love that . . .'

'Bitch,' said Jo, as Rhona dissolved into laughter. 'You've a one-track mind, Rho.'

'I know, "one track and it's a dirt track",' recited the editor. 'I couldn't resist it. Anyway, Jo, there's no point pretending there isn't something going on between you, even if the pair of you behave like complete strangers when you're in the office.'

'But there *isn't* anything going on,' protested Jo.

296

'Are you trying to tell me that all that bonding and having dinner in New York was totally platonic, because I won't believe you,' Rhona said.

'You know you fancy him, you're just too stubborn to admit it. You told me yourself how you thought something was going to happen between the two of you the first night until he got all businesslike.'

'Oh God, I don't know.' Jo took a sip of tea and looked at Rhona blankly. 'Yes, I like him, but I'm not exactly a bargain in the girlfriend department, am I?

'I'm pregnant with another man's baby, so what the hell would someone like Mark Denton want with me? He's only being kind,' said Jo in a resigned voice.

'Don't be silly, Jo,' snapped Rhona. 'You're one of my best friends and one of the nicest people I know, and Mark is interested in you, I know for a fact. He's always liked you.'

'What do you mean "always liked me"?' demanded Jo.

'Well, there never really was a right time to tell you . . .' the other woman said slowly, picking up her cigarettes and extracting one from the pack.

'Rhona, stop prevaricating and tell me!'

'Well, the first Christmas after you arrived at *Style*, Mark and I went out for lunch and he was very interested in you. He asked if you were going out with someone, that sort of thing.' Rhona lit her cigarette and took a deep drag. 'You were going out with Tim at the time, so I told him and that was it. Then, when you broke up with Tim, Mark was involved with a woman and well, the timing was just never right.' Rhona shrugged.

'Why didn't you ever tell me, Rhona?' asked Jo, completely stunned.

'I would have if Mark hadn't been the boss, but it would undoubtedly have made you feel very self-conscious to think that he fancied you. It would have been awkward.'

'That might have been better than being so openly hostile to him all the time,' Jo said ruefully, remembering all the times when she'd sparred with Mark at the weekly editorial meetings. How awful to think that he'd actually liked her enough to ask Rhona about her romantic entanglements while she'd been oblivious to him. Jo cringed at the thought of it all.

'You see,' commented Rhona, observing Jo's horrified face. 'Imagine what it would have been like if I'd told you before now. You'd have been mortified. I'm only telling you now, Jo, because I'm very fond of Mark, I'd love to see the two of you together and the timing is perfect. You'd be perfect for each other and, Lord knows, you deserve a decent man after Richard.'

'I don't know,' Jo muttered. 'This is so weird. I did think there was something between us when we were in New York, but then he seemed to withdraw into being the ice man again. I don't understand him . . .'

A knock on the door interrupted her.

'Rhona,' Annette stuck her head around the door. 'I've got Claire on the phone for you. I know you didn't want to be disturbed but she says it's urgent.'

'I'll take it, Annette,' Rhona replied. 'Listen,' she said to Jo in a quieter voice, 'do you really think Mark would be so eager to spend the entire day driving you around crumbling cottages in the mountains if he was just trying to be kind to a pregnant employee? No. Think about it, Jo. You deserve him.'

The phone rang and she picked it up.

'Hi, Claire, what's the problem?'

Jo silently gathered up the transparencies from Rhona's desk and manoeuvred herself out of the chair. She felt quite big, even though the girls in the office kept telling her she was in great shape for six months pregnant. The only problem was clothes. For someone who loved clothes as much as Jo, it was sheer hell to have to bypass all her gorgeous outfits in the morning and pick something from her limited collection of elastic-waisted outfits.

Today she'd worn a soft navy knitted dress which was stretchy enough to fit her, bump and all, and a long, skinny-knit cardigan in silky French blue over it. It looked great, especially worn with the matte gold pendant she'd bought from a stall in Turkey years ago.

But by next month she was going to have to buy some dressy maternity clothes or she'd be stuck with wearing jogging pants and big T-shirts until she had the baby.

Jo sat down at her desk and looked tiredly at the list of things she had to do. All her energy had vanished during the conversation with Rhona. Now Jo wondered how she was ever going to transcribe that morning's interview, *and* write it up.

For two hours she worked solidly, oblivious to the noise of phones, conversations about missing pictures and Annette's radio tuned to chart music. She had finally finished writing up her interview and was setting up a new file on the word processor to write up the *Top Ten Beauty Products We Love*, when Emma breezed into the office.

Enveloped in a cloud of CK One, wearing what looked like a very expensive cerise dress and holding a brand new briefcase, Emma dispensed smiles all round before dumping the briefcase on her desk.

'Hello all,' she said airily before turning to Annette. 'Did anyone ring for me?' she asked.

The cheek of her, thought Jo. She completely messed up an interview and she marches in like there's absolutely nothing wrong, with no apology or excuse for her behaviour. And there was she thinking that her attempts to turn Emma into a responsible member of staff over the past few months had actually worked.

She'd trusted Emma's declarations that she wanted to learn and had been so sure the younger woman had turned over a new leaf and really wanted to fit in. How wrong could you be?

'Emma,' Jo said coolly, interrupting the other woman's conversation with Annette about phone messages. 'What happened this morning?'

'Oh, that was a bit of a mix-up and I couldn't make it this morning. I thought Nikki could do it,' Emma said blithely.

'Nikki is sick, as a matter of fact,' Jo explained, determined not to lose her temper or raise her voice. 'And Rhona had to go to a lot of trouble to get someone else to do the interviews. If you were sick, or if there was some crisis and you just couldn't do something you'd arranged, I'd understand.

'But I'd expect some sort of explanation. Instead, you swan in here without either an explanation or an apology and that's just not good enough, Emma.'

'Well, it's all right now, isn't it?' Emma said dismissively. 'So don't fly into a fit. It was hardly the cover story, anyway.' She turned away from Jo and went back to her desk, leaving the deputy editor incandescent with fury.

Even Brenda, who'd heard everything, sank back in her chair nervously as though trying to avoid the inevitable storm. Annette was staring at Jo anxiously, while Tom had stopped tapping away at his keyboard and was listening expectantly. The whole office was waiting for Jo to say something, but she couldn't speak. How dare Emma behave like that?

Nobody else would be so unreliable and indifferent, but of course Emma thought she could do anything she wanted because she was the boss's niece. Finally, Jo found her voice.

'How dare you speak to me like that,' she said, her voice shaky with temper. 'I gave you a chance to make up for all the misunderstandings between us, I gave you a chance to work at being a journalist. And you have the nerve to screw up an interview – something you begged for – and now won't even apologise for it. Is that the thanks I get for trying to help you, Emma? What the hell are you doing in this office if you don't want to work? This isn't a haven for bored twenty-somethings, you know!'

'No, it's a haven for stupid pregnant women,' sneered Emma, her pretty face screwed up with spite. 'Don't think I don't know you're after my uncle. You just want to use him like you use all men. Are you trying to get a rich stepfather for your bastard?'

'Emma!' Rhona stood outside her office with her mouth open, outrage written all over her face. 'In my office now,' she barked.

For once, Emma looked worried. She was afraid of Rhona. 'Get back to work everyone,' snarled the editor. 'Are you OK, Jo?' she said, putting an arm around her friend. Jo didn't speak. If she did, she was afraid she would cry. She'd tried so hard with Emma for Mark's sake and she thought she was finally getting through to her. Then, to experience this blast of sheer, barefaced hatred was devastating.

Why did Emma hate her so much? Why did she say such a horrible thing about Jo using men? She didn't, did she? Is that what Emma would tell Mark, that Jo was after him for his money? It was all too horrible to think about.

'I think I'll go home,' she said blindly, afraid that the tears would fall.

'Stay here for five minutes,' Rhona said firmly. 'I'll deal with that little bitch and then you and I are getting out for a coffee. Don't pay any attention to what she said.'

Brenda made her coffee, Annette abandoned the switch to mutter comforting words to her and even Tom produced two miniature bottles of whiskey from his desk and poured one into her coffee.

'I can't drink that,' sniffled Jo.

'Jo,' said Annette firmly, 'I've three children and I know all there is to know about pregnancy. You have to be very careful about alcohol for the first three months but there's no harm in taking the odd glass of wine or a drink for medicinal purposes after that. And this is medicinal. So drink it, you're as white as a sheet, you poor thing.'

The spiked coffee hit Jo's system like a bullet, leaving her feeling utterly light-headed and totally exhausted. She drank it back and wondered how she'd ever get home. She felt like she wouldn't have the energy to put the car in first gear.

Rhona would probably be ages with Emma, listening to whatever cock-and-bull story the girl would come up with in her defence.

But true to her word, a mere five minutes had passed when Rhona marched out of her office followed by Emma, her face now blotched with tears. Everyone stared with hostility at the younger woman who immediately snatched up her handbag and fled to the bathroom.

'Little cow,' hissed Annette. 'Don't mind her, Jo. She can forget it if she thinks I'm ever taking messages from her boyfriend, her mother or her seven best friends ever again!'

'I doubt if she'll ask you for a while,' Rhona pointed out drily. 'Come on, Ms Ryan.'

They sat in the bar in the Berkeley Court Hotel and ate nuts from the deep bowl on the table in front of them.

'Very good for protein,' said Rhona with her mouth full.

'And very high in calories,' replied Jo mournfully, grabbing another handful.

'Well, you need an energy boost after today.' Rhona waved at a young waitress and ordered decaffeinated coffee for both of them and a brandy for herself. 'I can't believe that Tom had booze in his desk,' she added. 'When I think of all the times when I've dearly needed a drink in that bloody office and he never opened his mouth, the wretch! You do have an effect on men, my dear.'

'But not on women, it seems.'

'Emma isn't a woman. She's a nightmare in human form and don't forget it. You'll be glad to know that I savaged her for her appalling behaviour, both for being utterly unprofessional in not turning up for that interview, and for being equally unprofessional in her attack on you.'

'What did she say to that?' asked Jo.

'She whinged that you didn't like her and then I told her I didn't like her very much either, but that wasn't the point. That certainly shut her up. Anyway, pet,' Rhona patted Jo's knee, 'I finished up by telling her that I wouldn't sack her – I'd let Mark sack her after I'd talked to him about her behaviour. The pièce de résistance, I thought. You should have seen her spoiled little face when I said that. She went white and then she cried. Hhhmph.' The coffee arrived and Rhona poured a cup for Jo.

'I told her that crying might work with her uncle, but it cut no ice with me. I'm going to ring him tonight.'

Jo thought about Mark hearing two versions of the afternoon's events. No doubt Emma would be phoning him that instant, giving him chapter and verse on what a bitch Jo Ryan was, how manipulative she was and how she tried to make poor Emma's life a misery.

By the time he heard Rhona's version, he would have probably decided that Emma was right – that Jo was just a conniving, manipulative person. Why did that thought depress her so much?

She got home at half nine after having a Malaysian meal with Rhona in Kites in Ballsbridge. Satay lamb, chicken with cashew nuts and a large helping of ice cream made her sleepy but gave the baby a new lease of life.

I hope you're not going to kick all night, Jo said to her bump as she switched on the lights in the apartment. The answering machine's messages light was on and she pressed the 'play' button before closing the curtains.

Mark Denton's deep voice filled the room.

'Jo,' he said, sounding very tired. 'I'm in London and I've just got this dreadful message on the mobile-phone playback from Emma. She sounds very upset and says something awful happened in the office earlier. She says she's really sorry and she apologised to you, but you won't forgive her. And then she just cries and hangs up. Listen, Jo, I won't be home until the weekend, so can you talk to her and calm her down. I know she's difficult but she genuinely looks up to you and it's obviously killing her that you're angry with her.'

He paused. 'It's nine-fifteen and I'm going out to dinner with someone. I'll call you tomorrow . . .' It sounded as if he wanted to add something, then the machine clicked. He'd run out of tape time.

There was no other message so he hadn't rung back to finish whatever he wanted to say to her.

Damn. She thumped the machine. It wasn't its fault but she wanted to hurt something because she felt so hurt. He hadn't even given her the benefit of the doubt, he'd just believed Emma. So that was all he thought about her.

CHAPTER FIFTEEN

'I'm glad you decided to come in, Aisling,' Vivienne said, handing her a mug of very strong-looking coffee. 'You'd have regretted it if you didn't. Edward really wants to get this sorted out properly. Harassment is not something he takes lightly.'

Aisling sat down nervously and looked around Vivienne's office as if she'd never seen it before in her life. She remembered her first day at work when she'd sat in this same chair and quivered with terror. Would she be able to work the computer or how would she deal with working in an office after years away from one? It had never entered her mind that the actual job itself would be the least of her problems. That her boss would make her life hell.

How could she explain to someone as confident as Vivienne what it felt like to tremble when you heard your boss's footsteps on the stairs every morning?

Would the other woman be able to comprehend that someone would force a smile onto her face every time she entered her superior's office, as if that would stave off his psychotic flights of temper? Probably not. Aisling picked a bit of dust off her navy shirt and cursed Leo Murphy.

If he hadn't been such a pig this could have been any ordinary Monday morning at the office. Instead, she was waiting to see Edward Richardson who had heard about Friday's encounter from Vivienne. He wanted to talk to Aisling about it. All she really wanted to do was forget about the whole damn thing and wish she'd never lost her temper with Leo – or told Vivienne what had really happened, for that matter.

'It's been going on ever since I joined,' she admitted shakily to Vivienne on Friday evening when she rang to find out exactly what had gone on in Aisling's office after the partners' lunch. 'I didn't know what to do, Vivienne, I've never experienced anything like that before. Nobody tells you how to deal with men like Leo and I just didn't know what to do,' she repeated miserably. 'I'm sorry.'

Vivienne was furious. 'That bastard,' she said. Aisling started to cry silently with the relief of finally telling someone from Richardson, Reid and Finucane what Leo had been like. But her relief quickly turned to terror when Vivienne pointed out that she'd have to tell Edward Richardson what had happened.

'You can't,' said Aisling frantically. 'You can't!'

'I have to tell him,' Vivienne insisted. 'It's his responsibility to make sure that none of his staff have to experience harassment. Anyway,' she added, 'this isn't the first time this has happened.'

On the other end of the phone Aisling gasped. She was stunned. She *wasn't* the first woman Leo had harassed? The *bastard*!

'When Elizabeth was on holiday, earlier this year, we had a temp in because none of us could cover for Elizabeth at the time,' said Vivienne.

'The temp only lasted two days. When she left she claimed Leo had been scaring her by making all sorts of weird comments. I honestly thought she wasn't serious, but I can see now what must have happened. Aisling,' Vivienne continued earnestly, 'you should have said something to me about him. They're very serious accusations.'

The word 'accusations' hit Aisling like a slap in the face. Accusations! She hadn't needed to spend more than a week in a solicitors' practice to see that *accusations* were not statements to be tossed around lightly.

Aisling didn't want to make accusations, she didn't want Leo to tear her apart in public for daring to say that he'd tried to touch her and harass her. He was a *lawyer*, for God's sake! He'd make mincemeat out of her. She could imagine him telling everyone how she'd thrown herself at him, a lonely ex-wife with nobody to cling on to at night and a desire for vengeance on mankind in general. Oh God, she could see it all now.

When Vivienne rang back two hours later to say she'd spoken to Edward and he wanted her to come and talk to him on Monday morning, Aisling panicked. It didn't matter about the other woman Leo had harassed. She'd never told her story. The first person to accuse Leo Murphy of sexual harassment would be Aisling Moran. She wasn't even three months back at work and look what had happened. What a great way to kick-start her career.

Two Valiums meant she spent Saturday in a haze, staring blankly at the TV and not answering the phone. She knew Jo had promised to ring to see how she was, but Aisling really didn't want to talk to anyone.

After all her plans to say hello to Michael and show off her new-found figure, Friday had obliterated her self-confidence. There was no way she wanted to face him now. She stayed in her room when Michael picked up the boys and stared out the window at his car as he reversed onto the road.

She managed to burn the grilled cod and roasted vegetable dish she'd made from a low-calorie recipe in a magazine. And she blindly put her red silk blouse into the machine with the boys' soccer shorts and socks, turning the entire wash bright pink.

She downed most of a bottle of wine on Saturday night watching Pat Kenny, but she still hadn't been able to sleep. Instead she lay in bed, wide awake, turning Friday's awful scene over and over in her brain and wondering whether it really was her fault after all.

It was as if there were two voices in her head – one telling her she'd messed everything up, again. The other telling her that making a wax dummy out of Leo Murphy and sticking a few pins in him would be the perfect revenge. What am I going to do? She thought at half three as she sat up in bed with the light on and a barely read magazine propped up in front of her.

The only good thing was that the Finucanes were away for the weekend, so Pat – and therefore Fiona – obviously had no idea what had happened.

Oh God, she moaned over and over again, what sort of can of worms have I opened up? Why did I ever lose my temper with Leo? Why didn't I calmly and quietly tell Vivienne what was going on and let her deal with it? Why was I such a wimp? The whole bloody thing was a nightmare.

'I wouldn't have come in if you hadn't rung me, Vivienne,' she said, clutching her coffee cup tightly. It was the one with the poppies, her favourite. 'I never wanted to see this place ever again because of him.'

The other woman pulled up a chair beside Aisling's, sat down and clasped one of Aisling's hands in her own.

'I know it took a lot of guts to come in here today, especially after all the things you told me. You've no idea how guilty I feel about never saying anything to you about Leo before . . .' Vivienne looked at Aisling apologetically.

'If I'd known he would try the same trick with you, of course I'd have said something. But I honestly thought there was something going on with Leo and the temp, and *that* was why she'd left so abruptly.' Vivienne sighed deeply.

'She was very pretty, sexy and very sure of herself. That's why I didn't really believe her. I know that sounds awful – as if you bring harassment upon yourself if you're sexy or good-looking. But I never thought he'd try it again, on someone like you,' she added earnestly.

Aisling said nothing for a moment. There were so many bobbles on her skirt she realised absently. Maybe she could try shaving them off with a disposable razor. Vivienne was still looking at her intently.

'Poor girl,' Aisling said finally. 'At least she had the sense to get away from him. I've been thinking about it all weekend, you know. I was the perfect victim – I had zero confidence and was so scared I'd make a mistake in the job that I must have seemed like a heaven-sent opportunity to pick on,' she said quietly.

'Men like him gravitate towards twenty-one-year-old temps and terrified women returning to work. They know we haven't got either the experience or the nerve to tell them where to stick it.'

The grandfather clock in the hall outside struck nine. Aisling jumped, spilling coffee onto the pale carpet.

'Oh sorry,' she said. 'I'm very jumpy today.'

'Don't be sorry,' Vivienne urged, putting an arm around Aisling's shoulder. 'You've every reason to be nervy.'

Nervy was not the word. Terrified, apprehensive and anxious might just cover the feeling in the pit of her stomach. Vivienne's phone rang and she quickly picked it up.

'Yes, Edward. She's here. I'll send her in. I'll hold all calls.'

Aisling blanched. Hold all calls. How long was Edward planning to talk to her for? God, she wished she had another Valium with her. She'd gone through the stash Fiona had given her. She knew she'd have to see her own doctor for more. She walked along the thick grey carpet on the way to Edward's office and prayed silently.

She'd never been in his office before, only peered in the door on Caroline's whistle-stop tour of the premises.

'Go on in,' said Vivienne encouragingly, holding the door open.

'Hello, Aisling,' said Edward. He rose from behind his highly polished antique desk and held out his hand. Dressed in a dark pin-striped suit with his gold-rimmed glasses on, he looked very formal and more than a little forbidding.

During her months with the company, he always smiled and asked her how she was whenever they bumped into each other, his manner more like that of an old friend than an employer.

Today, however, the old friend-of-the-family persona was gone, to be replaced by a steely-eyed look. Edward meant business.

'Sit down, Aisling,' he said.

Aisling sat with her hands tightly clasped, her jaw locked with tension. She wished she were anywhere else in the whole world but here.

'I'm very sorry to hear that there's a problem between you and Leo,' Edward began. 'Naturally, I'd hate to think that any member of the staff felt they had been sexually harassed while working here and, if that is the case, this company will do their utmost to make sure that the full letter of the law is adhered to.'

Aisling listened intently. Edward seemed to be saying that he'd do anything to help her *if* Leo *had* harassed her. But there was a big question mark over the whole matter. She felt the faint stirrings of anger inside her.

'You understand that we have to listen to Mr Murphy's side of the story,' he said.

'Of course,' said Aisling automatically.

'Tell me everything.' Edward took an elegant fountain pen off the desk and opened up a legal pad.

Have you got all day? thought Aisling grimly.

When she'd finished, Edward rang Vivienne and asked her to bring in some coffee and biscuits.

'You need it, my dear,' he advised Aisling, looking at her pale face. She felt totally drained. Talking about Leo's advances was like experiencing it all over again. She'd told Edward that she didn't want any trouble and that she'd considered not coming back to the office.

'But I need the job,' she said candidly.

Vivienne was either psychic or listening at the door, because she arrived with a tray of coffee and a plateful of biscuits within sixty seconds. Grateful to have the spotlight off herself at last, Aisling took a cup and stirred in sugar and milk. She almost didn't hear Edward asking Vivienne to summon Leo Murphy to the boss's office.

'He's coming here now?' she asked in horror.

'Calm down, Aisling,' Edward said gently. 'Nothing's going to happen. I'm here. This is a very serious matter and I'll be honest with you, it won't go away until we can clear the air.'

He leaned across the desk and looked at her earnestly. 'I know that you don't want to create any problems, Aisling, but until this is resolved, it would be awkward for both you and

Leo. With my experience of these matters, a meeting between both parties, where the problem is discussed, is the best option. I want you to understand that you are fully entitled to take legal action if you so wish. This meeting doesn't preclude that.'

Even as Edward said he understood that she didn't want any sort of legal battle with Leo, a little voice in Aisling's head was repeating the same words over and over again. 'He's done it before, it wasn't your fault.' She couldn't make the voice go away, it kept nagging her. Did she want a quiet life or justice? Did she want to let him get away with it because she was too scared to fight him?

There was a sharp knock on the door. Aisling couldn't help turning to look at it.

'Come in,' Edward said loudly.

Vivienne walked in, followed by Leo, all smiles, in one of his black suits with the usual dusting of dandruff on his shoulders. His face fell when he saw Aisling. Instead of sitting on the chair beside her, he chose one to the far right of Edward's desk. She looked away. She didn't want to see his face.

'Leo, delighted you could come,' Edward said smoothly. 'We've a problem I want to discuss. Vivienne, could you stay and take notes.'

'What's this about?' began Leo, his voice a little loud.

Edward didn't beat around the bush. 'Mrs Moran has come to me with a complaint, Leo. She says that last Friday, a few hours after the partners' lunch, you sexually harassed her, both physically and verbally.'

Aisling noticed that Edward didn't suffer from Leo's long-windedness. He was precise and to the point.

'She also says that you have been making suggestive comments to her since she started working here. I wanted this meeting to decide whether this has to go any further, Leo, to hear your side of the story.'

The other man bridled. 'This is ridiculous!' he snapped. 'Utterly ridiculous! These accusations are totally unfounded.'

310

Aisling moved slightly further away from him on her chair. She kept her eyes firmly trained on Edward's face, but she could hear Leo's breath quickening, the way it did when he was about to embark on a fully-fledged tantrum. She hoped Edward noticed his junior partner's mood. This was not the way to win clients and influence people.

'Leo, I think I should point out to you that Mrs Moran did not want to come in to work after last week's incident,' Edward said. 'She has told me that she doesn't want to pursue this matter further. So far,' he added pointedly.

'She merely wants the matter cleared up. In fact, had it not been for Ms Hogan, who was looking for Mrs Moran at the time of the incident, I doubt that Mrs Moran would have ever sought this meeting. What I'm saying, Leo, is that I want this sorted out with as little trouble as possible.'

Thank you, Edward, said Aisling silently. He believes me. Vivienne must have told him about the temp. She allowed herself a quick sideways glance at Leo. He was now the colour of chalk. Behind him, Vivienne glanced quickly at Aisling and gave her the faintest flicker of a grin.

It was only then that Aisling realised what Edward was doing. He was cleverly giving Leo the impression that Vivienne had witnessed everything.

Leo didn't know whether she had or not, but he daren't risk denying everything, therefore forcing Aisling to take him to court, in case he was wrong. Leo had to own up, didn't he? She felt a flicker of triumph.

'I don't know what to say,' spluttered Leo. 'I mean, this is a ludicrous situation.'

'In that way?' inquired Edward silkily. Aisling could see how he'd built up such a successful practice. Charming and urbane, Edward Richardson was, nevertheless, every inch a tough lawyer when the occasion demanded it. She wondered if she could ask him to handle her inevitable divorce?

'Well, this whole situation is ludicrous,' protested Leo. He no longer sounded so cocky. 'Everything's been blown out of all proportion.'

Edward, Aisling and Vivienne all leaned a fraction forward in their chairs. Had Leo just thrown all professional caution to the winds or was he completely rattled?

'*What* exactly has been blown out of all proportion?' asked Edward. 'If nothing happened, how can anything have been blown out of all proportion?'

'I have to admit, I got carried away and kissed Mrs Moran . . .' stammered Leo, visibly shaken.

'*Kissed* her?' asked the other man sternly. 'Kissing implies that Mrs Moran was willing, Mr Murphy, and she says she wasn't.'

'It was a clumsy attempt, I'd had too much to drink,' Leo stuttered. 'I never meant to hurt or offend her.'

Aisling could feel the tension leave her body. She never thought he'd confess. She had won. Now she wanted him hung, drawn and quartered. No, that was too easy. She wanted him alone in a room with herself, Vivienne and Fiona wielding baseball bats. Maybe too bloodthirsty.

'But I deny ever having made advances towards Mrs Moran before,' Leo added sharply. 'This was a one-off occurrence for which I am profoundly sorry. In fact, I had planned to apologise to Mrs Moran today if I upset her with my clumsy advance.'

The way Leo was telling it, Friday's incident had become a love scene between a lovestruck admirer and his shy secretary, instead of an attempted grope. Aisling had had enough.

'Your behaviour was disgraceful!' she snapped at Leo. 'You are an absolute pig who made my life a misery. You deserve to be locked up and I shall see to it that you are!' she shrieked. 'How dare you try something like that on anyone. You completely abused your position and . . .'

'Mrs Moran,' interrupted Edward firmly. 'This is not the time for an argument which would only cause further distress. If you are willing to accept Mr Murphy's apology, we can leave it at that.'

'I will accept Mr Murphy's apology when he makes it to *me*!' said Aisling angrily. 'Apologising to you isn't the same.'

312

'Quite right,' said Edward. 'Mr Murphy?'

Leo's face was a picture. He was still pale under his tan but he had two red spots on his cheeks.

Leo turned to face Aisling. He could barely look at her and kept his eyes trained on some spot behind her head.

'I apologise if my attentions on Friday upset you, Mrs Moran. It won't happen again.'

'Good.' She smiled at him, a satisfied smile. 'Mr Richardson,' she said. If everyone was going to be formal, she might as well too. 'I'm afraid that I would find it difficult to work with Mr Murphy again and I would like some other position within the company.'

She hoped she wasn't pushing it too far. Her contract was still only temporary and, for all she knew, they could have booted her out of the company on the grounds that they only had one position to be filled and she was rejecting it. But she didn't think that was going to happen.

It was perfectly obvious to Aisling that Edward Richardson saw Leo as the guilty party. He would do his best for her, she was sure of it.

'I understand,' he said. 'If you'd excuse me, ladies, I want a word with Mr Murphy. I'll talk to you when I'm finished, Mrs Moran. Thank you.'

'No. Thank *you*,' replied Aisling, rising to her feet.

Outside the door, she hugged Vivienne with delight.

'We did it,' she whispered.

'I'm so glad,' Vivienne whispered back. 'That bastard deserved to be brought to court, so he got off lightly. Well,' she amended, 'maybe not. Wait till you see him when Edward is finished with him. Edward is furious about the whole thing. I told him about the temp who complained and he went ballistic. He's going to give Murphy a verbal warning.'

'Really?' Aisling asked.

'Yes. Sexual harassment is an extremely serious charge nowadays, Aisling, and the firm has taken on several harassment cases over the past few years. So think how damaging it would be to the firm if news of this got out? Come into my office and wait for Edward. But don't talk about what's happened. Caroline is there. She doesn't know anything about this. It would be better to keep it that way.'

Aisling arranged her spider plant so that the spindly leaves hung over the edge of the desk. She put a small framed photo of the twins beside it, and placed the little soapstone box, in which she kept paper clips, in front of the picture. The window was right behind her, so she adjusted the position of her VDU screen until it no longer reflected the bright sunlight streaming in the window. There. She was settled.

Vivienne had certainly been busy on Monday. She'd got a brand new desk for Aisling, a right-angled one which meant she had lots of space for both her computer keyboard and her wire baskets.

The senior secretary had despatched four of the filing cabinets in her office to the file room and had made enough space for Aisling's new desk. There were three desks in the office so there wasn't a lot of room, but Aisling couldn't have cared less. She was working with two women she liked and Edward had asked her to be secretary to Anthony Green, one of the firm's new partners. She'd met him at the fateful partners' lunch and immediately liked him.

What was more, Vivienne explained, he was just married and never stopped talking about 'my wife'.

'That's a relief,' said Aisling at eight forty-five on Tuesday morning as she finished arranging her belongings on her new desk.

'There's a price to be paid when you're irresistible to men,' Vivienne pointed out. She opened a black compact and peered at the mirror as she carefully applied some lipstick. 'I was afraid I'd have to ask you to wear a chador in to work.'

'Harassment is nothing to do with sex appeal,' Aisling shuddered. 'It's a power trip for the pig in question. Anyway, I haven't exactly been fighting admirers off with a stick since Michael left, you know.'

'I'm sorry,' Vivienne said. 'I didn't mean to be flip. I was trying to be complimentary. The only reason you aren't beating men off with a stick is because you don't get out enough.'

'Where am I supposed to go?' demanded Aisling. 'Most of the people I know are couples that Michael and I both knew and they don't invite me to be the odd one out at their dinner parties. My best single friend is Jo Ryan, and she's over five months pregnant.

'After a day at work, she just goes home and conks out on the settee – unless she's house-hunting. The only other option is to go to singles' nights out and I haven't the nerve.'

'Why don't you come out with me?' asked Vivienne. 'I've a couple of girlfriends I go out with once a week and we'd love to have you with us.'

'Would they mind me tagging along?' asked Aisling.

'I wouldn't have asked you otherwise,' said Vivienne sensibly. 'We're going out for a meal on Thursday. Probably just pizza and a glass of wine, nothing expensive. You'd enjoy it.'

'OK, I will come. I'd love to.' Aisling was delighted. She hadn't been out in ages – lunch in McDonald's with the twins didn't count – and the thought of a night out *and* adult conversation was bliss. She'd ask Fiona's baby-sitter to mind the boys.

It never rained but it poured, she thought that evening once she'd got off the phone with Fiona. After fifteen minutes listening to Fiona's shocked commiserations about the Leo Murphy affair – 'That bastard, Daddy should have fired him!' – the conversation turned to the party the Finucanes were giving on Saturday night to celebrate their tenth wedding anniversary.

'It's not going to be a big party,' Fiona assured Aisling. 'Only about fifty or sixty people.' Fiona and Aisling had wildly different views about how many people constituted a *big* party.

'I'm doing Marks and Spencer's dips and cocktails, which even *I* can organise so don't feel you have to volunteer to help. All I want from you is your presence at nine o'clock in a devastatingly glamorous outfit.'

'No problem,' Aisling replied cheerily. 'Should I wear the Dior off-the-shoulder number or would the Versace sequinned miniskirt be better?'

'Come in your bikini, darling. I'm inviting all the eligible single men I know, so I want you in something noticeable.'

'Me in a bikini would be noticeable, but not necessarily in the right way, Fiona,' Aisling said, thinking of her stretch marks.

'Don't knock yourself, Aisling, but do wear something sexy. I've told them all you're a red-hot career woman who wore out her last man, so don't let me down!'

Aisling hung up laughing.

There was absolutely nothing red-hot in her wardrobe and she couldn't see herself shopping for anything that would make her stand out from the crowd.

She wasn't *that* confident about her new figure. And she didn't have either the time or the energy to trawl the shops during lunchtime. But she could always get her hair done on Saturday morning when the boys were at soccer. Maybe she'd get a few inches cut off or have it styled differently.

Wednesday was manic. Caroline was sick so Vivienne and Aisling had to divide her work between them. Another new partner started work and he didn't like his new office, wanted help working his computer and required business cards *immediately*. And then the men putting in the new alarm system managed to turn off the electricity, losing all the computer files that people were working on and hadn't saved. The air in Aisling and Vivienne's office was blue with swearing.

Yet in the middle of all the power cuts, lost files and surprised yells coming from the people stuck in the windowless file room, Aisling felt happy, almost serene.

She didn't really mind if the power went off all day, as long as she wasn't sitting in Leo Murphy's office. She sang along to the radio going into work and tapped her fingers to the music blasting out of the canteen at lunchtime. Nothing could dim the relief she felt at the thought that her ten weeks working for that bastard were over. He'd stayed out on Tuesday, 'ringing his lawyer, no doubt', muttered Vivienne.

On Wednesday he kept his office door shut, an unusual occurrence unless he had a client in.

Buoyed up by her victory over him, she no longer quivered when she heard his step on the stairs. Aisling knew he wouldn't come near her ever again.

It was after six on Wednesday by the time Aisling left the office and hurried to the car in the pouring rain, a plastic bag held over her head to keep her hair dry. Her head was aching from working at double speed to make up for lost computer time, but she was still in good humour.

The twins waltzed out of the childminder's house each carrying a balloon, a small plastic bag and a party blower along with their schoolbags.

'Hiya, Mum,' they yelled in unison, obviously in the best of spirits.

'Where did you get the balloons and the sweets?' she asked as Paul thrust his small plastic bag at her and urged her to take one.

'Lorrie's party,' replied Phillip thickly as he chewed on a toffee. 'She's ten.'

'She's Phillip's girlfriend!' shouted Paul, dodging his brother's immediate kick.

'She isn't,' howled Phillip.

'Is! Is!' screeched Paul.

'Boys! Stop!' pleaded Aisling. 'I've got a headache. I hope Mrs O'Brien hasn't been giving you fizzy drinks,' she said once they were in the back seat of the car still squabbling energetically.

'Ribena,' said Paul, dodging Phillip's well-aimed thumps. 'I hate Ribena.'

'Well I love it,' Phillip answered.

They kept it up all the way home, scuffling and whispering threats at each other until finally Aisling told them she'd throw them both out of the car to walk home if they didn't shut up.

317

At home, they belted up the stairs together, leaving a trail of schoolbags, anoraks and sweets in the hall. Aisling just walked past the mess.

In the kitchen, she took a dish of lasagne out of the fridge and slid it into the oven. The was dinner organised. She quickly boiled the kettle, made herself a cup of tea and carried it into the sitting room where she slid off her shoes and sank into an armchair. She deserved a rest. She smiled to herself.

The lasagne would take around forty minutes and she wasn't budging until it was cooked. The terrible twosome could kill each other upstairs if they liked, but she wasn't going to investigate.

After dinner, the boys sat at the kitchen table and Aisling refereed while they did their homework.

'Phillip must work at his handwriting,' the teacher had written at the "teacher's comments" section of his homework notebook. Looking at the childish scrawl all over his English copybook where sentences rambled with little regard for the lines on the page, Aisling could see what Miss Devine meant.

'I'm trying,' he said sweetly, leaning up against his mother.

'Are you?' she asked.

'Yes.' Phillip nodded. 'I'm very good at maths. I got ten out of ten in my test yesterday. So did Paul. But Miss Devine took a mark off him because he broke Shane's pencil.'

'Why did you do that, Paul?' asked Aisling, astonished that the quieter of the two had been involved in any sort of argument. Phillip was the truculent one, the twin most likely to fight. Left to his own devices, Paul wouldn't have hurt a fly.

He was saying nothing. Eyes focused on his open copybook, he wrote slowly, his left hand bent awkwardly as he wrote.

'Paul. Talk to me!'

'Shane said you and Dad would get divorced and never live together again, so Paul took his pencil. It wasn't Paul's fault,' Phillip said defensively.

'Is this true?' asked Aisling quietly.

Paul nodded.

318

She put one hand on his dark head and ruffled his hair, trying her hardest to smile even though she wanted to cry. Poor Paul. He did his best to pretend everything was all right when, deep down, he was a miserable little boy caught in the crossfire of a marriage break-up. Phillip had coped so much better. Or at least, it seemed that way.

He was eager to see his dad every Saturday and loved being driven around in *her* sports car. The time spent with their father was always jam-packed with excitement, Aisling complained to Fiona, because he brought them to McDonald's, to the cinema or bowling. 'To make up for not being there all week. He gets the fun part,' she pointed out. 'Meanwhile, I get them up in the morning, dole out the Coco Pops, get them to school, pick them up at night, feed them, help them do their homework, wash their clothes and buy the groceries. I think we should swap now and again,' she added crossly, knowing in her heart that she would have hated it if the twins lived with Michael and not with her.

Both boys came back home happy and tired after the weekend, but the previous Sunday night Paul was very subdued. Would Dad ever be coming home to live with them again? He asked, staring at her with confused dark eyes. Aisling hadn't known what to say at first. She'd simply hugged him and said that Dad loved them and would see them all the time, but that he wanted to live somewhere else.

Now, Aisling put down Phillip's homework notebook and looked at them both earnestly.

'Boys, there's no point in getting upset when people talk about your dad and I splitting up,' she said. 'It happens to lots of families and the important thing to remember is that even though Dad and I aren't getting on well, we both still love you two, OK? You know,' she added conversationally, 'you're lucky because you have *two* homes now. That's special. I bet Shane won't get two lots of Christmas presents, either. Tell him that next time he bothers you, Paul.'

'I will,' said Paul, his jaw set as firmly as his father's. It was hard to put Michael out of her mind when the kids looked so

319

like him. Somewhat cheered up, Paul returned to his home-work and Phillip carefully tugged his notebook out from under Aisling's elbow.

'Work on your handwriting, brat,' she said, ruffling his hair affectionately.

When the boys were finally in bed, Aisling finished the ironing before mashing the potato for the following evening's shepherd's pie. It wasn't their favourite dish but she wanted something quick and easy to give them before she went out. She'd hoovered earlier in the evening and now she dusted the sitting room, cleaned the downstairs loo and put another wash on. Even though the baby-sitter was a seventeen-year-old Leaving Cert student who had more on her mind than untidy houses, Aisling's pride meant she didn't want the place looking messy the following evening.

As usual, she was halfway through bleaching the worktops before she remembered her rubber gloves lying untouched in the cupboard underneath the sink. That's why Vivienne has elegant nails and I have dry hands and flaky nails, she muttered. There was no point bothering with them now. She'd rub cream on her hands later. If she remembered.

It was half ten by the time she'd finished cleaning and polishing. Roll on tomorrow, Aisling thought, sinking into the settee with a small gin and tonic. If ever a woman deserved a night out, she did.

Thomas Read's was buzzing when Aisling ventured in, clutching the folds of her raincoat around her legs self-consciously. She was wearing a new on-the-knee black skirt which showed off lots of leg in her seven-deniers. The short skirt was a mistake, she decided passing the bus stop and getting a flash of herself tottering in her black suede stilettos. She loved short skirts but was never sure whether she had the legs for them or not. Definitely not.

As she stood, she scanned the pub anxiously. She couldn't see Vivienne anywhere. The place was jam-packed even though it was only after eight o'clock. The tables were full of well-dressed people, all looking at home in the trendy city-centre pub. Aisling felt totally out of place, as if she had a sign over her head proclaiming that she was thirty-five, separated and wasn't used to going anywhere more exciting on Thursday evenings than Quinnsworth.

She spotted Vivienne standing up and waving at her. Relief flooded through her as she wound her way through the crowd. It was *horrible* arriving on her own, trying to fit in and find people at the same time when she felt so self-conscious and out of place.

'Awful, I know,' said the dark-haired woman sitting beside Vivienne when Aisling arrived at the table and sat down, raincoat still on. 'There's nothing worse than arriving somewhere on your own.' Wow, thought Aisling, I really *must* have a sign over my head.

'Glad you made it.' Vivienne looked marvellous in a crimson velvet fitted shirt with her hair in an elegant topknot.

'Aisling, this is Maria.' She gestured at the woman who had spoken when Aisling arrived, a large brunette wearing a grape-coloured satin jacket which revealed an impressive cleavage. Maria was wearing a lot of make-up which emphasised full lips and high cheekbones and a jet pendant necklace which drew the eye directly down. 'And Annie.'

'Nice to meet you,' said Annie, pulling up a chair for Aisling. She was petite, blonde and wearing a rich brown lycra dress Aisling had already spotted in Dunnes.

'I'm afraid we've already started,' Annie said, picking up her glass of red wine. 'Maria, catch that waiter's eye, will you?'

'Hello, Aisling, welcome to our little gathering,' said Maria warmly, leaning over the table towards Aisling. 'When you walked in, you reminded me of myself four years ago just after I split up with my husband,' she confessed. 'I was terrified of going anywhere on my own after years of being part of a couple. Every time I went out, I felt so strange and out of place, being on my own and not being used to it. And now look at me!'

Several people did and Maria smiled at them, shooting smouldering looks at a handsome young man at the table beside them who was chattering in Italian to two girls.

'Maria likes to stand out from the crowd,' explained Vivienne gravely.

'It makes a change from all those times when I wanted to sit in the corner and die because I was a size eighteen and I wanted to be a ten,' said Maria, turning away from Mr Latin with a wink. She waved at a bar girl. 'Now, what's your poison, Aisling?'

'A gin and tonic, please,' said Aisling, feeling more at home in her little black skirt and silky grey wrapover blouse now that it appeared that the other women were dressed to kill.

'Enough about us. Tell us all about you. Vivienne has been filling us in on the boss with the roaming hands and I want to hear every gory detail of how you thumped him! I wouldn't like to tell you what I'd do if he tried it on me!'

Aisling burst out laughing. She'd love to see what the voluptuous Maria would do if she got her hands on Leo.

They talked so much that they were half an hour late for their table in Sinners, the Lebanese restaurant a few doors away. In between hearing about Maria's gorgeous new dentist, Aisling discovered how the three other women had met. They'd been doing a computer course five years before, had struck up a friendship during the first lunch-break and had remained friends ever since. They were all totally different – the extrovert and risqué Maria, down-to-earth Vivienne and Annie, a quiet woman with a wry sense of humour – yet they got on like a house on fire.

'This place is lovely,' said Maria as she squeezed into the pew-style seat at their table and dumped a bulging suede handbag onto the seat beside her. 'And so's the waiter, she whispered.

'Are we going to order or not?' Annie demanded ten minutes later, while Maria flirted with the waiter. 'I'm ravenous.'

'Sorry,' Maria said repentantly. 'He's so cute. It's a pity he's so young. He's just my type.'

On Vivienne's advice, Aisling ordered the house speciality,

Mezes, a selection of different types of Lebanese food.

'It *sounds* like lots of teeny-weeny dishes and you think you'll still be hungry afterwards,' said Maria, 'but wait until you see the amount you get. You'll be stuffed.'

They ate char-grilled lamb, stuffed vine leaves and beautiful deep-fried goat's cheese, and talked non-stop about what had happened to each of them over the past week.

As they chattered about everything under the sun, Aisling found herself joining in as if she'd known them all her life. Funny, down-to-earth and warm, the three women were the sort of people you could tell anything to.

She found herself talking to them about her separation from Michael in a way she'd never been able to do with her sister, Sorcha. It was a relief to talk about how scared she'd been at the thought of going back to work after so long.

'I was terrified of *you* at first, Vivienne,' Aisling admitted, now knowing the other woman well enough to actually say it.

'You poor thing,' Vivienne said apologetically. 'That was a dreadful day for me because Christine had been awake all night with a stomach bug and I hated leaving her with my mother that morning. I was a complete zombie with exhaustion. It took me five minutes to hide the dark circles with concealer. And when I met you for the first time I thought you were just some bored well-heeled housewife amusing herself with a job . . . Oh, I'm sorry, Aisling, I really am.' She leaned over and patted Aisling's arm. 'I'd always prided myself on not judging people until I knew them and I did just that with you.'

'Oh, it doesn't matter now,' Aisling said sincerely. 'Look how good you've been to me since.'

'I should have told you about bloody Leo, that's what,' Vivienne replied. 'I was thinking of how legally risky it would be to spread a rumour like that especially when I didn't really have any proof, so I said nothing and you had to deal with the consequences.'

'That's in the past, Viv. So let's forget about it.' Aisling patted the other woman's hand gently.

'You're absolutely right, Aisling,' Maria said firmly. 'We're not here to dredge up bad experiences. We're here to have fun.' She lifted her glass for a toast and the others followed suit. 'To us and to fun!'

'Cheers,' the others said in unison.

Maria was separated and had two teenage children, a fact which amazed Aisling as the other woman only looked about thirty-two or -three.

'Thirty-three and a few months,' confirmed Maria, with a cheesy smile. 'Ninety-six months, actually. It's my lifestyle, you see. Some people diet, drink lots of water and buy horrifically expensive moisturisers to stay young,' she confided to Aisling.

'Personally, I use the dairy chocolate bar method of staying young,' she continued. 'Eat lots of chocolate – yes, you do put on weight, but you're happy – only use water for making tea, coffee or hot whiskies, go out with plenty of nice men and make sure you've got two mad young girls around the house. That keeps me young.'

'Sounds like a great recipe,' Aisling said. 'How old are the girls?'

'Shelley was fifteen last month – I can't *believe* how fast she's growing up,' exclaimed Maria. 'Lynsey is seventeen. She's doing her Leaving this year and Shelley's doing her Group. The house is an exam time bomb waiting to go off. I'm afraid to have the telly up loud at night because they're studying so hard.'

'You're lucky they both want to study,' said Aisling.

'Shelley really looks up to Lynsey, she hero-worships her,' explained Maria. 'Because Lynsey got the best Group Cert results in the school, Shelley wants to do the same, which is wonderful. I'm delighted.'

Annie was in her late thirties, was married to Greg, a carpenter, and had one little girl. She told Aisling that she'd been engaged for five years to her childhood sweetheart until she was twenty-nine when she fell in love with a man she worked with. She left her fiancé to move in with Greg and had never looked back.

'I know because of your experience, you probably think it's a dreadful thing to do,' Annie said slowly, stirring sugar into her coffee.

'I was living with Ray for six years and I thought we'd get married and have kids eventually, you know, the whole nine yards. Then I met Greg and fell in love.' She paused for a moment, obviously thinking about him. Vivienne said she'd never seen a couple so incredibly in love. 'They hold hands when they walk,' Vivienne explained. 'How many couples do you know who do that after nine years together?'

'You don't choose who you fall in love with,' continued Annie. 'It was so dreadful at the time of the break-up, but I'm so glad I did it. I'm so happy now,' she added.

'Annie is proof that true love exists,' remarked Vivienne, pouring the remains of the third bottle of wine into their glasses.

'Well, you're not doing too badly in the love department yourself,' Maria pointed out.

'I don't know,' Vivienne said gloomily. 'I think Pat's getting cold feet about the whole thing. We're supposed to be going away next weekend and yesterday he phoned to say he might have to work on Saturday after all.' She took a gulp of wine. 'God, I'd love a cigarette. I always want to start smoking again when I've had a few glasses of wine.'

Vivienne was going out with a detective she'd met at a wedding ten months previously. Good-looking, kind, solvent and with a great sense of humour, he was almost too good to be true, Vivienne said. She kept waiting to discover some fatal flaw in him. Privately, Aisling thought Vivienne was probably right. What man *didn't* have a fatal flaw?

'Pat's job is hardly routine, Viv,' Annie said sensibly. 'He never knows what's going to come up or when he has to work, so you can't blame him for that.'

'And Christine loves him,' put in Maria. 'She may only be eight but she's very clever, cleverer than her mother when it comes to men!' She wagged a finger at Vivienne.

As the staff in Sinners seemed in no hurry to close the place up, the four women sat and talked until nearly one.

'Oh God, is that the time?' gasped Aisling, looking at her watch in alarm. 'The baby-sitter will go berserk. I didn't mean to be home so late.'

'You need to get out, Aisling,' Vivienne said quietly. 'Otherwise you'll go mad. Think of this evening as therapy. It's more fun and much cheaper than Prozac!'

Aisling and Maria shared a taxi home. The other woman lived in Sandymount, which was on Aisling's way home.

'You will come out with us again, won't you?' asked Maria when the taxi pulled up outside a pretty terraced house in a quiet street.

'Of course, I'd love to,' answered Aisling warmly.

After her night out with Vivienne, Annie and Maria, all of whom obviously enjoyed her company, Aisling felt more confident about going to the Finucanes' party. On Friday evening while the boys were watching TV, she tore her wardrobe apart looking for something that would live up to Fiona's description of 'red-hot'.

She found nothing. The evening clothes she'd worn for the past few years were generally size sixteen, black, navy or grey and all-encompassing to hide the tummy she hated and her fat thighs. All she found were long, A-line tunics, several sloppy jumpers and a pink silk overshirt that had always made her look like she was pregnant. Now that she fitted into a size twelve with ease, everything looked frumpy and far too big on her. There was nothing terribly sexy in the evening-clothes department apart from a black body with a low-cut neck. Worn with her new black skirt, the outfit looked nice but rather boring. She poked around in the drawer where she kept her costume jewellery, looking for something that would enliven the outfit. Nothing. She was about to strip it off in despair when the doorbell rang.

When she got downstairs, Phillip had already answered the

door and Fiona was standing in the hall.

'Looks like I came at the right time,' Fiona said gaily, waving a big Next bag.

'This is what I'm thinking of wearing tomorrow night,' Aisling said, doing a twirl in her stockinged feet. 'I can't find anything else, basically. Is it OK?'

'It's OK, but you want to look better than OK, my dear. That's why I came over. Come on upstairs. I've brought over a few gorgeous things for you to try on for the party. I knew you wouldn't buy anything new.' Fiona marched upstairs with Aisling following her.

Even though she had probably been having a mini-breakdown at home organising the house for the party, Fiona would still make time to make sure her friend was wearing something drop-dead gorgeous. She was a great friend, Aisling thought as she followed Fiona's petite jeans-clad bum up the stairs.

'I know you don't want to spend all day tomorrow buying clothes, which is a good thing as I can't come with you.' Fiona talked as she opened the bag and laid various items of clothing on Aisling's bed. 'One day we must go shopping together because I still don't trust you not to buy boring dark things because you think they make you look thinner. But until then, here are a few bits and pieces for tomorrow night. What do you think of this?'

She held up a bronze-coloured body with a wrapover front which was made of spray-on lycra and would undoubtedly reveal plenty of cleavage.

'It's very Maria,' Aisling said, holding the body up to herself and looking at the mirror. 'But it's also very small. How the hell can any of *your* clothes fit *me*?'

'It's all down to the Goddess of Lycra,' Fiona said. 'This stuff is stretchy, so it'll fit you, no problem. Is Maria one of Vivienne's friends?'

'Yes, she's a howl,' Aisling said, unzipping her skirt. 'She's a real individual, mad as a bicycle. She had us all in stitches the whole night. You'll have to meet the three of them.

You'll really like Vivienne and Annie as well. What do you think?'

She stepped back from Fiona and looked in the mirror. The body fitted her as if it had been made for her. It moulded her curves like a second skin and the subtle colour suited her much better than the black body she'd been wearing minutes before.

'Gorgeous. It's lovely.' Fiona eyed the outfit with her head at an angle. 'Try it with trousers or with your long black skirt. I think it'll look great with a long skirt and this gold chain belt.'

She was right. Aisling stood in front of the mirror, delighted with the slim and toned body she saw. Thank you Callanetics, she said to herself.

'Try on this,' ordered Fiona, handing Aisling a black lace top.

'This is perfect, Fiona,' protested Aisling, gesturing at what she was wearing. 'I don't need anything else.'

'Go on, Aisling. You need more than one sexy evening outfit now that you're turning into a party animal. Anyway, that top suits you much better than it suits me, so you'd be doing me a favour if you keep it . . .'

'I can't keep it,' Aisling said.

'Don't be silly. I never wear the bronze thing because I just don't have the boobs for it.' Fiona looked down at her rather flat chest ruefully. 'And you should take the black thing too. It never really suited me. Go on, take them. They're just cluttering up my wardrobe. Or rather Pat's wardrobe, since I've taken over most of his as well. I think I'll soon have to buy one of those clothes rails you see in shops.'

Aisling quickly tried on the lace top. Beautifully cut with a high neck and long sleeves, if it had been made of anything other than lace, it would have looked very plain. But because it only had a built-in bra lining the fabric under the lace around her breasts, the effect was of a very revealing and incredibly sexy outfit.

'Fiona, I cannot go out in this. You could see my bra at the back,' Aisling pointed out. 'In fact, you couldn't wear a bra with this at all.'

'That's the whole point.' Fiona sat back on the bed and gave her friend a mischievous grin.

'What do you mean? Am I supposed to break into *Patricia the Stripper* and undress when there's a lull in the conversation?'

Fiona looked cagey. 'Well, I've got a couple of nice single men coming and I *did* promise them a live strip show in the dining room . . .' She chuckled at the idea. 'No, Aisling, I just want you to live up to your potential. You're gorgeous and it's about time you realised it. There's no point hiding behind loads of clothes any more. I won't let you.'

Aisling was unbelievably touched.

'You're very good to me, Fiona. What would I do without you?'

Fiona considered this. 'Well, you wouldn't have an appointment with my hairdresser at ten tomorrow morning. I'm going in for a blow-dry and I thought it would be great if we went together.'

She looked at Aisling expectantly. 'What do you think?'

'That's a great idea,' Aisling answered. 'I didn't book anywhere because it slipped my mind today. Actually, I was thinking of getting highlights put in, just a few, nothing much,' she added hurriedly. She shouldn't have said that. Now Fiona would pester her unmercifully to get the full Marilyn peroxide look.

'Brilliant!' Fiona clapped her hands delightedly. 'I know you'll look wonderful with highlights. Watch out boys,' she said with a wicked laugh. 'The newly single and available Aisling Moran is going to hit the scene!'

'They'll think I'm really available if I wear this,' Aisling pointed out.

'All the more reason to wear it. You don't want to become a nun!'

Aisling couldn't think of a suitable answer to that.

★　★　★

The smell of ammonia filled Aisling's nostrils and she was glad when a cup of coffee was put before her. Taking a sip, she turned her attention to *Vogue* magazine and relaxed. It was lucky that Fiona had made an appointment for her as the salon was already buzzing and it was only a quarter past eleven.

'We're doing a wedding party with *six* bridesmaids,' explained the colourist as he painstakingly divided Aisling's hair into tiny sections, slipped tiny pieces of easi-meche paper under each section and painted different types of bleach on. 'They *all* want ringlets,' he whispered. 'It's like a Helena Bonham-Carter lookalike competition in here.'

An earnest young man wearing all black, the colourist chattered away as he worked on Aisling's hair. She was fascinated by the whole procedure. By using the meche method, he explained, he could apply different colours to her hair and this would make it look more natural than just being bleached with one colour.

She had a lot of hair and it took a solid hour to do her whole head. When he had finished, he gave her a pile of glossy magazines, asked her did she want coffee and put her under a rather strange hairdryer which looked like a three-bar fire more than anything else.

It felt wonderful to be pampered, to sit back, read magazines, drink coffee and let someone else run around like a headless chicken. She'd been up at eight, organising the boys' soccer kit which she hadn't done the night before, getting their breakfast and bringing them to soccer. She'd ended up putting her make-up on at traffic lights because she didn't want to go to the hairdresser's barefaced. Nothing accentuated lines more than the unforgiving light in a hairdressing salon.

But today wasn't like any of the other times she'd gone to the hairdresser over the last few years. Since she'd put on weight, sitting for ages in front of a mirror with nothing to do but stare at herself was painful. Not any more.

Today, the woman in the mirror was a slim, independent working woman.

She turned a page. She never bought *Vogue* so it was nice to read it for free at the hairdresser's. And it certainly gave you a glance into how the other half lived, she thought, marvelling at how a simple dress could cost over a thousand pounds, even if it was made by Gucci. For that money, it would want to be able to do the dishes, hoover the sitting room and cook the dinner.

She looked up to see how Fiona was getting on. Her neighbour was seated at the other end of the salon having her hair blow-dried into a sleek bob.

Aisling didn't know who was more pleased when she said she wanted her whole head highlighted – the hairdresser or Fiona.

'Well, how are you doing?' asked Fiona, appearing at Aisling's side suddenly.

'I'm doing marvellously,' said Aisling with a smile, holding up her coffee cup with her little finger crooked in a parody of the way her granny told her was ladylike. 'I think I should spend all Saturday mornings in the hairdresser.'

'Good, said Fiona, who *did* spend all her Saturday mornings in the hairdresser. 'You'd be great company for me. What time will you be ready?'

'About another hour, I reckon,' Aisling replied.

'I'll nip off to do some shopping then. I saw this divine little dress in Jackie Lavin's window yesterday and I'm going to try it on. Yes, I *know* I said I wasn't buying any clothes for ages, and I know Pat will murder me if he sees another shopping bag in the house. He says I'm a shopaholic,' Fiona added in a surprised tone. 'But this dress is lovely. It's silver-beaded and has a halter-neck . . . Divine. I'll be back in an hour, OK?'

You just had to laugh at Fiona, Aisling thought. If she knew anyone else who spent half her life shopping and the other half thinking about shopping, she'd think they were one of society's rich bitches. But Fiona was so kind and funny, you didn't mind the fact that she spent more on clothes in one week than many people earned in two. It must be nice to have an inheritance.

By the time Fiona returned with two large bags of shopping, Aisling was ready. The colourist was showing her the back of her head with a hand mirror and she was bursting with delight. The long lank mousy hair had gone, to be replaced by soft waves of shoulder-length glossy blonde hair which framed her face beautifully. The face was the same, Aisling thought, taking in the perfectly styled hair, but it looked totally different now.

Her skin glowed beside the soft gold and ash blonde strands of hair. Her eyes looked large and luminous now that her hair was swept back from her face.

'Aisling! Wow!' Fiona's voice was high-pitched with surprise.

'Well, what do you think?' Aisling swivelled around in her chair and grinned at her friend.

'You look amazing, absolutely amazing. You should have had this done years ago,' said Fiona. 'I'd probably walk past you on the street if I hadn't seen you here. You look so *different*.'

'I know. Isn't it wonderful?' Aisling couldn't keep the delight out of her voice. She felt transformed. She wanted to run outside and march into all the expensive shops in the Blackrock Centre. Now she looked as if she belonged in them, looked as if she was a stylish and attractive woman instead of the drudge she'd been for so long.

She shook her head slightly for the third time, enjoying the feeling of her hair rippling around her head. Aisling felt as if she'd never get tired of doing this, delighted with how light her hair felt and fascinated at the way it fell perfectly into place each time.

'Come on, we better get out of here,' she said. 'I have to pick up the twins and you have to organise the party of the year.'

Fiona grimaced. 'I love the idea of having a party until the actual day I'm having it. Then, I want to sit curled up on the couch with a dry Martini and a good book.'

'It'll be fun, Fiona, you know you'll start enjoying yourself

332

after the first half-hour. You always do.'

The twins loved Aisling's new hairstyle.

'You look great, Mum,' Paul said.

'Yeah, it's lovely,' added Phillip.

But they weren't the ones she wanted to impress with her new look. Once they got home, she raced upstairs to look at herself in her bedroom mirror. Maybe she only looked good in the hair salon, she thought anxiously. Maybe she'd revert back to her normal, boring self as soon as she looked in the mirror at home. The woman who stood in the centre of the bedroom was totally different from the woman who'd left that morning. A deep, slow smile spread across Aisling's face. She took her lipstick out of her handbag and quickly applied some. But the colour which had looked fine with her mousey long hair looked pale and uninteresting on the blonde Aisling.

She rummaged around in the dressing-table drawer until she found what she was looking for – a rich pink lipstick she'd bought ages ago and never worn. It went perfectly with the pink short-sleeved cardigan she wore with her jeans, jeans she needed to belt at the waist.

It was after two when Phillip roared down from his bedroom, 'Dad's here, Dad's here!'

Aisling put down the knife she'd been using to peel the potatoes and quickly washed her hands. OK, Michael, get ready to meet the new, improved Aisling Moran.

She fixed a smile on her lips and opened the door slowly, her heart thumping madly. He was standing a few feet away from the front door, obviously expecting the boys to run out to the car the way they usually did. Dressed in dark grey cords and his ancient marl grey Nike T-shirt, Michael looked tired and drawn. She'd have sworn that there were more grey hairs around his temples than there had been the last time she'd seen him.

'Hello, Michael,' she said coolly. 'The boys will be down in a minute. We had a late lunch and they haven't got their stuff ready.'

Ignoring the look of astonishment in his eyes, she turned

333

and yelled up the stairs. 'Come on boys, get a move on.'

When she turned back to Michael, he was studying her as if they'd only just met. His gaze came back to rest on her face and the look in his eyes was one of admiration.

'You look fantastic, Aisling,' he said slowly. 'Your hair is different, it's great.'

'Thanks,' she murmured casually, as though she didn't give a damn what he thought of her. She flicked back a tendril of ash blonde hair off her face, enjoying his discomfiture. Just because you left me, doesn't mean I turned into a one-woman disaster area, she thought.

'How are things? You're coping all right with the money I'm paying into your account?' he asked awkwardly.

Despite their earlier fight about money, he'd been generous with his maintenance payments. She was doing fine financially, what with his money and her wages, but Aisling was still nervous of splashing out on anything. The thought of the first few days when she'd found damn-all money in their joint account was still too fresh in her mind.

'Fine, we're doing great.'

'Good. How's the job?'

'Fine.'

They stood in silence for a moment. Michael seemed to be searching for something to say. Under normal circumstances, Aisling, who couldn't bear awkward silences, would have said something inane just to keep the conversation going. Today she was master of the situation. She said nothing.

'What are you up to tonight?' he asked finally. 'Any plans?'

Wow, she thought triumphantly, I *must* look good. A few months ago, Aisling wouldn't have had any plans for a Saturday night and he knew it. Now, she obviously looked good enough to merit an inquiry about her social life.

'Going to a party,' she said.

'Really. Who's having the party? Anyone I know?'

'No.' She was cool and calm on the outside, but on the inside she was laughing to her heart's content. He wanted to know where she was going, who she was going with and how the hell she was looking this good. But he wouldn't say a word. He didn't want to let on that he was consumed with curiosity about the newly blonde Aisling Moran.

After a full two minutes' silence, she mentally chalked up a point to herself. I bet you're burning up with curiosity, Michael. Hah!

'You look tired,' she commented. 'Lots of late nights?' Score two to Aisling.

'You know what it's like in the *News*,' he said wearily. 'To make up for the Saturdays I take off to see the boys, I'm working on Mondays now and end up working very late on Friday.'

'Dad!' roared Phillip, appearing beside his mother with a bulging hold-all. God only knew what he'd packed. Both twins were magpies who loved collecting junk and loved having it with them at all times, something they'd inherited from Aisling. Her handbags routinely had to be repaired when the handles broke or the stitching came undone from all the bits and pieces she carried around with her.

She gave Paul a hug before doing the same to his brother.

'Be good and take care, darlings.' She stood back in the doorway, making it crystal-clear that the conversation with Michael was over. Her smile was frosty.

'Bye. See you tomorrow,' she said.

'Yeah, bye.' Michael looked at her blankly for a moment, as if he wanted to say something but decided not to. Then he turned and walked to the car. She watched for a moment, waved goodbye to the boys and shut the front door. Her euphoria vanished instantly. It had been wonderful to give Michael a shock, wonderful to see him re-evaluating her. It had been a short-lived feeling. Without the boys the house felt empty. And so did she.

There was no point staying home and moping, she told herself firmly as she grabbed her handbag, her shopping list and her car keys. Get out of the house or you'll go mad. Show off your new look.

She dawdled around the Stillorgan shopping centre for over

335

an hour, browsing in the bookshop and running her hands along rails of clothes in A-Wear.

She picked up a couple of things and tried them on, but even the thrill of fitting comfortably into a size twelve didn't cheer her up. She'd felt great earlier. Why had meeting Michael for the first time in weeks plunged her into such despair? Was it because seeing him brought all the pain back, pain that she'd pushed to the back of her mind when she was working or with the twins? Or was it that she missed him? Damn Michael anyway.

In Quinnsworth, she shopped slowly, meandering between the aisles and picking up the ingredients for the pesto tagliatelle that Jo loved. She was coming to dinner on Sunday and Aisling wanted it to be a special night.

On the phone a few days earlier, Jo had sounded very miserable but couldn't talk properly because she was working late in the office and wasn't alone. The poor thing. She was obviously finding it hard coping with pregnancy on her own.

Aisling threw several packets of pasta into her trolley. The boys loved spaghetti and never tired of sucking individual strands of pasta into their mouths and seeing who could suck fastest.

Michael loved ravioli because his Italian grandmother had made 'the most delicious ravioli in the world'. Despite all her culinary skills, Aisling had never been able to match his granny's recipe. There'd been no pleasing him, had there? Why had she even tried? Why was she thinking about him, in fact? He was gone. There was no point crying over Michael. He had his own life and she had to get on with hers. Tonight was a good time to start. She'd get dressed early and go over to help Fiona with the party preparations. Then she'd chat up all the eligible men Fiona had promised to invite. Ciao, Michael. Hello new life.

'So, you work with Pat. Are you a lawyer?' Gary eased himself into the armchair beside Aisling and gave her the benefit of a gleaming white smile. He was tall, fair and quite overweight, dwarfing the armchair with his bulk.

For someone who'd only been introduced to her a minute ago, Gary was staring at her in a very familiar manner. His eyes were travelling over her body slowly and carefully as if he were a surveyor looking for dry rot.

'No,' she said loudly, to get his attention away from her chest. She loved wearing the slinky black lace top but it was very revealing and Gary was the second man to be transfixed by her boobs. What was more, he was wearing a wedding ring, although his wife had been nowhere in sight when Pat introduced him. This was her first party as a separated woman and she was very nervous about the whole thing. After twelve years married to one man, her socialising-with-men skills were, as she'd said to Fiona, nil.

'I'm a secretary at the firm,' Aisling said. 'I work for Anthony Green.'

'Really,' muttered Gary, his mind elsewhere.

'What branch of law do you specialise in?' she asked pointedly. 'Divorce?'

He sat up like a shot. 'Er, no. Conveyancing.'

God, she couldn't believe she had the misfortune to meet *another* leering conveyancing lawyer. She'd thought Leo was the only one, a freak of the legal system. She tried out a frosty stare on Gary. It had worked on Michael earlier.

Gary got the message. 'Excuse me,' he said. 'I must talk to my wife for a moment. I'll talk to you later.'

Not if I have anything to do with it, Aisling decided, abandoning her chair quickly and heading for the dining room.

It was nearly nine-thirty and most of the guests had arrived, mainly couples with a bottle of wine in hand. She'd spotted only two men arriving without female partners, one a very handsome Scandinavian type in his late thirties and the other slightly older, dark-haired and equally good-looking.

Arriving together, they'd brought champagne and a huge, feathery fern for Fiona who would, as Aisling knew, immediately kill it. The men hugged Fiona, shook hands with Pat and went into the dining room to get a drink. As Maria would have said, you wouldn't kick either of them out of bed for eating crisps. But the more Aisling watched them surreptitiously, the more she became convinced that they were a couple. She drained her glass of red wine and found Fiona holding court beside the bar, with four men around her.

'Typical, Finucane,' she whispered in Fiona's ears. 'The only blokes I'm interested in are gay and the only ones who are interested in me are lecherous or married!'

'The dilemma of the modern single woman,' Fiona whispered back. 'I did notice Gary move in on you. I decided not to rescue you because I knew he was *just* your type. Actually, his wife has known Pat since college which is why he's here, otherwise I wouldn't have him in the house. He's a pig.'

'You can say that again,' Aisling remarked. 'I don't think he actually looked at my *face* once during our entire conversation.'

'That's what happens when you flaunt yourself, you trollop,' Fiona said deadpan. 'Seriously, you'll love Anders and Peter. I'll introduce them to you. Anders is from Sweden, as if you couldn't tell, and they're both brilliant fun. But don't worry,' she added with a grin. 'I promise you, there are some lovely men coming later who aren't gay, married or devoted to their mothers. Now, have another drink.'

For the next hour, Aisling had a whale of a time. Fiona's clique of men friends were delighted to talk to the attractive blonde in the sexy outfit, while Aisling enjoyed a little flirtation, knowing that Fiona was there to bail her out if anything got too serious.

'If I wasn't married, I'd definitely chance my arm there,' one man said to Fiona.

'Giles, if you weren't married, you wouldn't be interested in her,' Fiona pointed out reasonably. 'You'd be running after some mysterious married woman. It's all the thrill of the forbidden, you know.'

Fiona dips, crudités and small bowls of black and green stuffed olives were going down a treat. Aisling had eaten far too much and was sitting on the corner of the settee talking to Fiona's sister-in-law, Sandra, when Fiona tapped her on the arm.

'Sorry to interrupt, Sandra, but I've got this divine man I want Aisling to meet.'

'Goody,' said Aisling getting to her feet. She felt very confident and quite tipsy thanks to five glasses of Australian red. She followed Fiona into the kitchen where a man in an open-necked denim shirt and chinos was sprawled on a kitchen chair laughing and joking with Pat. He looked up as she walked in and her first impression was that he had the same olive skin as Michael, but there the resemblance ended.

He had the most incredible bright blue eyes, a wide, mobile mouth which was curved into a grin and chestnut hair worn down to his shirt collar.

'Sam Delaney, meet Aisling Moran,' said Fiona.

Sam jumped to his feet and held out one hand.

'Delighted to meet you, Aisling. I've heard all about you and now I want to hear your side.'

Everyone laughed, especially Pat, who was well on his way to being plastered.

'Nice to meet you too,' said Aisling. She took his hand and looked down, seeing strong tanned wrists feathered with coppery hairs. Was she imagining it or had he held her hand for longer than was strictly necessary?

She looked into his face and smiled a five-glasses-of-red-wine smile.

'Are you gay, married or devoted to your mother?' she asked.

Fiona snorted into her gin sling.

'No,' breathed Sam, leaning forward so that his face was only a few inches away from hers. 'I'm available.'

'Me too,' said Aisling with a large grin.

'Sit down,' said Sam, pulling up a chair for her and positioning it close to his. Aisling sank onto the chair, put her empty glass on the table and turned to look at Sam. He was watching her, the blue eyes taking in every movement. Unlike

339

the lecherous Gary, Sam's eyes didn't linger too long on the curves revealed by her lacy outfit. But he looked long enough to tell Aisling he was interested. Very interested.

Stone-cold sober, she knew she'd have been nervous at the thought of chatting up such a handsome man. But the combination of wine, her new image and the compliments from Fiona's male friends made her feel ready for anything. As Sam filled her glass from a full bottle of red wine, her normal inhibitions drained away. She felt attractive, flirtatious and reckless.

'How come I've never met you before, Sam?' she said, savouring the sound of his name on her tongue. Sam. What a sexy name.

'I could say the same about you,' he answered.

'Sam's been abroad for five years,' interrupted Pat from the other side of the table. 'Working in Texas.'

'Texas. Wow. That must have been interesting,' Aisling said. She put her elbow on the table and propped her head up with one hand, letting silky strands of blonde hair hang between her fingers. She'd seen Jo do it and it had looked very provocative. 'What do you do?'

'I'm in computer software. I was in Texas for four years working for one company and in Louisiana for another two years,' Sam explained.

'That's six years,' said Pat, sounding surprised. 'I thought it was five.'

'I think we better mingle with our guests,' said Fiona firmly. She dragged Pat off with her, leaving Aisling and Sam alone in the kitchen. Their eyes met and they both broke out laughing at the same time.

'I get the idea that Fiona is doing her best to fix us up with each other,' Sam said.

Aisling flushed and took a deep slug of wine.

'I know. Sorry,' she said quickly. 'I'm sure it's a real pain in the ass having women thrown at you every time you come back to Ireland for a holiday.'

'I didn't mean it like that, Aisling,' Sam said softly. She liked

the way he said her name. 'I'm delighted they left us alone.
I'm enjoying myself. And,' he added, picking up his glass and
holding it towards hers, 'I'm not on holiday. I'm home for
good.'

They clinked glasses companionably.

'Tell me about Texas,' Aisling said. 'I've never even been to
America and Texas sounds so exotic, so *Dallas*!'

'It's not really like *Dallas*,' said Sam with a chuckle. 'It used
to be, or so they tell me. Houston, where I worked, is a very
cosmopolitan city, all mirror-windowed skyscrapers and Cadillacs. But the oil boom was over in the early Eighties and the
whole city suffered. So there aren't as many millionaires as
there used to be. None like J. R., anyway.'

'Damn,' said Aisling. 'You mean there isn't a Cattle Baron's
Ball after all?'

'There probably is. There are certainly enough people
wearing Stetsons and cowboy boots, but you don't see many
suede fringed jackets. It's too hot.'

'Really?' she asked.

'Oh, it's unbelievable. In the summer, you can't drive with
your windows open. You just keep the air-conditioning on the
whole time,' Sam said. 'Putting your arm out the window of
the car when you're on the freeway is like being hit with a
blast from a hot-air dryer.'

'Have some dips,' announced Fiona as she swept into the
kitchen with a tray of empty glasses. She took a bowl of
taramasalata and a large plate of cut vegetables out of the
fridge and left them in front of Sam. 'Are you having fun?' she
whispered into Aisling's ear.

Sam's mouth curved into a knowing grin as he looked
Aisling in the eye.

'Loads of fun,' she replied, never taking her eyes off his
face.

'Maybe we should just have sex on the table and then
they'd all be happy,' suggested Sam with a glint in his eye
when Fiona left with a tray of dips for the rest of the guests.

'I don't know,' replied Aisling, as though she were thinking

341

seriously about the idea. 'Maybe we should know a little about each other before that, what do you think? Sex on the first date is one thing, but I always find that sex within the first ten minutes is pushing it!' He laughed uproariously. Aisling couldn't believe she'd just said that.

What the hell, she didn't have to play Michael Moran's quiet little wifey any more.

They scraped the bowl clean as they sat at Fiona's spotless kitchen table and talked. Aisling found out that Sam was originally from Cork where his parents still had a small dairy farm near Clonakilty. He'd lived in Dublin for seven years before moving to Texas.

'The money was incredible,' he explained, 'even if the change of climate nearly killed me. I thought I'd feel at home somewhere like Texas because I had this idea that it was a rural sort of place, like home. Unfortunately, in Houston, the nearest you got to cows was in a steak house. For the first six months, I didn't see much apart from the office.'

'But you must have seen lots after that,' Aisling said.

'Yeah, I did. I loved Galveston, that was my favourite place. It's this old Victorian town on the Gulf Coast, all pretty wooden houses and ornate Victorian mansions. And miles and miles of sand covered with this sea grass you can't pick because it's the only thing holding the sand together and keeping the ocean out!'

'It must be wonderful to have travelled so much.' Aisling picked up the last bit of carrot off the plate.

'It was.' Sam sat back in his chair, his mind suddenly elsewhere. On whoever he left behind, Aisling thought to herself. Why else would a successful man leave the States to come home? He must have been married. He had to be forty or near it and he was charming, funny and good-looking. No way a man like Sam would have remained single for long.

God, how did I ever think I was the only person in the world to have their marriage break up? she wondered. That was just my self-obsession and self-pity.

It's happening all the time. Is there anyone out there who

342

doesn't carry the remains of their past around with them, memories of happier times, different times?

'You look like you're lost in time,' she said softly.

He smiled apologetically. 'Sorry. You're right. I was a bit.'

'You know, if I'd met you six years ago, we wouldn't be having this conversation in the kitchen,' she said. 'I'd have been in there with my husband and I'd never have flirted with you.'

'I know. Fiona told me you were separated. He must be mad.'

'So must she.'

He grimaced and drained his wine glass. 'That obvious, huh?'

Aisling pretended to consider it. 'Maybe not to most people, but let's just say, I'm sensitive to that sort of thing now. I find myself looking at people in the supermarket, staring at their ring fingers and working out if they're married, separated, whatever. It's my little game.'

'You still wear your wedding ring,' Sam said, almost accusingly.

She looked down at her left hand, at the sapphire surrounded by tiny diamonds and the slim wedding band she still wore. She was so used to wearing them that she couldn't imagine taking them off. But why, she thought? Michael was gone. He was living with somebody else and he wasn't coming back. So why was she still wearing his rings?

For a moment, she was back in McDowell's on the day he'd bought her engagement ring. Thirteen years ago.

'The sapphire ring suits you best,' Michael said, leaning on the glass-fronted case with her fingers held tenderly in his hand.

'I like the diamond solitaire,' she answered. 'I've always dreamed of having a diamond ring.'

'The sapphire one has little diamonds around it,' Michael pointed out, sensible as ever. In the end, he'd won. He bought her the sapphire ring and promised her a ring with a solitaire – sometime. He'd never bought it.

Aisling looked at Sam and shrugged. 'You're right,' she said, looking into his eyes, wondering how anyone could have eyes so blue. 'I don't know why I still wear them.'

She straightened out her fingers and slid the rings off. With all the weight she'd lost, they came off easily. She left them on the table beside her wine glass. Twelve years of marriage down the Swannee.

'We'll have to celebrate,' Sam said gently, moving his chair right beside hers. He put one hand around her neck and pulled her face closer to his, so close that she could feel his breath on her skin. Then his lips met hers, softly touching hers.

For a moment, Aisling panicked. This was happening so fast. Then she felt Sam's arms reach around her waist, gently holding her to him. She relaxed and let herself go, feeling her mouth open under his. He tasted sweet and faintly bitter, the wine on his breath mingling with something else. Her skin felt warm where he was holding her.

Nobody had held her like this for so long. She'd spent so many nights alone in the big bed, only Flossie or her books for company. Now, she was in a man's arms, a man who wanted her.

Suddenly, she wanted to go to bed with him. Now. This instant. Shocked, she wondered if she'd lost her mind, but no. She hadn't. She simply wanted him, hungered for him, as she used to hunger for jam doughnuts or ice cream. She didn't care if she never saw another doughnut ever again, all she wanted was Sam.

'Aisling,' he murmured into her hair, his lips brushing against her neck and her ear. 'I shouldn't have done that, but I couldn't help myself.'

She arched her neck back, leaving her skin exposed for him. He was a quick learner. 'I'm glad you did,' she said softly, as he moved along her neck to the soft hollow at the base of her throat.

'Oh!'

Aisling would have recognised Fiona's voice anywhere. She

344

made a sort of strangulated squeak and turned on her heel.

Aisling and Sam started laughing at exactly the same moment. She clutched Sam's head against her neck and roared.

'We've been caught,' she said between laughs.

'I feel like I'm fifteen again and my mother has just caught me groping my girlfriend in the dairy.' Sam could barely talk he was laughing so much. 'I don't think I enjoyed that so much.'

He moved up until they were face to face. He held her face cradled in his hands and kissed her again, gently on the lips.

'I never thought I'd be found snogging in the kitchen at a party at my age, but that was wonderful,' he said. 'I hope you don't regret this tomorrow, Aisling. I'd like to see you again.'

'I'd love that.' It was true. But Fiona's interruption had brought her to her senses.

A flirtation and a kiss in the kitchen was one thing. Going off with a man she'd just met for wild passionate sex was another.

It would be wild and passionate sex, she knew that for sure. The way he kissed sent ripples of excitement down her spine.

Aisling gently stroked Sam's cheek and smiled at him.

'I better go. It's late.'

It was nearly twelve and the baby-sitter said she didn't want to stay the night. Aisling got up from her chair. Sam jumped up instantly.

'Will you let me walk you home?'

'Of course. But I don't want the neighbours to think I'm a scarlet woman, so we better be discreet,' Aisling said quickly. She had a sudden vision of all the guests from the party craning their heads out of Fiona's upstairs windows for a better view of Sam kissing her passionately at her hall door. Or worse, the boys seeing her kissing Sam passionately.

'Damn, you've ruined my whole plan.' Sam put his arms around her waist and grinned. He wasn't as tall as Michael, she thought suddenly. Stop it, Aisling, she said silently. She didn't want to think of Michael. She kissed Sam again. He tasted just as good this time round.

'I'll just get my handbag,' she said. She hurried up to Fiona's spare room where she'd left her things.

Fiona caught her rushing down the stairs.

'Are you going?' Fiona was doing her best to conceal a smirk but she couldn't quite manage it. 'Both of you?' she asked meaningfully.

'Sam is walking me home,' Aisling said. 'Walking. That's all. So don't focus the telescope on my house!'

'I'm so pleased you like him, he's a dear man.' Fiona gave her a big hug. 'Phone me tomorrow and tell me *everything*, right?'

'I promise.'

CHAPTER SIXTEEN

Jo sat on a stool in the small dressing room and watched Frederick paint one last coat of ruby-red lipstick on the model's perfect mouth. The girl sat perfectly still in the chair. Dark arched brows framed pale blue eyes edged by expertly applied eyeliner, giving her an exotic, faintly Egyptian look.

'We want vampish make-up, dark, smoky eyes and dark lips,' Jo had explained to Frederick on the phone the previous week. 'I'm calling it the Christmas Glamour Look and I've got three long dark evening dresses, one black velvet tuxedo and a sequinned minidress for the shoot. The make-up has to be dramatic.'

Frederick was doing his best to be very dramatic, although the heavy make-up required for the camera looked out of place in a draughty photographic studio on a cool Monday morning in September.

Exhausted after a restless night, Jo didn't feel up to organising the shoot for the December issue. It was two months to the Christmas production day, but that edition traditionally carried lots of fashion pages and Jo knew that Ralph, the photographer *Style* used, had a catalogue shoot lined up for half of October and was going on holiday to Jamaica in November. That left September for everything – the skiing clothes shoot, the knitwear shoot, the working woman's suit shoot and the lingerie-to-get-your-man-to-buy-you-for-Christmas shoot.

She had to organise all those over the next two weeks, which would mean lots of dashing around the shops searching for the right accessories and perfect shoes. At least she'd got absolutely everything she needed today.

Several elegant dresses hung from the rail in the small

dressing room, ready for the two models to transform themselves into glamour queens. Boxes containing high-heeled suede and satin sandals were lined up on the floor, while packets of tights lay on the cupboard top alongside the simple silver earrings Jo had picked for the shoot.

Frederick's huge bag of tricks were spread out on the counter top, palettes of every colour under the sun, eye pencils, brushes, jars of foundation and cotton buds jostling for space beside the hairdresser's heated rollers, cans of hairspray, pins and brushes.

Outside the door, Ralph yelled instructions around the large, high-ceilinged studio. It was nearly eleven on Monday morning and they had to be finished by half two because Ralph was photographing a group for a business magazine at three. It didn't leave them much time for the *Style* shoot and as the other model was late, they were definitely in trouble.

The photographer's favourite Eric Clapton CD was belting out of the sound system and Jo could feel the stirrings of a thumping headache. This was shaping up to be a disastrous day. It had been a pretty bad weekend, as she'd waited for Mark to ring so she could explain exactly what had happened at the office.

She'd gone over it in her head many times, telling him how she'd really tried to get on well with Emma. How she'd worked with the younger woman to make her part of the *Style* team. How Emma had thrown it all back in her face in a fit of spite. But Mark hadn't phoned.

By Sunday night, Jo had convinced herself that he'd heard Emma's side of the story and had made up his mind not to ring her at all. She felt utterly miserable. The only bright spark on the horizon was the thought of her cottage, which Mark's contractor friend had told her was structurally sound even though it needed some work.

'Finished,' announced Frederick. He stood back and admired his handiwork. The model, Carol, unfurled her long, impossibly slender body, stood up and reached into her denim shirt pocket for her cigarettes.

'Don't worry, I'll smoke outside,' she said, patting Jo on the shoulder. The model pulled on a tatty leather bomber jacket over her jeans, careful not to dislodge the heated rollers in her dark hair and left the room, lighting up as she went.

'We're nearly ready,' shouted Ralph from the studio. 'Where the hell is Stephanie?'

'Here,' came another voice, as a tall blonde girl dressed in grey sweatpants and parka hurried into the dressing room, hair flying. 'Sorry I'm late,' she said to Jo. 'I got stuck in traffic.'

'Steph, your hair!' shrieked Alan, the hairdresser, pushing into the dressing room with a tray and four mugs of tea. Stephanie's high-cheekboned face was stunning even devoid of make-up, but her hair was definitely greasy at the roots. 'I won't have time to wash it now. It'll have to be sleeked-back hair,' Alan muttered to Jo.

'Fine.' Jo was tired, cross and ready to belt Steph's beautiful head. She didn't care what Alan did to the model's bloody hair. Damn Mark. Damn, damn, damn.

Thirty-five minutes later, Steph and Carol reclined gracefully on a leopardskin chaise-longue, looking as if they had been born in floor-length satin. With their hair beautifully styled, flawless make-up on their faces and perfect size-ten bodies encased in sleek designer clothes, they appeared a million miles away from the two casually dressed young women who'd rushed into the studio earlier.

Jo had been involved in the fashion business for years, yet she never ceased to be amazed at how a team of experts, with the right tools and lighting, could turn a pretty woman into a spectacular one.

Nobody looking at the finished photos would ever be able to tell that Carol had a spot on her chin and dark circles under her eyes or that Stephanie's hair had been slicked back into a knot because the hairdresser hadn't the time to wash it.

'Turn your head a little to the left, Carol,' ordered Ralph, squinting at the models through his viewfinder. 'A little more, that's good. Alan, fix her hair, there's a bit sticking out.'

349

Jo tried to relax while Ralph was shooting. She sat down in the leather armchair he often used as a prop, put her feet up on the arms and poked around in a pot of strawberry yogurt with a little plastic spoon. Frederick was up and down from his seat like a jack-in-the-box, powdering away the shiny faces brought on by strong lights.

'We'll never be out in time,' Frederick grumbled, sinking back into his chair after the tenth powdering break. 'I'll kill Stephanie if we aren't. I'm due somewhere at half three.'

'And I'm due in four months if I don't have a nervous breakdown first,' Jo answered glumly.

'It's not that bad, pet, is it?' asked Frederick in concern. 'You look wonderful and I thought everything was going so well. It's not Richard, is it? That pig, I don't know why you stuck with him for so long, he wasn't worth it.'

Ralph bellowed and Frederick leaped up with his powder puff at the ready.

Richard? thought Jo. She couldn't give a damn about Richard. He'd dumped another pregnant girlfriend before her and she'd lost every ounce of respect or love for him. He'd only phoned once in the past few months – a faltering message left on her answering machine.

'It's me, er . . . Richard. You're not here and I'll,' he paused, 'ring you some other time. Hope you're all right,' he added awkwardly.

Hope you're all right? Snarled Jo when she got home. What sort of a greeting was that to the mother of your child? she wanted to know. His lack of interest only hardened her heart even more against him.

When she went to the hospital on her own for her check-ups and sat, tears flowing down her face as she looked at the ultrasound picture of the baby, Jo felt immeasurably sad that she had no one to share the experience with. But she never regretted the fact that Richard wasn't with her. She couldn't imagine anyone worse as a father or would-be father. She and the baby were better without him. Now, when she thought about him at all, it was with a mixture of irritation and disgust. Irritation at his childishness and immaturity, and disgust that she'd been so stupid not to see through his lies and recognise him for the coward he truly was.

'Do you want another cup of tea?' Frederick asked kindly, perching on the edge of the armchair. Seeing Jo's look of misery, he took her hand. 'He's not worth it, pet,' he said, misinterpreting her sad face.

'Forget Richard, for your own sake. I didn't mean to tell you this,' he hesitated, 'but you better know.'

Jo sat up straighter. What news of Richard did Frederick have?

'I've seen him out with that Freeman girl, the tarty one with the little red Mazda and the vacuum in her skull,' Frederick continued.

Jo knew exactly who he was talking about. Rachel Freeman, a twentysomething model who'd materialised beside Richard at several parties, smiling at him coyly and completely ignoring the fact that Jo was holding his hand.

'She's just a kid,' he'd said to Jo, adding that he preferred mature, beautiful women to silly youngsters. His words had rung true at the time and she had believed him, foolishly, as it now turned out.

Had Richard been having a fling with the gormless Rachel all along? Had the last laugh been at *her* expense? Probably. She felt inexplicably tired all of a sudden.

'She was practically glued to him at the hip, all kissy-kissy and holding hands,' Frederick divulged, outrage popping out of him. 'You'd think they were Siamese twins. So just forget him, Jo. He doesn't deserve you.'

'Anyway,' he continued, with a smirk, 'I happen to know that one captain of industry is very smitten with you, so you won't be on your own for very long!'

Jo tried to smile but she couldn't manage it. If only you knew, Frederick, she thought. With my record for choosing men, I should start writing to a death row prisoner in America so I can fall in love with him.

'Phone,' yelled Ralph's assistant from the studio's dark-room. 'Call for Jo Ryan.'

351

'The Louisiana Penitentiary, no doubt, with a list of fanci-able prisoners,' she muttered, hoisting herself out of the seat.

'Jo,' said Rhona, sounding relieved. 'I thought nobody would ever answer the bloody phone.'

'That's because Ralph is attempting to blow all our ear-drums as well as his own with ten billion classic rock tracks. It's a miracle anybody answered at all. What's up?' she added, leaning against a counter top covered with contact sheets of tiny photos.

'Mark was looking for you,' replied Rhona in a softer voice. 'I can't really talk too loudly because my office door isn't shut, but he arrived this morning looking like a thunder-cloud.'

'So?'

'So, he'd got back late on Sunday and must have got an earful from dear sister Denise about her poor little Emmy Wemmy having a spot of bother at work.'

'Surprise, surprise,' said Jo sarcastically. 'Has he advertised my job yet?'

'No,' hissed Rhona, 'listen. He demanded a meeting with me and wanted to know everything that had gone on last week. I told him everything up straight and I said that it was virtually impossible to see how Emma had a future with the magazine since she's so incredibly hostile and unprofessional to my staff, *especially* my deputy editor.'

'Thank you, Rhona,' said Jo, suddenly tearful. The way she felt right now, she'd blub at the slightest hint of sympathy.

'Well, it's true,' stated Rhona. 'You're a fantastic deputy, a great fashion editor and a real pro. Not to mention a great friend. But our friendship isn't the point. The point is my editorial control – or the lack of it – when it comes to staff,' she added. 'I wanted Mark to know that we wouldn't take that kind of crap from any other junior and Emma has been trading on that fact. And I said that her personal attack on you was vitriolic in the extreme.'

'What did he say to that?' asked Jo quietly.

'He didn't say anything, actually, but the look on his face

was enough. I'd bet next month's salary on darling Emma getting an earful.'

'Well, what was the outcome? What did he say at the end?' Jo desperately wanted to know what Mark thought of her, whether he believed Emma's side of the story or Rhona's.

'He said he wanted a meeting with me at four and that he wanted to talk to you first.'

'Huh. To tell me poor Emma is his flesh and blood and that I can take a hike.' Jo knew she sounded bitter. 'I better go. We've still got three more outfits to go. We'll be lucky to be finished by half two.'

'Are you coming back to the office?' Rhona asked.

'I don't know,' Jo said sharply. 'I've got to get groceries and I have to buy some trousers because nothing fits me very well right now, so I probably won't come in today.' Or tomorrow. She didn't want to come in all week if it meant she could avoid Mark.

'Mark wanted to phone you after we talked, but I knew you were upset and I said I'd try and track you down,' Rhona explained. 'I didn't want you to fly off the handle with him. You should come in to the office after the shoot. He'll be here.'

'I might. Thanks for standing up for me, Rho,' Jo said. 'Bye.'

'Jo, don't go yet. You sound upset.'

Damnit, where had she hidden those bloody tissues? Jo looked wildly around the office, searching for a tissue in the midst of bits of paper, contact sheets, negatives and newspapers.

'I'm sorry, Rhona,' she muttered, wiping her eyes on the sleeve of her sweater. 'I have to go. Really.'

It was three by the time Jo finally left the studio, with Frederick walking beside her, arms full of plastic-wrapped dresses. He was bringing them back to the safety of the office because Jo had decided to go shopping and didn't want to leave hundreds of pounds' worth of borrowed clothes in the car at the supermarket.

'Brenda knows what has to go where,' she said, as she put two shoe boxes into Frederick's car. He stowed the dresses carefully on the back seat. 'I'm sorry to leave you with all this, I know you're in a rush.'

'Don't worry. I don't mind being a little bit late and you look as if you need a bit of time to yourself. Take care.' He reached out and threw his arms around Jo, giving her a warm hug. 'Listen to Uncle Frederick, go home and go to bed. Or read a trashy novel and eats lots of ice cream.'

Jo sniffed. 'I will. Thanks for being so good, Frederick.'

Mothercare was jammed. It took several trying-on sessions to find a pair of trousers she liked. She'd been hoping she wouldn't have to buy too many maternity clothes but it seemed that trousers were one thing you couldn't economise on.

She bought one black and one grey pair of trousers and three pairs of maternity tights. Worn with overshirts or jumpers, they ought to see her through the next few months.

Her answering machine's message light was winking at her when she got home. Had Mark phoned her? Rhona had left two messages asking her to ring the office. 'Mark wants to talk to you,' Rhona said the first time. Then, 'Please ring. He's driving me mad.'

'Let him phone, then,' said Jo crossly. Had his dialling finger seized up suddenly? Or wasn't he able to make a simple phone call unless his secretary did it for him? She unpacked the shopping and sank down onto the settee with the TV remote control.

When the phone finally rang at half seven, she was in the bath, relaxing in a cocoon of aromatherapy bubbles with a face mask on. Even if she'd wanted to answer it, she wouldn't have got out of the bath in time.

She sank back into the bubbles feeling cross.

She sat in the bath for another two minutes, then, consumed with curiosity to see who'd phoned, she got out and headed for the answering machine, wrapped up in a towel, rivulets of water dripping onto the carpet.

Mark's voice was formal. 'I'm going to a charity dinner in the Shelbourne at eight so call me back on the mobile before then.'

The barefaced cheek of him! Hell would freeze over before she'd bother phoning him. She pressed the delete button with venom and stormed back into the bathroom to remove the face mask.

After another restless night, Jo rang the office first thing.

'Annette, tell Rhona I'm not feeling well and I won't be in today,' she told the receptionist.

'Oh you poor dear, what's wrong?' asked Annette anxiously.

Hating herself for lying, Jo muttered that she was feeling very tired. 'I think I'll spend the day in bed,' she added. 'Tell Rhona not to bother ringing me unless it's urgent and then I'll have the answering machine on. I need some sleep.'

'Don't worry, Jo. I won't let anyone disturb you on pain of death.'

Does that apply to the boss? Jo wondered. Could she add 'pain and torture' to the prescription?

She spent a boring morning sorting out her wardrobe, Gareth O'Callaghan's mellifluous tones in the background. She tried on lots of things to see if they could accommodate her swelling belly, and was dismayed to see how few things actually did. I'll probably never get into any of this stuff again, she realised miserably, as she looked at all the beautiful slim-fitting outfits she couldn't even button up.

She loved that grey wool pinstripe. It would be awful not to be able to wear that ever again. And the black leather miniskirt. She'd bought it with one of her first freelance cheques and worn it almost to death for a year. It was in pretty good condition considering. She'd hate not to fit into it again.

Nibbling a Ryvita to keep the Hobnob pangs at bay, she stashed everything she couldn't wear in the left side of her wardrobe and arranged the rest on the right. The few items hanging in the wearable side of the wardrobe made her even more depressed.

The phone rang twice but the caller hung up abruptly when the answering machine answered. It must be her mother, Jo thought, she hated answering machines. When the doorbell rang loudly half an hour after the last hang-up, Jo peered out of her peephole. It was Mark.

Blast. She leaned up against the door, wondering whether he'd heard her stomping into the hall. He rang the bell again. Obviously he had.

She stood silently, hoping he'd go away. No such luck.

'Jo, it's Mark.'

Double blast.

'I was worried when you rang in sick today. Can I come in?'

She toyed with a whole range of answers. 'No.' 'No, you pig.' 'Not until Hell freezes over.'

'Jo. Please let me in. I know you're there.'

She wrenched the door open. 'Yes?' she said icily.

'Can I come in?' he asked, grey eyes serious as they stared down at her brown ones.

'Why do you want to come in? Can't you sack me in the office like normal despots? Or do you like the personal touch?'

'For God's sake, Jo,' he muttered, running a hand through his hair. 'Let me in, won't you?'

'Five minutes,' she announced. She stood back to let him enter. He walked in, looking strangely out of place in his navy pinstripe suit, blue shirt and yellow tie. His hair was rumpled and so was his face.

'You've got five minutes,' repeated Jo. 'I'm updating my CV, you understand, and I don't have any time to waste.'

Refusing to rise to the bait, Mark walked into the small sitting room and stared around for a moment before sitting down on the settee. He stretched long legs ahead of him and looked up at her. 'Sit down, Jo.'

'This is my house, smart ass,' she hissed. '*Don't* tell me when to sit down.'

'Sorry, sorry.'

She sat. The sheer *nerve* of him. Marching into her house and taking over.

356

'So?' Jo arranged her cotton jumper over her blue jogging pants to hide the ink stain on the front. She was angry and she hated being caught out wearing a dreadful outfit. And this – ancient white hand-knitted jumper with threads hanging out and threadbare jogging pants with no socks – was pretty dreadful. The carpet could have done with a good vacuum into the bargain and the weeping fig had wept a new batch of dead leaves onto the fireplace . . .

'I've come to apologise.'

Jo blinked.

'I should have rung you but I was in the car, I'd left your number in the office and,' Mark paused and tried to look her in the eye, but she avoided his gaze, 'I didn't think it was that important. At the time.'

'It wasn't important at all,' she replied coldly. 'Just your average day in the office when nepotism runs amok. There's nothing to apologise for.' Jo knew she was pushing it but she didn't care. For once she felt gloriously like flinging caution to the wind.

'I just can't work under those circumstances, that's all. I've worked in journalism for thirteen years and I've never been treated with the sort of disrespect Emma showed me. What's more,' she was beginning to enjoy this, 'I've certainly never treated anyone else that badly, either. It just isn't in my nature and it certainly isn't the way to win friends and influence people, or get the best out of them. But your niece is a law unto herself and quite frankly, I won't work with her any more.' She snorted. 'Anyway, you've made it quite plain what way your allegiance lies.'

'What way is that?' he asked calmly.

'*What way is that?*' she mimicked.

'Do you honestly want me to answer that?' Mark looked tired.

'No.' Jo was really angry now. 'I don't. You've already answered it by your silence. When I thought you'd want to talk to me to find out what had happened, you simply didn't bother ringing. When I thought you and I had a friendship, a . . .'

'A what?' he prompted.

She'd been on the verge of saying 'a relationship', and he knew it. Damn him, but he wasn't getting her to play his bloody games. She didn't want to be his amusement for the evening.

'A *nothing*,' she said angrily. 'We have nothing, I can see that now. And I can see I can't work for you any more.'

'Don't be rash,' snapped Mark.

'Don't tell me what not to be!' she shrieked. 'You're just like all bloody men, telling me what not to be. Just get out! Get out of here and stick your bloody job where the sun doesn't fucking shine!'

He stood up slowly and sighed. 'Jo, I'm sorry. I came here to apologise, I wanted to explain what had happened.'

'I don't want your apologies,' she said, feeling her eyes smart. God, she didn't want to cry in front of him. What sort of whinging idiot had she turned into, always crying at the drop of a hat? 'Just go.'

'Please, Jo. Listen to me.'

'Just go.'

He said nothing, but he didn't move either.

Jo poked around in her sleeve looking for a tissue. Why wasn't he going? Was she going to have to throw him out?

'Jo, just let me say one thing, all right?' His eyes were alight with something she couldn't identify. It was probably amusement, she thought, since it felt as if the rest of the world's male population were laughing at her for her naïvety and sheer stupidity. Jo Ryan falls for another man's lies, *again*. Ha bloody ha.

'I'm sorry I didn't ring you over the weekend, but believe me, I didn't take Emma's explanation at face value,' Mark said in a low voice. 'And I'm sorry if I sounded angry with you when I rang you from London about it, but it had been a very bad day. Emma's latest crisis was all I needed and I thought you'd be able to handle her until I got back.' He leaned against the back of an armchair tiredly and folded his arms. 'I trust your judgement, Jo, that's why I wanted you to sort things out. Please believe me.'

Jo stared at him fiercely, determined not to be swayed by any trumped-up explanation.

'The problem was that I had no idea what Emma had actually said and done until Rhona told me and since I've heard, I've been trying to get hold of you to apologise for her behaviour. Please understand,' he said, looking at her intently. 'I wouldn't hurt you for the world.'

He stood up and fished his car keys out of his trouser pocket. 'I'm going to go now because I've upset you. And let's just forget about where I can stick the deputy editorship.'

Jo flushed.

'Take as much time off as you need, Jo. Bye.'

He went, leaving behind him a scent of cologne, the same one she'd smelled when they sat together on the plane, when they'd gone out to dinner, when he'd brought her looking at the house in Redwood Lane.

She stared at the door for a moment, feeling the anger subside as rapidly as it had erupted. In the kitchen, she got a glass of water and drank it quickly, her hand shaking.

Hell, what had she said, what had she done? Jo felt her face flame when she thought about it. She told *the boss* that he could 'stick his job'. Oh God. At least he hadn't accepted her resignation.

How would she ever face him again? How could she sit in at the editorial meetings and have him look at her with those grave, sad eyes as if she'd hurt him deeply? And she must have. He'd been trying to say the right thing and she'd flown off the handle and ruined it all. As usual. It wasn't Mark's fault that she was utterly at sea emotionally. That was Richard's fault. Richard and the pregnancy which was responsible for mood swings like tidal waves.

And Mark wasn't just the boss, anyway. He was more than that, much more, if she admitted it to herself.

She had a sudden impulse to phone him on his mobile. She had the number, although she'd never used it before. If she rang and apologised now, maybe he'd come back and she could say she was sorry properly.

Tell him that she simply felt alone and miserable at the thought of having the baby on her own and that he'd arrived when she was at her lowest. Then she thought again.

Face facts, she told herself. Mark is your boss, not your lover. Phoning him would look stupid, desperate even. You've messed everything up. Think about what you're going to do now.

When she'd made a cup of sweet tea and taken the last couple of chocolate digestives from the packet, she phoned Rhona. Rhona would know what to do. Or, at the very worst, she'd know what sort of hat Jo could wear into the office for the rest of her life so she wouldn't have to either look at Mark Denton or let him see her face puce with embarrassment.

'Rho, you won't believe what I've done.'

'I can't imagine, Jo,' Rhona replied. Jo could hear her take a deep drag of a cigarette. 'But you don't sound the best. Are you feeling OK?'

'Apart from a hollow feeling in the pit of my stomach, I'm fine,' Jo explained. 'Mark's just been to see me,' she added, more slowly.

'Why do I get the feeling that all did not go well on this visit?' Rhona inquired.

'Because you're psychic?'

'Nope. It's probably because I can always tell when you're gearing for a complete blow-out,' Rhona said. 'You do get to know people when you've worked with them for three years. So what happened? Is he still breathing?'

'Oh Rho.' Jo sat on the edge of the settee with the phone balanced on her knees. 'I've known myself for thirty-four years and even *I* wouldn't have predicted this one. I've been such a fool. Within the space of about five minutes I managed to insult Mark, tell him where to stick his job, *and*,' she grimaced at the thought of it, 'I nearly said that I thought we had a "relationship" before he messed it all up. I didn't say it but he knew I was going to. You've no idea how I feel,' wailed Jo. 'What is it about me that I can't be normal where men are concerned?'

'It's impossible to be normal when men are involved because they're impossible,' Rhona replied. 'They give the phrase "mission impossible" a whole new dimension. Now look, Jo, this is hardly the end of the world. You're just overwrought. I'm sure Mark knows that.'

'Oh, so he thinks I'm hysterical and that's supposed to be good?'

'It's better than him thinking you meant it about sticking his job. He didn't accept, did he?' Rhona said knowingly. 'Course he didn't. You know he likes you. What am I saying *likes* you, he fancies you like *mad*. He's just unfortunate to have been caught in the crossfire of pregnancy hormones.'

'Do you think he'll understand?' Jo finished the second biscuit and licked the crumbs off her fingers.

'Honestly, Jo, for a woman who *looks* as if she should have the entire male population slavering at her feet, you really haven't a clue about men, have you?'

Not waiting for an answer, Rhona ploughed on. 'It's obvious to me that Mark is crazy about you. But because he's trying to tread carefully, and because you're hopeless at reading the situation, you're making a complete mess of the whole thing.'

'Do you think so?' Jo said doubtfully. It all sounded so much more reasonable when Rhona said it.

'Yes. Now listen to your auntie Rhona – or Madame Rhona the psychic as I want to be known in future – and go off and have a nice swim, or something energetic like that. Then go home, relax and come in here tomorrow morning as if nothing ever happened. OK?'

'OK. What about Emma? I simply couldn't face her tomorrow.'

'You won't have to. I've suspended her. Actually, I've never suspended anyone before,' the other woman said thoughtfully, 'so I had to make it up as I went along. It went pretty well, though.'

'What did you say?' demanded Jo, dying to know every gory detail.

'Well, remember that time we were at the Prêt A Porter

première party in the Chocolate Bar and that drunk pulled me onto his lap and tried to stick his hand down my Ben De Lisi shirt?' Even in times of crisis, Rhona was exact about clothes.

'Oh my God yes, I'll never forget it! I didn't think you knew how to be so vicious.'

'I was worse than that with Emma,' Rhona said. 'That girl will think twice – actually, she'll think three or four times – before ever speaking to anyone in *Style* like that ever again. I pointed out that word quickly gets around about someone who's trouble to work with. It's one thing to be pig-ignorant and rude if you've made it, if you're a damn good journalist or whatever.'

She took another drag of her cigarette. 'But if you're trouble and you're only a junior with no evidence of any talent whatsoever, forget about a career in journalism, I said. There are thousands of freelances out there just waiting to step into your shoes, Emma, so wake up and smell the coffee.'

'I'm impressed.'

'So was I,' Rhona said smugly. 'I gave Ted a brief version of it at home afterwards and he was shocked, I can tell you. He says he's going to disown me when the kids get into trouble at school and I have to go down to give the headmistress a piece of my mind. He couldn't face the carnage, he said.'

Jo suddenly realised she was laughing and that the knot of tension in her belly was loosening.

'Thanks, Rhona, you're great at getting people to forget their problems. Can I stay in your house until I have the baby so you can stop me going berserk every second day?'

'With three under-tens running around constantly, you'd really go mad, I can tell you,' Rhona replied.

'You're right.' Jo managed a weak laugh. 'If I take lots of deep breaths tomorrow morning, I think I'll be able to face the office. Mark's not due in, is he?'

'Nope. Anyway, he's not going to bite you.'

'No, but I may pass out with embarrassment when I see him,' Jo pointed out.

'No you won't.' Rhona's voice was firm. 'Go and do something energetic so you don't have a second to think about it. I'll be in the office at half nine tomorrow morning with the kettle boiled.'

Nerves got Jo out of bed early, so she was the first person in the office and had already made a cup of tea when Rhona arrived.

'How come I always have so much junk with me?' demanded Rhona, staggering into the office weighed down as usual by a capacious handbag, a bulging briefcase and the fat black velvet make-up bag she could never fit in her handbag.

'Get pregnant, split up with Ted and you'll be able to spend many happy hours at home feeling exhausted and bored, and you'll end up tidying your handbag/wardrobe/kitchen cupboards/whatever,' said Jo, pouring water on a tea bag for Rhona.

'Did you do all that?'

'Yes. I feel very virtuous, I can tell you. I even threw out all the saggy knickers I never wear, found and binned the tights with holes in them and rounded up all the black socks and found them partners, or the closest thing to a partner.'

'I'm impressed. Will you do mine?'

'Do what?' inquired Nikki, the beauty editor, who'd just arrived in a cloud of Opium.

'Jo has turned into a living, breathing "de-junk your life" feature,' Rhona explained, taking her tea into her office so she could smoke.

'Oh please de-junk my life.' Nikki shrugged off her black suede coat. 'I spent half of yesterday afternoon writing an article about the beauty essentials and how you only needed blusher, lip gloss, concealer and mascara in your emergency make-up bag. While I, naturally, carry half of Boots around with me every day and it necessitated a ten-minute search this morning to locate my new eyebrow make-up. By the way,' she said to Jo as she switched on her computer, 'you haven't forgotten the make-over session this morning?'

'Shit,' said Jo, who had. 'It just slipped my mind. What time are they coming in at?'

'Ten-thirty. We're going to the hairdresser's at eleven and Michelle – she's the new make-up artist I was telling you about, Rhona – she's doing their make-up in the salon. Then we've lunch in Spinelli's at one and the photographer will take the pics there.'

'Oh no, I forgot to remind Annette to get the clothes picked up yesterday,' shouted Jo in horror.

'Don't panic, I did it,' said Nikki. 'I knew you were sick,' she added. 'How are you today?'

'Fine,' Jo replied. 'I just needed a few days in bed.'

'Ah yes, but with whom?' called Rhona from her office, winking lewdly at Jo.

'Watch it McNamara,' she replied. 'Just because you can take on headmistresses, don't try anything with me.'

'What's this about headmistresses?' inquired Nikki.

Jo, Nikki and Michelle, the make-up artist, all tilted their heads sideways and looked at the second make-over candidate through narrowed eyes. It was hard to see where to begin. They were in Peter Mark's Hair and Beauty salon in the Stephen's Green shopping centre and the day was deteriorating rapidly.

The first woman to be made over was an already stunning redhead in her early forties who needed a make-over like Ivana Trump needed dresses. With a fabulous figure, perfect make-up, glossy hair and an outfit that must have cost a week's wages, there was absolutely nothing any of them could do to improve Helen.

'How the hell did we pick her?' whispered Nikki into Jo's ear when Helen was brought off to the washbasins.

'Her letter said she was a mother of four with kids ranging in age from twenty to four, that she worked part-time as a nurse and helped her husband run a garden centre outside Cork,' replied Jo. 'The picture was blurry and she said she'd love a change of image and I thought she deserved it . . .'

364

'*She* could probably give us lessons on changing our image,' groaned Nikki. 'I don't know what we can do to improve her.'

The second make-over candidate, however, was going to be a huge headache for the hairdresser. As a result of a perm gone wrong, twenty-nine-year-old Sharon – who had long mousey hair in the passport-sized photo she'd sent in – now sported layered hair that sat at an unflattering length between her ears and her jaw. The hairdresser was nearly tearing her own hair out at the thought of doing anything with Sharon's hair in its present state.

'You'll have to think of something,' Jo hissed at the hairdresser and make-up artist. 'The poor girl travelled miles to be here and she's going to have a wonderful day and look beautiful if we have to buy her a bloody wig!'

To make matters worse, Sharon wasn't the size fourteen that she'd claimed in her letter. Instead, she was an eighteen at least which meant that the elegant wool jacket and skirt Jo had carefully picked for her definitely wouldn't fit.

'I've seen some fabulous suits in the shops that would have looked really gorgeous on her,' groaned Jo, 'if only she'd said she was a size eighteen in the letter, I could have brought her off and we'd have picked something amazing. There just isn't the time now!'

'Well, what will we do?' demanded Nikki.

'I'm going to race down to Marks and Spark's to get her a different outfit because they have great clothes in right now and we simply don't have the time for a proper shopping trip. Damn,' she added, 'I'd have *loved* to have gone shopping with Sharon.'

Marks was blissfully empty and Jo spent an enjoyable fifteen minutes browsing, wishing she could buy something instead of saving her money for the new house. Now that she'd rung an estate agent about selling her apartment, the idea of moving had finally become reality and she knew she had to economise. She'd stuck her credit card at the back of her dressing-table drawer and vowed to keep it there no matter what sort of mid-season sales started.

She'd have to be very careful with money until she was settled in her new home. Luckily, the woman from the estate agent's said apartments in her block were always in demand and she'd have no trouble selling, despite the time of year.

'It's such a pretty complex and the apartments are quite spacious compared to the ones being built now, so I doubt if you'll have to wait long,' the estate agent said.

Jo was so busy working out how much money she'd need to borrow to buy the cottage and wondering whether she could afford a sloppy chenille jumper to hide her bump, that she totally lost track of time.

Oh no, she thought looking at her watch in horror. It was half eleven and she hadn't even started looking for clothes for Sharon.

But Jo wasn't a clothesaholic with an encyclopaedic knowledge of where to get what in her favourite shops for nothing.

It was just twelve as she rushed up Grafton Street with a large M & S bag in each hang. Jo really wished she hadn't worn the long caramel wool cardigan over the cream silk shirt and black trousers. As she hurried past the crowds ambling along the pedestrian street, she was soon roasting hot and felt ready for a make-over herself. Or at least a chance to redo her foundation which had undoubtedly disappeared with sweat.

She struggled up the escalator and into Peter Mark's to find Nikki relaxing on a couch, reading a magazine and leisurely sipping a cup of coffee, oblivious to the controlled chaos of the salon. Nikki's blonde hair was immaculate, her face wasn't shiny and red, and her off-white trouser suit looked as fresh as if it had just been returned from the dry-cleaner's. Hot, sticky and convinced that she smelled like a jockey's armpit, Jo felt like bag lady by comparison.

'You got the clothes all right, then?' Nikki got up and took the two large bags from Jo. 'You look wrecked. Sit down and I'll get you a cup of tea.'

'Thanks,' panted Jo, sinking gratefully onto the seat Nikki had just vacated. 'I *feel* wrecked. But I got this beautiful crimson Mandarin jacket and matching palazzos that will look great on Sharon. How's it going?' she asked anxiously.

'Brilliantly,' said Nikki enthusiastically. 'You wouldn't believe how Sharon's hair has turned out. That hairdresser has worked miracles. And Helen looks amazing. Mind you, she looked amazing in the beginning.'

'Well,' said Jo, relieved to find that the make-over had been a success after all, 'we'll just make her "before" picture very, very small. Or else say she didn't really get a make-over but just wanted to feel pampered for a day.'

Nikki had been right. Sharon's new look really suited her. The hairdresser has shaped her hair, added a rich chestnut rinse to make it glossy and given her a short, feather cut. 'The only thing I could think of,' she told Jo, 'and it worked!'

Sharon looked a million dollars thanks to the elegant crimson suit that Jo had picked for her, teamed with the right make-up and a new haircut which emphasised her beautiful dark brown eyes.

'It's fantastic.' She beamed at Jo. 'Thank you so much. I never thought I could look like this.' She threw her arms around the fashion editor.

'I'm so pleased for you,' said Jo with a big smile. 'This is my favourite part of make-overs,' she added as the photographer took a couple of quick pictures, 'when people are pleased with what we've done. Normally we just take the pictures and go. But today we've got a wonderful lunch lined up where you two ladies can show off your amazing ladies-who-lunch look!'

'Have you got any deodorant?' Jo whispered to Nikki in the restaurant loos. She'd managed to tone down her red face, but she still felt sticky after her run up Grafton Street.

Nikki handed Jo some deodorant and a bottle of Opium.

'Thanks,' said Jo gratefully, spraying herself liberally. 'I've left my perfume in the office by mistake and I'm sure all my Trésor has worn off.'

She glanced at Nikki as the other woman expertly applied a fresh coat of subtle beige lipstick and wished, for once, that she didn't work with such a paragon of style and beauty. Nikki was always perfectly turned out, never wore chipped nail varnish and never got lipstick on her teeth. And today was no exception.

Jo ran a brush through her tortoiseshell curls and wished she had something to tie it back with because it was greasy at the roots. Then she followed Nikki into the restaurant. Helen, Sharon and Nell, the photographer, were at the table getting stuck into pre-lunch gin and tonics, the other two laughing at some filthy joke Nell had just told them.

Jo was just manoeuvring herself around the table into her seat at the wall when she spotted them. The woman wore a figure-hugging black shift dress and an eye-catching red jacket which a very suave and elegant Mark Denton was helping her out of. He must have said something funny because she laughed suddenly, the sleek dark hair rippling as she leaned her head back. Even her laugh was warm, husky and sexy.

Bitch. Jo felt jealousy spear her as she watched Mark, very attractive in a steel grey suit to match his eyes, pull out the woman's chair before sinking into his. He took the menu and wine list from the waiter almost without looking at him, eyes on the woman all the time. Not surprising, Jo thought maliciously, when the bitch was wearing a dress with a deep vee in the front showing a Grand Canyon cleavage that had to be thanks to a Wonderbra. Who the hell was she? thought Jo venomously, taking in the glint of serious gold bangles.

'Madam?' inquired a voice. Jo came to her senses to find a waiter smiling down at her, pen and order pad in hand.

'Oh er . . . I'll have, what will I have . . .' she muttered, casting a quick glance at the menu she'd been dying to get her hands on ten minutes earlier.

'Today's specials are Dublin Bay prawns in Pernod and monkfish tails in a Provençale sauce,' said the waiter hopefully.

'Fine.' Jo shut the menu with a snap and handed it to him. She didn't care if she ordered rats' tails in Pernod at that precise moment.

Nikki was filling Helen, Sharon and Nell in on the finer

details of the party she'd been to at the weekend where one woman turned up with her husband and left with somebody else's.

'She's Dublin's Zsa Zsa Gabor.' Nikki giggled. 'Ask her how many husbands she's had and she'll say "Mine or other people's?"'

Jo craned her head to see what Mark and the mystery woman were up to in the far corner of the restaurant. Laughing a lot, she thought grimly, watching the dark head shake with mirth yet again. He doesn't waste any time, does he?

'You know her, don't you, Jo?' asked Nikki, breaking off mid-story to include Jo in the conversation.

'Know who?'

'The Zsa Zsa woman at my party, Lizzie Something-or-other. Lord, you're a million miles away, aren't you, Jo?' Then, noticing Jo's face, which had gone quite pale, Nikki said, 'Are you feeling all right? Are you ill?'

Jo grabbed the glass of water in front of her and took a huge gulp. 'Fine,' she lied, 'fine. I'm just hungry. Hand me a bread roll, will you?'

She sneaked a glance at Mark's table just in time to see the waiter arrive with a bottle of champagne and an ice bucket. What the hell were they celebrating? Jo half-listened to the conversation going on around her as she nibbled at her bread roll listlessly. Who was that woman? She thought murderously.

She was very quiet during the meal, barely touched her prawns and poked the monkfish around the plate in a desultory fashion.

The others drank three bottles of wine and were so merry that Nell had to use up three rolls of film before she got any pictures where the two newly made-over women weren't laughing hysterically.

The waiter was serving coffee when Nikki finally noticed Mark and his companion.

'Look who's having lunch with his ex,' she murmured to Jo

with a smirk. 'I thought that liaison was finished.'

Jo dropped her teaspoon with a clatter. 'What?' she asked.

'It's Eva Marot,' said Nikki. 'I thought they'd broken up a long time ago.'

Trying not to look as though it mattered to her, Jo asked who Eva was.

'You must know.' Nikki raised one perfectly shaped blonde eyebrow in amazement. 'He was involved with her for years, even after she got married. She married some filthy-rich French guy and lives in London most of the time. But she comes back to Ireland a lot – she's an artist and she often paints here. The light is wonderful, apparently.'

Nikki took a sip of brandy. 'They were quite an item for a long time. Up to a year or so ago, I think,' she added thoughtfully. 'I can't believe you never heard of her. She was Eva Ward before her marriage.'

'No, I didn't hear anything,' said Jo faintly.

'She's half-French on her mother's side and very chic. Always wears the most gorgeous clothes.' The other woman took another long look at Mark and his companion. 'That *has* to be Armani she's wearing, don't you think?'

'Mmm, you're probably right.' Jo toyed with the brown sugar crystals in the bowl in front of her. Stop looking at them, Nikki, she pleaded silently. Or else Mark'll come over and I couldn't bear to meet him like this, with me looking like hell and him with Ms Epitome of Chic with the sexy laugh. I bet she whispers sweet nothings in French in bed, she thought jealously.

The waiter arrived with more brandy for everyone except Jo. Nikki turned her attention to Helen's story about Brandy Alexanders and how the first one she'd ever had made her instantly drunk – and madly sexy.

'Have one,' squealed Nell. 'You're getting the train home and both you and your husband will have something to remember today by!'

Jo smiled but her mind was miles away. *She* was the woman Suzanne had told her about at the party in New York. The mystery woman who'd broken Mark's heart, the one Suzanne assumed Jo knew all about. Eva Marot. Jo said the name to herself several times, wondering why she'd never even heard the tiniest piece of gossip about her and Mark.

To cap it all, Rhona must have known all along. Jo would just kill her when she got her. Imagine not saying *anything* about Mark's past love? She was staring blankly into her half-drunk cup of coffee when she heard that deep, rich voice she'd recognise anywhere.

'Hello, ladies,' Mark said warmly. 'Did you have a nice lunch?'

Jo looked up sharply. He was standing at the other side of the table, smiling at the five of them. *She* stood just behind him, an elegant vision straight out of the pages of *Vogue*. Jo could have sworn that the string of pearls around her neck was real, they had that expensive real-pearl lustre.

'This is a lunch for our make-over ladies, Mark,' Nikki was saying. 'Helen and Sharon, meet Mark Denton, *Style*'s publisher. And you know Nell, don't you?'

'Yes, hello, Helen, Sharon and Nell. And how are you, Jo?' he asked, looking directly at Jo's startled face.

'Fine!' she said brightly. 'Marvellous! How was your lunch?' she inquired in the same high-pitched tone.

'Very nice,' Mark answered, looking at her curiously.

'The food is just wonderful here, isn't it?' Eva said in her faintly accented voice, as she slid one arm through Mark's. 'It's hard not to eat too much.' She patted a stomach flat as a pancake.

Cow, thought Jo. Just because she's skinny, she doesn't have to look down on the rest of us.

'Eva, this is Jo Ryan,' introduced Mark, '*Style*'s deputy and fashion editor, Nikki Ahearn, our beauty editor, Nell Deane, who's a photographer and Sharon and Helen who've just had a make-over and look gorgeous, if I may say so.' Sharon went pink with pleasure.

'How nice to meet you all.' Eva's smile looked remarkably genuine, Jo thought sourly. But then it would, wouldn't it? A husband *and* a lover – she was having her cake and eating it too.

'I'm glad to see that you're back at work, Jo,' Mark said gently, looking her straight in the eye. Jo glared at him. Was that some sort of dig?

'I have felt better,' she snapped.

'I can see that,' he replied. 'You look worn out.'

The bastard. Just because she wasn't done up like a dog's dinner, he didn't have to be so smart.

'When is your baby due?' inquired Eva politely, gazing at Jo's stomach.'

'Four months – well, four and a half, actually.'

'Is it your first?' Eva asked next.

What was this, Jo fumed, bloody *Mastermind*?

'Yes.'

'Oh.' The other woman appeared to notice her coolness. 'We should go now, Mark,' she murmured, her dark glossy head close to his. Eva was tall, Jo realised, around five ten if she could talk to Mark without craning her neck the way Jo had to.

'Of course, Eva. We don't want to be late,' he said. 'Bye, ladies, it's been nice meeting you.' Mark looked at Jo briefly. 'I'll see you next week at the editorial meeting.'

'Yeah, bye.'

'So nice to meet you all,' Eva said warmly.

Jo took a sip of her coffee even though it was practically lukewarm. She was determined not to watch them leave. But she couldn't resist. As she glanced up they were at the door, Mark's strong arm opening the door for Eva to walk through. Chivalrous as ever.

The waiter brought the bill along with a small plate of After Eights. Nobody touched them. No point wasting them. Jo reached in and took three. What was the point of watching her figure anyway? Nobody noticed.

'I can't believe you never told me about her!' Jo's voice was angry. She stood in Rhona's office and stared crossly down at her friend. Rhona, who'd been working on her monthly editorial when Jo stormed in after lunch in Spinelli's, leaned back in her chair and looked at Jo.

'Listen, Jo, Mark told me about Eva in confidence.' Rhona's voice was very firm and very serious. 'He told me one night a long time before you joined *Style* and he told me as a friend, asked me not to tell anyone about it. I'm not saying it was easy to keep it to myself, especially that day when I told you Mark had been interested in you for a long time. But honestly, Jo,' Rhona said earnestly, 'by then I thought you could do without hearing about his beloved ex-girlfriend, a woman he'd adored for years. That would hardly have made you feel very special, would it?'

'I suppose . . .' said Jo slowly. *A woman he'd adored for years*? What hope had she against that sort of competition?

A pregnant woman who flew off the handle at the drop of a hat could hardly compete with an exotic artist who'd loved him for years.

'Anyway, it's over. They split up a long time ago,' Rhona said.

'They looked very much together at lunch today,' Jo pointed out. 'They were all over each other.'

'Believe me.' Rhona's voice was serious. 'They're not together any more. Look Jo, I'm sorry I couldn't tell you about her, but that would have been breaking a confidence and I couldn't do that to Mark. I've known him a long time and he trusts me. He's also very perceptive. If I'd spilled the beans to you, he'd have worked out who told you in two minutes flat. And he'd have gone mad.'

Rhona lit up a cigarette, then stubbed it out hurriedly. 'Sorry, I keep forgetting not to smoke in front of you,' she said. 'Jo, I wanted to tell you loads of times, but when you really became interested in him, you wouldn't have appreciated it. And I knew Mark would want to tell you himself if he was serious about you. Can't you understand the dilemma I was in?'

Jo sighed and sat down in the chair opposite Rhona.

'Sorry, Rho,' she apologised. 'I've no right to barge in here and screech at you. I'm angry at myself really, for even thinking he could be interested in me. And if he was,' she added quickly, seeing that Rhona was going to interrupt, 'I've screwed it up myself. I should have business cards made up – "Jo Ryan Incorporated. Will Destroy Any Relationship in Ten Minutes Flat." '

'Don't be daft,' said Rhona impatiently. 'You've just had a bad couple of weeks. He's not still involved with Eva, I'm sure of it.'

'Even if he isn't, he's definitely not interested in me any more,' Jo said sadly. 'So, now that I'm no longer an interested party, is there anything else I should know about Mr Denton? Has he ten kids hidden away somewhere, or a mad wife locked in the attic, perhaps?'

She tried to sound flip but Rhona knew her too well for that.

'No,' Rhona said. 'He has remarkably few skeletons in the cupboard. A lot less than I have,' she added with a wry grin. 'But let him tell you about Eva.'

'He's not going to tell me anything.'

'You have it your way,' Rhona replied. She changed the subject. 'So tell me, is the November issue too early for the "I know we all want to go on a diet for Christmas, readers, but let's be grown-ups and accept the way we are" editorial?'

'No, November is fine,' Jo said. 'Let's leave the "diet your way to beauty" until the January issue and I'll be one of the guinea pigs when I have to lose the two stone I'll have put on by then.'

She had just switched on her computer and was looking at the Christmas Glamour Look photos that Ralph had delivered, when her phone rang.

'Jo. I wonder could I have a word with you?' Mark said.

'I'm busy,' she snapped.

'I'm sure you are,' he replied. 'But this is important.'

'Fine. Talk.'

'I want to *see* you, Jo, not have you talk in monosyllables on the phone.'

Oh no, she thought, she couldn't handle that, she couldn't handle actually *seeing* him. She didn't want to see him ever again because she knew she'd just break down and cry if she did. If she could keep away from him for a while, then she'd be fine, she knew it. She'd get over Mark Denton. She'd have to.

'I can't see you right now, Mark,' she said firmly. 'Can't you talk on the phone? Anyway, I thought you were tied up for the afternoon?' she added smartly.

'I'm not busy,' he said slowly. 'I think we've got some unfinished business and I want it sorted out right now.'

'Oh, you mean me calling you names and telling you where you could stick your job. I'm sorry,' Jo said in a low voice. 'I apologise, I had no right to say those things.'

'That's not really it,' Mark said, 'that's just part of the problem. I want to know what's behind it, what's going on. There seems to have been some sort of misunderstanding between us . . .'

Jo froze. She knew exactly what he meant. He was talking about her feelings for him, her 'infatuation'. *She'd* all but chatted him up in New York, flirted shamelessly with him and behaved like a spurned girlfriend when he hadn't rung her over Emma's little explosion. Now he was going to warn her off. Of course he was. He was back with the love of his life and he wanted all the loose ends tied up. He didn't want to subject poor Eva to any more of Jo's ferocious stares, did he?

What a mess. She couldn't let him think that she really fancied him, that would be too cringe-making. She had to say something.

'I'm sorry,' she gabbled at high speed. 'I know I've been acting strangely, but it's the baby. The baby,' she paused, before inspiration struck, 'and Richard. He's back and we're talking, and I'm going through a difficult time, sorting everything out. You know.'

'Oh.' Mark's voice sounded different, remote. 'I see,' he said coolly. 'Of course, I understand. Sorry to bother you, Jo, I'll let you get back to work.'

He hung up. Jo sat with the phone against her ear and wished Brenda wasn't sitting at the desk opposite, gabbling away to her boyfriend, so that she could cry.

CHAPTER SEVENTEEN

'Tell me all about Sam. Is he drop-dead gorgeous? Or,' Jo curled her stockinged feet up under her on the armchair in Aisling's sitting room and adjusted her huge grey woollen cardigan until she was comfortable, 'does he have any brothers?'

'Not that I know of,' replied Aisling, 'but then, there are lots of things I don't know about him.'

It was true. Since the party seven days ago, Aisling had spoken to him on the phone twice and both conversations had been funny, jokey and absent of any information. It had been so blissfully unlike all those stilted boy/girl conversations she'd had years ago when she started going out with boys. You talked about what school you'd gone to, or what courses you were doing in college and where your parents came from. So you could 'place' the person and figure out if it was safe to bring him home.

She'd been married so long that she could barely remember life before Michael, life when she had gone on dates with a variety of men – who were always unsuitable in her father's opinion. Dating as a grown-up was much more fun. No one had to approve of her choice, except herself.

'No,' she said thoughtfully, 'I'm pretty sure Sam has a couple of sisters but no brothers.'

'That's perfect.' Jo reached for another chocolate-chip cookie. 'If he has sisters, he'll understand women. Not like those MCPs who've grown up with an adoring mammie and no female company to educate them about the ways of the world. These biscuits are delicious,' she added, taking a big bite. 'Did you make them yourself?'

Aisling laughed. 'These days I'm lucky if I get to make the bed in the morning, never mind bake biscuits.'

'Well, they look home-made.'

'They *are* home-made but not from *my* home. I got them at the boys' school fête along with a ton of apple tarts and fairy cakes I've frozen so I can drag them out and impress people with my home cooking all year long. Pity I never copped on to that when I was a housewife,' Aisling remarked drily.

'You're not having any,' said Jo. While she'd been enjoying a mug of frothy hot chocolate and biscuits, Aisling had been sipping black coffee.

'I never eat biscuits any more, unless I can see the pack and know exactly how many calories there are in each one,' Aisling explained. 'It took me long enough to get the weight off, so I'm not putting it back on again.'

'You look great,' Jo said with sincerity. The slightly plump, out-of-shape Aisling was a thing of the past. She was svelte in a pair of slim black trousers and a soft angora jumper in a caramel colour which matched her newly dyed hair. It wasn't even how Aisling *looked* that made the difference, Jo realised. She had changed from the inside out.

The nervous, miserable woman of four months ago, constantly on the verge of tears, had gone to be replaced by an attractive woman who had learned to live life on her own terms.

Jo remembered when she'd felt that she was living life on her terms. That had been before she'd become pregnant, before Richard had showed his true colours, before she'd fallen, disastrously, for Mark. Now, she hurtled along a path she hadn't chosen, scared and exhilarated at the same time.

She felt Aisling's hand on her shoulder and looked up to see her friend sit on the arm of the chair with a concerned expression on her face.

'Are you all right?' Aisling asked gently.

'Yes.' She snuffled. 'I was thinking about this time over three months ago when I thought everything was fine. When I first got pregnant and I thought he'd want the baby as much as I did.' She stroked her belly lovingly. 'I want the baby so much, I can't understand how he didn't. I thought it was all going to be so perfect.'

'But it wasn't, he wasn't. Richard was lying and sooner or later he'd have shown his true colours,' Aisling said earnestly. 'You couldn't have lived with the sort of man who'd want you to have an abortion so you could both go abroad to work with no strings attached.'

'I know,' Jo said simply.

Aisling wasn't finished. 'The life you had was a house of cards, Jo. Mine was the same and it was bound to tumble down sooner or later. I know it was agony when it all fell apart, but let's be honest, there's no easy way to break up a relationship. And we've passed that horrible, depressing stage, both of us,' she insisted. 'We're on to the next stage. I know you're in bits about having the baby on your own and of course it would be better to have a father for him . . .'

'Her,' said Jo with a grin. 'I know it's a girl, I just feel it. Aren't you, my darling?' she cooed at her bump. 'I understand what you're saying, Ash, I really do. No father is better than a father like Richard,' she recited, as if she was repeating a mantra she'd said to herself many, many times before.

'At least if you're on your own, you've got the chance of meeting someone else and finding a good dad for her,' Aisling said.

'I thought I'd found him,' Jo explained.

'Mark Denton?' asked Aisling.

'Yes. Dear, dear Mark. And I screwed it up. Oh God, I hate to even think about it.' Jo leaned back in the chair and massaged the bridge of her nose with her right hand. She felt tired, exhausted even. It had been a horrible week. She hadn't even had to avoid Mark because *he* studiously avoided the office. He phoned Rhona when he needed to talk to her instead of dropping in as he usually did. To make matters worse, she couldn't go home until late every evening as the estate agent was showing the apartment to prospective buyers. So she'd ended up sitting in the office with a takeaway until eight on Wednesday, Thursday and Friday.

If she hadn't promised to visit Aisling this Saturday morning, she wouldn't have got out of bed at all. Even then she'd only managed to drag on her ancient woolly cardigan, a faded pink T-shirt and her grey jogging pants. She hadn't had the energy to wash her hair and knew it fell in lank waves around her shoulders.

Aisling contemplated her for a moment and then got up. 'Come on into the kitchen and I'll make you something decent for lunch,' she said firmly. 'You can tell me all about Mark while I'm cooking.'

The scent of the herb and mushroom omelette she'd made Jo still lingered in the air as Aisling hurried round the house that evening, collecting tights, socks, knickers and jumpers off the radiators. Sam was picking her up at half seven and she only had an hour to dry her hair, dress and put on her make-up. It was her own fault for spending too long planning the menu for her first catering dinner.

When Rachel Coughlan had rung on Monday morning, tentatively booking Aisling for a dinner party for twelve, she'd been so stunned she'd been speechless for the first minute.

'I thought I'd book early in case you're really busy,' Rachel said on the phone, not sounding anything like a high-powered businesswoman who'd just set up her own PR agency. 'Jim said everyone was thrilled and very impressed with your cooking and he's sure you're already madly busy. I do hope you can fit me in. It's for my brother's forty-fifth birthday. He's coming home from the States and his wife is so fussy, I'd love to outshine her.'

Thrilled to be asked, and even more thrilled that Jim Coughlan thought so highly of her that he assumed she'd be snowed under with work, Aisling said she'd dream up a very posh menu if that's what Rachel wanted.

'Yes,' the other woman said enthusiastically, delighted to have found an ally. 'You can't imagine what it's like to feel like a second-class citizen to this New York career woman who can whistle up a four-course meal at the drop of a hat and still look like something from a fashion magazine at dinner.'

'Oh yes I can,' said Aisling grimly. 'Don't worry, Rachel.

She'll be dumbstruck when she sees what we'll do.'

'Unfortunately, my sister-in-law has never been dumbstruck in her entire life, more's the pity,' muttered Rachel.

Aisling had been so engrossed in deciding whether rack of lamb would be suitably classy for the meal, or if she should try something more difficult like pheasant in Calvados, that she hadn't noticed the time. When she finally looked at her watch, she abandoned the menu and raced upstairs to the bathroom.

An hour later, wearing the crossover bronze body Fiona had given her, she sat in the kitchen picking cat fur off her long black skirt. Flossie, disgusted at the prospect of being left alone, wove herself in and out between Aisling's ankles, leaving enough fur on her owner's sheer black tights to knit another cat.

'I'm sorry, Flossie.' She stroked the cat's silken chin and wondered how Flossie always knew when she was going out. 'I won't be out late. Wait till you see the treat I've got you.'

She checked her make-up one last time, gave herself a blast of Magie Noire and got up to feed Flossie.

'Isn't that nice?' she asked as the cat tucked into a bowl of tinned salmon.

When the doorbell rang at a minute after half seven, her stomach was rumbling with nerves. She had no idea how she was going to be able to eat anything at all, but she didn't care.

Sam stood on the doorstep, holding a small bouquet of flowers in his hands. For a moment Aisling was stunned. She'd forgotten how heart-stoppingly attractive he was. He wore a pale blue cotton shirt that brought out the bright blue of his eyes and set off his tan. A well-cut dark jacket and jeans showed off a physique that spoke of many hours in the gym. He looked like a Calvin Klein aftershave advert come to life, from the tips of his brown suede boots to his all-American grin.

'You look lovely, Aisling.' His eyes glinted in admiration. 'Can I come in?' he added.

'Oh God, yes, I'm sorry.' Blushing bright pink, Aisling stood back and let him in. She'd been so busy staring at him that she'd quite forgotten to ask him in.

'These are for you,' he said, handing her the bouquet, 'for making me feel at home in Ireland again.'

To hide her red face, she buried her nose in the flowers, breathing in the heady scent of pale yellow roses and the fragrance of the forest green ferns. She couldn't remember the last time anyone had given her flowers, apart from Michael's guilt-ridden garage forecourt arrangements.

'They're beautiful,' she said fervently.

'So are you.' Sam looked deep into her eyes and gave her another slow, lazy grin.

Aisling felt the fluttering in her stomach move lower. God only knew what it would feel like if he actually touched her.

'The table is booked for eight,' he said. 'Do you want to go out or aren't you hungry?' he asked, one eyebrow raised in amusement.

'Oh, of course. I'll just put these in water,' she muttered. She wondered if he could tell what she was thinking. She hoped not.

He held the door for her to climb into the taxi. She'd been sure he'd have a car.

'Can't drink and drive,' he said. 'I thought we'd have champagne and you simply couldn't drive after drinking that.'

'No, of course not,' replied Aisling in a knowing tone, as if she had champagne all the time. She wasn't sure she believed that stuff about him not drinking and driving. Sam had the air of a man who never did anything by the rules. There was something about him, a sense of recklessness, that made him very, very attractive. And just a little bit dangerous.

He'd chosen a small French restaurant, with dim lighting and small tables set far enough apart from each other to allow couples to talk privately. Their table was in one corner, the golden glow of a candle cast flattering light on the snow-white damask tablecloth and gleaming silverware. Good, thought Aisling. Candlelight was much more flattering to crow's feet than harsh lighting.

The waitress handed them the menus and then disappeared, leaving them alone. The place was jammed with couples, obviously enticed in by the fact that the restaurant was dark and dim, making it perfect for illicit encounters. Probably the sort of place Michael had taken that cow to.

The staff kept firmly in the background while Ella Fitzgerald's rich voice crooned love songs in the background.

'Do you like this place?' asked Sam softly.

'I love it,' she answered.

'Good. We should come here every Saturday night,' he replied.

Aisling's pulse raced. It was only their first date and he was already talking about a future together! She couldn't wait to tell Fiona and Jo.

She shot him what she hoped was a sexy smile, and looked at her menu. Who needed food on an occasion like this?

They drank Moët from elegant crystal champagne flutes and Sam told her all about working in Texas and Louisiana.

'I'd love to bring you to New Orleans,' he said, sliding his hand past his empty soup bowl to grasp Aisling's hand. 'You'd love it. It's so atmospheric and European, it's the most European city I've ever been to in America. You can walk along the streets in the French Quarter and it's like being in Paris or Budapest.'

'You've travelled so much,' said Aisling enviously. 'I've been to Greece, Portugal, France and Britain, and that's it. You've been everywhere.'

He shrugged. 'I travelled for a couple of years after leaving college, that's how I've seen so much. You simply didn't have that chance, you were bringing up two kids.'

'I can't wait for you to meet them,' Aisling said eagerly. 'They'll love you.'

Oh no, she thought in horror. She couldn't believe she'd just said that. Single men were not fascinated by the notion of other men's children.

'I can't wait either,' Sam said. 'I love kids. My sisters' children are fantastic and the two older ones – Jerri's boys – came out to stay with me last year for a month. They went wild for New Orleans and had me down at the aquarium for two days solid.'

'It sounds fascinating,' said Aisling, mentally giving him ten out of ten for loving children. Handsome, kind, funny, romantic *and* dying to meet the boys. What more could a woman ask for?

'It *is* fascinating,' Sam was saying. 'It's got every sort of sea creature you can imagine, apart from whales, that is. You walk along these corridors with glass overhead and around you and you can see sharks, stingrays, giant squid swimming around these massive tanks.'

He stopped as the waitress placed their main courses in front of them and refilled their glasses with Moët.

'Anyway, that's enough about sharks. My favourite sort of wildlife doesn't reside behind glass.' Sam flashed her a killer smile.

'What do you mean?' Aisling asked demurely.

Sam slid one hand across the table and grasped hers, his fingers putting gentle pressure on the palm of her hand.

'That I enjoy life, in every sense of the word. I've always believed that you've got to live life to the full, take all the pleasures and passion from life while you can. That can mean being a little wild sometimes,' he said, gazing at Aisling intently, leaving her in no doubt as to what he meant.

She felt herself grow pink under his scrutiny.

'I don't get much of a chance to be wild,' she said, picking up her glass with the hand he wasn't holding. 'Work, kids, exhaustion – none of it leaves time for acting wild. Coming out to dinner instead of staying at home doing the ironing is my idea of wild these days!'

Aisling knew that this wasn't what he'd meant but she wanted to change the subject rapidly. The whole conversation had taken a distinct dive into territory she wasn't either comfortable or familiar with, and she wanted it back on track. Until she'd had another couple of drinks, anyway.

'Of course, there was another reason for the boys' fascination with the aquarium,' Sam said with a smile, returning to

384

their original conversation. 'They came during their summer holidays in July and in the summer walking around New Orleans is like being baked in a hot oven with ninety per cent humidity thrown in to make it worse. After an hour meandering around the markets by the river, the aquarium is beautifully cool!'

As they ate he told her about his two years of travelling with a college friend. Aisling listened wide-eyed as he recounted tales about backpacking in India – 'an unbelievable experience' – driving across America in a rent-a-wreck – 'New Mexico has got to be one of the most beautiful places on earth' – and working on a kibbutz in Israel.

He made her laugh telling her stories about ending up in cockroach-infested motel rooms, and how he ended up in hospital in Ecuador thanks to a virulent stomach bug.

Aisling couldn't help but notice that he never talked about his feelings. There was no mention of the woman he'd been involved with in Texas, or of their split-up. Still, Aisling thought, there was plenty of time for those sort of confessional conversations later.

Accustomed to being a listener after years of marriage to Michael, she sat in rapt silence as Sam talked her through all the places he'd seen in his thirty-nine years. Everywhere he went, he tried some new sport or pastime to fulfil his love of danger.

His favourite had been rock-climbing in Colorado.

'That sounds terrifying,' she said with a shudder, as he explained how difficult it was to scale a two-hundred-metre cliff-face with a deadly overhang at the top which had claimed the lives of two climbers.

'The adrenaline buzz is something else,' Sam said, his eyes distant as if remembering. 'I can't explain it, it's primeval, the feeling that it's just you, one man, against nature. When you're up there, you can imagine what it must have felt like for primitive men battling the earth just to survive.'

For a moment he stared into space. Then, just as quickly, he came back to her.

'There's a climb in Arizona every year, in one of the canyons off the Grand Canyon,' Sam said. 'I've never done it but I'd like to. You see, I always dreamed of being a stuntman when I was a kid,' he explained. 'It was all those years of watching Steve McQueen movies or Clint Eastwood ones. But my mother told me not to be stupid and to go to college. Still, I think I would have made a pretty good stuntman, what do you think?'

Aisling didn't even need to consider it. The more Sam talked, the more apparent it became that he'd love risking life and limb every day with lots of people watching. For a moment, she wondered why Sam had come back to Ireland since he loved the States so much. But she didn't want to ask him difficult questions, any more than she wanted him to ask her awkward ones. Tonight, she merely wanted to feel good, sexy and wanted.

'It was the biggest goddamn shark I'd ever seen in my life,' Sam said, telling her about the weeks he'd spent shark-fishing the previous summer, when he'd caught a monster shark.

A little voice in Aisling's head reminded her that Sam in 'action-hero mode' was not a million miles away from Michael telling her about the brilliant political profile he'd just written. But then Michael wouldn't have been feeding her strawberries from his plate while he did it.

She loved the way Sam carefully coated each strawberry in cream before gently holding it to her lips, letting her take a huge bite before he finished the half-eaten fruit. There was something very sensuous about the whole thing. Aisling found herself responding to it. Her inhibitions drained away as she tasted strawberries and champagne, and enjoyed the heady atmosphere between them.

When Sam went to the bathroom, she sat back in her chair and took a quick glance around the restaurant. She was enjoying herself hugely. It had been a long time since she'd enjoyed a meal out like this, an intimate dinner where she didn't feel frumpy, boring and, eventually, plastered. When Michael brought her out to dinner, she felt so depressed at her size and miserable because she hated whatever dreadful outfit she was wearing that she ate everything put in front of her and drank like a fish.

It was a glorious change to feel confident and slim, to dine with an attractive man who looked deep into her eyes.

They worked their way through a second bottle of champagne and four Irish coffees, by which time Sam was gently playing with Aisling's fingers across the table and giving her veiled looks from heavy-lidded eyes. 'Do you miss your husband?' he asked suddenly.

Three months ago, Aisling would have burst into tears at that question. Now she watched Sam's fingers gently stroke the fleshy part at the base of her palm and answered, 'Yes and no. I miss him because we were together so long, I miss the person in the bed beside me at night, the man who put out the bins. Sometimes,' she added, 'sometimes, I don't even think about him, when I'm very busy and I don't have time.'

'That's not quite what I meant,' Sam whispered, increasing the pressure with his fingers.

She looked up at him. It was strange and exciting to watch his want for her. Curiously liberating. It made her feel free from the past, free to say what she wanted instead of saying the right thing.

'I haven't even thought about sex since he left,' she replied candidly. 'Until I met you.' She gasped. 'I can't believe I said that,' she said, laughing. 'That's the effect you have on me, Sam Delaney.'

'I'm glad to hear it. Didn't you ever feel the need to break out when you were married? The desire to do something different?' Sam asked idly.

'Or do *someone* different? Isn't that what you mean?' Aisling said. 'That's not me. Well,' she corrected herself, 'that wasn't me.' It is now, she thought silently.

She caught the waitress's eye. 'Could I have a brandy? Do you want one, Sam?' If she was going to do this, she needed some more liquid confidence. Her head was definitely going to ache in the morning.

'Is the new Aisling ready for something different?' Sam asked in a low voice when the waitress had placed two brandy balloons in front of them.

It was now or never, she told herself. Go for it. She finished her brandy in a couple of burning gulps before answering. 'Yes.'

Sam grinned and drained his glass. 'Shall we go and continue this conversation at home?'

'Sure.'

Amazed at her own audacity, she sat in the back of the taxi and held Sam's hand. Hand-holding wasn't what he had in mind. He didn't seem to care what the taxi-driver saw, he simply slid his arms around her and kissed her passionately. Once, Aisling would have died of shame thinking about the driver watching them in his rear-view mirror, two adults behaving like sex-mad adolescents. But, insulated by alcohol, she didn't care, even when Sam's hand slid up her skirt to stroke between her thighs.

When she fumbled with her keys before finding the right one to open her front door, Aisling briefly wondered if the neighbours were watching her arrive home with a strange man.

At least they wouldn't know how late he stayed, she reflected, since he hadn't brought his car. Nobody could squint out of their windows and tut-tut if a strange car was parked outside the Morans' in the morning.

Fiona was probably peering out, Aisling realised and stifled a laugh. She should have come up with a secret signal with her neighbour – two flashes of the torch from the master bedroom if Sam made mad passionate love to her, and one flash if he fell asleep on the settee after too much booze.

Sam ambled into the sitting room and lounged on the settee.

'Nice place. Sit down, darling,' he said patting the space beside him.

Suddenly, she felt stone-cold sober. Here she was bringing a strange man into her home, the home she'd shared with

Michael and the boys, and this man was sure that they'd make love. So sure, that he was making himself completely at home, taking over her settee possessively. What am I doing? She thought.

'I have to let the cat out,' she muttered nervously, backing out of the room and into the kitchen. 'Flossie, Flossie, where are you?' she called.

Typically, Flossie had vamoosed when she was required. She wasn't in her wicker basket beside the double radiator. She couldn't be used as an excuse or plonked on Aisling's lap so Sam couldn't drag her onto his.

'D'you have any brandy?' he asked, appearing behind her in the kitchen.

'Of course,' she answered. 'Funny, I always thought I was the only one who wanted another drink after a meal out.'

'Me too. Brandy makes me want more brandy,' he added, looking around the kitchen. 'No cat, huh?'

'She must have gone upstairs to the hotpress.' Aisling rummaged around in the cupboard for decent glasses. 'She loves snuggling up on the socks at the bottom. Here we are,' she said triumphantly. She took two whiskey tumblers made of heavy glass with a green tint. 'Damn, I've just remembered I've no brandy. There's whiskey in the cupboard beside the notice-board.'

She rinsed the glasses and turned to find him examining the photos and notes stuck to the cork notice-board. There was a picture of the boys in Portugal, sliding down a huge water slide, their hands in the air and their mouths open as they shrieked in delight. It was three years old, but Aisling loved it. There was a picture of the boys and their soccer team after winning a cup match, faces dirty and proud. And there was a photo taken at a barbeque in Fiona's garden the summer before, a shot of Fiona dancing with Nicole with Pat in the background wearing an apron and waving a large fork with a sausage on each prong. There weren't any pictures of Michael. There had been a really nice one of him and the boys in Portugal, lying on the beach pretending to pose like

389

body-builders with white zinc striped down their noses to protect them from the sun.

She had taken it down and stuck it at the back of the drawer in the dining-room sideboard. She had briefly thought of cutting Michael out of the picture altogether, but decided that was a bit childish.

Sam stared at the photos and notes, looked at the postcard from Sorcha in Istanbul and the Mickey Mouse one from the Finucanes in Disneyland, and Aisling's shopping list reminders to get loo roll and fabric softener.

'There are none of you here,' he remarked, turning to her.

Aisling took a half-full bottle of Jameson out of the cupboard and sloshed some into each glass. 'I'm not photo-genic.'

'Don't say that,' he said firmly. 'I'm telling you, Aisling, you mightn't think so but you're one gorgeous lady.'

She was about to contradict him when she remembered an article she'd read in a magazine about compliments and how to take them graciously. *You'll never have confidence in yourself if you can't take a compliment. Your lack of confidence will eventually convince people that they're wrong – and you're right about yourself.*

'Thanks,' she said. That wasn't so hard, now was it? she thought.

'I guess nobody's told you you're beautiful often enough,' Sam said.

He leaned back against the worktop and took a long draught of whiskey. Aisling did the same. The fiery liquid hit her system with a jolt.

'Come here,' Sam said.

Still holding her glass, she stood in front of him. He stroked her cheek and let his hand lazily slide down her face to caress her neck. She could feel her skin burn where he'd touched her and she unconsciously leaned forward so he could touch her some more.

'You are beautiful,' he murmured, taking her glass away from her. He slid both arms around her waist and pulled her forward. Their lips met and it was as if Aisling had never been kissed before. His mouth was hungry on hers and she pressed her body close to his, throwing reservations to the wind. They clung together, bodies melting into each other. His body was solid, from all that rock-climbing, no doubt.

She held his head close to hers, her fingers running through his chestnut hair while she kissed him open-mouthed. He tasted good. Fantastic, in fact. She kissed him again, lots of small kisses melting into one long one.

It was the previous week all over again. Her nervousness had gone and she felt greedy for him, eager to feel his body pressed up against hers, inside hers.

'You're something else, Aisling,' he breathed, pulling his mouth away from hers for a moment. 'Should we continue this upstairs?'

'Yes.' Aisling couldn't believe what was going to happen. Here she was, a separated woman of thirty-five clinging to a man she barely knew – ready to have sex with him. On the first date, too. Did that make her the ultimate trollop, a complete slut? Probably. But who cared? She could do what she wanted. But it had to be safe. If she was going to do something this crazy, she'd better think about pregnancy or AIDs.

'Do you have condoms?' she asked bluntly, amazed at her own daring.

'Yes. Are you sure you want to do this?' he whispered, as he covered her in tiny, hot kisses.

'Yes. Come on.'

She'd made the decision, there was no going back. So what if she was about to have sex in her marital home with someone who wasn't her husband. Her bloody husband had shagged off with someone else. God, she needed a drink.

She moved out of Sam's embrace and picked up her glass, draining it. He smiled and drank his down too, proffering his glass for a refill. She poured two more huge whiskies, then took him by the hand and led him upstairs.

The bedroom was in darkness. Before she'd had a chance to

turn on the bedside lights, more flattering than the overhead one, he put his glass down and took hers away from her, then put his arms around her again.

They fell on the bed and rolled over until she was on top of him. He kissed her ardently while one hand burrowed under her skirt, sliding it up her thighs. Stockings and suspenders, Aisling thought, I should be wearing stockings and suspenders. Not tights.

Sam tried to reach the waistband of her black sheer tights but couldn't manage to hoist her skirt up high enough.

They'd be there all night if she didn't help.

'Hold on,' she whispered. Why am I whispering anyway? She wondered. There was nobody to hear them.

Aisling kissed him again and then wriggled off him, getting to her feet shakily. God, she'd had too much to drink. She was pretty pissed.

He gazed up at her expectantly as she unzipped her skirt slowly. Damn. There were few sights more unerotic than a pair of tights worn over knickers. Or a body. She didn't want him to see her like that.

'I'm waiting,' Sam sounded amused. 'Turn on the lights so I can see you.'

Aisling walked around the bed to turn on her bedside lamp. As she switched it on, Sam grabbed her, one hand unzipping her skirt. It slid down to her ankles and she quickly dragged off her tights before he pulled her into his arms. They kissed again, his tongue exploring her mouth while his hands gently explored her body. Thank God she'd shaved her legs earlier.

'Can I take this off?' Sam asked, fingers at the snap fasteners at the crotch of her bronze body.

'Only if you take everything off as well.'

Aisling unbuttoned his shirt, her fingers clumsy as they fiddled with the small buttons. She'd nearly finished and was sliding her hands under the fabric to touch his chest, when she felt him unpop her bronze body. She shuddered with pleasure as she felt his fingers on her bare flesh, stroking and probing her intimately.

'Oh Sam,' she murmured.

'Is it good?' he asked.

'Wonderful,' she replied, giving herself up to sheer pleasure. Sam pushed the body up until he'd exposed her breasts encased in a cream cotton bra.

'You're gorgeous,' he said, nuzzling the soft flesh of her breasts. 'Help me get this thing off.'

Aisling sat up and pulled the body off over her head. Sam reached behind her back and unclasped her bra swiftly.

'Now you,' she demanded, pulling his shirt tail out of his jeans. He stripped off quickly, then pulled down the duvet, and slid into the bed. Aisling got in beside him and snuggled up to him, loving the sensation of his warm silky skin on hers.

'You're beautiful, Aisling,' he repeated, tracing soft kisses down to her breasts, kissing her until Aisling was wild with pleasure.

'That's wonderful,' she said softly. 'Your turn.'

'No.' He propped himself up on one arm and gazed at her. 'Tonight I'm in charge and my job is to make you come over and over again,' he added. 'So lie back and think of the Empire!'

He kissed her breasts again as one hand gently stroked the sensitive skin on her inner thighs.

Aisling moaned with pleasure.

'If you insist, Mr Delaney,' she said.

'I do.'

Wow, thought Aisling for the second time as she lay propped up on the pillows with Sam sprawled out in the bed beside her. He was snoring, not loudly but still enough to keep her awake.

After two orgasms, she should have been out for the count, but she couldn't sleep. Even though it was four in the morning, she felt incredibly awake, utterly relaxed and totally sated. She hadn't realised quite how boring and mundane sex with Michael had become until now.

393

He'd been unstoppable, determined to send her into parox-ysms of pleasure twice. Twice. Wow.

She slid out from under the covers. Sam wouldn't miss her. Even if he did, she just had to have a drink of water. All the alcohol she'd consumed was taking its toll and she was madly thirsty. She took her dressing-gown off the hook on the door and went downstairs for a drink of water.

After draining the second glass, she refilled it and crept quietly into the downstairs toilet.

Aisling was amazed to find that she actually looked good. She glowed. That was it. Her hair was tousled, her lipstick had been completely kissed off, her eyes were red-rimmed with rivulets of mascara under them and she felt very tired, but the face in the mirror shone back at her.

She'd done it. She'd broken the curse of Michael by sleeping with another man in their bed. Thank you so much, Sam, she whispered to her reflection.

When she slid carefully under the duvet, Sam grunted and moved till he was curled up against her, his body moulded to hers. He moaned again, wrapped one arm around her and nuzzled into her neck.

'All right?' he muttered sleepily.

'Wonderful,' she whispered back, cuddling into him hap-pily. 'Wonderful.'

He woke her by kissing her gently, starting on her mouth and working his way down her neck until she opened her eyes groggily.

'This is your wake-up call, Aisling.' Sam moved further down her body to cup her full breasts in his hands.

'What time is it?' she asked, closing her eyes.

'Twenty to two.'

'Two! In the afternoon?' She shot up in the bed. 'The boys will be coming soon, you've got to go, Sam,' she said urgently.

'Relax.' His voice was amused. 'They're not coming home until six, you told me that last night. So what's the rush?'

'I know, but . . .' Aisling couldn't explain her panic. Last night, it had been different. How could she explain that she wanted Sam out of the house because she felt guilty, as if she'd done something wrong. She wanted him out so she could sort out her muddled feelings, so she could wash up the glasses, change the sheets and rinse him off her body. The boys mustn't see him yet, it was too soon.

'Please understand, Sam,' she began, 'I've never done anything like this before and it feels strange. I can't let the boys meet you yet. It would be too confusing for them, you must see that.'

'Did you enjoy last night?' he asked softly. His fingers played with her hair. He had the most amazing eyes.

'Of course . . .'

He stopped her words with a kiss, a gentle kiss which turned into a long, deep passionate one. Aisling couldn't help responding. The stubble on his chin grazed the soft skin on her neck as he moved down to nuzzle her breasts.

'I love your breasts, Aisling,' he said huskily. She couldn't resist him. He was so sexy and he seemed to know exactly how to turn her on. Before she knew it, they were wrapped up in the duvet, limbs intertwined as they made love.

'I'll go at three. That'll give you loads of time,' Sam murmured.

An hour later, she lay in the bath and watched him finish shaving. He splashed water on his face, dried it and looked at his reflection in the mirror, turning sideways to make sure he hadn't missed a bit with her old razor. Satisfied with what he saw, Sam ran a comb through his hair before pulling on his shirt.

'I'll see myself out,' he said and leaned down to caress one breast.

'God, you feel great. I want to drag you back to bed again. But not that bed, of course.' He straightened up abruptly. 'It's got to go, don't you agree?'

'Why?' asked Aisling, completely at a loss to know what he meant.

'We can hardly make love in the bed you shared with your husband,' he replied in astonished tones.

'Oh. I see,' Aisling said, although she didn't. Making love in Michael's bed hadn't worried him too much the night before. But then, they'd both been so plastered that they could have been making love on O'Connell Bridge with a paying crowd watching.

'We could go shopping next weekend,' he said. 'We've got to get some decent booze as well. I've got a real taste for bourbon after living in the States.'

'Fine,' Aisling said automatically.

Sam leaned down and kissed her gently on the mouth, a lingering gentle kiss.

He blew her another kiss from the bathroom door.

'See you soon,' he said.

She heard him slam the front door and sank happily back into the bubbles. Who cared if he wanted a new bed or bourbon instead of whiskey? He was wonderful, he was crazy about her. Hell, he could redecorate the bedroom if he felt like it. Aisling closed her eyes and thought about Sam making love to her. She'd get up and tidy the house later.

'Well, how was dinner?' demanded Fiona, the moment Aisling picked up the phone. 'Where did you go? Tell me *everything*.'

'Everything?' asked Aisling innocently, trying not to burst with excitement. 'Sam arrived at just after half seven and he was wearing a blue shirt . . .'

'Bugger the blue shirt!' said Fiona in exasperation. 'How did you get on? Did he kiss you, did you kiss him, did you have mad, passionate sex to Ravel's *Bolero*?'

Aisling snorted down the phone. 'The answers to those questions, in order, are, Marvellously, Yes. Yes and Yes – although we didn't have any music. You know I don't have a stereo in the bedroom.'

'Aisling Moran,' shrieked Fiona. 'I don't believe you. You slept with him? You didn't, did you?' she asked.

'Yes, I did. I know I'm a trollop but who cares, it felt absolutely wonderful and I'm glad I did sleep with him. Not that we got that much sleep . . .'

'Has he gone?' asked Fiona.

'Yes.'

'Right. Put the kettle on, I'm coming over. If you can walk into the kitchen without crutches, that is!'

'He's very attractive, of course,' Fiona said five minutes later, as she sat in Aisling's kitchen and lit a cigarette. 'And let's face it, straight, good-looking, single men are practically extinct in this country these days. Since you have me to thank for introducing you to him, I want all the juicy details. I mean *all.*'

'Thank you, darling Fiona, for introducing me to him,' Aisling said with a giggle. 'I certainly owe you. Sam is a fantastic lover. Not that I have anything to compare him with,' she added. 'But it was wonderful. Three times, Fiona, *three times.* I'm exhausted.'

'You don't look exhausted, Fiona remarked wryly. 'You look like they've turned a light on inside you.'

'I know. It's amazing, isn't it?' Aisling sat back in her chair with a practically untouched cup of coffee in one hand.

'We were awake till at least four and I should have a thumping great hangover after all we drank, but do you know what?' She grinned at Fiona. 'I feel fantastic. And different. I can't explain it, but being with Sam, it was as if all this pressure that's been building up inside me since Michael left was suddenly released, I could relax and let go. It was amazing.'

'You're in love,' Fiona said with a laugh.

'No,' corrected Aisling. 'I'm not. I fancy Sam and he fancies me, but that's not love. I don't want to be in love again, not for a long time.' She was suddenly serious. 'Love is just trouble. If you love someone, they have the power to hurt you and I don't want to go through that ever again.'

'That's perfectly understandable,' the other woman said. 'But don't think you can control love, Aisling. You can't.'

'I know that.' Aisling got up and filled up the kettle. The washing machine shuddered to a stop beside her, ending its final spin. She really should hang out the clothes but she couldn't be bothered. Tomorrow would do.

'Getting a job, losing weight and learning how to live on my own – they were all important things, but no matter what I did, I was still tied to Michael,' Aisling explained. 'Now I'm not. I was tied to him even though he wasn't tied to me. He'd escaped but I couldn't. Sam helped me to escape.'

'When are you seeing him again?' Fiona asked.

'Next weekend, for dinner. He wanted to see me tomorrow but he's got to go to Cork for the week. He's ringing later.'

Fiona raised one eyebrow expressively. 'He's keen.'

The last globule of cream squelched out of the piping bag onto the strawberry cheesecake. Aisling dumped the bag in the sink and carefully carried the plate over to the fridge.

Dizzy, the Coughlans' fat black spaniel, watched Aisling's every move, big brown eyes fixed on the woman who'd been cooking all sorts of delicious things in the kitchen all afternoon.

'No, you can't have anything, Dizzy,' Aisling admonished the drooling dog. 'You're on a diet.'

'*I'm* the one who should be on a diet,' wailed Rachel. She hurried into the kitchen wearing a pink candlewick dressing-gown with a wet towel wrapped, turban-style, around her head.

Rachel was short, plump, very pretty and looked at least ten years younger than her husband, who had to be around forty-five. She was also very disorganised, as Aisling had found out when she arrived in the Coughlans' kitchen a few hours earlier and started a lengthy search in hopelessly untidy cupboards for a large plate for the cheesecake.

'The zip on my black crêpe dress won't close. I know I should have bought those tummy-flattener pants,' Rachel said miserably. 'Have I time to race off to Spar and get a pair of control tights, do you think?'

'You have the time,' Aisling said slowly, thinking of the calorie-laden meal she'd been preparing. 'But you'll be awfully uncomfortable by the time you've eaten dinner if the dress is too tight in the first place.'

'You're right.' Rachel stomped over to the fridge and took out a bottle of white wine from the half-dozen on the bottom shelf.

'Oh, the cheesecake looks delicious!' she squealed as soon as she saw it. 'I can't wait to try it. Let's have a glass of wine, Aisling,' she wheedled. 'You've been busy all day and you need a break.'

Aisling had been working hard in Rachel's huge old-fashioned kitchen for over two hours, slicing vegetables, finishing off the cheesecake she'd made at home and preparing the pheasant with apples and Calvados. She'd nearly gone mad making the fiddly timbales of smoked salmon with dill salad Rachel had wanted to impress her snooty American sister-in-law, Antonia.

'When she's gone, I'll tell everyone else that you cooked the meal. Antonia will want to leave early, she always does. Doesn't like spending too much time with her in-laws,' Rachel revealed. 'But I want to pretend that I did everything just to shut that cow up. Do you mind awfully?'

'As long as you sneak my cards into everyone else's pockets when they're going,' Aisling replied, fishing several cream printed cards out of her handbag.

Reservations
*Why slave over the cooker when you can relax at your own
dinner party? My team and I can cook you an exquisite,
mouth-watering menu from fresh ingredients and you won't
have to lift a finger. Phone Aisling Moran for details.*

This wasn't strictly true. Aisling's team was herself and herself and herself. Still, she *could* get help if she really needed it. Her mother had offered to give her a hand with desserts.

'This looks very impressive.' Rachel admired the rich creamy paper and the elegant copperplate lettering Aisling had picked in the printing shop.

She'd had a hundred made up and was now crossing her fingers that they'd pay for themselves. She took a cautious sip

399

of wine from the glass Rachel handed her. Catastrophic if she ruined her first dinner by getting tiddly with the hostess before the meal.

'Is there anything I can do?' Rachel sat down at the kitchen table and took a bottle of flamingo-pink nail varnish from her dressing-gown pocket.

'No thanks, you relax,' said Aisling quickly. She'd seen Rachel's hopelessly untidy cupboards and the large collection of ready-made microwaveable meals in the freezer. The other woman was obviously not a dab hand in the kitchen.

By half seven everything was ready. The guests were due, the pheasant was cooking gently in the oven, the damned timbales were perfect and even Rachel was ready, resplendent in an expensive-looking gold silk blouse, black trousers and plenty of gold jewellery.

Her daughter, Amy – sixteen and pretty despite the sulky expression on her face – had been pressed into service to help serve the meal. Either Rachel had been around fifteen when she had Amy, or she used lots of miraculous wrinkle-preventing eye cream, Aisling decided.

In a tattered pair of 501s, a skinny black polo neck that was turning grey, and black suede boots with stack heels, Amy looked like a younger, slimmer version of her mother.

'You could have dressed up, Amy.' Rachel marched into the kitchen to find her offspring enjoying a sneaky vodka tonic. 'You certainly shouldn't be drinking. I said one glass of wine, if you remember. And those jeans are dreadful.'

Amy shot Rachel a venomous look.

'Don't look at me like that, Madam,' started Rachel crossly. Aisling knew that a row was brewing. Maybe I should cook the stuff at home and just drive it over, she thought silently. Maybe I should forget the idea of running a catering company at all.

The doorbell rang loudly. Row instantly forgotten, Rachel roared for her husband to answer the door and hurried out to welcome her guests.

It was eight by the time everyone was seated. Jim was on

wine service and winked at Aisling when he rushed past her with two bottles of white and the corkscrew under his arm. Rachel bustled back into the kitchen to help Amy carry in the twelve plates.

'I don't want Antonia to see you,' she whispered to Aisling.

Aisling was grateful that she didn't have to go in and serve the guests. Cooking a meal *and* looking fresh as a daisy when serving it, simply wasn't possible. Her grey T-shirt was damp with sweat and her hair had flopped in the heat of the kitchen, strands stuck to her forehead. She longed for a long warm bath, a nice book and a glass of sweet white wine.

But it would be at least half ten when she got home and she knew that she'd barely have the energy to slump onto the settee and watch some mindless rubbish before going to bed.

When the guests were all eating, she pushed the door between the kitchen and the dining room open just a fraction, and listened.

She heard murmurs of 'Delicious, Rachel' and 'This salmon is fantastic, how did you do it?' They liked it. She only hoped the pheasant went down as well.

'Would you like some pheasant?' she asked Amy when the girl returned to the kitchen after delivering the last plate.

'I'm a vegetarian,' Amy said, then added, 'but everyone in there is gobbling the pheasant up like mad. Even Aunt Antonia.'

'Not a woman easily pleased, I believe.' Aisling filled the sink with hot water.

Amy grimaced. 'She's a cow. I hope she chokes on it. Not because of your cooking,' she added quickly. 'No offence.'

'None taken. If you're hungry, I could make you some nice cheese sauce for the broccoli and cauliflower, or an omelette?' Aisling had noticed that the girl looked tired and pale under her heavy pancake foundation.

'No, but thanks anyway.' Amy was really very pretty when she smiled. 'D'you want a hand with the washing-up?'

Aisling scrubbed and Amy dried.

'Do you cook all the time, for a living, I mean?'

401

'Actually, this is my first dinner party,' Aisling explained. 'I work as a secretary in a legal firm and I ended up catering for a special lunch when the original caterers made a mess of things. That's where I met your father and he said your mother would love some help with parties and dinners for her new business.'

'That's true. She can't even make tea. So you never did anything like this before?'

'I love cooking and I've done cooking courses but I never actually thought of doing it professionally. Until this year, anyway.'

'Why is that?'

'I was a housewife and I went back to work when my husband and I split up earlier this year,' Aisling said matter-of-factly. She didn't feel her heart ache when she said it, didn't feel the lump in her throat at the thought of Michael. Thank God. She rinsed a copper-bottomed saucepan and placed it on the drainer.

'When people congratulated me on my cooking after the lunch, I decided to do something about it and then your mum rang. With a bit of luck, and if people get my cards when they're leaving, I'll get more jobs like this.'

'Wow, that's amazing. You're a career woman.' Amy dried a wooden spoon carefully.

Aisling smiled at the girl. 'I suppose I am. Strange, I never thought I'd be one.'

'That's what I want to be,' Amy said. 'I don't want to sit around like Mum did for years waiting for something to happen before Dad pushed her into doing something.'

'That's hardly fair, Amy,' Aisling rebuked gently.' If your mother hasn't worked for a few years, it's very, very difficult going back. I should know.

'My first few months back at work were a nightmare. Imagine if you'd been off school for two years and then had to go back to class with girls two years younger and start again . . .'

'I suppose you're right,' Amy said reluctantly.

'I *know* I'm right,' Aisling said firmly. 'You'd feel totally threatened and stupid, because they'd know more than you. You'd be paranoid about not fitting in. It's a horrible feeling, believe me. Take it from me, your mum's been really brave setting up this PR company and I'm sure she could do with your support.'

'Suppose.' Amy dried a saucepan.

'Everything's going wonderfully, Aisling.'

Rachel rushed into the kitchen clutching four empty bottles of wine.

'It is if you've gone through all that booze already,' reproved Amy, as if she hadn't been drinking herself. 'That's nine bottles at least.'

'It's a party. And there are twelve of us,' Rachel retorted. 'They love the pheasant, especially Antonia. She says she's "amazed it's so good". Bitch. Can you put cyanide on her cheesecake, Aisling?'

Aisling grinned. 'I'm not sure how good that would be for my reputation as a dinner-party cook. I'll do salmon timbales but I draw the line at cyanide.'

'They were gorgeous,' Rachel sighed. 'Everyone wanted to know how I did them. And the pheasant too. I think they're all convinced I cleaned out Marks and Spencer's food hall. As soon as Antonia is gone, do come in and I'll introduce you, won't you?'

Aisling didn't really want to but then she thought about her business. 'Of course. I'll need to freshen up first.'

'Use my room,' volunteered Amy.

It was half twelve when Aisling turned the key in her front door lock. The pots and pans would just have to stay in the hall overnight, she decided, dumping everything onto the hall carpet.

Antonia and her husband had stayed at the Coughlans' until eleven, so Aisling and Amy had sat in the kitchen watching Tom Cruise in *Top Gun* on the small TV beside the microwave until they'd left.

When Aisling finally walked into the dining room, everyone clapped.

403

'The best meal I've had in years,' said one woman, holding up a large glass of port as a toast. 'I do hope you can cook for me sometime.'

'Of course,' Aisling said. 'I'll give you a card.'

The meal had been a huge success and, as she went into the kitchen to look for Flossie, she felt elated but dog-tired. She switched off the lights downstairs and went to bed, not even bothering to take off her eye make-up. Just before turning out her bedside light, she switched the alarm clock off. She was going to have a lie-in in the morning. She deserved it.

'Aisling, that really isn't you. It doesn't suit you.' Sam stood a few feet away from the changing cubicle, eyes narrowed as he looked at the fitted navy dress Aisling had just tried on. She sighed in exasperation. This was the third item she'd tried on and he'd hated the other two as well.

The cream woollen dress with a matching long cardigan was 'too tight', the elegant black shirt was 'too short', and she'd thought he was going to have a seizure when he saw the clingy red lycra top that went with it. They'd been shopping in the Stephen's Green Centre for just an hour and Aisling was already wondering what sort of illness she could fake so she could go home. She'd been so thrilled with Sam's present of a clothes voucher to celebrate their first month of going out together. It was such a thoughtful gift, she'd told Fiona happily.

Aisling cooked a special dinner for the occasion and she was delighted when Sam gave her the voucher which was hidden in a big box of chocolates. It was the sort of gesture Michael would never have made.

'We can go shopping next Saturday,' Sam had said, unwrapping a coffee creme for her.

'I'd love that,' she said truthfully, wondering how to avoid eating too many chocolates without upsetting him. A whole box of Dairy Milk would mean she couldn't eat a proper meal for at least a month. 'I'd love to go shopping with you.'

Famous last words.

'What *would* look good on me, Sam?' she demanded now,

irritated beyond belief. 'A yashmak?'

'Honey, don't get upset.' He looked pained, his eyes troubled, as if she'd really upset him. 'I just want you to buy something suitable, that's all.'

'Suitable for *what*?'

'For going out to dinner with me, for the office. You needn't be so defensive. I'm only trying to help.'

'Listen, Sam.' Aisling looked at him with eyes blazing. 'You and I have very different ideas about what's "suitable". I have the sort of figure I can show off. And I want to show it off!' she hissed. 'Have you got that?'

'Fine. I just want you to look nice.'

The cheek of him, Aisling thought crossly as she retreated into the changing room and pulled the curtains. As if she didn't look nice before.

Men always thought they knew better than you. She hoped this particular phase turned out to be just that – a phase – a brief one. For all his faults, Michael had never been particularly interested in her wardrobe. Then again, maybe that had been part of the problem. Perhaps men were supposed to be fascinated by what their women wore. Perhaps it was a caveman thing, a flattering thing.

Aisling stood in her bra and knickers and looked at the three very nice outfits that Sam had condemned. They all *looked* nice. But after years of wearing sloppy T-shirts and elastic-waisted trousers, she probably wasn't the best fashion expert in the world.

Wearing anything clingy was a thrill for her. But maybe Sam was right and she shouldn't indulge her taste for spray-on lycra garments in case she ended up looking like mutton dressed as lamb.

'Aisling.' The curtain shook. 'Look what I've found.'

She stuck her head out of the cubicle.

'This,' Sam produced a clothes-hanger from behind his back, 'would be lovely on you.'

'This' turned out to be a long, highly patterned pale peach dress that flowed and billowed like a sail, a dress which would undoubtedly make her look like an over-the-hill bridesmaid. Six months ago, Aisling would have loved it, mainly because it was big enough to accommodate a size sixteen. However, she wasn't a size sixteen any more and she wanted to wear something which showed off the fact. Sam didn't know anything about this. He had no idea she'd lost so much weight, she hadn't told him. Aisling had felt it might change his opinion of her, as if he'd go off her if he found out she hadn't always been the slim blonde she was now.

It wasn't fair to expect him to understand her hatred for anything baggy. Keep calm, she told herself. Don't let the sins of Michael Moran be visited on every man after him.

She reached out and took the dress from Sam. His face creased into a smile and she grinned back at him. She impulsively leaned out and kissed him on the cheek. There was something utterly charming about Sam's smile, that mischievous grin which lit up his face. He was quite irresistible standing there in a snow-white cricket jumper and faded denims which clung to his long legs. One of the shop assistants had eyed him up the moment they walked into the shop until Aisling shot her a proprietorial 'hands off' look.

'Bet you a tenner it looks lovely on you,' said Sam confidently, as she slipped back behind the curtain.

His attitude to clothes was probably because he'd lived in the States for so long, Aisling decided as she took the dress off the hanger and stepped into it. Apart from places like California, people in the US dressed in a much more conservative manner than their European cousins, didn't they? Aisling wasn't sure. But she ought to give Sam the benefit of the doubt. Definitely.

'It's beautiful, Aisling.' He held one of her hands high and made her turn so he could admire the dress from every angle. Privately, she thought it made her look like some sort of child-woman instead of a mature woman of thirty-five. But Sam loved it.

'It's so sexy,' he cried with delight. 'You look amazing.'

He grabbed her in a bear hug and whispered in her ear. 'Good enough to eat. Let's take it.'

'And then we can stop shopping?' Aisling asked.

'Absolutely.'

'I'll take it.'

CHAPTER EIGHTEEN

'Sit down.' The builder dragged up a paint-speckled stool for Jo to sit on. He covered it with a newspaper and Jo sat down gratefully. For once, it wasn't tiredness, an aching back or her recently developed varicose veins that made her want to sit down rapidly. It was the state of the cottage.

She'd expected a clean, newly refurbished place but she'd walked into a disaster area, with dust everywhere and the sound of a kango hammer blasting in her ears.

Rhona had often asked her whether she was insane to sell her cosy, modern apartment in Malahide to move into an old, ramshackle cottage in the Dublin mountains.

'You won't be in before Christmas,' Rhona declared when Jo explained that there'd be a two-week gap between moving out of her apartment and moving into the newly painted, renovated and rewired house in tranquil Redwood Lane.

'The contractor's a very reliable man and he says it'll all be finished by the fifth of November,' Jo replied. 'Honestly, Rho, it's not like you to be so pessimistic.'

Rhona looked at her friend shrewdly. 'Jo, if it's finished by the tenth of November, we'll go out to celebrate – you can have dinner and I'll eat my hat. It's a pity you hadn't joined *Style* when Ted and I bought our house. I distinctly remember being told the house would be ready by the end of August. We moved in during a torrential downpour in October. I never got the water stains out of my mother's old cream armchair.'

It looked as if Rhona was going to be proved right. It was already the second week in November, the builders had been working for three weeks and the cottage looked worse than ever.

The tiny hall was filthy with muddy footprints. A week of

rain had stopped work on the roof. The garden had turned into a bog and roof still hadn't been fixed. All the cottage needed was rewiring, central heating installed, a bit of work on the plumbing and a small job on the roof, or so Mark's contractor friend had said.

So why, after three weeks, was the entire place like a building site?

'It's not as bad as it looks,' the builder roared over the din.

'Really, Tom? Well, that's a relief because it looks bad, very bad.' Jo's head throbbed in time to the kango hammer.

'Turn it off,' roared Tom in the direction of the kitchen.

When nothing happened, he left Jo in the tiny hall wondering what the hell she was going to say to the painters who were due to arrive tomorrow.

'Tea?' asked Tom, poking his head around the kitchen door. 'We're just brewing up.'

'OK. Now tell me what's happened?' Jo asked wearily. She got off the stool, walked into the kitchen and stared at the big hole where the sink used to be and at the gash that ran across the recently concreted floor.

'Plumbing problem. We've had to rip up the floor. I did ring you at the office yesterday evening to tell you,' he added, 'but when I couldn't contact you, I just went ahead and sorted it out. It'll add another two days onto the work. We'll be finished by Tuesday, latest.'

'The painters are coming tomorrow,' Jo said in a faint voice.

'I know, I know. I'll ring them up and tell them not to come until Tuesday afternoon.'

'Sugar?' inquired the man who'd been working the kango hammer.

'Two, please,' said Jo, 'and do you have any biscuits?' Or Prozac?

They drank their tea and talked about how the rain had delayed the work, how the plumbing had delayed the work and how there was some problem with the phone-line according to the man from Telecom.

'Oh, did I tell you that he came?' asked Tom.

Jo speed-munched her way through three fig rolls and drank a cup of very sweet tea before climbing the stairs. The pale wooden banisters were thick with concrete dust, lumps of plaster had found their way onto the steps. Jo ignored it.

As she walked into the second bedroom, she realised that the painters would have to spend days cleaning the walls and woodwork.

At least the cork tiles in the bathroom would only need a wash. But the pale green carpet in the smaller bedroom was so dusty Jo knew she'd have to replace it. She thought about the mounting bills and decided that judicious hoovering would have to do for the moment. Maybe she could rent one of those industrial carpet cleaners and do it herself. Then again, she thought gloomily, at seven months pregnant she was hardly in any condition to hoover anything except food up from her plate. She felt *huge*. Even her gynaecologist said so. Huge, broke and with a half-finished cottage hanging around her neck like a millstone. She poked at a bit of carpet with her shoe. A cloud of dust rose like white smoke from the Vatican. Blast.

If anyone asked her what she wanted for her birthday in a couple of weeks, she'd ask for a carpet-cleaning voucher.

The kango hammer started up again, the noise practically drowned out the thoughts in her head. God, what a waste it had been coming up here today. But she had to do something on her day off instead of slobbing around Aisling's house. It was lovely of Aisling to have offered her spare room for the two weeks when Jo was homeless – make that six weeks – and lovely to spend time with her friend, the first time they'd actually lived together since their flat-sharing days. But she preferred her own space to living with someone else, even if that someone was as easy-going as Aisling. And now that Sam was there every minute of the day, Jo was beginning to feel like a gooseberry. An enormous gooseberry.

She went into the main bedroom and idled away a few moments imagining how she was going to decorate it. She'd picked a rich yellow paint to go with the cream and butter-milk curtains she fancied. But the curtain material would have to wait. God only knew how much extra the contractor would charge.

She was staring out at the muddy wasteland at the front of the cottage wondering how it could possibly be transformed back into something resembling a garden, when the baby kicked. Jo's face grew soft as she stroked her belly lovingly.

The baby was always kicking these days, but Jo didn't mind, except when it happened all night. On those days when she felt depressed, miserable and lonely at the thought of having the baby all by herself, all it took was a gentle reminder from her little passenger to cheer her up.

'I'm off,' she said to Dick, the kango-hammer man, who'd stopped the machine once he saw her making her way carefully down the stairs.

'Bye, Tom,' she called into the sitting room.

'He's gone,' Dick said.

Charming, thought Jo. Rips up the kitchen floor and buggers off. What a worker.

It had started to rain. Again. She trudged through the mud where she and Mark had once negotiated nettles and long grass, and got into her car.

She'd had to push the driver's seat back so she could fit her bump behind the steering wheel. Her size also meant she'd outgrown practically everything she owned, including her maternity trousers. Aisling was going to bring her shopping tomorrow, 'early, so we'll avoid the Saturday crowds', she'd said. Aisling was great. She'd even sorted through her old 'fat' clothes to find something to fit Jo.

A flowery overshirt Aisling had produced, her own black maternity skirt and a pair of pale grey ski boots were today's deeply unflattering outfit. Wedged into the driver's seat, Jo couldn't see her feet, but she just knew that the ski boots were filthy from the muck outside the cottage.

There was no way she could go into the supermarket in this state. Damn and blast.

She turned the key in the ignition. The engine made a high-pitched whirring noise, gave a little shudder and then died. Damn, damn, damn. She turned the key again. Same outcome. I do not believe this is happening, she shrieked. She tried again and when the engine made a third half-hearted attempt to get going, she thumped the steering wheel angrily. Bloody car! This is the perfect time for you to pack it in!

She levered herself out of the car, marched back into the cottage and gave Dick the fright of his life when she tapped him on the shoulder.

'Jesus!' he yelled.

Jo was not in the mood for conversation. 'My car won't start. Will you have a look at it?'

By the time Dick had pulled off his dusty overalls, tried the car a few times and spent ten minutes with his head under the bonnet poking around, Jo was at boiling-point.

'It's your starting motor,' he pronounced finally.

'Which means *what*, exactly?' Jo asked irritably.

'It's not going anywhere today,' he replied.

Jo felt as if she'd been deflated. 'What will I do?' she asked. 'Can you give me a lift to a garage or something?' she pleaded.

'Tom's got the van and he's not coming back for a couple of hours. He's running over to check on a job in Bray. But I've got a mobile. You can ring someone.'

Rhona's mobile phone squawked that she was either out of coverage or had her unit turned off.

Rhona was out all day, Nikki was in London and everyone else in the office was at lunch, Annette said when she answered the phone.

'I can't go anywhere,' Annette said, deeply apologetic, 'the man's coming to fix Tom's word processor and I've got to be here. I'll get someone to pick you up as soon as . . . oh, hold on, Jo, will you.'

Jo sheltered from the rain under the porch of the cottage. She wouldn't be able to hear a thing Annette was saying from *inside* the cottage since Dick had started kango-ing again.

412

She'd have to get her own mobile phone. More money. Why hadn't she bothered joining the AA? Why, why, why?

'Jo?' said a man's deep voice. She gasped. It was Mark. 'What's happened?'

She'd managed to avoid him for ages, had been frostily polite in the office, disappeared as fast as a heavily pregnant woman could whenever he seemed to be walking towards her desk to talk to her. Now there was no escape.

'My car's broken down. It's the starting motor, apparently. I've got no one to bring me home,' she wailed. 'And I don't know who to ring. It's never actually broken down on me before.'

'Where are you? And how do you know it's the starting motor?'

'I'm at the cottage. Redwood Lane. One of the builders looked at it for me. It's his phone I'm using but he doesn't have the van because Tom's gone to Bray.'

If Mark was confused by this explanation, he didn't let on. 'Leave it to me,' he said firmly. 'I'll arrange for a tow truck to pick the car up and I'll come and get you myself. Give me three-quarters of an hour.'

He must have really pushed the Porsche to the speed limit. Only twenty-five minutes later his car roared down the lane and stopped outside the house.

'Nice car,' said Dick appreciatively, sipping another cup of tea. Too much tea, that was why the cottage was like a disaster area, Jo thought testily. Maybe she should swipe the tea bags and see how much Dick got done without a tea break every half an hour.

'Your fella, is he?' Dick inquired with interest.

Jo sniffed. 'No.'

'Mmm,' Dick muttered, as if he'd noticed the eyeshadow, mascara and lipstick she'd carefully applied in the bathroom mirror. She hoped his nose was too bunged up with cement dust to smell the liberal application of Trésor. If only she'd been able to find her brush. Not that she could have done much repair work when her hair was so damp and frizzy.

413

Mark swept up the path, a dark brown waxed raincoat flapping around his long legs. He looked far more at home in the wilds of the Dublin mountains than she did. Apart from her ski boots.

He also looked healthily brown after two weeks in the Maldives, the honey colour of his skin made the grey streaks in his short hair stand out even more. He was sickeningly attractive, sexy and most definitely not 'my fella', thought Jo desolately.

'Hello,' she said in a small voice.

'Come and sit in my car while I have a look at the engine.' He put a strong arm around her. They walked slowly down the path. He pushed the passenger seat back, helped her in carefully and said, 'I won't be a moment.'

Jo watched him stride back to her car and lift the bonnet capably. Mark did everything capably, everything from running several businesses to fixing the coffee maker in the office when Annette said it couldn't be fixed.

He'd made her feel safe, comforted and special for a few months. And she'd pushed him away and into the arms of his old girlfriend. Well, he'd hardly gone to the Maldives *alone*.

A few minutes later, Mark opened the car door, threw his raincoat into the back and eased his big frame into the driver's seat.

'It's the starting motor, all right. Someone from my garage is coming to get it. They'll have it for you tomorrow afternoon.'

'Will it be expensive?' she asked tiredly.

Mark shot her a glance.

'No. I doubt it. It's just a small job.'

'Really?'

'Really. I don't suppose you've had any lunch, Jo, have you?' he asked kindly.

Nobody said her name like that but Mark, with that mixture of warmth and something else, something she could never define. Tenderness. Was that it? Couldn't be. Why would he bother being kind to her when she'd been such a bitch to him?

Jo bit her lip and looked out the window at the small patchwork fields speeding by, dark with mud. Cows huddled together in the rain, monotonously chewing silage from big metal troughs. They looked as wet as she was. They looked depressed too. Being a cow couldn't be much fun.

She felt a hand on hers, a warm, strong hand clasping her small, cold one for a moment.

'Let's go to Johnny Fox's. I could do with a decent pint of Guinness and some lunch, how about you?'

Jo couldn't say anything. She just nodded.

'Good. And you can tell me why you're still up to your eyes in builders a month after they started.'

'Don't get me going on builders,' said Jo, brightening up. 'Honestly, I don't know what they're playing at. They know I'm in a hurry to move in but they don't seem to be working any faster to make up for lost time.'

'Have you spoken to Brian recently?' Mark put his hand back on Jo's after negotiating a sharp bend. 'He's the best contractor I know. He usually runs a pretty tight ship.'

'He's away all this week.' Jo was almost afraid to move in case she dislodged his hand from hers. It felt lovely to be touched, so comforting to have his fingers gently curled around hers.

'I'll ring his office later,' Mark said, 'and put the skids under those boyos at your house. Brian must be paying them too much if they've all got mobiles, and I don't want to make them millionaires at your expense.'

'Thanks,' Jo said gratefully. 'I know I should be tougher on them myself, but I'm just not up to it right now. If they said anything back to me, I know I'd cry.' She was sick of acting hard-as-nails with Mark. He didn't have to know that when she felt like crying, it was because she'd messed up her chances with him. Nobody knew that, not even Rhona.

Jo had lost count of the times when she'd lain in bed and wondered what he was doing, who he was doing it with.

She still had the ticket stub from their trip to America in her purse and sometimes she took it out and touched it,

415

remembering the few days they'd had together. When anything seemed possible, even a love affair between a pregnant woman and her boss.

Jo had searched the gossip columns relentlessly, keeping an eye out for mentions of glamorous half-French painters or wealthy businessmen. But there'd been nothing.

Once or twice, she'd thought of telling Rhona what had happened, that she'd lied to Mark about Richard. Then she'd stopped herself. Mark had to be in love with Eva and Rhona knew about it, Jo was sure. Telling Rhona that she was in love with Mark would put the other woman in a difficult position.

Jo could almost hear her words, 'They're getting married, Jo, as soon as she can get a divorce.'

Mark looked over and grinned at her, the tiny lines around his grey eyes crinkled up attractively.

'I have tissues in the glove compartment if you feel like a good sob,' he offered. 'But I hope I can cheer you up.'

You sure could, Jo thought silently.

He stopped the car outside the highest pub in Ireland and hurried around to help Jo out of her seat.

Oh God, she thought, remembering the muddy ski boots.

'I look a mess,' she sighed. 'These horrible boots and everything.'

Mark took her face in both hands and kissed her gently on the lips. 'You look absolutely beautiful, as always, Jo.'

Still holding her upturned face, he stared at her carefully, eyes taking in her huge dark eyes fringed with thick lashes. She stared back at him, wondering if she'd dreamed the last moment. She looked an absolute mess with her frizzy hair and her awful clothes. Had he really kissed her and told her she was beautiful? It was like some glorious dream.

Mark was watching her intensely, fingers warm on her skin and suddenly she knew what he was waiting for. A response. He wasn't sure, he'd taken a chance. What a fabulous, marvellous, perfectly timed chance.

Jo smiled at him, feeling the warmth deep inside her spread onto her face.

She stretched one hand up and touched his cheek gently. She stood on her toes and arched herself towards his lips, not easy in her condition. He slid one arm around her, supporting her back as he bent down to kiss her. This time, it was no gentle, platonic kiss: it was deep and passionate, yet somehow full of love and understanding.

Mark pulled away first. 'I should have done that a long time ago,' he said. 'I've wanted to for long enough.'

Jo couldn't speak. She stood looking up at him, her eyes strangely filled with tears.

'Come on.' He took her by the hand and led her towards the pub's front door. 'It's starting to rain again. We can't have you getting soaked twice in one day.'

He found a pew-style seat for her near the fireplace and banked up cushions behind her to protect her back. After months of looking after herself, this act of tenderness was nearly her undoing.

'Don't cry, Jo,' Mark said softly, sitting beside her and kissing her on the cheek. 'I know you're all emotional. But I'm here to look after you now.'

This finished her off completely. 'It's so wonderful,' she sobbed, the tears finally racing down her cheeks. 'You're being so nice, after I was such a bitch to you. I don't deserve it.'

'Of course you do. It's me who doesn't deserve you.' He handed her his handkerchief. 'Blow.'

'I'm always stealing your handkerchiefs,' she snuffled tearily. 'Sorry.'

'My handkerchiefs are all yours, everything of mine is yours.'

He meant it too, she realised, looking up at his face through the tears.

'What about Eva?' she asked.

'There's been nothing going on between Eva and myself, not for a long time. Certainly not since I fell in love with you.'

'What about the Maldives?' asked Jo anxiously. 'You couldn't go *there* on your own, could you?'

417

Mark's look of amazement told her he hadn't a clue what she was talking about.

'Your holiday,' she prompted.

'I went to Spain with some friends to play golf. Male friends, I should add. I couldn't stand a beach holiday. Unless you were with me,' he added, planting a gentle kiss on her forehead. 'Think of the fun I could have rubbing sun lotion onto you.'

She drank hot tea and he fed her smoked salmon on home-made brown bread. He only started on his plate when hers was finished.

'You're so good to me, Mark,' she said simply, leaning comfortably against his shoulder as he ate.

'I've wanted to be good to you for a long time but you wouldn't let me,' he answered, taking a bite of bread. 'You're very good at that "I'm an independent woman" thing, very good at scaring people off.'

Jo grimaced. 'I know, I'm sorry.'

'There's no need to be sorry, I can understand exactly why you'd want to scare people off.'

'Can you?' she asked uncertainly. She desperately wanted him to understand everything. 'I was so lonely and on my own when Richard left. I felt like a one-woman disaster area. I couldn't bear to let anyone close.'

'I can see that now,' he said with a low laugh. 'When you split up with him . . . I didn't know if that was the right time to make my move. I was afraid you were still in love with him.'

Jo let her right hand rest on Mark's neck, her fingers stroked the back of his head. She loved feeling the breadth of his shoulders, the sheer physical size of him. He made her feel petite, even now when she was as big as a whale.

'When I asked you to go to New York, it was a gamble. I hoped you'd go. I wanted to find out how you really felt about him despite the break-up.'

'You knew we'd split up?' she asked in astonishment.

He grinned and fed her a sliver of salmon drenched in lemon juice.

'Yes. I haf good informants, *Fräulein*,' he said in a mock-German accent. 'I needed to know if you could ever think of me. And I thought you could – and maybe even did – until you told me about the baby.' He shrugged. 'At that point, I felt like such a heel, as if I was trying to take advantage of you.'

'That's why you started treating me like your long-lost little sister,' she said, finally understanding.

'I didn't feel very brotherly towards you.' Mark stroked her thigh with one hand. 'Not at all.'

Jo felt a warmth in her belly at the thought of Mark harbouring unbrotherly desires for her. She remembered the dream she'd had about him that night in the Manhattan Fitzpatrick, the dream where they were naked and entangled in bed.

'I thought you were disgusted with me, that's why we couldn't talk except on the phone,' she explained, dragging her thoughts away from the picture of them in bed.

'Disgusted? Never. You've got to understand something, Jo,' Mark said, turning to face her, 'the way I felt about you, I couldn't bear to see you alone, alone and pregnant thanks to that bastard, when you should have been loved and your baby should have been loved.'

She loved hearing him talk this way, loved it.

'Christ, I couldn't bear to see you facing everything on your own.' He tucked back a few damp strands of Jo's hair behind one ear.

'So you mean you fancied me when you brought me out to lunch ages ago, before we went to New York?' Jo demanded.

'Yes.'

'And you fancied me when we went to New York?'

'Fancied you? I wanted to drag you into bed and never let you out again. When you wore that brown painted thing, I couldn't take my eyes off you.'

'That's my Mary Gregory dress, not some "thing"! But you liked it?' she added, with an arch smile.

'I loved it.'

419

'Good. I was beginning to think I'd lost my touch,' she added triumphantly.

'And I love you too, Jo. I just needed the chance to tell you. Today was it.'

'Oh Mark.' Jo leaned against him contentedly. 'I love you too. I thought I'd never be able to say that – to your face, that is.' She sat up straight. 'Do you think we should ask the garage to keep the starting motor for us as a sort of memento?'

'One we can look at on our silver wedding and feel indebted to?' he asked, kissing her again.

'Exactly!'

'We should keep Rhona's telephone as a memento as well,' he added.

'Why?'

'Because yesterday she told me that you weren't really with Richard, that he hadn't come back. Why the hell did you say he had?'

'I didn't want you to think I was pining for you when you were obviously in love with Eva,' Jo said defensively. 'I couldn't bear you to pity me or think I was a foolish pregnant woman.'

'I've never met anyone as imaginative as you in my life,' Mark said. 'Does this mean that if I don't ring you first thing tomorrow morning, you'll suddenly decide that I've gone off to the South of France with someone else?'

Jo didn't answer. She was thinking of the most important question of all, the one thing she had to ask.

'The baby. The baby is the most important thing in my life, Mark. I have to think of her first. Can you love my baby, even though she's Richard's?'

'She *won't* be Richard's baby,' he said simply. 'She'll be *our* baby, *our* child. If I hadn't wanted both mother and child, do you think I'd be here? I'm not like him. I don't just want the beautiful journalist and nothing else, no ties, no commitments. I want the woman, the mother, you.' Mark turned on the seat, held her hands and looked at her.

'I know you've been hurt, Jo, but you've got to trust me. I'll never let anyone hurt you ever again. And as for that bastard . . .'

She placed a finger over his mouth. 'Don't ruin it by even talking about him,' she said. 'He's bad news, always has been, although I didn't realise it for a long time. Let's just forget about him.'

They sat in front of the fire for an hour. Jo warmed her toes after Mark had carefully taken off her ski boots.

'I can't remember when I last saw my feet,' she said cheerfully, as the warmth of the fire sank into her bones.

'Was I always really horrible to you?' she asked, hating to think of how she'd been fatally drawn into disagreeing with every second word Mark had said at the editorial conferences.

'Brutal,' he replied. 'You were so argumentative, always determined to have your say because you had such strong opinions about everything. But I liked that. You were never afraid to have your say. And if you were proved wrong, you always said so, which I like even more.'

'Like the posters with the three words wrongly spelled?' she asked.

'Like the posters,' he agreed. 'You were so angry with yourself that day when you realised they'd nearly gone to the printers incorrectly. And you were twice as angry with me for mentioning it at the meeting. I remember you were wearing that pink cardigan thing, it was really quite see-through.'

Jo grimaced. 'I know, I only realised how transparent it was later.'

'I noticed,' he said with a small smile. 'You came back into the boardroom after the meeting to get your notebook, all barely concealed temper.' He paused and grinned. 'I was trying not to stare at your breasts because I could see the faint outline of your bra through the cardigan . . . It was quite a feat to talk at all.'

'I thought you were a pig and I was waiting for you to make a sarcastic comment!' Jo exclaimed.

'I was trying not to grab you and tell you I was crazy about you there and then,' Mark said.

'Really?' she asked in delight. 'I was going to throw that cardigan out.'

'Don't you dare,' he murmured. 'Next time you wear it, I want to take it off.'

'I might not fit into it ever again,' Jo said ruefully, looking down at herself.

'It doesn't matter. We'll just have to find something else for me to rip off,' Mark said gently.

It was nearly four when Mark looked at his watch.

'I'm afraid that we have to go, darling,' he said, smiling down at her as if he couldn't quite believe that she was his. She knew how he felt.

'I've got to go to this business dinner in town at eight and I've got a meeting in Jurys beforehand.' He got to his feet.

'Oh.' Jo couldn't hide her disappointment. She'd hoped that they could spend the evening together and now he was telling her about his plans, plans that had nothing to do with her.

'You're invited, my pet, so don't get upset. I'll pick you up at half six,' he added, tickling her under the chin.

Jo beamed at him. 'You've certainly got me figured out.'

'I've been doing research for over three years,' he said. 'My God, are you all right? Is it the baby?' he asked suddenly, as Jo let out an anguished squeak.

'No. I've nothing to wear!' she wailed. 'Nothing glamorous that will fit me, anyway.'

'Is that all?' Mark gave her a hug. 'Rhona's bound to have something glam from her three pregnancies and we're not far from her house. We could drop in and pick something up.'

Rhona answered her mobile with her characteristically brusque, 'Yes!'

'Hi, Rho, it's Jo here. Where are you?'

'Stuck behind a bloody truck on the dual carriageway. You sound as if you're on a car phone, Jo.'

'I am. I'm with Mark.'

She was rewarded with a triumphant roar on the other end of the receiver.

'With Mark as in with him in the car, or *with* Mark?' Rhona demanded.

'*With* him,' answered Mark, who could hear his editor's roars.

'Yahoo! Thank you for ringing me to tell me,' Rhona said in a quieter voice.

'Actually, I'm ringing because I need something sexy in the maternity-dress line for this dinner Mark is bringing me to tonight,' Jo said apologetically. 'We're only a few miles away from your place . . .'

'Typical. I personally co-ordinate the match of the decade and you just want to rifle through my wardrobe!' Rhona did her best to sound outraged but failed. 'I'll be home in twenty minutes. Ted will be there so tell him to put the kettle on. Better still, I'll phone him myself.'

When Rhona swept into her sitting room half an hour later, she brought a bottle of rosé wine with her.

'We've got to celebrate,' she said, kissing Jo warmly on the cheek. 'It's only sparkling wine but it's better than tea. I'm so happy for you, Jo,' she whispered. 'You deserve him. He's a wonderful man.'

Mark got up from his seat beside Jo and held Rhona in a bear hug. 'Thanks for everything.' He turned to face Jo. 'If it wasn't for this lady, we'd still be freezing each other out every time we met.'

'My wife is a formidable woman,' Ted agreed, handing them all glasses of frothy pink wine.

A second bottle of rosé had been consumed by the time Rhona and Jo finally made it upstairs to rummage through Rhona's wardrobe with five-year-old Susie and eight-year-old Lynne eagerly accompanying them.

'Do you want to see our room?' inquired Susie, who was holding Jo's hand.

'Of course. Will you show it to me?' asked Jo.

After five minutes admiring Susie's teddies, her dolls and Lynne's latest potato-print picture, she followed Rhona into the spare bedroom.

423

'I shouldn't drink on an empty stomach,' hiccuped Rhona, heaving open the old pine wardrobe door. 'You had half a glass, and Mark only had one – that means that Ted and I drank practically two bottles on our own.'

'Well, it's not as if you're going anywhere,' Jo pointed out sensibly. 'Oh Rhona, this is lovely,' she said, taking out a long cream silk dress with tiny buttons all the way from hem to neck.

'Lovely if you're six foot and six stone,' said Rhona, sitting down on the bed. 'This is my spare wardrobe, the one the girls like best,' she added. 'And it's where I keep all the stuff I should never have bought because I can't fit into it. Lynne, show Jo the stuff at the back beside the sequinned dress. There's a nice velvet thing I wore when I was having Susie.'

'Can I try it on?' asked Susie. She looked up from the basket of lipsticks she'd taken off the dressing table.

'No darling. It's for big people only.'

'Really big people,' said Jo when she saw it. On the hanger, the long-sleeved empire-line dress in midnight blue looked big enough to fit Rhona and Jo together.

But when Jo put it on, she found that it was amazingly flattering. The high waist drew the eye to her cleavage so that you didn't notice her huge bump, while the long, tapered sleeves gave it a faintly medieval air.

'Perfect,' Rhona said, looking at her deputy editor through narrowed eyes.

'Purfect, purfect,' sang Susie, admiring the broad pink smile and bright red eyebrows she'd drawn on herself with lipstick.

'If Susie does your make-up, you'll look stunning,' added Rhona gravely.

'Thank you, Rho,' Jo said suddenly. 'Thank you for this and for what you've done for Mark and me.'

'Well, I knew that if I didn't do something, the pair of you would never sort things out. Of course, this means I have to sit up at the top of the church for the wedding and I get to wear an enormously mad hat.'

'Anything you want,' replied Jo with a large grin. She sat down on the bed. 'Come on, Susie, put on my lipstick!'

CHAPTER NINETEEN

The answering machine switched on seconds before Aisling reached the phone. She'd only had the machine for a month and she still found herself racing out of the shower or hurrying from the depths of the settee when the phone rang, having forgotten that people could leave messages. She decided to wait to see who was calling before she picked up the phone and carried the groceries over to the fridge and began to unpack what felt like a ton of cat food and an equal weight of the fromage frais that the boys were currently eating by the bucketload.

'This is Carla De Paor,' said the caller, in a high, rather posh accent. 'I'm phoning to see if you can cater for a party before Christmas. Do give me a ring if you can help. My number is . . .'

'Hello, Ms De Paor,' said Aisling, snatching up the phone and turning the machine off. 'This is Aisling Moran. You want to book *Reservations* to cater for a party? When is the party?'

'Friday, December thirteenth. For about fifty people. I know it's terribly short notice, only asking you two weeks before, but my friend Yvonne recommended you so highly. I do hope you can help me,' the caller added.

Aisling looked at the *Cat's Companion* calendar hanging by the phone and did some quick calculations. She had a midweek dinner party for ten that week, her second for Jim and Rachel Coughlan, and a buffet to get organised for the following Saturday, a day after the De Paor party. But the buffet would be very simple and she could always rope someone in to help with the party catering. She'd need to get off work early, of course, but she was owed plenty of time off.

'Yes, I can probably fit you in, Ms De Paor,' she said in the cool, businesslike manner she'd learned to use on the phone.

'A lot depends on how elaborate the party is. What are you planning?'

'Nibbles, a finger buffet really,' the other woman replied. 'The party isn't until nine and it's not dinner, you know. Just something to have with the booze. Oh you're so good to take me on,' she gushed. 'My other people said they couldn't do it at the last minute. If Yvonne hadn't told me about you, I don't know what I'd have done!'

'*Reservations* won't let you down,' Aisling said firmly. 'Once we've taken a client on, we provide a first-class service.' Unless I get sick, she thought privately, in which case the whole thing falls apart at the seams.

'I'd like to meet you to go over exactly what menu you'd like,' Aisling continued. 'Could you meet me on Monday at one-fifteen in the Harcourt Hotel?'

'Yes, yes, no problem. How will I recognise you?'

I'll be the one with the bags under my eyes and the rose between my teeth, Aisling thought mischievously. She said, 'I'm blonde and I'll be wearing a navy suit.'

'Marvellous, thank you so much,' said the other woman. 'Ciao.'

Ciao? Did people still say that? Aisling wondered as she hung up. A mental picture of Carla De Paor came to her – a cosseted wealthy wife with bobbed burgundy hair, a year-round tan from too many hours in the sun and enough gold around her neck to settle Bolivia's national debt.

Once, that type of woman would have overawed Aisling, made her feel gauche and dowdy. But not any more. In the last few months, she'd met more society types than she'd ever dreamed of as *Reservations* made a name for itself as a small but exclusive catering business.

She'd learned that the ones with the posh voices and the expensive clothes were just as likely to have grimy kitchen utensils and mice droppings in the saucepan cupboard. And, when she'd changed her clothes in a bedroom of one luxuri-ous mansion in Foxrock, she'd passed the master bedroom and realised that the elegant lady who dressed in chic clothes and sported French-manicured nails, left the same tangle of tights, discarded outfits and clutter of toiletries on the bed as any woman did. There was no doubt about it, Ireland's most glamorous people were decidedly unglamorous when you got past the façade. Dealing with the De Paors would be no problem.

Aisling had just unpacked the shopping when the phone rang again. This time she picked it up.

'Hiya, Aisling. How are you, honey?' Sam's voice hadn't lost its faint transatlantic twang, a subtle variation on his native accent that made the endearment 'honey' sound deliciously sexy.

'I'm fine, Sam. Just been shopping and I'm going out to pick up the boys in half an hour. We're going to have lunch with my mother.'

'Still on for tonight?' he asked.

'Of course,' she replied. 'It's not every night I get brought to a charity ball, so I'm not going to miss it.'

'Are you finally going to tell me what you're wearing, or is it still a big secret?' he asked.

Aisling stifled her irritation. Ever since Mark had asked them to accompany himself and Jo to the fund-raising ball for Chinese orphans, Sam had been wheedling away to find out what Aisling was going to wear.

'It's a surprise,' she said. 'I want to dazzle you.'

'*Dazzle?*' said Sam suspiciously.

'Yes, dazzle.' Aisling could feel herself getting agitated. What was the matter with him? Every time he mentioned the ball, he wanted to know what she was wearing, even though she'd told him it was a surprise at least four times. Which word was he having difficulty with, she wondered? Dazzle or surprise?

'I just want to know, that's all.' Sam sniffed. Nobody could sniff like Sam. Each one was an Oscar winner, laden with meaning.

'Why?' Aisling couldn't stop herself. She was annoyed by the implication that she couldn't pick something suitable for a posh ball in the Shelbourne without his help. She wasn't some hare-brained bimbo who couldn't tell a black-tie affair from a beery barbeque in somebody's back garden. She was a working woman who'd just arranged *another* booking for her catering business. A business she'd set up thanks to her own cooking skills and entrepreneurial ability. So why the hell was Sam treating her as if she was an imbecile with no clothes sense?

Damn him. He was so square when it came to clothes. Not satisfied with buying her a ludicrously little-girl dress the first time they went out shopping, he'd subsequently surprised her with another maidenly outfit – a ruinously expensive white Ghost dress that made her look like a milkmaid. He probably expected her to wear that to the ball. Well, he could forget it.

'I'd love to see you wearing *my* dress.' He sniffed again. 'You look beautiful in it, so elegant.' There was a pause. 'I'm sorry,' he added in a low voice. 'It's childish to want you to wear my present.'

It was Aisling's turn to sigh. Don't be so hard on him, she told herself. You're just out of sync with normal man/woman relationships. Most men probably want their girlfriends to wear feminine outfits instead of knock-'em-dead sexy dresses. Perfectly normal, wasn't it? She'd ask Jo, just to be on the safe side.

'I love the white dress you bought me,' she said. It was only a half-lie. She *did* like it, but it wasn't the sort of thing you could wear into the office and it was far too impractical to inspire confidence in her catering clients. 'But I've bought a lovely dress for the ball and I want to wear it. You'll like it when you see it, I just know it.'

He'll hate it, she thought as she hung up. It was very sexy – the complete opposite of the white dress he'd bought. A year ago, she wouldn't have dreamed of wearing anything like it. Mind you, a year ago she wouldn't have fitted into a long oyster-coloured halter-neck dress. Especially one that moulded her body like surgical gloves. Still, Jo said it was going to be a very over-the-top affair, so Aisling had felt

428

justified blowing two and a half dinner parties' worth of takings on the dress.

'Hello, Ash,' murmured Jo, walking into the kitchen rubbing her eyes sleepily. Eight months pregnant, Jo was very big and in her towelling dressing-gown worn over a large T-shirt, she looked as if she had a beach-ball tied around her middle.

'Did you sleep?' asked Aisling, pulling out a chair for her.

'Not really. I keep having to pee all night and she's kicking like mad,' Jo sighed.

'I'll make you a nice cup of tea and some toast,' offered Aisling, 'and you can sit inside and watch telly.'

'Thank you. What would I do without you, Ash?' Jo asked.

'You'd get out more,' Aisling replied, filling the kettle. 'I'm afraid the boys will soon think you're their mother. You're here more often than I am.'

'I don't mind baby-sitting at all. I love being with them. Anyway, when you're building up a business you've got to accept lots of work, at least that's what Richard always told me,' she added drily. 'It'll be easier when you've got someone to help full time.'

Aisling put brown bread into the toaster and placed a tray with Flora, marmalade, milk and sugar on it on the table in front of Jo.

'I'll need to hire someone sooner rather than later,' she said. 'I've just got another job, a party for fifty on Friday week. For an awfully jolly-hockey-sticks-sounding woman called Carla De Paor.'

'Well done! That name's familiar, though,' Jo said thoughtfully. 'Aren't they the ones with the huge pile in Greystones and the garage business?'

'Don't know,' said Aisling, making the tea. 'The only problem is that Sam will go ballistic when I tell him because Michael was taking the boys that Friday night and Sam and I were going to drive to Wexford and spend the night in a hotel somewhere.'

'You can do that another time,' Jo pointed out. 'You've got

to make as many contacts as you can now to get yourself established.'

Aisling looked out of the kitchen window at the bird-table where a tiny robin daintily pecked at the nuts she'd put out earlier. It was a freezing November day, the last vestiges of frost still sparkled in the pale wintry sun.

'I know,' she said slowly. 'But Sam doesn't seem to understand that. He knew what I wanted to do when we met, but now he really seems to hate me working at night. I don't know why.'

'I'm afraid that's a typical male reaction,' Jo said. 'Independence is wonderful, an attractive quality in fact. Like wearing sexy clothes, miniskirts or low-cut blouses. Until you become an item. Then, it's "don't go out wearing that dress, cover up your boobs, your legs, whatever, and turn into Little Miss Stay at Home.'

'You said it,' muttered Aisling, thinking of Sam's fascination with her wardrobe. 'Mark isn't like that, is he?'

'No. Not at all. I think it must be because he's so confident and secure in himself.' Jo took her toast out of the toaster and plastered it with Flora. 'He loves the fact that I've made my own way in the world. But not all men are like that,' she added, licking a piece of margarine off her fingers.

'Why do I get stuck with the ones who want to turn me into the bloody housewife from hell?' demanded Aisling.

'Come on, Ash, give him a chance,' begged Jo. 'He's probably trying to protect you. He can see that you're stretching yourself by doing two jobs as well as looking after Paul and Phillip.'

'You're right. It's just that . . .' she paused.

'What?' asked Jo through a mouth full of toast.

'I'm beginning to feel claustrophobic,' Aisling said finally. There. She'd said it, actually said what had been rattling around in her head for the past two weeks.

In the three months since she'd met Sam, she'd had a marvellous time. Most of the time. Nearly all the time, really. He was a handsome, attentive lover and that had doubled her confidence, made her feel happy, relaxed and as secure as a recently separated woman could be.

Sam stayed at her house on the nights when the boys were with Michael and they made passionate love, before falling asleep wrapped in each other's arms. On Sunday mornings, they sat in bed reading the papers – never the *News* – and had breakfast, before making love again, usually with toast crumbs sticking to their bodies.

Aisling was amazed at how quickly she'd got used to his presence in her life and her bed. When Michael left, she'd genuinely thought that she'd never want another man ever again. And here she was in a serious relationship with Sam.

He'd certainly improved her life, made her feel better about herself in every way. But there was something not quite right about their relationship lately. She'd first noticed it one day when he rang her from his office to tell her that his trip to London the following day had been cancelled.

'I thought we could have a romantic dinner for two,' he suggested. 'Just you, me and a bottle of nice Chablis.'

'Sorry, Sam,' Aisling said. 'The boys have to finish a project by Thursday morning, so I said I'd help them with it tomorrow night. It's on "Space", which is great because they love watching *Star Trek*. They're mad about anything to do with astronauts. Anyway,' she added, 'I'm not really able to do late nights in the middle of the week. I'll fall asleep at my desk if I don't get a decent seven hours' sleep. I do hope you understand.'

'It's all right, I understand,' he said sharply. Clearly, he didn't understand at all.

She could imagine how it looked from his point of view. He'd offered her a lovely night out and she'd turned him down, rejected him.

Well, tough, she thought to herself. The boys are more important than a night out, they need me. There's been enough uncertainty in their lives during the past year. They need a stable home life. I'm out often enough because of the catering business, so they need to know that I'm there when they want me to help them with something.

Sam had become even more annoyed the following weekend when Aisling couldn't spend Saturday afternoon with him. She was cooking twelve huge vegetarian quiches and had to make a smoked trout pâté which a client was picking up that evening.

'You can't work all the time,' he growled. 'You've got to stop working so hard. This bloody business means I never see you.'

Aha, thought Aisling. That's more like it. You're not upset at the idea of me working too hard, you're just cross because it means you can't get what you want. Typical man. She'd been prepared to promise him a romantic evening at home when she'd cook his favourite peppered steak with all the trimmings. But she was damned if she'd do it when he was going to behave childishly.

He'd been so cold towards her the next time they met that Aisling found herself apologising for Saturday. She told him she'd consult him in future so her cooking didn't infringe on their time together.

'I'm sorry, Sam,' she'd said. She sat beside him on the settee and cuddled up close. 'I didn't think. I'm trying to make the business a success and when I get an order, I hate to turn it down. But I'll check with you in future in case you've anything nice planned, all right?'

Even as she said it, Aisling knew she was making a big mistake. Making a rod for her own back, her mother used to say. She didn't explain any of this to Jo, who was eating her toast hungrily.

'All relationships have their ups and downs,' Jo said comfortingly. 'It's a bad patch you're going through, that's all.'

'So says the woman who is blissfully in love and hasn't said a cross word to Mark for the past six weeks,' joked Aisling.

Jo beamed at her. 'Are we sickeningly in love?' she asked.

'You're a living, breathing Danielle Steel storyline.'

'That bad!'

'No, I'm kidding. I'm thrilled for you both. Now, more tea?' asked Aisling.

'I'd love some.'

Aisling topped up the teapot with hot water and listened to Jo read something funny from the newspaper. But her mind was elsewhere.

'Well, what do you think?' Aisling twirled around in her oyster-coloured evening dress in front of Jo who was sitting on the bed in Aisling's bedroom, sipping a glass of milk.

'Absolutely amazing. Fantastic,' praised Jo. 'You'll be the belle of the ball. I wish I looked like that!' she added wistfully, patting her vast belly in Rhona's velvet dress.

'You'll get your figure back in no time,' said Aisling comfortingly. 'You're naturally slim for a start and the weight will just fall off when the baby is born, I know it will.'

Jo grimaced. 'I do hope so. I feel like a supertanker in velvet.'

'You look great, Jo. Your skin is fantastic, your hair is so shiny and the dress is very flattering.' Aisling hugged her friend.

'It would want to be,' pointed out Jo, 'seeing as how it's the only thing I can wear out at night. This is the third outing it's had in the last few weeks and if I meet anyone I know at the ball, they're going to think I only have one dress,' she added gloomily.

'Mark certainly thinks you look great.'

Jo's face softened. 'He does, doesn't he? He's such a wonderful man. So different from Richard. Actually, talking of Richard . . .'

The doorbell rang loudly, cutting across Jo's voice.

'They're early.' She glanced down at her watch.

Aisling hurried to the stairs, holding up the skirt of her long satin dress as she ran.

'I'll let them in. Take your time coming downstairs, Jo.'

Mark and Sam stood at the front door, handsome in their dinner jackets.

'Aisling, you look . . . great,' said Sam in an astonished voice. He stood back. His eyes travelled the length of her

433

body, as he admired the clinging dress which showed off her curves. She'd spent an hour coaxing her blonde hair into soft waves and it rippled as she moved, the silver and golden colours perfectly matched by the shade of her dress.

In fact, the only spot of colour were her eyes, which Jo had carefully made up for her, their denim blue accentuated by smudged brown liner and thick dark brown mascara. Against the pale fawn colours of her hair and dress, her eyes looked hypnotic and intensely blue.

'You look beautiful, Aisling.' Mark leaned over to kiss her warmly. 'Sam's going to have to spend the entire night fighting off competition from love-stricken admirers.'

Sam didn't look pleased at the thought. 'They can look but they better not touch.' He slid one arm around Aisling possessively and kissed her.

'Is Jo upstairs?' asked Mark.

'Mmm.' Aisling couldn't talk properly with Sam glued to her.

Mark took the stairs two at a time and met Jo as she walked out of the bathroom stuffing spare tissues into her handbag.

When he hugged her gently, careful not to squash her bump, Jo experienced that sense of complete happiness she felt whenever she was with Mark. 'How's my favourite mum-to-be?' He dropped a kiss on the top of her head.

'Huge.' Jo snuggled her head into his chest. 'I'm afraid that someone's going to come up to me tonight, break a bottle of champagne on me and say "God bless her and all who sail in her".'

She could feel Mark's deep laugh vibrate in his belly.

'Don't be silly. You look great. You're only a tiny little thing. Will I carry you downstairs to prove it?'

Jo slapped him playfully. 'Only if you want to end up in casualty with a slipped disc, Mark.'

Downstairs, they found Aisling trying to set the video to record something while Sam stood boot-faced in the hall, holding her coat and looking at his watch.

'We'll be late,' he said testily.

'I'm coming,' called Aisling. 'I just want to tape a film later.'

She reached the front door just as Mark opened it and both she and Jo gasped.

'A limo!' Jo said in astonishment. A gleaming black stretch Mercedes was parked in the drive, a black-suited driver holding open one of the back doors.

Mark grinned as he put on his black wool overcoat. 'I thought we should do it in style tonight,' he said, 'because it's a special evening. A very special evening,' he added, glancing at Jo.

He and Jo sat facing the front of the car with Aisling and Sam opposite them.

'We could have had champagne, but since Jo can't drink any, I didn't order it,' Mark said, stretching out his long legs.

'I could have half a glass.' Jo leaned comfortably against him. 'Do you know what this reminds me of?' she said in a much softer tone so only he could hear.

'No.' Mark put his arm around her.

'Remember when we arrived in New York and the hotel limo was there to meet us? I'd never been in one before but I was determined not to appear unsophisticated and say so.' She settled herself even closer to him. 'I kept wanting to open the drinks compartment to see if there was actually anything in it.'

'You never cease to amaze me, Jo,' Mark said. 'I've never met anyone who can act as marvellously sophisticated as you do when you put your mind to it.'

'Acting comes in very handy sometimes,' she whispered. 'Especially when you're chatting up the boss . . .'

When the limo pulled up outside the Shelbourne, Aisling was amazed to see three other equally long limos parked in front of the hotel. Their driver double-parked, ran around to open the door and helped her out as she stared at a tall woman in floor-length fur who was getting out of the limo beside her.

'Get a load of that coat,' Aisling whispered to Jo.

'Definitely ranch mink,' Jo whispered back.

435

'I bought her a mink and she wouldn't feed it,' Mark pointed out to Aisling, doing his best to sound serious.

The two women burst out laughing. Madame Mink stared at them frostily.

'Silly cow for wearing fur in the first place,' said Aisling.

She walked into the ballroom with a spring in her step. She felt beautiful, sexy and gloriously confident. She could see people glancing at her, men openly admiring her beautiful, elegant outfit. It had to be the dress.

'It's the dress,' she whispered to Jo.

'It's you,' whispered Jo back. 'You look amazing.'

They found their table and the two women were just sitting down beside each other so they could gossip, when Mark arrived with their cloakroom tickets.

'Your lady in mink had a tantrum at the cloakroom. She insisted that they find somewhere extra safe for her coat,' he explained.

'Goodness.' Aisling fanned herself with the small dinner menu. 'I do hope you asked for the same treatment for mine. It's a family heirloom and I know Dunnes are unlikely to ever have anything as gorgeous ever again. I'd be distraught if anything happened to it. I mean, *where* would you get your hands on anything *that* nice for sixty pounds?'

'Was it only sixty quid?' asked Jo, astonished. 'It looks much more expensive.'

'Fiona picked it out for me,' Aisling explained. 'She has the most amazing eye for clothes. Nearly as good as you.'

Sam excused himself to talk to someone he'd spotted at another table. Aisling amused herself by looking around, gazing at the people at other tables. Men looked so handsome in dinner jackets, she thought, as she watched beautifully dressed couples weaving through the tables. Even the ugliest, scruffiest man looked better in a black tuxedo.

The women had obviously pulled out all the stops. Sleek blondes and brunettes in elegant black sheaths, vied for attention with women in flowing ballgowns. A couple of very young and very slim women sashayed across the room in spray-on lycra creations, one bronze and one a startling white that contrasted with the girl's pale golden skin.

You had to be young and slim to get away with that type of dress. Aisling wondered what sort of underwear the girl in the white dress was wearing. All-in-one, vacuum-packed underwear? No, she was thin enough to get away with ordinary undies.

A balloon floated into view, an oversized cream balloon with swirly gold writing on it saying something she couldn't make out. Someone had gone to an awful lot of trouble with the decorations. The entire room was done in gold and cream, gold and cream balloons hung from the ceiling. Glass vases of tiny cream roses, tied up with gold ribbons, stood on the tables, and wreaths of gold and cream silk flowers were garlanded around the room and on the raised dais where seats and music stands were laid out for a band.

There was plenty of gold on the ears, wrists and necks of the female guests, Aisling noticed enviously. She fiddled with her plain gold bracelet and wished she had a gold and diamond necklace like the statuesque blonde in pink satin who was batting heavily mascaraed eyes at her companion.

Then Aisling saw him. He was walking towards their table, talking to another man, not really watching where he was going. He looked handsome, if a little tired, in the expensive tuxedo she'd helped him buy just over three years ago.

'It would be handy to have my own instead of renting one every time I need it,' Michael had said as they trawled Dublin's most expensive men's shops to find what he was looking for.

It certainly suited him, Aisling had to admit, although he'd put on weight and the buttons were ever so slightly strained across his stomach. Her gaze shifted to the two women who walked a couple of steps behind the men chatting animatedly.

Both were dark-haired. One had short, jet-black hair, offset by a brilliant ruby ballgown, the other's brown bob swung as she walked. She wore a strapless white silk dress with a tight bodice which flared out into a full skirt much too wide for

437

someone of her height. Pearl earrings and a pearl choker completed the outfit.

The dress must have looked stunning on the shop dummy. But it was a major fashion mistake on the dumpy, short-legged woman who wore it.

Aisling stared at her husband's girlfriend and wondered why she didn't want to grab her wine glass and smash it over the other woman's head.

So that was Jennifer Carroll. *The* Jennifer Carroll. It was funny, Aisling realised, staring at her in an almost removed state of mind, but Jennifer didn't look anything like the femme fatale she'd imagined. How had Fiona described her?

All red talons, glittery gold outfits and skirts cut up to her thighs. Something like that.

The woman who was now only a few yards away from her bore no resemblance to the predatory manhunter that Fiona had described.

In the flesh – the not inconsiderable flesh, Aisling noticed in amazement – Jennifer Carroll was short, verging on plump. Her pale skin looked pasty against the gleaming white dress.

Aisling hated the smell of fake tan but, as she glanced down at her golden arms, she was pleased she'd put it on the night before. Jennifer didn't look as if she'd bothered with anything much, apart from having her hair salon-blow-dried.

But maybe Jennifer just hadn't had the time to bother, Aisling reflected, because she was ironing Michael's dress-shirt, finding his cuff links – 'They *must* be there somewhere, Aisling!' – and trying to put her make-up on in front of the mirror while he poked about in the drawers underneath the mirror looking for a particular pair of black socks.

A cork popped loudly beside her. Aisling turned to see a waiter pouring frothy liquid into Jo's glass.

'Let's have a toast.' Jo turned to face Aisling with a half-full glass of champagne held aloft. 'To all of us and . . . omigod! It's . . . it's Michael and . . . her!' Jo's mouth formed a pale pink oval as she stared at Michael and Jennifer. 'I don't believe

438

it!' she gasped. 'Oh Ash,' Jo laid a warm hand on her friend's shoulder, 'are you all right?'

'Yes,' said Aisling, still not sure exactly how she felt. 'Stunned, yes. It's strange but, I'm OK, honestly.'

'He looking at us,' hissed Jo. 'Look the other way!'

Aisling obediently twisted around in her chair and smiled warmly at a surprised Miss Pink Satin who obviously felt obliged to smile back.

'Have we had our toast?' Aisling said brightly to the whole table. 'Let's toast the future!'

Everyone raised their glasses and drank. Aisling drained her glass in a couple of frothy gulps.

Jo's mouth fell open again.

'If I drank that fast, I'd hiccup for a month,' she said. 'Are you sure you're all right, Ash?'

'I'm not sure,' whispered Aisling, a fixed smile still glued to her face. 'In a few minutes, I'll either be over at their table battering Michael and Jennifer with your handbag – yours is bigger than mine – or I'll be perfectly fine. I don't know which. Now, are they sitting down yet? Where are they sitting?'

'What are you two whispering about?' said Mark, leaning towards them.

'It's Michael and his girlfriend,' hissed Jo, 'over there.'

'Where?' demanded Mark.

'The second table on the left, beside the dance floor.'

Aisling turned her head slightly. She had no idea whether she wanted to talk to Michael or not.

'The woman in that dreadful white meringue dress,' Jo told Mark, bridling like a mother hen seeing someone hurt her favourite chick. 'It's a dreadful dress. Doesn't she have a full-length mirror in her bloody house? I can't *believe* anyone would go out looking like that.'

For the first time since she'd spotted Michael, Aisling smiled properly.

'You're a howl, Ryan,' she said affectionately to Jo. 'You're so protective.'

'Well, she ran off with your husband,' said Jo indignantly. 'I mean, really!'

'You can only run off with someone who wants to run off in the first place,' Aisling said, in the tone of someone who'd spent an awful lot of time turning the whole situation over and over in her head. 'Look what's happened to me as a result. Michael's leaving changed my life. It was brutal, and not the sort of experience I'd recommend, but it worked. It changed my life and, boy, did it need changing. And now look at me.' She smiled and flicked back a lock of blonde hair.

'You're one hell of a woman, Aisling,' Mark commented. 'There can't be many women who've coped the way you have.'

'Not to mention losing practically two stone and starting a new business,' put in Jo.

'How about a toast to you, Aisling – and to *Reservations*?' said Mark.

'Hello, guys.' Sam slid into his seat beside Aisling. 'What have I missed?'

'Oh, we've just been gossiping.' Aisling shot a warning glance at the other two.

'So I asked him why it was going to take two weeks to put down a wooden floor in the kitchen,' Jo said, 'since it had only taken one week to replaster all the downstairs.'

'What exactly are you having done to the cottage now?' inquired Sam idly.

Aisling stifled her irritation. Sam spent hours in her house and had listened to Jo and herself discussing the renovation of the cottage often enough to know precisely what was going on, down to the last nut and bolt. He obviously hadn't listened to a word they'd said.

'It's nearly finished apart from a few minor details,' explained Jo patiently.

Aisling remembered when she'd indulgently repeated herself every time Michael muttered. 'What?'

He usually said 'What?' halfway through dinner when Aisling was regaling him with details of her day or telling him about the funny thing she'd heard on the radio that morning.

Dinner *chez* Moran. Michael indifferently munching his way through Aisling's delicious stuffed pork with one eye on the newspaper and one eye on his ratatouille – to make sure that his fork didn't miss his mouth and spill food down his shirt front.

Aisling couldn't suppress a shiver. Had she really lived her life like that? Repeating herself endlessly. When Michael hadn't been bothered to listen? Had she really been that quiet little mouse? A mousey mouse, she realised with a grin, running one hand through her blonde mane. A mouse with no confidence, no conversation and no waist. She took a sip of champagne to calm herself down.

Even her hands looked better nowadays, she realised, admiring the fingers that curled around her glass, the short, well-shaped nails painted with a soft opalescent pink. They were never going to look like Vivienne's perfectly manicured hands. But they were improving. She'd been stirring chocolate sauce one night at one of her catering jobs when she noticed that, though her hair, clothes and figure were much improved, her hands let her down completely.

Now she made herself wear rubber gloves when she was cleaning the bath and scouring saucepans, something she hadn't bothered with for years.

Aisling glanced over to Michael's table.

Thank you, Jennifer, she said silently. Thank you. If you hadn't come along, I'd still be living on automatic pilot, still worried about what to cook for dinner, still utterly depressed. You've no idea what a difference you've made to my life. Or my hands.

'Aisling, honey, what are you going to have to eat?' Sam asked. 'I think the lamb sounds nice.' Sam was looking at the menu hungrily, the subject of Jo's cottage obviously closed.

Aisling picked up the small menu. Each course of the five-course meal offered at least two choices. Raw oysters or roast pepper salad, two types of sorbet, consommé or five-mushroom soup, rack of lamb, salmon cutlets or aubergine

441

lasagne, dessert trolley or Irish cheese board. A wonderful menu.

'Oysters make me sick and I hate peppers,' Sam muttered.

He sounded just like Phillip when he was sulking for some reason or other, Aisling realised. And Sam was certainly sulking. He'd been shocked at the sight of her daring dress, but he hadn't been able to make a fuss in front of Jo and Mark. Instead, he was being charming to all and sundry, while being very cool with her. She hated childish adults.

Stop it, Aisling, she told herself sharply. He's funny, kind, very sexy and crazy about you. Don't ruin it. 'Maybe they can rustle up something else, a salad perhaps?' she said in a placatory tone.

'I hope so.' He sniffed.

Aisling reached over for one of the bottles of white wine that had just been placed on the table and filled Sam's glass to the brim. When he drank half, she filled it some more. If that's what it took to keep him amused, then she'd keep filling his glass all night. It was like giving the boys 7-Up when they were sick, or Calpol when they were babies.

Could they rustle up a green salad or some alternative to the two starters? Aisling inquired.

When the waitress promised to bring a mixed salad for the gentleman, Sam didn't even say thank you. Aisling felt her temper rise. If there was one thing she couldn't bear, it was people who couldn't be civil to waitresses, bar staff, whoever. It drove her mad. She looked down to find that she'd shredded her cloakroom ticket.

By ten o'clock, the meal was practically over. A few people were still forking up the remains of some wonderful profiteroles. The classical music, which had been piped through the room all through dinner, was turned off and a woman with a microphone announced that the charity auction would shortly begin.

'We've got a raffle for some marvellous prizes,' she explained. 'The top prize is a luxury holiday for two to Tunisia.' Everyone clapped appreciatively. 'Tickets are five pounds each, or six for twenty-five pounds.'

'Oh, gimme a hundred, then,' Jo said under her breath to Aisling.

The classical music was slapped back on and the organisers started to work their way around the tables, bearing books of tickets and cash boxes.

'What were you going to tell me about Richard earlier?' Aisling whispered to Jo.

'He rang me,' Jo whispered.

'He didn't!' said Aisling, aghast.

'Shush,' hissed Jo. 'I haven't told Mark yet.'

'Why didn't you tell me?' demanded Aisling. 'What did he say?'

Jo leaned back in her chair and said nothing for a moment.

'Sorry. I just felt very faint suddenly,' she said. 'He rang me at work yesterday and he upset me so much, I didn't want to talk about it. The pig. Hand me that menu, would you?'

Aisling gave her the menu and Jo immediately began fanning her face. 'He wanted to see me. He said he was sorry he'd left me and he wanted to try again.'

Aisling was stunned. 'I can't believe it.'

'Neither could I. I told him he could get stuffed,' Jo said with relish. 'And I have to say,' she added, a triumphant smile hovering around her lips, 'he was absolutely gobsmacked when I said it. He honestly thought I'd welcome him with open arms and when I said "Get stuffed", he was speechless.'

'*I'm* almost speechless at the sheer nerve of him,' Aisling said. 'Imagine phoning you for the first time in six months and having the temerity to think you'd have him back!'

'That's Richard for you,' Jo said, still fanning herself. 'He lives in a fantasy world where nothing ever goes really wrong. If it does, he walks away. And to think I wanted him to be a father to my baby.' She shuddered.

'I'm so glad you have Mark,' Aisling said gently.

'Me too. He's involved, he wants to know how I feel and how the baby is doing every moment of the day.' Jo couldn't keep the happiness out of her voice. '*He's* the real father.

443

Richard may be the biological father, but he'll never be her real dad.'

Aisling didn't want to upset Jo, but she knew she had to ask. 'What if he demands access to the baby?' she asked.

Jo absent-mindedly fiddled with a curl of her dark, glossy hair. 'I'm not sure,' she said. 'He'd have a right to see her, of course, but I'd hate it. I'd hate him having anything to do with her when he didn't want me to have her in the first place.'

'Have you talked all this over with Mark?'

'Yes,' Jo replied. 'We talk about everything – apart from this latest bit of news,' she added hastily. 'I'm trying to find the right time to tell Mark so he won't go ballistic.'

Knowing the sort of straightforward and honourable man Mark was, Aisling could well understand how this fresh example of Richard's appallingly selfish behaviour would send him into a cold, controlled rage.

'We've talked about Richard wanting access and visitation rights,' Jo explained. 'Mark wants to do what's right for the baby. He knows that she's entitled to see her real father. But,' she broke off to emphasise the point, 'he absolutely *loathes* Richard for what he did to me. If Richard has to come to my place to see the baby, I'll need to lock Mark into the hotpress beforehand so he won't murder Richard.'

'Did someone mention that bastard's name?' Mark turned to face them.

Jo blushed. 'I was just telling Aisling that we've been talking about Richard's rights to see the baby.'

The muscles in Mark's face tightened and his grey eyes grew icy cold.

'Ladies and gentlemen,' boomed a voice, 'the auction is ready to begin.'

Saved by the bell, thought Aisling. The loud voice of the auctioneer drummed out of the speakers around the room and made conversation all but impossible. Aisling squeezed Jo's hand affectionately before turning to face the dais.

'What am I bid for this football jersey?' roared the auction-eer. 'A jersey signed by all the members of the Irish team, a perfect Christmas present for the soccer-mad teenager.'

Aisling watched with interest as people bid outrageous
sums of money for the oddest things. Two china plates with
butterfly designs hand-painted in nail varnish made £1,000
because the artist in question was the lead singer of a rock
band. Just as well she'd chosen singing instead of art for her
career, Jo said with a giggle.

A beautiful piece of driftwood made into a piece of
sculpture went for half that, even though Aisling felt it was
ten times more beautiful than the garish butterflies.

'I know the money is being raised for charity, but why do
the items have to be so bloody daft?' she asked Jo when the
auctioneer was giving his vocal chords a brief break.

'I think it's supposed to be more fun for the seriously
wealthy bidders if the stuff is totally useless,' Jo replied.
'Presumably, there's a certain cachet in being able to tell all
your rich pals that you spent £2,000 on a biscuit tin which
Oscar Wilde's cleaning lady swore belonged to him!'

It was when a man at the next table successfully bid for a
tiny watercolour painting, that Michael finally saw Aisling.
They'd both turned to look at the purchaser and their eyes
locked. Though she was quite a distance away from him,
Aisling could have sworn he went pale with shock. Not
surprising. The very idea of his estranged wife and new
girlfriend meeting at a party would be enough to give any
man an ulcer.

Michael probably expected her to race over to his table and
throw something at him, or to scratch Jennifer's eyes out.
Well, she wasn't going to do that.

Aisling allowed herself a little pat on the back. She'd come
a long way from the enraged, grief-stricken wife of six months
ago. Let Michael panic. She wasn't about to lose her cool.

Sam had loosened up after numerous glasses of wine and
two brandies. He wanted to dance with Aisling.

'Do you think they'll play the tango?' he murmured into
her ear. 'I'm quite good at Latin American dancing.'

'We better wait till the auction stops and the music starts,'

445

CATHY KELLY

Aisling advised, as he started nuzzling her ear.

She could feel one hand moving stealthily up her thigh, gently caressing her through the fabric of her dress.

'So you don't hate the dress after all,' she couldn't resist saying.

'It's very nice. I'd prefer it if I was the only one to see you looking this sexy,' Sam said. 'You're mine and nobody else's. Remember that.'

She wasn't likely to forget it from the way he was holding onto her.

'Sam,' she began, 'you've got to understand, I'm not a *thing*. I'm a person. I don't *belong* to anyone except myself.'

He wasn't listening. The band had just launched into the first bars of Glenn Miller when Sam caught Aisling's hand and pulled her out of her chair.

'C'mon, honey. Let's show them how it's done.'

Normally Aisling couldn't have thought of anything worse than being practically the first couple on the dance floor, but for once she didn't mind. She and Sam made a handsome couple and she wanted to give Michael the opportunity to see what he'd dumped.

When Sam spun her around, she could see Michael's poker face. Jennifer sat a little apart from him, looking strained. Let them watch, thought Aisling, bestowing a warm smile on Sam. She'd put him straight about the question of 'ownership' later.

Sam may have looked good, but he was no dancer. After two fast numbers, she was ready to sit down and rest her bruised toes when the tempo of the music slowed. Sam immediately slid one arm around her waist and started to waltz clumsily, her body crushed against his.

'You look wonderful,' he murmured through boozy breath.

'Thank you,' Aisling replied with the sexiest smile she could muster. Now was not the time to remind him that he'd hated her outfit a couple of hours ago. She closed her eyes and kissed him, a long, passionate kiss more suited to the bedroom than the dance floor. God, but she was enjoying this.

446

She opened one eye and took a surreptitious look in Michael's direction, delighted to see that he looked as if he'd just had a root canal done at the dentist – and been presented with the bill into the bargain.

Another kiss, I think, she decided. Poor Sam was going to be beside himself with passion if she didn't stop.

'We should go home early,' said Sam huskily when their lips finally parted.

That wasn't part of Aisling's plan.

'We can't just go and leave Jo and Mark after they invited us,' she said hurriedly. 'Anyway, we've all tomorrow morning to lie in bed and . . . read,' she added with a meaningful grin. 'I've had enough dancing, Sam. I want to go to the ladies' room, OK?'

They walked leisurely back to their table. Aisling deliberately chose a route which avoided Michael's table. She'd go over to say hello in her own time – when she'd powdered down her undoubtedly shiny nose and put on more lipstick.

In the ladies', she decided against giving herself another blast of perfume – it would look too obvious. But she brushed her hair and slicked on plenty of the coral lipstick which made her lips look full and glossy.

'Hello, Michael, how are you? Aren't you going to introduce me to your friend?' she practised. No, that sounded wrong.

'Michael, darling, so nice to see you again.'

Too false. How about. 'Hi, Mike, nice to see you. Can't stop. My boyfriend's insatiable and we have to get back to bed immediately. Bye.'

There had to be a right way to do it. Maybe there was a book – *How to Behave When You Meet Your Ex and His Lover for the First Time*. And if there wasn't a book, perhaps she would write it. It would be a bestseller, she was sure of it.

A woman washing her hands at the basins looked at Aisling enviously, a quick peep when she thought Aisling wasn't looking. She was tall and heavily built, and wore the sort of size sixteen dress that Aisling herself would have had to wear a year ago. Poor thing, Aisling thought, sympathetically.

She held the door open for the other woman as they left and smiled at her.

'That's a lovely dress,' the woman said longingly. 'I wish I could wear something like that.'

'Thank you,' said Aisling with a friendly look. 'I'm still not used to being able to wear it myself, you know. Six months ago I wouldn't have been able to get away with this, but I've lost loads of weight.'

'Really?' asked the woman, with the fascinated gaze of the eternal dieter who knows the calorific content of every single type of chocolate biscuit.

'Really,' Aisling repeated. 'And if I can do it, anybody can. See you.' She walked off, thinking about the smile which had spread across the other woman's face – a there-is-hope-for-me-after-all sort of smile. I'd be great as a diet counsellor, Aisling thought happily. She was so busy thinking about how satisfying it would be to help other depressed and miserable women lose weight and regain control of their lives, that she almost didn't realise she had walked straight up to Michael's table.

Here goes, she decided. There's no backing out now.

'Hello, Michael. How are you? You must be Jennifer.' She was amazed at how calm and steady her voice sounded.

'H . . . hello,' stuttered Michael in shock.

Aisling didn't know which of them looked the more stunned. Jennifer stared up at her with wide, frightened eyes, like a rabbit caught in the headlights of an oncoming juggernaut. Michael looked utterly horrified.

'Relax,' Aisling said. 'I'm not going to bite. We're adults, after all.'

'Of course,' Jennifer said breathlessly. 'Nice to meet you, Aisling. The boys are always talking about you.'

'I'm glad to hear it,' Aisling said. Close up, the other woman looked tired and drawn, plenty of crow's feet around her pale blue eyes. She had to be thirty-five or thirty-six.

'Would you like to sit down?' Jennifer asked politely, gesturing to the empty chair beside her. Michael shot her a withering look and she flushed. Her eyes glistened with what looked suspiciously like tears.

They were having a *row*! Aisling couldn't believe it. She hoped it was about her. She sat down gracefully, determined not to spoil the effect of her perfectly styled hair and beautiful dress.

'How are you both?' she asked graciously, feeling rather like the Queen at a garden party. All she needed were the elbow-length white gloves and the tiara.

'Fine,' said Michael sharply, shooting Jennifer another meaningful look. The other woman's face fell and, for an instant, Aisling felt sorry for her. Michael had always been very talented in the withering-look department.

'Sorry.' Jennifer pushed back her hair clumsily and left, rushing towards the ladies'.

'Was it something I said?' asked Aisling, still with the serene smile on her face.

'No.' Michael sounded as weary as he looked. The band struck up The Carpenters' *Close to You.*

'You always loved that song,' he said absently.

'And you hated it,' Aisling answered.

'Did I? I quite like it now.'

Aisling's eyebrows shot up. 'Are you mellowing, Michael?' she asked.

He snorted. 'No. Yes. I don't know.' He ran one hand through his hair, leaving it standing up in dark peaks. Once, she'd have cried at this point, the point where she realised that she'd never smooth his hair down for him again. Not any more. Her hair-smoothing days were well and truly over.

'Did I interrupt an argument?'

'Sort of. It was a bit of a shock seeing you here, that's all,' he admitted.

'Why?'

'You know why,' he said. 'You've never met Jennifer and she feels so guilty about everything.'

Typical, thought Aisling, *she* feels guilty but you obviously don't.

'We have to meet sometime, why not now?' she said.

'I suppose,' he said, reaching for his cigarettes. Silk Cut purple, she noticed. Amazing. She'd tried to get him to stop smoking Marlboro for years. It took six months with another woman to have him down to a lighter brand.

'Things have been difficult recently and Jennifer got a shock when she saw you. You look amazing,' he added. 'You do, you know.'

'I know.' Aisling gave him her cat-devouring-a-meringue smile and prayed that she wouldn't be struck dead for lying so blatantly. When did any woman ever say *I know* to a statement about her looking good?

'Jenny's been sick, she had a bug and she doesn't look very good, so she was a bit freaked out to see you here looking like some bloody superstar.' He took a deep drag of his cigarette.

Score *dix points* to Aisling. He thought she looked good and so did 'Jenny'. Marvellous. Make it *douze points*. At least that explained why Jennifer didn't look like the stunner she'd expected. Perhaps she had better days. She'd want to.

'I shouldn't be telling you any of that, I suppose,' Michael added gloomily.

'I'm afraid that there aren't any rules for this type of situation,' Aisling said, a touch of sarcasm in her voice. 'So we'll have to make them up as we go along. I'm sorry I don't fit in with your version of the dumped wife – a thirteen-stone heifer with a bit of a booze problem,' she sniped. 'It would have been easier for you if I still looked like that, wouldn't it? So you could tell "Jenny" that you couldn't bear to live with me any longer and she'd have believed you. It's not so easy when I look better than she does. Tough, Michael.'

Aisling gazed at him angrily. She hadn't meant to lose her temper but she couldn't help herself.

'It wasn't like that,' he protested weakly. 'You know that!'

'I didn't know *anything*,' she said. 'That's the whole point. You never gave me a chance. But,' she gazed at him contemptuously, 'you did me a favour. After all those years of telling me I'd be no good going back to work, I did.'

'Aisling,' begged Michael, 'let's not go into this now, please.'

'Why?' she demanded. 'Am I causing a scene?' She glanced around. Despite the loud music, people were staring at them. But she didn't care. She'd waited a long time to tell Michael what she really thought and now he was a captive audience.

'Thanks to you, I had to go out and get a job. And thanks to *me* and *my* skills, I started up a catering business. *Reservations*. It's very successful actually,' she hissed. 'But I doubt if you and "Jenny" would be able to afford to hire me. It's an exclusive business, no riff-raff.'

'For God's sake, Aisling, let's be adults about this.' Michael looked shattered.

'Adults? If you want to behave like an adult, why did you bite *her* head off when she was behaving like one? Don't tell me,' she snapped. 'I know. It's because that's the way you are, Michael, isn't it? Difficult. That's the polite way of putting it, anyway,' Aisling added sarcastically. She looked at him with disdain. 'If Jenny's worried that I'm going to steal you back because I'm no longer the frumpy wife, I can put her mind at rest. Our relationship is over, dead as a dodo, *finito*, finished, gone.' Aisling enunciated each word clearly and crisply.

'So she can stop worrying. Get her to come back and I'll tell her,' she offered.

She was pleased to see that Michael looked hurt. There wasn't a thing he could say.

'In fact, I'll get her myself.' Aisling got to her feet abruptly. She walked out of the ballroom. Jennifer wasn't in the ladies'. Aisling found her at the bar, gulping a gin and tonic as if her life depended upon it. Slimline tonic, too, Aisling noticed.

'You didn't have to leave,' Aisling said. 'There's nothing we have to talk about that you can't hear. All we need is to wait another four and a half years and Michael and I can get divorced. So don't worry about me wanting him back. I don't.'

Even as she said it, Aisling knew it was true. She didn't want Michael back – under any circumstances. She'd had twelve years of marriage and that was enough. It had taken many hours of sobbing to figure it all out. But she knew what she wanted now. Aisling had tasted freedom and she liked the taste. Loved it, in fact. There was no going back. Jennifer would find that out for herself. Sooner rather than later, Aisling reflected, if Michael was true to form.

'Would you like a drink?' Jennifer asked tentatively.

'No thanks. I've got to get back to Sam. He's so possessive, he hates it when I leave him,' Aisling couldn't help adding. Was she really here, talking calmly with the woman who'd stolen her husband? No, not stolen, she corrected herself. The woman who'd been there when he decided their marriage was over and that he wanted out. 'You know, new lovers can't wait to get you home to bed!' Aisling smiled wickedly. She idly wondered if the wild start-of-the-affair sex between Jennifer and Michael had dimmed. Definitely, if the strained atmosphere between them was anything to go by. 'See you soon.' She walked away with her head held high.

'Where've you been?' Demanded Sam when she sat down between him and Jo.

'Talking to my husband,' she replied sharply.

'What!' he screeched, pushing back his chair and getting to his feet. 'Where is he?'

'Calm down, Sam,' said Aisling tiredly. She'd had enough trauma for one night without Sam's histrionics.

'What did he say to you? If he upset you, I'll kill him! I'll kill him, anyway,' Sam raged. His face was flushed with alcohol, his eyes were angry and he was actually balling his hands up into fists. 'What did you talk to him for?' He glared at Aisling.

She'd had enough. This was ridiculous. Sam was going to fight Michael over her, probably because he didn't like the idea of Michael seeing her in a sexy dress. Or merely because he wanted to fight with *anyone* who dared to look at her.

Aisling stood up until they were face to face. She didn't even raise her voice.

'Listen, Sam. Who I talk to is none of your bloody business. Michael is still my husband, not even my ex-husband yet, so

452

we have a lot of things to talk about. Like our children, for instance. Do you understand what I'm talking about?' she asked him as if she was talking to a five-year-old.

'Aisling!' he shouted.

'Shut up,' she hissed. 'This is *none of your business*. Do you understand?'

'No. It *is* my business. I'm with you, I'm responsible for you!' he snarled.

'You're not responsible for me, Sam. You never were and you aren't now. Accept that or leave now!'

Shaking with controlled rage, Aisling sat down again.

'I'm so glad you're back,' panted Jo.

'Are you all right?' asked Aisling, Sam forgotten as she took in her friend's pale, damp face.

'No. I don't think so. I feel very strange all of a sudden. Mark went to the loo five minutes ago, and I've been feeling very strange since then.'

'I'm so sorry. I was so busy with Sam, I never noticed . . . Why didn't you come and get me?' Aisling hissed at Sam.

'I didn't know where you were!' he retorted.

'Oh Ash!' Jo's cry was loud and scared. Her eyes were huge as she looked at her friend. 'My waters just broke!'

CHAPTER TWENTY

Mark held Jo's right hand tightly as the limo raced towards the Coombe.

'Don't worry, Jo,' he said encouragingly. 'You're going to be fine, I promise.'

'But you've never had a baby,' sobbed Jo. 'How do you know?'

'*I* have and you're going to be fine,' said Aisling reassuringly, squeezing Jo's left hand.

'The baby's early. I'm not due yet,' wailed Jo. How could she be having the baby so soon? She'd another three weeks to go, the baby was premature. Maybe she wasn't in labour at all. She'd read the pregnancy books and she hadn't had the hours of contractions she'd expected. It had to be a false alarm.

'Aaagh,' she screamed as another contraction hit her.

'Oh God,' groaned Mark. 'Hurry up,' he yelled at the driver.

'He's going as fast as he can,' Aisling said in the calm and controlled voice she used when the twins had nightmares. 'We don't want to end up in the casualty room before we get to the delivery ward, do we?' She glared at Mark.

'You're right, you're right,' he said. 'You've got to stay calm,' he added to Jo.

'I don't want to be calm,' she yelled. 'This hurts.'

And it's going to hurt a hell of a lot more, Aisling reflected. Wait till they got to the bit where Jo screeched that she was never going to let a man get within a fifty-foot radius of her ever again. Aisling remembered that one. Listening to a woman screaming that sex was off the agenda *for ever* was enough to put the fear of God into any man. Never mind one who wasn't even the father in the first place.

Once she'd realised that Jo was going into labour, Aisling sent Sam to her house in a taxi to get Jo's hospital suitcase.

They'd packed it a few days before.

Jo already had a large collection of baby clothes, including beautifully knitted matinée coats and shawls her mother had made, and a selection of pastel-coloured babygros Rhona had given her. Packing for the baby was no problem, she said, reading from the list.

'Nappies, vests, babygros, cardigans, soft towels, a hat, gloves, breast-feeding bras, sanitary towels, nipple cream, the list goes on and on. It's like bringing an entire department store into hospital,' Jo laughed.

'Breathe deeply, Jo,' Mark said in an encouraging voice.

'That's later,' hissed Jo.

'All right, Jo. Don't get upset,' Aisling said. 'You've got to stay calm.'

'Calm? Shrieked the expectant mother. 'How can I stay calm? I'm having the baby in a car!'

'You're not, Jo.' Mark held her gently. The pain of the contraction faded. They sat quietly for a few moments, Jo's eyes closed again, one hand lay gently on her bump, the other tightly clasped in Mark's.

Jo was so glad it was Mark who was with her right now. She couldn't imagine what Richard would have done. Phoned his mother, probably, before retiring to the nearest pub for some Dutch courage. He wouldn't have been much help, wouldn't have been *any* help.

Mark wasn't like that. He loved her and that meant he wanted to be with her all the time. Wonderful, wonderful Mark. She could feel his hand warm and strong around hers.

He seemed to understand that she didn't want to talk. She wanted to stay silent. If she could keep her eyes closed and stay very, very still, she mightn't have another contraction. Then they could all go home.

'Aaagh!'

The pain was intense. And terrifying. There was no doubt about it, Jo thought as she clenched her teeth, she was having the baby. It was going to happen very soon.

'Thank God,' breathed Aisling as the limo pulled up outside the hospital. 'I thought we'd never get here.'

'You and me both,' muttered Jo, between deep breaths.

Within minutes, she was being examined by a midwife who pronounced her as three centimetres dilated.

'Di-lated to meet you,' Jo joked weakly.

'You're wonderful, do you know that?' said Mark quietly. 'Even now you're able to make me laugh.'

'Fear,' said Jo. 'I'm bloody terrified. I'm trying to make both of us laugh . . .' Another huge contraction gripped her.

The midwife, a down-to-earth woman named Paula, took Jo's blood pressure, temperature and pulse before listening to the baby's heartbeat.

'Both you and your baby are doing fine,' Paula said calmly. 'You're definitely in labour, but it could be a long time before you reach the second stage. You've got to relax, Jo.'

'I'm in labour, really?' asked Jo in alarm.

'Yes, but you could have a long wait,' Paula explained. 'I'll be monitoring you all the time to see how you're doing, but you've got to relax.'

Jo felt as if a tight band was being wound around her chest, squeezing her heart and lungs until she could barely breathe. In labour. She was in labour. There was no stopping it, there was no turning back. The baby was coming. She was terrified.

'Mark!'

'Yes, Jo, I'm here.'

She squeezed his hand in terror. 'Oh Mark, it's happening and I'm not ready, I'm not ready at all.' Her voice became a sob.

She clung to him, sobbing with a mixture of fear and pain. Mark looked at Paula in anguish, not knowing what to do.

'You might feel better if you walked around for a while,' Paula advised Jo. 'Would you like to do that?'

Jo nodded through the tears. Anything was better than just lying back on the pillows in pain. She'd love to walk if only she could. It was all so terrifying, so utterly terrifying.

★ ★ ★

When Sam arrived with Jo's things half an hour later, she was feeling more relaxed.

'She's calmed down a lot,' Mark told Aisling when he left the labour ward to get Jo's nightie. 'They gave her an injection of pethidine. She refuses to have an epidural, as you know. I wish she'd have one.'

'Jo's terrified of the idea,' Aisling said. 'I did my best to convince her. Told her *I'd* have had one if I could when I was having the twins, but she won't hear of it.'

Mark rubbed his eyes tiredly. 'She says you should go home, Aisling, and get some sleep.'

'Sleep! I don't think I could,' Aisling exclaimed, pulling her coat tighter around her shoulders. 'I feel so useless out here, I wish I could do something.'

'*You* feel useless,' Mark said, his voice strained. 'At least you've gone through this. I don't know what to do at all, except tell her to breathe deeply. I can barely breathe myself when I see her in so much pain!'

Aisling gave him a hug. 'You're doing great. She simply needs you with her, the hospital will do all the rest. Don't worry.'

'Thanks.'

Aisling watched him go. He looked utterly haggard, but then, they all did. Her eyes had been bloodshot the last time she looked in the ladies' mirror and even Sam, who always looked in the prime of health, was white-faced with tiredness.

'What time is it?' murmured Jo when Mark went back to her. 'I think I dozed off.' She sounded almost drunk. Paula had explained that pethidine could do that to you.

'It's nearly three.' He stroked her face softly. He was glad that she was dozing off, glad that the injection meant she slept between each agonising contraction. He sat beside her, watching her eyelids flutter as she slept. She seemed to be having mini nightmares, tossing restlessly and waking screaming when the pain hit her. Mark held her hand while she slept and wiped her hot face and neck with a cool facecloth when she woke up. Paula was fantastic. She soothed Jo when he couldn't.

·'The baby's heartbeat is very strong,' she told Jo. 'It won't be too long now.'

The hands on Mark's watch had crawled around to half four when a red-haired nurse popped her head around the door.

'Mr Ryan, Paula said you should grab a cup of tea and I'll stay with Mrs Ryan,' she said.

'Thanks, but I couldn't leave her,' he replied.

'Go on,' the nurse insisted. 'It could be a long night.'

Mark gulped his scalding tea, not really wanting to wait until it cooled. He was afraid to be away from Jo for more than ten minutes. Who knew when she'd go into the second stage?

'Mark!!' He heard her long before he reached the ward. She was screeching in pain, her face contorted as a powerful contraction hit her. Her eyes were red with exhaustion and sweat had matted strands of dark hair to her forehead.

'Jo, I'm sorry, I'm sorry I was gone,' he cried.

'I've got to push!' she screamed.

'Don't push yet.' Paula's voice was calm and controlled. 'This isn't the time to push. Take two short breaths and then breathe out slowly,' she advised, checking Jo's cervix. Another nurse monitored the baby's heart through the machine they'd connected to Jo's belly.

'You're nine and a half centimetres dilated, Jo. You're nearly ready. How do you feel?'

'Bloody awful,' panted Jo. 'Aaagghh!'

They propped her up with a pile of pillows, getting her into the most comfortable position.

'You're doing great, Jo,' Mark said.

'Ten centimetres,' said Paula.

Jo screamed with pain. 'Now I know why they call it "labour".'

'OK now, push!' commanded Paula. 'A long, steady push.'

Jo pushed, tucking her chin down onto her chest. That was

the right way to do it, she was sure. That was what they'd said at the classes. Oh God, the pain, she couldn't take it. How could the baby come out? How would it fit?

'You're doing brilliantly, Jo,' said Mark encouragingly, one large hand clasped tightly in Jo's small one.

'Take a deep breath as you feel each contraction beginning,' Paula said. 'Ready . . .'

Jo did her best and pushed as hard as she could. She could feel the baby, feel the baby coming out.

'That's great, one more push. It's crowning. Jo, we can see the baby's head.'

Mark squeezed her hand and Jo felt the tears swell in her eyes. The baby, her baby.

'Don't push for a moment, Jo. The baby's head is stretching the birth canal. We don't want you to tear,' Paula said.

'Relax,' Mark said.

'And pant,' added the red-haired nurse.

Jo panted, feeling the pressure lessen.

'Oh Jo, look, the baby's head!' yelled Mark in excitement.

She could barely see, couldn't stretch any farther. She so desperately wanted to see the baby's head.

'Push,' commanded Paula. 'Just a couple more pushes, just two more!'

With one last push, Jo felt the baby ease out. She gasped with relief, and as Paula held the small bloodied body up for her to see, she gasped with joy.

'She's a beautiful little girl,' Paula said triumphantly.

Tears blinded Jo. She watched Paula expertly check the tiny infant. She'd read all about the Apgar score to assess the baby for breathing, heart rate and response to stimulation. Before, the Apgar had been words on a page – now it was the most important thing in the world to her.

'Oh Mark.' Jo held her breath with terror. Please let the baby be all right. The baby let out a loud wail, a healthy sound that brought colour to her mother's cheeks.

'Is she all right?' Jo asked, barely able to speak with fear.

'You've got a beautiful little girl, Jo,' said Paula. 'She's seven pounds one ounce, very healthy. She scored an eight on her Apgar.'

Paula laid the baby, all wrapped up in a soft towel, in Jo's arms. Jo gazed down at the huge blue eyes, the downy dark hair clinging to her head, and the small pink mouth screwed up with crying. She'd never felt anything like it before, Jo thought, the powerful and intense love she felt for her tiny, fragile baby. She held the baby's delicate little hands, marvelling at the tiny fingers.

'She's so beautiful,' said Jo, holding the fragile baby close to her chest. Mark sat on the edge of the bed and stroked the baby's head. His huge hand dwarfed the infant's red face.

As if she had responded to his touch, the baby stopped crying and snuggled instinctively closer to Jo's breast. She made little sucking noises with her mouth and Jo was about to open her hospital gown to feed her when Paula appeared beside her.

'Because she was premature, we've got to make sure that she's healthy,' the midwife said, gently taking the baby from Jo. 'The paediatrician wants a look at her. I'll be back with her as soon as I can.'

Jo felt as if a part of her was missing. She laid her fingers over the mound of her belly, still huge from carrying her little passenger all those months. If something went wrong, if the baby was sick, Jo didn't know how she'd cope. She'd die if anything happened to the baby, she just knew it.

'She'll be fine, Jo.' Mark leaned over to kiss her forehead. It was no good. She loved Mark to pieces, but he couldn't comfort her when it came to her darling baby.

After fifteen of the longest minutes of Jo's life, Claire, the red-haired nurse, returned with the baby and the paediatrician in tow.

'She's fine,' explained the doctor. 'Perfectly healthy. She's quite big for a pre-term baby at seven pounds one ounce. And she's perfect.'

'I know, isn't she?' Jo beamed up at him.

'You hold her, Mark,' she added. When Mark took the

infant into his arms, she mewled like a kitten at first and then snuggled peacefully into his chest.

'She's fantastic,' Mark said in awe, staring at her as though he'd never seen a baby before.

'A daddy's girl already,' said Jo with a smile.

Half an hour later, the baby was sleeping peacefully in her crib when Claire came into the brightly painted hospital room Jo had been wheeled into.

'You need to get some rest,' she told Jo.

'I'm exhausted,' Jo admitted, 'but could I have a cup of tea, please?'

'Yes. Do you want one too?' Claire asked Mark.

'I'd kill for some tea,' he replied gratefully.

'She's so beautiful, isn't she?' Jo gazed into the cot beside her bed where the baby lay sleeping.

'How could she be anything else when she's got the most gorgeous mother in the world?' Mark sat on the edge of the chair beside Jo's bed and leaned over towards her. 'I had this all planned,' he said. 'We were going to leave the Shelbourne early and get the limo to drive us up to the cottage, where I have candles, champagne, flowers and the CD player with your favourite Mariah Carey CD all ready to swing into action. And then,' he paused and looked at Jo intently, his grey eyes warm with love, 'I was going to ask you to marry me. So will you marry me?' he asked softly, so as not to wake the baby. 'I think this is the perfect moment, with our daughter asleep beside us.'

He fumbled around the inside pocket of his dinner jacket which lay on the chair behind him. A moment later he produced a small navy leather box, opened it, and offered it to Jo.

'Oh, it's beautiful,' she breathed, stunned by the square-cut emerald surrounded by tiny diamonds. As she moved the box, the little diamonds twinkled in the light.

She looked up at Mark.

'Oh Mark, thank you so much. I do. I will. Whatever!'

She'd never loved him more than at this moment, with

stubble darkening his jaw, eyes red-rimmed, his face pale with tiredness and strain. He'd been with her for the birth of the baby, *their* baby. *She* was Mark's child, there was no doubt in her mind about that. He leaned forward and kissed her gently on the mouth.

'I'm so glad. I've wanted to ask you for a long time, but it had to be the right moment.'

Jo grinned tiredly as she lay back on her pillows.

'I think we can safely say that we'll never forget this moment,' she said.

The door swung open and Claire arrived in with a small pot of tea and two cups.

'Your friend is still outside. She can come in for a moment if you'd like.'

'Mark, go and get Aisling,' said Jo. 'Tell her we've some news for her.'

CHAPTER TWENTY-ONE

'Do I look OK?' Jo twisted and turned in front of the mirror in her bedroom. Did her bum look too big in the cream brocade suit? The slim fitted jacket flattered her curves and the combination of the long straight skirt and high-heeled cream boots made her look like an elegant Edwardian lady. Or at least it had when she tried it on in Amanda Wakeley's shop in London. But now she wasn't so sure.

It wasn't the traditional wedding dress, but as she and Mark weren't having the traditional church wedding, she preferred a low-key outfit to go with the simple civil service. A ceremony attended by their close family and a small reception in the beautiful estate in Enniskerry's Powerscourt was what they'd both wanted.

The ceremony was at three. It was still only half one, there was plenty of time for last-minute panic attacks about whether her outfit looked all right and would she have to insist that Ralph, the photographer, doctor the wedding pictures to make her look slimmer.

Jo examined herself in the mirror. She was still a little pale, even though she'd used at least half a ton of bronzing powder. But at least she'd lost most of the weight she'd put on carrying Isabel.

If only her bum was as slim as it had been before she'd got pregnant, then she'd be totally happy. But you couldn't really tell thanks to those lycra-panelled knickers that sucked every-thing in.

Her dark hair was piled up on top of her head. A few tendrils clustered around her face. Jo fiddled with these curls restlessly.

'You look great, stop worrying.' Aisling looked up from the bed where she was trying to undo Isabel's babygro to change her nappy.

At three months old, Isabel Ryan was a very energetic young lady and enjoyed nothing more than wriggling madly when she was having her clothes put on or taken off, kicking the undresser in lots of painful places.

'Let me, Ash.' Jo got down on her knees beside the bed and took over from Aisling. 'How's my Isabel?' she cooed, kissing her daughter's snub nose. The baby squealed with delight and kicked harder as Jo tried to ease her tiny feet out of the cream towelling outfit.

'Don't kick Mummy in the tummy, pet. Now you've got to be very, very good while Mummy gets ready to marry Daddy,' murmured Jo, as she expertly undid the babygro and unfastened the nappy. 'Won't you be good, Isabel?' she asked.

Isabel responded with another couple of unco-ordinated kicks and a happy gurgle.

'She's a love.' Aisling sat on the edge of the bed and watched, with more than a hint of longing in her own voice.

'Isn't she just?' Jo said proudly. 'We've been so lucky with her. When I went to the crèche for the first time last week, three of the mothers there couldn't believe it when I told them how good Isabel is. I think they think I'm making it up to make them jealous.'

'Not many babies sleep solidly for eight hours at night.' Aisling opened her handbag and pretended to search for her lipstick. She *had* to get over the maternal feelings which tore at her heart every time she held Jo's little daughter in her arms.

'The twins were awful for sleeping. I'd get Phillip off to sleep when Paul would wake up, or vice versa.'

Aisling outlined her lips with lip pencil and then applied the deep pink colour which went perfectly with the fitted dusky rose wool trouser-suit she was wearing.

It was just as well she'd worn the long-sleeved pale pink body underneath, she thought. It was the coldest day in February, freezing winds whipped around Jo and Mark's cottage in the Dublin mountains.

464

'Come on, darling, help Mummy put your dress on,' Jo was saying softly.

'I'll help,' Aisling offered, seeing the difficulties Jo was having trying to slip the cream silk overdress, the same colour as her own elegant suit, over Isabel's head. By the time Jo finally managed to put the cream bonnet with the silk ribbons on her daughter's dark hair, Isabel looked like a baby from an eighteenth-century French painting.

'All we need are Marie Antoinette's shepherdess's dresses, bonnets and a couple of sheep and we're all set to be hung in the National Gallery,' Aisling said with a laugh before extracting a camera from her handbag. 'Smile!'

'We've got half an hour before the car comes so I decided to open one of the bottles of champagne Mark left in the kitchen.' Laura Ryan appeared at the bedroom door with a tray, three glasses and a bottle of Cristal.

'Champagne,' cried Jo in delight. 'My favourite. Mum, I didn't know there *was* any champagne in the house.'

'Your husband-to-be is highly organised,' her mother replied with a smile. 'He told me about the case before he left and said he'd hidden a Chocolate Orange in the cupboard under the sink for you to go with it.'

'Oh.' Jo sighed appreciatively. 'He knows I love Chocolate orange.'

'With champagne?' asked Aisling.

'With *anything*.' Jo and her mother laughed at exactly the same time. Aisling was struck again by how alike the two women were. There was no way you'd ever think that the lithe and dark-haired Laura Ryan was a grandmother, never mind the mother of grown-up children.

'Let me take Isabel.' Laura picked up her granddaughter with delight. Isabel gurgled happily and blew bubbles at her adoring granny.

Jo draped a towel across her mother's shoulder so she could cuddle Isabel without ruining her wedding outfit with dribbles.

'Granny has to look good in front of your daddy's relatives,'

Laura explained as she adjusted the towel.

'You look fantastic, Mum,' said Jo sharply. 'There won't be anyone there to hold a candle to you. Anyway, I told you that Mark's family is very nice. His sister, Denise, is lovely, although I have no idea where she got that little bitch Emma from,' Jo added thoughtfully.

'She's the only one I was worried about. I could picture her making snide remarks all day, but not any more. She knows what side her bread is buttered on now,' Jo added vehemently.

'Tell me, what's happened?' demanded Aisling, agog.

Jo abandoned all pretence of putting on her eyeliner.

'Well,' she said with a definite glint in her eye, 'I went into the office last week with my copy and I had Isabel with me, of course. That little cow was there, sitting in my seat as cool as a cucumber and she'd dumped all my stuff on top of my filing cabinet. She didn't expect to see me, I can tell you.' Jo grinned triumphantly. 'She went puce and started moving her stuff off the desk quickly. I went in to talk to Rhona and when I came out she was on the phone bitching about me.'

'I don't believe it!' said Aisling. 'How stupid can she be, talking about you like that when you were there.'

Jo shrugged. 'That girl is a real mystery to me. Sometimes she's so smart and bitchy, and other times she comes across like a complete fool. Anyway,' she took a sip of champagne, 'I waited until she was off the phone, let Rhona take Isabel, then I called Emma into Rhona's office. I told her that I knew exactly what sort of person she was, and I said that even though I didn't believe in throwing my weight around normally, she'd better watch out when I came back to work. "You may be Mark's niece," I told her. "But *I'll* be his wife. You figure it out." That shut her up.'

Aisling and Laura howled with laughter.

'Well done,' Laura said, 'I'm proud of you.'

'That's priceless. I'd have loved to have seen her face,' said Aisling.

'You will. She's going to be at the reception,' Jo pointed out. 'But just wait till you see how nice she is to me. She didn't think I had it in me to be hard, but she knows better now.'

'You could never be hard, Jo,' Aisling said. 'Not in a million years.'

Jo considered this as she screwed the lid off her mascara tube. 'I've wisened up, maybe that's it.'

'Haven't we all?' Aisling thought of the past year and all the changes it had brought to her life. In a short period of time, she'd gone from being a depressed married woman to being a fulfilled working mother who'd managed to set up her own company, *and* hold down another job, *and* look after her beloved twin sons on her own into the bargain. She'd certainly toughened up.

She'd even managed to exorcise Michael's memory thanks to Sam. The affair had been wonderful at first. It had turned into a bit of a nightmare at the very end. Aisling cast her mind back to the day after the charity ball, the day she'd told Sam to get out of her life for good.

She'd just got home after dropping some things into the hospital for Jo and was about to start dinner when the doorbell rang. It was five in the afternoon, the boys were watching TV and she wasn't expecting any visitors.

'It's Sam,' announced Phillip. He stuck his head around the kitchen door.

Just what she didn't need. After last night's confrontation, she could do without another one. She was sick and tired of Sam Delaney. She opened the freezer to see what she could defrost for dinner and waited for Sam to come looking for her. When he didn't appear, she went into the sitting room.

'Where is he?' she asked in a puzzled voice.

'Outside,' Phillip said innocently.

Aisling glared at him. 'Why didn't you open the door?' she demanded. Before Phillip could answer, the doorbell rang again.

'I thought you weren't going to let me in,' Sam said, when she opened the front door.

'That was just Phillip playing games,' she said tiredly,

leading the way into the kitchen.

'Little brat.' Sam's voice was harsh.

Aisling whirled around in fury. 'Don't you dare call my son names! Who the hell do you think you are?' she yelled.

'Jesus, Aisling. Don't fly off the handle,' Sam said, taken aback. 'It's only a comment, I'm sorry. Look, I'm here to apologise for last night, so why don't I do a double apology? Sorry for flying off the handle last night and sorry for saying your son is a b . . . sorry,' he said lamely.

'What's wrong, Mum?' demanded Paul, rushing into the kitchen with Phillip on his heels. The pair of them stared at Sam accusingly. 'What's *he* said now?' Phillip's furious face was so like Michael's, it was uncanny.

'Will we throw him out, Mum?' asked Paul.

Aisling felt her heart burst with pride. Her little heroes, ready to take on a grown-up three times their size just to protect her. She went over and hugged them both. They were growing up so quickly, in a couple of years they'd be as tall as she was.

'No, boys, it's OK.'

Paul relaxed at her words, but Phillip's body was still tensed as if he was ready to fight. He moved out of her embrace and looked up at Sam steadily.

'Our dad isn't here, but don't think you can boss Mum around,' he hissed. 'We don't like you. Why don't you go back to America?'

'Yeah, why not?' said Paul.

Aisling was stunned. She had no idea that the twins disliked Sam so much. She'd thought they got on all right with him. But when she cast her mind back over the few times when the four of them had been together, she realised that when they all went to McDonald's or the cinema, both boys sat on her side, never beside Sam. Funny, she'd never thought about that before.

'It's all right, boys,' she said. 'Everything is fine, everything is going to be fine.' She smiled at Phillip. 'Go on and watch the TV. We'll have dinner in an hour.'

As they left, Sam dragged out a kitchen chair from the table and sat down with a thump.

'You're ruining those boys, ruining them because you're guilty about being separated,' he said in his mid-Atlantic drawl. Aisling realised that she hated the way he spoke, his American twang suddenly sounded so false. 'When I was their age, I'd have been given a good beating for speaking to an adult like that. And that's what Phillip wants. A few slaps would be good for him.'

She turned to look at him, taking in his flushed face and angry eyes. He was a bully, all right. Why hadn't she noticed it before? She'd been seduced by the way he made her feel. She'd wanted to get her own back at Michael by having such a sexy, handsome boyfriend.

She'd let that, and his amazing ability in bed, blind her to his faults. Not any more.

'You're entitled to your opinion about children,' she said evenly. 'But don't think you're going to try your theories out on *my* children, because you aren't. And you're not going to try it out on me, either, Sam. It's over between us. So if you could leave, I can get back to living my life without you telling me where I'm going wrong every five minutes.'

Sam stared at her open-mouthed. 'You can't mean that, Aisling,' he said. 'What about us, about our plans . . .?'

'There is no *us* any more. It's over.'

He grabbed her arm and tried to pull her onto his lap, his words cajoling. 'Please, Ash, don't say that.'

'Let me go!' She wrenched herself free of his grasp.

'Aisling.' Sam stood up and tried to put his arms around her, but she backed away.

'Just go, Sam.'

'Yeah, go.' Phillip and Paul were back, standing at the door like small sentries. For a moment, Aisling felt her chest tighten as Sam's face grew dark. His jaw tensed.

Jesus, he wasn't going to hit them, was he?

'Boys, come here!' she cried. They ran to her and stood in front of her.

469

'Go!' she said again.

He shrugged. 'I'll go, but you'll be sorry. I know you will. You'll want me back.'

Yeah, when hell freezes over, she thought silently. Nobody said anything as Sam turned and walked out the door. He slammed the front door behind him.

How predictable.

'Well boys, what do you want for dinner?' Aisling asked brightly, determined to hide how shaken she was by the encounter. 'Or should we go to McDonald's for a treat?'

'*We'll* cook,' Phillip announced. He pulled up a chair for her at the table. 'We can defrost just as well as you can.'

Aisling had to laugh. She got herself a glass of icy white wine from the fridge and sat down at the table. 'OK, boys, what are we eating?'

'Are you thinking about Sam?' asked Jo.

Aisling looked at her friend and smiled. 'You know me so well, Jo,' she said.

'Well enough to know that you've done the right thing,' Jo said quietly.

'Oh I know that.'

'I'll take Isabel downstairs while you finish getting ready, girls,' Laura said, taking the baby out of the room.

'Now I know where you get your perceptiveness from,' Aisling said. She sat on the pale yellow duvet and looked up at her friend. 'I'm not upset, Jo. To be honest, I'm very happy. I love my life now, I love the freedom. OK, juggling work, more work and childminders isn't easy, but there's this huge sense of freedom in everything I do. *I* make the decisions, *I* decide what I'm going to do every day, every week,' she explained earnestly.

'It's incredibly liberating. Sam was great for my self-confidence, at the beginning anyway,' she added wryly, 'but being around him made me realise that I don't want another man to worry about. Not for a long time. And when I do want someone else, it has to be on my terms.'

'So you're happy?' asked Jo tentatively. 'I know it's childish, but I want you to be happy on my wedding day.'

Aisling got up and wrapped her arms around Jo.

'I am happy. I'm so happy for you and Mark too. It's wonderful seeing how happy you both are with Isabel.'

'Thanks for everything, Ash,' Jo said. 'Thank you for being here today and thank you for being so good to me when I needed you.'

'What are friends for?' Aisling asked with a shrug. 'Now tell me, this photographer, Ralph, who's taking the wedding pictures. Is he handsome? Is he single?'

'Yes and yes,' said Jo, a tad too enthusiastically. 'He's drop-dead gorgeous. Dark hair, brown eyes, great body. There's only one problem – he's gay.'

'Is he a mature adult?' demanded Aisling.

'Absolutely,' Jo replied.

'Fine. We can work on everything else. Just as long as he's grown-up, that's all I want. Now, shall we go to a wedding?'

'You bet.'

SHE'S THE ONE

To John, with all my love, always,
and to Kate, I'll never forget you.

Writing acknowledgements is almost harder than the book because I know I'll leave somebody out! But here goes: my heartfelt thanks to my darling John for everything; to my dear family for their help and support, especially my ever supportive Mum, Dad, Lucy, Fran, Anne, Laura and Naomi. And of course to my beloved Tamsin.

Thanks to my dear friend Sarah Hamilton and my favourite nephew Jamie; thanks to Ros Edwards and Helenka Fuglewicz for being marvellous agents; thanks to my girl friends Lisa, Esther, Liz, Joanne, Mairead, Annie and Moira for constant encouragement and thanks to all my colleagues and friends at *Sunday World* – you know who you are; also thanks to Patricia Scanlan for wonderful phone calls and Sally Hamwee for legal expertise.

Special thanks to my wonderful publishing families at Headline and Poolbeg. It's a pleasure working with all of you.

Thanks to dear Clare Foss who is the most marvellously kind editor. Special thanks to Amanda Ridout, Frances, Rebecca, James, Sarah, Ros and all the other people I just know I'm leaving out at Headline who have been so welcoming.

Thanks to Paula, Gaye, Elaine, Emer, Conor, Sarah, Nicole, Phillip, Connor, Kieran and everybody at Poolbeg who have been so marvellous to me and thanks to Margaret Daly for publicity.

Thank you to all the journalists and reviewers who said such lovely things the last time; I really appreciated it all. And thanks to the lovely booksellers I've met throughout Ireland and the UK who were so helpful and kind to me during my first terrifying tour.

Thanks to family friends John and Mary Kelly, John and Joan Gourley and Liz, Arthur and everyone at Kilmurray for their support during Dad's illness, and thanks to Professor Brian Lawlor, all the amazing staff at the Delaney Ward, St Patrick's Hospital, the staff at the Kylemore Clinic and the Alzheimer Society of Ireland.

Thank you so much to the people who liked *Woman to Woman* and to those who sent me fantastic letters telling me so. I hope you like this.

Finally, thanks to Kate Cruise O'Brien who tragically died earlier this year. A wonderful editor and an incredible person, she was a huge loss to everybody. Like everyone who knew Kate, I miss her and I will never forget her.

CHAPTER ONE

Dear Annie,

I hope you can help me. I've been married two months and my marriage is already a disaster. We didn't live together before we got married so I never dreamed it could be like this. I have a demanding job and so does my husband, but he still leaves all the housework to me. It doesn't matter what time I get home, I'm supposed to get dinner and I end up spending all my weekends trying to sort out the house, wash the clothes and iron his shirts. He always leaves the shopping to me, even when he has a day off. He says his mother always did that sort of thing. I can't believe that I didn't know he was like this before we got married.

What can I do? I'm going mad about this and I can't talk to anyone because everyone thinks we're the perfect couple. Please help before my marriage is ruined.

Depressed

Dee paused, fingers poised over the computer keyboard as she looked at the handwritten letter again. Sometimes it took ages to think up replies to the *Dear Annie* letters, especially those from people who needed a

1

miracle by way of an answer, instead of advice on how to improve their relationship with a child-free weekend away somewhere romantic and a bottle of sensual massage oil.

Dee couldn't always get her brain working properly when it came to composing her replies, so she frequently took refuge in the biscuit tin. Today wasn't one of those days. Today she didn't have to think twice because, ironic though it was, she knew exactly how to answer this one.

Dear Depressed,

You've no idea how common your problem is and my postbag is full of pleas for help from women who thought they were marrying Mr Right and found out too late that they'd in-advertently got hitched to Mr-My-Mother-Always-Did-It-That-Way-And-Reared-10-Kids, Four-Goats-And-Still-Made-Her-Own-Bread.

You've got to take action or you may as well buy an apron with the word 'Slave' on it.

First, stop doing all the shopping, hoovering, washing, ironing – and wait until he notices. Believe me, he will . . .

Dee stopped typing. She leant back and massaged her neck with one hand. She was completely exhausted after spending the whole week in the Central Criminal Court reporting on a murder trial and really didn't feel up to spending Saturday, her first day off in ten days, working on her agony column.

She wanted to laze in a bath filled with relaxing aromatherapy stuff, with a thirst-quenching Bacardi and Coke, and a fat, juicy novel by her side. If she felt up to

2

it, she might even shave her legs before they started looking as if they belonged to a Greek taxi driver. Then again, maybe she'd stick to relaxing. Who the hell was going to see her legs? Not Gary, that was for sure. The only legs he noticed these days were incredibly hairy, wore shorts topped with sports jerseys and their owners answered to the name of Manchester United Football Club.

She sighed. The bath would have to wait until she'd finished her column. *Dear Annie* ran in the *Sentinel* on Mondays and Wednesdays and, short of phoning the women's editor from an ambulance bearing her to hospital with a bout of pleurisy, Dee had to produce a column by eleven on Sunday. It would take at least three hours to write. Maybe Gold Blend and a digestive or three would loosen the knot in her neck. Or maybe she'd have one of those Weight Watcher mini cheese-cakes she'd hidden at the back of the bottom shelf in the freezer.

They were practically calorie-free. Well, they *had* to be or they wouldn't be called Weight Watchers. One cheesecake wouldn't be too bad. And she'd had Special K and anaemic skimmed milk for breakfast, so she was due a treat.

Dee left the tiny spare room that doubled as her office and made her way past the overflowing wicker linen basket. She tried to ignore it but she couldn't.

Somebody had to do it, she thought crossly, grabbing an armful of wet towels, Gary's soccer jersey and several of his greying T-shirts.

Arms full of laundry, she negotiated the stairs, ignor-ing the wisps of marmalade cat-hair which covered the dark mulberry carpet in fetching little balls of fluff. Why did Smudge insist on completing her laborious

3

grooming routine on the stairs instead of doing it in the kitchen on the lino? Dee wondered gloomily. To make matters worse, the hoover was kaput and she didn't have the energy to take it to the electrical shop to get it fixed. She stepped over a dusty pile of Gary's soccer magazines which he'd stacked haphazardly at the bottom of the stairs.

'I'll take them up later!' he'd snapped on Thursday night when she'd tripped over what had to be six months' worth of *Soccer Fanatic* magazines. 'For God's sake, Dee, give me a break! I can't spend my whole bloody life cleaning up, can I?'

Then he'd stomped off into the sitting-room. Dee had barely dropped her bulging black briefcase on the floor beside the coat stand before she heard Sky Sports blaring from the TV.

She was too exhausted to argue. Gary's version of cleaning up meant emptying his ashtrays before they overflowed. *Just* before they overflowed, at that. Whoever said 'If you want to know me, come live with me' was right.

Four years ago, when she'd met Gary Redmond, she'd thought he was the answer to her dreams. After several failed relationships with fellow journalists, Dee had decided that she was never going out with a reporter ever again. Neurotic, obsessed with *their* stories all the time and terminally jealous if she got a better scoop than they did that week, her three failed flings with reporters had put her off male reporters as a species.

She'd dumped her last ex's belongings – the toothbrush he'd left in her flat, the sweater she'd bought him for his birthday and the notebook she'd found with his new girlfriend's phone number scrawled in lipstick – on to his desk in the newsroom a mere month before she met Gary. The lithe, dark-haired man in the expensive-looking grey suit who spilled Guinness over her in the Shelbourne's Horseshoe Bar was so apologetic, so charming and so obviously not a journalist, that she found herself agreeing to have a drink with him, 'to make up for my being so clumsy'.

While Gary did his best to charm her, Dee sipped the champagne cocktail he'd insisted on buying her and thanked her lucky stars that she'd spent the past, boyfriend-less month on a severe diet, had lost ten pounds and was a skinny size fourteen verging on size twelve. Otherwise she wouldn't have felt confident enough to have a drink with such an attractive man. And she certainly wouldn't have fitted into the tight-as-a-tourniquet black dress that showed off her generous cleavage and great legs.

Of course, the combination of control panel sheer tights and Marks & Spencer's vacuum-packed knickers meant she felt like an Egyptian mummy, and two champagne cocktails, complete with lots of fizz, were almost too much for the black dress to bear. Dee felt her stomach groan inside its sexy Lycra casing. But you had to suffer to be beautiful. Well, suffer to be reasonable-looking. Other people – mainly her best friend, Maeve – were always telling Dee that she was pretty, sexy and had marvellously expressive dark eyes. But she'd never been too keen on voluptuous curves, a bosom that needed a government health warning because men were always staring at it, mesmerised, or dark rippling curls that needed a gallon of anti-frizz serum applied every single day. She liked her eyes, of course, but what Dee really wanted to be was a classy Nordic blonde, effort-lessly chic and effortlessly skinny, with legs up to her armpits.

After an hour in Gary's company, she was charmed by his intelligence and dark good looks, flattered by his obvious interest in her and, even though accountancy had never been high on her list of desirable occupations in a mate, Gary was nothing like any accountant she'd ever known.

'You remind me of those beautiful pre-Raphaelite women in nineteenth-century paintings,' he'd murmured as he leant over her at the bar. She got a waft of Armani aftershave combined with healthy male pheromones. 'They've got long, rippling auburn or chestnut hair, big dark eyes, and always look like they're waiting to be lured away to some shady meadow to do something nineteenth-century girls weren't supposed to do.'

If one of the lads in the newsroom had said anything like that, Dee would have burst out laughing *before* thumping him. But Gary Redmond's deep voice made the words sound like the sexiest thing she'd ever heard. He had a way of looking at her with those strange almost hazel eyes that melted Dee's insides.

'Really?' she'd said, looking up at him and calculating that, as she was five foot three, he had to be over five nine which made him tall enough but not too tall. She hated really tall men. You got a crick in your neck talking up to them all the time. 'So how do you know so much about art?'

'My mother loves improving herself,' he replied with a wry grin. 'When we were kids she insisted we went on holiday to Italy and France so we could visit the Louvre and just about every chapel in Florence.'

'Sounds marvellous,' Dee said, thinking of the O'Reilly family's annual two weeks in a caravan somewhere on the Irish coast. The only gallery they ever visited was the shooting one in the local amusement arcade. She'd preferred the swing boats herself until she was fifteen and realised that you could fit *two* people into a dodgem – perfect for getting close to boys.

'Do you think it's too late to teach art appreciation to a complete philistine?' Dee inquired silkily, giving him the sultry look she'd perfected after years of practice in front of her bedroom mirror. 'I don't know anything about art.'

'I'm sure you're a quick learner,' he'd answered.

Two hours later, they were giggling over a bottle of wine in the Unicorn. A week later, they were in love. Dee still remembered their third date. She'd been convinced that she loved him by then.

Gary had turned up at her flat with a picnic basket jammed with cold chicken, French bread, potato salad, a six-pack of Budweiser and strawberry ice cream in a cooler bag. After three days eating nothing but grapefruit and consuming endless low-cal chocolate drinks in order to keep those damn' ten pounds off, Dee could have polished off the entire basket herself in ten minutes. She felt faint from lack of food and the scent of French bread was driving her insane with hunger.

'We're going on a picnic,' Gary said, grabbing her in a bear hug as soon as she opened her front door.

'Picnic? But it's half-eight!' she said in surprise.

'A late-night picnic, Dee.' Gary kissed her passionately. 'Now bring your fleece jacket. It might be cold.'

They sat cuddled together in his red Mazda at Dollymount with the roof down and soft music on the car stereo. It had been freezing at first. But the beer warmed their blood and when Gary unzipped her blue fleece jacket in an exploratory way, Dee began to feel very hot.

'Who said accountants aren't romantic?' she whispered into his ear as he slid a hand under her jumper.

But romance had certainly gone out of the window the last few months, she reflected. In fact, she couldn't remember the last time Gary had done anything even vaguely caring. He'd nearly forgotten Valentine's Day, for God's sake. Mind you, she would have given a shopful of red roses if he would occasionally remember to put the toilet seat down.

She stuffed the armful of dirty clothes into the machine, sloshed in some detergent, the last dribble of fabric conditioner, and switched the machine on. Then she took a mug from the pile of unwashed china in the sink, cleared enough room to rinse it under the hot tap and briefly considered giving in and washing up. No, damn it. She wasn't going to. Bloody Gary could do it.

Eventually, he'll get tired of seeing the dishes piled high and he'll do them himself. The secret is not to nag him – let him decide to do the housework off his own bat. He might let the sink reach Everest proportions before he thinks of washing up but, give him a week of unironed shirts, no socks and underpants that the Laundry Fairy has somehow missed, and he'll start doing housework. Wait and see.

Giving advice and actually acting on it were two very different things, Dee thought. She knew what the depressed letter writer *should* do about her housework-shy chauvinist. But since Dee still hadn't managed to get her own lazy fiancé to wash up so much as a single plate, she felt a complete hypocrite telling *Depressed* what to do.

She'd been operating the let-the-dishes-pile-up policy for the last week and the only fact that was becoming

8

apparent was that Gary would rather buy a new shirt than wash a dirty one and that he was completely oblivious to a mountain of dirty dishes in the sink, green mould in the fridge and no clean underpants in his drawer.

It was all his bloody mother's fault. She'd ruined him, never let him lift a finger around the house so that he was now convinced that only women knew the secret to cleaning the toilet and hoovering the sitting-room. Or at least, he *pretended* he didn't know the secret. As she constantly moaned to her best friend, Maeve, Dee should have known exactly what she was getting into when she met Gary's mother for the first time. They'd been going out for three months and he was practically living in Dee's flat on the South Circular Road when he'd asked her home to meet his mother.

'She's nothing like your mum,' said Gary who'd been introduced to Dee's parents and younger brothers at a traditional music night in the Submarine pub. The O'Reillys had welcomed Gary into the fold and had done their best to make him feel comfortable. By closing time, he and her dad were best pals and Gary had been invited to Sunday lunch that weekend.

By way of contrast, his mother had invited Dee to afternoon tea which she served in dainty cups after asking her guest to be careful because it was 'my best china'.

Convinced that the snub hadn't been intentional, Dee smiled and said how lovely the royal blue three-piece suite was.

She *should* have noticed that Gary sat comfortably in an armchair and let his mother hurry in and out of the kitchen bearing china cups, scones, sponge cakes and his favourite gingerbread without once offering to help.

And she should also have wondered why her charming, attentive lover turned into an eager-to-please mummy's boy in his mother's presence.

But she was too busy trying to smile sweetly – and, later, too irritated by Margaret's unsubtle probing – to notice.

'How long have you worked on the . . . er . . . the paper, Deirdre?'

'Six years.'

'I see. And you work in news, Gary tells me. That must be interesting. Have you thought about moving on to another publication perhaps?'

'No.'

'Oh. More cake, darling?' Margaret said to Gary, her voice warming up about a hundred degrees. She handed another lump of cake to her son and turned back to the inquisition. 'What does your father do, Deirdre? Is he in journalism as well?'

'He's a mechanic,' Dee answered, toying with the idea of saying that he played piano in a brothel in between acting as the getaway driver during an occasional armed robbery.

'He *runs* a garage, does he?'

'No. He's a mechanic. Specialises in exhausts.'

'Oh.'

It hadn't taken Dee long to realise that Margaret Redmond was one of those Irish mammies who thought nobody, *absolutely nobody*, was good enough for her youngest boy.

An expert cook, skilled seamstress and the first person in the queue for Communion at daily Mass, Gary's mother was a much-admired member of the Clontarf community and was desperately religious. She didn't drink, smoke or swear and never sat down to watch mindless television – unless it was an educational documentary – when she could be baking a lemon sponge for the church fête or painstakingly rubbing Vanish into the boys' shirt collars. She went to art appreciation classes although Dee was convinced she only did it to show off, and once a week played pitch and putt with a ladies' group.

She'd reared five boys, married four of them off to suitable girls, buried her accountant husband and was now biding her time waiting for the first daughter-in-law to get pregnant so she could crochet endless pram blankets and baby-sit religiously.

Short, rounded – from too many lemon sponges – and boasting a tight grey perm and bi-focals, Margaret Redmond was a million miles away from Dee's mother and a very tough cookie underneath it all.

If Dee had realised that going out with Gary meant getting lumbered with his horrible, social-climbing mother on a regular basis, she wasn't sure that she'd ever have fallen for him – despite his sexy eyes, great body and the charm that he could switch on like a light bulb.

He could switch it off just as easily. She sighed. The only spoon left in the cutlery drawer was the ancient soup spoon she'd used to mix the terracotta and mustard paint together when she'd attempted to colour-wash the bathroom walls. The paint was hard. It couldn't be poisonous, could it?

Who cared anyway? Instant coffee and emulsion might taste nice. The last frozen cheesecake had mysteriously vanished. Dee took the Argos catalogue, six plain biscuits – the twenty-five per cent less fat ones that everyone in work was raving about – and sat down at the pine table that wobbled madly when the piece of

11

cardboard under one leg was dislodged.

Outside the patio doors, a pale May sun broke through the clouds, making the raindrops on the whirly clothesline glitter like crystals. The grass in the tiny back garden was at least six inches high. Last year's nasturtiums had greedily outflanked a couple of stunted heathers to take over the entire flower bed by the patio. Dee knew she had to do something with the garden, soon, but she didn't have the time. Next weekend, she'd cut the front grass and pull up a few dandelions. Nobody but the engineering students next door could see the back garden and since *their* garden looked as if it needed to be nuked, they had no right to complain about hers.

When the phone rang a few minutes later, she was gazing at the catalogue's kitchen utensils, wondering whether a gleaming green plastic vegetable rack would look nice in one corner of the kitchen. A rack would also put an end to the problem of the potatoes sprouting shoots in the damp part at the bottom of the fridge. Must do that, she promised herself.

'Dee,' barked Ian Mahon, the *Sentinel*'s news editor. His bad-tempered, forty-Marlboro-a-day voice never failed to make her stand up straighter, even when he was just on the phone. In person, he was much worse. Very tall, stooped and mean-eyed, Mahon was universally loathed by the reporters, who called him Stalin in their kinder moments.

He was very good at his job, but Dee was convinced he'd be better at it if he didn't terrify the younger reporters with his habit of appearing beside their desks and reading their stories over their shoulders before screeching at them for doing something wrong. After six years in the newsroom at the mercy of Stalin's rages, Dee was used to him. More or less.

'There's a story breaking,' he growled now. 'That young Australian pop star, Chazz . . . we've got a tip-off that he's trashed a room in the Conrad Hotel. We've got a snapper down there now but he hasn't got any pictures. We want you to blag your way in. You've a contact there, haven't you?'

'Yes,' sighed Dee. So much for her day off. Typically, Stalin hadn't asked her if she was busy. No. He'd just assumed she'd jump to attention.

'Who's down there?' she asked, professionalism taking over. She grabbed a biro and scribbled down the details on the reporter's notebook she kept by the phone.

'Kevin Mills. I gave him your mobile number and he's going to ring you.'

Dee brightened up. Kevin Mills was a great photographer, who never lost his cool and always got the shot. Plus, he was extremely good-looking in a dark, gypsyish way.

A freelance photographer with his own agency, Kevin specialised in staking out celebrities. As Dee usually covered straight news stories, she'd rarely worked with him. But he had a reputation for being totally committed to the job and was certainly better-looking than Seanie Keane, the *Sentinel* staff photographer she usually worked with.

Kevin was unlikely to bore her to tears the way Seanie did when he wittered on about the painfully slow progress he was making on the crumbling nineteenth-century house he was renovating himself.

'If you can't get any pictures of Chazz, at least try and get into a similar room or suite for pics. Ring me in an hour,' Stalin commanded before hanging up abruptly.

Dee stuck out her tongue at the receiver. Pig!

Upstairs, she changed her comfy grey sweat pants and her favourite blue tie-dye T-shirt for something suitable for mingling with the rich and famous in the Conrad, one of Dublin's plushest hotels.

The severe black trouser suit looked best with her brown corkscrew curls loose but, as she hadn't washed her hair that morning, she'd have to tie it back. The trousers were too tight so she had to leave the top button open. Damn. There was no avoiding the issue by refusing to weigh herself or by wearing her black baggy trousers and sloppy overshirts – she was putting on weight again.

It was all Gary's fault. When Dee was upset, she turned to food for solace, and she was always upset these days. Yesterday she'd eaten three Mars Bars before lunchtime, and had still managed to consume a huge plate of *tagliatelle carbonara* for lunch. Why couldn't she be like her friend Maeve? A beanpole who ate like a horse, Maeve had eaten the *carbonara* and apple crumble afterwards and *she* never needed to leave her waistband buttons open.

In the bathroom, Dee stared at her reflection gloomily. As usual, she didn't notice her pretty, rounded face with its creamy pale skin, dark, expressive eyes and curly chestnut hair that framed her face beautifully.

Instead, she saw a short, plump woman squeezed into a pair of size 14 trousers when she really needed size 16. Dee turned sideways to see how far her stomach stuck out.

'Oh, God,' she groaned in misery.

She was *huge*. How could she even leave the house looking like she did? Her boobs bulged out of the bra under her clean pale pink T-shirt and her waist was almost non-existent. She looked like a pig, Dee thought. A short, dark-haired pig.

She hadn't time to put on the Number 7 foundation that covered up her freckles but she couldn't go out without lavishing a heavy coat of dark brown mascara on her eyelashes.

After a good spray of Opium, she grabbed her shoulder bag, snagged her mobile phone from the charger, and hopped into her white Corolla a mere ten minutes after Stalin's call.

Wait till he got the expenses, she promised herself grimly as she reversed out of the drive. That would teach him to drag her out on her day off. The extra money might be useful for buying the sort of tent of a dress she was going to have to wear soon.

'I'll meet you on Hatch Street at half-twelve,' Kevin said in a low voice over his mobile phone, the line crackling with static. 'I can't talk now.'

The traffic was very heavy. She'd never make it in time. Damn it, Dee thought, adjusting the rearview mirror so she could put on her lipstick at the Sundrive Road lights. Then the rush hit her, that amazing adrenaline rush she got when she was on to something good. It never failed. The buzz of working on a hot story even pushed her misery over her weight problem to the back of her mind, which was saying something.

She hoped another reporter hadn't got there before her. That was the problem with these anonymous tip-offs: people didn't just ring one paper, they rang them all. And nobody was more annoyed than the reporters who arrived to catch their scoop only to discover a representative of every other major paper there.

Kevin was waiting on Hatch Street, smoking a cigarette as he leant up against the silver Porsche he'd bought with the proceeds of selling last year's sunbathing shots of Liz Hurley on holiday in West Cork. His dark green waxed jacket concealed the two cameras which hung around his neck, the tell-tale telephoto lenses pointing downwards. He was gazing at the side of the hotel, eyes narrowed in contemplation.

'What's the story?' Dee asked as she eyed the photographer. Around six two – you had to be tall to reach over everyone's heads to get good pictures – with a rangy frame, dark eyes and a permanent five o'clock shadow on his square jaw, Kevin could have made as much money in front of the camera as behind it.

Even if he knew how gorgeous he was, and Dee reckoned he *had* to because office gossip insisted that there was always a queue of women lining up to date him, Kevin never behaved as if he was the best thing since George Clooney. Dee hated men with big egos.

She tried to arrange her jacket in a flattering way so she'd look as thin as possible. Sucking in her stomach, she stood up straight in the manner magazines were always advising. 'Lose five pounds instantly' the head-lines screamed, advocating the imagine-you've-got-a-string-pulling-your-head-up method. Dee craned her neck and did her best to look as if she'd lost ten.

Kevin took a long drag on his cigarette before he dropped it to the ground and stubbed it out with his Timberland boot.

'He's in there and the cops were called, according to my source. But she's not saying anything else. She was supposed to meet me outside half an hour ago and she never showed. Mahon said you knew someone on the staff.'

Dee gave him an apologetic look. 'I don't. I don't know why he thinks I have a source in there but I wasn't going to correct him. You know what he's like.'

'Fair enough. Let's take a walk round the front,' Kevin said.

As luck would have it, they didn't have to do anything else to get their story. They were walking around the front of the hotel when a dark blue car sped up the ramp from the hotel's underground car park.

The two men in the front were unmistakably detectives. It didn't take a telephoto lens to establish that the man in the back seat, flanked by two more burly cops, was Chazz.

The rock star looked the other way as the car hit the street, which gave Kevin the chance he needed. He ran towards it, his Canon clicking madly, and rolled off twenty shots in as many seconds.

The singer bent his head to escape being photographed but it was too late. Kevin had nailed him!

'Fantastic!' Dee caught up with him as the blue car sped out of sight. 'That was great. Let's hope nobody else gets it before Monday.'

'They won't have those shots anyway,' he replied with a big grin. 'I'm going down to the hotel bar to see if I can arrange to get pictures of the room he trashed. Want to come?'

It was the best invitation Dee had had all day. Gary was away for the weekend, ensconced in Old Trafford, probably pissed as a newt already. The only thing waiting for her at home was his laundry, which he was never going to do no matter how long she left it, and her agony column. The thought of a drink with an attractive man who wouldn't talk for hours about the Premier League was very inviting.

But she had to say no. If Kevin got the pictures of the hotel room, she could describe it from his shots. And the most urgent task was to talk to the cops about the

17

arrest of Chazz, aka Charlie Leonard, lead singer of Panic Zone. Since she was feeling more than a little fed up with Gary, Lord knew what a few stiff drinks with Kevin Mills could lead to. The last time she'd been this angry with her fiancé, the time he'd forgotten the dinner they always had to celebrate the anniversary of their first meeting, she'd been so cross that she'd gone drinking with the crowd from work and ended up flirting drunkenly with the happily married chief sub-editor, Bill. What a mistake that had been.

The next morning at work had been hell. Ribald jokes about her behaviour kept everyone in stitches until lunchtime, never mind the pain of her murderous hangover. Dee shuddered at the memory.

'Can't, sorry. Some other time?'

Kevin grinned down at her.

''Bye.' He touched her hand. 'Some other time. I'll hold you to that.'

Dee couldn't help smiling to herself as she walked back to her car and rang Harcourt Street cop shop on her mobile. Even though her legs were positively furry and her hair was a mess, Kevin Mills had asked her for a drink. Well, it *was* work, she amended. But he'd still asked her.

Dear Annie,

I've been going out with my fiancé for six years. We got engaged two years ago and we live together, but the other day a male colleague asked me out for a drink and I really wanted to go with him. What's wrong with me? I love my fiancé and feel so guilty about wanting to go for a drink with this other man.

I didn't go, of course, but now I can't stop

thinking that there must be something wrong between me and my boyfriend for me to have felt this way. I'm devastated by this.

Confused

Dear Confused,

This is more than likely just a phase you're going through. Now that you're engaged to be married, you probably think that you're 100 per cent 'safe', that you'll never fancy anyone else again. That's not necessarily the case.

Plenty of happily married people occasionally fancy someone else and the test of the relationship is whether they actually do anything about this momentary feeling or not. Don't feel guilty for merely being attracted to someone else. You haven't done anything wrong, you're a perfectly normal woman.

If your relationship is going through a rocky stage, that could contribute to your feelings of confusion. All relationships have bad patches, you've just got to make more of an effort to make your relationship work at these times. It's so easy to get bored with someone but think of all the reasons why you fell for your fiancé in the first place . . .

It was late afternoon by the time Dee got home. She'd finally got her story confirmed by a police contact and Kevin had rung while she was parking the car outside the supermarket to say he'd got the pictures of the room Chazz had ruined.

'He hadn't done very much, actually, but my source says the management called the police when he tried to hit one of the room-service guys. The hotel won't stand for that sort of thing. They don't know I was even in there, so don't phone them for a comment until tomorrow in case they give the story to someone else.'

'Of course.' Dee knew the rules of the game. If you told them what you were going to do, then somebody in the hotel might tip off another journalist they were friendly with, thereby ruining the *Sentinel*'s scoop.

'I'll have the pictures on your desk first thing tomorrow morning, OK?' Kevin's voice was brusque with none of its earlier warmth.

'OK,' answered Dee brightly. ''Bye.' She must have imagined that he was interested in her. She carried the grocery shopping into the hall, the six heavy Superquinn bags dragging her down like a pack pony.

At least she had something nice for dinner, she thought, as she stowed the chicken stir-fry ingredients in the fridge. She jammed two packs of mini strawberry cheesecakes in the freezer. The kettle had nearly boiled but Dee changed her mind about having a cup of coffee and poured herself a glass of white wine to take upstairs while she worked on her column. It was a bit early for a drink but she felt she deserved one. Gary would be phoning later and she'd tell him she was sorry they'd rowed and that she loved him.

At ten o'clock on a Sunday morning, the offices of the *Sentinel* were usually very quiet. Even though there was a full staff working on Monday's edition, people still came in slightly later than on other days. On Sundays they wanted to lie in bed longer, eating toast, drinking coffee and reading the papers from cover to cover, especially when it was raining so hard that the raindrops bounced off the pavement.

Dee hated working on Sundays. Today, she was tired,

she'd got a spot on her chin and knew she was heading into her PMT danger zone. She was also utterly depressed to discover that she now weighed eleven stone four pounds, most of it on her stomach. She'd just made a pot of percolated coffee and was searching for milk in the fridge in the tiny kitchen when her best friend, Maeve Lynch, hurried past, clutching her bulging briefcase with one hand and dragging a drenched black PVC raincoat with the other. Tall, thin and with short hair that she was always dyeing a variety of wildly unnatural burgundy colours, Maeve was one of the paper's sub-editors, responsible for laying out pages and coming up with headlines.

'Coffee. Thank God,' she breathed, like an addict in need of a fix. 'You're an angel, Dee.'

'At least *somebody* thinks so,' Dee muttered gloomily. Gary hadn't rung the night before and she'd gone to bed fuming. She'd spent the restless night hours planning exactly what she'd tell him when he got home. Most of it involved swear words and copious amounts of shouting.

'What's wrong?' asked Maeve sympathetically. 'Gary?'

'When is it ever *not* Gary?'

'What happened?' Maeve put three spoons of sugar in her coffee. Dee could never understand how her friend could consume so much sugar and still remain positively anorexic-looking. 'I thought he was away for the weekend, anyway?'

'He is. Hasn't even bothered to phone me.'

'Oh. Well, you know what men are like,' Maeve said sagely.

'No, but I know what Gary's like.'

They took their coffee into the newsroom, a large and untidy open-plan office with computer terminals on

21

every desk, fax machines in one corner and four TVs high on the walls.

There were none of the potted plants and tasteful prints you saw in other offices: the *Sentinel*'s newsroom was a no-go area for horticulture. Once six o'clock came, everyone who smoked got out their fags and lit up eagerly.

By then, the editor's executive secretary, a hard-nosed anti-smoker who was a born-again tyrant, was gone and they could do what they liked. No plant had ever lasted more than six weeks in this atmosphere, even the gossip columnist's trailing ivy that she'd religiously fed with Bio-Gro.

Dee had never smoked, apart from the odd one when she was in the pub with Maeve and wanted something to do with her hands. But sometimes she wished she did – nicotine was supposed to suppress your appetite. She had visions of herself as a very thin, very soignée woman with ribs like a greyhound's and an elegant cigarette holder constantly held aloft in one slender hand. Then she realised that cigarettes or no cigarettes, she loved food. That was her problem.

Dee plonked the coffee down on her desk which was still covered with the previous week's newspapers. She made a space by pushing all the junk to one side, opened a reporter's notebook and wrote the date on the top of a fresh page. She'd always done that. Her first news editor had said it was the best way to keep track of what you were doing – to write *everything* in one notebook so you never lost valuable phone numbers on bits of paper.

'Here.' Maeve handed her a brown paper bag with three sugary ring doughnuts inside and dragged a chair over to Dee's desk.

Dee did her best to ignore the doughnuts. She felt fat enough.

'We won't talk about your crappy weekend if you don't want to,' Maeve said. 'I'll bore you senseless telling you about mine.'

Dee sat back in her chair, put her feet up on the desk and sipped her coffee mournfully. 'I have to talk about it to *someone*, Maeve,' she said. 'Otherwise I'll go mad. Contradiction – madder.'

'What's he done now?' mumbled Maeve, her mouth still full of doughnut.

'It's what he *hasn't* done that's driving me mad. We had a huge row on Friday morning about the housework. And he said he was sick to the teeth of me nagging him about it. I mean, honestly, he barely washes a cup these days. The sink has been full for nearly a week, we're completely out of cutlery and he still won't touch it . . .'

'So you've cleaned up?' interrupted Maeve.

'I haven't!' said Dee firmly. 'But I'm going to,' she added. 'I can't face the house looking like a tip for one more day. But what's made it worse is that he hasn't even rung me once since he left. He's so thoughtless!'

Maeve reached into the paper bag, took out another doughnut and offered it to Dee, who looked longingly at it for a millisecond and then took it.

'Well, if it's any consolation, my weekend was a complete disaster too. That charming TV producer, the one who asked me last week where I'd been all his life, never phoned to arrange our evening out.'

'Oh, that's awful. What did you do?'

'Went out with the girls from the flat downstairs. They're mad, that pair. Every time I go out with them we end up standing outside some nightclub at four in

23

the morning trying to remember where we live so we can tell the taxi driver.'

Dee couldn't help feeling mildly jealous. Maeve had been having a whale of a time knocking back tequila slammers while she'd been stuck at home waiting for bloody Gary to ring. It hit her once again that she'd made the classic female mistake. She'd lost touch with her girlfriends when she became seriously involved with a man.

But Gary continued to go out with his pals as though he were still young, free and single.

It wasn't as if he stopped her going out with her friends; Dee just felt that they should do things together because they were a couple. She fancied meandering round Habitat at the weekend looking for nice pieces of bedroom furniture or buying books and then spending hours in quaint Dublin pubs, drinking Irish coffees and reading. But Gary preferred to go boozing with his pals.

'Let's forget about men,' Maeve said suddenly. 'I'm taking you out for a drink after work and we aren't going even to *talk* about the weaker sex. But first, I've got some great gossip for you.'

Dee perked up. Like all reporters, she loved gossip. 'What?'

Maeve grinned wickedly. 'Antonia's leaving! Hubbie has got a job with a London pharmaceutical company. An offer he couldn't resist, apparently. He was going to commute every weekend but he's been offered so much money that Antonia feels they can survive on his salary, no problem, so she's going with him and plans to freelance for a couple of the British women's magazines. The kids are grown up so she doesn't have to worry about them any more.'

Dee was stunned. 'I can't believe it!' she said. 'When I

think how hard she fought to get the women's editor's job, I can't believe she's giving it up this easily. How did you find out? She didn't tell you, did she?'

Dee knew that Antonia and Maeve weren't the best of friends. But then nobody had ever managed to hit it off with the highly strung Antonia who made every crisis into a grand-scale drama and who never let anyone forget that she came from a wealthy Anglo-Irish family with a duchess for a cousin.

'One of the sports guys told me. I met him last night when the girls and I were in Slattery's. He heard it from the temp in advertising, who overheard her boss on the phone to Antonia's husband – they play golf together – talking about buying property in London. But you're not to tell anyone yet,' Maeve warned. 'The temp was pissed when she told Tom. Nobody else knows about it yet.'

'I see,' said Dee slowly. With Antonia out of the running, the way was clear for her to escape from the newsdesk into the challenging world of the women's pages. She was sick to the teeth of hard news and longed for the chance to prove that she was a natural features writer. She'd only worked as a news reporter in the beginning because it was much easier to get a job there than in features.

But she was eager to get away from brutal murder trials and stories about drug barons and pushers. And it wasn't as if Nigel Burke, the editor, didn't know that she was a good features writer. She'd worked in features all over Christmas when half the staff had been laid up in bed with a brutal 'flu virus. Everyone had raved about her *Unsung Heroes: People Who Save Lives Over Christmas* series which had run for a week. This was the chance she'd been waiting for. Antonia, who had no interest in harder-edged stories, had only ever written about the next season's fashions or what sort of lipgloss lasted longest on your lips without transferring to either a wineglass or your boyfriend. Dee was keen to transform the women's pages from eight pages of beauty hints into a part of the paper which dealt with serious women's issues.

'I know what you're thinking. And you'd be perfect for Antonia's job,' Maeve said. 'You could do it in your sleep and probably make the women's pages a thousand times better.'

'I could hardly make them any worse,' Dee remarked.

'You said it,' Maeve added fervently. 'I can't begin to tell you the times I've wanted to strangle that bloody woman when she'd insist on changing her fashion pieces after I'd already laid them out because she'd found this "fabulous new designer we must write about, darling". And as for the arguments we'd have when I'd rewrite some of her stuff because she went off on tangents that made no sense whatsoever . . .'

'Now, Maeve, don't sit on the fence about this one,' joked Dee. 'Tell me what you *really* think about Antonia?'

'She thought she was far too good for this paper. We're well shot of her.'

'I know. Would you like to work with me?' Dee inquired, her mind racing. This was it, her big chance.

'I'd love to work with you,' Maeve said, before adding more cautiously, 'but don't forget, Dee, you won't be the only one after Antonia's job.'

'The only person who's got a chance is Phil Walsh and she loves being features ed. She wouldn't even go for women's editor,' Dee said dismissively.

Maeve scrunched up the paper bag the doughnuts

had come in and pushed back her chair. 'There'll be plenty of people outside who'd kill for the job,' she pointed out. 'I mean, who wouldn't?'

'Nigel would never bring in anyone from outside,' Dee answered, lowering her voice as she saw the editor unlock the door to his office. 'You know he wouldn't.' She got up and clutched her friend's arm excitedly. 'This is fantastic news. I can't wait to tell Gary!'

CHAPTER TWO

Isabel pulled the clothes out of the washing-machine and groaned. One of the girls had left a tissue in a pocket and the entire load was covered in bits of shredded tissue paper.

'Shit!' she muttered crossly. The moment she'd ripped a giant ladder in her last pair of new ten deniers that morning, Isabel had known it wasn't going to be her day. She'd been right.

She'd stopped to get petrol on the Stillorgan dual carriageway which meant it took ten minutes to nose the car back into the early-morning traffic. So she'd been late for the editorial meeting.

As a result, her new boss, Richie Devine, who was clearly in a bad temper, icily demanded to know why she thought she could waltz in fifteen minutes later than everyone else, especially since she was only temporary. Meaning 'temporary, never to be made permanent', Isabel knew. She'd flashed him the winning smile her husband had once told her lit up her face like a hundred-watt bulb, but it had no effect.

Winning smiles worked quite well when you were a twenty-something student with pert boobs, zero experience of life's tragedies and no crow's feet. But not when you were thirty-nine and the combined stresses of marital separation and moving house meant that you'd lost so much weight your cheekbones were hollow and your collar bones more prominent than your cleavage. At that stage, no amount of smiling had the slightest effect.

'At *Motor 2000*, we have deadlines and we expect all our staff to adhere to them,' Richie Devine said bossily, before he went on to discuss the 'high concept of an advertising supplement on jeeps'. Isabel couldn't think of anything more boring than designing the pages for the jeep edition but she smiled brightly at Richie and tried to remember that she really, really needed this sub-editing job even if the pay was dreadful and the work about as thrilling as watching an extended version of *Prisoner Cell Block H*.

Designing the layout of pages and writing headlines was interesting when you worked as a sub-editor on a women's magazine, which was what Isabel had done for ten enjoyable years. But doing the same thing on a third-rate car magazine, where any evidence of origi-nality was treated with suspicion by a mercurial boss, was utterly draining and very depressing. To put the icing on the cake, the bank had just rung her about her overdraft, which was 'way over your agreed limit, Mrs Farrell'.

My life is way over my limit, Isabel thought gloomily as she poked around all the wet pockets trying to find the culprit responsible for messing up her washing.

'Mum, where are my Levis?' yelled a shrill voice from upstairs.

'Wet and covered in the tissue you left in your bloody pocket,' she yelled back as she found the sodden remains in the Levis in question.

Her elder daughter didn't reply, but Isabel could hear

Robin stomp into her bedroom and slam the door loudly. This was standard behaviour for her fifteen-year-old daughter. Well, standard behaviour nowadays.

Isabel could still remember when Robin had been her best friend, closest ally and biggest admirer. That had been a mere three months ago, before they'd left the leafy suburbs of Oxford to move to Isabel's parents' home in Wicklow. She knew it hadn't been easy for the girls to leave their comfy home, private school and lots of friends, but she'd had no choice.

David had left them with no choice, she thought darkly, as she picked bits of tissue off everything. It hadn't been easy for *her* either. She'd left a home she'd lovingly renovated from a shell and a job she really enjoyed. And all because her damned husband had lost every penny they owned trying to drag his stupid advertising agency out of trouble. That had been the final nail in the coffin of their marriage.

Broke and with the building society on the verge of repossessing their home, Isabel had felt she'd no option but to leave both David and Oxford and start again. And she'd never forgive him for it.

They'd weathered so many storms together that she had actually thought there was nothing about David Farrell she didn't know. After sixteen years of marriage, she was convinced there wasn't anything else he could do to shock her. And she'd always hoped the love would eventually come back into their marriage. Somehow. She should have known better.

They'd recovered from his affairs – three of them – his two years of unemployment, and even his disastrous flirtation with the stock market. But when Isabel found out that he had gambled, and lost, their home on a business that was shaky to start with, she knew she had

31

to leave him. It wasn't just for her sake, it was for the girls'.

If David could gamble *their* home and threaten the security of their young lives, without even thinking about it, then Isabel couldn't stay with him though she had known that Robin and twelve-year-old Naomi would be devastated by the break-up.

David had stopped loving her a long time ago, round about the time she'd lost the baby. Isabel hadn't known which was worse: losing the baby boy she'd longed for, or enduring the months of depression afterwards when her husband hadn't been able to communicate with her and didn't seem to want to anyway.

It had been August, nearly five years ago, a gloriously sunny month when Isabel had spent her days off sitting in the garden, sipping iced water and trying to read while eight-year-old Naomi and ten-year-old Robin waged war on each other. She didn't have the energy to shout at them, so they rampaged through the garden, into the kitchen and up the stairs, screaming blue murder while Isabel lolled in her deckchair with a magazine on her lap and thought up babies' names. She was fourteen weeks pregnant and convinced she was having a boy. After much consideration, the girls in the office agreed. Isabel had been thrilled. After two girls, she wanted a boy and knew that David secretly longed for someone with whom he could discuss football and carburettors in the future.

She'd never forget the pain of losing that baby, her precious little boy. It had all happened so quickly. One minute, she was washing a lettuce in the cracked old Belfast sink: the next, she was doubled up in pain, the sort of pain that meant only one thing.

David brought flowers to the hospital when he got

back from London the next day. He couldn't meet her eyes. All she wanted was to be held, to be told that it would be all right. And to be allowed to grieve for the baby she'd lost; not told that they could 'have another one soon, to make up for it', as one thoughtless doctor had said the day before. You couldn't make up for a baby you'd loved, Isabel had thought, and howled with pain.

David would understand, she told herself. Yet, when he came to see her, it was as if they were separated by a thousand miles of icy water. He held her hand for ages but couldn't speak, except in platitudes.

'They say you can come home tomorrow,' he'd said in a low voice. 'The girls will be thrilled. I bought Robin this fantastic doll in Regent Street. You can do her hair and put make-up on her. I bought a painting-by-numbers set for Naomi.'

'Great.' Isabel sat back against her pillows, feeling hollow. There was a gaping hole inside her, a part of her missing. And David was talking about dolls and paints as if she was in hospital after spraining her ankle!

He never did talk about the baby. At first, she wondered if he didn't care. Or if he felt guilty for not being there when she'd had the miscarriage. By the time she realised that he was distraught at the loss of his son, it was too late. She was crippled by depression and unable to mother him to recovery. For God's sake, she was only able to mother Naomi and Robin on autopilot. Her grown-up husband could deal with his own pain while she tried to survive hers. Their marriage had limped along like a lifeboat with a hole in it. They shared the same house, the same bed and the same dinner table. And that was it.

Maybe she should have left him then, when she was

thirty-four and had an energy for life she certainly
didn't have now. Then, Robin had been a malleable ten
year old who might have coped with her parents'
separation better than she did now. But then, Isabel was
worn out with grief and didn't have the energy for the
hassle. And who the hell knew the right time to split up
anyway? Isabel didn't feel that she knew anything any
more.

She slammed the washing-machine door shut, stood
up wearily and leaned against the gleaming white for-
mica worktop that her mother spent hours scrubbing
with Dettox. The whole kitchen gleamed, from the
cooker top to the spotless white windowsill where a
single geranium sat in splendour, without a brown leaf
in sight.

Isabel hated her mother's kitchen, hated its cold,
clinical feel, the way it looked as if nobody ever left
toast crumbs on the table or as if little hands never left
jammy handprints on the fridge.

The sterile environment of 23 Sycamore Avenue was
in direct contrast to Isabel's Oxford kitchen.

That had been warm and cosy with distressed
wooden cupboards and worn terracotta tiles on the
floor. An entire oasis of plants on the window trailed
leaves untidily over the draining-board. Unhygienic, her
mother would have said. The cork notice board had
been jammed with school photos of Robin and Naomi,
shopping lists and cartoons the girls had cut out from
comics.

The worktops were cluttered, the iron permanently
upright beside the kettle from Isabel's usual early-
morning ironing session. It was a family kitchen, but
they weren't a family any more.

She'd told David she was leaving him in that kitchen,

during a last, dreadful row. He'd been sitting in the den watching soccer with a can of beer in one hand and the remote control in the other when she'd come downstairs with the letter from the building society.

It was brusque and terrifying. The recently extended mortgage on the house hadn't been paid in six months and, unless funds were forthcoming shortly, they would take legal proceedings. Reading those threatening words had made Isabel sick to her stomach. She'd felt weak, exhausted, stunned. And then, she'd felt angry.

'How could you do this to us?' she'd yelled at David. 'How could you? And why the hell didn't you tell me? Did you really think I wouldn't be interested in knowing we haven't a penny to our name?'

'Relax, Izzy,' he'd said, in the laid-back tone he always used when she was angry with him. It simply made her even more angry.

'Relax!' she yelled. 'How can I relax? The building society is going to repossess the house! I know there isn't enough money in the current account to pay those kind of arrears. Have you any idea what that means?'

'Yes, of course I do.' David stood up slowly, unfurling his long, lean body with the languid grace that Isabel had once loved. Now, it merely irritated her.

His height and his handsome, smiling face had drawn her to him all those years ago. She'd been the tallest girl in her class at college, a willowy five foot eight with long blonde hair and hippie-ish clothes. She'd never been sure whether it was her height or her faintly distant air – to disguise a crippling shyness – that had put men off. But something had. So when the six-foot rugby winger asked her to partner him at the end-of-term dance, she'd accepted his offer joyfully and had never looked back.

Eighteen years later, while she watched him asleep beside her, his girlishly long lashes resting on remarkably unlined cheeks, she'd wondered how she had ever fallen in love with him.

Why hadn't she seen past the good looks and the charm that masked a habitual liar? David had had more pie-in-the-sky dreams than a sixteen-year-old would-be rock star with an air guitar.

She could see past the mask now and she could see that if she stayed with David Farrell, one-time insurance salesman and currently broke advertising agency boss, she and the girls would live to regret it.

He'd walked past her into the kitchen and took another Budweiser from the fridge, brushing back a curl of the dark hair that reached his blue polo shirt collar.

'Why didn't you show me the letter?' Isabel had demanded. 'When were you planning to tell me? When the bailiffs arrived? Or when the estate agent stuck a For Sale sign up outside?' She waited for his answer, waited for some shred of hope that this wasn't really happening.

But as David sipped his beer slowly, before turning to look at her with those pale blue eyes, she'd known that it *was* happening. He had lost everything.

'Izzy, honey,' he'd said softly. He'd put down his can and tried to hug her. Isabel pushed him away angrily.

'Don't lie to me, David. Don't butter me up. Just tell me the truth, will you?'

'Izzy,' he'd said again, in hurt tones, 'it's not as bad as it looks . . .'

'Don't lie!'

'OK, OK,' he'd replied quickly. 'It's still not as bad as it looks. I've got a contingency plan. Freddie says we should declare ourselves bankrupt and start again. Maybe in London this time . . .' He'd stared into space, as if his mind was already on the new business.

Isabel knew what he was thinking of – a new agency, called Farrell Ellis instead of Ellis Farrell. Well, they'd have to have a new name if they went bankrupt.

So they'd put Freddie's name last, instead of the other way around. New premises in a smart area of London, expensively decorated in muted tones, with chrome and glass coffee tables strewn with copies of *Time* and *Campaign*, and a sexy receptionist with a silly name and legs up to her armpits for the clients – and the boss – to fancy.

Bay trees in expensive containers outside the front door. A genuine oil painting or two in reception to show that the agency men knew what 'real' art was even if they prostituted their talent for £100,000 accounts and new BMWs. Leather armchairs scattered around reception, of course, those intricately designed ones that were uncomfortable but chic. And fresh flowers every second day.

All paid for with cash from another mortgaged house. A house that Isabel, Robin and Naomi would never feel really safe in because the carpet was always in danger of being swept from under their feet. If the VAT man blinked, they'd be homeless. If the agency lost a big account, they'd be homeless. Well, not any more, Isabel had thought fiercely. She'd never again wager their future on a man who couldn't keep a tenner in his pocket for five minutes without an overwhelming urge to spend it.

From now on, Naomi and Robin would be financially secure if Isabel had to work her fingers to the bone to make sure of it.

She'd looked around the room slowly, her eyes lingering on the bits and pieces she and David had bought over the years when they'd had the money to go abroad on holiday. She especially loved the two large painted plates they'd brought home from Portugal one year. She'd adored those plates – a riot of blue and pink flowers handpainted on gleaming white china – the day she saw them in a street market in Lisbon. David had insisted on buying them for her.

Naturally, when it was time to bring them home, Isabel had ended up dragging them with her in a huge plastic bag, while she held on to Naomi's small hand and her own bulging suitcase at the same time. David was carrying six bottles of sparkling rosé. He was convinced he could make a fortune by importing that particular brand to the UK. All he needed was the go-ahead from a pal of his who was a big name in the import/export business and they could have their own villa on the Algarve this time next year! Six bottles ought to convince him, surely . . .

Isabel also loved the Russian dolls he'd brought back from a trip to Russia. They'd sat on top of the freezer, bright crimson touched with gilt. They were totally gaudy but so sweet, five little figures each smaller than the one before. Naomi had loved playing with them when she was little and, more than once, Isabel had rescued the smallest one from being stuck up her daughter's nose. From the age of three onwards, she'd tried to push *everything* up her nose, from pasta shapes to peas. After the second trip to the doctor's surgery, Isabel had thought of buying her own nasal forceps.

'I'm leaving you, David,' she'd said, tearing her eyes away from the Russian dolls. 'I can't take this any more.'

'Don't be stupid,' he'd replied scathingly, as if this was the latest in a series of idiotic ideas. 'Where will you go?'

'Home. To Ireland. Anywhere but here.'

'Izzy, don't be ridiculous. Why do you want to leave?' he'd demanded.

'Because we don't *have* a marriage and, since you've just lost our home, I've suddenly realised I can't stand the uncertainty of life with you, David. That's why.'

She was suddenly utterly sure that she was doing the right thing. It was a bizarre, liberating experience. As if she'd finally tidied out a room she'd been meaning to dejunk for years and found that, without the clutter, she felt like a new woman.

Amazingly, she didn't even feel like crying. She felt strong and brave. She should have done this a long time ago, six months ago to be exact. Maybe then they'd actually have had some property to sell in order to split their assets. Now, all they had were the furnishings she'd painstakingly restored because they'd never had the money to buy new stuff.

As if he'd suddenly sensed a sea change, David crossed the room to touch her.

'Don't do this, Isabel,' he'd urged. He'd tried to wrap her in his embrace, fitting her body close to his in the old familiar way. Isabel couldn't remember a time when they hadn't been together, a time when his body scent hadn't been as familiar to her as her own. That was the problem.

Gently and without speaking, she'd moved out of his arms. She'd leant against the scrubbed pine kitchen table and looked at her husband who hadn't moved. Head bent sorrowfully, hair falling forward and obscuring his face. It was his James Dean pose. But however well it had worked eighteen years ago, it certainly wasn't working now.

'There's no need to make this difficult, David. We

both know it's been over for years, since the baby . . .'

He didn't even flinch. Isabel thought of the times she'd sobbed into the night thinking about the lost child.

She remembered what it had been like to look at the unneeded baby clothes and to realise that no tiny baby would wear them, that no downy head would nestle against her breast wrapped in this soft white cardigan or that fluffy old blanket with the rabbits on it.

It was a tragedy that they'd never been able to talk about it, and a double tragedy that David had seemed to stop caring about everything else afterwards. But Isabel had no intention of spending the rest of her life living with the aftermath of that tragedy. Especially with a man she realised she no longer really loved, a man who'd forgotten about the most important people in his life – his daughters.

'I'm going back to Dublin with the girls,' she said quietly. 'We can't pay the school fees for next term and I'm not putting them through the torture of staying in Oxford and watching all their friends go back to school, when they suddenly can't. We might even get a refund for the months they'll miss.'

It was simpler to talk about practical matters. Simpler to reduce their relationship to a series of financial transactions and travel plans instead of talking about the emotional side of things.

'You should go to London and do your own thing – it's what you've always wanted.' She couldn't resist saying it. 'I'll get a job in Ireland. I want to go back, I've always wanted to. You didn't.'

David didn't say anything. Isabel wondered whether he was trying to think of something clever, something to get him out of all the trouble he was in. Or whether he was relieved and thought it unwise to say anything in case she changed her mind.

Then he got angry.

'What the hell are you talking about, for Christ's sake? You can't leave me. What about the girls? What about them?'

'You should have thought of that when you and Freddie were spending money like it was going out of fashion,' Isabel had said contemptuously. 'You didn't worry about the girls then, did you? How many trips abroad with important clients was the house worth, anyway? Three or four? I'd love to know how much of my hard-earned cash went into impressing people who didn't spend enough with the agency to cover their bloody trips to the Monte Carlo Grand Prix, despite all the champagne you poured down their throats!'

David had started yelling at her then.

'What gives you the right to be so high and mighty, Isabel? Did you work your butt off to make this family a fortune? Well, I did, *I did*, and I wanted it to work. And it will! But you, you stupid bitch, you just can't wait. We *had* to put money into entertaining. That's the way business is done. It takes time, we were nearly there . . .'

She'd walked out of the kitchen, picked up her car keys and got into the car. She had to pick up the girls from friends' houses later on but couldn't bear to wait in the house with David until then. Her battered Volkswagen was going to have to last a bit longer, she'd realised grimly as she reversed out of the drive after the usual fiddling with the gear stick to find reverse.

The moss that had spread through the lawn in the front garden wasn't going to irritate her the way it had for the past few months, she remembered thinking idly as the car shuddered backwards.

41

She'd be gone soon and another woman would look out of the front window past the lavender bush and promise herself she'd apply moss killer. That was one thing fewer for Isabel to worry about.

Those last few days before they'd left Oxford had been dreadful, with constant recriminations from David and crying fits from the girls.

'Why are you doing this?' screeched Robin when she heard. 'You can't break up our family, Mum, you can't!'

Even though Isabel felt she really hadn't any choice but to go back to Ireland, she couldn't explain to Robin, the teenager who adored her feckless, charming father, that it was go home or stay in Oxford and endure the painful process of bankruptcy. Isabel knew she couldn't bear to watch strangers march through the house, complaining about the damp in the downstairs loo and trying to knock a couple of thousand off what was already a knock-down price.

She'd thought about what would happen if they stayed in the UK. The indignity of relying on charity from friends and renting some squalid flat, which would be all she could afford as she certainly didn't have the deposit for a new home. The girls would have hated it, she knew.

'You can stay with us. Please stay,' begged her friend Anna, whose family published *Today's Woman*, the magazine for which Isabel worked. They'd sat in Anna's kitchen and made inroads into a bottle of wine. Neither of them bothered with the cheese and salad sandwiches Anna had made. 'We've lots of room, you and the girls can stay in the granny flat. And you'll soon be back on your feet.'

Isabel had tried to explain why she had to leave. It

wasn't running away, she'd said. But she needed to be as far away from David as she could in case she ran back to him when she got afraid or lonely. She'd read about other women who did that and didn't want to be one of them. She couldn't afford to be, for the girls' sake.

'What about *your* sake, Isabel?' Anna asked quietly.

Isabel had shrugged helplessly. She didn't know what to say. 'I've lived so much of my life here but I need to go somewhere different,' she'd said finally. 'All my married life, I've gone where David wanted to go. Belfast when he wanted to, London, and then Oxford. He picked where he wanted to work or where the next big business opportunities were happening. I think I finally need to go somewhere *I've* picked. And the only place I can go right now is Ireland. We can stay with my parents – not that I'm looking forward to that because my mother and I don't get on,' Isabel added wryly. 'But it's somewhere I can go to think about things. And, when I get a job, I'll be able to save some money for a deposit on a house or apartment. I think it'll be good for the girls. You know, a new country and a new school. It might take their minds off the separation.'

But her plan had backfired. Robin had barely spoken to her mother for a week before the move. And when she did speak, it was to demand that she be allowed to stay and live with David. Isabel couldn't explain that his plans didn't include having his daughter to live with him.

He was already checking out flats in London – bachelor flats, perfect for a man setting up a new business. His earlier rage had gone, to be replaced by enthusiasm for a fresh start. Freddie knew just the man they needed to see, apparently.

'You know, I can make this work, Izzy,' David had

said. 'Maybe it's best if I'm on my own for a while – it'll keep the bills down. I can live very cheaply. I can't imagine you in the sort of crappy flat I'll get. You'd hate it.' He was still trying to charm her, trying to get round her.

Isabel watched his face grow animated as he talked about setting up again on his own and wondered again why she'd stayed with him so long. It wasn't as if his reckless behaviour was a surprise to her. She'd realised exactly what sort of man she'd married by the time Robin was born. He'd just lost money on a 'surefire' deal. The computer software systems he'd bought in bulk through a 'friend' had proved impossible to shift.

It was a miracle he'd had any money to buy the expensive champagne he'd insisted on to toast their first child. That was typical of David. No matter how broke they were, he always insisted on buying the best of everything – like gold earrings from Tiffany's for Isabel on her thirty-third birthday, the same year they'd abandoned their plans to replace the oil-fired central heating in the house because they didn't have the spare cash. As they all shivered through a bad winter, she knew she'd have preferred cheap earrings, a bit of scrimping and saving – and heating that worked.

'The only problem is the girls . . .' David stroked her hand as he talked. It was one of his ploys and it worked, but only with women who didn't know him. Isabel had had enough hand-stroking to last her a lifetime.

'I doubt if I'll get anywhere nice enough for them to stay. Me, I don't care what sort of hovel I live in. It'll work out, Izzy,' he said again. 'Freddie has a pal who's interested in investing in us. When I've got the business going, you'll come back, won't you?'

She'd never asked him why this mysterious investor

44

hadn't bailed out the existing firm instead of waiting for two bankrupts to start their second ad agency before arriving with lorry loads of cash. What was the point? David would have had some excuse for that too.

So she'd said nothing and instead packed up everything she could afford to transport back to Ireland. And, somewhere in the laborious moving process, around the same time as the packing case containing all her saucepans and pots went missing, Robin had changed from caring daughter into the teenager from hell. After two weeks at her new school, St Clodagh's, all the clothes she'd previously liked suddenly became 'crap'. She wanted highlights in her hair because 'everyone has them' and her language had deteriorated at a frightening rate.

Isabel found it exhausting and infuriating coping with a girl who was bolshy, difficult and moodier than a roomful of hormonally challenged women. Dealing with Robin was almost worse than working with Richie Devine.

Robin had an excuse – she was a teenager – while Richie was the grown-up editor of a car magazine, even though he behaved more like an adolescent than any spotty fifteen year old Isabel had ever met. At least twelve-year-old Naomi was still the same – funny, sweet and accident-prone. The last time Isabel had laughed had been on Tuesday when Naomi had broken into giggles after tripping over her schoolbag in the hall.

Naomi was a funny child with such an off-beat sense of humour that you had to laugh with her. And, if Isabel hadn't found something to laugh at, life at her parents' home would have been completely unbearable. The anti-depressants helped, too, of course. Not that anyone knew she was taking them. She'd gone to the doctor after the first week at home, when she'd cried at least twice each day.

Two months later, she wasn't crying much at all and, apart from the fact that she was so sleepy in the morning, nobody would have a clue she was taking anything.

Isabel had picked up the clothes basket and opened the back door when the phone rang loudly. She dropped the basket quickly but before she had time to reach the phone in the hall, she could hear Robin pound across the landing to answer it in her grandparents' bedroom.

Pound, pound, pound, went Robin again.

'It's for you,' she roared down the stairs.

Wonders will never cease, thought Isabel, astonished that it wasn't another of Robin's new best friends, the ones who'd told her all about the correct, horrendously expensive trainers to buy, the right place to have her highlights done and what sort of utterly cool top she 'just had to have' before next Saturday's disco.

'Hello.'

'Isabel – I've got the most amazing job for you.'

Suzanne sounded as breathless as ever. But then her cousin had always sounded out of breath whenever she had news to impart, be it about her latest – dull – boyfriend or how well she'd done in the French exam – always better than Isabel.

'What sort of job?' asked Isabel, convinced it would be something daft, like running a community paper for a pittance. Suzanne hadn't grasped the fact that Isabel and David would not get back together, that she was broke because David's firm had gone belly-up, and that Isabel therefore needed a proper, full-time job so she could buy a house and move out of her mother's.

'Tim heard about it in the office.'

Isabel perked up slightly. Suzanne's husband was an estate agent and, even if Isabel couldn't figure out how he'd heard about a sub-editing job for her, she knew that Tim was about ten times more practical than her scatty cousin and would not mention jobs unless they were at least vaguely suitable.

'What sort of job?' she asked.

'It's because of the house in Sydney Parade. A mansion, Tim says. They want a quick sale, you see, that's why he got it instead of Anthony, because Anthony is up to his eyes with the Ailesbury Road auction . . .'

'Suzanne,' said Isabel with more patience than she felt, 'what the hell are you talking about?'

'The FitzSimonses! They're selling up to move to London and you know what she does, don't you?'

'*She? Who's she?*'

'Antonia FitzSimons! She's the women's editor of the *Sentinel*!'

The penny dropped. Clanged, in fact. A job vacancy! The position of women's editor on a paper like the *Sentinel* was the stuff of which dreams were made. The *Sentinel* was an upmarket tabloid with a huge readership. Before Robin was born, Isabel had wanted to work on a publication like that.

But it was a top job and she'd been out of the country for ten years, which meant she now knew nobody on the *Sentinel*.

Experience in journalism had shown her that complete strangers rarely walked into the best jobs – those generally went to people on the staff or who'd freelanced for the paper for years.

Isabel knew she had the experience for the job but it mightn't count as she'd worked abroad for so long. She'd worked as deputy editor of a top – well, medium

47

– UK women's magazine and before that had spent five years as chief sub-editor on a local Oxford paper. She'd still be working for *Today's Woman* if bloody David hadn't forced her to run home to Mother and Father. Getting Antonia FitzSimons's job would transform her life. But did she have a hope in hell?

'When did all this happen?'

Isabel dragged one of her mother's spotless white kitchen chairs across the black and white lino so she could sit and talk at the same time.

'They rang the agency yesterday and Anthony – that's Tim's boss – only put him on to it today. Anthony's raging he can't handle it himself but he really can't because he's up to his eyeballs with Ailesbury Road. Tim says the commission on Ailesbury will nearly pay for Anthony's conservatory . . .'

'Suzanne,' interrupted Isabel, utterly confused, 'just tell me about the FitzSimonses.'

'He rang yesterday, said he wanted the house sold ASAP because they're moving to London next week and want everything sorted because they need the cash to buy a new house. Holland Park, he said, apparently. Tim says the house prices there are astronomical,' Suzanne rambled on. 'It sounds wonderful. Six bedrooms, three en suite, a conservatory and granny flat . . .'

'In their house in Sydney Parade? Wow, that'll make a bomb!'

'No,' said Suzanne. 'The house they want in Holland Park. He told Tim all about it. Boasting, really.'

Isabel gave up. 'I've got to go, Suz. Can I ring Tim at work now or will he be out?'

'Ring him,' urged Suzanne. 'He'll tell you everything.'

After she'd talked to Tim, Isabel rang a friend on

Style, one of Ireland's top fashion magazines. Rhona McNamara was the only person from her college days whom she'd contacted since she'd come home. It was embarrassing to have to explain to everyone why she'd left Oxford, and why David wasn't with her. So Isabel decided not to bother.

Their old friends would find out eventually so she'd be spared the pain of telling them about the bankruptcy and all the other miserable details of her marital break-up. Rhona was different. She could be relied upon not to pry, nor to lord it over Isabel although she had a husband, three adorable kids *and* a career.

'Wouldn't mind Antonia's job myself,' said Rhona now. 'The *Sentinel* crowd get paid buckets, have expense accounts better than an MEP's *and* they all get company cars. You'd better get your oar in quickly, Isabel. That job will go like a shot.'

'I know, Rhona. But do you think I've a chance?'

Isabel absently fiddled with the fraying cuff of her faded grey sweatshirt. She'd only unpacked about a quarter of the black plastic sacks in which she'd transported her clothes. So far, she was getting most use out of the ancient casual stuff that was too worn or too wrecked to wear outside the front door. What was the point of unpacking her elegant work clothes when nobody but *Motor 2000*'s deeply demoralised staff would get to see them? Anyway, her hair needed highlighting badly as the mousy roots were showing through and she was too broke to get them redone. Getting all dressed up and still having two inches of mouse showing would be too depressing.

Rhona's voice broke into her thoughts. 'The downside of the job is that you haven't worked for the paper before and most newspapers like to employ people they already know. But,' she added, gleefully, 'I hear there are huge problems at the *Sentinel*. Circulation figures are going down and the editor, Nigel Burke – who's been there for ten years and is either burnt out or verging on insane, according to gossip – is keen on the idea of bringing in outsiders to shake up the staff.

'You never know, being a complete outsider who's worked abroad for ten years could swing it in your favour. Send in your CV today and ring tomorrow.'

'Oh, God, I don't know,' said Isabel slowly. 'Everything's been so awful for the past few months, I'm totally messed up. Robin's barely talking to me, I'm on the verge of being fired by piggy Richie Devine, and I can't even stop my own mother from telling me where I've gone wrong and how to run my life. Am I insane to think of applying for a job like women's editor of a national paper?'

'Don't be silly, Isabel. You'd be perfect for the job,' Rhona said briskly. 'Anyway, a chaotic personal life is a necessity for a women's editor today. How else would you write all those "juggling your life" editorials if you weren't juggling yourself?'

'I'm not even juggling, I've dropped everything,' protested Isabel, half-serious.

'So? You'll be able to empathise with your readers, won't you?'

Afterwards, Isabel went upstairs, found her old portable typewriter and spent an hour working on a CV.

Painfully putting all the details on paper made her feel even more unsure about applying for the job. How had she done all those things – run magazines and papers and actually enjoyed it? Now she felt tired all the time; tired and lacking in confidence. Could she really do a job like the one on the *Sentinel*?

The old Isabel could have. The pre-break up Isabel who was used to getting compliments about her style, her wonderful taste in clothes and her ability to stay calm in the face of any office catastrophe.

'How do you do it?' Penny Southark, Isabel's old editor on *Today's Woman*, had demanded when a new and inexperienced sub-editor managed to wipe out half the magazine on her computer hard disc and only Isabel had remained composed enough to sort things out.

She'd just smiled. 'Simple. My mother is such an organised person that my entire childhood was spent listening to her telling me how to do things right. In my mother's book, panicking about anything meant you were definitely doing it wrong. Calm was her favourite word – she should have been a Buddhist.'

Isabel didn't add that growing up with such a perfectionist was very, very difficult, especially when the perfectionist in question lost all her much-vaunted calmness when her daughter did things wrong.

Lately, Isabel felt that she'd lost her ability to be calm in the face of disaster. She'd also lost a lot of her hard-won confidence, as if the gradual erosion of the important parts of her life had somehow eroded part of her spirit at the same time. She felt sad, weary and more unsure of herself than she'd been for years.

Always quite slim, she'd lost weight over the past few months and it didn't suit her. Her face was pale, emphasising a fine bone structure a little too near the surface for comfort. The large blue eyes looked haunted, and without make-up – she hadn't really bothered wearing any for months now – her shoulder-length dark blonde hair combined with darker roots made her face look even more wan.

She could always unearth that fake tan, Isabel

thought, as she examined herself critically in the bedroom mirror. She had to do something. Nobody would hire her looking the way she did now. And she just *had* to get a decent job. Maybe Rhona was right – maybe she was well able to work for the *Sentinel*.

Pamela Mulhearn thought it was a shade ambitious when her daughter Isabel mentioned applying for the job on the *Sentinel* that night. Just back from her bridge club, Pamela walked into the kitchen and took off her cream linen jacket, eyeing herself in the mirror to check that her short, frosted curls were perfectly in place.

Tall, slim and still able to fit into the clothes she'd worn when she was twenty – a fact of which she was very proud – Pamela's posture was ramrod straight. She still climbed in and out of cars with the ladylike precision her own strict mother had drummed into her nearly sixty years ago.

'It's a good paper, Isabel, but are you sure you're ready for such a demanding job right now?' Pamela said doubtfully, wrinkling up the elegant nose that was so like her daughter's. She sat down and crossed slim legs, smoothing down the cream plaid skirt she'd bought in Harrods thirty years ago. 'Surely you'd be better off staying at the car magazine? Being women's editor would be very difficult and you're getting on all right where you are now. I doubt if you're ready for it.'

You doubt if I'm able for anything, Mother, Isabel thought with irritation. Why the hell couldn't her mother be supportive? Just for once. But that would be breaking the habit of a lifetime. No matter what Isabel did, it wouldn't be enough. It wouldn't measure up to anything Luke had done.

Lucky old brother Luke, living thousands of miles

away from Ireland and still the apple of his mother's eye and the yardstick by which everyone's achievements – mainly Isabel's – were measured. If he'd lived round the corner, perhaps Pamela would have realised that even her precious surgeon son made mistakes. Not as big as the mistakes her daughter had made, like going off with David, but mistakes nevertheless. Anyway, for all they knew, he could be busking on Hollywood Boulevard instead of working in a plush private clinic as an ophthalmic surgeon. Who knew what he was really up to since he phoned about twice a year and they'd only visited him a couple of times in the last decade?

If only her mother had had a career, something to occupy that rapier mind, life at home would have been so much better, Isabel thought. But a lifetime of watching other people struggle with tasks that Pamela Mulhearn could have done in her sleep, had made her bitter, frustrated – and always ready to leap down Isabel's throat.

Totally unaware of the bitter thoughts rattling through her daughter's head, Pamela flicked open her handbag with tapering, pearly pink-tipped fingers, took out a tiny silver pill box and extracted two of her migraine tablets.

'Be a dear, Harry, and get me some water, will you?'

Even though Pamela phrased the sentence as a question, she wasn't actually *asking* her husband to get her some water – she was ordering him. As she ordered everyone from him right down to the packer at the supermarket, who would be pointedly told to unpack the shopping if he'd inadvertently stuck a tin of consommé on top of the asparagus tips. Her mother was so good at ordering that she should have been in the army, Isabel thought privately. She even had a driver. Harry didn't play bridge but he faithfully drove his wife to her friends' houses three times a week and was content to return four hours later and pick her up.

He handed her some water and looked briefly towards the garden. Isabel knew her father desperately wanted to slip out to his shed, put on his ancient gardening clothes and leave the women to it while he tended his vegetables.

'What do you think, Harry?' asked Pamela. 'I think Isabel has been through too much lately, what with David,' she hissed his name, 'and having to move jobs and sell that beautiful house. A new job is too much to take on as well.'

'I agree with you, love,' Harry said, as he always did. Harry Mulhearn would have said that the moon was made of blue cheese if his wife asked him to. It was easier that way, as he'd learned after forty-five years of living with her. Isabel had never been able to stop herself from arguing.

Duty done, Harry went out of the back door to look round his beloved garden, the pride and joy of his life. Isabel loved gardening too, probably because she'd spent so many enjoyable hours with her father in the sun-filled back garden when she was young, watching him prune, plant, dig – and stay out of his wife's way.

The garden was a credit to his effort and skill, a curving lawn with three separate areas: the rose garden, the vegetable patch, and Isabel's favourite, the wild flower garden, a mass of cowslips, bluebells and dog roses, which her mother disliked.

'Mother,' Isabel argued now, 'it's a fantastic job and it would be wonderful if I got it. Of course it'll be demanding, but that's what I want right now. Something to take my mind off David and the separation.'

'Separation?' erupted her mother. 'I do hope you mean divorce? That's the only way to get rid of that weasel.'

Isabel ignored the interruption. 'As I was saying, the only problem is that there'll be incredible competition for the job.'

Her mother shrugged coolly, angry because Isabel had ignored what she'd said about getting divorced. 'You don't have to take my advice, Isabel. You never have before,' she said sharply.

Isabel dug her nails into her palms. She was sorry she'd ever mentioned the job.

'But when you have a nervous breakdown, *I'll* be the one picking up the pieces. I'm not the sort to say "don't come running to me" when that happens, Isabel, but that's how I feel.'

Isabel sat grinding her teeth. After three difficult months, she was desperate to get away from her parents' house. Please God, or whoever was up there, let her get a decent job so she could buy a three-bedroomed house or flat and then the girls wouldn't have to share a room. And *she* wouldn't have to listen to her mother's endless litany of Isabel's mistakes.

Her errors included getting into journalism in the first place: 'I wish you'd done medicine, Isabel, like your brother. It's not as if you didn't have the brains. You just didn't try hard enough.' Marrying David: 'I knew he was a wastrel the moment I set eyes on him.' And leaving the country when David got a job in sales with a large computer firm in the UK: 'Very stupid.'

'Well, if you *are* going for an interview, you'd better get your hair cut,' her mother said disapprovingly. Pamela Mulhearn felt that women over thirty should have short hair. At thirty-nine, Isabel was far too old to have hair past her ears. A nice sleek short style would be more suitable, more mature. 'Gordon would love to do your hair, Isabel,' Pamela added.

'Thanks, Mother. But I like my hair the way it is.'

Isabel couldn't afford to get her hair highlighted, which it badly needed, so she wasn't going to bother coughing up £25 for Gordon to butcher it into a frosted helmet like her mother's. She was convinced he could only cut hair one way, the way he secretly wanted his own to look.

'Have it your own way,' Pamela said. 'But I think you could do with a more suitable cut. Claudia's is so nice.'

Claudia was Luke's wife, a paragon of elegance and the sort of woman who wouldn't dream of leaving the house without wearing the entire Estée Lauder range, French-manicured nails and at least half a can of hairspray welding her gamine haircut in place.

'We haven't seen her *or* Luke,' Isabel emphasised, 'for so long that she could have Rapunzel-length hair by now, Mother.'

'Don't forget, Isabel, your brother invited your father and me over to Los Angeles last year. It wasn't his fault we couldn't manage to go the only week he was free.'

Isabel grabbed the kettle, shoved it under the tap and filled it up. There was no point in arguing that it seemed odd that a successful man like her brother could only take *one week* off during the entire summer. Dear God, please, please let me get the job so I can move out of home, she prayed.

Anything, anything, would be better than grinding her teeth every five minutes. No wonder she'd jumped at the chance to leave Ireland when David had suggested moving to London ten years ago.

Robin slouched into the kitchen wearing no bra and a

skin-tight black T-shirt – which Isabel had never seen before – with her black jeans. Her hair, the same dark blonde as her mother's, hung straight around her face and the heavy, over-long fringe almost obscured blue eyes that were sooty with Isabel's mascara. The combination of her height – she was nearly as tall as her mother now – and the sort of slender body that a supermodel would envy, meant Robin looked a lot older than fifteen. With make-up, she could have passed for nineteen or twenty, a fact that worried Isabel more and more.

The sweet, conscientious Robin of old wouldn't have given her mother a moment's worry about her whereabouts or her friends. But this sullen stranger was a different proposition altogether. Visions of her heavily made-up daughter hitting nightclubs with a dangerous, older crowd haunted Isabel.

She wanted to ask Robin where the T-shirt had come from, but knew that if she said anything her mother would go into outraged overdrive. Family rows were magnified tenfold when Pamela was involved. Robin pulled open the fridge, poked around until she found a yoghurt, and started eating it, completely unconcerned about the effect she was having on her grandmother.

'See ya,' she said once she'd finished her yoghurt. She dumped the spoon in the sink and tossed the pot blithely into the bin.

'Where are you going at this time of night?' asked Pamela.

'Out.' Robin stared at her grandmother insolently.

'It's half-eight on a school night! You've got homework to do,' Pamela said tartly. 'I don't think that's a very good idea, young lady . . .'

'You're not my mother!' retorted Robin.

57

'Don't you talk to me like that!' shrieked Pamela.

'Robin! Mother! Stop it!' Isabel intervened. 'Mother, this is between Robin and me. And, Robin, don't talk to your grandmother like that.'

'She can't tell me what to do, she's not my bloody mother! Or my father,' yelled Robin. 'I hate her, I hate you, I hate this place. I want to go home to Dad!'

Eyes blazing and tears running down her cheeks, taking plenty of mascara with them, Robin ran from the kitchen, sobbing loudly. They heard the door to her bedroom slam shut.

Pamela turned on Isabel. 'I didn't take you in to be treated like that,' she hissed. 'You know what these arguments do to my nerves. And it makes me wonder how you've brought that girl up when she speaks to me in that tone of voice.'

Isabel didn't point out that her mother started a fair percentage of the said fights. But she knew that didn't excuse Robin's appalling behaviour for one moment.

'I know, Mother. I'm sorry,' she said wearily. 'All this has been so hard on Robin.'

'It certainly hasn't been easy on the rest of us,' snapped her mother. 'I'm going to lie down. My migraine is getting worse.'

Pamela marched out of the kitchen and upstairs while Isabel leant against the sink. Her legs felt like jelly and she could feel the beginnings of a brutal headache throbbing at the base of her own skull. She hated arguments of any kind, always had. And unless she and the girls found somewhere else to live, there were going to be plenty more.

CHAPTER THREE

The office was like an oven. A great gust of hot air greeted Dee when she walked into the newsroom. The windows were open and the editor's secretary had positioned a huge electric fan right beside her desk, blowing papers and wafts of Chanel No. 5 towards the sub-editors' desks in the middle of the room.

'The air conditioning's bust,' muttered one of the sports reporters as he hurried past Dee. 'I'm going to a match,' he yelled to the sports editor who was just coming out of the editor's office, his face pale, no doubt after one of Nigel Burke's legendary tellings-off.

'He's probably going home to sit in front of the box and watch Sky Sports,' grumbled Maeve at the reporter's departing back. Dee pulled up a spare chair and sat beside her.

'Lucky sod. The heat's killing me and the smell of that damn' perfume is making me sick,' Maeve whispered. Nobody ever complained too loudly about the editor's secretary, Sheila Smyth, because she had ears like a rabbit, heard everything and reported it straight back to Nigel.

Dee cast a quick glance at Sheila and caught her staring beadily in Maeve's direction.

'Drill Sergeant Smyth is looking this way,' she said

under her breath. 'I'd better let you go back to work or she'll send her thugs round to nail your kneecaps to the floor.'

Dee got up. Maeve put a hand on her arm.

'Hold on,' she whispered. 'Since you couldn't make it, I had lunch with Phil Walsh and she's got the latest on Antonia's resignation. Come to the kitchen and I'll tell you – I need a break anyway.'

In the tiny kitchen, Maeve made a speedy cup of instant coffee.

'Antonia told Nigel first thing this morning. That's why he's going round like a bear with a sore head. He's already bawled out all the photographers for not getting pictures of Johnny Depp in the Clarence last night. And he was brutal to that poor trainee reporter from Cork. She's hiding in Advertising, sobbing her heart out.'

'God, he's such a bastard!' Dee said. 'But I can't believe Antonia didn't tell him immediately. You know how cross he gets if he doesn't hear everything straight away.'

'Well, you know how dense she can be. It probably never occurred to her that the editor would like to be one of the first to know she was going to resign. Or that her eighteen-carat golden handshake could very quickly turn into a gilt one if she left him in the lurch. Anyway, according to Phil, she ended up in floods because he called her every name in the book and then she went home – without finishing her bloody column, I might add. It's only half-written so I'll have to stick loads of bloody pictures in . . .'

'What did Nigel say to her?' demanded Dee. 'Did he say anything about a replacement?'

Maeve raised one eyebrow. 'From what Phil told me, I

don't think Antonia took in much of what he said apart from, "You stupid cow!" '

'Sorry I missed it,' said Dee regretfully. 'Should I go in and ask for the job today? I spent all last night working on my ideas for the women's section. All I need to do is print them out and I'm ready.'

The sports editor came into the kitchen with a cup in one hand and a mournful expression on his face. Normally an incorrigible flirt, he didn't even smile at the two of them. Nigel Burke's tirades did that to people.

As editor of the *Sentinel*, Nigel was the man in charge and had six people directly below him in the paper's hierarchy – his deputy editor and the women's, sports, news, features and pictures editors. Of those six, only one was just as bad-tempered and aggressive as Nigel, and that was the news editor, Ian Mahon.

Between them, they made more noise and had more rows than the rest of the staff put together, and their fights meant that sparks, and occasionally ashtrays, were always flying in the office.

'I've been thinking, Dee,' Maeve whispered, 'you'd better not go in and say you want the job yet. Give him a day to settle down. Because if you go in with your ideas today, it'll be obvious that you heard about Antonia leaving before he did, and he's quite likely to consider you the worst kind of traitor for not telling him.'

'Good point. I'll go in tomorrow.'

They were walking past Nigel Burke's office as they made their way back into the newsroom when his door burst open and he emerged, red-faced.

'Mahon!' he shouted in the direction of the news editor's office, which was right at the back of the newsroom, behind thirty or so reporters' desks. 'I want

61

to know who's responsible for all these libel writs that have just landed on my desk!' he yelled, brandishing a sheaf of faxes in one hand.

'We're being sued by every bloody solicitor in the country. *You're* supposed to make sure we don't libel anyone, so *you're* not doing your bloody job right! And it's costing this newspaper a fortune!'

Nigel pounded past the subs' desks like a bull in a china shop.

Dee followed him into the newsroom, where all the reporters who'd been making personal phone calls and flicking idly through the papers while waiting for stories to break, hastily attacked their keyboards like people possessed.

The gossip columnist, whose desk was nearest Stalin's office, dropped the Yves St Laurent powder compact she'd been using to touch up her make-up, snatched up her phone and started talking at length to the engaged tone. 'Really, how interesting. And which member of the Royal family is coming to the ball? Ooooh, Princess Anne! Lovely!'

Nigel Burke didn't notice. He strode through the newsroom, marched into Stalin's office and slammed the glass door so hard the panels shook.

Unfortunately for the news editor, the glass front that let him watch every move the reporters made from the comfort of his own office wasn't soundproofed. The entire newsroom could hear everything Nigel yelled at him and the sports department listened in delight, thrilled to see another department in trouble.

'You stupid bastard . . .' Nigel screeched.

The news reporters kept their heads down and prayed *they* wouldn't be called in to explain exactly why a story of theirs had resulted in the paper's being sued for libel.

'*More* libel cases?' Dee asked Gerry, the political correspondent.

'That's the third today,' he replied, never taking his eyes off his computer screen. 'Nigel is going out of his mind about them. He's only just recovered from shelling out fifty grand to that bloke who was wrongly named as a drug pusher last year.'

'Did you hear about Antonia?' Dee inquired, as she switched on her computer.

'Heard last week. Just as well she's going. She'd never stick the next six months.'

Dee was surprised. 'But Nigel's always adored her – apart from today, of course – no matter how dreadful her column was. Why do you say that? Do you know something I don't, Gerry?' she added suspiciously.

He typed another sentence before answering. 'Let's just say that the powers-that-be aren't too pleased with our beloved Nigel. If the circulation figures keep dropping the way they've been for the past year, the paper's going to start losing money.'

'Wow!' Dee was stunned. 'I didn't know it was that bad.' She blanched as she thought of the massive mortgage she and Gary were saddled with, the holiday to Florida they'd been discussing for months and the expense of their wedding the following year. Well, she *hoped* it would be the following year.

'Nigel had better get his finger out if he wants to keep his job,' Gerry remarked, turning back to his story. 'So, you're thinking of going for Antonia's job, are you?'

'Do you know *everything*, Gerry?' Dee asked, startled out of her nightmare over finances.

He grinned at his screen. 'Most things.'

The first thing that struck Dee as she opened the front

door was the delicious scent of garlic and lamb wafting out of the kitchen. Fantastic. Gary had decided to cook after all. So he *had* listened last night when she'd complained about having to do all the washing, cooking and cleaning.

'I'm home, Gary. That smells fantastic. Is it really my favourite garlic and rosemary lamb?'

'Deirdre, you're home at last,' her future mother-in-law said sweetly from the kitchen. 'Dinner's nearly ready. I've sent Gary out for some milk as you didn't have any in the fridge except that dreadful skimmed sort which really isn't good for you at all. Oh, and some proper coffee. I do hate instant.'

Shit! When the hell had Gary's bloody mother decided to come over? And why hadn't he warned her? Dee dropped her briefcase on the floor and marched upstairs. No way was she going into the kitchen to say hello to Margaret Redmond wearing this outfit. Margaret always said that she hated women who wore 'vulgar, tight clothes' and Dee's clingy top was both. Not that Margaret could talk. Her clothes might all have been expensive stuff bought from chi-chi little suburban boutiques, but she still looked like a Sherman tank in every single one of them. Mumsy didn't just enjoy baking lorryloads of cakes and meringues – she loved eating them too.

'I'll be down in a minute, Margaret,' Dee said loudly, taking the stairs two at a time. Give you a chance to hide your broomstick, you old battleaxe.

'Take your time, Deirdre. I've everything under control. Where do you keep the napkins I gave you for your engagement? I can't find them anywhere.'

'That's because they've been at the bottom of the linen basket for the last three months with red wine stains on them,' Dee muttered to herself. Bloody bitch is just checking up on me.

'They're dirty, Margaret,' she yelled down the stairs. 'We'll have to use the tissue ones in the third drawer down.'

Another black mark. Dee didn't measure up to her future mother-in-law's exacting criteria. The daughter of a wealthy butcher, Margaret Redmond considered herself to be upper middle class and Dee, with her working-class roots and propensity for speaking her mind, didn't conform with Margaret's idea of the sort of woman her beloved younger son should marry.

Dee could see it all: the social-climbing Mrs Redmond hadn't been grooming her son with trips to art galleries and expensive violin lessons for him to go out with a mechanic's daughter. Only a huntin', shootin', fishin' gel with a lineage like a racehorse's and at least one parent with a posh accent would do for Mumsy.

'Interfering old cow,' Dee muttered as she changed clothes.

She pulled her comfy old black ski pants out of the wardrobe and had one foot in before she realised that her usual evening outfit – ski pants and a huge jumper which covered her bum – wouldn't be suitable for dinner with this particular guest.

Damn Gary! He could be so bloody insensitive. If he'd known his mother was planning to come round, he could at least have phoned the *Sentinel* to warn her.

The front door slammed.

'I got Rombouts filtered coffee. Is that OK?' Gary was clearly talking to darling Mumsy and not to Dee. Whose bloody house was this? Hers or theirs? And what was wrong with instant coffee?

Dee gritted her teeth and pulled a silky yellow

polo-neck jumper from a drawer and dragged it over her head before adding a voluminous black shirt. The last thing she wanted this evening was a forced conversation over dinner while her future mother-in-law bitched about everything from her missing linen napkins to the lack of decent food in the fridge.

'Hi, Dee. Did you have a good day?' Gary called up the stairs in a slightly tense voice. He had every right to be tense, Dee thought crossly as she ran a comb through her hair.

'Lovely, *dear*,' she replied.

She flounced into the bathroom to slap on some more make-up. As she reached for a bit of loo roll to remove a smudge of mascara, she realised there was none left.

She opened the cabinet under the sink to look for more loo roll and the box of strawberry condoms she'd bought Gary as a joke a few months earlier fell out. They'd used one but that was it. Dee stuffed them hastily at the back of the cabinet and was about to close the door when she changed her mind.

She took the box out and left it on the windowsill where Mumsy was sure to see it. About time she realised her son wasn't a saint, Dee thought with a wicked grin.

Dinner was hell. Gary avoided looking Dee in the eye and she noticed that he'd changed into the white cotton sweater his mother had bought him for his birthday the year before. He normally slobbed around in ancient T-shirts and threadbare jeans, but he had to dress up for his mother. It suited him, the pure white showed up the tan he'd got from playing lots of soccer in the evening sun. But Dee wasn't in a mood to appreciate her fiancé's finer points when he'd let his mother come over unannounced. *And* was sucking up to her like mad.

The cardboard that stopped the dining-room table from rocking was still missing, so Gary spent ages wedging bits of the cornflake box under the wonky leg. A lengthy grace was said and then Margaret dished out the vegetables like some Biblical princess distributing shekels to the poor.

'Some potatoes, Deirdre?' she said coolly. Then, in a much warmer tone, 'I've made your favourite cheesy ones, Gary.'

Margaret could certainly cook and the smell of succulent lamb was enough to make Dee drool with anticipation. But it was hard to enjoy the meal when her future mother-in-law was at the same table, ostentatiously holding up her knife to the light before breathing on it and polishing it with her napkin. Tissue napkin. To Margaret, paper napkins were on a par with having tea served in mugs and sticking the milk carton on the table instead of using a jug.

'Is your dinner all right, love?' Margaret asked her son anxiously.

'Beautiful. There's nothing like home cooking.' Gary smiled warmly at his mother and shovelled another forkful of lamb into his mouth.

Traitor, thought Dee. She stabbed a pea with her fork and a splash of gravy sailed on to the red place mat. I could make bloody lamb and cheesy potatoes every night if I didn't have a job. Or if I didn't spend so much of my time at home doing extra work or hoovering because your bloody son doesn't.

'He loves his lamb,' Margaret said fondly, her mean little eyes softening. 'All my boys love my cooking. I've got a great cookbook at home I could lend you, Deirdre,' she added with saccharine sweetness. 'It's got some of

Gary's favourite meals in it. He loves shepherd's pie, you know. Only with good mince.'

Dee simmered. This woman had marched into *her* house, stuck her nose up at the contents of Dee's fridge and the state of the place, and now she was insinuating that Dee couldn't – or wouldn't – cook! She clenched her jaw and imagined what she'd *like* to say . . .

'*You do spoil your boys, Margaret. In fact, you've spoiled poor Gary so much, he doesn't know how to boil an egg for himself and hasn't a clue how to do anything more complicated than phone the pizza delivery people, do you, darling?*' Dee smiled to herself, imagining the look of shock on her future mother-in-law's face. '*But he's marvellous in bed, of course. He nearly broke the chandelier the other night swinging from it on to the mattress!*'

She could visualise Margaret spluttering into her half glass of mineral water. What a howl it would be. Dee wouldn't let her get a word in edgeways.

'*In a modern relationship, people work together. Last night we decided to split all the housework and the cooking, didn't we, Gary?*'

'More wine, Dee?' his voice broke into her little daydream. He was holding up the bottle with a self-satisfied smile on his face. Of course he was pleased, she thought crossly. He'd made Mumsy happy and that was what counted. Who cared what Dee felt?

She barely spoke during the rest of the meal and left when Margaret started to dish up the rice pudding, pleading that she had to work on her agony column. Dee hated rice pudding with a vengeance; it was nearly as bad as tapioca, another nursery food staple that Gary unaccountably loved. Margaret probably had a cookbook full of recipes on thrilling things to do with tapioca and sago. Yeuch! If the stupid woman stopped fussing about her boys and had the odd glass of wine, she might be slightly more human. Then again, it'd take more than a glass of Chianti to turn Margaret Redmond into anything approaching a human being.

Upstairs, Dee turned on her computer but couldn't bring herself to write a word. She felt so angry. Angry and hurt. Gary *could* have told her Margaret was coming over. To add insult to injury, he'd never made it so plain that he'd hop to his mother's bidding when he wouldn't lift a finger for Dee. When was the last time he had gone anywhere near a shop unless he wanted to visit the off-licence or drop a video back to the shop? But once Mumsy clicked her fat little fingers, he hopped to it like a soldier on parade. So much for a relaxing evening at home watching the Tuesday movie. It was Woody Allen's *Hannah And Her Sisters* too.

Dee got the detective novel she was reading from her bedside table, sat in her tiny office, feet propped up on the desk, and ate an entire packet of butterscotch sweets. That was two big meals, five chocolate digestives in the office, four glasses of wine *and* a pack of sweets. Damn and blast. Nothing but black coffee and fruit tomorrow, she vowed.

The waistband of her size fourteen jeans was getting painfully tight. That was the problem with living with someone who could eat what he liked and still stay whippet-thin. Gary regularly brought home chocolate bars and giant tins of Pringles and left them lying around where Dee couldn't resist them. And then he had the temerity to say *she* had better watch her figure!

Dear Annie,
 I've been big all my life. Not fat exactly, just plump. I could lose a stone and a half. Well, two

stone. I've also spent most of my thirty-two years on a diet. My problem is my boyfriend.

When I met him, I was somewhat thinner. He said he loved the way I looked, but he hated women who dieted. He says you should eat what you want and you won't put on weight because that's what he does and he's slim.

So I eat what I want and I've put on weight, which he hates. I have to hide the dieting books and my low-calorie stuff at the back of the saucepan cupboard because he says I should throw out 'that rubbish'. He also says I look better slimmer and now our love life is non-existent. I know it's because he doesn't find me attractive any more. I can't look at the bathroom scales and I'm eating more than ever. I'm beginning to hate myself. What should I do?

When Dee heard the front door slam at half-ten, she switched off the computer and marched downstairs. Gary was stacking clean plates in the cupboard. The sink was empty, a tea towel was draped over the mixer taps and the worktops were spotless.

If Gary had done it, Dee would have been thrilled, but since his bloody mother had tidied up – no doubt, muttering that the whole place could do with a proper spring clean – Dee was irritated by the gleaming surfaces and cutlery-free dish rack.

Totally ignoring Gary, she filled the kettle and angrily got a cup from the mug tree. She didn't trust herself to speak even though she had a million things to say.

'I'm sorry, Dee, I should have told you she was coming. But she sounded so down when she rang today, I had to ask her over,' Gary said in a pleading voice. 'You know how cut up she is over its being Dad's anniversary. She's all alone in that big house . . .'

I wonder why? thought Dee savagely. She wrenched the lid off the coffee jar with some force. The old cow has completely alienated most of her neighbours, *all* of her daughters-in-law, and the only people who bother talking to her are her besotted little boys, five chauvinists who blindly worship the ground she marches on.

'She's lonely,' Gary repeated.

Dee turned around angrily to face him.

'I don't mind having your mother here if she's really lonely and miserable, but I *do* mind that she spends every moment of her time here criticising me! I don't cook proper food for you, I don't have decent food in the fridge, I use skimmed milk, instant coffee and, perish the thought, I even expect you to get your lily-white hands dirty doing a bit of housework! *That's* what I object to,' Dee hissed. 'Her constant harping.'

'She's not like that,' protested Gary.

'But the worst thing is the way you back her up. *Don't worry Mumsy, dopey Dee will never be able to cook like you, so why don't you come over every week and inject a little home cooking into our humdrum lives!* How the hell do you think that makes me feel? You won't even back me up in front of your bloody mother!'

'Oh, for God's sake, Dee, give it a rest,' he said wearily. 'I don't know what your problem is with my mother. God knows, she doesn't have much pleasure in her life these days and if cooking my dinner makes her happy, then I'm happy.'

'But I'm not!' shrieked Dee. 'Are you deaf or something? Don't you hear the way she puts me down constantly? And doesn't it occur to you that she has no right to march into my kitchen and start slagging off the

71

way I run this house? Because,' Dee paused for breath, '*I* run this house. *You* certainly don't.'

He put a calming hand on her arm but Dee shrugged it off.

'Don't try and placate me, Gary. This isn't a joke, it's serious. I'm sick of you treating me like a skivvy. I work just as many hours, and sometimes more, than you do, I earn as much money and yet you still expect me to tidy up after you and wash your clothes. Well it's not on. I'm not doing it any more.'

'OK, OK, I'll help. But I don't see the need to tidy up as often as you want to,' he said mildly.

Dee clenched her teeth to stop herself from thumping him. He was so bloody stupid sometimes. He'd missed the whole point.

If Gary limited his tidying-up duties to the times he felt it was necessary, they'd live in squalor. Because he *never* saw the need to tidy up. They'd be back to square one in a week, with her screaming at him to wash the bloody dishes.

'There's no point talking to you, Gary. If you can't respect me enough to do your share of the housework, how can I expect your mother to? *She* puts me down because you put me down, and she knows she can say whatever nasty things she likes and you'll never stop her.'

'Don't be ridiculous,' he said. 'We're only talking about the washing up, not the future of the civilised world!'

'You just don't get it, do you?' Dee said tiredly. What was the point of talking about it all? Gary was never going to see her point of view.

'By the way,' he said in a calmer voice, 'Mum asked me could we take her to Simon's wedding because she doesn't want to drive her car.'

Dee raised her eyes to heaven. It was bad enough that Gary had accepted his cousin's wedding invitation without mentioning it to her until the previous week. But the idea of carting bloody Margaret all the way to Ashford in Wicklow was worse. At least an hour each way of bitching and smart comments. Dee groaned inwardly.

'Yeah, fine,' she snapped.

Simon was the son of Margaret's sister – another sharp-tongued, bossy harridan. His wedding to a wealthy solicitor's only daughter was 'the society wedding of the year' according to his doting Auntie Margaret. Dee was dreading it. She'd heard quite enough of how the Delahuntys were having the reception in the four-acre grounds of their stately Georgian pile in Ashford. Grounds that contained a rose garden bordered by a box hedge, several statues, a fountain and a tennis court.

'Yvonne's parents are charming. I think it's a wonderful idea to hold the reception in their grounds. They've even got an indoor swimming pool,' Margaret had explained.

God only knew what she was going to wear, Dee thought morosely. She'd have to buy something new or she'd look quite out of place among all the identikit pastel pink, blue and yellow £500 suits from Brown Thomas that all the other female guests would doubtless be wearing with the family pearls. More expense. Well, Gary could buy the wedding present. It was the least he could do.

'Tell you what,' he said, sitting down behind her at the table and massaging her bare neck, 'let's go out to dinner on Friday night, just the two of us to somewhere romantic. What do you think?'

She turned to face him. 'OK. That would be lovely.'

'I *do* love you, Dee,' he said gently, tracing the contours of her cheek with one hand.

He looked tired, she realised with a jolt. There were shadows under his eyes and he'd been stifling yawns all evening.

'I know it's difficult having Mum to dinner, but I feel so guilty when she rings and I say she can't come over,' he said. 'You'd want to do the same if your mother was in the same position, wouldn't you?'

'Yes,' Dee said, relenting. Maybe she *was* being a bit of a cow. Work was getting to her lately. Although all that would change if she got Antonia's job. Who knew? On Friday she could be celebrating her new appointment as women's editor. Now that *would* be a celebration!

CHAPTER FOUR

Nigel Burke slammed the door of the MD's office shut behind him.

'Would you like a cup of tea?' asked Ted Holt's secretary, a frosty-faced, fortyish brunette, seated behind an imposing desk.

Isabel sat down on a large black leather armchair and immediately slid uncomfortably into its depths.

'Sorry, er, no.' She tried to pull herself up in the chair. Why did so many offices have waiting-room chairs that you sank into without a trace? It was hard to look dignified when you were struggling to get out of a chair, your tights and knickers on view, your knee-length skirt hoicked up.

Isabel's feet touched the ground once more and she tried to smile at the woman opposite her, a confident, I'm-not-fazed-by-sliding-into-chairs look. The secretary stared determinedly at her word processor. A yellow mug with steam rising out of it stood on the desk beside her and Isabel wished she'd said 'yes' to that tea.

She'd have killed for a cup after her fifty-minute interview with the *Sentinel*'s managing director, Ted Holt, and Nigel.

They'd certainly grilled her thoroughly. Every aspect of her previous career was discussed, from 'Why did you leave Ireland in the first place?' to why she'd decided to leave her job in the British women's magazine. They'd wanted to know how she'd develop the women's pages if she was appointed. Isabel had been prepared for all these questions and had spent two hours the night before running through every possible answer, as calmly and professionally as possible, with Naomi standing in for Nigel.

As she sat on a hard chair in front of Nigel and Ted, Isabel had been very grateful for the previous night's practice run. Of course, she hadn't told Naomi that she'd come home to Ireland because she had split up from her husband and was thinking of getting a divorce.

Nigel's eyes had warmed momentarily at the words 'divorce'. *He* might have been impressed by her on-the-knee black skirt, her slim, seven-denier-clad legs and the elegant red jacket she wore. But it was impossible to tell if Ted Holt liked her as a person or, more importantly, as a job candidate. His sharp little eyes gave nothing away. He sat back in his chair, arms folded across a vast blue-striped chest, another question on his thin lips as soon as she'd finished answering the last one. The way he'd looked at her, Isabel didn't feel she'd a hope in hell of getting the job.

The secretary's phone rang. Isabel jumped in her seat nervously.

'Mr Holt's office,' the secretary said, winding a stray strand of hair behind her ear. 'No, he's not to be disturbed. He'll ring you back in half an hour.'

Half an hour? marvelled Isabel. Was that how long she'd have to wait outside the MD's office while they considered her for the job? It was already eleven-forty-five and she was due in at work by twelve.

She'd got the morning off by pleading a dental

emergency. Her *Motor 2000* boss, Richie, would be furious if she arrived any later, especially if she didn't look as if she'd spent the morning having a filling replaced. Maybe she could suck a big boiled sweet for the first hour back at work so her mouth would look swollen.

Isabel grinned to herself. But if she got the women's editor job, it wouldn't matter how cross Richie was. She wouldn't need his crummy job any more. Still, it was a big 'if'.

She tugged her skirt down towards her knees and wondered if she'd made the right choice in wearing something shortish instead of a skirt down to her ankles. Could a short skirt be construed as too sexy or flirtatious? It felt like a million years since she'd last gone for a proper job interview. The job in the car magazine hadn't counted because they'd only been looking for a freelance sub-editor and any sub with half a brain would have got it.

The *Sentinel* wanted a woman with fashion experience, so she could hardly have turned up looking drab, could she?

Forget about the skirt. The interview is over, it's immaterial what they think of your bloody outfit at this point, she told herself. She sighed and cast a desultory look at the daily papers which were spread over the table in front of her. The waiting was agonising – she might as well have been in the dentist's having a major bit of drilling done. At least he gave you an injection before he hit a nerve.

Suddenly, the inner office door swung open and Ted Holt appeared. He didn't waste time on pleasantries like nodding at Isabel or addressing his secretary by name – he just barked out orders.

'Get my car sent round and phone the restaurant and tell them we'll be late. I've got to call into the lawyers' on my way.'

The secretary was obviously used to his brusque manner and didn't bat an eyelid. 'Right. Do you want your messages now, Ted, or will I give them to you later?' she asked.

'Later.' He turned to Isabel. 'Come in,' he said, his voice warming.

Isabel did her best to smile and followed him back into the office where she'd been interviewed. Her heart was thumping so loud she was sure he could hear it and her mouth was as dry as the Sahara. Ted looked friendly for the first time. But was he lulling her into a false sense of security before telling her she hadn't got the job – or were they going to offer it to her? Who knew? And if he treated his staff the way he'd treated his secretary – with a bluntness that was verging on rude – then did she really want to work for him?

Isabel sat in the same hard chair she'd taken before and forced herself to clasp her hands gently in her lap instead of squeezing them tightly. That's what all the self-help articles told you to do when you were nervous. It didn't work.

Both men smiled expansively.

Ted leant against the front of his vast mahogany desk, opened a polished wooden box and extracted a cigar as fat as a frankfurter.

'We want to offer you the position of women's editor,' he said, 'and I think that calls for a celebration!'

'Hear, hear.' Nigel leant over to proffer a lighter.

Isabel didn't know what to say. She couldn't believe it. They'd offered her the job! *She* was the new women's editor of the *Sentinel*!

'Thank you. I accept, of course.' She beamed at the two men. 'You won't regret it, I promise you,' she added fervently.

'Nigel and I never regret anything, isn't that right, eh?' Ted winked at his editor. 'Now, can you join us for a spot of lunch, Isabel? We've got some important details to discuss, such as your salary, naturally, and I enjoy doing business over a glass of wine, especially when the company is so attractive!'

She flushed at the remark and thought of *Motor 2000* and the three-page article waiting on her desk to be transformed into a thrilling feature on buying the correct van for a small business. Much as she disliked Richie Devine, she hated to let anyone down.

Still, she reckoned, it would be a mistake to say no to her new bosses on day one, even if it did seem a little presumptuous to expect she'd be free for lunch at a moment's notice.

Isabel liked to be able to pencil in a date in her diary at least a week before the event. David used to drive her mad when he asked friends over for dinner at one day's notice. It was one of the many things they'd argued about.

'How the hell am I supposed to knock up dinner for six tomorrow evening when I'll be working late? I won't have time to get any groceries at lunchtime and the house is a disaster area,' she'd yelled the last time this had happened.

Maybe Ted Holt was just another man who did everything on the spur of the moment, particularly as he'd called her in for an interview a mere two days after she'd applied for the job.

'I'd love to,' Isabel said, giving her new boss the benefit of the ultra-confident smile she'd practised in

79

front of the bathroom mirror the night before, 'but I must make a phone call first.'

'Sure, sure. Use the phone outside.' Ted waved one hand in the direction of the door. 'We'll be leaving in ten minutes.'

'Ted said I could use your phone,' she said to his secretary by way of explanation. 'We were never introduced. I'm Isabel Farrell,' she added.

'I'm Marion,' the other woman replied. 'Dial nine for an outside line. Would you like a cup of tea or coffee this time? Ted won't be leaving for a while and I've got a pot of coffee brewed.'

'I'd kill for a cup of coffee,' Isabel said gratefully. 'Thanks.'

Marion left the room with two cups and Isabel quickly dialled the office. Thankfully, Richie wasn't there.

'Tell him I'm really sorry and I'll be in extra early tomorrow morning to finish the pages I'm working on,' she told the other sub-editor. 'Yes, I *know* he's going to go berserk but I can't help it. I'll see you tomorrow.'

She hung up.

Marion came back with a small tray containing coffee, sugar, milk and some chocolate digestives.

'Welcome to the *Sentinel*.' She put the tray on the coffee table.

'Thanks.' Isabel had no idea how Marion knew she'd got the job, but then how had the secretary known she was going to lunch with Ted and Nigel? Perhaps she was psychic.

'They never leave on time for lunch,' Marion added. She took a couple of chocolate biscuits over to her desk with her coffee, sat back in her chair and prepared to chat.

'This really is a great place to work. I've been here ten years – I worked for the previous MD before Ted – and I'm telling you, I wouldn't leave here for anything. This office has a buzz about it. Not like some places I've worked in.' She took a bite of digestive and went on talking with her mouth full. 'It's lovely to have new people coming on board, a bit of excitement is good for all of us!' She smiled matily. 'Antonia was very nice, but a bit posh, if you know what I mean.'

Isabel didn't but was too interested in the gossip to say so. She nodded encouragingly.

'Everybody liked her – well, most people,' Marion continued. 'She'd been here since the paper started and she'd got great fashion sense. Always perfectly turned out. Have you always worked in fashion yourself?'

'No, not really. I've worked in women's magazines in the UK for a long time, but I've never really covered women's issues for a newspaper before,' Isabel explained.

'Really? And why did you leave your other job?' Marian inquired, leaning forward intently.

'It's a long story . . .' Isabel hesitated. Should she be going into this with the MD's secretary?

'Oh, go on, Ted won't be out for ages.' Marion glanced at her phone. A red light indicated that her boss's line was busy. 'I love a good chat.'

When Nigel and Ted emerged from the office fifteen minutes later, Isabel had drunk a second cup of coffee and was left with the feeling that Marion now knew an awful lot about her, while she knew next to nothing about Marion. Except that she was fond of both gossip and chocolate digestives, which probably explained why she wore a vast patterned overshirt that could have doubled as a maternity smock any day. Isabel

81

cursed the nervousness that had made her chat away to the secretary.

'Sorry to keep you waiting, Isabel.' Ted buttoned up his jacket and headed for reception. 'I won't be back this afternoon,' he said over his shoulder to Marion. 'I'll be on the mobile if you need me.'

In the restaurant, they started with glasses of white wine – 'To keep us going while we order,' said Nigel, taking a deep sip – and moved on to two bottles of wine – red, to go with Ted's *filet mignon*. Determined to look cool and collected no matter what, Isabel barely touched her wine during the meal. The last thing she wanted was to get drunk at lunchtime, but it was obvious that Ted and Nigel had no such reservations.

They drank like it was going out of fashion, in between eating enough to stuff a small mattress. While Isabel enjoyed her grilled sole with salad, Nigel and Ted tucked into the sort of cholesterol-laden meal that had heart attack written all over it.

'I hate all that fancy French cooking – one bit of meat and two tiny bloody potatoes on a huge plate,' Ted said unnecessarily, as he speared a large piece of rare steak with his fork. 'Good Irish cooking, that's what I like.'

And lots of it, Isabel noted. Finally, Ted ordered horrendously expensive port to go with the selection of Irish cheeses.

Nigel and he were certainly entertaining company, and the editor's stories of the people he'd worked with were genuinely hilarious. But it was clear to Isabel that no matter how jovial or friendly he was today, Nigel wasn't a good man to have as an enemy.

'It was the story of the year, the decade, maybe,' he explained to Isabel, his face animated as he spoke. 'The bishop with two young grandchildren nobody knew about. We all knew he'd a daughter in her twenties but he'd managed to live that one down. "A youthful indiscretion", he said. Nobody had ever managed to track down the daughter, and not a soul knew she was living in Canada with twin sons.' He took a deep slug of port.

'Those kids were the image of the bishop. I'd been working on the story for six months and just before we were going public with it, that bastard Dick Morgan scooped it from under my nose and ran it on the front page of *Ireland Today*. I said I'd get him back and I did.'

Nigel's face lit up with glee. 'His wife had a fling with an old crony of mine and I made sure Morgan, and every reporter in Dublin, heard about it. It nearly killed him!'

'What goes around, comes around,' Ted said solemnly.

'I'll drink to that,' Nigel said with satisfaction.

There wasn't anything they *wouldn't* drink to, Isabel thought as she grinned and raised her glass with theirs.

The meal was over before Ted began talking about her new job.

'We've had a lot of interest in the position, I can tell you,' he said, lighting another cigar. 'Antonia had barely left when we got six letters of application for the job.'

'Really?' said Isabel, gratified to know how many people she'd beaten.

'It's a hell of a job and it's very important for the paper,' Ted added, which is why we needed a replacement immediately. Tell me, I've been wondering how you knew about Antonia going? It wasn't common knowledge. I was very impressed that you knew about the vacancy so quickly, especially since you've been out of the Irish journalistic scene for so long. You must have some great contacts.' He smiled at her eagerly, obviously

83

dying to know exactly which *Sentinel* staffer had been feeding her information.

Isabel thought for a moment before replying. If they believed she was a red-hot journalist with her finger on the pulse, so much the better. They were never going to hear she'd discovered the job was up for grabs thanks to her cousin's estate agent husband. Or that her gossiping skills were so non-existent the MD's secretary now knew her life history while she knew nothing about the other woman.

Isabel smiled archly at them and tapped the side of her nose with her forefinger. 'Trade secret, gentlemen,' she said.

Ted burst out laughing. 'You'll be well able for them all on Tuesday,' he said confidently.

Isabel kept smiling, the sort of fixed grin that would hurt if she kept it up much longer. Able for whom? It sounded ominous.

'You see,' Ted drained his port and looked impatiently around for the waiter, 'there were six applications for the job – and you were the only outsider, or non-*Sentinel* person, to apply. Nigel and I both feel that the paper needs new blood, someone to shake things up a bit. We don't want people getting too comfortable, you know,' he added.

'It's bad for a paper when the staff get complacent and that's what's been happening recently. Another couple of these,' he said loudly to the waiter, holding up his empty glass. 'So, in getting the job, Isabel, you've pulled the rug out from under quite a few people. But I expect you already know that?

'I can't wait to see their faces on Tuesday morning when we introduce you at the editorial conference!' He smiled maliciously. 'You'll put the cat among the pigeons, I can tell you, Isabel.'

He and Nigel laughed, sharing the same joke. Isabel
didn't know exactly what was amusing them so much,
but she was beginning to get an inkling. Five *Sentinel*
journalists had applied for the job and she'd got it – an
outsider. What was worse, Nigel wasn't going to give the
people who had applied unsuccessfully the chance to
get over their disappointment in private. In fact, it was
quite possible he wasn't even going to tell them they'd
been unsuccessful. Oh no, he was going to introduce
Isabel as the new women's editor in a blaze of glory on
Tuesday morning and then stand back and watch jaws
drop.

To the staff, she would look like Ted and Nigel's hired
hand, their stooge, someone to keep an eye on a staff
they clearly mistrusted. What the hell had she let
herself in for?

'I've changed my mind,' Isabel said to the waiter
who'd just brought over two more glasses of port. 'Can I
have another too?'

'Mum, you're brill!' shouted Naomi when she heard. A
slight, freckle-faced girl with her father's cool blue eyes
and hair the same rich brown colour as his, Naomi had
inherited David's sunny disposition – without his reckless, devil-may-care attitude.

She danced into the kitchen singing her favourite All
Saints' song until she reached the cooker and slid her
arms around her mother's waist. Isabel hugged her
younger daughter warmly.

Thank God for Naomi, she thought for the thou-
sandth time since the break-up.

'I'm glad *somebody* thinks so. Your sister barely spoke
to me this morning. She's still sulking about being told

she can't go to that overnight party on Friday. And your grandmother's in a mood because I told her not to interfere.'

'Don't mind them, Mum,' Naomi said indignantly. 'They're so childish.'

Isabel grinned wryly. Naomi was right – the other pair were far more trouble than this wise and kind young girl who wouldn't be a teenager for another two months.

'Robin will get over it. She wants to be angry with *someone*, that's all.'

'Oh, I know.' Isabel sighed. 'I just wish she didn't always have to be angry with *me*.'

She turned to stir the onions and chopped garlic she was sautéeing on the cooker. She was making real *Provençale* sauce for her special chicken dish to celebrate getting the job. If she let the onions and garlic burn, it would ruin the sauce. It was half-five and she was enjoying a few minutes alone with Naomi before her parents got back from their shopping trip into the city.

That was one of the things Isabel hated about living in this house: she never had any time alone with the girls. Not that Robin seemed to care these days. She spent hours with her friends, supposedly studying in their houses, although Isabel suspected that schoolwork was way down her elder daughter's list of priorities.

But it was lovely to be on her own with Naomi so they could chat the way they had at home in Oxford.

'When do you start?' asked her daughter, shrugging off the faded denim jacket she'd inherited from Robin. She perched on one of the kitchen chairs, long skinny legs folded under her.

'On Tuesday. I haven't actually seen the office I'll be working in because the editor didn't have time to show

me. The managing director's office, where I was interviewed, is on a different floor from the newsroom.'
Isabel didn't mention that showing her the office would have ruined Nigel's malicious plan to shock the other journalists by introducing her for the first time on Tuesday morning.

'Will you have your own office?' Naomi inquired.

'No. Well, I don't think so. Nobody mentioned it.'

Isabel added the tomatoes she'd chopped up and the mixture sizzled.

'Did you meet any of the other journalists?'

'No, I didn't, but . . .'

Isabel broke off as she heard the front door open. Her mother's carrying tones could be heard even in the kitchen.

'Thank the Lord we're home! I can't stand travelling on the DART. All that pushing and shoving, and horrible people with those Walkmans turned up so loud I get a headache from the hissing noises. And they won't give up a seat for anyone . . . I don't know what the world's coming to.'

Isabel and Naomi exchanged knowing looks. Their 'quiet time' was over. Naomi raced out of the kitchen.

'Hello, Granny. Did you have a nice time shopping?' she asked in an innocent voice as if she hadn't just heard her grandmother moaning a moment earlier. Isabel smiled as she bent over the steaming saucepan. The little minx!

'It wasn't too bad, pet.' Pamela, like most people, couldn't resist Naomi's cheery good nature. 'Where's your mother?'

'Cooking, Granny. She's been dying for you to come home so she's got someone to talk to. She gets bored talking to me.'

When her mother marched into the kitchen, Isabel was conveniently facing the other way, trying not to snigger out loud.

'Hello, Isabel. What *are* you cooking?' Her mother sniffed the air.

She felt her hackles rise.

There was something about the way her mother spoke to her that constantly reminded Isabel of her childhood. Even now, it was as if Pamela was speaking to a wayward twelve year old instead of a thirty-nine-year-old separated mother-of-two. Her mother was just so *bossy*. Isabel sometimes half-expected Pamela to order her to tidy her room and not to leave the house wearing make-up.

As the head of a high-powered corporation, she would have reigned supreme and won countless Businesswoman of the Year accolades. As a woman bored both with her family's company and running a home, she was positively shrewish.

Isabel stuck a forced smile on her face for what felt like the tenth time that day and turned around.

'Mother,' she acknowledged, 'buy anything nice?'

Her mother sighed heavily. She put her navy leather handbag on the table and went straight to the kettle, patting a few non-existent stray hairs into place.

'There's nothing but rubbish in the shops. I don't know why I bother. And your father couldn't keep up with me, kept saying he was out of breath and needed to sit down.' She sniffed. 'That's why we're so late. What is that you're cooking? It smells strange. I've some bacon and cabbage for tonight.'

Which nobody likes but you, Isabel muttered to herself.

'It's a French dish, Mother. Robin and Naomi love it

and, as we're celebrating tonight, I thought I'd cook it for them.'

'I hate to see good food going to waste,' her mother said crossly. 'You should have told me you were going to cook something else, Isabel. You just don't think, do you?'

Isabel ignored her and tasted the sauce from the wooden spoon, trying not to burn her mouth. It needed more basil, just a pinch. But it was still gorgeous. As the rich, garlicky aroma filled her nostrils, she could remember the last time she'd cooked it: Robin's birthday in February. David had given her a £50 voucher for Miss Selfridge and she'd been over the moon.

The four of them had eaten together, but Robin had finished quickly so she could phone her best friend and tell her that the wispy purple chiffon dress she'd admired for so long in Miss Selfridge window was no longer a daydream.

'I won't be long on the phone, I know you've got a birthday cake ready, Mum,' Robin had said, giving her mother a quick hug before she'd danced out of the room.

Isabel could barely remember the last time Robin had been so affectionate. That was what hurt the most about their relationship these days – the fact that Robin had always been a loving daughter before, the most affectionate kid you could imagine.

And now she was permanently sullen, never gave or looked for a hug, and was only even vaguely animated when she was angry. Which was often enough.

Isabel sighed. So much had changed.

'What are we celebrating?' demanded her mother. She refolded the tea towel Isabel had left scrunched up by the sink.

'I got the job on the *Sentinel*, Mother.'

'*Really?*'

'Yes, don't sound so shocked.' Isabel wrenched open the oven and took out the browned chicken pieces.

'I'm not shocked. I'm merely surprised you found out so soon. Didn't they have any other applicants?'

Don't lose your temper, Isabel. Stay calm.

'Of course they did but they've seen everyone else, Mother, and I was the one they wanted. I start on Tuesday and I'm thrilled.'

'Well done,' her father said abruptly.

Isabel hadn't even noticed him come into the kitchen. He usually stayed out of it, regarding it as his wife's territory and, therefore, giving it a wide berth.

'Thanks, Dad,' Isabel said warmly. Why couldn't her mother have said that?

'Here are your tablets, Pamela,' he said, handing his wife a pharmacist's bottle, 'for your headache.'

'I got a bottle of wine, Dad,' Isabel said. 'It's on the windowsill. Maybe you could open it and we could have a glass before dinner.' Or before I murder my bloody mother.

'I'll have a sherry, Harry,' her mother said with a meaningful sniff. 'You know I can't drink wine when I've got a headache. It makes migraine worse, as you know, Isabel,' she added pointedly.

All the more for me, she thought, and didn't mention the second bottle she'd bought. It might come in useful if the Mulhearn family dinner proved as tense as usual.

Her mother wasn't to be deflected by a glass of sherry, though.

'I hope it's not one of those contracts where they can fire you after six months? You should get a lawyer to look at it for you, Isabel, you're hopeless with things like that. You could ask that nice lawyer friend of Luke's, he's got his own firm now,' Pamela advised. 'I'm sure he wouldn't charge you too much under the circumstances. And I hope they're paying you a decent wage? After all, you're a deserted wife with two children . . .'

'Mother, I'm not a deserted wife. I'm separated. David didn't desert me, we split up. There's a difference, a *big* difference. And I'm not *hopeless with contracts*. How the hell do you think I held down two decent jobs in the UK? Because they all felt sorry for me?'

'Don't get on your high horse, Isabel.'

'I'm not.' But her hand shook as she slopped the tomato sauce over the chicken pieces. Calm down, she told herself. 'They'll be paying me a very good salary but it's nothing to do with my circumstances. Salaries don't work like that, Mother. Otherwise, there wouldn't be any *poor* people in the world.'

'Well, I don't know, Isabel. It's a pity you've got to support the children on your own now. Not that David was ever much of a breadwinner but at least he was a father and contributed *something*.' Pamela paused to sip her sherry. 'And it's not as if you're going to meet anyone else at your age, is it? I was talking to your Aunt Janet this morning and she said that Annette had split up with her latest man, which is no surprise to me. If you haven't got married by the time you're thirty-five, there's no hope for you.'

'Here.'

Her father shoved a very full glass of wine under Isabel's nose.

'Thanks, Dad.'

'Have a sip.' His eyes were warm with understanding.

To hell with a sip. Isabel took a good gulp and winced slightly. It wasn't the best wine she'd ever tasted. But

91

she was on such a tight budget that anything over a fiver was too expensive. David knew enough about wine to pick something good no matter what the price – a skill she'd never had. Well, she'd learn. She didn't need him any more.

'This will be ready in another half an hour,' she announced, determined not to be goaded into losing her temper. 'Mother, you have a rest this evening. Put your feet up and I'll lay the table. Naomi can help me.'

Pamela smiled for the first time. 'I *am* tired,' she said. 'I think I'll have a lie down then.'

'Great.'

As soon as she was alone, Isabel picked up the newspaper her father had left on the kitchen table and riffled through it until she found the property section. Big, small, indifferent, infested with vampire bats or painted acid yellow all over – she didn't care what sort of place she bought so long as she could get out of her mother's house.

Dinner was not a roaring success. For a start, Robin was half an hour late. The chicken was practically cremated by half-six, so Isabel had served it, mentally cursing her daughter for not turning up in time.

'I told you I'd netball practice this evening,' Robin said when she marched into the kitchen and met her mother's angry glare. Robin's ponytail still looked as silky and fresh as it had that morning after she'd hogged the hairdryer for thirty minutes. She didn't look as though she'd just spent an hour running around on the netball court. But Isabel decided not to say anything. She couldn't face another row.

Pamela was too busy pushing her chicken around her plate to comment. The look on her face said dried up chicken *Provençale* was not her idea of a proper meal. Certainly not in the bacon and cabbage league.

'Robin, it's your favourite,' Naomi said helpfully, pulling the chair beside her out for her sister.

Robin sank moodily on to it.

'I'm not hungry,' she announced.

'Mum got the job,' Naomi added.

'I was hoping you'd be pleased for me,' Isabel said drily.

Robin had the grace to look ashamed.

'That's great, Mum,' she said. 'Well done.'

Isabel smiled, got up and put a small portion of chicken and baked potatoes on a plate for Robin. Robin gave the chicken the same sort of glance her grandmother had given it.

'I made chicken *Provençale*, specially for you, love,' Isabel said. 'Not that it resembles anything *Provençale* any more, it's so dried up.'

'I can't believe you did this,' said Robin in a strange, high voice. 'This is Daddy's favourite. You *know* the last time we had this – on my birthday. How *could* you?'

She pushed the plate away from her, scraping her chair on the floor in her haste, and ran out of the kitchen sobbing.

'Don't mind her.' Isabel felt her father's hand on her sleeve as the tears threatened to fall. 'You know what young girls are like. I remember you at that age.' He patted his daughter's sleeve. 'You were an awful handful.'

'Disgraceful, that's what it is,' Pamela snorted, and took the opportunity to push her untouched dinner away from her. 'You've ruined that girl. Mark my words, you'll have nothing but trouble with her. Wayward, that's what she is . . .'

'Give it a rest, Pamela!'

The sound of Harry Mulhearn's raised voice gave them all a shock. Isabel couldn't remember the last time she'd heard her father speak angrily.

'She's just a confused young girl. She can do without your interference, Pamela. Leave Isabel to rear her family on her own.'

Enraged, Isabel's mother launched another attack. 'I won't have that kind of behaviour here. I open my home to Isabel and the girls and look what I have to put up with. That child is a disruptive influence. She's rude, she's inconsiderate, and I don't know why I put up with it.'

Isabel remained standing and put her head in her hands. She wanted to block out all the shouting and yelling forever. She wanted to climb into bed, pull the duvet over her head and wake up to find it had all been a horrible dream, a nightmare.

She'd come to in her comfortable bed in The Gables, with the light streaming in through the pale green-sprigged curtains and the scent of her rambling rose drifting in from the open window. Robin would be singing along to the radio in her bedroom as she carefully applied the little bit of eye-shadow allowed in school, Naomi would be trying to stay in bed for a few minutes longer, and David would have just come into the bedroom with a steaming cup of tea for Isabel . . .

No, that wasn't a dream – that was a fantasy. David had never got up to make her a cup of tea in their entire married life. *She* had to make the tea for him, never the other way round.

Her mother was still muttering, but she was doing it quietly.

'Mum, are you OK?' Naomi stood beside Isabel, her eyes wet.

'I'm fine. Fine, darling.' Isabel put an arm around the trembling child. This wasn't fair on poor Naomi. Whatever happened, she just had to get out of this house.

It was bad enough coping with Robin on neutral ground, but in the explosive atmosphere of her parents' house, it was impossible.

'Everything's going to be fine, Naomi,' she said, resting her cheek on the top of her daughter's head. 'I promise. This weekend, we'll go house hunting,' she whispered. 'It'll be our secret, yours and mine. All right?'

CHAPTER FIVE

Dee swung into the *Sentinel* car park at high speed and drove to the parking spot near the front door which she usually occupied if she was in early enough. A rather battered, British-registered green Volkswagen she didn't recognise was parked there. Blast! It was raining heavily. The only other spot left was the one in front of the security hut which was as far away from the entrance as you could get. She'd be drowned in the torrential downpour before she reached cover. And, naturally, she didn't have an umbrella or a raincoat with her.

'The wet look really suits you,' said one of the photographers moments later as Dee stood in reception and shook the rain off her hair.

'Ha, bloody ha,' she retorted as she ducked into the ladies to see how frizzy her hair was. It didn't matter how much non-frizz serum she sloshed on – all it took was a bit of rain and her carefully styled hair was like a pile of dirty brown straw.

She was rummaging through her bulging handbag for a brush and her small can of hairspray when a loo flushed and a tall slim blonde came out of one of the cubicles. Taller than Dee and around three stone thinner, the woman was very pretty with a delicate, fine-boned face, large blue eyes and a cupid's bow mouth that was curved into a shy smile.

'Hello,' she said. She turned nervously towards the mirror and carefully washed her hands. Married, Dee observed, noticing the slim gold wedding band and antique diamond ring. And definitely well-off. That beige trouser suit hadn't cost less than £300 and the cream suede handbag and matching pumps were hardly chain store stuff either. What's more, *her* hair hadn't been ruined in the rain. Dee fluffed her own mop resentfully as she eyed the other woman's blonde wavy hair – not a strand out of place.

'Awful weather, isn't it?' the stranger said hesitantly with another shy smile.

'Yeah,' Dee agreed. And wondered why anyone stylish, elegant-looking and so *slim* could be lacking in confidence.

'Trust me to forget my bloody umbrella,' she said, to put the other woman at her ease. Maybe she was one of the interviewees for the advertising secretary's job, Dee thought. Poor dear, she looked far too reserved and quiet to cope with the banter and ribald jokes in that department. The blonde woman took out a lipliner and shakily outlined her lips with a pale pink the same colour as her nails. God, she was nervous.

Dee decided to do her good deed for the day. 'That's a lovely suit,' she said kindly. 'Where did you get it?'

'Thanks.' When she smiled, the blonde woman's face lit up. 'I got it in a sale in this little boutique in Oxford about two years ago. It's my favourite shop . . . well, it *was*. I moved home a couple of months ago and I doubt if I'll be going back,' she added sadly.

'Oh,' Dee said, aware that she'd somehow said the wrong thing. 'Well, it's lovely. I'm always on the look out for nice suits for work but I keep buying boring black ones, like this.' She laughed, indicating the fitted black velvet jacket and matching mini skirt she wore with a cream lacy T-shirt. She'd felt so enormous when she'd looked in the mirror that morning that she'd decided to dress so outrageously over the top that nobody would notice how fat she was. Her make-up was expertly applied, she'd worn her favourite dangly jet earrings and, with spindly suede mules accentuating her black-clad legs in the mini skirt, she hoped she'd achieved the desired effect.

'Black suits you,' the other woman protested. 'Your hair is so vibrant you can get away with it. It just makes me look washed-out.'

'Thanks,' said Dee, thrilled at the compliment. Vibrant, huh? Gary had been too grumpy and too interested in the paper over breakfast to notice what she'd been wearing or what she'd looked like, which was nothing new.

She sighed. Maybe they needed a weekend away, somewhere secluded and romantic. That was it. She'd get some holiday brochures later and they could pick where to go tonight.

''Bye.' The blonde woman smiled shyly.

'See you,' Dee replied. 'Oh, and good luck.'

Isabel was still smiling when she walked along the corridor to Ted Holt's office. What was she worrying about? That woman in the loo had been so kind and friendly, exactly the opposite of what she'd been expecting.

Isabel was almost certain she was Dee O'Reilly because she'd seen Dee's picture byline in the paper the day before. The photograph didn't do her justice. Dee was much better-looking in real life, no black and white picture could do justice to her stunning colouring. She was incredibly attractive with creamy pale skin, a smattering of tawny freckles and big, dark eyes. And she had the most amazing hair. Isabel would have killed for those lustrous, chestnut corkscrew curls. Dee was certainly a big girl but she could carry it off. She had a wonderful sense of style, was very sexy and obviously bursting with self-confidence. What a pity all bigger women weren't as assured, Isabel thought. *Of course!* What a great idea for her first fashion spread – clothes for women over size sixteen.

Pleased that she'd added another idea to her list, Isabel stopped for a moment before going into Ted's secretary's office. With a look around to make sure nobody could see her, she hoisted up her bra straps and boobs with one quick movement. There. She was never going to be Dolly Parton, but a padded, plunge bra certainly helped in that department.

She hoped the bronzing powder she'd brushed on liberally didn't come off on her jacket.

Ted and Nigel were waiting for her. Nigel had abandoned the smart suit and tie he'd worn at the interview for an open-necked shirt in a bilious green, and black, slightly shiny trousers.

At least Ted was well dressed in a grey pinstripe suit even if he was openly eyeing her up through his piggy little eyes.

'Ready?' asked Nigel. He reached into his shirt pocket, took out a cigarette and lit it in one practised movement.

'Yes,' Isabel answered. 'I'm ready.' Almost. It was a long time since she'd been in a daily newspaper office. The noise and bustle hit her as soon as Nigel pushed open the big door and showed her into a massive room that took up an entire floor of the building. It was buzzing with activity. People were talking on phones, sitting at desks scanning the day's newspapers and writing furiously on screens.

Two televisions droned in the background, one turned to the teletext service, the other to CNN, while raucous laughter came from a little group at the far end of the room. From the door, Isabel could barely make them out.

A couple of people turned and looked at the three of them, staring curiously at Isabel for a moment. But no one else took any notice. They were too busy following up stories or talking animatedly on the phone. She could feel her legs trembling. It had been so long since she'd worked in a daily newspaper, so long since she'd been a part of that frantic world where everyone's lives depended on getting the story before the deadline.

To judge by the number of desks, at least sixty people worked in this office alone. No, probably more. God knew how many worked in the rest of the place. It didn't look like the sort of office where you'd make firm friends for the rest of your life. Unlike her last permanent job, where, in the tiny magazine office, they'd all lived in each other's pockets.

'The newsroom is the hub of the place,' Nigel explained. 'We don't have lots of different journalistic departments on different floors here. I like to keep an eye on things, so everyone is based here – the sports department, features, you name it, it's all here, right in front of me. Apart from the photographic department, which is in the basement. This is my office,' he added, as he opened a door into a very untidy room, dominated by a big desk. The walls were stained brown with nicotine and the air was stale with the smell of old cigarette smoke. Newspapers were stacked higgledy-piggledy on the floor, on a coffee table and on the low, grey couch against one wall.

Yellow post-its with phone numbers scrawled on them littered the desk, along with curled up sheets of fax paper and several uncapped biros.

'Have a seat.' Nigel sank into the chair behind his desk.

Isabel cleared a section of the couch and sat down nervously. Be calm, she told herself fiercely. You've just earned yourself a great job, don't panic now. Think of Robin and Naomi – you're doing it for them, too. You've got to get a place of your own for the girls.

Nigel riffled through the heap of paper beside the phone. His face darkened.

'Jesus, look at this,' he said angrily, holding up a sheet of fax paper. 'The lawyers say we haven't a hope in hell of getting away with an apology for a fraud story where we named the wrong effing person. I'm going to kill that stupid reporter for putting an extra initial in the man's name. Smyth P. Mitchell became Smyth P.J. Mitchell,' he explained to Isabel, 'and Smyth P.J. wasn't very pleased to see his name wrongly splashed over our front page last week.

'The lawyers say we're going to have our asses sued,' he added to Ted.

Ted sat down heavily. 'I thought you'd talked about this to Mahon?'

'The news editor,' interjected Nigel for Isabel's benefit.

'The soon-to-be-*ex* news editor if he keeps this up,' snarled Ted. 'Next time we get sued, he can bloody well pay the damages himself. That might make him a bit more careful about checking stories for libel. We can't afford another big case, not now.'

'Nigel,' said a female voice on the editor's phone intercom, 'I've got a call for you on line one.'

'Can't you take a number? I'm busy,' he snapped.

'It's Simon Walsh. He says it's urgent.'

'I'm in a meeting.'

'He wants an answer now, Nigel.'

'I'll call him back at twelve, right?'

'Fine.'

'Stupid bitch never knows when to interrupt me and when not to,' he said testily.

What a charmer. Isabel fought to keep a neutral expression on her face.

She'd only been on the premises ten minutes and the editor and managing director had already slagged off two members of staff in her presence. Nigel handed both Ted and Isabel a stapled sheaf of pages.

'This is a list of the subjects we'll be covering at the editorial meeting,' he said. 'I'll get everyone into the conference room. You two can make your grand entrance in half an hour when we're nearly finished.' He grinned maliciously. 'Let's ruffle some feathers!'

Isabel didn't even bother to smile as he left. She flicked through her pages but she couldn't read them, could barely focus at all. This was going to be a nightmare, she knew it. A meeting that would include the five furious journalists who'd wanted the job she'd just got.

She could have coped with that but she was beginning to think that the *only* reason she'd been brought in was to do just what Nigel had said – to ruffle their feathers. Or, worse, to completely undermine them.

'I'm going to talk to Nigel today. Antonia's only doing

the rest of this week as women's editor and we need a replacement, which, hopefully, will be me. What do you think?' Dee perched on the edge of Maeve's desk and looked at her friend anxiously. 'I'm going berserk wondering what he's thinking. If he hasn't mentioned the job to me so far, do you think that's a bad sign?'

Maeve keyed in another command on her word processor before swivelling her chair around.

Today, she wore a sloppy deep red jumper and matching lipstick, neither of which did a hell of a lot for her pale skin and short, dyed burgundy hair. Sometimes Dee longed to take her friend aside and give her a complete makeover, starting with throwing out all of Maeve's rather eccentric wardrobe. But she wouldn't have hurt Maeve for the world and to point out that her dress and colour sense were non-existent would have been very hurtful indeed. She'd just have to keep buying Maeve jumpers and shirts in the pale, subtle colours that suited her for Christmas and birthdays and hope that she might suddenly realise what looked good on her.

'With Nigel, *everything* is a bad sign, whether he's mentioned the job to you or not,' Maeve remarked. 'He loves to play games, Dee, you know that. Making you wait while he figures out who to give Antonia's job is just another of his little tricks.'

She reached into a drawer for a packet of Silk Cut and a lighter. 'Right now, I bet you a tenner he's working out exactly *who* he can give the job to in order to irritate the maximum number of people.'

Dee sighed. Maeve was probably right. Nigel made Machiavelli look like a boy scout leader. Stabbing people in the back was his forte.

Maeve got up. 'C'mon, I need a cigarette before the editorial meeting.'

Smoking was banned in the building but the diehard smokers like Maeve still smoked in the loos and, if they could get away with it, in the long corridor outside the conference room.

They stood there beside an open window while Maeve smoked and Dee fretted. Blast Nigel. Why the hell couldn't he tell her whether he was considering her for Antonia's job? All this waiting would give her an ulcer. It was *days* since she'd sent in her application. How long did it take to compile a list of suitable candidates – a month?

Nigel sauntered down the corridor whistling, a folder under his arm. He looked positively jaunty. 'Hello, girls,' he said with a nod, before going into the conference room.

Girls! Dee hated it when he said that. They were women. Not girls. What bloody age did he think girls became women – fifty?

'He looks very pleased with himself,' muttered Maeve out of the side of her mouth.

She was right. Nigel did look happy. And what did he have to be happy about? Dee wondered. She was still wondering five minutes later when the editor finished lacerating both Mahon and Henry, the unfortunate reporter who'd added an extra initial to the defendant's name in the fraud story.

Dee shifted in her chair and for the second time rearranged her notebook and pen on top of the conference table. She resisted the impulse to doodle on her notebook because Nigel took a particularly dim view of people not paying one hundred percent attention to what he was saying – or shouting, as the case may be.

Doodling was a sure sign of not paying attention and

could get you sent off to do some horrible rats-in-the-neighbourhood story which would involve hanging around a housing estate all day while each and every resident complained about the rat invasion and the lack of council help in getting rid of them. Photographers who got on the wrong side of Nigel also got rat duty but they had to hang around and try to get a *picture* of a rat, which was even worse. One reporter insisted he knew a photographer who kept a dead rat in his freezer for that sole purpose.

The editor finished bawling out poor Henry and smiled slowly. Dee shifted uneasily in her seat. Expenses – that had to be it. Everyone's expenses claims were too high and they were all going to get a telling off. Nigel loved telling people off.

But he didn't say anything about expenses. He worked his way down the news list, in his usual bullying way. Everyone and their granny was told they were incompetent, useless and destined for the high jump if they didn't get some decent stories that could be printed without libelling too many people. In other words, it was business as usual.

The only strange thing was that neither Nigel, nor the news editor, assigned Dee any stories. She couldn't figure out why. And then a glimmer of hope came to her.

Maybe Nigel was going to appoint her women's editor after all! That's why he hasn't given me anything new to work on, she thought joyfully. They've finally recognised what I can do, after six years!

She desperately wanted to blurt it out to Maeve but thought she'd better wait. She could be wrong after all. Nevertheless Dee sat through the rest of the meeting in a state of complete and utter joy.

She could see herself telling Gary. He'd always hated her working in news because the hours could be so anti-social. Now he'd be thrilled. And to think of telling her parents that the first member of the O'Reilly family to go to college, had been given a top job at the age of thirty-two! Dee remembered how delighted mum and dad had been when she'd got her first full-time job in journalism. They'd been so happy and proud. Wait till they heard she was women's editor.

When the meeting ended, Nigel didn't dismiss the assembled journalists with his usual: 'Scram! You won't get stories sitting on your backsides.' Instead, he left his place at the top of the table and opened the conference-room door to usher in the managing director and the tall blonde woman Dee had met in the ladies a little earlier.

The woman smiled uneasily at the thirty people who sat around the polished table and quickly sat down in the chair beside Nigel's.

'He's either going to tell us that circulation is up – which is why Holt is here – or he'll explain that they've got to economise by reneging on the last pay scale deal and the blonde is the accountant with the figures to back it up,' Maeve whispered.

Belinda, the gossip columnist, who'd just bought an horrendously expensive new house, groaned at the remark.

'Doesn't look like an accountant to me,' said the sports editor, Tony, appreciatively. 'If she *is* an accountant, I think I definitely need to hire one!'

'Me too,' added one of the news team.

'I bet she's a time-and-motion spy sent to see how long it takes us to write stories in between making cups of coffee. And you boys don't need accountants,' whispered Dee, who was so happy she couldn't care less what bad news the accountant or time-and-motion woman was ready to impart.

'Anyway, *I* can do your accounts, boys,' she added with a laugh. 'I'll show you: you spend all your money in the pub. QED. That'll be two hundred quid and I expect the cheque in the next post.'

'Hilarious, Dee. Can you do mine too . . .'

'Shush!' hissed someone.

Everyone shushed. The news editor, sitting near the top of the table, fiddled with his tie and looked anxious. So he bloody should, Dee thought. If he wasn't pushing all the reporters to track down six or seven news stories every day, Henry wouldn't have made such a stupid mistake in the fraud story. He was simply overworked, like everyone else on the news team. That was how costly errors were made.

'Good morning,' said Ted Holt loudly. He gazed smugly around the table like Solomon about to impart a pearl of wisdom. 'I'm sorry to barge in on your editorial meeting but there's someone I'd like you to meet.'

Maeve and Dee exchanged brief glances.

'Accountant,' mouthed Maeve.

'Time-and-motion expert,' whispered Dee.

'As you all know . . .' intoned Ted gravely.

Dee raised her eyes to heaven. They'd be here all day if Holt started one of his sermons.

'. . . a valued member of staff is leaving the *Sentinel* for pastures new and she'll be sorely missed.'

Dee stared at the managing director in shock. What was this? Ted was hardly about to arrange a party for Antonia. In his mind, once a member of staff left the paper, they were useless to him and, therefore, not worth the time or the money a leaving party demanded. No, that wasn't it.

The only other possibility was that he was announcing Antonia's replacement. He couldn't be doing that, could he?

'But we're not the sort of paper to let the grass grow under our feet, so today I'm introducing you to . . .'

Omigod, he *was*!

'Isabel Farrell, our new women's editor.' He gestured to the woman sitting beside him. 'Stand up and say hello, Isabel.'

Isabel rose to her feet slowly. This wasn't the time for nervousness, not any more. She had the job and that was that. There was no going back and definitely no hope of the earth swallowing her before the five disgruntled would-be women's editors got their talons into her. It was up to her to make the first move.

As she stared at the curious faces who must be wondering where she'd come from and whether she was a management stooge or not, Isabel felt a surge of courage.

She could do the job, she was sure of it. She was a damn' good sub, a good writer and had always enjoyed great relationships with the people who worked under her. Her head was buzzing with ideas to freshen up the women's section. All she needed was the self-confidence to do it. She took a deep breath and told herself to keep it simple.

'I'm delighted to meet you all,' she said, pitching her voice a fraction lower to hide her nervousness. 'I'm sure you're wondering where I've come from and why you don't know me, but I've been living in the UK for the past ten years where I've worked almost exclusively in women's magazines, always at management level. I was deputy editor of *Today's Woman* for five years.'

She paused and, out of the corner of her eye, saw a

flash of chestnut curls that made her notice Dee O'Reilly. A very thin woman with almost purple hair sitting beside Dee was speaking softly to her. Neither woman was looking at Isabel.

Dee was a dedicated news reporter, Isabel knew. The appointment of the new women's editor was probably of no interest to her. Lots of news reporters thought that their part of the paper was by far the most important; the features and women's sections trailed behind miserably in their opinion. Isabel pushed on with the little speech she'd been rehearsing all weekend.

'I've come back to Ireland for good and I can't tell you how pleased I am to be joining such an excellent paper and such a great team of journalists. It may take me some time to get to know you all.' She smiled warmly around the table. 'But I'm confident that I'll settle in pretty quickly and I'm sure we're going to work very well together.'

She gave them another smile and sat down, her heart belting along like a racehorse heading for Becher's Brook. Thank God that was over. The job would be a cinch compared to addressing a crowd of people she didn't know.

'Well done!' cried Nigel. He got up and patted her on the back. 'As you can see, folks, Isabel is going to be a great addition to our team. I'll bring her around and introduce her to you all later. But first, a toast to our new women's editor!'

Dee sat stunned as Nigel's secretary, Sheila, unceremoniously plonked a tower of plastic cups and four bottles of sparkling wine on the table.

'We won't get drunk on that,' muttered a voice. 'Four lousy bottles! What cheapskates.'

When everyone had at least half an inch of wine sloshing around in the bottom of their plastic cup, Nigel shouted 'Cheers!' enthusiastically.

'Bastard,' Dee said fiercely to Maeve. 'He's such a bastard. He could at least have told us. He could have shown us that courtesy. I mean,' she added, her face pink with rage, 'I spoke to that bloody woman in the loo earlier. I was *nice* to her, for Christ's sake! And I guarantee she knew exactly who I was.'

Dee pushed back her chair savagely and stood up, flinging back a strand of hair that had swung over her face. 'I bet Nigel told her exactly who applied for the job, so she knows who she's swiped it from. Well, if she thinks she's going to lord it over me, she's deeply mistaken. I'll never ever talk to that bitch!'

'Dee,' cautioned Maeve, 'calm down, will you?' She grabbed her friend's arm. 'Don't give him the satisfaction of seeing you're angry. That's what he wants.'

'Well, if that's going to please him, I'm going to make him very bloody happy today,' Dee hissed. She grabbed her notebook and marched out of the room, hair swinging behind her.

All she wanted was to sit quietly somewhere before she broke down and sobbed.

Dear Annie,
    I've been passed over for a job I was sure I'd get and now I'm devastated and hurt. I don't know how I can face anyone in my office, or the person who got the job. I was convinced I'd get it and, now that I haven't, I feel like a balloon that's had all the air let out. What do you advise me to do?

Surrounded by people at the top of the conference

111

table, Isabel didn't notice Dee's rapid departure. People were being really nice to her, she realised, after ten minutes of being introduced to various reporters, subs and photographers. Even the sports editor seemed pleased to see her.

'Tony Winston,' he said in a suave voice. He stretched out one tanned hand and held hers for longer than was strictly necessary as he gazed down her cleavage.

Latin-looking and dressed in a bright pink polo shirt to show off his tan, he was incredibly handsome and knew it. 'We must go out to lunch,' he added, giving her the benefit of a salacious grin.

'Hello, I'm Maeve Lynch.' Isabel looked up to see that the woman who'd been sitting beside Dee O'Reilly was staring at her intently. *She* didn't look too pleased. Maybe she'd applied for the job.

'Nice to meet you, Maeve,' said Isabel.

'Maeve's the sub-editor who works on Antonia's . . . well, *your* pages,' explained Nigel's secretary who had taken a shine to Isabel and was introducing people to her. Yes, if Maeve had worked on Antonia's pages she had almost certainly applied for the job.

'Oh, I'm looking forward to working with you,' Isabel said with a smile. Maeve must hate my guts, she thought silently. That's all I need – a sub-editor who absolutely loathes me. She'd better try the friendly approach. Maeve was friends with Dee, she'd try that angle.

Isabel looked over Maeve's shoulder inquiringly. 'I saw Dee O'Reilly with you – I spoke to her earlier in the loo. Is she still here?'

'Er . . . no, she had to leave in a hurry,' Maeve improvised.

'Pity. I'd really like to meet her properly,' Isabel said earnestly.

'You will, Isabel,' interrupted Nigel smoothly. 'Come on, I'll show you your desk. Sheila, will you find Dee and tell her I want to talk to her in my office in,' he looked at his watch, 'fifteen minutes?'

Maeve checked the newsroom, saw that Dee wasn't at her desk and then ran down the back stairs as fast as she could. She found her friend around the back of the printing works, smoking a cigarette as she paced up and down miserably.

'I can't believe you're smoking!' exclaimed Maeve.

Dee turned reddened eyes towards her friend. 'At times like this, I wonder why I never started,' she murmured. 'Although Camel are too strong. I got this from the security guard. They're supposed to relax you.' She took another deep drag and then tossed the cigarette away. 'Gimme one of yours. They're milder.'

'I'll give you one and then never ask me again. Only yesterday you were giving out stink to me for not stopping smoking,' Maeve remarked as she proferred a Silk Cut.

'Yesterday was different,' snuffled Dee. 'Yesterday I thought I had a great job and a chance of promotion. Today, I'm a has-been.'

'Don't be daft,' said Maeve, lighting up. 'Think of this as a minor glitch in your plans. You can still get promotion.'

'Not to the job I really want, though,' protested Dee angrily. 'I want to be women's editor or features editor, and unless that Isabel bitch or poor Phil Walsh drops dead tomorrow, there's no hope of me getting *their* jobs, is there?' She paced some more.

'No,' admitted Maeve. 'Come on in, Dee, it's starting to rain and you're going to get drenched.'

Dee could feel tears in her eyes again. Damn. Why

the hell was she so emotional? Why couldn't she be one of those women who never cried, no matter what happened? She sobbed at everything from *Gone With The Wind* to TV shows where abandoned guinea pigs were given loving new homes. And now she'd have red eyes. Everyone in the office would know she'd been upset and would also know why. How horribly humiliating.

She gingerly wiped away the tears under her eyelashes, hoping not to smudge her mascara.

'Do I look awful?' she asked Maeve. 'I do, don't I?' she answered without giving her friend a chance to reply. 'Will you do me a favour? I can't go back looking like this, so will you discreetly grab my handbag and I'll go to the pub for a coffee until I look normal, which could take some time.'

She'd love a big gin and tonic to calm her nerves, but that would be fatal. There was no such thing as one drink in Magee's Lounge. One led to two, then three, and before you knew it, it was closing time and one of your less drunk colleagues was grinning at you smugly, making you wonder exactly whom you'd insulted or, worse still, what dark secret you'd inadvertently revealed.

'Bad news, kiddo,' Maeve said. 'Nigel's looking for you. He wants you in his office pronto. That's why I came looking for you – I didn't want Drill Sergeant Smyth to find you first.'

'Shit! Give me another fag.'

'What are you like?' demanded Maeve. 'One minute you're Ms-Anti-Smoking, the next you're Dennis Leary. Are you sure you don't want a cigar?'

It worked. Dee couldn't resist laughing.

'If Demi Moore and Sharon Stone can smoke cigars, I

can too. Maybe piggy Ted Holt will graciously give me one of his Romeo y Julietas to make up for not giving me the job.'

'Somehow I doubt it,' said Maeve. 'You only get one of those if you do some serious sucking up, which is why Nigel always has one stuffed in his mouth.'

'Maybe I *should* have done a bit of sucking up.' Dee took a long drag of her cigarette. 'At least then I'd have got the job I wanted. And I bet that's why Ms Prim, Butter-Wouldn't-Melt women's editor got it. She's probably an expert sycophant.

'You wait, Maeve,' Dee said bitterly, 'she won't be in the place five minutes before she's going up and down, to and from Holt's office like a bloody yo-yo spilling the beans on all of us. She *could* be having a fling with him. They're probably having a torrid groping session in Nigel's office right now. I can see it all – Nigel standing outside like a good little yes-man, telling them when someone's coming . . .'

At that precise moment, Isabel was admiring her new desk which was opposite the features editor's. Sheila explained that Antonia had moved her stuff out of the office and was working from home during her last week with the *Sentinel*. But she was coming in on Wednesday to fill Isabel in on who did what on the women's pages, apparently. She'd also give her a list of contact numbers for everyone from fashion PRs to battered wives' shelters. As Isabel hadn't worked in journalism in Ireland for ten years, her Irish contacts were nil, so she really needed Antonia's help.

'Nice to meet you,' said Phil Walsh, the phone clamped between her jaw and shoulder. 'Welcome to the mad house.'

115

'It doesn't look too mad to me,' Isabel said with a grin.

'Oh, don't mind me,' said Phil, 'I've been here years and I'm jaundiced. Ten years of Nigel Burke would drive anyone insane. Yes,' she said into the phone, 'I've been holding for five minutes and I'm sick of "Greensleeves".'

Isabel examined her surroundings with pleasure. The people in the middle of the room had to make do with an open-plan office, but she and Phil had a mini 'office' by the windows all to themselves, neatly separated from the rest of the room by grey partitions. Their little dogbox was totally private and very cosy. Phil was clearly into horses and children in a big way. Half of her section of the office was decorated with pictures of a huge brown horse with various rosettes pinned to its bridle. The other half was crowded with pictures of four smiling teenagers, nearly all in jodhpurs, clinging to one horse or another.

Antonia's side was bare. Isabel thought it looked nicer without too much clutter. Pictures of Naomi and Robin on her desk and a calendar on the wall, she decided. That was all she needed.

The view from the second-floor window wasn't exactly inspiring, it looked out on to the car park. But Isabel didn't care. She loved being able to see out of a window, even if the view was only of rows of dusty cars, a couple of motorbikes and a skip.

She had brought a few things from home – the large yellow spotted ceramic mug she'd always used as a pen holder, the Rolodex with all her now-useless phone numbers on it, and the cactus Naomi and Robin had given her that morning.

'Is this a not-so-subtle hint that I'm prickly these days?' she'd joked when she'd opened the carefully wrapped parcel.

116

'No,' giggled Naomi. 'You got it because it was the only thing we could buy yesterday. The big flower pots were too dear and Robin said you'd like this.'

'Thank you both so much.' Isabel had hugged her daughters, happier with her odd-shaped little present than she would have been with a diamond necklace. The fact that Robin had bothered to buy her anything at all for her first day at work had meant a lot. She tried the cactus on each side of her computer to see which way looked better. On the left.

At least she knew how to work the computer. It was the same as the ones in *Motor 2000*. Poor Richie Devine, she thought, remembering her previous boss.

'I was going to make you permanent,' he'd raged when she'd told him she was leaving.

'Really?' Isabel said mildly. 'Then you should have told me, Richie, and I wouldn't have bothered applying for other jobs.' She still felt a bit mean about leaving him in the lurch but he'd get over it.

'I thought I'd bring you some stationery,' said Sheila. She struggled into Isabel's little cubbyhole with a load of notebooks, A4 pads, boxes of pens and a stapler.

'I'll order you some business cards once you've decided which ones you want. You and Phil share a secretary but she's out this week. I'll do any typing you need.'

'Thanks,' Isabel said, bemused by the other woman's attentiveness.

Phil hung up the phone. 'I don't know what you've done to deserve that,' she said as Sheila left, having made Isabel promise to call her if she needed *anything*. 'She rarely bothers with the rest of us.'

'What's her name again?' asked Isabel.

'Sheila Smyth, or Drill Sergeant Smyth, depending on how well she treats you. And I should point out that she's Drill Sergeant Smyth to everyone else except her boss and Ted Holt. Which means you are privileged to have her being nice to you.'

'Is it good or bad having her like you?'

'Scary. She only likes you if you're flavour of the month. So if they're going to fire you, you'll have advance warning. Sheila will start treating you like dirt as soon as she finds out. Which will be before you, I might add.' Phil grinned.

'Charming.' Isabel liked Phil who was straightforward at least.

She obviously wasn't interested in making a fashion statement. She was around fifty, rotund, and wore a man's grey cotton cardigan over a navy T-shirt and jeans so old and worn they were almost white. She wore her long, dark hair tied back in a neat ponytail and obviously never bothered with make-up.

Shrewd grey eyes examined Isabel from behind wire-rimmed glasses.

Isabel wondered if she dare ask Phil which of the other members of staff had applied to be women's editor. But she wasn't sure if it was too soon to ask. After all, Phil hardly knew her.

Her phone rang. It was Nigel, all charm and politeness.

'Isabel, dear, could you pop up to my office for a few minutes? There's someone I want you to meet.'

'Of course.' Did he call all the women 'dear'? she wondered.

Nigel didn't want to talk about Isabel's ideas for the paper, even though she'd brought the carefully typed up sheets she'd been working on all weekend. He wasn't interested in new ideas. He wanted to talk about appointing a deputy women's editor.

'We've never had a deputy women's ed before,' he said, twiddling a biro in one hand. 'But I think we need one now. The paper's getting bigger and there are more freelances than ever working for us, so it's a good idea to have someone else to help you with the day-to-day running of your section.'

Isabel nodded, wondering where all this was leading. He was the boss and she was the new employee. If Nigel wanted to appoint a lobotomised gorilla to the position of deputy women's editor, there wasn't a damn' thing she could do about it.

'You and features share a lot of the same writers and you'll have to liaise with Phil Walsh to make sure you don't overlap. Another helping hand would be useful. Don't you think that's a good idea?' he asked.

'Sure,' Isabel replied. 'I'd appreciate some help, especially until I settle in. Who were you thinking of appointing?'

A sharp rap at the door stopped Nigel from answering.

'Come in,' he yelled.

Dee stepped into the room. She didn't see Isabel seated on the couch nearest the door.

'You wanted to talk to me, Nigel,' she said shortly.

'Yes, Dee.' He smiled. 'I want you to meet Isabel Farrell, the new women's editor.'

Dee wheeled around rapidly.

'Hello.' Isabel stood up and reached out her hand.

'Hello,' Dee said coolly. There was no 'Welcome to the *Sentinel*' or anything like that.

'I wanted you girls to meet because you'll be working

very closely with each other in future,' Nigel said. 'Dee has been interested in moving out of hard news and into features for a long time, and I know she really wants to work in the women's section. That's why I've come up with a plan that should please both of you – I'm appointing her as deputy women's ed.'

Silence. Isabel watched Dee's pale face flare into a vivid pink. Oh, God, what the hell was going on here?

'Don't you think that's a good idea, Isabel?' asked Nigel silkily. 'Dee is a very experienced news reporter and a good writer.'

'It's a great idea if she wants the job,' Isabel said evenly. She couldn't think why the other woman looked so angry unless Nigel was pushing her out of news reporting for some reason.

'Dee *is* very interested in this area of the paper, and in fact she's wanted to get out of news for some time now.' Nigel paused to take a sip of coffee. 'I know you'd set your sights somewhat higher, Dee, but I think we need someone with Isabel's experience in the top job and as there are no openings in features, I figured you'd like working with her . . .'

So *that* was it, Isabel realised. Dee *had* applied for her job and now Nigel was offering her second prize as a sop. How awful. And what a pig he was.

Couldn't he see how insulting this was to Dee, to offer her a lesser job in front of the very woman who'd won what she wanted?

Dee still hadn't said anything.

Isabel got up.

'I'll leave you two to talk,' she said. 'I'd love to have you as my deputy, Dee,' she added, 'if you're interested?'

Outside the editor's office, Isabel leant against the wall tiredly. She'd won the job of her dreams but she'd jumped out of the frying pan and right into the fire. A fire hot enough to melt gold, at that.

Still, there was no point brooding. She had a lot of work to do and there was nobody to rely on but herself. The usual story, Isabel though wryly.

CHAPTER SIX

Maeve had just poured the last drop of slimline tonic into Dee's glass when she grabbed it. She took a couple of huge gulps and coughed as the power of a double gin hit the back of her throat.

'You all right?' asked Maeve.

'Fine.' Dee settled back into her seat at the bar. 'Can I have two bags of cheese and onion crisps, please?' she asked the barman.

It was just after five and the roomy, mock-rustic bar in Magee's was empty. The after-work rush wouldn't happen for another hour when the second shift at the *Sentinel* – Magee's best customers – left work. The barman was taking what he felt was a well-deserved rest before the thirsty hordes arrived, demanding beer and whiskey chasers, toasted cheese sandwiches and the odd bottle of champagne if a major story had worked out.

Dee handed Maeve one of the bags, ripped open the other morosely and ate as if she hadn't had anything for a month. She had – but lunch didn't count. She'd been too shocked to eat more than a few bites of her tuna fish sandwich.

She hadn't gone to the kitchen for her daily half a dozen cups of coffee because she couldn't face passing Nigel's office in case she either screamed at him or started crying. The rat! Thankfully Maeve had been able to skive off work early to have a drink with her, otherwise Dee would have gone mad. Her phone hadn't stopped ringing all day, so she'd finally told the switchboard operator to say she wasn't in to any callers. She particularly wanted to avoid personal calls.

No matter how successfully she could put on a cheerful act to business contacts, there was no way she'd have been able to do it if a friend had rung. One kindly 'How are you, Dee?' would have sent her into floods.

She ate another handful of crisps and took a sip of gin to wash them down.

'I still can't believe he did that to me, I just can't believe it,' she said blankly, gazing at the bottles lined up behind the bar. The overhead lights glinted off whiskey and scotch, lighting them up like polished amber.

'I can,' Maeve replied. 'Nigel is a Grade A bastard and his idea of fun is making everyone else's life a misery, you should know that.'

'But why me?' wailed Dee.

Maeve patted her friend's arm. 'Remember what someone said about why they climbed Mount Everest? The answer was "because it was there". Well, that's Nigel Burke for you. He shafted you because he *could* and probably because he wanted to teach us all a little lesson along the lines of "I can do what I want because this is my empire".'

Dee finished her crisps. 'I can't believe he had the audacity to offer me the job with Isabel Farrell sitting there. That was practically the worst thing. It was as if they'd planned it together.'

'At least she left the office,' Maeve pointed out.

'Only because she could tell I wasn't going to say

anything until she did. I'd love to have told Nigel I wouldn't touch the deputy editorship with a barge pole. I should have . . .'

'No, you shouldn't.' Maeve waved at the barman for two more drinks. 'If you'd done that, you'd be spending the rest of your days covering beauty contests and school board elections. At least being made a deputy editor is promotion.'

Dee nodded gloomily.

'A springboard to other things,' insisted her friend. 'You never know what this could lead to.'

'Possibly me getting life imprisonment for murder. I just haven't figured out exactly *how* to kill Nigel. Which would be more painful – that "death by a thousand cuts" thing I've read about or just stabbing him with my blood transfusion service pencil?'

Maeve laughed. 'I know you're getting better when you can joke like that, O'Reilly.'

Dee looked at her mournfully. 'I wasn't joking. Well, maybe a little.' She drained her drink and picked up the next one. 'More crisps,' she announced. 'That's what we need.'

Three-quarters of an hour, two more bags of crisps and three more drinks each later, Dee felt a lot more cheerful.

She'd taken off her jacket and hung it over the back of her seat, no longer bothered about the fact that the lacy T-shirt showed her bra plainly and was only wearable with a jacket over it. Her mascara had run so much that Maeve had given her a tissue to wipe it off and her hair was a mess.

But as she peered woozily at her reflection in the mirror behind the bar, Dee thought she looked pretty good. Big, yes, but good. Sexy, almost. Definitely not fat.

And the amazing thing was, she reflected, ripping open the packet of dry roasted peanuts Maeve had kindly bought her, she didn't feel at all drunk. Not a bit. She was quite sober, really, considering.

'How long have you been here?' Gerry Deegan, pulled up a bar stool beside the two women.

'Not long.' Dee smiled hazily at the political correspondent. 'We've only had three drinks.'

'Four,' said Maeve. 'Or was it five?'

'Could we have had five?' Dee asked in surprise.

'We could. And your first two were doubles.'

'Ooops!' Dee giggled.

'What are we celebrating?' Gerry asked, one eye on the barman who was slowly pouring him a pint of Guinness.

'I'm leaving journalism to become a nun,' announced Dee. She twirled a ringlet around one finger and smiled dreamily at Gerry. 'I'm thinking of one of those enclosed orders where you don't have to talk to people. I don't feel up to talking to people at the moment.'

'That'll be the day,' said a voice. It was Tony Winston with one of his sports freelances in tow. 'What would we do without gorgeous creatures like you, Dee, to brighten up the office?' He gave her a peck on the cheek. 'I can't see you in a nun's habit, unless you wear stockings and stilettos under it and are on your way to a fancy dress party.'

'Get out of here, you walking hormone,' said Maeve loudly, hitting him across the arm with Gerry's evening paper.

'You didn't waste any time chatting up our new women's editor, did you?' said Dee sharply, who'd heard all about Tony's attempts at charming Isabel.

'I believe you were on the verge of asking her round

to your place to show her your World Cup mementoes there and then.'

'Ah.' He nodded sagely. 'So that's it.'

'That's what?' asked Dee.

'That's why the two of you are over here getting plastered. You wanted that job, didn't you, Dee?'

She ignored him.

'Tell your Uncle Tony,' he coaxed, putting his dark head close to hers. Dee could smell his aftershave. It was cloying, horrible stuff although he obviously thought it rendered him irresistible.

'Bugger off, Tony.' She gave him an almighty push that sent him cannoning into Gerry and his barely touched pint of Guinness. Beer went everywhere – all over Tony's prized pink Lacoste shirt and Gerry's shoes.

'Sorry, Gerry,' Dee apologised.

'What about me?' demanded Tony, holding his dripping shirt away from his body in disgust.

Dee gave him a scornful look.

'I think we should get out of here before Tony gets really pissed off,' Maeve whispered.

He stalked off to the men's room, cursing as he went.

'C'mon.' Maeve grabbed her rucksack, Dee's enormous handbag, and her friend by the arm.

'Sorry, Gerry,' Dee said again. 'I didn't mean to get you.'

'It's OK. My shoes got most of it. I'm fine. I'm sorry about you not getting Antonia's job,' he said surprisingly. 'I had an idea Nigel would pull a trick like that. He's made you deputy, hasn't he?'

Dee nodded. The office gossip machine was obviously working as efficiently as ever.

'A word of advice from someone who's been round the block more than once, Dee. Get back there and do it, and remember to do it well. Don't give Nigel Burke the satisfaction of thinking he's won. He loves that. Do your best and you'll get a hell of a lot more out of the job than if you do it half-heartedly.

'Besides,' Gerry added with a wicked smirk, 'I don't know if Nigel will be around that much longer anyway. Think of the party we'll have when he goes!'

'Thanks, Gerry.' Dee smiled.

Maeve dragged her off. 'Ring Gary and tell him to pick you up as you can't possibly drive home,' she instructed once they were outside Magee's.

Dee clumsily dialled her home number on her mobile phone. The answering machine kicked in after three rings.

'He's not home,' she said forlornly. Suddenly, she desperately wanted to see Gary, to let him hug her and tell her it was going to be all right. That he loved her even if she wasn't appreciated by her boss. And now he wasn't there. He'd rejected her too. Dee felt tearful all over again.

'Was he going out tonight?' Maeve asked.

'Can't remember,' she muttered.

Maeve slid an arm around her. 'Let's get a taxi to your place. I'll cook us something and we can watch *Thelma and Louise*. How does that sound?'

'Wonderful. Thanks, Maeve. What would I do without you?'

'Don't thank me,' her friend replied briskly, and stuck out her arm at an approaching taxi. 'Just wait till you get my bill!'

Maeve was a good cook. Given a few withered mushrooms, an elderly onion, tomatoes, surprisingly fresh cheese and some eggs, she could make a Spanish omelette any chef would be proud of.

128

'I *was* going to make a salad to go with the omelette,' she said, poking around in the salad crisper part of the fridge, 'but everything's gone off somewhat.' She threw the dripping remains of an iceberg lettuce into the bin.

'It's Gary's week for cleaning and shopping,' muttered Dee from the depths of the settee.

'Surprise, surprise!'

Dee got up, put knives and forks on the coffee table, added napkins – paper ones – and inexpertly uncorked a bottle of red wine.

'I don't know if I could drink anything else,' said Maeve when she brought the plates into the sitting-room to find Dee filling two huge wineglasses. 'I've got to be in early tomorrow and I couldn't face another hangover.'

'That's OK.' Dee smiled crookedly. 'All the more for me.'

The film was one of her favourites and she'd often watched it when she was depressed. They sat side by side on the settee, ate Maeve's succulent omelette and empathised.

'That's it, Maeve,' Dee mumbled. 'Thelma has crossed over, she can't go back. That's just like me. I can't go back into work and do that stupid job with that horrible woman.' She gazed at her friend through bleary eyes. 'I just can't.'

At half-ten, Maeve called a taxi.

'Please go to bed, Dee. You'll feel better in the morning.

'My head won't,' she said darkly.

'True.' Maeve hugged her. 'Now go to bed. I'm going to turn the TV off and I want you up those stairs before I leave.'

'Right, officer,' Dee clumsily climbed up them.

'Thanks, Maeve. You're a great friend,' she mumbled when she reached the top. 'I'm going to bed now. Very tired. I'll think in the morning.'

Isabel sank down on to her mother's uncomfortable Chesterfield, leant back and closed her eyes. What a day! She felt as if she'd run a marathon. And she would never wear those bloody cream Roland Cartier slingbacks ever again. They looked good but they hurt like hell. That was what you got for buying sale shoes which were too tight.

She levered them off her feet, struggled out of her jacket and allowed herself to imagine what it would be like to be able to sit there all evening, watching soaps and stupid game shows until it was time for bed. She wouldn't have to talk to anyone, other than Naomi and Robin. She wouldn't have to make forced conversation with her mother.

'Hiya, Mum.' Naomi raced into the room. She jumped on to the settee beside her mother.

'So, how was it?'

'Great, darling. Everyone was very nice to me. I've got a lovely desk beside the features editor, Phil Walsh, and she's very friendly.'

'You don't have your own office?' Naomi sounded disappointed.

Isabel smiled and smoothed her daughter's unruly hair.

'Nobody has an office, darling. Except for the editor. We all work in a very big room with lots of desks in the middle. I'm one of the lucky ones because I sit beside the window and I've got a big partition which stops everyone from seeing what I'm doing.'

'When can I come and see it?'

Naomi had been a frequent visitor to Isabel's other offices, apart from *Motor 2000*, but somehow she didn't think the *Sentinel* was the sort of place where the staff's children would be made welcome.

'I don't know, maybe during the summer.'

Naomi's face fell.

'Or I suppose I could take you in on Saturday,' Isabel relented. Nobody would be at work then because there wasn't a Sunday edition of the paper.

'Cool! Robin told Granny she was going to make dinner this evening,' Naomi announced. Isabel's eyebrows shot up. 'She made a casserole thingy in home economics and we're having that with rice.'

Isabel hoped that Robin was more talented in the rice department than she was. It always ended up either too hard or a slushy mess, no matter how she weighed rice, water, whatever. Hopefully, Robin would be a better cook. She certainly seemed to like home economics and had concocted a delicious vegetable lasagne in her class a couple of weeks previously.

'I'm making dessert,' Naomi added proudly. 'It's a surprise. You don't have to do anything, Mum. It's chocolate mousse,' she whispered, 'but you're not supposed to know.'

'My lips are sealed. It all sounds delicious, Naomi, and so long as I don't have to do anything, I'm happy.'

'Do you want a drink, Mum? I told Granny you'd need wine because you like some at dinner and because it was your first day at work.'

Isabel groaned inwardly. That was all she needed. Her mother would think she was on the verge of becoming an alcoholic.

One sherry per evening and brandy after disasters – that was Pamela's idea of drinking. There was no use in trying to explain that Isabel and David had always enjoyed wine in the evenings. Or that she'd quite enjoyed those evenings when he wasn't around for dinner, so she could decide whether she wanted red or white and drink a couple of glasses in blissful solitude with her feet up.

'How did Granny look when you mentioned the wine?' she asked Naomi. 'What did she say?'

Her daughter shrugged. 'Nothing. Why, Mum?'

Isabel smiled at her. 'No reason. Now tell me, what was school like today? Did you get your English essay back?'

Naomi pulled a face. 'Yeah. I got a D. I always got Bs at home, Mum.'

'I know, love. It's very difficult to get used to a new school, new teachers and a new syllabus. It's going to take time before you settle in.' She gave her daughter's hand a squeeze. 'I already know you're going to be a world-class journalist, Naomi.'

Her portable typewriter was her most prized possession and she longed to be in the same business as her mum. Isabel hoped to buy a decent computer for the girls before the end of the year as David had kept his Mac when they'd moved away. She was still broke, though.

'But it may take St Clodagh's some time before they realise it too. Now go and see if you can persuade your big sister to make me a cup of tea, would you?'

Naomi grinned and jumped off the settee. Isabel made a mental note to ring St Clodagh's the next morning and talk to the headmistress.

When she'd enrolled Naomi there a couple of months previously, she'd told the headmistress that her shy twelve-year-old daughter was going to need some gentle treatment before she found her feet in a new country and school. Mrs Robinson, the headmistress, had claimed to understand that.

Isabel knew that no matter how long it took Naomi to settle into her other classes, she was always instantly at home in English, her favourite subject. She was an avid reader and devoured everything from Enid Blyton to the Brontës. Which was why the news that Naomi had got a D for an essay she'd worked hard on made Isabel realise that not everybody in St Clodagh's had listened to her.

You didn't understand at all, Mrs Robinson, Isabel thought angrily. But you will by the time I've finished with you.

Still, ringing the school would give her the opportunity to find out how Robin had been getting on too. Her elder daughter had to cope with a totally new syllabus for exams in June, which she was dreading.

If only Robin would talk to her! Isabel despaired of ever having a conversation with her daughter that didn't involve phrases like: 'You *never* let me do anything' and 'If Dad were here, it would be different'.

And, as if all that wasn't bad enough, Isabel knew she'd have to face Dee O'Reilly in the morning, who, if her enraged expression when she'd finally left the editor's office was anything to go by, loathed Nigel and Isabel equally.

Not for the first time, she sent up a silent word of thanks to the good people who made anti-depressants. Without a little chemical back-up, she'd have gone to pieces by now, she was sure of it.

'Tea.' Robin came into the room with a china cup and saucer, and a bourbon biscuit on a tray. Isabel was thrilled. Not because of the tea, but because Robin had

133

made an effort for her. She beamed at her daughter.

'Thank you, Robin, you're a pet.'

She took a sip, then nibbled her biscuit.

'How was work?' Robin perched on the edge of an armchair. She was still in her school uniform – grey skirt and jumper, white blouse and royal blue and grey striped tie. Robin looked like a schoolgirl again and not the minxy madam she could pass for in her clingy tops and figure-hugging hipsters.

'Hard going,' Isabel answered honestly. 'My deputy wanted the job I got. So I don't think we're going to be bosom buddies. Everyone else was nice, but it's going to be a demanding job, that's for sure.' She stretched her arms and yawned. 'I have to say, I *am* tired.'

'Well, you don't have to do anything this evening, Mum, I've made dinner.'

'So Naomi was saying. What is it? Something certainly smells delicious.'

Robin smiled with pleasure. 'Lamb with tomato and haricot beans.'

'Gorgeous! I'm famished.'

'It won't be finished for another twenty minutes because I just put the rice on,' Robin explained. 'Gran is having a rest – she's got another of her migraines. She wanted me to cook boiled potatoes but I hate them so I did rice. I'll call you when it's ready.'

Isabel sank back into the settee, turned on the TV and relaxed. She might as well enjoy this evening of blissful peace because, as Scarlett O'Hara once said, tomorrow was going to be another day.

As she drove into work the following morning in the late-May sunshine, Isabel felt ready to tackle anything. It didn't take long for her good humour to disappear. After five minutes in the office and just one call, she slammed down the phone angrily. Antonia FitzSimons had promised to help her in her new job but now she'd backed out. She wasn't pleased with the far-from-golden handshake Ted Holt had offered her.

'Obviously I feel under less of an obligation now,' she'd said when Isabel rang to find out what time Antonia would meet her in the office.

'Antonia, this is only my second day here. I need some back-up,' Isabel insisted, doing her best to ignore the feeling of panic rising in her chest.

'I'm afraid that's out of the question,' she snorted. 'Talk to Nigel and tell him how upset I am about all this, that's all I can suggest.'

Isabel stared at the phone grimly. What she wouldn't do to that lazy, spoilt cow if she ever got hold of her! Just because Antonia could afford to give up a full-time job, thanks to her husband's fat salary, didn't mean that everyone else was so privileged.

Isabel glanced anxiously at the big clock on the wall beside the nearest TV screen.

It was half-nine on Wednesday morning, she was due in an editorial meeting at two, and without any contact numbers or helpful information from Antonia, her hands were not just tied, they were virtually handcuffed.

Shit, shit, shit!

Antonia had even managed to sabotage her further by taking home all the fashion transparencies and press releases sent in by fashion companies. So there was damn-all to write about.

None of the freelances had rung to say hello or that they were sending in articles. Isabel had to get moving on tomorrow's women's pages or there'd be a very big gap in the paper. Hardly the ideal way to start her new job.

And, to add insult to injury, Dee O'Reilly, her supposed deputy, was nowhere in sight. Even Phil Walsh, who would probably help if she could, was out.

'It's Phil's day off,' muttered Jackie, the assistant Isabel shared with her. Jackie was not the sort of assistant to inspire confidence. She was around twenty, with coal-black dyed hair, a Band Aid-sized mini skirt, Doc Marten's, and an air of complete apathy.

'D'ya want coffee?' she asked when she came back from the loo with newly applied thick black eyeliner that made her look like an ancient Egyptian.

'Yes. Black, no sugar, please,' Isabel said.

Jackie ambled off and Isabel watched her dispiritedly. She needed at least one energetic, enthusiastic person on her side. It didn't look as if Jackie was going to measure up.

Ten minutes later, she returned with a cup of milky white coffee and a batch of post for the women's editor.

Ignoring the coffee, Isabel fell on the post with delight. Several of the large envelopes carried personalised mailing stamps from the large retail chains and designers' studios, so she knew that these were press releases and, hopefully, pictures, of the latest ranges of summer clothes.

She didn't give a damn whether they were actually meant for Antonia who had shown that she couldn't care less what happened to Isabel and the women's pages. Isabel was bloody well going to open the post that had been sent to the *Sentinel*'s women's editor because that was now her job, and stuff Antonia.

Anything private would be sent on to her, but Isabel needed to fill six empty pages for Thursday's paper.

'Wonderful!' she cried as she ripped open an envelope and found pictures of a range of bikinis, a new line of summer knitwear being launched the following day, and some elegant suits from Paul Costelloe's collection. That was the fashion pages covered for a few days at least.

The post also yielded a feature about infertility from one of the paper's regular contributors, Jane Wood, as well as ideas for a couple of other articles.

Thank you, Jane! Isabel grinned and put the extremely well-written piece into her 'in' tray. She wrote down Jane's number in her diary before rummaging through the rest of the post. That was four pages pretty well covered.

'Sorry, I gave you the wrong coffee,' said Jackie, swopping Isabel's cup for another one. 'I'm never very awake until I get my first cup,' she added apologetically.

Isabel smiled at her. Perhaps Jackie was nervous about working for a new boss and that was why she'd made the mistake. Maybe things were going to work out after all.

'Get up, Dee, get up! You're going to be late.'

What was wrong with Gary? she wondered numbly. He sounded as if he was at the bottom of a tunnel. What was going on? It was the middle of the night, surely?

The duvet was rudely ripped off the bed. Dee opened her eyes gingerly to stare blearily at her fiancé. He was already dressed in a blue suit and white shirt and looked very, very cross.

'This is the last time I'm calling you, Dee. I've called you five times already and you're going to be late for work if you don't get up now!' he snapped.

'Whaddya mean, you called me before?' Dee muttered. 'I'd have remembered if you'd called me.'

She sat up in bed and immediately felt horrendously sick.

'Ohmigod,' she sighed, lying down again. She felt as if she'd vomit if she sat up. Maybe lying down and breathing gently would do the trick. 'Omigod, what happened?'

'That's what I'd like to know,' hissed Gary. He looked incredibly angry. His hair, still wet from his shower, was slicked back from his face and he'd cut himself shaving. A little bit of loo roll was stuck to his cheek where he'd nicked it. 'I came home last night to find you pissed out of your brain, screaming at the top of your voice about Nigel Burke and some woman called Farrell. When I tried to calm you down, you slapped me and said you weren't taking orders from anyone ever again!'

'Oh, I'm so sorry.' Dee burned with shame and remorse. 'I'm so sorry, Gary. I just got drunk with Maeve . . .'

'I knew it would be Maeve,' he interrupted triumphantly. 'She's bad news, that woman. Can't get herself a man so she wants you out drinking with her till the middle of the night. It's just not on, Dee!'

She did her best to protest. 'Gary, you've got it wrong. It wasn't Maeve's fault. It was mine.'

'And that's supposed to make it better?' he yelled. 'It's a quarter to nine and I didn't sleep for hours, what with your drunken rambling, so I overslept and now I'm late for work. I'll see you tonight.'

And he was gone, leaving Dee miserable, exhausted, and very, very hungover. She dragged the duvet back over her head and stifled a sob. All she'd wanted was a little comfort and Gary hadn't been there. If he knew why she'd got so drunk, surely he'd have understood?

She felt so sick, so awfully ready to puke at any moment, she'd just lie in bed for a little while longer and then she'd feel better.

Ten minutes later the phone rang, making Dee jump in her duvet cocoon.

'Hello,' she said miserably, after inadvertently pushing a couple of books and her hand cream off the bedside locker in her attempts to pick up the receiver.

'You're not still in bed, are you?' demanded Maeve.

'Don't shout,' said Dee weakly. 'I've got an awful headache.'

'I'm not surprised. You got through a lorryload of booze last night.'

'I remember. I didn't say anything awful, did I?' Dee asked, pulling the phone back under the duvet with her.

'Not at all, you were hilariously funny until the very end when I thought you were either going to pass out or head off into the night to give Nigel a do-it-yourself vasectomy with a sharp kitchen implement.'

'So long as I was amusing.'

'Are you up yet? Maeve asked. 'Stupid question. You sound like you're speaking from a coal mine so I presume you're still in bed. It's nearly nine and you've got to get in for your first day of deputy editing along with the bitch from hell.'

Dee groaned. 'Don't remind me! I just don't feel up to it. You'll never guess what I did last night?'

'What?'

'I slapped Gary. I don't even remember it but he's very cross. I think he wants to divorce me.'

'He can't. You're not even married yet. Now, are you getting up? Last night, you vowed to show everyone what a brilliant women's editor you'd have made so that

Nigel and Ted would be desperately sorry for appointing Isabel. Come on,' Maeve cajoled, 'get up. I'll book a taxi for you for nine-forty-five, right?'

Dee groaned again. 'All right. I don't know if I can stand up though.'

'That's no excuse. See you in work later.'

Every bump the taxi went over made Dee feel even more nauseous. She prayed she'd feel a bit better when she got a dose of percolated coffee inside her at the office. And a Twix might help. Or perhaps it wouldn't.

She hadn't been able to face breakfast and anyway, she'd needed the time to shower and put on enough make-up to look even halfway decent. Despite wearing full war paint and lots of blusher, she was still very pale.

Clutching a polystyrene cup of coffee, she walked delicately up to her desk before remembering that Nigel had given her a new one – in the features department – only a few feet away from Isabel's.

Her old desk was still cluttered with her filing trays, papers, notebooks, small scraps of phone messages lying everywhere and little black marks where the after-six smokers had kindly left their butts filter-first on the desk until they burned down. She'd move properly tomorrow. There was no way she could face it now.

Dee plonked a few things down on her new desk and grabbed that day's copy of the *Sentinel*. The office was still quiet and, thankfully, there was no sign of bloody Isabel.

Dee was flicking through the paper and drinking her coffee when she heard a voice address her.

'Morning, Dee.'

Isabel stood in front of her, sickeningly cheerful, incredibly slim and beautifully dressed in a navy linen trouser suit. Her blonde hair was silky and fell perfectly to her shoulders, her large blue eyes were expertly made up. *She* didn't look as if she was dying of a hangover. Smug bitch.

'Good morning,' Dee replied, although she couldn't see what was so good about it.

'Dee, Phil's away so maybe you could sit at her desk while we talk about this week's pages and what we need to do?' Isabel said. 'Antonia hasn't left me any information about who does what or which articles are being written for the women's section. Maybe you could help me sort through that.'

'OK,' she mumbled.

'Great. Jackie's getting me some phone numbers and each of us can phone half of them, just to make sure we've enough stuff to fill the next few editions. Then we can talk about how we're going to work together. And you can tell me what you're interested in doing,' Isabel added.

'Right,' Dee said warily. She wasn't sure she trusted all this '*we'll* talk about it' stuff. She suspected it was a ploy to catch her off guard before Isabel started laying down the law about exactly who was boss.

She reluctantly got out a pen and notebook and sat down on Phil Walsh's chair. Isabel's phone rang almost immediately and, while she answered it, Dee surveyed Isabel's side of the cubbyhole.

She obviously had children because she'd a photo of herself and two girls on the far side of her computer. One was a very pretty teenager and the other was a few years younger. You wouldn't think she'd had kids judging by Isabel's figure. She was slim, verging on too thin. Not that Dee ever thought anyone could be too thin, but Isabel was practically model-girl underweight. Dee could see her collarbones jutting out above her simple white camisole top and her wrists and ankles were very skinny. Still, she looked good, classy.

The only thing that revealed she wasn't a wealthy lady of leisure were her nails. Cut short and filed straight across, they weren't even polished. Which was odd because, from the look of her, Dee would have guessed that Isabel Farrell had both the money and the time to spend in beauty salons. She probably had a filthy rich husband who paid all the bills, while her salary was spent as 'pin money', buying little designer numbers.

Dee glanced at her own nails. The chocolate brown varnish was a bit chipped, which was how she felt herself. Compared to Isabel's elegant ensemble, Dee felt that in her straight brown skirt and slinky coffee-coloured blouse – worn loose to hide her bulges – she looked drab and cheap. And fat. No, *the outfit* didn't make her look fat, *she* was fat, end of story. She sighed miserably.

'Dee, you look a little tired. Do you want a coffee or something?' Isabel asked kindly, as she hung up.

Startled, Dee nodded. She was probably just going to yell at Jackie to get the coffee, Dee figured. Isabel would hardly get it herself. But she stood up.

'Black, white, sugar?' she asked.

'Er, white with two sugars,' Dee replied. 'Thank you.'

Isabel came back a few minutes later with coffee for both of them and a Danish pastry in a paper bag for Dee.

'One of the runners got it for me in the shop across the road. I thought you looked as if you needed an energy lift. You don't have to eat it if you don't want to,' she added hesitantly.

'Thanks,' said Dee, amazed. 'I don't really know if I could eat it. I'm feeling a little off-colour today.' She didn't want to say that she was dying from a hangover as a result of a misery drinking session because Isabel had got the job she wanted.

'Oh. Are you up to doing any work?'

'Of course,' said Dee, stung by the implication that she'd run home on her first day as Isabel's deputy. 'Right, where'll we start?'

As Isabel talked about the article she'd received in the post and when they should use it, Dee drank her coffee but didn't touch the pastry. She could smell its sweet, buttery scent through the bag and her stomach began to feel better and very empty all of a sudden.

But she hated eating in front of people she didn't know. She hated eating in front of people full stop. If Maeve wasn't around to have lunch with, Dee nibbled fruit at her desk and ate a yoghurt virtuously. She saved her lasagne-and-chips binges for lunch with her friend.

There was no way she was going to eat that Danish in front of Isabel, even if it was screaming 'eat me' at her. Isabel probably thought Dee lived on cream buns and tubs of ice cream. If she saw Dee shovelling down a calorie-laden Danish, Isabel would think, 'That's why she's enormous – she can't stop eating.'

Dee shoved the bag away from her and started to work.

With Jackie's help, Isabel and Dee tracked down all the freelances whom Antonia used for her pages, and at twelve o'clock two of the staff journalists who worked between features and the women's pages arrived.

The only problem was that neither Carol-Anne nor Emily appeared to have been given anything to do by Antonia for weeks.

'I've got an article on famous divorces that I started doing for Phil but I can give it a women's pages slant, if you like?' offered Emily, a sweet-looking twenty-something brunette with almond-shaped green eyes.

'Great. We can use that on Saturday,' Isabel said, pleased at Emily's enthusiasm. 'Don't forget to get plenty of famous, attractive movie-star couples in there so the subs can use glamorous photos.'

'No problem.' Emily sat down at her desk and started rummaging through a pile of brown folders.

Isabel turned to the other woman. 'Carol-Anne, do you have anything you can write quickly for Friday's paper?'

'No. Not really.' Carol-Anne stared at her blankly. A thin, taut-faced woman with a swathe of ash-blonde curls and bags under her eyes from incessant partying, Carol-Anne prided herself on being the ultimate in glamour – red nails, red lips and a sporty car – and believed that, as a longstanding member of staff, she didn't have to take orders from anyone.

Dee watched with interest. In her opinion, Carol-Anne was as lazy as sin and Dee had once heard a rumour that she had actually been fired from her last job for writing a review of a play that had been cancelled at the last minute. But she and Antonia had been best pals since college and Antonia had always given Carol-Anne cushy jobs like writing the beauty notes from press releases. Dee knew for a fact that Carol-Anne had applied for Antonia's job too, and you didn't need to be a Mensa member to figure out that she'd got it in for Isabel.

'Nothing?' asked Isabel, surprised.

'No,' said Carol-Anne. The crimson lips curved smugly and turned back to her desk and her morning paper. Dee wondered for the millionth time why the other woman didn't get out of journalism when she daily made it clear to the world that she hated her job and did her best to do as little work as possible. Unlike Antonia, however, Carol-Anne didn't have a husband to support her, so it was either the *Sentinel* or the dole queue.

Dee glanced at Isabel. The other woman stared at Carol-Anne's back and seemed to be thinking.

'Carol-Anne,' she said suddenly, 'as you've nothing to do, I've a great idea for you. I'm sure there's a file somewhere on this sexual harassment case in America. Do a feature on it, updating the story with current Irish legislation. Give me a thousand words.'

Oooh, Dee thought, with a grin, that was a killer article to write. She had to hand it to Isabel. She had the measure of Carol-Anne and was obviously determined to get her to do some work.

Carol-Anne looked up, eyes narrowed as she stared at the woman who thought she could order her around.

Round one to Isabel, thought Dee. But she doesn't know Carol-Anne. If she gets that feature by next Wednesday, she'll be lucky.

'And, Carol-Anne,' Isabel said in a louder voice, so that everyone nearby could hear, 'I want it by tomorrow at ten.'

Game, set and match to Isabel! Carol-Anne wasn't going to be in for such an easy ride with *this* boss.

'You should have seen Carol-Anne's face, Maeve, she was *livid*!' laughed Dee. 'It was priceless.'

They were sitting in the coffee shop across the road from the office. Dee was eating chips because she needed carbohydrates for her hangover. Maeve had chosen lasagne because she was always ravenous at lunch.

'I have to hand it to Isabel, she's well able for Carol-Anne.'

'This is the same woman you were never going to speak to again last night?' inquired Maeve, as she dug into her lasagne.

'I know, I know,' Dee said irritably. 'I can hate her guts and still see her good points. And she *was* tough with Carol-Anne.'

'I wouldn't be too sure her methods will work,' Maeve cautioned. 'Wait and see. Tomorrow morning at around nine-thirty Jackie will most probably get a call from Carol-Anne to say she's very sick, the doctor wants her to lie down for at least a week, poor dear, and she can't *possibly* come into work. She won't phone Isabel, of course. She'll phone a naive assistant who'd swallow a brick and readily believe she's at death's door.'

'You're right. I forgot about the hypochondriac defence. "Poor me, my leg/stomach/head/big toe hurts so much I can't come in for a month." Delete where applicable.' Dee grinned.

'So are you going to tell Isabel how Carol-Anne's mind works, or are you going to let her figure it out for herself?' Maeve asked.

'I'm not going to tell her anything! She stole my job.'

'Two minutes ago you were saying "fair play to her". Now she's back to being a bitch again. Come on, Dee at least be consistent.'

She looked hurt. 'I thought you were on my side?'

Maeve put down her fork. 'I am. But I don't want to see you start a big fight that's going to last years. Isabel has been fair with you . . .'

'So far,' interrupted Dee.

'So far. But perhaps this is a little test, like Carol-Anne's. And if you end up fighting her, it could last as long as she's women's editor. And that could be a long time. Do you want that?'

'No. But I don't trust her, either.'

'Fair enough. Just give her a chance, Dee. That's all I'm saying.'

'But what about the Danish pastry?' she demanded. 'I've been thinking about it all morning. Maybe she bought it to suck up to me, because she thinks I'm a great big tank of a thing that she can wrap round her little finger by giving her cakes.'

'*Dee*!' said Maeve. 'Sometimes a Danish pastry is just a Danish pastry, right? Stop being paranoid and analysing things so much. I bet she'd have got one for me if I'd looked bad.'

'Maybe.' Dee wasn't so sure. 'She's so thin, Maeve. She makes me feel like a giant hippo beside her. I wonder, does she diet? If she does, I'd love to know what diet she's on.'

'She might be like me and not need to,' Maeve said as she started on her apple crumble.

'Oh, great,' Dee grumbled. '*Two* women in the office who can eat what they want and never put on an ounce. I swear I'm going on a diet tomorrow. The F-Plan always works well for me.'

'I don't know how you can eat all that horrible bran for breakfast,' Maeve pointed out. 'It tastes like cardboard.'

'That's the whole point. It's so tasteless you don't want to eat anything else and it fills you up like cardboard too. Tomorrow, definitely,' she said firmly. 'This is the diet that's going to change my life.'

★ ★ ★

After lunch Dee and Isabel spent two hours going over new ideas for the women's pages. When Isabel talked of having a serious interview piece every week, Dee couldn't hide her enthusiasm. That was exactly the sort of thing she'd wanted to do for years.

'It's a brilliant idea,' she said, eyes shining.

'Would you like to do the first one?' Isabel asked. 'We'll run it this week, so you've got until Monday evening to write it.'

'I'd love to do it.'

'That's settled then.'

Around four-fifteen, Dee's hangover went into the exhaustion phase. She suddenly felt dog-tired and barely had the energy to write. She'd love to go home early, but could hardly do that two days in a row.

Isabel passed her desk with a bundle of old copies of the paper and gave Dee a broad smile. Maybe she should go home early . . . She wasn't going to be much good for the rest of the day and at least Isabel knew she'd been working like a slave since morning.

Hell, she'd go home. A couple of hours in bed before Gary came back was just what she needed. She'd cook him a lovely dinner to apologise. There was nothing to eat in the house, so she'd nip into the Superquinn and buy something. Shepherd's pie, that was it. He loved it. She'd never made it before but it couldn't be that difficult, could it?

Dee quickly tidied her desk and switched off her computer. At that precise moment Nigel Burke appeared beside her, grinning like a Cheshire cat who'd just been lapping double cream.

'How's it going, Dee?' he asked. 'Settling in under your new boss?'

'Er, yes,' she muttered.

Nigel looked pointedly at his watch. 'Going a bit early, aren't you?'

'I told her to,' said a calm voice. Isabel held his gaze. 'Dee will be working late tomorrow night doing an interview and we've already got through an incredible amount of stuff today.'

There was nothing he could say to that.

'So long as you girls are getting on all right, that's all that matters,' he said quickly. 'I want to have a meeting with you both tomorrow.' He walked away briskly.

'Thanks,' Dee said to Isabel in amazement.

'You really have done so much today, Dee, and I've never believed in clocking in. Flexi-time works much better in a job like this,' Isabel replied. 'See you tomorrow morning.'

Dee got into her car slowly. Nothing was going as planned. Instead of being hostile, caustic and ready to argue with Isabel about everything, she'd actually worked hard for her all day. And had ended up looking so wrecked that the new women's editor had actually stood up for her!

On the surface at least Isabel Farrell was nothing like Dee had expected her to be. Still, it was early days yet.

CHAPTER SEVEN

Dee twisted round to see herself from every angle in
the changing-room mirror. There was no doubt about it
– the dress looked hideous on her. The forest green silk
had looked like the answer to all her prayers when it
was hanging up. It was obviously expensive and had
'class' written all over it, which she'd thought would
make it perfect for the Delahunty/Thomas nuptials in
Wicklow the following day.

But on Dee's now size sixteen body, it appeared to
have shrunk several sizes. It made her bum look like a
bean bag, not to mention what it did to her stomach.
There was only so much those control top tights could
do, let alone the fact that the middle seam would be
visible under the sliver-thin silk.

Dee managed to undo the zip, thankful she'd come to
one of Dublin's poshest shops. Because even though a
lot of the clothes cost more than an average worker
earned in a week, at least the changing rooms were
private and for one person only.

Nothing put Dee off clothes shops more than having
to wriggle in and out of things in communal changing
rooms. In her experience they were always jammed
with stick-thin girls who demanded to know if they
looked fat in little bits of Lycra. People like Dee were

doomed to look on in misery then try to struggle out of clothes without exposing any flesh so nobody could see their fat stomachs.

In Brown Thomas, the sales assistant hovered discreetly outside the cubicle. She asked if Dee needed anything instead of sticking her head around the curtain at inopportune moments.

'How does it look?' the sales lady inquired tactfully.

Like I've been sprayed with green cling-film, thought Dee gloomily. 'Er, it's not very me.'

She couldn't face the thought of pulling her clothes back on and going outside to hunt desperately through rails and rails of garments. She loved the luxury of buying clothes, normally, but never when she had to buy something for a specific event. Then, all the lovely, ultra-slimming things she'd drooled over but hadn't bought because she was broke mysteriously disappeared and she was left struggling to find anything even vaguely decent.

That was exactly what seemed to have happened today. What was even worse, Dee knew she was getting so enormous that she hadn't a hope in hell of buying anything that wouldn't look like a marquee. She stuck her head out of the cubicle.

'Could *you* take a look and see if you've anything that would suit me?'

The assistant's face lit up at the challenge. 'I have a couple of dresses you might try, but what I'd really suggest is a suit.'

'I don't want one of those on-the-knee, pastel suits you can only wear for a wedding,' Dee said firmly, with visions of herself fading into a sea of such outfits the following day.

'Don't worry, it's nothing like that,' the sales lady assured her.

152

Half an hour later, Dee marched up Grafton Street to the Stephen's Green car park, holding a large Brown Thomas bag triumphantly in one hand. The suit was beautiful and looked marvellous on her. All she needed now was a bit of fake tan to give her that just-back-from-Marbella colour.

The suit was a rich terracotta, its perfectly cut long jacket flattering her curves. The skirt showed off her great legs and the white camisole – which she'd picked because of Isabel's – was cut low enough to be seriously sexy when she took off the jacket. *If* she felt thin enough to take it off.

Of course, it had been horrifically expensive – all the best over-size-fourteen clothes were. But it hung so well, and made her look slimmer than she felt, that it was worth it.

Even crabby Margaret Redmond couldn't complain about her future daughter-in-law's taste this time. And Dee would be able to talk about her promotion to deputy women's editor and how she was the youngest person ever to get the job. Wonderful!

Well, she *was* the youngest person ever to get the job. Margaret didn't need to know that Dee was also the *only* person ever to get it.

Dee would have whistled if she'd been able to. What a great day it was turning out to be! She'd spent two hours that morning interviewing one of Ireland's female business tycoons and the interview had gone really well.

Donna Fratelli was friendly but as tough as old boots – she'd needed to be to bring her family's ailing pasta business out of the doldrums and into the Irish food business as a major player. But she was also very down-to-earth, very clever, and possessed the sort of sense of humour that would come across really well on paper.

When Dee had asked whether there was a man in her life or not, she wasn't too forthcoming but did point out that many men were frightened off by successful, independent women.

'Listen, if I had a penny for the number of guys who proudly tell me how successful they are, and then take a big step backwards when I tell them exactly how prosperous *my* business is, then I'd have a much bigger house and a Ferrari to boot,' Donna had told her drily.

Despite all her money and success, Dee felt sorry for Donna. She was nearly forty, very good-looking with dark Italian skin and eyes, very rich – and, evidently desperately lonely.

'Believe me,' she had said at the end, 'a woman's success manages to neuter men quicker than a surgeon performing a vasectomy.'

It was a brilliant quote and the perfect way to finish off Dee's article. But it was also a sad and telling comment.

Dear Annie,

All my friends think I have everything – money, success, good looks, you name it. But I'm so lonely. All the men I meet are either married or scared of commitment and, when they discover how successful I am, they run away. Am I really an 'ice maiden', as one guy called me?

Career Lady

Dear Career Lady,

You're no ice maiden. That's a sign of this particular man's inadequacies – not yours. He's wary of women who are independent and in control of their own lives. That's what he's afraid of – so he does the only thing he can and belittles you.

The real problem is that you are rich and successful. You are moving away from Mr Average's picture of the sort of woman he can cope with. You need to meet a man who isn't threatened by your success and power. Unfortunately, this will probably have to be a guy who is successful and powerful in his own right. But there is a man like that out there, somewhere . . .

'You're engaged, I see.' Donna had noticed Dee's engagement ring.

'Yes,' she'd said with a wry smile. It was incredible, really. Donna wore beautiful jewellery, including several platinum rings on her long, tapering fingers, yet she'd looked longingly at Dee's simple solitaire.

'And your fiancé is happy that you've got such a great job and your own independence?'

'Absolutely,' Dee said.

It was true, she mused now, as she paid her parking fee and drove out of the city centre to the office. Gary had been thrilled that she'd been promoted. He'd forgiven her drunken escapade – even the fact she'd hit him – and immediately went to the off-licence to buy a bottle of champagne to go with the shepherd's pie she'd attempted to make for dinner.

'Think of it – we'll be the success story of the year,' he'd said, one arm around Dee, a glass in his other hand. 'I reckon I'll make partner in the firm next January and you're at executive level on the paper. What a team, eh?'

Dee had snuggled up to him happily. He'd forgiven

her and was thrilled about the job.

His enthusiasm was infectious. They'd ended up making love in the sitting-room with half their clothes on. It had been months since they'd done anything so spontaneous. The memory of that passionate session made Dee feel sexy just thinking about it.

The one blip in their improved relationship was her weight. Gary had added that they really ought to join a gym, possibly one of the trendy and ultra-expensive ones in the city centre.

'It would do us good,' he'd said, giving Dee a gentle poke in the ribs. 'And if you're going to be the rising young executive, you'd better get rid of that extra weight you're always talking about. I can just picture you in one of those clingy chiffon dresses at my firm's Christmas party, all slim and sexy. All the other guys will be mad for you.' As he nuzzled into her neck, Dee had frozen in misery.

'Aw, come on, Dee,' he'd protested, feeling the tension in her body. 'I love you the way you are, you know that. I've always adored your Rubensesque figure. But *you're* the one who's always saying you want to lose weight – I'm just backing you up. Don't you understand that, darling?'

When Gary stared at her beseechingly, those hazel eyes in that handsome face just begging her to agree with him, Dee couldn't resist. He was only trying to help, she knew that. And she *was* always going on about her figure – he was right about that, too.

'I know,' she said slowly.

'You could do step aerobics? All the girls at the office are obsessed with step classes,' Gary said. 'I'll phone around tomorrow and check out a few gyms.'

Dee *was* lucky and it was about time she appreciated

it. She resolved to stop bitching about how Gary never did any cleaning. Her constant nagging hadn't worked. In fact, all it had done was create an icy atmosphere at home. From today on, she vowed, she'd be different – cool, calm and most definitely not the sort of woman to fly into a fury when she found the toilet seat up or the laundry basket full of dirty soccer kit. Yes, that was it. There was going to be a new Dee O'Reilly, a new woman who wouldn't get stressed out when office politics upset her and who would be able to speak to Margaret Redmond without immediately being overcome with an urge to hit the other woman with her handbag.

She was just too emotional, too fiery, Dee decided. It was the red O'Reilly hair that did it, her father had always joked. Dee was the only member of the family to have the rippling, chestnut curls of her paternal grandfather, a Corkman with an explosive temper.

Grandad O'Reilly had died a very unhappy man. None of his family had been on speaking terms with him. She didn't want to end up like that. So what if Gary was useless around the house? Her father didn't know one end of a tea towel from another and her mother coped. It was just a matter of how you handled things.

CHAPTER EIGHT

Dee smiled as she watched the smallest flower girl carefully pull a pink satin hairband off her head and fling it carelessly into the rose bushes before sitting down to take off her tiny pink ballet shoes. The operation complete, the four year old raced off into the garden, screeching with delight. The Delahuntys' pedigree Dalmatian ran after her.

It was about the only natural thing that had happened at the wedding so far. The whole event was an exercise in pretension. Dee wondered if Yvonne Thomas, *née* Delahunty, had asked a professional events organiser to copy *Bride's Magazine*'s version of the perfect wedding.

She could just picture it: Yvonne, brushing a skein of long, perfectly bleached hair back from her face with one plump manicured hand, saying: 'I don't care what it costs – I want it to be *the* society wedding of the year. I want it to be a work of art.'

But it wasn't so much a work of art as very artful, Dee thought sourly. The ceremony had been directed like an opera, with the choir all dolled up in flowing robes, Simon and his brothers in morning suits and three priests in front of the altar. As if Yvonne had wanted to be triply sure that she was married.

The church had been a riot of pale pink roses with

posies at the end of each pew. Yvonne's dress had a train so long it took six bridesmaids clad in pink silk meringue dresses to carry it, with three adorable flower girls and one outraged-looking page boy wearing velvet knickerbockers to help.

When the wedding party arrived at the Delahuntys' substantial country house, a string quartet was energetically working its way through Vivaldi's *Four Seasons*. Black-suited waiters brought around an endless supply of champagne – in real crystal glasses, Dee noticed. Smoked salmon niblets were provided for the two hundred or so guests. It would be at least an hour before lunch because two photographers were taking endless society pictures in the garden.

Dee just hoped they had plenty of Vaseline for the camera lenses to give the pictures that smudgy look. For Yvonne, despite all the tennis lessons, membership of an exclusive gym, endless sessions at the beautician, and a dress that probably cost as much as a small car, was definitely no raving beauty.

Nor had she succumbed to the usual pre-wedding nerves which made most brides lose half a stone. In her voluminous Brussels lace gown, she looked as if she'd put *on* weight since Dee had last seen her.

If she'd had one ounce of modesty, or wasn't so desperately spoiled, Yvonne could have been much more attractive. Dee would have sympathised with her about hips that spread when she just *looked* at cheesecake, because Dee understood that feeling very well. But Yvonne was so smug and self-satisfied, convinced she really was the greatest thing since sliced bread, that it gave Dee a perverse pleasure to criticise her.

Especially as she was still smarting over a remark Yvonne had made about 'that awful newspaper Deirdre works for'. Gary couldn't stand her and insisted that his cousin was only marrying her because Yvonne's father was a senior partner of Simon's legal firm.

'She's such a snob,' Gary said under his breath as he handed Dee another glass of champagne. He was the most handsome man in the room, she thought proudly. His wavy hair was brushed back from his strong face, winged eyebrows arched over eyes that glittered as he looked at Dee in her beautiful and very expensive new suit.

'Well, if Yvonne is a snob, so's Simon,' Dee countered. She refrained from adding, 'And so's your mother.'

'He's not that bad,' Gary demurred. 'But she's the limit. Apparently she went ballistic last night when she realised the caterers were serving Möet instead of Cristal.'

Dee stared at him in amazement. 'What a spoilt brat! She's just unbelievable. Doesn't she have a clue about the real world?'

He shook his head. 'I doubt it. But Simon will be well able for her. He's quite tough and she'll have to understand that once Daddy's not picking up the tab any more, she'd better economise.'

'*Economise!*' Dee exclaimed. 'Yvonne thinks she's slumming it if she spends less than a hundred and fifty quid on a skirt. She probably thinks "the real world" is the name of some cute boutique in London where they won't let you in unless you wave an American Express gold card at them and say you're a close personal friend of Nicole Kidman.'

Gary laughed. 'You're priceless, Dee, you know that?' He leant over and kissed her gently. 'And you look stunning in that outfit. Good enough to eat.'

Dee gave him an arch look. 'Maybe we could sneak

upstairs and find a spare bedroom?' she suggested. 'Your mother keeps telling me this house has ten, so we may as well use one of them.'

'Don't tempt me,' he murmured. One hand slid surreptitiously under her jacket and reached inside her camisole. Dee leant against him, feeling a wave of desire sweep over her. The combination of champagne, no lunch and the warm sun made her feel languorous and sexy.

What's more, she knew she looked great in her elegant terracotta suit, and looking good was one of the most powerful of aphrodisiacs.

'Gary and Deirdre . . .' Margaret Redmond appeared with a horsey-looking woman in tow. Gary whipped his hand out from under Dee's jacket.

'. . . have you met Mrs de Vere-Smyth? Her son is doing a degree at the London School of Economics. You've a couple of pals there, don't you, Gary?' Margaret lowered her voice a fraction and said meaningfully, 'And her husband is in banking, a merchant bank.'

'Really?' said Dee, cross at having been interrupted when she and Gary were sharing the only private moment they'd had all day. 'How interesting. You'll have to excuse me for a moment, I see someone I must talk to.'

She left Margaret open-mouthed and hurried towards Millie, a lovely Donegal girl who was married to Gary's older brother, Dan.

Millie was sitting alone on a white-painted iron bench, with a plate of smoked salmon parcels and tiny cheese nibbles on her lap. Dan was one of Simon's groomsmen and was off having endless photographs taken with the happy couple.

'I saw you escape,' Millie said indistinctly, her mouth full.

'I had to,' sighed Dee as she sat down. 'An hour and a half with that woman in the car this morning as we drove down was torture enough. I don't want to spend the entire reception listening to her boasting about her marvellous boys, her marvellous house, all the marvellous things she does for charity and the last art exhibition she went to. Horrible woman wouldn't recognise a decent painting if it bit her. She's such a pseud.' Dee took a cheesy thing off Millie's plate.

'I thought you were on a major diet for your holiday in Portugal next month,' she added. 'Wow, these are yummy.'

Millie grinned. 'Don't say anything – especially to Mother-in-law – but I'm eating for two.' She looked down at her stomach.

'Wonderful!' cried Dee. 'Congratulations, Millie. How far gone are you? You can't see anything.'

Millie looked her normal sturdy self in a gauzy cream jacket worn over a matching long dress. The pale colour suited her pale complexion and strawberry blonde bob.

She smiled ruefully. 'I'm three months gone and I've already put on eight pounds. You wouldn't notice in this outfit but I do look pregnant in my work clothes.

'We didn't want to say anything until at least three months. I knew Margaret would drive me insane if we told her before today. Can't you just imagine it? Everything I put in my mouth would be bad for the baby, everything I did would be wrong, and as for carrying on working while I was pregnant . . . forget it!'

The two women laughed in mutual understanding. Millie had been married to Dan for five years and worked in a bank. Dee had become good friends with the merry Donegal girl. They'd both had their fair share of snide remarks from Margaret who felt neither of them was good enough for her beloved boys. But Millie had a tougher hide than Dee, and rarely let her mother-in-law's barbs strike home. Dee, on the other hand, was often deeply hurt by Margaret's cutting remarks, although she tried to hide it.

'I'm due at the end of November so I'm going to work till around the beginning of the month,' Millie explained. 'Margaret will freak when she finds out that I'm not giving up work to sit at home with my feet up awaiting the birth of the first Redmond grandchild. But I'd go mad at home and it's not as if I'm delicate or anything.'

She took another salmon parcel and swallowed it whole. 'I think she likes to imagine all her daughters-in-law are little fragile things. Thinks we sound posher that way. She's never quite got over the fact that I'm from such a big, country family.' Millie was the youngest of eleven children. 'Apparently large families are provincial.'

'At least your family have a big farm and *some standing in the local community*,' Dee mimicked Margaret's marble-in-the-mouth accent. 'I'm never going to be forgiven for having a mechanic as a father and a mother who cleans the local school.' She didn't mean to sound bitter, but she did. Dee was actually very proud of her family.

'All the O'Reillys work damn' hard, we always have,' she said. 'None of us has ever sponged off the State, and just because my mother doesn't have bloody pastry forks and my dad goes down the local to watch football matches instead of listening to recitals in the Concert Hall, doesn't mean stuck-up Margaret Redmond can look down her crabby nose at us!' She finished abruptly, aware she'd suddenly become too emotional.

Millie patted her knee kindly. 'Don't let her upset you. She's not worth it. And, I promise you, when I tell her I'm going to keep working in the bank until a few weeks before the baby's born, I'll make sure you're there to see the look on her face. She'll go bananas! It'll be priceless. But Dan won't let her get a word in edgewise.'

That was the difference between the brothers, Dee reflected. Dan stood up to his mother and wouldn't let her pick on Millie. But Gary wanted to be his mother's pet, the youngest, the most devoted. Which meant he wilfully blinded himself to her faults – even when she was a cast-iron bitch towards Dee.

The musicians had done Vivaldi to death by now and had moved on to a rather kitsch version of 'Here Comes the Bride' to greet a beaming Yvonne who'd arrived from the rose garden with her entourage of bridesmaids.

'How many million photos have they taken?' Millie asked. 'I'm starving. Pregnancy does that to you,' she added with a grin.

Dan loped towards them with a champagne flute in one hand. His long legs looked even longer in stripey morning suit trousers. He wasn't nearly as good-looking as Gary and was slowly losing his hair. But he was very kind, a total gentleman and obviously adored his wife.

'How are you, Millie?' he asked, planting a kiss on the top of her head. 'Did you save me anything to eat?'

'I'm sorry, Dan, I've been a greedy pig and nearly polished off the lot. But it must be time for lunch soon.' Millie popped the last salmon parcel in her husband's mouth. 'I'm ravenous. I've told Dee the good news. We'd better tell your mother tonight, so she can start knitting.'

'Congratulations.' Dee gave him a kiss on the cheek. Dan beamed down at her.

'If you will all move into the marquee, lunch is served,' announced a waiter grandly.

'Will my two favourite ladies let me accompany them?' Dan held out both hands.

'We'd better hold on for a moment or we'll be squashed in the rush,' said Dee, as the wedding guests, ravenous after waiting so long for lunch, made for the striped marquee like starved piglets bustling towards the trough.

'There's no hurry, anyway,' Dan said. 'There are place names.'

'Written in copperplate on ivory parchment and held by silver place-name holders, I presume?' inquired Millie wickedly.

'Of course,' Dee said. 'What sort of wedding do you think this is, Millicent? Something common, or what?'

They all burst out laughing.

'I expect the same sort of thing from you and Gary,' Millie joked. 'Champers, string quartets and lots of gorgeous nibbles, plus seventeen bridesmaids who'll shower you with rose petals as you walk up the aisle.'

'Don't hold your breath,' Dee answered. 'My family wouldn't be into this type of party.'

'But Margaret would,' whispered a grinning Millie as the three of them walked into the marquee.

Robin ran one finger along a window ledge and then scrutinised the finger with distaste.

'This place is filthy,' she announced.

Isabel closed the airing cupboard door and looked tiredly at her daughter.

'Robin, it's only dirt. We can clean up. You've got to look beyond a bit of grime to see what you think of the house.'

'Only grime?' said Robin crossly as she marched across the room in her patent platform mules. 'I'm not sleeping in a house this filthy.'

To stop herself from saying something she'd regret, Isabel left the small kitchen and went back into the sitting-room. Robin was right about one thing – 12 Eagle Terrace was filthy. A small three-bedroomed terraced house in Bray, it could have been very pretty if the previous owner had ever bothered to paint or clean any part of it.

The peeling window frames outside and dirty grey façade gave the house a run-down look and inside it wasn't much better. The kitchen was 1960s, complete with swirling purple wallpaper which reminded Isabel of the once-cool Pucci designs that looked so good on leggings and shirts, and so bad on walls.

The sitting-room was painted a dark crimson colour and matching carpets gave it the look of a dilapidated brothel. The upstairs bedrooms were all painted off-white and had carpets that could only be called dirty brown. The small bathroom was a hideous pink.

All in all, you'd need to wear sunglasses to walk around the house, and even then you'd still get a headache, Isabel thought.

She struggled with the sitting-room window, trying to open it so she could see what the back garden looked like from a different angle. From the kitchen door, it was a long, narrow wasteland with a horrible clump of red hot pokers bang in the middle, spreading out like some giant, ugly spider. The window flew up suddenly and Isabel was able to see that the view wasn't any better from the sitting-room. Dispiritedly, she pulled the window shut.

The house was pretty awful and needed to be totally redecorated. But it was cheap and didn't seem to have any structural problems. It had gas central heating and on-street parking. The small terraced street it was situated in was quiet and in a nice area, so she wouldn't have to worry about the girls walking home in the dark winter evenings. And, because the house was in Bray, they could stay with her parents if Isabel had to work late.

Robin flounced downstairs. 'The bedrooms are tiny,' she pointed out.

'They're not,' Isabel sighed

'Well, they're not as big as the ones at home,' Robin said sulkily.

And whose fault is that? Isabel wanted to snap. Your bloody father's, that's who. If he hadn't mortgaged our lovely house against his business, we wouldn't have had to sell The Gables or leave Oxford.

And I wouldn't have to take a loan from my parents to put down even the tiniest deposit on a house, and I wouldn't be putting myself to the pin of my collar trying to get a mortgage because I'm a single woman now with no husband to share the bills.

She said nothing for a moment and let her blood cool.

Poor Robin, it wasn't fair on her at all. Naomi was her mother's girl and happy to be with Isabel, no matter how much she missed David. But Robin idolised her father.

She was deeply upset about the separation and wanted to lash out at someone. Isabel was that someone.

At that moment the estate agent walked back in after seeing out other prospective buyers.

'What do you think?' he asked urbanely, as though he'd just shown them a penthouse flat in Dalkey instead of a house that was so dirty it was a health hazard.

'We'll think about it,' Isabel replied coolly.

'Well, I should point out that it's not often a property comes on the market at this price,' the estate agent said smoothly. 'It's only because the new owners want a quick sale, and because the place needs a bit of work, that they're asking such a low price.'

Isabel hoped that Robin didn't pick up the words 'new owners'. If she knew that the previous inhabitant of 12 Eagle Terrace had died in his sleep in the sitting-room in front of the fire, she'd have run out of the place.

The estate agent shrugged. 'Those other people are pretty keen, I feel I ought to tell you.'

'Thank you,' Isabel said again. 'I'll be in touch. Come on, Robin.

'Let's go and have a cup of coffee and a sticky bun,' she suggested once they were outside.

'Yeah!' Robin's face lit up. She was still a child, even if she tried so hard to be grown-up, Isabel thought fondly. It was just as well that Naomi was in bed with 'flu. Being alone with Robin meant Isabel could talk to her on a different, 'us adults' basis that just might work.

Over a coffee slice, an éclair and two cappuccinos, Isabel explained the way she was thinking.

'Robin, we need a place of our own, you can understand that. Your dad isn't here and I'm looking to borrow money from the building society on my own, so it's very difficult. Normally they loan couples money by working out what both of them earn but they're only prepared to loan me money based on what *I* earn, so it's less. Do you understand?'

Robin's face was pale and taut. 'Yes.'

'That's why I'm looking at cheaper houses than the one we had in Oxford. I can't afford anything else.'

'What about Dad?' protested her daughter. 'Isn't he coming here?'

Isabel took another sip of coffee.

'Robin, your father and I have separated. You know that. I can't say what will happen in the future. I love him and I know you do too,' she began.

Tears glistened in her daughter's eyes.

'But he lost all our money. And that's not the worst thing,' Isabel hastened to add. 'The worst is that he lost the home we'd made for you and Naomi. That's what I can't accept, that's why we split up. He gambled with your security and safety.'

'You didn't have to leave him,' said Robin shakily. 'He would have worked it out.'

'There was no way to work it out, Robin. We were bankrupt. If I'd stayed, we'd have been completely broke. I couldn't do that to you and Naomi. Coming back to Ireland was the only choice. Please understand that,' begged Isabel.

Robin shoved her éclair away and stared at her mother mutinously. Isabel gave up. Robin was just like her father. There was no talking to her in this mood.

Isabel was doing the ironing when the phone rang at seven that evening. Robin had gone to see her friend, Karen, with strict instructions that she was to be back by half-eight, while Naomi was cuddled up in her duvet in the sitting-room watching TV. Isabel's parents were visiting a friend in hospital.

As there was nobody to yell, 'I'll get it,' Isabel answered the phone herself. It wasn't one of Robin's monosyllabic girlfriends as she'd expected. It was David.

'Hello, Izzy,' he said. 'How are you? And how are the girls?'

'Fine, we're all fine. I got a new job.'

'The one Robin told me about?'

'Yes. In the *Sentinel*. I'm the new women's editor,' she said flatly.

'Sounds like fun.'

'*Fun?*' She couldn't believe he'd said that. 'Working my fingers to the bone in a tough new job because it's your fault I had to leave the last one is hardly my idea of fun,' she snapped.

David ignored her outburst. 'Good money, I hope?'

'Enough for me to afford to pay a mortgage,' Isabel answered, bitterness in every syllable.

'Unlike me, is that it, Izzy?' he asked.

'Since you ask, yes, totally unlike you,' she said bitterly. 'It's going to be a couple of weeks before I can get the mortgage sorted out on the house I want but, when I do, that money's going to be in the building society every month without fail. No "Oh, dear, I'm overdrawn at the bank, darling Izzy, so let's skip a month's mortgage and get the building society to stick it on at the end of the mortgage. They don't mind doing that".'

'That only happened a couple of times,' he protested.

'*Couple of times?*' Isabel said incredulously. 'Oh, please, David. You may be able to fool other people but you can't fool me. Well,' she amended, 'you can't fool me *now*. There was a time when I believed your bullshit about our finances. But not any more. I learnt the hard way. The we-can't-get-the-heating-fixed-because-I've-blown-the-money hard way.' Even after a few months

171

away from David, Isabel was stunned by how bitter she still was. Just one phone call and she wanted to kill him; wanted to choke him for all his empty promises and denuded bank accounts.

'Don't be like that, Izzy,' he said in that infuriatingly relaxed way of his. 'Please calm down. Your mother's getting to you, huh? She always got on your nerves.'

Isabel fought for control and lost.

'It's not my *mother* that's the problem, David. It's you,' she hissed. 'And, by the way, I haven't heard from you for over two weeks, and while *I* can certainly spend the rest of my life without ever needing to set eyes on you again, your daughters, unaccountably, don't feel the same way. They love you and miss you. And *you* can't even be bothered to ring . . .'

'I've been busy setting up the new business. I had to go to Germany, I'm just back. You know how it is,' he protested.

'Oh, I know. What's her name? Heidi? Bettina?'

'Jesus!' David said in exasperation. 'You always shift the conversation around to that, don't you?'

'And why do you think that is, David? I know exactly what you're like when there's something, or *someone*, new on the horizon. I know the signs. And no new business ever keeps you that enthralled.' Isabel suddenly felt very tired. Why did she even bother to go through all this with him. She'd left him; it was over. He could do what he wanted to, whether it involved Heidi, Bettina or both at the same time. He could have a *ménage à gang* for all she cared.

What was important now, was how he treated the girls. It would be great if he'd occasionally remember the only two people in the world who genuinely loved him. He hadn't seen them for over a month, since he'd visited Dublin on a flying twenty-four-hour visit.

Typically, he'd arranged it as a sort of teenage sensory overload that included ten-pin bowling, lunch in McDonald's, a blockbuster movie in the Savoy in the afternoon and dinner at Planet Hollywood. No wonder Robin had been wretched when he'd gone. In a day spent with her beloved father, they hadn't had one single unoccupied moment in which to talk. A typical David day. He hated to talk.

'I'm not a kid, Mum,' Robin had told Isabel tearfully afterwards. 'I wanted to speak to Dad. I don't want to spend a day playing.'

Yeah, but your father does, Isabel had thought wryly. And a day jam-packed with activities had the added advantage of making deep, meaningful conversations completely impossible. Deep, meaningful conversations are his idea of hell, as you'll find out soon enough.

'Listen, David,' she said briskly. 'Let's stop arguing. I want to talk about the girls. You're going to have to be in touch more frequently, and you've got to come to visit them soon,' she added firmly. 'Robin is taking the separation very badly and needs to see you.'

'They can come to London next weekend,' he said.

'They bloody well won't,' Isabel said immediately. 'I can't afford the plane fare for both of them and, even if I could, I don't want them travelling on their own. Naomi's too young. Be realistic, will you?'

'OK, OK. I'll come the weekend after next. The good news is I've managed to get enough money together to pay off the mortgage arrears and the building society isn't going to repossess The Gables. Isn't that great?'

Isabel was stunned. They still owned the house after all? That was fantastic. They'd make some money selling it. She'd be able to put a deposit down on a house with her half. David might even be able to start paying maintenance for the girls. But where had he got the money from?

'I know what you're going to ask me, Izzy, and it's legal, I promise. It's a long story . . .'

'Tell me,' she ordered.

'I'll tell you when I see you.'

'Tell me now!' Isabel said sharply. 'What do you mean "it's legal"?'

'Izzy, I can't talk now, I'm in a rush. I'll phone next week with details of my flight. Now, are the girls there so I can say hello and give them the good news?'

'Robin is out but I'll get Naomi for you,' she said resignedly. She knew that when David didn't want to tell her something, nothing could induce him to do so. 'Naomi has 'flu, poor thing, and hasn't been getting on too well in school, so cheer her up, will you?'

'I wouldn't need to cheer her up over the phone if you hadn't walked out on me,' David said softly. 'She was getting on very well in her old school.'

'Don't start that,' Isabel groaned.

'Do you miss me, Izzy? I miss you. A lot. And there's no Bettina or Heidi, I promise.'

'Sure. 'Bye, David,' Isabel put down the receiver and called Naomi to the phone. She went back to her ironing but couldn't concentrate.

There's no Heidi or Bettina. I promise.

Since when had any of David's promises actually meant anything?

I promise you, Izzy. She didn't mean anything to me. It just happened. We were drunk and the shoot had gone so well. The crew were celebrating. It only happened once, I'd never do anything to hurt you. You're the one I love . . .

Next year will be better, I promise. Business is great.

You'll probably be able to give up work in a couple of years, we'll be doing so well. Imagine it – we could buy a house in Portugal. What do you think?

The iron hissed over one of Robin's school blouses as Isabel ironed vigorously. Damn David. Damn him and all his stupid, money-making schemes that had gone wrong. And he never seemed to learn from his mistakes.

But then neither had she.

Isabel hung the blouse on a hanger and started on another one. She was as bad as David, she reflected angrily.

After eighteen years, you'd think she'd have been smart enough to figure out that he'd never change, that he'd be a dreamer all his life. But no. She'd spent years convincing herself that one day it would all work out. Or that one day David might actually grow up and settle down to some boring nine-to-five job that would give her and the girls the security they desperately craved.

She was the stupid one. He wasn't going to change. And she'd never been strong enough to walk away. Until this time. She was broke and things were tough, but at least she'd actually done the right thing. She hoped.

CHAPTER NINE

'This was a brilliant idea, Gary,' said Dee. 'I love Wexford. I love drinking wine in the sun. And,' she leaned over and gave him a gentle kiss, 'I love you.'

She sat lazily back in her chair and stretched out her legs to give them a better chance of getting a sun tan. It was incredibly hot. The August sun was beating down on the verandah of the Ferrycarraig Hotel, toasting everyone who sat outside on the wooden deck as they gazed over the tiny bay and enjoyed their lunch. Seagulls swooped and dived over the water. A small boat slowly made its way out to sea, laughter coming from on deck.

Dressed in shorts and T-shirts, Dee and Gary relaxed facing the sun, letting the blissful warmth sink into their limbs.

The remains of two crab salads lay on the table in front of them and they'd got half way through a bottle of deliciously cool white wine.

Soft music drifted out from the bar, mingling with the conversation of people enjoying their lunch in the sun. Only a couple of marauding toddlers threatened the peace and even they were getting sleepy, if a little fractious, in the heat.

'We should do this every weekend,' Dee said happily.

'I agree. Now that you've got normal working hours, we can go away more often,' Gary pointed out. 'What do you think about going to Amsterdam in October? One of the guys from work went there for a weekend with his wife and they had a fantastic time.'

'Yes, I'd love it,' Dee said enthusiastically. 'But can we afford it? We're supposed to be saving for the wedding. If we can ever pick a date, that is,' she added.

'No, I've had a better idea,' Gary said seriously. 'We're going to go to Vegas to get married by an Elvis impersonator in a drive-by chapel of lurve. It'd be cheaper.' He leaned over and poked her gently in the ribs. 'Only kidding. I know you want the full works.'

Dee sat up. 'I don't,' she protested.

'You do, you know you do. I've seen all those copies of *Bride's Magazine* under the bed. I know you fancy yourself in one of those enormous lacy dresses with half a dozen bridesmaids and a veil with a tiara.'

'Perish the thought,' Dee said, poking him back. 'If you think I'm wearing one of those meringue dresses, you're mad. I'd look like a tank done up in net curtains.'

'Stop that, Dee. You wouldn't. You haven't got much weight to lose.' Gary sounded annoyed. 'You've got such a hang-up about your figure. Stop going on about it, for God's sake, right?'

Chastened, she nodded. She knew Gary hated it when she went on about her body. But he didn't understand what it was like to be an overweight woman, constantly tormented by the feeling that you'd look much better three stone lighter and with a washboard stomach. Gary could eat as much as an entire rugby team and never put on an ounce. Dee only had to look crossways at a chocolate biscuit to gain two pounds. She surreptitiously slid a hand under her T-shirt and pinched a bit of her stomach.

What did the diet cereal commercial say? *If you can pinch more than an inch . . . blah, blah, blah.* She could pinch more than an inch. She could pinch several inches in fact, she thought ruefully. God knew how many years she'd have to be eating Special K and skimmed milk for breakfast before she looked like one of the women in their adverts.

It was so unfair. She'd been so good all week in preparation for the weekend. She'd cut down on the sugars in her coffee and had only eaten salad sandwiches for lunch, despite the fact that she normally ate with Maeve who had a two-course meal twice a day and retained the physique of a long-distance runner. Dee had even given up ordering Mars Bars when the office runner went around at eleven asking everyone what they wanted for coffee break. But she couldn't resist the odd chocolate ice cream. Cornettos were her downfall.

Gary poured more wine into her glass.

'D'you fancy dessert?' he asked. 'They've got cheesecake.'

Dee's mouth watered. Cheesecake. She adored it. But they were going out to dinner later and she couldn't have two big meals in one day. Her favourite black trousers were now very tight around the waist and she hadn't bothered to pack the black velvet dress Gary loved her to wear because she looked three months pregnant in it.

'No, I'm full,' she lied. 'You have some. And get two forks.'

'Oh, yeah,' Gary said with a grin, 'so you can eat all mine? I'll just get two cheesecakes.'

What the heck? thought Dee. I'm on holiday. 'Yeah, I'd love some cheesecake.'

After lunch, she suggested a meander down by the bay to walk off the eight billion calories she'd just consumed. They held hands as they walked, happy, relaxed and totally contented. A family were a little ahead of them, three children and a bouncy Red Setter running around energetically.

'This is wonderful,' Dee said again. 'It's so relaxing.'

Gary picked a poppy from a drift of red flowers and handed it to her. 'Mademoiselle, a leetle present for you to tell you how much I luv you.'

'I think we should move down here,' Dee said dreamily. 'Wouldn't it be wonderful to have a walk like this every day, away from the hustle and bustle of the city?'

'This from the woman who gets withdrawal symptoms if she's away from the office for more than two weeks?' Gary asked incredulously.

'I don't,' Dee insisted. 'Not any more.'

He put an arm around her shoulders. 'I apologise. Now it's *three* weeks before you get withdrawal symptoms.'

He ducked as Dee swatted him with her flower. 'All right, I admit it – you're about a hundred and fifty times more relaxed since you got the new job,' he said.

'Do you think so?' she asked, surprised.

'Of course. When you worked in news, you were like one of those drumming bunnies they use to advertise batteries. "Use our batteries and the bunny never stops drumming, ever." You never stopped, Dee. Now you're much more laid-back. I think working with Isabel Farrell is good for you.'

'I suppose,' she conceded. She still hadn't quite forgiven Isabel for taking her job, even though the two of them got along very well.

Dee had taken the big interview slot as her own and

loved picking subjects for it and interviewing them. She also had more time to work on her agony column which meant she wasn't always under so much pressure at work.

Isabel was a surprisingly good boss, calm, considerate and always ready to give praise where it was due. She had slowly changed the whole look of the women's pages, with Maeve, Emily and Dee's help. After years of Antonia's tantrums and mental block when it came to grammar, working with Isabel was a welcome change. Maeve said she enjoyed it.

So did Dee, if she could have brought herself to admit it. Since their first frost moments in Nigel's office, both women had been ultra-polite to each other. Isabel always inquired after Gary, whom she'd never met but had spoken to on the phone, while Dee tried to be equally polite by asking after Isabel's daughters.

Thanks to Ted Holt's gossipy secretary, Marion, Dee knew that Isabel was either separated or divorced and that her ex still lived in the UK. But that was all she knew. Isabel was reserved and never volunteered any information about her life. Dee had no idea where Isabel lived or if she was involved with anyone else. And for someone as curious as Dee, that was very annoying indeed.

All in all, the new women's editor was quite mysterious. The only time Dee had extracted anything personal from her was a few weeks previously when she came back from lunch early to find Isabel at her desk, studying her bank statement with a worried expression on her face.

'I hate that job,' remarked Dee as she took off her jacket and sat down at her desk. 'I always overspend, particularly on clothes.'

Isabel looked up. 'It's a long time since I had the chance to overspend on clothes,' she said wryly. 'Two teenage daughters can spend your salary faster than the speed of light. Not to mention how quickly the bills mount up when you buy a house.'

'Oh, you've just bought a house. Where?' asked Dee, interested.

'Bray. Well, when I say house, I mean terraced hovel,' Isabel explained. 'It needs a lot of work. Work I can't afford, I might add.'

'I'm supposed to be saving for our wedding,' Dee said. 'But I'm not very good at saving.'

'Have you decided on a date?'

'No,' admitted Dee. 'I know we should have but we haven't got round to it yet.'

She didn't want to say that Gary had proved to be noticeably reluctant to settle on a date, apart from saying 'September sounds good', which he'd said the previous year as well. Dee wanted to know *which* September.

'I got married in a rush and it was a very small affair,' Isabel recalled. 'My dress was hideous, now that I think about it. I bought it in a hurry. It was all frills and ribbons, neither of which suit me.' She looked down at her classy white chinos, white linen blouse and cotton cricket jumper with a smile. 'That's why I stick to such simple clothes these days. My wedding photos put me off frills for good.'

Dee gazed at Isabel's figure enviously. There was no way in hell *she'd* ever be able to wear a pair of white trousers. Her bum would look like an elephant's and, with a matching sweater, she'd be a dead ringer for the Michelin Man.

It was very difficult working alongside someone with

Isabel's figure and dress sense. Always flawlessly turned out, she made Dee feel like a fat, frumpy matron. Apart from that, Isabel was really quite nice, though.

Not that *everyone* liked her. Carol-Anne still loathed her and took every opportunity to make smart remarks behind the women's editor's back.

Dee had been fascinated to see how Isabel would deal with someone of Carol-Anne's calibre, someone for whom bitching wasn't so much a habit, as a way of life.

'Wait till Madam has to deal with Nigel in one of his tempers,' Carol-Anne said when she saw how incredibly, and uncharacteristically, polite the editor was to Isabel. 'That'll wipe the smile off her self-satisfied face!'

If Isabel ever heard Carol-Anne's repeated vicious comments – and she must have – she never said a thing. Instead, she treated the other woman politely but firmly. And she made her work. Carol-Anne was doing three times the amount she'd done pre-Isabel.

And I'm doing less but I'm much happier, Dee reflected. She'd only acknowledge it to herself but she *did* like working for Isabel.

The sun went behind a patch of cloud and a soft breeze wafted across the bay. Dee shivered in her light T-shirt.

'Let's turn back,' she said, as she peered up at the sky. 'There's a huge patch of cloud and the sun won't be out for ages.'

'Spoilsport,' Gary said. 'I thought you said you'd like a walk? Come on, it'll do you good to get a bit of exercise.' He playfully swiped her on the behind. 'You might shift a couple of pounds off your rear end.'

'What do you mean by that?' demanded Dee, stung by his remark. 'Ten minutes ago you were telling me I was too hung-up about my figure. Now I'm heap of the week who needs a brisk walk to shift the fat off her behind!'

Gary threw his hands into the air in exasperation. 'This is why we can never talk about your weight problem. You just fly off the handle immediately.'

'*My weight problem?*' shrieked Dee.

'Come off it, Dee,' Gary said irritably. 'You know you have a weight problem. When I met you, you were miles slimmer. You were *thin*, for God's sake. Now look at you! You've just let yourself go and I hate it. But,' he looked at her coldly, 'I daren't say anything about it.'

'You're talking now,' Dee hissed.

He ignored her as he got into his stride. 'You wouldn't believe the number of times I've thought of buying you a piece of sexy lingerie or a nice dress when I'm away with the lads from the football club, but I can't. And why not? Because you'd have a fit if I came home with something that had a size sixteen label on it, that's why.'

Dee stared at him, dumbstruck.

'*You* know you're a size sixteen, *I* know you're a size sixteen, but we can't possibly mention it. Oh, no.'

He was enjoying this, she thought. He really was enjoying it, getting stuff off his chest that he'd been harbouring for months, years maybe.

And how did he know what size she was? She'd been hiding it from herself for weeks now, determined not to push all her size fourteen stuff to the back of the wardrobe in favour of her emergency tent-like clothes. If she did that, it'd be giving in to the fat instead of convincing herself she'd lose it.

'Oh, no, we have to pretend that the extra weight you've put on is just an unfortunate phase you're going through. When in reality, it's nothing of the sort. You're fat, Dee, have been for at least three years. How do you think that makes me feel, huh?' Gary demanded.

'How do you think I feel at my office party when everyone else's wife or girlfriend is done up in slinky little dresses and you're in some shapeless jacket with a ton of make-up on so you have something to hide behind? When you're not hiding behind ten vodka and oranges, that is. I mean,' he continued hotly, 'I thought you'd cop on when you got promoted. I thought you'd realise that a deputy women's editor should look elegant, well-groomed and slim. But no. You just started using more bloody make-up.'

He stopped suddenly and took a deep breath. Dee wanted to say lots of things. Like, '*Run out of steam, darling?*' But she couldn't. Her mouth was frozen, like her heart.

People had called her fat before. Kids in school. She'd been Ten Ton Deirdre or Mars Bar O'Reilly. She'd hated games in secondary school, loathed putting on the deeply unflattering gym skirt to trundle heavily up and down the netball court, sweating profusely and missing the ball all the time. There was always someone ready to tease her, to call her names, to humiliate her.

Only this time it wasn't some spotty fourteen-year-old girl being venomous because the fat O'Reilly girl was clever and got better marks in the English exam. No, this was her boyfriend, her *fiancé*, who was saying all these nasty things to her. Dee simply couldn't believe it.

'Well, aren't you going to say anything?' Gary asked. 'Or are you just going to stare at me and blub?'

Dee felt like bawling her eyes out but she wouldn't crumble in front of him, not after what he'd just said.

'What can I say?' she asked simply. 'You've said it all – I'm nothing but a fat, stupid bitch you're ashamed of. I can't think of any answer to that.'

She turned on her heel and walked away as swiftly as she could. She wanted to go back to the hotel, collect her stuff and go home. She couldn't spend another minute with Gary, not after this.

He caught up with her and stood on the path in front of her, blocking her way. He looked mildly repentant.

'Dee, I'm sorry. I shouldn't have been so blunt, so brutal. But I *had* to say it, you know that. It's because I love you.'

The tears came then. '*Because you love me?*' she said shakily. 'All that was done for love? Because it certainly didn't feel like it from this angle.'

'Dee . . .' He grabbed her and wrapped his arms around her.

She stiffened. 'Don't touch me. I can't bear it, not after what you've said.'

He held on firmly. 'I love you, Dee, you know that. But I have to be honest with you. I've wanted to say all that to you for so long. Wouldn't you prefer me to be honest?'

Dee couldn't answer – she was sobbing into his shoulder.

'I want the best for you and that includes making you look your best. *Helping* you look your best,' he amended. 'Please don't cry, Dee.'

He took her hand and led her back up the winding, grassy path to the hotel and into the bar.

'I can't go in, I look a mess,' she mumbled, head down and hair obscuring her tear-stained face.

'There's nobody in here, everyone's sitting outside in the sun,' Gary pointed out. 'Two brandies. Doubles,' he said to the barman.

'I don't want it,' said Dee tearfully when the barman

put the balloon glass in front of her.

'Drink it,' Gary said firmly.

She took a sip of the amber liquid and then a gulp.

Refusing to look at Gary, she stared out at the beautiful bay, a scene that had delighted her such a short time ago. Before Gary had completely decimated her world.

How had that happened? How had they gone from utter happiness to utter misery in a few short minutes? It had been such a wonderful weekend away, she'd been having such a lovely time, thinking about how she was enjoying work and about how fantastic it would be to have a mini-holiday in Amsterdam in a couple of months. And now this – total annihilation. Gary hadn't simply destroyed her confidence, he'd destroyed *her*.

He'd picked on the one subject that was guaranteed to tear her apart – her weight. Her horrible, fat, lumbering body that couldn't fit into half of her clothes any more; the body that had betrayed her all her life. It was still betraying her. And so had Gary.

She felt his hand on her knee.

'Don't be angry with me, Dee,' he said softly. 'I only wanted to help. Somebody had to say it.'

But why did it have to be you? You traitor, the one I loved the most. She bit her lip.

'Finish your drink, darling.' He pushed the glass towards her.

Dee turned to face him, her eyes dark and glassy. 'A moment ago, I was the woman who got plastered at office parties to give herself Dutch courage,' she said bitterly. 'Now, you want me to down a double brandy in two minutes because you've just insulted me, you haven't got any smelling salts handy and you hate people seeing me cry in public. You couldn't bear them to think you'd been so nasty you'd made me cry, isn't that it?' she said harshly.

'It's not like that, Dee. You've . . . you've . . . had a shock,' Gary said. 'I'm sorry about that, but we can get over this, I know we can.'

Yeah, right, thought Dee. There'll be snowballs in hell first. Well, if he wants me to finish my drink, I bloody well will. She grabbed her glass and drained it. The pain stayed in her heart but the brandy numbed it ever so slightly. She felt lightheaded suddenly. It was better than feeling totally devastated.

'Order me another. I'm going to the loo to fix my make-up – and put another ton on,' she added caustically. She pushed past him, shoving a spare bar stool out of the way with her knee. As she strode out of the bar, Dee was conscious of every single stone she weighed. She felt enormous, like a 747 manoeuvring itself through a small space. Was everybody in the hotel looking at her? Were the guests and the staff wondering why such a fat lump of a woman didn't simply stay at home with the fridge for company instead of coming out into the open along with 'normal' thin people?

All the old, hateful remarks flooded into her mind.

The last time I saw something that big, the ISPCA were trying to push it back into the water. Ha, ha, ha.

What's the similarity between a 50cc moped and a fat girl? They're both fun to ride until somebody sees you. Ha, ha, ha.

In the toilets, Dee stared at her red-rimmed eyes and red nose with disgust. She looked dreadful when she cried. She rummaged in her make-up bag for her foundation and was just about to open the tube when she changed her mind. Why bother? Gary was the only person who was going to be looking at her and he'd already made it plain he wasn't impressed. Why waste make-up on him? Anyway, he'd accused her of hiding behind her pancake foundation. She wouldn't do that again.

Instead, she slicked on some lipstick and scrubbed away her smudged mascara. She didn't bother putting any more on. Fat women could wear all the mascara in the world and they'd still be fat.

A fresh brandy was waiting for her.

'Are you all right?' Gary asked.

'Wonderful,' Dee said tightly. 'There's nothing I enjoy more than being savagely criticised by my own boyfriend. I could do this all day. Let's sit outside. You might get some inspiration for more insults because I'm sure there's a ferry due along in a minute. You could work out how much more weight I have to gain before I'm ferry-sized.'

She grabbed her glass and headed for the open door. 'Can we have two more of these?' she called to the barman as she passed him.

'We don't want to get pissed or we'll never be able to drive into Wexford this evening for dinner,' Gary said.

'You can drive where you bloody like, *darling*,' she said. 'I'm going to sit out in the sun and get drunk.'

After three more doubles, consumed in total silence, they were both quite drunk. Dee felt sleepy, lightheaded. But she could still remember every word Gary had said.

The sun had gone in by four o'clock and Dee decided she wanted to go back to their hotel bedroom and put on something warmer.

'I'll come too,' Gary said, getting off his seat.

'Suit yourself.'

He turned on the TV in the room, slumped down on

an armchair and watched football. Bloody typical. Dee sat on the bed, wrapped a cardigan around herself and picked up her latest novel. A murder story was exactly what she needed to keep her mind off what Gary had said.

And it might contain a few hints on how to kill someone without getting caught, she thought darkly.

She woke at half-seven, her head muzzy from a mixture of sleep and brandy. Gary sat beside her, gently kissing her face.

'How do you feel, my love?' he asked tenderly.

'Dreadful,' she muttered.

He kissed her cheek, her forehead, her nose, and then her mouth. His tongue slid inside, questing and passionate. 'I love you, Dee, you know that,' he murmured as he moved one hand under her T-shirt to caress her breasts through her bra.

'I've got a headache,' she said rudely. He wasn't getting away that easily. A quick grope and she'll be eating out of my hand? No way. How could she let him touch her or see her body after all he'd said? Every caress would feel like torture, as if he were measuring how huge she was.

'OK. Let's have dinner. I'm starving,' he said. 'I've booked a table here since neither of us is in a fit state to drive.'

'Fine,' Dee said shortly.

She didn't bother dolling herself up. Her black trousers and silvery grey velvet overshirt would do. She gave her hair a desultory comb and put on more lipstick and a dab of eye-shadow. She was having dinner with Gary because she was hungry and because there was no way she could get back to Dublin tonight. That was all.

They sat silently in the restaurant, both staring at the

menu. Dee was ravenous but wasn't about to order a huge meal. She'd have salad and more salad. That'd show him. She'd just decided on avocado salad for a starter and seafood salad for main course when a waiter arrived with an ice bucket containing a bottle of champagne along with a single, long-stemmed red rose.

'To say sorry,' Gary said softly.

Dee had always been a sucker for a romantic gesture. Roses and champagne! He must have arranged it all while she was asleep. He *did* love her, she knew that. And she loved him, madly and desperately. But could she ever forgive him for what he'd said? Or forget, for that matter. She didn't know if she could. Those hateful words spun in her head, every syllable as crisp and clear as if he'd just spoken.

Dee stared at the champagne bottle. The waiter opened it with a flourish and the people at a nearby table clapped, obviously thinking Gary and Dee were celebrating something. An engagement, perhaps. How bloody ironic.

How she'd love to have been able to talk to Maeve, to ask her if she agreed with all the things Gary had said. Maeve was a very truthful person, she wouldn't lie. She'd say if she thought Dee was a fat pig, if Dee really had let the side down with her loud clothes and too much make-up.

But then, Dee knew she'd never be able to tell Maeve about this. She'd be too ashamed to tell her. Too ashamed to admit that her loving fiancé had insulted her viciously.

It was odd to think she'd felt slightly sorry for Maeve recently, sorry for her beloved single friend who never seemed to be able to keep a man for longer than a weekend, while Dee was effortlessly happy with a handsome fiancé, a lovely town house and a wedding looming somewhere in the future. Hilarious. Now *she* was facing a ruined life thanks to the same handsome fiancé, while Maeve was probably spending a riotous Saturday night with her girlfriends, drinking pints of Guinness and drunkenly discussing why they didn't need men anyway.

'Dee?' Gary was looking at her. So was the waiter who'd just filled her glass with bubbles.

She was expected to drink it, Dee realised blankly. So she did.

Gary smiled warmly at her. Dee smiled back. She curled up her mouth at the edges and crinkled up her eyes the way she always did when she smiled. It had never been a mechanical effort before, it had always reached her eyes. But not this time.

'What are you ordering?' Gary asked sweetly. It was business as usual for him. Everything was back to normal. No, it isn't, Dee wanted to yell. She didn't. She gathered all the pain and the hurt back inside her heart where she could hide it, only to emerge when she could cope with it.

'I'll have the avocado and then the seafood salad for main course,' she told the waiter.

'Good girl,' said Gary encouragingly when the waiter was gone. 'Let's enjoy our weekend as if today never happened.'

'Yeah, let's.' Dee practised her mechanical smile again.

They clinked glasses.

Gary was asleep, snoring loudly as usual. Careful not to wake him, Dee turned in the bed and squinted at the small alarm clock she always brought with her on holidays. It was quite dark but she could see the luminous numbers: ten to two in the morning. She'd had a lot to drink, so had Gary, but she couldn't sleep.

She'd pretended to the moment her head hit the pillow. It was easier to feign sleep than to get into an argument with an amorous Gary who wanted to be forgiven.

She turned and lay on her back, staring at the outline of the pretty watercolour print on the far wall of the bedroom.

'Deirdre, you can't stay at home today. You missed a day last week and there's no way the principal is going to believe it if you have another day off sick.' Elizabeth O'Reilly tried to look severe and failed. It was hard to be angry with her fourteen-year-old daughter when she was such a sweet-natured, responsible and very kind girl. Normally, she didn't give her parents a moment's bother. She had only one problem – she was too heavy for a five-foot teenager.

'I'm not overweight, I'm under-tall,' Deirdre used to joke bravely.

But Elizabeth knew that no matter how hard her daughter attempted to make fun of her size, she was, in fact, utterly depressed about it. You could hear her at night when she sobbed miserably into her pillow. There was no point trying to comfort her – Dee would immediately rub her eyes and claim that nothing was wrong.

Elizabeth didn't know why Deirdre was heavy. None of the others was overweight. Her younger brother Shane, was a rail-thin, lanky ten year old, her father was positively thin, and Elizabeth herself had always kept her figure.

'Please, Mum, it's sports day and I just can't face it. Please let me take the day off,' begged Deirdre.

She knew exactly what sort of day she'd have if she went. The sports teacher would insist on getting every single third year on the pitch for the relay race or the five-a-side-soccer, and Deirdre dreaded it.

She couldn't run for more than a minute without going puce in the face and having to rest. That cow Julia Myers would run alongside her, taunting her.

'What's wrong, Ten Ton Deirdre? Eaten too many cream buns to run?'

Dee gazed unseeing at the hotel bedroom wall. *Ten Ton Deirdre.* No wonder she'd shortened her name when she started in journalism college. She'd told her family it was because she wanted to reinvent herself with a snappy new name suitable for newspaper by-lines. But it was really to stop her remembering all those horrific nicknames. Not that everyone in school had been horrible. She'd had lots of friends, pals who'd told bitches like Julia where to stick it when they called Dee names. But she remembered Julia and her vicious gang of four acolytes far better than she remembered all the friendly people. She felt the burning sensation in her eyes, the sting of hot, angry tears. Dee thought she'd spent enough of her life sobbing into pillows when she was a fat teenager. Obviously, she'd been wrong.

CHAPTER TEN

'Any messages, Jackie?' asked Isabel as she walked briskly past her assistant. She slung her handbag on to the desk and picked up the empty mug that sat beside her computer. She was dying for a cup of tea, something hot, liquid and comforting. Her throat felt raw and she was sure she was getting 'flu. Two hours in a stuffy, windowless room jammed with fashion journalists, who all seemed to smoke like troopers, hadn't helped.

Isabel was sorry she hadn't simply left in protest at having to wait until half-eleven before the fashion show, which was actually scheduled for half-ten, started. She couldn't stand being late and loathed bad time-keeping in others.

The clothes had all been dreadful too, lots of flimsy baby doll dresses that made skinny eighteen-year-old models look like jail bait and would make anyone else look completely ridiculous.

Jackie still hadn't answered.

'No messages then?' Isabel inquired again, looking at her for the first time. Jackie looked more like a rock chick than the features/women's department assistant. She wore her customary black mini, her long hair was done up in a thick plait and a heavy silver cross hung from her neck on a black satin ribbon. Usually, she was alert and ready for work. Once she'd had her first blast of caffeine, of course. But today her heavily kohled eyes were doleful and red.

'What's happened, Jackie?' asked Isabel, shocked at the girl's expression. She crouched down beside Jackie's chair. 'Are you all right, love?'

'We've been bought. Ted Holt's gone, Nigel's gone, and there are going to be huge staff cutbacks, I'm sure of it. And since I've only been here since January, I'll be fired.' Jackie started to cry.

Astonished, Isabel stared at her. 'What do you mean, "we've been bought"?'

'The *Sentinel* has been sold,' Phil Walsh said as she put a cup of very strong tea on the desk in front of Jackie. 'It's been sold to Roark International. We now belong to one of the biggest publishing companies in the world.'

'Oh,' said Isabel blankly. 'But that doesn't mean you're going to lose your job, Jackie. Does it?' she asked Phil.

The features editor shot her a glance over Jackie's head.

'Of course not,' said Phil with a bright smile. 'You're great at your job, Jackie, and Isabel and I won't let anyone fire you, we promise.'

'Absolutely,' added Isabel. She put her arm around Jackie. 'Nobody's going to fire you with us around. You're the best assistant I've ever had and I'll make them fire me before I let them fire you, right?'

Jackie nodded and gave her a tearful smile. 'Thank you,' she said in muffled tones.

Phil produced a tissue for her.

'I'd better go to the loo,' Jackie mumbled. 'I must look awful.'

'No, you don't,' Isabel and Phil assured her at the same time.

'Take your time,' said Isabel kindly, giving Jackie a quick hug. 'I'll answer the phones.'

When Jackie had gone, Isabel turned to Phil anxiously. 'No bullshitting. Tell me exactly what all this means. Do you think they'll fire us?'

'Who knows?' said Phil honestly. 'But we've got the National Union of Journalists behind us. People like Jackie aren't so lucky.'

'Are you serious?' Isabel was shocked. 'I mean, Roark International own the *Irish Telegraph* and *Ireland Today*, and I've never heard anything about mass firings.'

'Pity you weren't in Ireland two years ago, then. They gutted *Ireland Today* within a week of taking it over. Not that it didn't need a bit of pruning staff-wise,' Phil added reflectively. 'They had enough staff to run a couple of Cunard liners as well as bring out a daily paper. But the sackings were pretty brutal. They called it Night Of the Long Knives in Mulligan's. When they sobered up, that is. Which was two days later.'

'Oh, God,' said Isabel weakly. She sat down in Jackie's chair. 'Phil, what if they *do* fire people on the basis of "last in, first out"? I've just bought a house I can barely afford, I've the girls to think of and it was hard enough getting this job, never mind another one. What the hell am I going to do?'

She was panic-stricken. However the new bosses got rid of staff, however the sackings were dressed up, she could easily be out of a job in a week. She still owed the solicitor half of his conveyancing fee and the second month's mortgage was due.

To make matters worse, Robin insisted that she needed expensive new trainers and Isabel had just bought a washing-machine on the electricity bill. God only knew how she was ever going to pay any of it back.

Phil sat on the edge of the desk and folded her arms. That was a lovely pale blue cardigan she was wearing, Isabel thought idly, her mind desperate to think of something other than impending doom. It was a woman's cardi at that. Phil normally wore huge men's ones because she liked roomy clothes.

Stop it! she raged at herself. Why the hell am I thinking about cardigans at a time like this?

'Look, nobody knows what's going to happen,' Phil was saying. 'It depends on who Roark puts in here as managing director. Jack Carter – he's the chairman of Roark's Irish division – has a few guys he's groomed for this type of job and we could get a nice one, someone who wants to build the paper up and increase the staff. Or,' she paused, 'we could get a real hatchet man.'

'What are the chances of us getting a hatchet man?' Isabel asked.

Phil grinned. 'Don't panic, Isabel. You're doing a great job. They'd need to be crazy to fire you, surely you can see that?'

Isabel stared at her helplessly. 'Phil, if there's one thing I've learnt over the past year, it's that what you *see* and what is *really* going on are often two very different things. Just because you and I think I'm doing OK as women's editor doesn't mean diddly squat if the powers that be have someone they want to appoint instead.'

'On that basis, no job is safe,' Phil interrupted. 'They could get rid of us all but it would cost them a fortune in redundancies and they're not going to rush into anything, I'm telling you. Relax.'

If only I could, thought Isabel wryly.

'What's Jack Carter like? Is he a ruthless corporate

raider – or a sweet little pussycat of a man?' Isabel asked with a dash of sarcasm.

'I've never met him,' Phil said. 'He's one of those "left school at fifteen and started working as a post boy before crawling up the ranks" sort of guys. He's late-forties, very well off, and married to this real high society queen, Elizabeth Carter. There's no charity ball in this country she isn't at, fundraising for everything from one-eared donkeys to bewildered chimpanzees.'

'I met her once,' interrupted Jackie, back from the loo with red eyes but a brave smile on her face. 'It was at that TV telethon thing. She was lovely. Really beautiful, sort of like Cindy Crawford but older.'

'A lot older,' put in Phil. 'She's pushing fifty though she doesn't look it. Must be either good breeding – her uncle was Lord something or other – or a quick nip and tuck job. She's the high-profile member of the family. You never see Jack at the charity balls and premières.'

'Maybe he'll feel charitable towards us,' Isabel said hopefully.

'I've never heard anything bad about him,' Phil said. 'Although I did hear that she's partial to the odd recreational pharmaceutical – cocaine, in other words. He's supposed to be OK, one of the tough-but-fair school.

'Listen, ladies, I don't know about you but I've got some work to finish. If we can't produce a decent paper tomorrow, we might all be for the high jump.'

By three that afternoon, the rumours were flying. One common theory was that Eugene 'Slasher' Flynn would be leaving his post as MD of Roark International's flagship paper *Ireland Today*, in order to rip the *Sentinel* to pieces before rebuilding it as a very different sort of paper.

'Let's go to the pub, lads,' muttered the deputy sports

editor glumly when he heard this. Slasher hated both sports and sports reporters, having been the smallest and least athletic guy in his class at school, which had led to constant bullying he'd never forgotten.

The other rumour flying around was that Jack Carter would import some young blood from the company's Australian papers to give the *Sentinel* the benefit of some antipodean expertise. This was a much better prospect.

'Brilliant!' said the picture editor, a native of Sydney.

'Brilliant and then some!' smiled Maeve, her mind already picturing a few hunky Mel Gibson-lookalike executives brightening up the office – and her life.

There was very little work done that afternoon. Stalin bellowed loudly as usual but nobody paid much attention to the news editor's rantings. They were in deep enough shit without worrying about an irate boss. And anyway, as Phil remarked, the new bosses would undoubtedly change the pecking order so the management from the old regime could easily end up sweeping floors under the new one. The idea of Stalin on his hands and knees, scrubbing the canteen floor, cheered up quite a few people.

Isabel was so uptight about the whole takeover that she stared blankly at her computer and tried not to listen to all the rumours.

She was writing a piece about the latest skin cancer statistics but, no matter how many times she read and re-read the report from the Department of Health, she kept thinking about all the bills she had to pay and about the chance that she'd be made redundant a mere three months after getting the job.

By six o'clock, half the office had gone to Magee's to discuss the latest rumours, while the other half were pretending to work while mournfully discussing the chances of some descendant of Atilla the Hun's arriving to manage the paper.

Isabel couldn't take any more of it. She grabbed her briefcase and left, trying to remember if she'd defrosted the pork chops she'd planned to cook that night or if she'd have to go to the supermarket on the way home. Blast it, she thought wearily as she drove out of the office gates, she might as well go to the supermarket and get something anyway. She wasn't in the mood for cooking and could pick up some more tonic for the remains of the gin while she was there. An enormous drink was probably the wrong thing to have in this moment of crisis, but that's just what she felt like. A huge, huge gin to blot out all the terrifying fears in her head.

The late-night supermarket was jammed with after-work shoppers in a rage after being bossed around all day in the office and therefore determined to reassert themselves with some aggressive trolley manoeuvring. Isabel's trolley was crashed into three times before she reached the safety of the checkout.

It was then she realised she'd forgotten the tonic. She felt like crying. The queue had quickly built up behind her and the checkout guy had just started on her groceries. There was no way she could make a dash for the drinks section without being screeched at by the shoppers behind her. After her awful day, Isabel felt like sitting down in the middle of the supermarket and sobbing. Why couldn't things ever go well for her? What the hell had she done wrong for her life to be permanently screwed up?

'Are you paying by credit card or cash?' asked the assistant for the second time.

Isabel's mind focused.

'Cash,' she said, hoping she had enough in her purse. She smiled at the assistant. There, she'd done it again. Smiled as though everything was going perfectly when inside she was in despair.

That's my problem, Isabel thought grimly, stuffing her groceries into plastic bags. I smile when my heart is breaking and never let anyone know what's really going on. My brave smile never lets me down. She chuckled mirthlessly. At least *something* never lets me down.

At home, Robin was on the phone, perched on the bottom step of the stairs.

'Hiya,' she mouthed as her mother staggered in, weighed down with shopping bags, her briefcase and the pile of papers and articles she hadn't got round to reading in the office.

Still clutching all the bags, Isabel leant down awkwardly to kiss Robin on the cheek and went into the tiny kitchen where Naomi was curled up on the brown squashy settee. She was watching *Neighbours* on the portable TV which sat on the breakfast bar. A half-empty bowl of Rice Krispies was in her lap.

'Hiya, Mum,' she said cheerfully. 'I was too hungry to wait for dinner.'

'Sorry I'm late, Naomi,' Isabel said, as she unloaded her cargo with relief. She flexed the hand that she'd been carrying the plastic bags with, to get the circulation back. 'Has Robin eaten?'

'She had toast.'

'And is that all you've had to eat?' Isabel asked, indicating the cereal Naomi was eating.

She nodded.

'That's not enough, love. I'll fix up something light for us all. Robin can't exist on toast alone any more than you can live on Rice Krispies. How was your day? Did you both walk home from Granny's or did Grandad drive you?'

They talked as Isabel unpacked the shopping. Naomi put everything away and laid the breakfast bar neatly with plates and cutlery.

Isabel washed lettuce, tomatoes, mushrooms and cucumber and quickly assembled a salad. With the French crusty bread she'd bought, some Cheddar cheese and the remains of the salami in the fridge, they'd have a nice meal.

'Call your sister, will you?'

Robin took one look at the salad and turned up her nose. 'I'm not hungry. I've eaten,' she said, taking a Diet Coke from the fridge. She pulled the evening paper out of the pile on top of Isabel's briefcase, sat down on the settee and flicked through it aimlessly.

'Toast isn't enough for dinner,' Isabel said evenly. She could tell that Robin was ripe for an argument, which was the permanent state of affairs these days. Her perfectly shaped cupid's bow mouth was set in a pout, and her brows were heavy under the curtain of blonde hair which hid most of her face.

'Have a little bit of salad, Robin,' coaxed Isabel. 'There aren't any nutrients in toast.'

'I don't want anything else,' she said stubbornly, refusing to lift her head out of the paper.

Isabel took a deep breath. 'What did you have for lunch?'

'Oh, please. What is this, the Spanish Inquisition?' demanded Robin angrily. She threw the paper on the floor and stared at her mother defiantly. Naomi kept her eyes on her plate and nibbled a bit of cucumber.

'There's no inquisition. I simply want to make sure you eat properly, Robin. That's all. If you don't want to eat, I can't make you. And after the sort of day I've had, I don't want a fight, got it?' Isabel stared hard at her elder daughter. If Robin made just one more provocative remark, she'd explode.

For once, Robin seemed to realise that her mother was not in the mood to be crossed.

'Fine,' she mumbled. She left without slamming the door and ran upstairs. Isabel and Naomi heard her bedroom door bang shut and almost immediately the sound of Oasis could be heard from Robin's portable CD player.

At least she didn't have the music turned up to eardrum-splitting level.

Isabel shoved her fork into a bit of mushroom, not feeling very hungry any more.

'This is lovely, Mum,' said Naomi, trying to be helpful.

Isabel relaxed. 'Thanks, Naomi,' she said. 'What would I do without you?'

After dinner, Naomi washed up while Isabel reluctantly went into the sitting-room to tackle the wallpaper stripping. Since they'd moved into 12 Eagle Terrace a month ago, she'd been taking it room by room, stripping off the disgusting wallpaper and painting at the weekends. She'd taken four days off work to make the girls' rooms habitable. Robin had found a picture in *Homes & Gardens* of the sort of bedroom she wanted, so Isabel had done the basics, painting it the cool apple green her daughter wanted, and had left the rest to her.

With the magazine as her guide, Robin had then carefully painted her old chest of drawers, dressing-table and bedside table in a rich forest green before stencilling a fleur-de-lys design in gold paint all over her handiwork.

With the addition of a plain cream carpet and heavy cream curtains sprigged with an apple green leaf design, the room looked very pretty.

Robin had stencilled the same gold pattern as a frieze around the walls, just below ceiling height, and she'd even found some bronze brocade cushions in a local charity shop. Isabel had to hand it to her – she was very inventive and artistic.

'You've done such a beautiful job of your bedroom, you should pick what we'll do with the sitting-room,' Isabel had said, wanting to encourage Robin in her interior decorating skills. Unfortunately, she had been so grouchy for the past fortnight that Isabel hadn't been able to bring the subject up again.

With her father's help, Isabel had papered Naomi's small bedroom with a pretty and romantic floral paper in rose and peach shades. She'd spent some of her meagre budget on a brass bedhead and, with the addition of a ruinously expensive white broderie anglaise duvet cover and pillowcases, the effect was just as feminine and girlish as Naomi could want. She still needed a better bedside lamp than the old wooden one. Isabel was determined to get her a brass one and had decided to save until she could afford it.

She hadn't done anything with her own bedroom, apart from painting the walls with cheap magnolia paint and giving the woodwork a couple of quick coats of white gloss.

Old yellow curtains from The Gables, which didn't fit properly, covered the windows and she'd put down a couple of large burgundy cotton rugs to hide the horrible dirty-brown carpet until she could afford to replace it. Carpeting, papering and painting the girls' rooms had cost more than she'd intended.

It took hours, but she'd painstakingly stripped and painted the kitchen and replaced the ancient lino until it was the only room downstairs that was fit to sit in, which was why she and the girls watched TV there instead of in the horrible sitting-room.

Tonight, Isabel had planned to tackle the wallpaper over the fireplace in the sitting-room. But when she'd changed into her ancient leggings and an old T-shirt, she simply didn't feel up to it.

She sighed and pulled on the ancient Marigolds she'd been trying to remember to use for the wall-stripping. She was exhausted from double jobbing – working by day and decorating by night. Naomi wanted to help but Isabel refused point blank.

'You can help me tidy up, but I don't want you wearing yourself out. It's far too tiring for you. Besides,' she added, putting an arm around her slender daughter, 'who else is going to make me endless cups of tea if you're stuck in the middle of a difficult patch of wallpaper?'

Robin hadn't offered to help for ages, not since they'd first moved and she'd been struggling with maths homework she didn't feel like doing. Isabel remembered the last time the knotty subject of maths had come up in the Farrell household. It had been an astonishing conversation.

'I don't see the point of maths,' Robin had moaned. She was studying for her summer exams. 'It's not as if I'm ever going to want to work out the equation of a line in normal life, now am I? Yeah, knowing that's really going to come in handy if I'm travelling round the world working.'

Isabel had blanched. 'What do you mean, "travelling round the world working"?'

'That's what Susie's older sister is doing. She started off in India, now she's in Thailand and she's going to Australia next.' Robin's eyes lit up as she described the traditional back-packer's itinerary. 'She sent Susie a brilliant Gucci watch – fake, of course, but it looks real. And she's only nineteen,' she added.

'Is that what you'd like to do, Robin?' asked Isabel weakly. 'What about college and getting some qualifications when you leave school?'

Her daughter's expression was dismissive.

'That's what *everybody's* parents say. Taking a year off is *like* going to college, only you're learning things by going round the world. It's experience. You can go to college when you get back.'

'Well, you've a few years of school to get through first,' Isabel pointed out. 'You might have changed your mind about what you want to do a dozen times by then.'

'I won't.'

Robin was growing up so fast. It was hard to believe that only a couple of years ago, her biggest ambition had been to have a pony. Robin would be eighteen in three years, Naomi would be fifteen and Isabel would be nearly forty-three. *Forty-three!* It seemed so old. She was beginning to feel old too. Her fortieth birthday loomed ahead of her next month, like a huge stone wall she couldn't climb over.

Being thirty hadn't bothered her the way it had some people. David had practically gone into a decline on his thirtieth. He'd announced he was out of his wild twenties and it was all downhill from now on. Isabel had just laughed and told him she quite fancied older blokes.

She'd never been scared of aging. No cosmetics

company had ever seduced her into buying their 'use this and look like a seventeen year old forever' moisturisers because she knew it was all bunkum. People got old, that was that.

Women who stayed thirty-nine for years had always amused her. But now that she herself was on the verge of entering her fortieth year, she felt sick at the very idea. A divorcée in her thirties didn't sound quite so scary as the notion of one in her forties.

She went into the hall and peered at herself in the mirror. There were definitely more lines around her eyes. She'd always been proud of them – a pale aquamarine the colour of the sea on white sands, as David had once poetically said. He was an expert at that sort of rubbish – all talk and nothing to back it up. Well, her eyes didn't look particularly aquamarine now, she thought glumly. They just looked tired, surrounded by wrinkles, smudged mascara and coffee-coloured eyeshadow that had worn off. She looked tired, full stop.

'Who's looking at me, anyway?' she said out loud to the mirror. 'Nobody.' The last person to give her a flirtatious smile had been the security man on the office gate, and he looked young enough to be going out with Robin. He was probably flirting with her for a bet: 'See if you can chat up that blonde forty-something, the tall one with all the wrinkles and no boobs.'

There was no point moping about it. Isabel was going to be forty in September whether she liked it or not. Armed with a scraper and a bottle of water and washing-up liquid, Isabel went back into the sitting-room and started to spray the paper over the chimney flue. The fireplace had obviously been there since the house was built in the thirties and probably hadn't been swept since, if the dirt was anything to go by.

Sadly, it wasn't one of those fabulous Art Deco ones that thrilled do-it-yourself-TV-show presenters were always finding in architectural salvage yards. It was a horrible beige tiled affair that Isabel simply hated. Whatever happened, she thought, gazing at it with dislike, she had to get a new fireplace. Of course, getting a new one depended on whether she actually had a job or not by the next day. Shit! She'd almost managed to forget about the takeover. Who the hell knew what was going to happen?

But worrying wouldn't help. Isabel checked her watch. It was a quarter to eight. She'd work till half-nine and then have a drink and a bath.

The thought of sinking into a steaming bath filled with bubbles and that relaxing neroli oil she'd got in the Body Shop would keep her going. If she *had* to be a forty-year-old divorcée with more wrinkles than a linen shirt, at least she could be a beautifully relaxed, very clean, and – if she could ferret out some orange juice for the gin to make up for having no tonic – a slightly tipsy one.

By half-nine the following morning, the newsroom was packed to capacity. Everyone, from staff reporters to columnists who worked from home and rarely ventured into the office, had turned up, all awaiting the death knell or the celebratory news, as the case might be.

'I didn't get a wink's sleep,' confessed Belinda, the gossip columnist, nervously. '*Today* doesn't have a social column so they mightn't want one here either. I don't know what else I'd do – I mean, I've been writing a diary page for the past ten years. I'm hopeless at news.'

Dee would have liked to have consoled her, but she couldn't. She felt pretty inconsolable herself. Since

Maeve had rung her with the news that Roark International had bought the *Sentinel*, Dee had been feeling terribly anxious. She'd desperately wanted to go to Magee's that evening where everyone would discuss and rediscuss the takeover endlessly, and where there was a possibility that the odd pertinent piece of gossip would be dragged out of someone.

Instead, she'd spent the evening at a terminally boring surprise fortieth birthday party for one of Gary's colleagues. She'd smiled lots of hard, bright smiles at the people who'd tactlessly asked about her position on the paper now that the legendary Roark had bought it.

'I was amazed when I heard it on the news this evening. Will you all keep your jobs?' inquired one of the accountants' wives nastily. She'd had it in for Dee ever since her husband had drunkenly chatted Dee up at the last Christmas party.

Knowing this, Dee had given her what she hoped was a smug smile and tapped her nose enigmatically. 'I'm afraid I can't talk about it now, but you'll know soon enough.

'Cow!' she'd raged to Gary on the drive home, quite plastered from all the screwdrivers she'd drunk to cheer herself up. 'Honestly, if her bloody company had been taken over, I wouldn't be pleased as hell and practically asking her if she was going to be fired, now would I?'

''Course you wouldn't,' Gary replied, keeping his eyes on the road. 'She's just green with envy because you're gorgeous and sexy, and she's an anorexic crone with no personality.'

Dee stiffened. *Anorexic crone*? Was it possible that he'd finally realised how devastated she was after the Wexford incident? She'd tried to be normal on the outside, even though her insides felt as frozen as a Lean

210

Cuisine. But then, Gary had been at the back of the queue when God had been handing out intuition. He put one hand on her knee, edging up under her wrap-over skirt to stroke her thigh. The crash diet that had made her lose five pounds in a week had had a good effect, she thought wryly. Suddenly she was irresistible again.

'Anyway, Dee, they aren't stupid enough to get rid of someone with your talent and enthusiasm.'

'You never know,' she fretted.

Perched on the edge of her desk with a barely touched mug of extra strong Rombouts in one hand as she listened to the latest hypothesis on the takeover, she was still fretting.

'Can I have a cigarette?' she begged Maeve.

'All right.' Maeve gave her a Silk Cut and they stood outside in the corridor, along with a group of other nervous smokers.

'I can't tell if my hand is shaking from nerves or from a hangover,' said a green-faced news reporter, sucking on a Marlboro.

'Hangover,' Dee pronounced. 'Nobody would fire you, Noel. You'd sell your granny for a good story, so you're way too valuable to lose.'

Noel grinned with pleasure.

The newsroom door swung open.

'They're on their way up,' yelled someone.

'Who's on their way up?' demanded Maeve.

'Several blokes in suits.'

'Anyone we know?'

'Yeah, Slasher Flynn.'

'You're kidding?'

'I'm not.'

★ ★ ★

211

Eugene Flynn cleared his throat and looked at the assembled staff from behind thick glasses. Short, skinny and bald, he looked quite harmless. His suit, which had to be expensive, was a fraction too big and at first glance he appeared to be the sort of man whom women loved to mother.

Then he started to speak.

'I'm delighted to announce that I'm taking over the running of the *Sentinel* as managing director from today.' His voice was smug as he looked around for a reaction. Everyone was too shocked to give one. 'I can understand that you're all worried about your jobs but I want to reassure you, Roark International will not be purging the company. All the staff will be staying on and there'll be no redundancies. Certainly for the next year,' he added swiftly.

'Naturally, we can't speak for the future, but I want to point out that we will honour the job security agreements you had with the past management.'

The ripple of relief that went through the newsroom was palpable. Dee felt herself relax in her chair for the first time all morning.

'There will be changes, of course, and one vital change is the appointment of a new editor. Malley McDonnell from the group's Melbourne office will be taking over.'

Malley who? wondered Dee. She'd never heard of any journalist of that name before.

Everyone craned their necks to see which of the five suit-clad men behind Eugene Flynn was the new editor. The only woman in the group, a tall striking brunette in a mannish grey trouser suit, strode forward to stand beside Flynn. She dwarfed him, in height and build. The lines on her broad, strong face meant she had to be in her mid-forties, but she had a lean athletic body that belied her age.

'Hello, I'm Malley McDonnell,' she said, in a husky voice with just a touch of an Australian accent. 'I know this is all a bit of a shock to you – one day you're working for one group, the next another. It's pretty scary. But,' she looked searchingly around the room, 'this takeover is for the good of the paper. Once you get to know Roark International, and especially me, you'll see we have your interests at heart. We want to bring the *Sentinel* up-to-date, make it a newspaper for the twenty-first century. It's been losing circulation and all you guys could have been out of a job in a couple of years. But not any more,' she said passionately.

'I'm proud of the work I've done with the group's titles in Philadelphia and Hong Kong. Now I want you all to work with me to make us proud of the *Sentinel*, and to strengthen the paper's position so you're all sure of your jobs in ten years' time.'

When Eugene Flynn started clapping, everybody joined in enthusiastically, if a tad manically.

Malley stood back with her arms crossed and smiled.

'Either that's the most genuine "one for all and all for one" speech I've ever heard or we've just been given a dose of grade-A bullshit from a real expert,' Maeve whispered in Dee's ear.

'I hope it's the first,' she replied fervently. 'I'm not able for this takeover stuff. If I didn't have an ulcer over the whole women's editor job shenanigans, I've got one now.'

After half an hour of speeches from both Malley and Slasher, a clearer picture was forming. No changes were to be made until the new management had had a chance to inspect the paper closely.

Malley and Flynn would hold a series of meetings with the different section editors over the coming days. Their opinions would be sought.

And just to let people see that Roark International believed in the future of the paper – and, more importantly, had faith in the existing staff – the editors and deputy editors were invited to a charity bash at Jack Carter's home in Dalkey the following Saturday night where details of the new management would be formally announced.

'We want you to see that we're not here to rip the organisation to pieces, but to build it up to the very successful paper we think it can become,' Eugene Flynn added in sincere tones. 'I know that Mr Carter wants to meet you all personally to assure you we value your help and expertise, and that we want to safeguard your jobs.'

'Why does it sound more convincing when Malley McDonnell says it?' asked Phil Walsh cynically.

'Because he's so crooked that if he ate a six-inch nail, it'd come out a corkscrew, that's why,' Dee replied. 'But we haven't any option but to trust him. I just hate it when he talks about the paper *becoming* very successful. What the hell did he think we were already? A disaster?'

'I think he means to turn the *Sentinel* into something three times as successful as it already is,' interrupted Gerry Deegan.

They rounded on him. 'Where have you been for the last two days?' demanded Maeve. 'I bet you knew all about the takeover last week, you crafty pig. Why didn't you tell us what was going on?'

Gerry shrugged. 'I knew something but I was sworn to secrecy.'

'Well, tell us everything now,' said Dee. 'I can't

believe you let us all suffer yesterday without telling us what was happening. I didn't sleep a wink worrying about it,' she said, untruthfully. In fact, after all the vodka she'd had at the party, she'd been out like a light once her head hit the pillow, which hadn't pleased a lustful, stone-cold-sober Gary.

'Sorry, girls, no can do, I'm afraid,' Gerry said. 'I'm due to meet my old pal Malley McDonnell any minute now, and we'll be closeted together for hours while she asks me whom she should fire.'

Maeve looked at him suspiciously. 'You mean, you know her already?'

'Yes. But I'm kidding about me telling her who to fire. She's a good editor, I worked with her in Philadelphia. There's nothing to be afraid of with Malley, I promise you. She's a real professional and as straight as an arrow.'

'She's not the one we're worrying about,' Maeve snapped. 'It's the thought of Slasher running this place that gives me the creeps.'

'Join the club,' said Gerry. 'I know him from years ago and he's not exactly my favourite person either. I've got to rush, ladies, see you later.' He gave them an apologetic grin and left.

'What next?' demanded Maeve. 'Lord knows who else knew all about this, or who else knows Malley like the back of their hands. Ten to one we'll find half the photographers went to school with her and Tony Winston's slept with her . . .'

'Yeuch! I think she's got better taste than that,' Dee insisted. 'That was a lovely suit she was wearing. Definitely Calvin Klein. Anyone who has such nice clothes isn't going to be taken in by Tony's greasy flirting. And talking of clothes, whatever will we wear to this party on Saturday?'

CHAPTER ELEVEN

As Phil manoeuvered her ancient, dog-hair-covered estate car on to the grass verge between a gleaming black BMW and a silver Lexus, Isabel gazed out of the windscreen at the house in front of them. The moon glittered in a midnight blue sky, burnishing the ornamental pond in front of Jack Carter's house with silver. A graceful Georgian mansion set amidst several acres of trees and shrubs in one of Dublin's most expensive suburbs, Temple Isis had to be worth a small fortune.

'Some place, huh?' Phil remarked. 'He's done well for himself.'

'I daresay you could fit my house into this one about ten times and still have room for a swimming pool,' Isabel remarked, as she extricated her foot from a bit of horse's bridle that was jammed under the passenger seat. 'I wonder if they have a pool?'

Phil climbed out of the car. 'Haven't a clue, but Belinda will know. She's been frantically mugging up on Elizabeth Carter's endless charity committees so she can impress the boss's wife. It's all part of a grand scheme to keep her job.'

'I think it'll take more than a bit of flattery to safeguard any job once Eugene Flynn has made up his mind to axe it,' Isabel remarked. 'If his reputation is

217

anything to go by, we'd better all update our CVs.'

Conscious that she sounded a bit too gloomy for a party, Isabel changed the subject. 'I wonder what Belinda's going to wear? Yesterday, she told me she couldn't figure out whether to go for a long black silk dress that looks great but isn't made by anyone famous, or some second-hand pink silk Yves St Laurent cocktail dress with frills everywhere that sounds hideous.'

'Knowing Belinda, she'll go for the YSL. She can't resist the lure of designer labels. Neither can I,' Phil joked, picking Red Setter hairs off the navy chain-store shirtdress that made her stocky figure look heavier than ever. 'It was either this or the little Chanel number. Decisions, decisions.'

Isabel laughed. 'I had the same problem myself, wondering how many hundreds I should spend on a designer ensemble for this evening,' she said in a put-on posh voice. 'Or whether I should spend the money on the mortgage and the gas bill instead, and just pluck something from the back of the wardrobe.'

'You look lovely,' Phil said, admiring the amber silk palazzo pants and matching evening jacket Isabel wore with a black and amber *devoré* bodice.

'It's ancient,' Isabel protested, shaking her trousers in a vain attempt to loosen the coating of red and golden dog hairs. 'I bought it in the January sales eight or nine years ago for next to nothing and the bodice is Marks & Sparks underwear.'

'You've a real way with clothes,' Phil said. 'I gave up bothering twenty years ago when I got involved with horses and the kids were small. We were always totally broke in those days and preferred to spend any spare cash on upgrading the stables or buying new tack. And it's hard to be fashion conscious when you've got three very hairy dogs,' she added, plucking a wisp of rough collie fluff off Isabel's jacket. 'I normally keep Sellotape in the car for getting the hair off but the roll is empty.'

'We'll do.' Isabel slammed her door shut. 'The guest list is probably so full of the rich and famous that nobody will notice if you and I are wearing dresses made *entirely* from dog hair. And, believe it or not, there actually *is* a woman who makes coats and jumpers from knitted Red Setter hair.'

'She'd love my house, then,' Phil said. 'The dining-room carpet has several coats, a couple of jumpers and a very big bedspread's worth of hair on it. The kids are supposed to hoover but they never do.'

They were still laughing when they entered the vast, ornate hallway and followed the noise past a big, curving mahogany staircase with massive red Chinese urns set to either side of the first step.

The party was spread between a huge Chinese drawing-room and an airy ballroom. Guests spilled out on to the terrace from the French windows. Outside, fairy lights twinkled in the trees. Waiters cruised through the throng noiselessly, bearing hors d'oeuvres and booze.

Inside, the ballroom walls were covered with pink watered silk, and hung with oil paintings in Gothic-style gold frames. Giant flower arrangements on spindly gilt tables made the room look like a hothouse.

'I think Belinda may have made the right choice with the YSL number after all,' Isabel whispered, as they gazed at the plethora of very definitely designer outfits. 'And to think they say designers don't really make that much money any more. It's like having a ramp-side seat at Milan fashion week in here.'

'No dress should cost more than a horse,' Phil said

briskly. 'It's sinful. I don't recognise a single person here,' she added, peering at the crowd of dark-suited men and women in bright jewel colours, real rocks glittering on their necks and fingers. Blondes and brunettes of a certain age, with frosted helmet hairdos, little nipped-in cocktail dresses and spindly heels, stood cheek by jowl with stunning twenty-something models who wore breathtakingly little and sipped champagne.

The whole effect was very elegant, but very formal. Nobody looked as if they were keen to let their hair down or start limbo dancing after too many gins.

'I don't recognise anyone, either,' Isabel said as she looked around for a familiar face. 'Will we stay here until we see someone we know, or will we scout around for people from work?'

'Girls, where have you been, you latecomers? You've missed the Thai dancers.' He might have been the first person they recognised in the entire room but Tony Winston was, as usual, almost instantly annoying. 'Our crowd are all over the far side of the ballroom, beside the kitchen.'

'Surely you mean beside the bar?' said Isabel wickedly.

'No.' Tony brazenly put one arm around her waist as he led them towards the other side of the crowded room. Isabel stiffened at his touch. His dark hair gleamed with some sort of gel and he must have poured at least a pint of Boss over himself. 'The food's so good, nobody is drinking much at all yet.'

'Wonders will never cease,' remarked Phil.

'Lovely perfume you're wearing,' Tony said, his face very close to Isabel's neck as he inhaled. 'What's it called?'

'Piss off,' said Phil sharply.

Isabel moved away from Tony.

'Funny name for perfume,' he drawled, deliberately not taking the hint.

'You think *that's* funny? They're bringing out one soon that's called Come Too Close And You're Dead,' Phil retorted. 'I think it was created with you in mind.'

'Narky tonight, aren't we, Phil?' he said maliciously. 'Is it PMT? I bet Dick was delighted to get you out of his hair for one night.'

'Tony, if that's the only level of conversation you're capable of, please leave,' Isabel said frostily.

'Only if you leave with me, darling,' he purred. 'We could go home to my place . . .' He leant towards her with a suggestive grin.

'I didn't know two people could fit under a rock,' Isabel said smoothly.

Tony's face flushed with anger and he strode off.

'Well done,' Phil said admiringly. 'I've been watching him make cow's eyes at you for months now and I was wondering when you'd crack.'

'I feel like cracking his head open with a bottle,' said Isabel. 'He really is the limit. As if I'd be turned on by him! You've no idea what he's like, Phil.'

'Oh, yes I have.' Phil swiped two glasses of champagne off a passing waiter and handed one to Isabel. 'Prehistoric Man Vulgaris. He was all over one of the freelance sub-editors like a rash earlier this year – until she got vexed, threw a cup of cold tea over him and said she was taking him to court for sexual harassment. She didn't, but he got the message.'

'I suppose I should have said something sooner,' Isabel sighed. 'He's been driving me mad every day for months now, and if I go to the kitchen to make a cup of coffee, he's behind me in a flash saying, "Oh, sorry to bump against you, Isabel, it's such a tight squeeze in here, ha, ha, ha!" He's a creep.'

She took a sip of her drink. 'I'm not very good with men. Well, on a personal level,' she amended. 'If we were working together and disagreed on something, I'd be able to stand my ground and argue my case. But when it comes to somebody like Tony . . .'

'Harassing you?' supplied Phil.

'Yes, I suppose, harassing me, I'm just not very comfortable being rude with them. Although that's the only sort of treatment the Tonys of this world understand.'

'You amaze me, Isabel. You always *look* as if you could handle anything.'

'Looks can be deceptive,' she said dryly. 'Being married for so long means you forget everything you ever knew about men.'

'How come I've been married longer than you and I don't have any problems with lecherous men chatting me up?' joked Phil. 'Only kidding. You're gorgeous, Isabel, and now that you're single, you'd better get used to handling lots of men, lecherous or otherwise.'

'But I'm going to be forty next month,' she protested.

'So what?'

'A forty-year-old single mother, Phil, is hardly every man's dream date. Especially one with a mortgage she won't have paid off until she's sixty-five, which means I won't be able to save up for a face lift until it's too late.'

'Don't be so negative,' Phil said. 'You could always meet some sweet, very lonely, eighty-year-old millionaire with no dependants, a house on every continent, a Zimmer frame and the life expectancy of a mosquito. There are bound to be loads of them here tonight. And you know what they say – "I never met a millionaire I didn't like".'

Isabel laughed out loud. 'If I do meet one, you'll be the first to know. But I don't hold out much hope. And even if I did find one, ten to one he'd have a twenty-year-old "actress/model" welded on to his arm, glaring hands-off at every woman who came within a fifty-foot radius.'

'Come on.' Phil moved through the throng. 'Let's find the rest of the crew and see if Tony has started spreading the rumour that you're a lesbian yet.'

It wasn't hard to find their colleagues. The thirty or so journalists were in full party mode, a startling contrast to the rest of the partygoers who were behaving in a much more restrained manner, sipping their champagne rather than guzzling it.

Stalin, who was still – 'astonishingly', as Phil put it – a member of staff, looked uneasy as he smoked a cheroot standing beside Belinda, wearing his best outfit – a dark blue Western-style suit complete with one of those leather string ties held together at the collar by a turquoise and silver clasp. The suit's shiny patches matched his perspiring face.

'Isabel – Phil!' squeaked Belinda delightedly, quivering with excitement in a fuchsia taffeta confection that reminded Isabel of one of the costumes Naomi's old Barbie doll had come with. 'You'll never guess – I met Elizabeth Carter and *she knew who I was!* Isn't that fantastic?'

'Yeah, Jack Carter was here with Slasher Flynn and he met us all,' put in Fred, the head photographer.

'She's so nice, beautiful but very friendly,' gushed Belinda. 'And Jack was very polite, he shook my hand for *ages* . . .'

'Listen,' interrupted the chief sub, Tom, a stalwart of the union and a professional pessimist to boot, 'don't count your chickens till they're hatched. Just because the management is nice to you tonight, doesn't mean diddly squat. They could be as nice as pie to your face tonight, and *still* fire you on Monday. Although I'd like to see them try.'

For half an hour they stood and talked, eating endless won tons and sesame prawn toasts from the trays of passing waiters and drinking whatever they felt like. Beer, wine, vintage champagne or spirits – they had it all, according to a glassy-eyed Stalin, who'd obviously tried a bit of everything and was now knocking back shots of tequila. There was no sign of Dee O'Reilly, which Isabel thought was odd as she'd seemed quite excited at the idea of the party only yesterday.

Isabel sipped a second glass of champagne and looked around her warily. She was tired after a busy week and felt distinctly uncomfortable. The wealthy guests were obviously of the 'don't have to work ever again, what is a mortgage anyway?' league – a million miles removed from the *Sentinel* staff.

She wondered had any of *them* felt the icy grip of fear at the news that their company had been taken over and their jobs could be on the line? Not in a long time, she reckoned, eyeing the gold chains and diamond necklaces.

What was the point of this party anyway? If Jack Carter wanted to tell the staff about the new management, he could have done it in the office without all this palaver. But no, he wanted to admit them to his mansion and let them take a one-off look at his world of wealth and privilege.

It was as if he *wanted* the journalists to feel like complete outsiders, so he could make them see exactly who was boss. It was an exercise in arrogance, an act of supreme condescension. At that moment, she hated the very idea of Jack Carter. No matter that everyone said he was decent, he'd have to try very hard to impress her after tonight.

Isabel glanced at her watch. It was five to nine. *ER* would be starting soon and she could have been curled up on the couch watching it, with a glass of wine and some of that cheesy popcorn she was addicted to.

Naomi had a friend to stay and they'd be giggling in her room, pretending to get the sleeping bag ready for Joanne and secretly having no intention of sleeping for hours. Robin was keeping an eye on them, in between watching *Good Will Hunting* on video and gazing longingly at Matt Damon, her current hero.

It would have been so nice to be there with them, instead of standing aimlessly in a ballroom listening to fragments of conversations and watching people get drunker.

What was more, it was getting hotter by the minute. There were just too many people crammed together. Isabel had once read that charity hostesses invited at least twenty-five per cent too many people to functions on the grounds that most of them wouldn't be able to make it. If the jammed ballroom at Temple Isis was anything to go by, nobody turned down an invitation from Elizabeth Carter. Though Isabel fervently wished she'd been able to do just that.

She picked up a napkin and fanned herself with it. She could feel her pale skin turn a deep, unbecoming brick red, and knew that it didn't matter how much Ô de Lancôme she'd sprayed down her cleavage, it wouldn't be much good if she started to sweat like a racehorse. She tried to listen to the conversations around her. Phil was in the middle of a long, convoluted

225

story about someone whom she and Belinda both knew – Belinda could be interested in horse stories so long as the people involved were rich enough to have their own stables, their own trainer, and at least one Cheltenham-going racehorse.

Tony was telling blue jokes in between glowering in her direction. Stalin swayed happily, not talking to anybody. He was clearly on the verge of passing out.

'This is getting to me,' Isabel said finally. Nobody was listening. She turned and slipped through the crowd, making for the French windows. People moved to let her through and more than a couple of the male guests stared at her, taking in her tall elegant figure, the fragile, almost sad face and the swathe of dark blonde hair that was swept up into a classic French pleat.

Plenty of people had had the same idea as Isabel and the terrace was nearly as full as the ballroom. She walked down stone steps into the garden, walking carefully so her heels wouldn't sink into the grass. The cool night air was like a balm to her hot skin and she breathed in deeply.

Twenty yards away from the terrace and the party-goers, she came upon a wooden seat framed by a sweet-smelling rambling rose. She sat down gratefully and wondered how soon she could slip away from the party completely without being noticed.

'Enjoying yourself?' inquired a voice. He moved out of the shadows towards her, a tall, powerfully built man. Lights from the terrace lit up tanned, weathered skin and narrow eyes that seemed to bore into her. In a dark, beautifully cut suit with a pale tie, he wasn't handsome but he was certainly striking.

'It's so warm inside, I needed to get some fresh air,' Isabel replied. 'And I had to get away from the party.'

'I know what you mean.' The man crossed the lawn to stand in front of her and a small furry dog of indeterminate breed followed him. It scurried over to Isabel and immediately put wet paws on her knees.

'I'm sorry,' the man said. 'Kerry, down.' He moved as if to grab the dog's collar, but Isabel spoke first.

'It's OK. Leave her,' she said, smiling genuinely for the first time since she and Phil had arrived at the party. 'I love dogs.' She bent forward, ruffling the dog's grey ears, letting its soft shiny black nose burrow into her sleeve inquisitively.

'Good,' he replied, a hint of dry humour in his voice, 'because there's another one on the way.'

As if on cue, a large Golden Retriever belted up the lawn excitedly, tongue hanging out. The dog headed straight for Isabel.

'Duke, steady!' warned the man. 'Sit.'

Duke blithely ignored his master and rushed towards Isabel, burying his nose in her crotch.

'Duke! I warn you, he's very friendly,' the man said apologetically.

'This sort of friendliness is allowed in dogs,' she said, giggling as Duke's insistent nose investigated her. 'Though not in humans,' she quipped.

His laugh was a rich, throaty sound that seemed to come from deep inside his large frame. And when he laughed, the haughty look disappeared and the deep lines around his mouth curved up with good humour. He was very attractive when he smiled.

All male and very predatory, like a wolf. That was it. His hair was the same colour as a wolf's pelt, rich brown shot through with paler shades of burnt umber and gold. She'd bet it was as soft as Duke's fur to the touch . . .

Isabel's eyes widened in shock. She couldn't *believe* she'd just thought that! Talk about thinking like a lovestruck teenager. The readers' stories in Robin's *Just Seventeen* were more mature.

She bent over Duke in embarrassment, running her hands over his rippling honey-coloured fur. Kerry squeaked in abandoned indignation and wriggled closer for more attention.

'I'm not forgetting about you, love,' Isabel crooned, stretching her right hand out to the small dog, her left one rubbing Duke's ear as he almost purred with pleasure.

'You've made two conquests there,' said the man. 'Or maybe three.'

Isabel could feel herself blushing but kept her head down as she talked gently to the dogs.

'They get very restless when there's a party on,' he said, sitting down on the bench beside her. He took up the rest of the seat and stretched out long legs in front of him. He really was a big man, taller even than Isabel. She could smell the tang of Armani, about a zillion times more subtle than Tony Winston's drenched-in-aftershave smell. Duke shuffled his furry rear end over towards his master so they could both pat him at the same time.

'They're beautiful dogs,' Isabel said, still stroking Kerry's ears. 'They're so friendly.'

'Duke is a bit of a rake, he loves everyone, but Kerry's much more discriminating. She's very particular about whom she cuddles up to. You must have a magic touch with dogs.' He turned to face her and Isabel sat up.

Now that he wasn't facing the lights any more, his face was half in shadow and she didn't feel so self-conscious looking at him. He couldn't see her very well

228

either, she reckoned. Well, she hoped he couldn't. Her face was undoubtedly quite pink from a mixture of heat and embarrassment and she probably reeked of over-heated perfume and the remainder of Robin's Impulse deodorant. Not to mention the fact that her unsmudge-able mascara was probably halfway down her cheeks already.

'My mother isn't very keen on dogs, or any animal for that matter,' Isabel explained. She leant back against the seat to keep her face in the shadows. 'My father got me a Cocker Spaniel one Christmas but when he chewed the leg of the dining-room table, she insisted we get rid of him.' Isabel's eyes still filled with tears at the thought of Sasha, the puppy she'd loved with all her ten-year-old heart, until her mother had insisted he was given to another family.

David hadn't been much of a dog person either. He'd bought the girls two goldfish once, although he soon forgot all about Jaws and Flipper, so that Isabel was the one who had to race to the pet shop for a replacement each time one of them died. By Flipper Number Six, both girls were bored with fish and David said he hated rodents and wouldn't have a hamster in the house.

'I'd love a dog,' she said fervently, as Duke and Kerry looked up at her with adoring eyes, 'but I'm out all day and don't have the time to walk one.'

'What about your husband?'

'I'm separated,' she said shortly.

'Sorry,' he said, not sounding it.

'And you?' asked Isabel, determined not to let him get away with all these questions.

'Yes, I'm married.'

'So why are you outside chatting up strange women

in the garden?' she asked with a grin.

He replied instantly, 'I have a better chance of success in the dark. That way, you can't see my hump, my lazy eye and the facial tic. My left eyebrow does forty jumps a minute, you see. I'm in the *Guinness Book of Records*. It puts women off.'

Isabel burst out laughing.

'You're quick, I'll give you that.'

'But it's the truth.' He sounded wounded for a moment. 'Actually,' he added, 'I had to get away from the heat and the crowds myself. I can only take so many charity balls. I couldn't cope with meeting another ambassador or making polite chit-chat with people I really can't stand. Right now, I'd prefer to be sitting back after a decent dinner ready to watch something good on the telly. That would be luxury.'

Isabel nodded. 'Exactly what I was thinking myself. I love *ER* and it's on now.'

'I rather fancy a Western, something forty years old with John Wayne in it. I didn't really come out here to chat up strange women,' he added, his voice very soft. 'I was walking the dogs and saw you . . . and I just had to talk to you. That's my excuse.'

'That's very flattering,' Isabel said quietly. 'But isn't that a bit dangerous at a party? Couldn't your wife appear and wonder what you're up to with some stranger in the garden?'

He laughed. Bitterly, Isabel thought.

'At this precise moment, my wife wouldn't notice if I were out here sandwiched between Kim Basinger and Michelle Pfeiffer.' He glanced at her wryly. 'Although you're more beautiful than both of them.'

Before Isabel even had a chance to turn puce again, he added: 'I'd better introduce myself while I'm at it.

I'm Jack Carter.' He stretched out one large hand and Isabel stared at it, shocked.

Of course he was Jack Carter. The party was in the Carters' home and he was walking dogs in the garden, dogs that got restless when there was a party. Who the hell else would be walking them but the man of the house? What sort of idiot are you Isabel? *And* you said you had to get away! Talk about putting your foot in it.

'Isabel Farrell,' she said, and took his hand tentatively.

He certainly didn't give the sort of limp handshake she loathed, those damp, weak ones with all the backbone of a dead kipper. Jack Carter's handshake was a strong, warm one.

When he let her hand go, she got up quickly, leaving the dogs gazing up at her curiously.

'I'd better go back inside,' she said. Now that she'd met him, talked to him as if they were on the same level, she didn't want to have to tell him who she was. That she wasn't one of the party guests who'd brought a ten-thousand-pound cheque for his wife's favourite charity but one of his employees, one of the 'little people' she was sure he hadn't time for.

''Bye,' she said stiffly. Reaching down to pat Duke and Kerry goodbye, she quickly turned on her heel.

'I'm sorry, I should have told you who I was earlier,' Jack said. 'I hope I didn't embarrass you?'

Isabel didn't turn around. 'Not at all,' she said crisply, her heels getting stuck in the grass in her hurry to get away. Inside, she made her way back to the *Sentinel* crew who were gathered around a stunning dark-haired woman in a figure-hugging red silk dress.

Tall, curvy and with the creamy skin of someone who lived on mineral water and fruit, she was a dead ringer for an older Cindy Crawford, complete with full red lips, dark arched eyebrows and voluminous curls courtesy of at least half an hour with the Carmen rollers. All she needed was the mole, thought Isabel. And then it hit her – this was *his* wife.

'Isabel, this is Elizabeth Carter.' Phil took Isabel's arm and propelled her into the centre of the group alongside Elizabeth, exactly where she didn't want to be.

'De-lighted to meet you,' Elizabeth drawled. Her smoky, upper-class voice made even the shortest word sound at least two syllables long.

'Hello,' said Isabel stiltedly. The word was barely out of her mouth before Elizabeth quickly turned away to address the men in the group, all of whom were clearly very impressed by their hostess's overt sex appeal. 'We're thrilled you could all make it tonight,' she said throatily, gazing at each man in turn.

'The Cancer Ball is usually held in a hotel but we decided to keep costs down and have it here instead. The only problem is space.' She airily gestured around the massive ballroom. 'There simply isn't enough here. Does anyone have a cigarette?'

Immediately every man who smoked, and quite a few who didn't, felt frantically in their pockets for something to offer her.

'Thanks,' Elizabeth purred, after selecting a cigarette from Fred who kept his Dunhills in a silver cigarette case.

After inhaling as if she was underwater sucking on a diving respirator, Elizabeth then took a hefty swig from the crystal tumbler in her left hand.

'So what do you do?' she asked Fred.

'I'm the paper's head photographer,' he said, blossoming under her gaze.

'Fascinating. Could you do some shots of the house

for me sometime? I've been meaning to get someone in . . .'

Phil raised her eyebrows at Isabel and they moved discreetly away. 'She's something else,' Phil remarked. 'She could flirt for Ireland in the Olympics.'

'You can say that again,' Isabel replied. 'It's certainly working. The boys all look like they'd crawl on their hands and knees across the Kalahari Desert to get her a cup of tea. Tony's practically drooling.'

'That's nothing new. But I doubt if she'd want a cup of tea. More like a few lines of finest Colombian cocaine,' Phil remarked. 'Unless I'm mistaken, she's out of her tree.'

'What do you mean?' asked Isabel in amazement. Elizabeth had looked all right to her. She'd looked wonderful, in fact.

'She's stoned, high, whatever,' whispered Phil, looking around her in case anyone was listening. 'Which isn't the sort of behaviour you normally see in society hostesses at their own charity parties.

'My brother-in-law was heavily into drugs – he was a cocaine addict, actually – and I can spot the signs a mile away. Mrs Carter's very good, mind you. She can obviously cope without most people suspecting. I doubt if many of them here could spot that she's high. And the worse she gets, the posher her accent will be too, I guarantee it.'

'Wow!' Isabel was stunned. She craned her neck to look back at Elizabeth Carter. In her eye-catching dress, she looked the epitome of chic. Isabel bet that she wasn't feeling as hot and sweaty as everyone else on the premises.

'I could be wrong, of course,' Phil whispered. 'But she's pretty hyper for this type of party. Normally, the society queens sip the odd glass of champers when they're working the room and save their gimme-a-big-drink-quick mode for when the guests have gone. I reckon our hostess did a couple of lines in the bathroom before anyone arrived and now she's backing it up with booze. Let's hear it for excess, as my poor brother-in-law used to say.'

'Is he still doing coke?' whispered Isabel.

'No. He bankrupted himself and my sister in the process and when the cash ran out, he had to stop. Nearly killed him, of course.'

'Darling!' said Elizabeth, loudly summoning a passing waiter. 'Another vodka martini, no olive and only a little ice.' She carefully placed her glass on his tray and returned to her conversation.

Phil gave Isabel an 'I told you so' look.

Elizabeth's next drink, a full-to-the-brim tumbler, lasted precisely ten minutes. She was ordering a third when Dee O'Reilly arrived, chestnut curls flying and a sheen of perspiration glistening on her face as she reached the group.

Dressed in a clinging black velvet dress that molded every one of her voluptuous curves, she looked stunning, Isabel thought a touch enviously. Big but very sexy. Like Elizabeth Carter, Dee simply exuded sexuality and there was no doubt that men adored them both.

They were so different – one model-girl slim; the other a Rubensesque beauty. But they both had that indefinable *something*. Isabel felt like a dull older sister beside them. A very unsexy, dull older sister. She thought of the man in the garden and how she'd felt about him for the brief moment before she knew who he was. He'd certainly *seemed* to be attracted to her, or maybe she was imagining it.

'Sorry I'm late,' gasped Dee. 'Gary was driving me out here in my car when the bloody thing got a flat tyre. It took him ages to change it because I've misplaced the jack.' She grimaced. 'Still, it was just as well he was there. I'd have spent hours trying to work out how to get the car up without a jack, but he just rang the AA. And I told him that if he hadn't pranged his precious Alfa Romeo, he wouldn't have been driving mine and it would never have happened.'

'Well, you're here now and you haven't missed that much.' Isabel smiled at her. 'Do you want a drink? You look like you could do with one.'

'Oh, please, yes,' Dee said fervently. 'I could murder a drink and I'm ravenous. Who's that?' she asked, gesturing at Elizabeth.

'Our hostess,' said Phil, 'and host.'

Isabel looked up to see a tall figure join the group. Jack Carter's hair looked even more tawny under the lights and she could see that the eyes that had bored into hers so intently were a clear, gun-metal grey.

'How are we doing, everyone?' he asked.

'Marvellous,' said Stalin, raising a glass jerkily.

'I'm glad you're all enjoying yourselves. Have you tried anything from the buffet yet?'

'We love the salmon sautéed in vodka,' said Tony.

Elizabeth giggled. 'Have we got that? I didn't know. A bit of a waste of vodka, don't you think? The only thing I like to be sautéed in vodka is myself. Isn't that right, darling?' she said to her husband, her voice suddenly brittle.

He smiled woodenly at her.

'Ooh, something's going on there, don't you think?' whispered Phil in Isabel's ear.

Isabel didn't hear her. She was looking at Jack, still a

little shell-shocked after their encounter in the garden. Her stomach fluttered. She couldn't understand the feelings he'd aroused in her, couldn't believe that a man could make her feel like this again.

And here he was, standing by his wife in his palatial home with his friends and employees all around him, and she was wondering whether he was interested in *her*. What sort of a fool was she turning into? Did being on the verge of forty turn you into a complete idiot or was it just Isabel?

Dee introduced herself to her host and hostess.

'Sorry I'm late,' she apologised. 'Car trouble.'

'No problem,' Jack said calmly. 'It's nice to meet you, Dee. I've heard a lot about you.'

She went pink.

'All of it complimentary,' he assured her.

She went pinker.

His eyes moved from her face to Isabel's. Wordlessly, he stared at her for an instant. He was waiting for her to say something, she realised with a jolt.

'Isabel Farrell, women's editor,' she said formally, her voice as cold as she could make it.

His gaze never faltered. 'Hello, nice to meet you,' he said before turning away.

So that was the way he wanted to play it, she thought. The I've-never-met-you-before way. Fine. She could do that too.

'Come on, Elizabeth. It's time for your speech,' Jack said crisply. 'I'll see the rest of you in the *Sentinel* offices during the week.'

'God, isn't he gorgeous in the flesh?' Dee remarked as she drained her glass. 'Lucky old Liz.'

'Yeah,' Isabel replied quietly. 'Lucky old Liz.'

CHAPTER TWELVE

Where the hell were they? Dee fumbled through her handbag, clumsy fingers finding lipsticks, a Twix, pens, tissues, a half-unwrapped tampon and scrunched up petrol receipts. But no house keys. She must be drunker than she'd thought. It was all the champagne Tony had poured down her. She should have said no, but she was enjoying herself and it was nice to have an attentive man at her side, even if he was the ever-so-slightly-sleazy sports editor who kept looking down her dress. *He'd* obviously been turned on by her figure, even if she wasn't a Kate Moss clone.

And at least he hadn't tried anything on the drive home. Apart from putting his hand on her thigh and she'd belted him across the chest for that. What sort of a girl did he think she was anyway?

Dee shivered. It was very cold for August. She'd forgotten her coat. It must be in Tony's car. Blast.

Her mobile phone fell out of the bag, making an awful racket when it hit the ground. Double blast. Gary was bound to hear it and wake up. She didn't want to wake him because he'd go ballistic when he saw how drunk she was.

He'd told her he had something very important to discuss with her when he was driving her to Jack

Carter's party. And then the car had got that flat tyre so he hadn't been able to tell her what it was. So she'd promised to be home early and then they'd talk.

Since it was now very late, she was very drunk and definitely not in a state for serious conversation, Gary would undoubtedly be furious if she woke him.

Got them! Dee held up her keys with a triumphant rattle. Now all she had to do was creep in quietly, undress downstairs and sneak into bed without disturbing Gary. Oh, yeah, and bring up a big glass of water for the morning when she just knew she'd wake up dreaming of slurping entire bottles of 7UP to quench her burning hangover thirst.

Her plan didn't work out. When she half-crawled, half-walked up the stairs wearing only her underwear, clutching her dress in one hand and a glass of water in the other, Gary wasn't asleep. He was sitting up in bed reading, with his clock radio facing the door.

According to the clock, it was half-three, around three hours later than Dee had told him she'd be home.

'Did I wake you?' she asked, wide-eyed with assumed innocence. 'I was trying to be quiet.'

'If your idea of "quiet" is spending ten minutes outside the front door dropping things and swearing so loudly the whole street can hear you, then yes, you were quiet,' he snapped. 'Unfortunately, your definition and mine don't correspond.'

'Sorry,' mumbled Dee. Why was he so cross with her? She'd only been at an office party, not living it up at a nightclub or anything. And she'd *had* to go to the Carters' house, it wasn't as if she'd wanted to.

She'd have preferred an evening at home with Gary. Because she still loved him, despite everything he'd said. She'd felt frozen in anguish since their disastrous weekend in Wexford, devastated by what Gary had said. But an evening of constantly flowing champagne and plenty of compliments had defrosted her icy heart. After too much to drink, Dee felt warm, loved and happy again.

She decided to tell Gary all this.

She dropped her dress, banged the glass of water on the bedside table and lurched into bed on top of him, squashing his copy of *Arena*.

'Sorry,' she muttered again. 'But I love you, Gary, I really, really do. I know you were horrible to me, but I'm crazy about you. Can't live without you.'

Gary didn't respond.

Straddling him, she planted a big sloppy kiss on his forehead before moving down to his mouth. She'd make love to him, that would cheer him up. It always did. She nuzzled his neck hopefully.

'Will I take off my bra or will you?' she asked archly, as she sat up and provocatively slid down one of the straps of her black Wonderbra until she was spilling out of it. 'Ooops,' she added, as she nearly fell off the bed. She wasn't *that* drunk. Gary was pushing her off him.

'You're pissed, Dee. Again.' His face was dark as thunder and his mouth was set in a tight line as he dragged his legs from under both the duvet and Dee, and got out of bed.

'I can't believe you went out and got drunk tonight. You knew I wanted to talk to you about something important. "*Don't worry about me, Gary, I'll be home by twelve at the latest, so wait up and we'll talk.*" Does that sound familiar?'

Dee flinched at the sound of Gary angrily repeating her words. She *had* meant to be home earlier but it just hadn't worked out that way. Phil and Isabel could have

239

given her a lift if she'd wanted it, but they went home at around half-ten and she'd only just arrived. It would have been rude to go then. She started to say that but Gary was speaking to her.

He was standing by the bed, looking at her angrily, obviously not even slightly in the mood for sex even though she was sitting on his side of the bed, wearing her sexy undies and the sheer black hold-up stockings he loved.

'I wanted to discuss something important . . .'

'We can still discuss it,' she pleaded.

'No. We won't,' he said tightly. 'The time for discussion is over. In the light of your behaviour, I've made up my mind, Dee. I've been offered a six-month stint in the firm's office in London and I'm going to take it.'

She gazed at him in shock. London. Six months. Away for six months. He couldn't be serious? Her brain couldn't cope with the idea.

'B . . . b . . . but you can't,' she wailed. 'Why? Why and how? How can you leave me? What does it all mean?' Her face crumpled as she began to think about what Gary had just said.

'You're too pissed to think straight,' he said coldly. 'Pass out, why don't you, and I'll talk to you in the morning.'

He left the room and Dee could hear him rummaging in the airing cupboard. Wriggling off the bed, she hurried on to the landing to find Gary dragging the spare duvet downstairs.

'Where are you going?' she bleated.

'To sleep on the couch,' was his reply. He slammed the sitting-room door behind him. Dee was left hanging over the banisters miserably, wondering what had gone wrong. He couldn't mean it, could he? Fighting back the urge to bawl her eyes out, she padded back into the bedroom, climbed into Gary's side of the bed and curled the duvet around her. She could smell his aftershave on his pillows and it comforted her.

He couldn't leave her, surely? He knew she needed a couple of drinks to make her feel relaxed because she was self-conscious at parties. Stone cold sober, she was convinced she was unbearably fat and ugly. She liked a couple of drinks to loosen her up. That was all.

Gary had no idea what it was like to walk into a room crammed with bloody size ten supermodels staring at you superciliously, all with handspan waists and boobs that didn't spill over the top of their bras. Being big in a skinny world was her worst nightmare. Gary just didn't have a clue.

Her hangover wasn't the first thing that hit Dee on Sunday morning so much as the sensation of being alone in the double bed. The foot she sent over to the far side to test for Gary's body didn't hit anything except empty bed. She opened one glued-up eye and looked at the alarm clock. Half-eleven. He'd obviously gone off to play soccer without waking her.

If she wasn't working, Gary usually brought her a cup of coffee on Sunday mornings before he went off with the lads for a couple of hours of footie. Once upon a time, Dee had gone with him to important matches, standing on the sidelines in the freezing cold, cheering his team on and screaming at the other side if they fouled.

But his team didn't play league matches in the summer and she'd got out of the habit of getting up early on Sundays if she didn't absolutely have to.

Hopefully Gary would have cheered up by the time

he got home and would have got over his bad temper about the night before.

And as for moving to London, he couldn't possibly mean it. He was doing far too well in Dublin to risk even six months in another office, surely?

She'd promise never to drink again, she'd promise to stop nagging him about housework and she'd go on a diet. Anything to make everything all right again. Whatever Gary wanted, she'd do it. *Anything*. She'd make him see that they were meant for each other. How could he leave her then?

Dee kicked off the duvet and stretched before getting up. She felt quite OK really, not too hungover but very hungry. There probably wasn't anything in the house to eat. Wait a minute – she had some of those croissants that came in a tin. She could buy eggs when she went out to get the papers, cook the croissants, scramble some eggs and have a lovely brunch waiting for Gary when he got home. That was it. That'd cheer him up.

Delighted with her plan, Dee showered, washed her hair and got dressed, singing along to the radio. Visions of the reinvented Dee O'Reilly came into her mind – a slim, elegant Dee in a sleek size-ten trouser suit, with her hair straightened into a shiny bob, not the usual mess of tumbling, wayward curls. Subtle make-up. She could get made up at the Lancôme counter in Arnotts and learn how to apply eyeliner so she didn't look as if she'd gone four rounds with Mike Tyson.

She'd dump her usual enormous handbag for one of those classy little bags that looked businesslike. And she'd diet like a mad thing, resolve *never* to touch a Mars Bar again, eat fruit and drink eight glasses of water a day, the way you were supposed to, instead of hoping her usual eight cups of coffee covered the daily required liquid intake.

Yes, a new Dee would make Gary fall madly in love with her all over again so he'd forget about going to London.

When she'd dressed, Dee thought she looked the ultimate in cute – fat cute, but cute all the same. She wore blue jeans and a teeny weeny pink velour T-shirt that clung provocatively to her boobs. Her hair was tied on the top of her head like Pebbles from the Flintstones and she'd drenched herself in delicious vanilla Angel perfume. Gary wouldn't be able to resist her, she was convinced of it.

By five o'clock, she'd read all the Sunday papers, eaten both Gary's and her portions of scrambled egg and had polished off most of the croissants into the bargain. Smudge's belly was swollen up like a balloon with all the scrambled egg leftovers and she was fast asleep on one of the armchairs, only moving one paw as she swatted the occasional dream mouse.

Dee threw down the third TV supplement in exasperation. There was still no sign of Gary. He hadn't phoned. His mobile phone was gone but he didn't have it switched on. Dee had discovered his football kit and bag lying under the stairs. He obviously wasn't playing football so where the hell was he? And why hadn't he phoned? He couldn't still be cross with her, surely?

Dear Annie,

My boyfriend and I had a terrible fight, and he stormed off. He wouldn't even listen to my side of the story, which was extremely unfair of him because I had to go to an office party and you can't go to a party without having a drink, now can you?

243

The problem is, he hasn't come home and I'm not sure whether I'm worried or very, very angry. How dare he do this to me? What do you suggest – screaming at him when he does come in or giving him the silent treatment?

Dee made another cup of coffee and read her horoscope for the fifth time in a different paper. Scorpios in relationships were having a very bad week, whichever way you looked at it.

Prepare to let go of something you've dreamed of for a long time. This Tuesday's planetary movement suggests that you are at a crossroads in your life and what you do next will have extreme significance for your future . . . said one.

Your lucky colour is green, your lucky number is ten and single Scorpios are destined to meet the love of their lives on Tuesday. Scorpios with partners should expect some bad news on the romantic front, said another.

It didn't look good. Dee flicked through the TV channels. Nothing on but news and she was sick to the teeth of news.

At six she was seized by a fit of energy and manically tidied the kitchen, dried up all the dishes in the drainer, industriously cleaned the cooker top and bleached everything in sight.

By seven, she had flopped back on the settee and was looking around miserably. Something was definitely wrong. Gary would never stay out this late usually without at least phoning her.

Maeve answered the phone after about fifteen rings. 'I was in the bath,' she said breathlessly. 'I'm shaving my legs, de-fuzzing my moustache and dyeing my hair.'

'All at the same time? Isn't that dangerous?' asked Dee.

'Probably. But Karl is going to pick me up in an hour, so I've got to do it all at the same time. If I don't dye my hair, he'll discover I'm not a natural redhead. How was the posh party? Did anyone embarrass themselves hideously?'

Dee grimaced. 'Only me.'

'What did you do?' demanded Maeve, agog.

'Well, I didn't do much at the party exactly. It was more a matter of how long I spent at it, how much I drank while I was there and what happened when I got home.'

'Don't tell me.' Maeve sounded scathing. 'Sweet adorable Gary went ballistic because you got plastered and now he's in a major bad mood?'

'Sort of.' Dee was surprised at how quickly Maeve had diagnosed what was wrong. 'He was offered a job in London and wanted to talk to me about it but . . .'

'But you rolled up at half-four in the morning, incapable of intelligent conversation, giggling madly, and with a handbag-full of men's telephone numbers scrawled on bits of paper,' Maeve finished.

'Half-three, actually, and no phone numbers. Although I slapped Tony Winston when he drove me home . . . but no, that's too long a story to go into,' Dee said hurriedly. 'When I got home, Gary said he'd wanted to talk about the job in London and ask me what I thought. It's only for six months. But he said he'd decided to take it anyway because he's so fed up with me. He slept downstairs and I haven't seen him all day,' she added mournfully.

'Oh, you poor thing,' Maeve said sympathetically. 'Don't panic, Dee. You know he's only milking this for all it's worth. He probably wanted to take the job in London anyway and just wanted an excuse.'

'That's worse!' said Dee in a strangulated voice. She started to cry. 'It means he wants to leave me. But I love him, Maeve, you know that. If he wants me to change, I will. I can't bear to be without him.'

'Dee,' Maeve said in measured tones, 'don't do this to yourself. You can't change who you are any more than Gary can. And, let's face it, you'd love him to change. But he won't. Because he's a man and men don't change.'

'But I *don't* want him to change,' Dee wailed. 'I just want him back!'

'You wanted him to change last month. You wanted him to take his turn at the housework and stop being such a lazy slob. And you wanted him occasionally to say nice things to you, not purely when he was horny.'

'That was *last* month. Oh, Maeve, where is he? Why isn't he coming back? What'll I do?'

'His mobile phone is switched off?'

'Yes.'

'Where do you think he might go?'

'I don't know. Maybe to Len's flat. Or to the pub near Len's place, the Bleeding Horse.'

'Well, phone Len's place or phone the pub.'

'I can't.'

Maeve sighed. 'Give me the phone numbers and I'll do it.'

Gary was tracked down in Len's house. 'He sounded smashed out of his mind,' Maeve reported. 'They've been drinking whiskey all afternoon. Len even went so far as to invite me over. They must be desperate. The last time I saw Len, he told me he wouldn't go out with me if I was the last woman on earth. Mind you, that was because I'd told him he obviously has a small willy because he's so obsessed with his Porsche. A ten-year-old Porsche at that . . .'

'What did Gary say?' asked Dee in a small voice.

'He wouldn't talk to me,' Maeve replied. 'I could hear him in the background yelling that he'd "be home when he felt like it". Charming.'

Dee couldn't say anything. She felt crushed, as if all the breath had left her body. She sat down on the bottom step and hugged her knees into her body. This was a nightmare, a complete nightmare. Her life was crumbling apart in front of her and there was nothing she could do about it.

'Are you all right?' Maeve asked.

It wasn't fair to lay all her troubles on her friend. She'd been so utterly thrilled when Karl, an instructor at the gym she'd just joined, asked her out. Dee couldn't ruin Maeve's longed-for date with the first man in months who'd told her he'd phone her and actually *had*.

'I'm fine. Thanks, Maeve, go back to your de-fuzzing. I'm OK, honest.'

'You're not . . .'

'I am,' Dee said firmly. 'Get ready for your big night out. I know how much you've been looking forward to this. After all, I don't want to be the one responsible for Karl finding out that you're not a natural redhead,' she said, attempting to joke.

'I can't leave you like this.'

'Like what? Hell, I'm like this all the time,' Dee said brightly. 'You know Gary and me – always fighting. We never mean it. He'll come home when he's ready.'

She tried to sound flip, composed.

'Are you sure?' Maeve didn't sound terribly convinced. Dee longed to shout 'No!' and to have Maeve spend the evening with her, consoling her with stories about feckless, uncaring men and how they always came home in the end. But she knew she'd have hated herself if she was responsible for Maeve's cancelling her first date with Karl. Apparently good-looking, a vision of rippling muscles *and* solvent – a rarity for Maeve, who always picked the most dreadful, unemployable men – he sounded wonderful.

'Maeve, don't be ridiculous. Now that I know where Gary is, I'm satisfied. Absolutely not worried any more. Actually, I think I'll go out this evening just to spite him. I haven't seen Mum and Dad all week,' she added for authenticity. 'I'll visit them. Mum has the 'flu and could do with cheering up.'

'Good.' Maeve sounded relieved. 'You shouldn't sit in the house on your own all evening. It'd be bad for you.'

'I won't,' said Dee, privately planning to do just that. There was an unopened bottle of Absolut Citron Vodka in the freezer, a container of orange juice in the fridge and an entire pack of mini Mars Bars in one of the cupboards. Dee was going to have a wonderful evening.

'Have a brilliant night out and I want to know all the gory details tomorrow,' she instructed. 'Inside leg measurement, bank balance, job prospects and . . . is there anything I've left out?'

'No. That covers every eventuality.' Maeve laughed. 'Take care, Dee. I'll see you in work tomorrow. Everything will be OK, I'm sure of it. Gary loves you.'

'I know, I know,' she said. ''Bye, and thanks for everything. You're a great friend.' She was glad that Maeve couldn't see her or the fat tears that had started to roll down her face.

''Bye.'

Dee sat on the bottom step with the phone on her lap for a long time. Then she went into the kitchen and took the vodka out of the freezer. If she had to sit up all night until he came home, then she would.

When Gary finally arrived home, Dee had drunk only two small screwdrivers. She'd planned to get absolutely smashed so she wouldn't think about all the things Gary had said the night before. But she didn't feel like drinking. The memory of her own drunken antics were clear in her mind and she was astonished to realise that she didn't want to be that plastered ever again. She'd tried to hide her misery and insecurity in a flood of champagne but all she'd done was create even more problems.

Alcohol was not the answer, Dee thought wryly, remembering all the times in her life when she'd thought it *was*.

Without booze to take her mind off things – and she desperately wanted something to take her mind off things because she couldn't cope with facing the ugly thoughts that lurked in the recesses of her brain – she'd decided to watch some of her collection of *Absolutely Fabulous* videos. They were guaranteed to make her howl with laughter and she wouldn't have time to think while she was laughing.

But memories of Gary telling her he was leaving flickered on and off in her head, along with his taunting voice telling her she was fat – fat, ugly and shameful. Every time the voices threatened to spill over from her subconscious to her conscious mind, Dee forced herself to focus on Edina and Patsy's adventures in Harvey Nichols. Joanna Lumley was so *thin*, she thought enviously. She smoked – that had to be the secret.

The Christmas special was so rib-crackingly funny that Dee had managed to quell her misery quite successfully when she heard Gary open the front door at half-ten. At the sound of his arrival, she turned off the TV nervously.

Gary didn't shout 'I'm home!' the way he usually did when he was late and wanted to reassure Dee he wasn't a cat burglar. He simply slammed the front door and marched into the sitting-room.

'Hi,' she said anxiously. 'I was worried about you.'

His eyes were slits of disgust as he took in the Absolut Citron bottle on the coffee table.

'Drinking again?' he said harshly.

'Actually, no . . .' began Dee.

'Don't bother with excuses,' he snapped. 'You can do what you like: drink and eat yourself into oblivion for all I care. I'm leaving in the morning.'

He left the room abruptly and marched upstairs.

Dee exhaled slowly. He was going after all. There was nothing she could say to change his mind. She sat and stared at the blank TV screen for a few minutes. It was happening – what she'd dreaded all day. Gary was leaving.

Dee didn't know why, but she didn't break down and cry. Normally she cried at the drop of a hat. But for some reason she was totally calm now that the earthquake she'd feared had actually hit. In the kitchen, she made herself a cup of tea and drank it sitting at the kitchen table while she made a list in a reporter's notebook.

When was he going to London and what were they going to do with the house? Did he want to keep paying the mortgage or should she sell it and split the money?

Protracted banging noises from the spare bedroom told her Gary was sleeping there tonight. Dee felt strangely relieved. She felt too fragile for a night in the same bed, cold shoulders at either edge of the bed, determined not to touch. He hated her, really loathed her.

She had seen it in his eyes when he'd come home, his face a mask of hostility as he stared at her in disgust. Sleeping on the street was preferable to sleeping in the same bed with a man who was repulsed by you.

When Gary arrived downstairs a few minutes later, Dee nervously handed him the list of topics to be discussed.

He looked suspiciously at her tear-free face before he glanced at the notebook.

'I thought we should talk about the practicalities,' she said calmly.

'Er . . . yes,' he stuttered.

'What do you want to do with the house?'

'Sell it,' he said, quickly recovering his composure. 'I'm moving out tomorrow. If you want, you can arrange things with the estate agent and phone me to keep me up to date. The sooner we sell it the better.'

'When are you going to London?' Dee asked, amazed at how cool she was being.

'The end of September.'

'Oh,' she said. Around about the time they were supposed to be going to Amsterdam. Dee thought briefly about wandering around the pretty Dutch capital and visiting Anne Frank's house, somewhere she'd wanted to go since reading the famous diary when she was a teenager. What a terrible life it had been, living in fear all the time, scared that the Nazis would find the family and drag them apart forever. Imagine losing the people you loved most in the world like that.

Losing people you loved . . . Dee felt a lump in her throat and, terrified that she was going to blub after all, dumped her cup in the sink and ran upstairs. She didn't want him to see her crying.

Dee hardly slept that night. She heard Gary go to bed at one, after a couple of hours watching soccer on TV. She heard him brushing his teeth in the bathroom, familiar noises that normally meant he'd soon climb into bed beside her. Tonight, he switched off the landing light and went into the spare room instead.

She lay in the dark, worn out with misery but unable to sleep. Sometimes she cried, hot, hopeless tears that burned her cheeks as they slid down her face. Dawn was creeping into the room when she finally dozed off, her eyes heavy with exhaustion.

At seven in the morning she woke up, feeling instantly awake. Most Mondays she blindly thumped the snooze button and staggered out of bed at half-eight to be in work by ten. Today, she made coffee and toast and brought them back to bed in order to avoid Gary, who worked more traditional office hours. She couldn't face him; couldn't face his fierce, implacable loathing. Not with puffy, red eyes.

She heard him shower at half-seven, have breakfast at ten to eight, and leave the house at five past. When he was gone, she got up, tuned the radio to a loud, energetic rock station and got ready for work. She didn't feel like putting on much make-up. Why bother? Her face was pale and exhausted; her eyes sad and swollen from lack of sleep.

Dee half-heartedly applied eye-shadow and mascara. No make-up could make her look even halfway decent, she decided, gazing at herself sourly. Her dark eyes were dull and lifeless and her usually creamy skin pasty and unhealthy-looking.

She hadn't the energy to iron the grape-coloured silk blouse she'd planned to wear that morning, so she pulled on an old white shirt she hardly wore any more

252

along with the inevitable black palazzo pants. A long-line black velvet waistcoat that covered a multitude of sins pulled the outfit together. It wasn't exactly *Vogue*'s Ten-Most-Enduring-Classics, but it'd do.

Her hair was still damp and frizzy from the shower but it was too much trouble to tame it with anti-frizz stuff. So Dee clasped it back in a scrunchie without bothering to free a couple of strands to hang flatteringly around her face. She'd looked better, she thought as she passed the hall mirror and saw the pale face with the scraped back hair. A lot better.

Maeve danced up to Dee's desk, her face aglow. 'Hello. Isn't it a wonderful morning? And, no,' she said with a broad grin, 'I'm not this happy because gorgeous Karl bonked me senseless all last night. I'm happy because I've found him – *the* one, the man of my dreams! Knock on wood.'

She looked properly at Dee for the first time and her smile faded. 'Dee? Oh my God, what happened? Are you all right?'

Dee managed a wry grin. 'I'm fine. Single, disengaged – or is it un-engaged? – and looking for a new place to live. But otherwise I'm fine.'

'Oh, no.' Maeve put her arms around Dee and hugged her tightly. 'You poor thing. What happened? Or do you not want to talk about it?'

'I don't know if I could talk about it,' Dee explained. 'I don't want to burst into tears in the office *again*. It's becoming a bit of a habit. I'll tell you everything at lunch.'

'OK. Can I get you a cup of coffee or something?' Maeve asked solicitously.

'Yes, that'd be lovely.'

After sitting on her own for a moment while Maeve went to get the coffee, Dee realised that she desperately wanted to tell her friend everything at once. She took her handbag – if she blubbed, at least she'd have her make-up bag handy for repairs – and headed for the kitchen.

Maeve met her halfway with two cups of steaming coffee.

'Have you got your fags?' Dee asked.

Maeve nodded.

'Come into the loos. I'll be able to tell you everything if I can have a smoke.'

The story took three Silk Cuts each. Various women went in and out of the six-cubicle toilet, while Maeve and Dee seamlessly switched to mundane topics of conversation when there was anybody else present. To her amazement Dee still didn't cry, even when she got to the bit about selling the house immediately.

'Jesus, he's a cold bastard,' breathed Maeve.

'I was pretty cold myself,' Dee pointed out.

'That was shock. You cry your eyes out when you see a dead cat on the side of the road. The only reason you didn't go hysterical was because you were in shock. But it'll hit you like a sledgehammer later, I'm warning you.'

'Maybe.' Dee thought about it for a moment. 'I feel sort of frozen, as if none of this is really happening.'

'Like it's a dream sequence? You've been watching too much *Frasier*.'

They both laughed weakly.

'That's pretty true,' Dee said. 'He's a psychiatrist with a disastrous personal life. I'm an agony aunt with a disastrous personal life. Do you think I could sell my story as a sit-com script?'

'I don't see why not.' Maeve glanced at her watch. 'Look at the time! I'd better do some work or I'm history. I'm not like you lucky deputy editor types who can swan in and out when you please,' she said, giving Dee an affectionate hug. 'Please tell me if you feel bad later. I'll get an hour off and we can go to Magee's for a quiet chat, all right? I don't want you suffering in silence, Dee. Promise?'

Dee hadn't another moment to think about Gary until lunchtime. The new editor, Malley McDonnell, spent the morning in Ted Holt's old office – now Eugene Flynn's office – with him, meeting various departmental heads and discussing the changes that were to be made. Apart from the absence of Nigel, Ted and his gossipy secretary, Marion, who had left with her boss, everything was to be the same. *For now*, was the unspoken comment.

'We're bringing in a few new departmental heads,' Eugene explained smoothly when Isabel, Phil Walsh, Maeve, Dee and the other features/women's pages team were getting their pep talk. 'We're appointing two editorial directors – one responsible for the news side of the paper and one for the features/women's/ miscellaneous sections.'

Miscellaneous? So that's all they were, Dee thought crossly. She really didn't like Eugene Flynn. He looked like the sort of man who'd pull the legs off a daddy longlegs. And exactly what sort of new managerial system was he creating? *Editorial directors*?

That was a new title. Where did they fit in – directly under the editor and above the different departmental editors? Who knew? The way Flynn was organising the *Sentinel*, there'd soon be ten chiefs to every Indian and nobody would get any work done because there'd be so much executive squabbling about who was in charge of what.

'Jack Carter wanted to be here to tell you how the place was going to be run but he had to go to Belfast on business,' Malley interrupted.

Dee noticed that for some reason Isabel relaxed in her chair at that point. She'd been sitting bolt upright since they'd been in the MD's office, as if she was preparing for a deportment exam and was practising sitting ramrod straight with books balanced on her head.

'Chris Schriber is the editorial director of news, while Tanya Vernon is the editorial director in charge of you lot,' Eugene said. He buzzed his secretary. 'Send Tanya in.'

The door opened. The combined features and women's pages departments looked at their new boss with interest – and amazement.

Tanya Vernon was everything Dee longed to be but wasn't. She was tall, slender, striking-looking, and could have stepped straight off the pages of a high fashion magazine. Her shiny jet black hair was cut into an elegant crop that clung to her perfectly shaped skull and made her Slavic cheekbones stand out. The picture of elegance, she wore a very up-to-date white suit with spike-heeled grey suede shoes, a silver choker, and nothing visible under the buttoned-up jacket. The skirt was short, emphasising the sort of legs that sent grown men into a frenzy. On anyone less striking, the effect would have been that of sex kitten extraordinaire. But Dee sensed that only a very foolish man would ever assume Tanya Vernon was a bimbo.

Her pale grey almond-shaped eyes, dusted with charcoal grey shadow, surveyed the waiting journalists as if she was figuring out who to fire first. Then she smiled, a cool and utterly confident smile.

'I'm Tanya Vernon. And you are?' She held out a hand to Phil, who introduced herself and the rest of the group.

Dee tried to analyse her neutral accent as Tanya politely shook hands with everyone. She couldn't quite place it. Tanya wasn't American but there were traces of the West Coast there – or was it a hint of Australian?

There were no empty seats in the office so the new deputy editor leant against the wall behind Dee and Isabel while Malley and Flynn talked about their plans for the paper.

Dee didn't know if she was being paranoid or not, but she could feel Tanya's hard eyes boring into each of them in turn, sizing them up.

When the meeting was over, she and Isabel were the first to leave.

'I hate someone standing behind me like that,' Dee whispered as they went upstairs to the newsroom. 'I could feel her staring at me all the time.'

'Me too,' whispered Isabel. 'And somehow, I don't think she was very impressed with what she saw. She looks like one very tough lady.'

Dee was amazed. She hadn't thought Isabel would share her opinion. Isabel always seemed so confident and self-assured, not the sort of person to let anyone bother her, even someone as intimidating as Tanya Vernon.

'Have you heard of her before? Has she worked in journalism in this country?' Isabel asked in a normal voice once they reached the newsroom.

'No. And I can't figure out where she's from either,' Dee replied. 'Her accent is weird. In fact, she doesn't have an accent. Maybe she didn't grow up on earth at all,' Dee joked. 'She just dropped down from space one day, shaped like a supermodel.'

Isabel laughed. 'If she's an alien, I hope she's one of the ones who come in peace. I've been having nightmares about vicious new bosses firing half the staff and giving the rest of us coronaries with an increased workload. I'm praying the real thing is nothing like my nightmares.'

By three in the afternoon, Dee had reached the conclusion that Tanya Vernon hadn't been sent down to earth in a spaceship – she'd been sent up in an express elevator straight from hell.

Five minutes after stalking into the newsroom, Tanya had taken over the cubbyhole beside the windows that the photographers used for making phone calls and doing their expenses. 'There's already a photographic office downstairs,' she dismissively told Fred, the head photographer, when he arrived to find her dumping his stuff haphazardly into a document box. 'You don't need this.'

She cancelled lunch for the features and women's departments – 'We're having a meeting in the conference room. Send out for sandwiches.' And she commandeered Jackie as her assistant until her own arrived. 'I only need her for a week,' Tanya coolly told Phil and Isabel. 'You can manage until then.'

Phil's eyes narrowed at this but she said nothing at the time.

'*Her own assistant*, my backside! If she's going to behave like this all the time, I can foresee either a mutiny or mass redundancies,' Phil muttered to Dee when Tanya had gone off in search of a swivel chair that suited her.

'No time for lunch, huh?' Maeve said as she walked by Dee's desk. 'Do you want to go for a drink tonight?

I'm meeting Karl in town at eight but we've got at least an hour to talk.'

'Great,' said Dee weakly. She'd thought of asking if she could stay in Maeve's flat. She wasn't sure if she'd be able to face going home. Gary had said he was moving out today and Dee could imagine how bare the place would look with all his stuff gone.

The more she thought about it, the more depressed she got. The coffee table was his, a reject from his mother's house. So was the Waterford crystal lamp in one corner of the sitting-room.

The curtains had come from one of his elder brothers' houses. When Dee and Gary had bought their house a year ago, they'd been too broke to have curtains made, so Dan had donated brown brocade ones from his old house. Dee had hated them at first but she'd grown so used to them she'd never bothered to replace them.

Without all Gary's stuff, the house would look empty. Without Gary, it would feel empty.

'Dee.' Tanya's crisp, slightly sarcastic voice was impossible to ignore. 'We're having our meeting now. Are you interested?'

She jumped. 'Of course.'

Jackie had bought the sort of sandwiches Dee adored. Soft brown bread filled with chopped egg saturated in mayonnaise, chunks of Cheddar cheese accompanied by generous helpings of coleslaw, and salad sandwiches filled with cherry tomatoes, potato salad and cheese slivers. None of it exactly low-fat thanks to thickly spread full-fat butter and lots of mayonnaise.

It was ages since breakfast so Dee tucked in, heaping her plate with sandwiches. What was the point of dieting when her boyfriend had left her? If food comforted her, she might as well eat.

Tanya barely touched her cheese sandwich. But she drank several cups of black, sugarless coffee as she ran through a list of new ideas.

Dee found it hard to concentrate. As Maeve had said, the shock of Gary's departure had left her numb. Now, a day and a half after he'd announced he was leaving, it was finally hitting her. She stuffed the rest of her last egg sandwich into her mouth.

Tanya was talking to her again. 'If you're quite finished, Dee, perhaps we could continue our meeting?' she said in a chilly voice. 'I just asked you a question.'

Dee felt like a fat child who'd been caught with one pudgy hand in the biscuit tin after eating every single biscuit in it. Her face flamed.

'Tanya, pass the coffee, please,' said Isabel in a voice a few degrees colder than their new boss. 'If we're having lunchtime meetings, let's actually have some lunch.'

With eyes as hard as agates, Tanya shoved the coffee pot down the polished table.

'I'm not a big lunch eater,' she said snidely, gazing at Dee.

'*Chacun à son goût,*' replied Isabel in a flawless French accent.

Tanya stared at her blankly and then two pinpoints of crimson appeared in the otherwise impassive, high-cheekboned face. She hadn't a clue what Isabel had said, Dee realised with delight. She herself had loved French in school and had translated the remark easily.

'Each to his own. *In French,*' said Phil with a smile as she patted Tanya's arm in a glorious gesture of condescension. 'I think I'll have another cup of coffee too. Isabel's right, Tanya. If we're going to work during lunch, we may as well eat.'

Everyone relaxed, the sandwiches were passed around

again and Phil sent one of the office runners out to buy a packet of biscuits. 'Chocolate ones OK?' she inquired genially, as if they were all about to go on a picnic and were keen to discuss the merits of Hob Nobs versus chocolate digestives.

At the top of the table, Tanya glowered.

She soon got her revenge.

'I think we need more lively articles in the paper, ones aimed at younger women,' she said. 'I'd like to run a series on the modern Irish woman, her goals, her heroines – that sort of thing. I want to start with a lifestyle piece on gyms. You know, which are the most popular. Interview women who are committed to keeping healthy, slim, that sort of thing.' Tanya looked directly at Dee. 'That's your assignment for the next couple of days – a two-part feature on the gym industry and young women in particular.'

Dee could feel her insides somersault. Go to gyms and talk to slim, fit women about why they worked out? Her? All eleven stone four pounds of her? Or was it five now? She hadn't had the heart to stand on the scales that morning.

'Bring along a photographer and get some pictures of yourself talking to the subjects,' Tanya added. 'I like that touch in an article – seeing the person who wrote the piece gives it a kind of immediacy and credibility.'

Dee knew exactly what a picture of her beside a couple of Lycra-clad, size eight aerobics addicts would do. It would make her look like a fat, ugly heifer, which was exactly what Tanya intended.

'I'm not sure that's necessary for a feature like this,' Isabel said smoothly. 'This won't be an article about Dee's reaction to the subject, it's about the *women's* reaction to it. I hate the sort of journalism where the journalist is pushed forward more than the interviewee. It's presumptuous. Readers don't want to know about us,' she stressed. 'They want to know about the people we're supposed to be writing about.'

Dee felt a glimmer of hope. Maybe she'd be let off the hook.

But Tanya wasn't having any of it. 'No,' she said decisively. 'I want pictures of the interviewer.'

Dee kept her head down and scribbled endless notes on her A4 pad for the rest of the meeting. Tanya didn't bother addressing any more remarks to her and Dee tried to keep as low a profile as possible. By three everyone was worn out, apart from Tanya who unfurled her long, lithe body, smiled at the pale-faced women around the table, and marched out of the room at her usual fast pace.

'I didn't think you could power-walk in stilettos,' remarked Phil, watching Tanya's slim departing figure. Emily, the features freelance, grinned. 'She probably practises walking all over her staff in them, so marching around on office carpet isn't too difficult.'

They all laughed, but quietly. Nobody wanted Tanya to hear them.

Isabel gently touched Dee's arm as they returned to their desks.

'I hope you didn't think I was interfering earlier, Dee, but I got the impression you weren't all that wild about posing for the gym pictures,' she said quietly.

'You can say that again,' muttered Dee. 'I can't think of anything worse, apart from wearing a sandwich board walking down Grafton Street with Tell Me If You Think I Need To Lose Weight written on it in big letters. What a bitch that woman is. This really isn't my day.'

Isabel looked at her with kind eyes. 'If you want to

talk about it anytime, I'm here. I mean that,' she emphasised, 'I'm not just saying it.'

'Thanks,' Dee said, 'and thanks for sticking up for me at the meeting. I've got the feeling you've made yourself an enemy. Ms Vernon doesn't look like the sort of woman who's used to people disagreeing with her. Or making a fool of her, for that matter.'

They both grinned, remembering Tanya's face when Isabel had embarrassed her by speaking in French.

'Don't worry,' she said, 'I can handle Tanya. She's a bully and you've got to stand up to bullies. She may be in charge but it would be a mistake to say "How high?" when she says "Jump".'

'She could recommend us for the high-jump,' Dee joked.

'*She* might but I'm not so sure about the new editor. Gerry Deegan reckons Malley is a decent, hard-working woman so I can't see her letting Tanya rule with an iron fist in her Gucci glove.'

'I don't share your optimism,' Dee replied gloomily. 'The way my life is turning out, Tanya Vernon is probably already figuring out how soon she can fire me. Or perhaps she's going to humiliate me so much I'll resign first, which will eliminate the need for any severance pay.'

The moment she opened the front door, Dee knew that Gary had moved out. His assorted jackets and raincoats were no longer hanging on the overloaded coat stand. Only Dee's pink velvet floppy hat and her black mac hung there limply.

He'd taken all his stuff from under the stairs apart from a battered sports bag with an empty shower gel container in it. He couldn't even be bothered to put the bag in the bin, Dee realised.

At least he'd left the curtains in the sitting-room. The coffee table was gone along with his CD player, most of the CDs – Dee only owned five of her own – and the video machine.

She sat down heavily on the settee and stared at the mantelpiece. What was missing? Of course, the engraved silver frame with the picture of them at a New Year's Eve party.

Dee had loved that picture: she was at her thinnest in it, dressed in a slinky blue dress with her hair up. It was an incredibly flattering shot, taken at just the right angle so she had cheekbones and no hint of a double chin. Gary, handsome in a dinner jacket, clung to her, laughing at the camera and waving a glass over his head.

His mother had given them the frame as a Christmas present, which was probably why Gary had taken it. It was his, like the silver cutlery which he'd no doubt taken too, and the intaglio Indian blanket chest that had stood underneath the bookshelves.

He'd left the pottery hedgehogs Dee had bought in Kerry and the fat beeswax candles she liked to burn when planning a romantic evening in. There was something else there, she realised. A piece of paper, a note? Dee got up and walked over to the mantelpiece. Lying face down was the New Year's Eve photograph. Stripped from its frame, it lay forlornly on the bare wood.

He hadn't wanted the picture, hadn't wanted a reminder of them at their happiest. Gary had never been the sort of man to carry photos around in his wallet. And if he *had* been, it'd probably be a picture of his soccer team, victorious after winning some match or other.

Dee had two pictures of him in the credit card bit of her purse. They'd have to go, she decided firmly. There was no point being maudlin. Gary was gone, their relationship was over.

She tried to be positive. Think of all the extra wardrobe space. Think of the dieting possibilities – she need never keep fattening foods on the premises ever again. The 'Gary can eat what he likes and I can't deprive him of biscuits, butter and ice cream when I'm shopping' defence was gone. From now on, it was going to be Ryvita by the crate-load, raw carrots in the fridge for those snacking emergencies and plenty of mineral water.

Without him, she'd reinvent herself as a thin, organised, ultra-confident woman. That was it.

CHAPTER THIRTEEN

Isabel stood at the entrance to the Lionceaux restaurant's dining-room and looked around her in amazement. The usually spartan room had been transformed into a winter-cum-autumn scene. Fake snow-covered branches hung over the round tables at one end. Branches covered with russet-toned leaves dangled from the tables at the other. The tablecloths were in the blackberry and damson hues of autumn. Garlands of leaves and berries hung on the walls and a large basket of logs and pine cones stood beside a roaring fire. Even though it was August outside with blue skies, a sweltering sun and a temperature of at least seventy degrees, the interior of the city-centre restaurant resembled a cosy country house in the middle of November.

'Do you like it?' asked Penelope, the PR of the fashion company whose show Isabel had come to see. 'We thought it would be fun to make the autumn/winter show look . . . well . . . autumnal and wintry!'

'It's lovely.' Isabel admired the room. 'So long as I don't have to sit beside the fire, or I'll melt.' Most of the tables were full, apart from one right beside the blazing fire, where Isabel most definitely didn't want to sit.

'That's the only problem,' Penelope admitted, screwing up her pretty face in dismay as she looked around

267

for a spare seat. 'When I planned this in July, the weather was so awful and wet I couldn't imagine its ever being hot again. The poor models are going to roast in their winter coats. And I'm afraid the only table left is the one beside the fire,' she said apologetically. 'But I'll get the waiters to move it away a bit.'

By fanning herself with a menu and drinking iced water, Isabel managed to keep reasonably cool during the show. The models all looked a little flushed during the last minutes of the performance, she noticed.

'This floor-length suede coat with sheepskin lining will see you through the coldest December day,' purred the show's commentator, as a tall blonde girl sashayed across the room, perspiring heavily.

'That coat costs a month's pay,' whispered a scandalised Joe, the photographer who'd accompanied Isabel to the fashion show.

A gaunt and rake-thin fashion journalist at their table shot him a vicious look.

'You're not supposed to comment on the extortionate prices,' Isabel whispered back loudly, and winked at him. 'You're supposed to tell your readers that the coat is beautifully cut; that it's this season's *must-have*. And then you refuse to cough up the full price yourself and demand a huge discount from the designer because you wrote about it in your fashion pages.'

Joe grinned and the frosty-faced journalist sniffed loudly.

Isabel hadn't planned to stay for the lunch but Rhona McNamara, who'd arrived late and watched the show from the door, squeezed into the seat on the other side of Isabel and insisted.

'Otherwise, it'll just be me and those two harpies,' she murmured in Isabel's ear. 'They'll bitch about the entire show, complain about the food, the wine and the temperature of the room, and then smile sweetly at the PR person on their way out of the door in order to get their post-show pressie. Which should be a trowel for applying orange-tinged foundation!' she added wickedly.

Isabel had to smother a giggle. The 'harpies' were two notoriously bad-tempered fashion journalists who ruled the fashion journalism world and carried on like prima donnas. Only slightly older than Isabel, they'd both taken the dual cults of being thin and tanned to the extreme, so their gaunt, brown faces looked far older than they really were. They intimidated young fashion PRs, demanded massive discounts on everything they wrote about and whined for weeks afterwards if they didn't like the gift that fashion companies traditionally gave to fashion writers after shows.

Dressed today in little-girl pastel suits, with Barbara Cartland-style eyelashes over gimlet eyes, far too much blusher, vast paste earrings, solid helmets of big hair and unimpressed expressions on their emaciated faces, Vera and Linda had indeed bitched throughout the entire show.

Vera imperiously ordered one poor model to stop at their table so she could finger the material of the girl's brocade jacket. Her subsequent look of disgust showed she wasn't impressed.

Isabel loathed the pair of them. When they weren't busy snubbing her, they made disparaging remarks about the *Sentinel* and how the contents of the fashion pages had deteriorated since *darling* Antonia had left.

Isabel had groaned inwardly when they'd headed for her table and seated themselves ostentatiously opposite her, which had the effect of making every normal fashion writer avoid that table like the plague. *Why* they sat near her, Isabel couldn't understand – unless they actually enjoyed being bitchy.

'If you hadn't turned up, I wouldn't have stayed,' she told Rhona.

'Quite right,' she muttered out of the side of her mouth. 'The embalming fluid might have leaked across the table and the next time I saw you, you could have turned into a third Bride of Frankenstein.' She smiled sweetly at Vera and Linda and raised her glass in a toast.

While Joe went off to get photos of the models in outfits Isabel had picked earlier, she and Rhona talked – sotto voce, so Vera and Linda couldn't hear.

'How are Naomi and Robin?' Rhona asked, lighting up a menthol cigarette. She was always trying to give up smoking. 'If I didn't smoke, think how much weight I'd put on,' she always said whenever anyone criticised her twenty-a-day habit. A generous size fourteen with a wicked sense of humour and a down-to-earth manner, Rhona was great fun to be around. She'd been the life and soul of the party when the two friends were at college, and she hadn't changed a bit.

'Are they settling into Bray and the new house?' she asked.

'I think so,' Isabel answered. 'Mind you, after saying that, I'll probably go home tonight to find Robin in a right royal mood, giving out because I've dragged her away from her home, her friends, etc, etc, and ruined her life . . .'

'You poor dear.' Rhona patted her arm sympathetically. 'I'm dreading the day my lot turn into teenagers.'

'It's not necessarily anything to do with being a teenager,' Isabel pointed out. 'Naomi's nearly thirteen and she's wonderful. I don't know what I'd do without her, in fact. Mother was on the warpath the other night, something to do with Robin being rude to her. Naomi answered the phone and told her I was in the bath so I couldn't talk. Then she left the phone off the hook for the rest of the evening.'

'Clever girl. Perhaps she'd fancy being my secretary when she's older. I need someone who can lie at a moment's notice. Stressed out or not, you look good.'

Rhona admired Isabel's outfit, an indigo silk ribbed tunic she wore with navy trousers and a filigree silver and onyx necklace. 'And you're still slim! If I wasn't so fond of you, Isabel, I'd have to hate you for being exactly the same shape you were when we were in college. The only part of me that's still as slim is my bank balance.'

Isabel grinned. 'What about the mansion in Wicklow? And the designer wardrobe?'

'What designer wardrobe?' asked Rhona innocently, batting her eyelashes. 'Oh, this,' she exclaimed, looking down at her Lainey Keogh knitted dress. 'Is this designer stuff? Silly me!'

They chatted happily throughout the meal.

'What's this Tanya Vernon like?' asked Rhona.

'Spawn of the devil,' replied Isabel, as she cut into her monkfish. 'She picks on poor Dee O'Reilly dreadfully. I don't know why. She's just got a thing about her. The latest idea is to send Dee on a scuba diving holiday in Donegal.'

'Ouch!' Rhona said. 'Nobody looks good in neoprene and I know that Dee's like myself – on the voluptuous side.'

'Dee even said she'd already tried scuba diving and hated it,' Isabel pointed out, 'and that Emily – one of the feature writers – longs to try. But Madam Vernon has her heart set on sending Dee. The thing is,' she said thoughtfully, 'I'd love to stand up for Dee but I'm not sure she wants me too. She's always a little stand-offish with me, probably because she wanted the women's editor job. But she's so sweet, I'd love to help her.'

'Maybe you should talk to her about it,' suggested Rhona.

'I don't know. I think Dee's just broken up with her boyfriend. Sorry, fiancé. So she might simply be a little sensitive right now. Which is immaterial really, because Tanya Vernon would send even the most confident, happy person in the world insane and screaming for Prozac. She's amazing looking – tall, model-girl body, great cheekbones, the whole nine yards. But she's as hard as nails and she'd walk all over you.'

'Wow! She must be bad. I've never heard you talk so vehemently about anyone.'

Isabel raised her eyebrows. 'You have no idea what she's like. She's frighteningly ambitious – not that I'm saying there's anything wrong with that. It's just that ambition makes her ruthless. And she sucks up to Eugene Flynn like nobody's business. Mind you,' she added reflectively, 'at least when she's in his office, she's not harassing the rest of us!'

'You sure they're not . . . er . . . discussing Ugandan affairs?' Rhona asked, citing the old euphemism for illicit sex.

'I don't know. But she looks like the sort of woman who'd be into S and M and a dominatrix outfit. And as there are no manacles on the walls of Flynn's office, I'd rule sex out.'

'Why is it,' demanded Rhona, 'that so many tough, successful career women feel they have to pick on other women? I mean, we're all thrilled to see a female editor of an Irish national newspaper at last and the McDonnell woman certainly sounds decent.'

'She is,' said Isabel.

'Right, so that's one decent female boss. But her next-in-command *female* member of staff is a fascist cow. We've been complaining about horrible, sexist male bosses for years and yet when some women get a bit of power, they're just as bad as the old-fashioned male bigots.'

'Worse. I can't see too many male bosses sending a female reporter on a job purely to embarrass her about her size,' Isabel pointed out.

Rhona shuddered. 'That's low. I think we'll have to investigate Ms Vernon. You say you've no idea where she came from?'

'None.'

'Sounds suspicious to me. Let me dig a bit. She must have some dark secret somewhere and when you're as much of a bitch as she is, there's bound to be someone ready to spill the beans. Have you met Jack Carter yet?' Rhona inquired, abruptly changing the subject. She drained her glass of wine and looked around for a waiter. 'I've seen him a few times but never met him. He's very attractive, it must be all that power.'

Isabel suddenly became very interested in slicing up a spear of broccoli. 'Er, I met him briefly – very briefly at a party in their house.'

'Temple Isis, isn't it? Is it as grand as it looks in the interiors spreads?' Rhona smiled at the young man who was filling her glass with Burgundy.

'Just as grand,' said Isabel with relief, delighted to be off the awkward subject of Jack Carter. She'd thought about him many times since their first meeting. Far too many times. The man was her boss, married and obviously not interested in her.

'The ballroom is massive, very grand, and the place is awash with oil paintings.'

'Not prints in clipframes, I presume?'

'No. We're talking the real thing. And the floors are all marble. When I think how much the carpets for the girls' rooms cost me, my mind boggles to think of what marble floors cost per square metre,' Isabel added.

'I have heard,' Rhona lowered her voice, 'that Elizabeth Carter is over fond of nose candy.'

'You're the second person to say that to me,' Isabel said in astonishment. 'I wouldn't have noticed it myself, but one of the girls from work said she'd know the signs a mile away. Elizabeth certainly drank a good deal while I was watching her but she didn't come back from the loo with white powder all over her nose. Although she's hardly likely to be that dumb. Where did you hear that, anyway?'

'Jo Denton, my deputy editor, is married to Mark Denton – you know, the publisher? He knows Jack Carter quite well and has been at plenty of charity events with both of them. He told Jo that Mrs Carter is a regular coke head. It's not common knowledge, so don't spread it around,' she warned. 'The circles they move in are full of discreet people. You know, "I won't tell anyone about you if you don't tell anyone about me" sort of thing?'

'Dessert, ladies?' inquired a waiter.

'Oh, yes,' Rhona said enthusiastically.

'We've got Grand Marnier soufflé, strawberries and cream, champagne sorbet, almond tartlets with raspberries and Chocolate Surprise.'

'Chocolate Surprise sounds wonderful. What's in it?' Rhona asked.

'It's a surprise,' the waiter replied firmly.

'I love surprises and I love chocolate. I'll have it.'

'Dessert, Rhona?' asked Vera contemptuously.

Rhona smiled beatifically at her. 'Well, Vera, you know what they say – after a certain age, you've got to choose between your face and your figure. If you choose to keep your face looking good, you have to be prepared for a certain voluptuousness. If you choose your figure,' she gazed pointedly at Vera's skeletal limbs, 'you end up looking like a wrinkled old crone! I'll have cream on that chocolate surprise,' she added to the waiter.

'That's one way to get rid of the harpies,' Rhona said a moment later when Vera and Linda had departed in high dudgeon, clutching Kelly bags – 'Which they've had from the first time Kelly bags were fashionable,' as Rhona sniped.

Isabel was still shaking with mirth. 'That was priceless, Rhona,' she said, wiping her eyes with her napkin.

'I know it was bitchy,' her friend admitted, 'and I know that my wickedness on earth will undoubtedly result in my joining Tanya Vernon's beloved daddy in the bowels of hell when I die. But . . .' she grinned '. . . it was worth it!'

In the taxi back to the office, Isabel thought about Jack Carter. When she'd heard that he'd been called away on business and couldn't visit the *Sentinel* offices the week after the party, she'd been shocked at how let-down she'd felt. She'd *wanted* to see him again, wanted to see if she'd imagined that spark between them.

I do so want to see him again, pleaded one voice in her head. Forget him, said the voice of reason firmly. Back at her desk, she pushed Jack Carter out of her mind and concentrated on the feature she was writing.

'Tanya was looking for you before lunch.' Phil arrived at her desk with a fruit scone and a cup of coffee. 'Apparently, the captions for the bikini spread are all wrong, she needs to see you urgently about a holiday competition for next Saturday's paper, and she's all in a flap because Jack Carter is due in at half-three. That woman never stops – it's perpetual motion. She's been like a cat on a hot tin roof ever since she heard the big boss was coming into the office to meet the staff . . .'

Isabel wasn't listening. *He* was coming into the office in – she glanced at her watch – exactly twenty-five minutes. And she looked like a disaster area! Her face was probably flushed thanks to the glass of Burgundy she'd drunk at the fashion show, *and* she'd eaten that garlic mushroom thing for a starter. She must reek.

'Excuse me, Phil,' she blurted, shoving her chair back. 'I must go to the loo.' She grabbed her handbag and raced off, with Phil staring open-mouthed behind her.

In the loo, Isabel quickly rubbed on some fresh foundation to tone down her red face, sprayed buckets of Ô de Lancôme down her cleavage and did a repair job on her eye make-up. She didn't have a toothbrush with her, so she sucked the elderly Polo mint that had been lurking at the bottom of her handbag for days.

A loo flushed. Isabel hadn't thought there was anyone else in there but her. A cubicle door opened and Tanya emerged, handbag in hand. From the overpowering smell of Chanel No. 5 and her shine-free complexion, Isabel knew that Tanya had been primping in the privacy of the loo.

Phil was right. She *was* in a flap over Jack Carter's arrival. But then, aren't we all? Isabel thought wryly.

'You wanted to see me earlier?' she said.

'I'll talk to you outside,' Tanya said hurriedly.

Isabel shrugged. 'Fine.' She went to the door, glancing back in time to see Tanya extract a small bottle of mouthwash from her Moschino handbag.

Mouthwash? What the hell was she planning to do to Jack Carter? Isabel thought crossly. Snog him? The bitch! Was that how she'd crawled up the promotion ladder so quickly?

Isabel marched back to her desk, stopping off at the kitchen to get a Diet Coke from the drinks machine. She felt very hot for some reason and a cold drink might cool her down. Only the knowledge that her article on childcare was needed for the following morning prompted her to keep working, but her fingers felt clumsy on the keyboard and she kept typing words backwards.

Jack Carter *could* be one of those men who flirted with anything with a pulse and a skirt. Or perhaps he merely liked a bit of mild flirtation with women at parties.

A few teasing words in the garden hardly constituted an invitation to an affair, now did it? There were men who communicated with all women in that way – a bit of flirtatious banter and a smidgen of gallantry.

Anyway, he was married, Isabel reasoned. Her roots needed doing, she was hardly a sex symbol compared to his Cindy Crawford lookalike wife, and what man was going to be turned on by a tired, separated thirty nine year old with two kids? Well, practically forty year old with two kids. Jack didn't even have kids, probably hated them. Why would he be interested in her? Especially if he liked the Tanya Vernons of this world.

The more she thought about it, the harder she banged her keyboard keys. *Stop thinking about Jack Carter!*

'Isabel and Phil!' called Jackie breathlessly. 'Jack Carter has arrived. He's in Eugene Flynn's office and he's due up here in a minute.'

Isabel's glass of Burgundy started doing the tango in her stomach along with the garlic mushrooms. She stared blankly at her computer screen, willing herself to be calm.

She longed to glance in a mirror to see if she looked OK but couldn't, not with the resolutely vanity-free Phil sitting beside her. It was quite possible that Phil didn't look in the mirror before she left home in the morning, as her hair was often standing on end and she never bothered to remove the coating of Red Setter hairs. If she saw Isabel peering into her compact and doing things with lipstick, she'd definitely figure something was up.

'He's here,' said Jackie in a stage whisper.

The staff gathered in the newsroom, talking and joking among themselves. They were nervous at the thought of what the new boss would have to say, but no one would dream of showing it.

'Keep your wig on!' shrieked the news editor from his office.

'Some things never change,' remarked one of the young male reporters, who'd positioned himself near the features department so he could eye up Jackie.

'I hope our new lord and master has something interesting to say,' Maeve murmured as Isabel stood beside her.

'Mmm, yes,' she said absently, and craned her neck to watch Jack Carter enter the room. She needn't have bothered. She could see him perfectly. His big figure dwarfed Eugene Flynn's and he was even taller than Malley, who had to be at least five eleven.

The moment he walked into the newsroom, a hush descended upon the room. He had that effect, Isabel thought, almost proudly.

Dressed in a navy suit, blue shirt with a white collar and red tie, he looked every inch the successful, self-made man – and then some. The tawny hair was greying at the temples, she noticed, and the grey emphasised his tan. But it wasn't his height, the trappings of success or that vulpine tawny hair brushed fiercely back from his strong face that made him stand out. It was something else – something indefinable.

As Jack Carter scrutinised the staff with those piercing eyes slightly narrowed, you could have heard a pin drop. Isabel stared at him, longing for him to notice her. Then Jack's eyes reached hers. Her breathing stopped for the few seconds he stared at her, and then his eyes moved on, without even a hint of recognition.

She barely listened to his speech to the staff. She heard his voice, its low rich timbre filling the room. But if anyone had asked her afterwards to repeat even a word he'd said, she couldn't have.

However, she did see Tanya Vernon talking to him afterwards, standing much too close. And Tanya's suede mini-clad pelvis was thrust blatantly in his direction. Isabel watched icily as the other woman gave a girlish laugh, flicked back a non-existent strand of hair and put a hand on Jack's arm. He grinned down at her. The way he'd grinned at Isabel in the garden.

She turned away, deflated. Tanya's waft of Chanel had obviously had the desired effect.

'I like him,' Maeve said as everyone returned to their desks. 'He's a real no-bull-shit boss. Not like slimy Ted

Holt, who was always looking for someone to rub his greasy fat hands all over.'

'You mean, Ted was a groper?' asked Isabel, shocked out of her misery.

'Groper wasn't the word.' Maeve shuddered. 'He never went for me, mind you. But he loved Dee. He always made a bee-line for her at office parties. Said he "loved a girl with a bit of meat on her".'

'Charming!'

'Poor Dee, she doesn't have the best of luck with men,' Maeve sighed.

'I've been meaning to ask you about that,' Isabel said hesitantly, in a low tone. She wasn't sure if she should say anything to Dee's best friend, but she felt she had to do *something*. Her deputy had been red-eyed and quiet for the past week and Isabel wanted to help.

'Is Dee having some sort of problem at home? I'm only asking because I'm a bit worried about her. The way Tanya is picking on her can't help either.'

'That cow!' spat Maeve. 'If Dee wasn't so down in the dumps, she'd be well able for Bitch Vernon. But Gary, Dee's fiancé, has left her. She's devastated, although she's doing her best not to show it.'

'Poor Dee,' Isabel said with feeling.

'Yeah. She's refusing to face facts right now, living in cloud cuckoo land and hoping that if she doesn't think about it, it'll all go away.'

'I know you're her friend. That's why I asked you,' Isabel said quickly. 'But if there's anything I can do, please ask. I don't want to bulldoze through and tackle Tanya on Dee's behalf, but I'm very unhappy about the way she treats people . . . well, bullies them. I hate that sort of behaviour – it's not management, it's terrorism. I'd stand up for Dee, no problem.'

'Thanks.' Maeve smiled grimly. 'I know you mean it, too. Let's give Ms Vernon a little rope and see if she hangs herself.'

'With someone like Tanya, you could be waiting a long time.' Isabel's phone rang. 'I'll talk to you later,' she told Maeve, before hurrying to her desk. 'Hello, Isabel Farrell speaking.'

'Isabel.'

His voice made the hairs stand up on the back of her neck.

'I wanted to talk to you privately,' Jack Carter continued, 'but there was no chance of that a few minutes ago. What are you doing for lunch on Friday?'

Isabel didn't need to glance at her diary. On Fridays, she did the weekend grocery shopping at lunchtime and bought a sandwich to eat at her desk afterwards.

'I don't think I have any appointments,' she answered cautiously.

'Good. I'll meet you in the restaurant in the Herbert Park Hotel at half-twelve. I'm looking forward to it,' Jack added.

'Marvellous,' Isabel said. ''Bye.'

She put down the receiver and stared at the phone. Half an hour ago he'd practically ignored her at the meeting, plunging her to the depths of misery. And now he'd asked her out to lunch.

I wanted to talk to you privately . . . I'm looking forward to it.

Her heart soared. He wanted to meet her for lunch, was dying to take her to lunch. And it couldn't be about business, because whatever he'd wanted to say, he couldn't have said it to her earlier because they weren't alone! Isabel knew she was behaving like an infatuated schoolgirl but she didn't care. After all she'd been through, this was a wonderfully liberating sensation.

She tapped merrily at her computer as if she was playing the piano.

Phil glanced at her inquiringly. 'You all right?' she asked.

Isabel looked at her colleague with dancing eyes. 'I'm marvellous,' she said. 'Bloody marvellous!'

CHAPTER FOURTEEN

Dee stared at the picture in the paper, unable to take her eyes off it even though it was the most horrible picture of herself she'd ever seen. She stood, smiling cheerily in bright sunlight, on a tiny stone quay wearing a navy and red wetsuit as she held her diving flippers aloft. Damp hair streamed down over her shoulders, her make-up-less face looked scrubbed and clean, and every inch of her body was cruelly outlined by the clinging rubber wetsuit. It was like the 'before' picture in a slimming magazine – only there were no gorgeous 'after' shots of her in a size eight dress, grinning as she held up the wetsuit and saying she could now fit into it *twice*, she was so thin.

There were other pictures of Dee's diving weekend in the wilds of Donegal – underwater shots of astonishing, rainbow-coloured fish swimming through her gloved fingers, and pictures of the picturesque hamlet where she and thirty-nine diving enthusiasts had stayed when they weren't flinging themselves into the freezing Atlantic. There was even quite a nice picture of Dee and one of the diving instructors – the hunky one who looked as if he should have been a model – sharing a plate of cod and chips in the pub. She was wearing her black velvet T-shirt and with her hair fluffed out around her face, and low pub lighting, she'd looked almost decent.

But the picture that stood out was the one where she looked like a beached whale on the quay. It was so truly horrible that Dee couldn't keep her eyes off it. And, naturally, it was by far the biggest on the layout.

The freelance photographer, a keen diver and underwater photography expert, had promised Dee he'd send the photos straight to her so she could censor any awful ones before she sent them, and the article, to the sub-editors. But Tanya Vernon had rung the photographer, had somehow made him send the pictures to *her* first, and had picked a selection of the most horrific for Saturday's paper.

'What's wrong?' demanded Mick, the sub-editor, when Dee had cried out in shock as she saw which pictures he was using. 'They're top shots. The underwater ones are amazing, the colour is great.'

'That's not what I meant,' wailed Dee, horrified. She'd known the tight rubber diving outfit didn't suit her but, as the purpose-built diving hostel didn't have any full-length mirrors, she'd had no way of seeing how deeply unflattering it was. Until five days later in the *Sentinel* offices when she noticed Mick at work on her feature.

'Can't you use other ones?' begged Dee. 'There *must* be other ones. He took loads of pictures . . .'

Mick looked mulish. 'These are all I got,' he said, gesturing to the six photos on the desk in front of him. 'Tanya particularly wants to use these ones.'

'But I don't want you to,' Dee said tremulously. 'He promised he'd send them to me first . . .'

'Sorry, Dee. These are all I've got and Tanya wants them in the paper. She's not here so I can't ask her about them. You look great,' he added in a soothing voice.

'I'm so glad you think so,' she said tremulously before rushing from the newsroom.

Dee wasn't working on Saturday but she got up early and went straight to the newsagent's to get the paper, even before she'd had her first cup of coffee. She had to see how awful she looked. The pictures drew her like a magnet.

Once she'd bought the paper, she hurried outside the shop and riffled through the pages until she came to the diving article. It was worse even than she'd imagined. There she was in all her enormous glory – huge, lumpy and bulging out of her wetsuit. It might have been better, Dee thought miserably, if she'd looked even slightly gloomy or aware of her own bulk. But no, she was smiling as if she'd just been given the Hope diamond by a besotted boyfriend, blissfully unaware that she looked like the back end of a bus.

Maeve phoned while she was on her third bowl of Special K.

'Hiya, Dee,' she said with more-pronounced-than-usual cheeriness. 'What are you up to?'

'So you've seen the diving pictures?'

'Yeah,' Maeve admitted. 'Are you OK?'

'Delirious. I'm going on a diet tomorrow. I need to starve myself totally. Nothing but grapefruit, water and five-mile hikes. After six months of that, I might look halfway decent.'

'Oh, Dee, you look fine. You're so hyper-critical of yourself. Nobody but you would look twice at that picture.'

Dee shuddered. 'They wouldn't want to. I look enormous. No wonder Gary left me.'

'He left you because he's a spoilt brat who deserves to be colonically irrigated every morning with a kilo of Vindaloo powder,' Maeve told her vehemently. 'And I wish I could be the one to do it. Pig! Have you heard anything from him?'

'No. It's nearly two weeks since he left and he hasn't even rung me about selling the house. I don't know where I'm supposed to get the time to organise it,' Dee said. 'I haven't a moment to phone estate agents and all that.'

She didn't add that she'd been putting off phoning an estate agent, still hoping against hope that Gary would arrive on the doorstep with a bag of dirty laundry in one hand, a bunch of roses in the other and an apologetic expression on his face.

She'd pictured the scene endlessly, especially when she was lying in the big double bed at night, arms wrapped around herself so as to pretend she was being cuddled.

'Dee, are you still there?' asked Maeve. 'I was asking if you want to go out tonight with myself and the girls? We're going to get a pizza and go clubbing. Please say you'll come?'

She hesitated. She wasn't sure if she was up to a night out with the girls; a night where her newly single status would be highlighted every time the DJ played a love song and she had either to head for the loo or the bar in case she looked desperate for a dance with some neanderthal.

'I don't know,' she said slowly.

'O'Reilly, you're coming if I have to drag you out myself,' Maeve said firmly. 'You can stay with me tonight if you don't mind sleeping on the horrible sofa bed. The only problem is that Nancy and Ronnie refuse to sleep anywhere else, so don't get a fright in the middle of the night if you wake up with two heavy lumps taking all the space.'

Ronnie and Nancy were Maeve's beloved cats, one mink-coloured and one tabby.

'They don't have to sleep somewhere else,' Dee protested. Two warm, soft bodies curled up against hers would be a thoroughly enjoyable experience after a fortnight of singledom. Unfortunately for her, Smudge was one of those cats who hated sleeping with her owner. She preferred to snooze downstairs, no matter how often Dee tried to coax her into the lonely double bed. 'They can sleep on top of me, if they'd like. I'd love them to.'

'Brilliant. Will you come to my place then, say at about half-seven?' Maeve asked. 'And wear something devastating.'

'How about a wetsuit?' asked Dee wryly.

'Forget about that. Chalk it up to one of life's rich experiences, courtesy of Bitch Vernon. I swear that woman is just asking for trouble. Anyway, I've got plans for her.'

'You mean, you're making a wax doll to stick pins in?' inquired Dee.

Maeve sniggered. 'The thought *had* crossed my mind, I can tell you. Gathering bits of her hair for a doll wouldn't be hard, she spends so much time in the loo brushing it. You'd think she was auditioning for a hair commercial. She loves herself, doesn't she? Well, somebody has to. See you later or I'll come and get you,' she commanded.

Dee hadn't yet managed to summon up the energy to scan her wardrobe for something devastating when the phone rang again. It was Millie, her one-time future sister-in-law.

'Dee, I'm so sorry about you and Gary.' Millie's voice was full of warmth and sympathy. 'I just heard. How are you coping?'

Until that moment, Dee hadn't been doing too badly. That picture of herself in a disgusting diving suit had taken her mind off her other problems. But Millie's kind, familiar tones made her tearful.

'Fine,' she muttered, groping around in her pocket for a tissue.

'You don't sound fine. I'm coming over to see you.'

'No,' shrieked Dee, briefly shocked out of her misery. The house was like a pit. Smudge's fur was everywhere, the kitchen looked like the scene of a particularly wild heavy metal party, with dishes, glasses and cups everywhere, and she hadn't bothered cleaning the bathroom in ages because she was out of every cleaning fluid known to woman. 'Can we have a coffee somewhere instead?'

Millie was the picture of blooming pregnancy when she arrived at the Yacht. Her pale, freckled face glowed, her eyes sparkled and she looked very jaunty in a pair of pregnancy denim dungarees worn with a blue floral T-shirt.

'I know, it's a bit hippy-ish and the entire outfit is screaming "I'm pregnant",' she said, giving Dee a big hug, 'but the subtle, gathered-under-the-boobs maternity dresses make me look like I'm on my way to some very posh garden party. I hate all those interesting details on the collar meant to take your eye away from the bump. I mean, where else are you going to look?'

She pushed back a bit of strawberry blonde hair that had escaped from its casual ponytail. 'What'll you have? Tea, coffee? I know it's too early for lunch but I'm having a toasted cheese sandwich. I've got such a craving for cheese all the time. I ate an entire packet of mature Cheddar for my lunch yesterday, followed by two bags of shrimp cocktail crisps and some kiwi yoghurt.'

Ensconced on a curving bench seat at one of the picture windows with tea and coffee in front of them, Millie gave Dee's hand a quick squeeze.

'I didn't know you'd broken up with Gary until last night,' she began. 'Dan's been away on a course and his mother is barely talking to me because I didn't tell her about the baby immediately,' her hand slipped unconsciously to her belly, 'so she hasn't rung me. It was sheer fluke that Adrian rang us from London looking for some phone number or we'd never have found out.'

'Adrian knew?' asked Dee. He was the Redmond brother who came between Dan and Gary, a high-flying stockbroker who lived in Muswell Hill with his equally high-flying wife, Natasha, another stockbroker.

Dee had only met them a couple of times and had felt immediately intimidated by Adrian's glamorous half-Indian wife, who was petite, exquisitely beautiful and supposedly an amazing cook to boot.

'Gary's moving in with them next week when he starts work,' Millie continued. 'He was going to stay in a hotel when he moved to London but Margaret *had* to stick her big nose in, and begged Adrian to put him up for a month or so. I can't see Natasha being too impressed,' she added. 'Gary and a clutter-free minimalist apartment don't sound like ideal partners to me.'

Dee stirred her coffee silently and thought about how things had changed. Two weeks ago, she was getting married to Gary Redmond. Now, his sister-in-law was telling her what he'd been up to, filling Dee in on his life, his plans, where he was living and when he was going to start his new job. It was like some particularly nasty dream and she longed to wake up from it.

'Sorry, that was tactless.' Millie looked up from her tea to see Dee's frozen face. 'I thought you knew where he was. I thought you'd have spoken to Gary . . .'

'He hasn't rung me,' Dee said simply. 'Since he walked out of our front door, I've heard absolutely nothing. Zilch.'

'Oh, Dee, I'm sorry. I just can't believe you've split up, everything seemed to be going so well. What happened? No,' Millie said quickly, 'don't tell me. I'm not here on a fact-finding mission. I just want to help.'

'It's OK, I don't mind telling you,' she said.

But even as she said it, she realised that she *did* mind telling Millie. The things Gary had said to her still filled Dee with a secret, burning shame. She was fat, ugly, hopeless and an embarrassment to him. How could she tell that to a woman whose husband – Gary's brother, at that – worshipped her? Millie wouldn't be able to understand it. Dee certainly didn't. Telling her everything would be too humiliating for words.

For a brief second she almost hated Millie, which was unbelievable because nobody could hate her. It was just that she had everything Dee had once had. Well, to be honest, Millie had more. She had an adoring Redmond man for her husband, a man who wouldn't let his old biddy of a mother be nasty to her; she was pregnant with a much longed for baby; and she was loved. Loved, appreciated, treasured and adored.

Dee wondered if she'd ever understood how important those words were until now, when they didn't mean anything to her. Correction: when they didn't mean anything to the man in her life, the man who was supposed to make her feel loved, treasured, appreciated and adored.

'It's hard to talk about it all,' she admitted shakily. 'But Gary left me, not the other way around.' She blotted her eyes with a crumpled bit of loo roll. 'I'd still have him back, you know, but I haven't heard anything from him. I rang his mobile phone last week but he has it switched to the answering machine, so I left a message and asked him to phone me.' She hadn't even told Maeve that. 'He didn't return my call.'

Millie didn't say anything.

'So what does Dan think about all this?' Dee asked, anxious to change the subject. Telling Millie what she'd done made her feel even more hopeless and needy than ever.

Only the worst kind of losers rang their ex-boyfriends, begged for a phone call and then stared at the phone longingly for hours, willing it to ring.

Only complete failures would break their new diets by eating an entire tub of strawberry shortcake ice cream afterwards in anguish.

'Dan is shocked,' Millie said. 'He tried to talk to Gary about it on the phone but he wasn't too forthcoming. He's been staying with Margaret before he goes to London,' she added.

'I bet *she's* thrilled,' Dee said bitterly. 'She always hated me. I wasn't good enough for her precious son. Now he agrees with her. If she wasn't a tee-totaller, I'm sure she'd be breaking out the champagne.'

'Don't let Margaret come between you,' Millie said earnestly. 'You two were made for each other, you know it. You've got to get back together.'

'Millie, you don't understand,' Dee said fiercely. 'We didn't have some trite argument about who did the hoovering. Gary decided he was sick of me, he told me I was a fat bitch and he was ashamed of me.'

She heard Millie's sharp intake of breath but ignored it.

'He was offered the job in London and decided to take it. The engagement's now off and he wants me to sell the house. That's it, that's what happened. If you think we're likely to get back together despite all of this, then you're the only one who does!' Dee's voice broke and she sank her head into her hands.

'You poor thing.' Millie pushed her untouched sandwich aside and put an arm around her. 'I had no idea. I'll kill him. Dan will kill him.'

'I don't want people to know what happened,' sobbed Dee.

'It's OK, nobody else has to know, but I've got to tell Dan. He loves you and if anyone can give Gary a good kick in the behind, it's Dan. We won't sit by and let Gary ruin both your lives.'

Dee raised her head to look at Millie. 'Promise me you won't tell Dan? Promise me?' she begged. 'And I don't want *her* to know what happened, his mother. I couldn't bear it. She'd love to know exactly how I got my comeuppance, please don't tell her.'

'As if I would,' said Millie. 'I wouldn't tell that bloody woman what time of day it was if she asked. It's all her fault that Gary is as spoilt as he is. She ruined that boy. If he hadn't been Mumsy's little pet for so long, you wouldn't be having so much trouble with him. Now listen, Gary loves you, Dee, even if he's managed to forget it. He'll come back, I'm sure of it.'

'I'm not.' Dee had stopped crying. She'd been doing so much sobbing that her internal reservoir could only manage short bursts of tears, which was just as well or she'd have had permanently red-rimmed eyes. 'It's over, Millie. I know that for a fact. I simply don't know what to do about it or with myself. I'm lost.'

'Of course you're not lost,' she said briskly. 'You're not the sort of woman who's lost without a man.'

'I'm not?' Dee asked with a catch in her voice.

'You're not. You're going to dust yourself off, get out there and enjoy life. And when Mumsy's boy comes running home with his tail between his legs, you'll be the one calling the shots.'

It was a satisfying thought and one which Dee had regularly. Unfortunately, just as regularly, she had visions of herself as a greying, unwanted hulk that no man would ever look at again.

'I can't see it happening, Millie,' she sighed. 'I might have had some chance of getting back with Gary if he'd gone to stay with you and Dan when he left me. But Lord knows what Margaret has been filling his head with while he was staying with her. She's always thought I was a jumped up, lower-class scrubber who wasn't fit to clean her floors, never mind marry her son,' she said venomously. 'She's got the perfect chance to tell him that over and over again now. Did I tell you about the first Christmas I was going out with Gary and she gave me a pack of sports socks as a present? My poor mother saved up and gave Gary a beautiful designer tie.'

The memory still had the power to enrage her. That Christmas morning was engraved on her soul: the formal present-giving ceremony in the Redmond's equally formal house where even the Christmas tree didn't dare to shed its needles.

She'd carefully wrapped up Margaret's gift in gold wrapping paper. Typically, Gary had left it up to her to buy his mother's present.

After several months with him, Dee had finally got the measure of his mother and would have *liked* to have bought the old cow a book on manners, underlining any apposite sections on how to behave civilly towards your son's girlfriend. Instead, she kept her feelings in check and bought a big bottle of Joy, Margaret's favourite perfume.

Dee loved giving presents and had been happy to see how thrilled Margaret was to get the perfume, even if she did ostentatiously kiss Gary and tell him he was a wonderful son. He adored his striped polo shirt and had left the room to try it on while Dee ripped open her parcel and found two pairs of pink and white aerobics socks.

'I wouldn't have minded so much, but I think she'd figured out by then I wasn't an aerobics sort of girl.'

'My first Christmas present was a poinsettia, which promptly died,' Millie said. 'So the following year she bought me a book on how to care for houseplants!'

'Miaow!' laughed Dee.

'I knew I'd cheer you up. Tell me, what are you doing tonight? Please come round to have dinner with us? Although I should warn you that Dan is cooking Mexican food, so be ready for red hot chilli alert. Bring Smudge and stay the night with us.'

'Actually, I can't come tonight,' Dee said.

'You're not sitting at home on your own, I won't let you.'

'No, I'm not,' she protested. 'I'm going out with some girls from work. With Maeve actually. We're going clubbing.'

'Come and have dinner with us tomorrow night, then.'

'Can't. I'm going to my parents' house.'

'Have you told them?' Millie asked.

'Yeah. They were great. I thought they'd start giving out stink about Gary and tell me I was better off without him, but they didn't.' Dee grimaced. 'I think my mother doesn't want to say anything bad about him in case we get back together.'

'You will, I know you will,' Millie said enthusiastically.

Dee drank her coffee. She wouldn't put a bet on it.

'It's perfect for you.' Maeve tugged up the zip of her red Lycra top and looked at Dee, who was trying to figure out whether she should let the long, silky leopardskin cardigan hang open or close it with the tie belt.

'I've never seen you wear anything leopardskin before, it really suits you.'

'I went a bit mad in town,' she said, still fiddling with the cardigan's tie belt. 'It looked great in the shop but I'm not sure now . . . I look like an old, fat Spice Girl.'

'You look great.'

Dee examined herself critically in Maeve's bedroom mirror.

Worn over a clinging black knitted dress, the cardigan was very over the top and made her look like a voluptuous blues singer who was just about to burst into 'Cry Me A River' in a dark, smoke-filled jazz club. The sales assistant in Big Babes had been the sort of person who didn't believe bigger women should hide under vertically striped marquees.

She'd been very persuasive and insisted Dee swop the baggy shirt she'd been going to buy for the slinky knitted dress and cardigan. But what looked nice in a carefully lit shop with an admiring, size twenty sales assistant egging her on, wouldn't necessarily measure up in the cold light of a nightclub populated by *Elle*-slim girls.

'You're wearing it, you look great,' repeated Maeve, who could tell exactly what was going through her friend's mind. 'You don't look fat, I promise you. You look like a sex bomb and you'll need man repellent to keep the blokes away from you tonight.'

Dee grinned. She knew there was no chickening out. Maeve would insist she wore her new outfit. It was either that or the grey sweat suit she'd brought along for the next day.

'Tina Turner?' asked Maeve, poised by the CD player.

'Yeah. Play "Better Be Good To Me".' Dee loved that song. 'A special request for horrible bastard Gary Redmond!'

'You got it, girl!'

The music blasted into the room and Dee had to stop herself from moving to the beat as she applied a last coat of mascara. With plenty of sooty eye make-up for the heavy-lidded look, and a tiger's eye pendant just dipping into her cleavage, she was dressed to kill. Or would be by the time she'd consumed Maeve's Dutch courage concoction – a lethal mix of peach schnapps, vodka and orange juice.

'Is this a real cocktail or just the dregs of your drinks cabinet?' Dee took another sip and screwed up her face.

'It's a Vestal Virgin. Actually, I'm not totally sure if I've made it correctly – I've lost the cocktail booklet. But one of those will loosen you up a bit.'

'Loosen will be the word,' Dee pointed out. 'Maybe I'll give booze a miss till we order some wine in the restaurant. I don't want to drown my sorrows any more, Maeve. I've been doing that too much these days.'

'Don't let Gary dictate to you now that he's gone.'

Maeve stopped applying lip gloss to impart her warning. 'He's a bully and he's history,' she said crossly. 'So there's no need to pay any attention to all the rubbish he was always moaning about. You like the odd drink, so what?'

Dee decided that lip gloss was a good idea and swiped the tube off Maeve.

'He *was* right about that,' she said earnestly. 'I always got drunk at parties . . .'

'Because you felt self-conscious and unsure of yourself,' interrupted Maeve. 'Gary never even *knew* why you drank too much. The man had the sensitivity of a rhino.'

'Well, he sort of knew. He knew I was self-conscious. But that wasn't a proper excuse. Because I had one problem, I could have ended up giving myself a worse one, which would have been awful.'

Dee had been thinking about this for ages. She'd remembered all the times she'd had too many drinks to cover up her enormous insecurity complex. Pouring vodka into herself hadn't helped, and it certainly hadn't made her thinner. If anything, it had made her more depressed than ever when she woke up and remembered the daft, flirty things she'd said to people she hardly knew when buoyed up with five or six screwdrivers.

'I'm not drinking so much any more and I've got to do something about my weight,' she said decisively. 'There's no point hiding. I've got to *do* something. I'm joining a gym – I've got an introductory session next week. I'm going to do a step aerobics class.'

Maeve stared at her. 'Are you serious?'

'Deadly.'

'I'm thrilled, Dee. I'd love you to get some exercise

but you should do it because you want to be healthy not because you want to lose weight, in the hope,' Maeve hesitated, 'that Gary will come back to you. I'm sorry.' She sat on the bed and looked at Dee earnestly. 'I want to be a proper friend, so I don't want to see you throwing all your energy and dreams into this plan only for it to fail miserably.' Maeve reached for a Silk Cut. 'I want you to do this for yourself, not for some man who doesn't deserve it. Have I said too much?'

She looked up anxiously.

'No. You *are* a good friend, but I do know what I'm doing, Maeve. Honestly.' Dee sat down on the bed beside her. 'I think I need to change my life. And I do want Gary back. I know you think I shouldn't, not after everything . . .'

'Hey, it's your life and your decision,' Maeve interrupted, 'not mine. You love him and you want him back. I don't want to see you getting hurt again, that's all.'

Dee shrugged. 'I'm hurting now. I feel only half-alive, I can't work properly and I want to sit in the corner and cry every five minutes. What could be worse than that?'

Maeve took a deep drag of her cigarette and reached for the ashtray to stub it out. 'At least now, you're *hoping* Gary will come back. What happens if he makes it clear that no matter what you do, he won't?'

For a moment neither of them said anything.

'Let's talk about something else,' Dee said finally.

Romance was in the air, Dee realised mournfully as she peered over the top of her menu at the diners in Luciano's Pizzeria. The place was jammed with loving couples sharing twelve-inch pepperonis and bottles of Chianti. They all seemed to be gazing lovingly at each other over the garlic bread. She could imagine the conversations: 'I'll only have garlic bread if you have it, too.' 'OK, let's share . . .' 'Oh, you're *so* romantic!'

She sighed. Sitting in a restaurant on a Saturday night with a group of women was like shrieking out loud that she was manless. She might as well rent a small plane to fly over the city with an advertising flyer streaming behind it: 'Dee O'Reilly Is Single, Desperate And Gagging For A Man'.

It didn't matter that Chloë, Geraldine and Evie were single too. *They* didn't mind. They were in their late-twenties and genuinely preferred hanging around with their girlfriends. They didn't seem to feel the shame of being manless.

But then, Dee reflected, they didn't know the bliss of renting a video, ordering Chicken Tikka for two and sitting in front of the telly with their man, sharing connubial bliss and pitying all the people who didn't have what they had.

Dee used to pity Maeve and the girls, for God's sake! How often had she watched her friend tart herself up in the loos after work, for a fruitless night out on the pull?

Perfumed, painted and dressed up to within an inch of her life in the tightest of trousers and T-shirts you could buy in Morgan, Maeve would head off into the night and encounter nothing but the sort of pre-historic men who thought two whirls around the dance floor and a couple of Bacardis meant they owned shares in your Wonderbra. It was hell out there and Dee simply wasn't up to it.

Now Maeve had a boyfriend – one who didn't throw a wobbly when she went on her wild girls' nights out – and Dee was the manless one. Destined for endless parties where the main objective was quietly to size up every man in the room as potential boyfriend material.

What a nightmare. How could Gary do this to her? She desperately wanted to go home, back to the familiar four walls where she felt insulated from the horrible, dog-eat-dog world. But at home she missed Gary even more. She missed his soccer stuff dumped all over the bedroom floor, his voice in the morning telling her to get out of bed, and she missed his arms around her. She missed that most of all, his presence.

Dear Annie,

Last month, I thought I had everything. A great job, a great boyfriend, everything really . . . My boyfriend suddenly dumped me and it's as if my whole life has disintegrated. I've never had much self-confidence but I haven't a shred now. He gave me lots of reasons for leaving but what it all boils down to is he thinks I'm fat and he's ashamed of me. I always thought I was fat too, but he told me I was being silly and that he loved me as I was. Finding out that he didn't really love me for what I was has been like a huge slap in the face. It's as if everything we did together for four years was a lie, as if he was kidding me all the time.

I feel so let down, so hurt. I can't tell people how I really feel. I'm supposed to help others solve their problems and I can't solve my own. I feel such a failure, a fraud. And I'm lonely. My boyfriend and I were together for a long time and I'm scared stiff at the thought of being on my own again. I've tried talking to him but he won't even return my calls. What should I do? I've thought of simply turning up on his doorstep – even though he's moved abroad – but I'm not sure what he'd do. Should I risk it?

Lonesome

'That's a big pepper grinder,' remarked Maeve, as the waiter proffered a black pepper grinder that was at least two feet long.

The girls exploded with mirth. The handsome waiter, who was used to this reaction, gave her a saucy smile.

'Pepper?' he asked.

Maeve nodded and he ground some out on to her seafood pasta.

'Would you like some?' he asked Dee, giving her an appreciative look.

'Yes, thanks.' What was his game? she wondered. Was it the 'chat up the spinsters of this parish' night? Did the waiters get paid more if they flirted with the single girls, like the male dancing partners laid on for lonely older women on cruises? Well, she wasn't in the mood to be patronised. She sat stonily while he sprinkled far too much pepper on to her food.

'I don't think ground pepper was the only thing he was offering you, Dee.' Chloë nudged her in the arm when the waiter had left.

Cue another explosion of giggles.

'I told you that outfit would work,' Maeve said, raising her glass in Dee's direction.

'God, I wish I had boobs like yours, Dee,' groaned Geri enviously, adjusting her pink ruffle shirt over her non-existent bosom. 'Men love boobs.'

'Correction,' Mara said. 'Men love enormous boobs on stick-thin girls, which, as we all know, doesn't happen in nature. Except in California.'

'True,' agreed Geraldine. 'Nature gives us skinny top halves with flat chests and balances it with hips so enormous you need a "wide vehicle" sign on your bum.'

'You could always get a boob job,' Maeve suggested. 'What do you think, Dee?'

Dee, who hadn't been paying attention, blinked. 'Sorry, I was miles away.'

'Boob jobs. Are you in favour or not?'

Dee relaxed and grinned. 'I've never had to think about a boob job,' she joked. 'But I've thought about liposuction more than once.' She twirled some pesto sauce and mushrooms on to her fork. 'Perhaps the only surgery I need is having my jaw wired so I can't pig out on gorgeous Italian food.'

Chloë's eyes lit up at the mention of the word liposuction. 'Would you have it? I've often thought about it for my thighs.'

Maeve shuddered and reached for the bottle of red wine. 'I can't even bear to think about that.'

'That's because you don't need it,' Chloe pointed out. 'You're naturally thin.'

'You're thin too!' Maeve retorted.

'I've fat thighs,' Chloë said. 'You can't tell with bootleg trousers.'

'I'm not against surgery,' Maeve explained. 'I just don't like pain, blood or needles.'

'I could put up with a bit of pain to have all my fat bits vacuumed away,' Chloë replied.

'Liposuction does sound magical, so far as results are concerned,' Dee said. 'Imagine – one minute you're fat, the next you're a waif. Still, I always feel that if I'm ever going to be thin, I've got to suffer to do it. You know, spend hours on jogging machines.'

Geraldine ate the last morsel of her pizza and licked her fingers. 'Delicious! I must admit, I like fast results. I prefer the idea of exercise routines that promise you'll look five years younger after five hours of doing their exercises. Not that I've ever got round to actually *doing* any of those exercise plans. But when I need to, I'll go for the five-hour one rather than the lifetime-of-pain variety.'

'Call me a cynic,' Mara said, 'but so far as I'm concerned, the only five-hour process that'll make you look five years younger is one that involves a scalpel, a talented plastic surgeon and ten grand in cash.'

'Talking of fat, who wants dessert?' asked Maeve as she pushed her plate away and lit up. 'They do the most amazing cake with marscapone cheese here.'

'Grab the waiter and get the dessert menu,' Geraldine said.

Their waiter rushed by, again wielding the enormous pepper mill.

'What is it with the enormous pepper mill?' Chloë demanded. 'Is it a status symbol? Do Italian waiters fight over who's got the longest one?'

'It's a mating ritual,' Maeve insisted. 'See how he waved it at Dee. If that's not a strong come on signal, I don't know what is.'

'I don't think we should let her come out with us any more,' Mara said with a wicked grin. 'She's too sexy. There'll be no men left for the rest of us!'

Dee got an attack of the giggles. 'You're quite safe, you know. Maeve sprayed me with man-repellent earlier.'

'Brilliant!' whooped Chloë. 'That'll come in handy later when we decide which of the lads we fancy and which ones we want to get rid of. OK, who's for more wine?'

CHAPTER FIFTEEN

Isabel burrowed her head into the pillow to block out the sound of next door's dog barking manically. She was so tired, it was only around six in the morning and she really wanted to get another three-quarters of an hour of sleep. Especially as she'd spent hours staring at the luminous green numbers on her clock radio the night before, watching half-one crawl sluggishly towards two before she was able even to doze.

It was her nerves. Nerves at the thought of going out to lunch with the chairman of Roark International, the big boss; nerves because she felt like a star-struck teenager just *thinking* about him; and nerves because he was *married*, after all.

Stop thinking and go back to sleep, Isabel told herself. At your age, you need all the beauty sleep you can get.

Rudy yapped on. A sweet black mongrel who danced around her feet when he was out on the street, he had the most irritating bark imaginable when Isabel was at home or trying to sleep.

'Please stop, Rudy,' she moaned. She wished she could summon up the energy to drag her other pillow across the bed and cover her ears with it. But she was too tired to do anything.

What the hell was he barking at, anyway? It was too

late for burglars and too early for visitors. Rudy usually only got into his barking stride when the postman arrived at around eight-fifteen.

A dart of shock penetrated Isabel's brain. The postman . . . Eight-fifteen . . . Just then, she heard the familiar twang of the brass letter box banging shut. She sat bolt upright in the bed, stared at the clock and witnessed the little green number on the end change from five to six. Not eight-fifteen, eight-sixteen.

'Oh, no! I can't believe I've overslept, today of all days! What's wrong with you, you bloody clock radio?'

Isabel leapt out of bed and ran downstairs in her enormous marl grey T-shirt, flicked on the kettle, grabbed a yoghurt from the fridge and ate it on her way to get the post. More bills. And a flyer for an ironing and house cleaning service. Some hope of that, she thought wryly, wishing she could ignore the dust on the hall table.

She didn't have time to do any serious housework during the week and certainly didn't have the cash to get someone else to do it. Just as well neither she nor the girls was asthmatic. There was dust on the dust and the kitchen floor was screaming out for a good scrub. Isabel loathed dust and dirt. As she hurried upstairs, she promised herself she'd do a mammoth spring clean the next day.

Fifteen minutes later, Isabel was showered, her hair was half-dry and beginning to curl around her face, and she was panicking.

The fitted white cotton waistcoat she'd decided to wear wasn't in her chest of drawers. She'd been sure she'd washed and ironed it. She'd seen it only the day before. Cursing, she dragged out all the other white things and dumped them on the bed, anxiously sorting through them. This was ridiculous! It was bad enough that the house was over-run with dust mites, now they had clothes-eating gremlins as well. Isabel stood up straight. She didn't have gremlins after all. She had a fifteen-year-old daughter who loved her mother's clothes.

'Robin, have you seen my white waistcoat, the fitted one?' Isabel pushed open Robin's bedroom door and looked around at the clothes strewn everywhere.

'Whaa?' moaned her daughter, moving like a caterpillar in her duvet chrysalis.

'My white cotton waistcoat, the one with the eyelet embroidery.' It was a beautiful waistcoat, one she'd bought in a tiny boutique in Portugal. Almost prim in its pristine whiteness. Yet the eyelet embroidery could be ever-so-slightly revealing – and very sexy – if you didn't wear a slip underneath. Worn with her business-like fitted navy linen suit, Isabel thought the waistcoat would look wonderful. A perfect fusion of career woman and real woman.

Then she noticed it, screwed up into a bundle at the foot of Robin's bed, half wrapped in a pair of inside-out jeans. It must have looked great worn with them, she thought furiously.

'Robin, next time you want to borrow something of mine, could you please ask?'

'You weren't here,' Robin mumbled from the depths of her bed. 'I wanted to wear something nice yesterday, we went to Dalkey.'

'I wanted to look nice today,' Isabel said tiredly, 'and I'd decided to wear the waistcoat. Now I've nothing ironed and I'm late.'

The lump in the bed made no response. Isabel massaged the bridge of her nose and hoped the rest of the day wasn't going to be like this. She pulled a pale pink sleeveless cotton blouse out of her wardrobe. Verging on the frumpy and nowhere near as sexy as her beloved waistcoat, it'd have to do. Her multi-stranded necklace of seed pearls would finish the outfit and, Isabel thought as inspiration struck, rich red lipstick would add some glamour. With her usual pale pink, she'd look too boring for words.

She stuck her head in Robin's bedroom again before she left for work.

'Will you dust the house today? Just do the downstairs and run the hoover over. Get Naomi to wash up your breakfast things and water the plants. Mrs McCarthy is coming at ten to take Naomi and Julie to day camp and I expect you to be here when she gets back at five, OK?'

Isabel hated getting the girls to do housework in their summer holiday, but she needed a hand around the house. And at least if Robin was tidying, she couldn't spend too much time hanging around Bray with unsuitable girlfriends. Isabel was convinced she'd smelt smoke on her elder daughter's clothes the previous week. But she hadn't wanted to start an argument while Robin was so deeply uncommunicative.

If Isabel said one word about the link between cancer and smoking, Robin would almost certainly buy two hundred untipped coffin nails and smoke them until her lungs were frazzled. So Isabel was biding her time.

The newsroom was abuzz when she arrived at work, much later than usual. Tanya Vernon lounged on her swivel chair like an *Elle*-dressed piranha, phone jammed against one ear as she watched Isabel's progress across the office. If anyone else had arrived half an hour late,

Tanya would have berated them loudly. But she always trod carefully with the self-assured and poised women's editor.

'Did you bring the evening paper with you?' joked Phil, who had no such scruples.

'No, they were all sold out,' replied Isabel easily.

She switched on her computer, opened her briefcase and flicked open her Rolodex.

Jackie arrived with a sheaf of messages.

'I love your outfit, Isabel,' she said enthusiastically. 'That lipstick's very glam. I've never seen you wear red before. Are you going anywhere nice for lunch?'

Isabel coloured. 'Not really,' she replied, as off-handedly as she could manage. 'I'm meeting an old friend for a sandwich.'

The morning flew by. Isabel's phone never stopped ringing and she barely had a chance to drink the cup of coffee Phil brought her for elevenses. She'd only left herself twenty-five minutes to get to the hotel by the time she finally left her desk, and hadn't even had a chance to freshen up.

'I want to talk to you,' said Tanya as Isabel raced past her, handbag flying.

'I'll be back later,' she said, ignoring Tanya's snort of disapproval.

The traffic was brutal, the day was a scorcher and the fan in Isabel's car could only manage 'hot' or 'hotter'. She unwound the window the whole way down and hoped she wouldn't sweat on to her cotton top.

She nearly missed the turn into the Herbert Park Hotel car park and then almost bumped into a Mercedes coupé which was reversing out of a parking spot as she sped in.

Get a grip, Isabel, she told herself firmly. You're like a

lovesick teenager. She brushed her hair vigorously, glad that she'd recently had it cut and highlighted so that the tell-tale mousy roots were gone. It fell in silky blonde waves to her shoulders. She ran some blusher over her high cheekbones and slicked more lipstick on her full lips. Her naturally dark eyelashes framed her big blue eyes and meant she didn't need much mascara, so she simply brushed a subtle beige over her eyelids. Finished, she examined the results in the car mirror. She looked good. Or was the ruby red lip colour overdoing it?

In the lift up from the car park, she looked at herself nervously. The lip colour was too trollopy, she was sure of it. Certainly too much for a business meeting.

But then again, what sort of meeting were they having? Business or pleasure? Jack Carter hadn't said and she hadn't asked. She'd better not assume too much.

The lift opened and Isabel had taken one step towards the ladies' when she was confronted by the man himself. He stood like a prop forward blocking her way. He was immaculately dressed in a pristine white shirt and smart tie beneath a dark navy suit. Tall, handsome and very male. Isabel felt her pulse speeding like a racehorse.

'I decided to meet you here,' said Jack, holding out one large hand, 'as I guessed you'd be coming up from the car park.'

'Hello,' Isabel said tremulously. She shook his hand and drew hers away again quickly. Had she held on too long?

'I thought you'd like this place,' he added as they walked towards the restaurant. 'The food is good and it's never as crowded as some of the city-centre restaurants.'

The maître d' smiled, murmured 'Mr Carter, Madame' and led them to a quiet table for two.

Isabel sat down, fiddling with the collar of her blouse before making eye contact with Jack for the second time since they'd met.

His eyes looked different. They weren't the gunmetal grey she'd remembered from the meeting in the *Sentinel* office. Instead, they were a clear pewter colour, alight with interest and warmth. He was more attractive than she'd remembered too, the strong-boned face more relaxed and a smile playing around the corners of his mouth. He seemed a little nervous, almost edgy, Isabel thought. She was probably imagining it. Why would the head of a multinational corporation be scared of her?

'Does this meet with your approval?' he asked anxiously, eyes briefly sweeping over her. 'I wanted to find somewhere that wasn't too crowded or hot.'

He'd remembered *exactly* what she'd said that night in his garden, Isabel realised with a start. Then she noticed the glint in his eyes, an amused glint that told her he was teasing.

'This is perfect, although I quite like picnics,' she answered softly. 'Talking and eating outside can be so relaxing, and you could have brought the dogs.'

'Sir, a message came for you. It's urgent.' A waiter handed Jack an envelope.

He ripped it open and his face clouded.

'Sorry, Isabel. I didn't want to be disturbed but something always comes up. I just have to make one quick phone call, a *very quick* phone call,' he added. 'Do you mind?'

'Not at all,' she said, waving one hand. 'Would you prefer to be alone?' She pushed back her chair, ready to leave the table.

'No, please stay. I'll only be a moment.'

He fished a mobile phone from his jacket pocket and punched in numbers.

After a few minutes, it became apparent that when Jack Carter did something, he gave it his complete concentration. It was as if she wasn't there, as if he was sitting in his high-rise office at his desk having an important conversation, instead of a restaurant with a woman he barely knew sitting opposite.

Isabel studied him surreptitiously as he spoke on the phone. He ran one strong hand through his hair, raking the tawny strands back from his forehead impatiently, streaks of silver appearing under the rich brown.

His eyebrows were drawn down heavily over his eyes and Isabel noticed a faint, silvery scar running from his left eyebrow to his left temple. It hadn't tanned as well as the rest of his face.

She idly wondered where he'd got his tan. Lying beside a bronzed and oiled Elizabeth in the South of France? Or splayed out on a millionaire's yacht, with a gang of other wealthy pals, all sipping elaborate cocktails, Greek islands in the background?

'Sorry about that,' Jack apologised as he switched off his mobile phone. 'Have you decided what to order?'

The faint rapport they'd had when talking about picnics had evaporated. It was like talking to a stranger again.

They both studied the menu.

'Would you like wine?' he asked.

Isabel thought about it. If this was a business lunch, maybe she should stick to mineral water. But would he be offended if she said no to wine?

'A glass of red, perhaps?' she said.

'Are you racing back to work?' He stared at her intently as if the waiter wasn't standing beside them.

Isabel was sure she wasn't imagining it. His look said, 'Don't rush back to work.'

'No.' She smiled. 'I'm not.'

'A bottle of number thirty-five,' he said to the waiter. 'I'm not rushing either and we may as well have a bottle while we're at it. Doesn't Malley let you have long enough lunch breaks?'

'I don't have time for long lunch breaks,' Isabel said. 'I'm too busy.' She stopped, aware that she sounded like a sycophantic employee looking for praise. 'That sounded wrong,' she said. 'It's just that since I've taken over the women's editorship, I haven't had time for long, leisurely lunches.'

'I understand.'

They talked about the perfect length for lunch and ate their bread – well, Jack ate his and Isabel nibbled a corner of tomato and fennel bread. She'd felt ravenous earlier, now she wasn't a bit hungry. She felt confused, nervous and excited, all at the same time. No matter what banal thing she said – to her shame, she'd actually blurted: 'Maybe we should have a cookery section every week and tell people how to make delicious bread like this' – Jack listened to her intently, concentrating on her every word as if she'd just revealed some fascinating piece of insider information.

His eyes never left her face, he looked fascinated by her, enthralled. But all he wanted to talk about was business.

By the time their starters arrived, she'd come to the unwelcome conclusion that Jack Carter had invited her to lunch purely to discuss the *Sentinel*.

It was work all the way. For the first half an hour, they discussed women's magazines in Ireland and the changing face of the newspaper industry. Jack was very interested in what she had to say, particularly in relation to her experience in magazines in the UK.

By the time she'd consumed her Caesar salad and given him a description of the reader profile of the magazine she'd worked on in Oxford, Isabel had got her appetite back, even though the feeling of excitement inside her had dimmed from supernova brightness to forty-watt-bulb level.

'Where do you see the women's pages going?' asked Jack, his voice serious.

Isabel took a sip of wine. She enjoyed talking about her job but not when she'd been hoping to spend lunch gazing into the eyes of such an attractive man. Over her chicken and his Dover sole, they moved on to politics, which Isabel hated talking about. Jack wanted more political content in the paper. Not wanting to point out that political articles had absolutely zilch to do with her, Isabel nodded sagely and wondered why her romantic antennae had been so off target.

Not that she'd been exactly looking for dates recently. After splitting up with David, the last thing she'd wanted was another man. But she'd been so incredibly attracted to Jack and so sure that he'd felt the same way. And now they were talking about politicians and by-elections like a couple of world-weary political hacks in Buswell's hotel. Boy, had she got it wrong.

'Is your chicken nice?' asked Jack, suddenly.

Isabel looked at him in surprise. He sounded anxious again, as if he was genuinely worried whether she was enjoying herself.

Sitting in the garden with his beloved dogs at his feet, he'd been supremely relaxed, the master of the situation. Now, he was anything but.

'It's lovely,' she said, smiling at him. He smiled back.

He really was so attractive, she thought ruefully. She stared down at the table, eyes alighting on Jack's hands. She loved his strong wrists and the way the little hairs curled around them, dark beside the silver of his watch. You could tell a lot by a man's hands. His were workmen's, strong and capable. Not manicured and buffed to a high sheen. That wasn't Jack Carter's style at all. She dragged her eyes away.

'So, who do you think should tackle the increased political coverage in the paper?' she asked, determined to be businesslike.

'Er . . .' Jack appeared nonplussed momentarily. 'I'm not sure. Who do you think?'

Isabel racked her brains frantically. It was like being interviewed for her job all over again. She lurched into a conversation about different styles of political reporting, in the hope that Jack wouldn't think she was only interested in her section of the paper. As they finished the wine, Isabel realised that she'd better get back to the office soon.

She didn't want the boss to think she took incredibly long lunches given the slightest opportunity to do so.

'That was lovely,' she said briskly, putting her napkin on the table. 'But I really must be getting back to work.'

'You sure you don't want dessert?' Jack asked, his voice sounding panicky. 'They do a very nice mousse thing here . . .'

Isabel had been about to pick up her handbag from the floor. She stopped.

Jack leant forward across the table and put one large hand on her small one. 'Please don't go so soon.'

'Oh, OK.' She sat back in her chair while he called the waiter over.

'We'll have dessert now,' he said.

315

'Of course, sir.'

She wasn't in the least bit hungry any more, but Isabel ordered tropical fruit salad and Jack plumped for apple crumble. She couldn't see any mousse on the menu.

'I've been thinking,' he said, after taking his first bite of crumble.

Isabel's heart stopped for a second. What was he going to say now?

'I've been thinking of increasing the size of your department,' he said finally.

She couldn't keep the surprise out of her voice.

'That's wonderful, thank you, Jack. Is that what you invited me here to say?'

He dug his spoon into the crumble but didn't eat any. Raising his eyes to hers, he gave her a long, soul-searching stare. Then he pushed his bowl away, leant both elbows on the table and steepled his hands together thoughtfully.

'Actually, I didn't have any plans to give you more staff until a few seconds ago,' he admitted, taking a deep breath before continuing. 'I didn't know what else to say to you. I wanted to keep us talking, so that you'd stay here with me, but you're making me tongue tied, Isabel, and I don't know what to do. Can you believe it?'

He gave a low, ironic laugh and sat back in his chair, waiting for her to say something. Isabel gazed back at him, excitement flooding into her heart. *He liked her. She made him tongue tied!* She knew she hadn't imagined that spark of attraction after all. She hadn't been dreaming, she hadn't been wrong.

Her cheeks felt flushed and warm. 'I thought you asked me out to lunch to talk about business,' she said slowly.

Jack didn't hesitate. His eyes bored into hers. 'I asked you out to lunch because I haven't been able to stop thinking about you since that night in the rose garden.'

He gave her a long, scorching glance. 'I wanted to phone you first thing on Monday morning after the party, but urgent business took me abroad. Today was the first chance I've had to see you alone again. And as soon as I did . . .' He looked faintly sheepish. 'I didn't know what to say. You were so calm and composed sitting there, I couldn't think of how to say what I felt. Until just now, when I thought you were leaving and I knew that if I didn't come clean, I'd spend more sleepless nights thinking about you.'

Isabel felt the hairs on the back of her neck stand up and the butterflies in her stomach swooped, landing with a resounding thud, like a team of gymnasts who'd just performed the most difficult movement perfectly and were confident of full marks from the adjudicators.

'Did you really think this was meant to be a business lunch?' he asked.

She played for time and took a sip of luke-warm coffee before answering. She thought of lying, but changed her mind. Why hide the truth?

'Well, I had hoped it would be more than just business,' she answered simply.

They both laughed, the tension evaporating.

'What a captain of industry,' Jack mocked himself. 'None of the people I do business with would believe it if they saw me right now. I've got a reputation for being as tough as old boots.'

'So I've heard. But I'm going to hold you to that promise about extra staff,' said Isabel, smiling.

'You can have anything you want,' Jack said fervently.

'Anything? OK, I want a chauffeur-driven limo, a

corner office and . . . only kidding.' Isabel speared a bit of papaya. 'Somehow I feel as if I've been too honest about my feelings, but you look like the sort of man who respects honesty.'

'I do, but it doesn't always pay off. I had to be honest with you, though, Isabel. You know about me, you know I'm married. You know I shouldn't be here. But,' he looked at her helplessly, 'I couldn't stop myself.'

That was exactly the way she felt too. Drawn to him, knowing she shouldn't be, but unable to stop herself. 'I shouldn't be here, either.' Isabel abandoned her fruit salad. 'My husband was unfaithful and that hurt me. His affairs would have hurt me a lot more if I'd really cared, of course,' she added wryly, 'although I didn't know I didn't care until earlier this year. Our marriage broke down a long time ago but I couldn't accept it. But I know enough about how it feels to be betrayed to hate the idea of doing that to anyone else . . .'

Somehow, her openness felt right to her. It was as if she'd known Jack all her life.

'I know what that feels like too,' he said quietly. 'My wife had an affair once. It was a long time ago. It was so long ago but I still remember how much it hurt, even if she can't.'

Isabel said nothing. She was a little shocked by how bitter he sounded. Why wouldn't his wife remember?

The waiter arrived, looking utterly distraught. 'Was it not satisfactory?' he asked at the sight of their two practically untouched desserts.

'It was excellent,' Jack said smoothly.

'Lovely,' added Isabel, feeling guilty for leaving so much of such a delicious fruit salad. 'I think our eyes were bigger than our stomachs.'

The waiter whisked the plates away.

'I don't normally get into conversations like this,' Jack said suddenly. He leant back in his chair, and gently rubbed his fingers across his chin. 'I'm known for keeping my innermost thoughts to myself.'

Isabel smiled. 'That's pretty much what they all think of me in the *Sentinel*. No one really knows me.'

Having changed the subject, she thought it might be wiser to stay away from talking about partners and ex-partners. Especially when she felt she already knew too much about Elizabeth Carter. She wished Phil had never mentioned the rumours that Jack's wife was a habitual drug user. It was information she'd prefer not to have known.

'I want to know everything about you,' Jack said, leaning across the table and taking her hand in his. His skin was warm, his fingers gentle as they stroked her hand, exploring the soft skin, reaching up to encircle her slender wrist. 'I want to know about your life, your daughters, what you like, what you hate, what makes you happy, what makes you sad. Everything.'

'How do you know about my daughters?' she asked, suspiciously.

He looked guilty. 'I asked about you. But I did it subtly . . .'

'What do you mean, you asked?' she demanded, withdrawing her hand. 'It must have been a dead giveaway.'

'It wasn't, I promise you,' he protested softly. 'I talked to the editor about *all* the senior staff. I wanted to know more about you but I knew that would have been too obvious.'

Isabel relaxed. 'Sorry. I'm just so scared of causing a scandal in the office. Of course I'll tell you about the girls.'

She talked about sweet, kind Naomi, who longed to be a journalist like her mother, and about pretty, highly strung Robin who was going through a rebellious stage. 'You know teenage girls,' Isabel said wryly.

'I don't know any teenage girls,' Jack remarked. 'Elizabeth and I don't have children,' he added quietly.

Isabel waited, silently.

'We planned to have children, naturally. Who doesn't?' Jack sighed. 'But it never happened. It changed things between us. It wasn't the only thing that changed either,' he added enigmatically. 'That's the way it's been for around ten years now. Live and let live.'

'Is that why you're here now?' she asked gently.

'I'm here because of you, because you're unlike any other woman I've ever met.'

She gave him a questioning look. Was that a throw-away line, the pitch of an experienced Lothario who had so many notches on his bedpost that it resembled a Hindu carving?

'I've met plenty of women who wanted to become involved with me . . .' Jack said, fiddling with the stem of his wineglass.

'And did you succumb?' Isabel asked cynically. She didn't want to hear about other women. But there *must* have been others. Jack could have had his pick of scores of women and not just because he was a powerful man. He was attractive, charismatic. The sort of man who drew women like a magnet.

But while Isabel preferred to know the truth, it still cut her to the bone to think about the other women.

'No. Except once.' His gaze never wavered as he looked at her. 'I had an affair seven years ago, the first time I ever did. I was always faithful, anachronistic though that may seem these days,' he said.

320

'This woman was very special, she'd been my friend for many years and we ended up sleeping together one night . . .' he hesitated, searching for the right word '. . . because we were lonely, I suppose. That's the only way I can describe it. We were together for about six months.'

'Did you love her?' Isabel asked in a low voice.

'Yes, as a friend and a lover. She lived abroad and I could have moved and lived with her but I didn't.'

'Why?'

Jack shrugged. 'I don't know. I asked myself that question every day for a year when we broke up, every day when I felt sad and alone. But the moment was gone and there was no going back. She's married now herself,' he added. 'She's very happy, has twins. Little terrors, she says.'

Isabel fiddled with her napkins.

'I'm not telling you this because I still love her,' Jack said urgently. 'That's all in the past. I'm telling you because I don't want you to think that I have played around with scores of women. I haven't. What I feel about you is special; something I've never felt before. That's what I'm trying to say in my clumsy way.' The pewter eyes were earnest now, the proud face open and vulnerable.

'Isabel, look at me.' His voice was gentle and demanding at the same time. 'You're beautiful, fascinating, sophisticated, clever and more than a little reserved. But I feel as if I can see past all that, past it to the passionate woman inside. I want to know that woman.' His hand grabbed hers.

'I want to know you too, Jack. But this is madness, you know it is.' Isabel spoke quietly. 'I can't deny what I feel about you but I still can't believe we're here, why we're even thinking of doing this. Are we mad?'

'Probably.'

They drank more coffee and as they continued to talk, time flew.

When Isabel finally looked at her watch, she was horrified to discover that it was a quarter to four.

'Oh, God, I've got to get back to work!' she exclaimed.

'I wish you didn't have to,' Jack said earnestly. 'When can I see you again?'

Isabel felt flustered. She couldn't see him over the weekend. How could she hide this from the girls? It would be impossible. They were supposed to go to visit Rhona on Saturday and to her mother's on Sunday.

'The earliest I could see you is Monday,' she said, apologetically. 'I'm sorry . . .'

He held her hand across the table. 'It's OK. Let's not rush things. We could have a pub lunch on Monday, take a couple of hours to talk?'

'That would be lovely.'

He kissed her gently on the cheek in the lift down to the car park. When he touched her, Isabel had to quell the desire to put her arms around him and kiss him properly.

'I'll phone you on Monday,' he said tenderly, looking down at her, his face just inches away from hers. He walked her to her car and stood there, smiling until she started the engine. When she drove up the car park ramp, Isabel could feel his eyes on her still.

On Monday, Isabel felt ecstatic, joyous almost. She'd spent the weekend thinking about nothing but Jack, replaying their conversation over and over again in her head. She'd thought today would never come so she could see him again.

But now they sat side by side on a wooden bench in the Queen's in Dalkey, drank soup, ate toasted cheese sandwiches and went through several glasses of white wine.

Yes, she knew she was crazy to see him again, but she couldn't help it.

She felt utterly relaxed with him, chatting easily about her weekend, telling him about the funny things Naomi had done. He loved hearing her talk, even her story about the search for the perfect hamsters.

'Naomi wanted two females but it's impossible to figure out which sex they are and we went to three pet shops before we were guaranteed we were getting two girls,' Isabel explained. 'Even now, I'm not convinced. Cindy and Barbie will probably turn out to be Sid and Ben.'

'Or Sid and Barbie,' grinned Jack, 'which will mean a bigger cage.'

'There is no such thing as a bigger cage than the one we got,' she pointed out. 'We bought the penthouse-with-a-river-view of hamster enclosures. It's got about four different rooms, tunnels, a hamster gym and a big plastic ball for exercise outside.'

'A plastic ball?' he asked, confused.

'You put the hamster in the ball, close it – it has air holes – and she can run around on the carpet safely without escaping into the settee and living there forever.'

He laughed. 'You learn something new every day.'

Isabel swirled her wine thoughtfully. Jack's thigh lay beside hers on the bench. When he moved – or laughed – he touched her, his leg close to hers. She was intensely aware of it. Calm down, Isabel, she told herself. He thinks you're cool and collected.

By the time the waitress proffered dessert, they'd finished their wine and were too sated to think of eating anything else.

'Just coffee,' Isabel said. She glanced at her watch. It was half-two, time she was on her way back to the office. Time for the real world.

Jack leaned closer. 'What have you got to do this afternoon?' he asked softly.

Isabel sighed. 'Lots of little bits and pieces. Tidying up really.'

'Call the office and tell them you won't be back,' he said suddenly. 'For once in our lives, let's play truant. It's a beautiful day, we could go for a drive.'

Isabel gazed at him. His face was animated, eager. He looked like a kid dying for a long-promised trip to Disneyworld.

What the heck? Faced with an afternoon spent arguing with Tanya Vernon over some trivial matter in the meeting the other woman had demanded, or else spending it with Jack Carter, Isabel knew what she wanted to do. There really was no contest.

She was sick and tired of being the responsible one, of always doing the right thing and never letting her heart rule her head.

'I'd love to,' Isabel said.

They walked under the dark tunnel and down the sloping lane to Killiney beach, as gulls and guillemots wheeled above their heads. A couple of people walked their dogs along the sand; a small group of women and children sat on a bright red blanket, having a picnic in the August sun.

The tang of the sea hung in the air, reminding Isabel of summer days in childhood spent on the beach, running into the water and searching for shells among the pebbles.

Her shoes weren't built for walking here, so she took them off and walked in her bare feet.

'Give them to me.' Jack took her shoes in one hand and reached for her hand with the other. He stroked her palm gently with his fingers.

Isabel felt warm and content inside. It felt utterly natural to be walking along the beach with Jack, holding hands and letting the gentle sea breeze sweep over them.

She *should* have been in the office, and in fact couldn't believe that she'd taken an unannounced afternoon off. She, Isabel Farrell, the most conscientious person she knew, bunking off. But she was having such a glorious time with such a wonderful man, that she didn't care.

It might do Tanya Vernon good to be stood up. It might also do her good to see Isabel walk along a beach with Jack Carter, she thought with an evil little grin. Serve the other woman right for being such a vicious cow.

Isabel looked up at Jack and smiled, wanting him to know how much she was enjoying herself.

He grinned back and tightened his grip on her hand. He'd left his suit jacket in the car and had rolled up his shirt sleeves to feel the sun on his arms.

'I haven't been here for years,' he said. 'It's funny how you can live on an island and never go near a beach until you go abroad.'

'My parents sometimes brought us here when we were small, myself and my brother,' Isabel said. She kicked the sand with her feet, loving the sensation of it between her toes. 'Luke – he's a surgeon in LA – loved the sea and was always bringing boats down here to see if they'd float. I used to collect shells. Everywhere I went, I collected shells or pebbles. It sounds silly, doesn't it? I was always ruining the pockets of my clothes dragging pretty pebbles and rocks home in them. It drove my poor mother insane.'

Isabel couldn't resist looking down at the sand, keeping an eye out, just in case.

'There's a lovely one!' she exclaimed and stooped, still holding Jack's hand, to pick up a fragment of opalescent pink shell. 'Isn't that beautiful?' she said, showing it to him. 'I'd love to be able to paint my bedroom that colour – a pearlised pinky-purple. I've never seen anything like that in the paint catalogues.'

Jack let go of her hand, slid one strong arm around her waist and gave her an affectionate squeeze. 'You see, Isabel, this is what I like about you. If you were one of the women I normally meet, you wouldn't be happy wandering along the beach, picking up shells.' He kissed the top of her head. 'You'd be demanding to know when I was going to fly you to Paris in the company jet.'

'You mean, Paris in the company jet was the other option?' she joked.

'It's always an option,' Jack said. 'You simply aren't the sort of woman who'd want to do it.'

'Does that mean I'm a pushover?' she asked. Tanya would have been packing for Paris before Jack had managed to finish saying, 'Do you want to come to lunch . . .'

'No,' he said. 'It means you're one of the few unspoiled and truly genuine women I've ever met.'

Isabel shrugged off the compliment, faintly embarrassed.

'I don't know how I'd fit in a flight to Paris and still be home in time to cook dinner for my daughters tonight,' she said. 'Not to mention cooking up something for the two new members of the family, Cindy and Barbie.'

'Here's another shell for your collection,' said Jack.

Grateful for the change of subject, Isabel examined the shell, a perfect white scallop.

They walked and talked for half an hour, stopping occasionally to pick up interesting pebbles and shells. Then, tired thanks to a combination of lunch, wine and walking in the afternoon heat, they sat down on the high wall at the bottom of the cliff.

Isabel placed her shells on the bit of wall between them. They both bent at the same time to pick one up and banged their heads together.

'Ouch!' Isabel groaned.

'Sorry. Your poor head.' Jack put a hand on the back of her neck and kissed her forehead where he'd bumped into her.

Isabel caught her breath. His face was inches away from hers, she could smell his aftershave and feel the heat of his breath. He moved downwards. His lips touched hers, gently at first, then passionate and fierce.

Jack's arms slid around her and he held her tightly, pulling her closer, Isabel couldn't resist, she didn't want to. She clung to him, kissing him just as fiercely, just as passionately.

It was like being consumed by someone, feeling his mouth bruising hers. He moved away from her mouth, kissed her cheekbones, her eyelids, her jaw, her neck, like someone who'd been denied human contact for years. She leant into him, loving the sensation of his mouth on her skin. Her fingers splayed across his neck and shoulders, touching and caressing. And still they kissed, deeply, passionately, hungrily.

'Isabel.' He said her name raggedly as he pulled away abruptly. 'I'm sorry, have I rushed you?'

She cradled his face in her hands, amazed and yet not

amazed at what she felt for him. 'Don't be sorry. I've been thinking about this all weekend.'

'Me too.'

They fell on each other's mouths again, hungry for each other. When they stopped kissing, Isabel's mouth felt bruised. She was sure she'd have beard rash later from his five o'clock shadow.

Jack held her hands in his.

'I have to see you again,' he said, his gaze direct. 'Soon, not in three or four days' time.'

'It's difficult . . . with Robin and Naomi. Who do I tell them you are?'

'I don't know. I'm sorry, this isn't fair. I just want to see you again.' His fingers caressed her hands, gently stroking the delicate veins that showed through the skin. 'Can I phone you tomorrow?'

'Yes. I'm not working, though. I've got a day off in lieu of the Saturdays I've worked. We'd better go,' Isabel said. 'It's late.'

'Let me drive you home,' he said. 'You're over the limit and I don't want you to lose your licence.'

'Yes, please,' she said. More time to spend with Jack before he drifted back into his world and she sank back into hers.

Naturally, it was the one evening when Robin *wasn't* in her bedroom listening to her stereo. When her mother arrived home, she was at the front door saying a protracted goodbye to her friend Susie. As Jack's silver Jaguar pulled up outside number 12, the two girls stared at it intently. Isabel could see her daughter's eyes widen as she recognised who was sitting in the passenger seat.

'Robin?' Jack asked, looking at the tall, slim girl in faded jeans and Isabel's indigo silk cardigan.

'Yes. I can't imagine what she's going to make of this,' Isabel groaned.

'I'll resist the temptation to kiss you then,' he said. Instead, he slid one hand across to squeeze her thigh.

'I'll phone you tomorrow.' He stared straight ahead to all intents and purposes admiring the terraced houses on Isabel's street. 'Thank you for the most incredible afternoon.'

''Bye.' She got out of the car. 'Thanks a million for the lift. I hope I didn't put you too much out of your way,' she said loudly to Jack before she slammed the door as casually as she could.

Then, she arranged her face into what she hoped was a normal smile for the benefit of her daughter and walked nonchalantly to the door. It was hard looking normal after the sheer excitement of the day. She wanted to dance with delight, to yell from the rooftops that she'd fallen madly, desperately in love. But she couldn't.

'Hi, Mrs Farrell,' said Susie, a blonde vision in PVC jeans and a tiny black T-shirt. 'I'd better go, Rob. 'Bye, see ya tomorrow.'

'See ya,' Robin said. 'Where's the car, Mum?' she demanded, turning back to her mother. 'I wanted you to drive me to Cheryl's house this evening. She lives in Monkstown.'

Isabel thought of her car, sitting forlornly in the Queen's car park.

'I ended up having a couple of drinks with the gang from work,' she improvised. 'So I left the car there. I didn't want to drink and drive. One of the guys offered to drive me home, to save me the taxi fare.'

'But you promised to take me shopping tomorrow,' her daughter started indignantly. 'You know I need new stuff for autumn. Who was that, anyway?'

'Someone from work. We'll get the train to Dalkey in the morning, get the car and then drive into town,' Isabel said.

'I thought you said you went for a drink after work?' Robin said suspiciously. 'What's the car doing in Dalkey?'

Isabel gave up. 'It just *is*, Robin, all right? Now I've got a headache. Can you make something for yourself and Naomi for dinner?'

'I'm not surprised you've got a headache. It's very early in the evening to be plastered,' Robin sniffed disapprovingly.

'I'm *not* plastered,' said Isabel. 'I had a few glasses of wine at lunchtime. And, Robin, if one of us is destined to turn into my mother, it's supposed to be *me*, not you.'

'It's your life.' Robin stalked off into the kitchen.

That's supposed to be my line too, Isabel thought as she went tiredly upstairs.

'Hiya, Mum.' Naomi was at her bedroom door, clad in her school sports outfit and almost bouncing with excitement. 'I won my tennis match this afternoon! I'm through to the semi-finals.'

'Well done, darling. I'm thrilled.' Isabel gave her a huge hug. 'I've got an awful headache and I'm going to lie down. Come into my room and talk to me.'

She lay on the bed, propped up with pillows, and listened to Naomi recounting every shot.

'The summer camp coach thinks I should have private lessons at school this year. Could we afford them, Mum? I know it'll be expensive,' Naomi said earnestly.

Isabel felt her heart melt. Poor little Naomi. She was so scared they hadn't enough money, she was afraid to ask for tennis lessons.

Damn David! Isabel had worked long and hard to make a good home for the girls and thanks to his business disasters Naomi felt she couldn't have the sort of things all the other girls she knew had. Well, she'd have tennis lessons for the rest of her life, if Isabel had to slave for the money.

'Of course you can have tennis lessons, Naomi,' she said now. 'We're not broke at all any more. We've got plenty of money,' she lied. 'I want you to have the best of everything. And if you happen to turn into Martina Hingis, then so much the better!'

'Naomi!' yelled Robin from downstairs. 'Dinner. Now.'

'I asked Robin to make you something for dinner,' Isabel said. 'I'm sorry, I know I should be cooking . . .'

'Mum, you make dinner every night,' protested Naomi. 'You can't do it all the time. Will I bring you up some toast and tea?'

'No, Naomi. I'm not hungry. I'll just lie here and rest for half an hour.'

When Naomi raced downstairs, Isabel thought about Jack. How could they have a proper, normal relationship under such circumstances?

Do I want a love that's measured out in lunchtimes? she wondered. Do I want to be the other woman, always on the end of the phone but never fully with the one I love? And didn't know the answer to her own question.

CHAPTER SIXTEEN

'She put on nearly five kilos, can you believe that? If I ever got that fat, I'd kill myself.' Two lean, Lycra-clad women strolled into the gym changing room and dumped their towels and mineral water bottles on the wooden bench in the centre. The red-haired one slumped down on the bench, leaning back on the bare boards and stretching languorously.

'But that's what you get when you don't work out,' she added.

'I'm just amazed. I thought she was so into her body that she'd never let herself go like that.' The dark-haired girl slid her white leotard over shoulders damp with sweat and dragged it down her perfectly toned torso. Underneath, she wore a sports bra and grey cycling shorts that were moulded to slim thighs. The white G-string leotard bisected her behind into two flawless, taut globes.

Dee tried her hardest not to look and failed. She pretended to tie her laces but couldn't resist peering up at the other woman's body in amazement. It was like watching a ballet dancer rip off her tutu to reveal a physique crafted by years of sweat and effort. The red-haired girl executed an effortless sit-up and got off the bench.

'I put on four pounds once when I missed training for a month,' she said, reaching round for her water bottle. She glanced briefly at Dee, who was stuck in the corner, trying to hide her bulk behind several open locker doors.

Dee looked down at her trainers hurriedly. God, they'd think she fancied them if she stared any more. But she couldn't help herself. Both women were amazing looking, toned and beautiful. What she wouldn't give to look like they did! The little mermaid had given up her voice for legs – Dee felt as if she'd give ten years of her life for a body like theirs.

'Are you going out tonight?' asked the red-head, ripping off the rest of her workout clothes.

Dee gazed at her and considered crying. So that perfect body wasn't all thanks to the great god of Lycra. The red-head girl had *thighs* that were slim and a flat stomach, not just vacuum-packed cycling shorts making it look as if she did.

'Yes,' replied the other woman, 'one of the girls from work is getting married and we're going clubbing.'

Not content with looking perfect, they had boundless energy too, Dee realised mournfully. She'd only driven here from work and changed into her new sports clothes and already she felt exhausted. She couldn't imagine how shattered she'd feel *after* an aerobics class.

Shuffling down the corridor in her stiff new trainers, Dee began to get a sense of what the word 'humiliation' really meant. There may have been other overweight, unfit people wandering around the ultra-modern Fitness Studio, but she couldn't see them. Everyone appeared to be slim and glowing with health, instead of at least three stone overweight and glowing with embarrassment.

Eyes down, she negotiated the coffee bar and made it to the gym where her Fit For Life consultation was to take place. Fit For Nothing more like, Dee thought to herself.

The gym was packed. Dozens of shiny-faced, lean people jogged, cycled, stepped and rowed to a pulsing beat. Televisions suspended high up on one wall showed everything from *Emmerdale* to MTV and as she looked nervously around, Dee heartily wished she was at home watching her own television. Maybe she could just cut out the mini Mars Bars and she'd lose weight. She'd start walking, stop eating chocolate digestives, she didn't need a gym . . .

'Dee O'Reilly?' asked a kind voice.

Dee turned to see a tall, very muscular young man in an acid yellow polo shirt and shorts standing behind her. Twenty-something, around six four and incredibly attractive in a Scandinavian rock star way, he was the sort of man to make your knees go weak. As Dee's knees were already weak with nerves, she simply stared at him blankly.

'I'm James,' he said. 'I'll be doing your Fit For Life consultation because Danielle's out sick.' He took her hand in a firm, one-hundred-and-fifty-five-kilos-on-the-bench-press grip. Dee smiled weakly.

It wasn't enough that she was going to be officially shamed into finding out how unfit and slobby she was – she was going to be shamed by a very good-looking man into the bargain. What a perfect evening this was turning out to be. Why didn't she simply strip down to her bra and knickers in front of the entire gym and humiliate herself completely?

'How did you know it was me?' she asked, seconds before her brain realised this was a very dumb question

335

indeed. How the *hell* did she think he knew? Because she was the only person on the premises who looked like an opera singer as opposed to a fit, gym-going person.

'I didn't recognise you and I know everyone else in the gym tonight,' James said cheerily. 'C'mon, let's get started. This takes about half an hour.'

'Fine,' said Dee. 'So I'll be too late to make the step aerobics class,' she added hopefully. With any luck, she'd leave after the consultation without going anywhere near the aerobics department, could grab a video en route home and collapse in front of the box with some chocolate. And never go near the Fitness Studio ever again.

'No, you'll be in time,' James reassured her.

'Oh, goody.'

After five minutes' hard pedalling on the bike in the consultation room, Dee felt she'd had enough exercise for one night.

'Now that you've warmed up a little, I'll increase the resistance and you've got to keep pedalling at the same speed,' James explained, checking that the wrist bands reading her pulse were working properly before he fiddled around with the bike's control panel.

Warmed up? thought Dee. She already felt heated up to about gas mark five. How much hotter did she have to get?

James sat down at the computer again and watched Dee's pulse rate on the screen.

'How much longer do I have to keep going?' she panted. Her thighs were burning with the effort of moving the pedals and she didn't think she could keep it up much longer.

'Only ten minutes,' he said breezily.

Another ten minutes! Dee's energy flagged suddenly. The last time she'd done anything this energetic, she'd been hoovering the stairs when Smudge had moulted fur everywhere and dinner party guests were due any second.

'You're going below the speed limit,' James warned. 'Get those legs moving! You can do it!'

Dee really didn't think she could.

'I haven't done any exercise for a long time,' she wheezed, her thighs in agony.

'How long?' inquired her torturer.

'Never, really,' she said, biting the bullet in the hope that he'd stop the test on medical grounds. A totally unfit person could pass out with the strain of fifteen minutes on a bike.

'You're doing very well, Dee, in that case,' he said encouragingly. 'Most people who've never exercised before can barely cycle. You've done . . .' he glanced at his stopwatch, '. . . nearly nine minutes. Only six to go!'

When the time came for her to sit on the ground for the flexibility tests, she sank on to the carpet gratefully and wondered if it would be bad form to curl up on it and beg for a rest. She was sweating madly, the stray bits of hair around her face were plastered damply to it, and she felt weak from the unaccustomed effort of cycling.

'Put your feet together and stretch out as far as you can,' ordered James.

Stretching she could do, no problem. The only difficulty was that she might pass out on the floor when she was supposed to be reaching her feet. Next, James measured her inner arms and thighs with little callipers that pinched painfully. Then he tested her lung capacity.

Dee had just about stopped panting and had thought the test was practically over when the worst bit came.

'Hop on the scales, Dee,' said James, not even looking up from the computer screen where he was typing in her details.

She reeled in shock. 'The scales?'

'Yeah, and then we're finished. You're just in time for the aerobics class. It's a beginners' one, you'll be well able for it. You did very well on the exercise bike.'

'I don't want to be weighed,' Dee said suddenly.

His expression was sympathetic. 'I understand. Lots of people don't want to be weighed, but we have to do it. That's how we assess your physical fitness and we can't let you join the club properly until we do that.'

Dee said nothing. She felt like crying. It was bad enough weighing herself in the privacy of her own bathroom, away from prying eyes. But to be weighed publicly, in front of such a gorgeous man . . . He'd think she was a total pig when he realised how much she actually weighed. Then he'd put her weight into the computer and it would be official – Dee O'Reilly: Tank Girl.

Maybe other people in the gym would be able to look her up on the computer and see how fat she was. It was too awful for words. She shouldn't have come here.

'You don't have to look,' James offered. 'I'll just weigh you quickly and I won't tell you. C'mon, it'll all be over in a minute and you can get to that aerobics class.'

His voice was wheedling. He patted her shoulder.

'I'm not letting you out the door until we finish this, and I'm a strong bloke,' he joked.

Dee dithered for an instant. He was so nice, so friendly.

'OK.'

'Great.'

338

He kept his hand over the panel that showed her weight. Dee stared at the wall, not wanting to look in his direction. But he didn't gasp in shock or curl his lip in disgust.

'Off you go,' he said cheerily after a couple of seconds. He pushed a button and removed his hand from the now-blank panel. 'See, I told you I wouldn't let you see.'

Relieved, she got off the scales.

'I'll have your assessment in two days,' James said. 'If you want to come in then, I'll make out a programme for you – you know, gym work, what machines you should use and what areas you need to work on.'

'Everywhere,' Dee remarked wryly.

'It always seems so daunting at first, but it's not,' he said encouragingly. 'In six weeks, if you come regularly, you won't know yourself. You can achieve amazing results in that time. And, let me tell you,' he grinned at her, 'there isn't a woman in this gym who likes being weighed, so you'll fit right in.'

'Thanks for the encouragement.' Dee smiled. 'You've been really kind. I was dreading this. Now, which way do I go for aerobics?'

Dee's entire body was weak with exhaustion as she unlocked the front door and nudged it open with her hip. She dropped her gym bag on to the hall floor, followed by her handbag and coat.

All she wanted was an enormous plate of sausages and chips, something to give her back even a fraction of the energy she'd had earlier in the day. Step aerobics had been hell. How did women do it week in, week out, for years? She was shattered after a beginners' class and couldn't imagine what the advanced 'power workout'

CATHY KELLY

must be like. From the moment the throbbing beat had boomed out of the aerobics studio speakers, it had been torture. The luminous pink Lycra-clad demon at the top of the class had leapt around like someone on a particularly bad acid trip, merrily shouting commands to the assembled beginners.

At least they'd all been pretty dreadful too. There'd been several overweight women in the class, bundled into long, baggy T-shirts with long, baggy sweat pants designed to hide everything. Just like Dee.

Thankfully she wasn't the only person who didn't know what a 'jumping jack' was either. What felt like twenty million jumping jacks and a few billion grapevine steps later, she wished she still didn't know.

Dee bent, painfully, to pick up the letters on the mat inside the front door. Junk mail about discount oil refills didn't interest her, nor did a flyer for a crêche. Then she found a letter that shocked her out of her exhaustion.

She'd have known Gary's writing anywhere. That familiar sloping script that had decorated birthday and Valentine cards for four years.

To my darling Dee, love you forever, always, with all my heart, Gary . . .

Could he have had a change of heart? she wondered, staring at the envelope. Did he still love her desperately, want to come home and make everything the way it had been before?

For a moment, Dee held the precious letter close to her chest, longing for the words to be the ones she hoped to read. That *had* to be it. Why else would Gary write to her?

She ripped open the envelope, tearing through the London postmark. Inside was one thin sheet, only half-covered with Gary's almost illegible scrawl.

340

Dee,

I'm writing to find out why you haven't put the house up for sale yet? My mother says there's no estate agent's sign up. I want to sell it and unless you plan to buy my half, then see an estate agent.

If you won't, I will. I don't want my money tied up in a property I'm not living in. Sort it out.

Gary

She scrunched up the letter in one trembling hand. Why would he write to her, indeed? Because he was too much of a coward to phone her and demand to know why she hadn't put the house on the market. The bastard!

After four years together, he didn't even have the decency to phone her. All she got was a short, sharp letter that contained not one shred of kindness. After all they'd been through together . . . One lousy phone call, that was all she'd wanted.

It wasn't as if she'd bawl her eyes out on the phone or scream at him if he rang. No way. She simply wanted the chance to talk to him, person to person. What did Gary take her for? Some demented bunny-boiler who'd lost her mind because her man had dumped her and would screech down the phone, begging him to come back? Hardly. She was a successful career woman, the deputy women's editor of a leading newspaper, no less. Not a fool. Not the sort of woman to disintegrate in front of him. She wouldn't mind so much if he'd even made an effort to be polite on paper, but he hadn't. The letter was blunt verging on rude. Never mind verging, Dee thought angrily, it *was* bloody rude.

She stomped into the kitchen, opened the pedal bin and dumped the letter in it. Bastard! What she'd like to do to Gary-bloody-Redmond if she ever got her hands on him again! As for his bitch of a mother . . . Sneaking round looking for estate agent's signs, indeed. She'd bet a tenner the old cow had stuck her ugly head up to the front window to see if the house had gone to rack and ruin since her beloved Gary had left, to check if his investment had deteriorated.

In fact, it was much more likely to have deteriorated while he was living there, Dee thought venomously, since he was a lazy, useless sod who'd never cleaned up in his life.

She wrenched open the fridge, seeking solace. The large slab of Edam cheese, iceberg lettuce and family pack of diet yoghurts didn't fit the bill. Neither did the neatly stacked Lean Cuisines in the freezer. The small boxes of microwavable chips were another matter. So much for the diet to end all diets, Dee muttered to herself as she stuck one box of chips in the microwave and poked around in the cupboards for the ketchup.

After demolishing three boxes of chips, four chocolate digestives and a can of Diet Coke, Dee fished Gary's letter out of the bin and smoothed it out carefully. She re-read it several times, to make sure she hadn't imagined its nasty tone. She hadn't. *Sort it out.* Gary had managed to stop himself from adding *or else* but it was clear that was the message. Dee wondered what the 'or else' would be?

Would he send his mother round armed with a baseball bat, or would he simply get his lawyer to write a stinker of a letter threatening the courts if she didn't sell up sharpish?

Their lawyer, actually. Although he was Gary's friend, so it was obvious which of them he'd choose to represent in a battle. She'd better organise her own legal

342

adviser in case things got nasty. Dee sighed. Perhaps she and Gary should have drawn up some sort of pre-engagement contract to sort out the fine details in the event of a break-up.

But when you were madly in love, you didn't think about breaking up. You thought about picnics on the beach, sharing romantic dinners and spending the rest of your life with the man you adored. Sometimes you day-dreamed about having his babies. You certainly didn't anticipate the day when he'd hot-foot it to London, order you to sell the joint home immediately and then send his mother round on a reconnaissance mission to see if you'd started flogging the house yet.

Smudge's elegant marmalade-coloured face appeared at the kitchen window. She miaowed plaintively and Dee let her in.

'Where have you been, Smudgy?' she demanded, picking up the cat and trying to hug her.

Smudge was not the sort of cat who took kindly to hugs. She wriggled out of Dee's arms and landed daintily on the worktop beside the white ceramic dish with her name painted on it in black.

'You only come home for dinner,' Dee grumbled, opening a tin of cat food. 'Why can't you be more like Ronnie and Nancy? They love cuddles and they adore Maeve. Hell, they like *me* more than you do.'

Smudge looked the other way in disdain, arching her graceful neck to signify that she was bored with conversation and was waiting for her dinner. After breaking up the chunks of cat food to the consistency that Smudge required, Dee placed the dish in front of her.

The cat glanced at it briefly with amber eyes then shot off the worktop into the sitting-room. Dee sighed. Even Smudge hated her.

Making a cup of tea, she took another couple of chocolate digestives and followed the cat into the sitting-room. She flung herself tiredly on to the big armchair and thought of all the things she'd say to Gary next time she saw him. And it wouldn't be anything nice.

Dressed to kill and looking devastatingly slim, she'd throw a drink in his face before marching off with her new boyfriend, some six-foot hunk of pure muscle who worshipped her. A six-foot hunk who'd then spend the evening wrapped around her so tightly they practically qualified for Siamese twin status.

Dee smiled grimly to herself. A new boyfriend . . . that'd show Gary. She knew just how to make sure he found out about Mr Wonderful too. Millie was holding a dinner party in a couple of weeks' time and had begged Dee to go. Dee would – but not alone.

Dee could hear them shouting long before she reached the conference room. Tanya Vernon's voice carried the entire length of the corridor, its previously accentless quality coloured by rage.

'You piece of shit!' she screamed in a strong Midlands accent. 'Don't you ever dare to countermand an order I've given!'

'You have no authority over my staff,' yelled back Chris Schriber, editorial director for news. 'How dare you tell that kid that your assignment took precedence over mine?'

Dee belted past the conference room and into the safety of the newsroom where the early-morning staff were clustered near the door, necks craned, listening avidly to the row.

'I'm glad *somebody's* standing up to that bitch,' said

Noel, one of the young news reporters, fervently. 'She's a thundering cow.'

'What happened?' asked Dee, wriggling past the fascinated throng.

'She made the fatal error of bullying the new free-lance into doing an assignment for the features department when Chris had given him an urgent news story. Big mistake,' said Noel joyfully. 'Because Chris looks so easy going and laid-back, she thought she could walk all over him. She'll learn.'

Tanya's voice went up an octave.

'You fucker!' she screeched.

'Have you noticed her accent?' Belinda, the gossip columnist, was rubbing her hands together with glee. 'It didn't take long for the posh Dublin 4 sounds to disappear. I wonder how long she spent trying to lose her real accent?'

'I wonder why she bothered?' said Dee. 'She should be proud of where she comes from instead of trying to cover it up. Silly cow reminds me of my ex's mother, always trying to pretend to be something she's not.'

She walked past the empty desks to her own. Isabel was the only other person not listening to the Vernon/Schriber match. She sat at her desk, concentrating fiercely on her computer screen.

'Morning, Isabel,' Dee said.

The other woman looked up, her expression tense.

'Oh, Dee, hello. I didn't hear you come in. I'm supposed to have this damn' article finished and I just couldn't write for toffee yesterday.'

'I know what that's like,' Dee replied with feeling, dumping her bulging briefcase on her desk. She'd found it impossible to write even the simplest article recently. Staring at the blank computer screen was the perfect opportunity to dwell on all the misery in her life. 'You must have great powers of concentration, though, Isabel,' she added, 'as you're the only person on the premises not glued to the bout of the century.'

Isabel raised her eyes heavenwards. 'If I listened, I'd be tempted to rush in there and join in,' she said. 'That woman would try the patience of a saint.'

Dee was amazed. 'But you never seem the slightest bit upset by her. You're always so calm and cool.'

Grinning, Isabel swivelled the chair away from her computer and stretched her arms above her head to loosen the tension in her shoulders. 'I count to a hundred backwards, that does the trick. But one day . . .'

'One day you'll finish her with a sawn-off shotgun?' suggested Dee, laughing.

Isabel pretended to consider this. 'It's an interesting thought but I couldn't face the time in jail. You get life for premeditated murder. No, one day I'll give Ms Vernon a taste of her own medicine. And when I'm finished with her, she'll be sorry.'

'Can I watch?' Dee begged. 'I'll hold your coat. I hate her guts.'

'So you should,' Isabel said. 'Tanya's utterly vile to you, although I don't know why.' She left her chair to sit on the edge of Dee's desk. 'You let her bully you too much, you know. You've got to stand up to her. I'll back you up any time you want to do it, but you have to make the first move.'

Disconcerted by the suddenly serious tone of the conversation, Dee said nothing.

'Er . . . thanks,' she stuttered after a moment.

'I mean it,' Isabel emphasised. 'I hate seeing her pick on you but I haven't really discussed it with you before because . . .' She hesitated and looked around the office.

There was still nobody down their end of the newsroom, everyone was hanging around the door, glued to the ongoing row '. . . because I knew you resented my getting the women's editor job, and I didn't think you'd appreciate any interference from me. But we get on now, we work well together and I feel we should sort things out. That includes Tanya. What do you think?'

The concern on Isabel's face was so genuine that Dee knew she was serious. She wasn't surprised by Isabel's kindness, not really. Deep down, she'd always known that Isabel was a decent woman. She just hadn't wanted to face up to it. It was easier to hate her for taking Dee's job than to think about what sort of person she really was.

Dee stretched out a hand and patted Isabel on the arm. 'Thank you,' she said. 'I know you mean it.' In an instant, her eyes flooded. She could cope with rows and horrible letters from Gary. It was compassion and sympathy she couldn't take.

'Sorry,' she sniffled, looking blindly around her desk for a spare tissue. 'I've just been having a bit of an awful time recently and I feel all messed up. Your being nice to me sets me off.'

'You poor thing,' Isabel said fiercely. 'I know just what that's like.' She put her arms around Dee and hugged her, the way she hugged Robin and Naomi. 'I was just the same when my husband and I split up. All I did was cry.'

'You know about me and Gary?' Dee asked in surprise.

'Maeve told me. I asked her,' Isabel added hurriedly. 'She wasn't breaking a confidence, I'd just figured out that something awful had happened to you and I wondered if I could help.'

'It's OK, I don't mind you knowing. It's just . . .' Dee started to sob '. . . everything's so messed up. He hasn't contacted me since he left, then last night I got a letter from him wanting to know why I hadn't started selling the house,' she wailed.

'That's appalling,' Isabel said with feeling.

'I know.' Dee sobbed even harder.

The newsroom door slammed loudly and people started moving back to their desks.

'Come into my little cubicle,' Isabel urged, taking one look at Dee's blotchy face. 'I'll keep everyone out while you stop crying. Otherwise they'll all want to know what's wrong.'

She made strong, sugary tea while Dee sat facing the window and tried to repair her face with a fresh dollop of Number 7.

'Tanya's on the warpath,' Isabel announced, putting a mug in front of Dee. 'She's in Malley's office now and as soon as she gets out of there, she'll be down here like a shot, looking for fresh meat. Pretend you're on my phone and sit looking out of the window until you feel better. I'll get rid of her if she storms down here.'

But Tanya never came back into the newsroom. After fifteen high-decibel minutes in the editor's office, she marched out of the building to whoops of delight from the newsroom.

'Way to go, Chris, my man!' yelled Noel when Chris Schriber left Malley McDonnell's office a moment later.

'You socked it to that cow!' yelled another news reporter.

'Seems we're not alone in loathing Ms Vernon,' Isabel remarked drily to Dee.

'There are probably more people in the *Sentinel*'s We

Hate Tanya Club than there are in this branch of the NUJ,' Dee said, with only a trace of a snuffle.

She drank her tea gratefully and waited for her face to return to its normal colour.

'Thanks, Isabel,' she said warmly as she finally left the safety of the women's editor's cubicle to return to her own desk.

'What are you up to tonight?' Isabel inquired on the spur of the moment.

'Oh, I dunno. The men in my life are fighting about who gets to whisk me off to Guilbaud's for a slap-up four-course meal,' Dee quipped with a touch of her old sparkle.

'If you're not doing anything, I'd love you to come out to my house for dinner,' Isabel offered. 'It'd just be simple food in the kitchen, nothing fancy, I'm afraid. You could meet my daughters.'

Dee was touched. 'That would be wonderful,' she said. 'I'd love to.'

'It's a deal then. You can come out with me after work, if you want, then you can have a couple of glasses of wine and get a taxi home.'

Dee groaned. 'That sounds fabulous. Food, wine *and* company.'

Dee pottered around Isabel's kitchen, admiring all the little homely touches. She picked up the smallest of the family of crimson and gilt dolls that sat on the window next to a pretty variegated ivy.

'I love these little things,' she said. 'They're so cute. Are they Russian?'

'Yes.' Isabel turned round from the sink where she was washing mushrooms. 'David, my husband, brought them back from Moscow.'

For a brief moment, Isabel wasn't in the kitchen in Eagle Terrace. She was hundreds of miles away in her cosy kitchen in Oxford, with its familiar distressed wooden cupboards and the warm terracotta tiles on the floor. She was looking beyond David to the Russian dolls, concentrating on them instead of on the husband she was about to leave.

It all seemed like years ago; years since she'd seen his face. Now the face she dreamed of in the middle of the night was Jack's. *His* arms enfolded her in her dreams, *he* kissed her languorously and drove her insane with passion. Not David.

'The painted plates are lovely too,' Dee added. 'They suit the room perfectly. Where did you get them?'

Isabel dragged herself back to reality. 'They're Portuguese. We went on holiday there a lot.'

'Oh, God, I'd love to be on a beach in Portugal now,' Dee said dreamily. She sat on one of the stools at the breakfast bar. 'Can you imagine it – the sun on your skin, sand between your toes, and no work?'

Isabel thought of the last time she'd felt sand between her toes, that magical afternoon she and Jack had spent a mere three days ago on Killiney beach. Merely thinking about it sent shivers of excitement through her body. He'd phoned her twice since then but they hadn't managed to meet up because Naomi had developed a sore throat and Isabel skipped lunch every day so she could rush home early to look after her.

Isabel couldn't wait to see Jack again, to feel him hold her tight and kiss her passionately. What would it be like to make love to him, to be made love to by him . . .

'Are you *sure* you don't want me to help you with dinner?' asked Dee, seeing the way Isabel kept stopping washing the mushrooms to stare into space.

'No.' She flushed. 'I didn't invite you out here to make you cook your own dinner. You need a little pampering. It's only a simple pasta dish, anyway, so it's not exactly difficult to make. The girls will lay the table when they come home from the video shop. I want you to sit there and relax. Have another glass of wine.'

The front door banged shut. 'Sorry it took so long,' sang Naomi from the hall. She stuck her head round the kitchen door. 'Robin spent *ages* talking to the guy in the shop.'

'I did not!' she protested hotly, following her sister into the kitchen.

'You did. He's gorgeous,' Naomi sighed.

'Oh, no,' joked Dee. 'A battle between sisters for love of the hunky video shop guy! That was the one advantage of having a brother. No competition.' Robin and Naomi laughed. 'Not that the bloke in my video shop looked twice at me!' Dee complained.

'I'm sure he did,' Isabel said firmly. 'You just wouldn't have noticed. Girls, will you lay the table?'

It was lovely eating as part of a group again, Dee realised as she tucked into the delicious meal Isabel had whisked up. The three Farrells joked and talked easily. Even Robin, whom Isabel had warned was going through rather a spiky stage, was relaxed and chatty.

After dinner, the girls sat on the old squashy settee and watched their video, while Isabel and Dee sat at the breakfast bar and finished the bottle of rosé Dee had brought.

'That was delicious, Isabel,' she said. 'You are a marvellous cook. I couldn't conjure up anything like that in half an hour.'

'I love cooking. Well, most of the time,' Isabel amended. 'Sometimes it can be a bit of a drag, cooking every evening. I long to have toast and marmalade because I'm exhausted, but I've got to make something nutritious and interesting for the girls.' She lowered her voice. 'I'm so paranoid about Robin developing an eating disorder that I insist we eat together every evening. She doesn't show any sign of it so far but she's so aware of her body and very fashion conscious. You can't be too careful with girls of her age, I've read some awful health reports about bulimia and anorexia. The stress of the break-up could easily push her into it.'

'She ate everything and she didn't race off to the bathroom afterwards, either,' whispered Dee, who was familiar with the signs of eating disorders.

'I know, I just can't help worrying.'

'Listen,' said Dee, 'I do nothing but worry. If I didn't have something to worry about, I'd get worried!'

She got up to go to the bathroom and Isabel sat and finished her wine. She really was enjoying Dee's company. She'd forgotten how lovely it was to have a female friend over for the evening.

Since moving home to Ireland, she'd desperately missed all her close women friends in the UK and had more or less blocked everyone else out. It had been an instinct for self-protection, she imagined. She'd shut herself off from people to give herself time to heal from the pain of her marital breakdown. Now it was time to let people back in.

When Naomi went to bed and Robin retreated to her bedroom to listen to CDs, Isabel and Dee moved on to the settee. Isabel opened another bottle of wine and produced some bowls of cheesy popcorn.

'I love this stuff,' she admitted, kicking off her shoes and curling her feet up under her on the settee.

'So do I,' said Dee. 'The only difference is that you

can eat it and stay skinny, while I can't. But,' she added positively, 'all that's going to change now that I'm joining a gym.'

She kept Isabel in stitches telling her about the beginners' step aerobics class.

'I thought I was going to pass out with exhaustion. The instructor was like Barbie's taller, slimmer, better-looking younger sister while most of the class were the same shape as your little Russian dolls, all wearing far too many clothes. From what I saw yesterday, the slimmer you are, the tinier your sports clothes become. So if you've a size eight figure, you wear precisely four inches of leopardskin Lycra. I think I'd better purchase four metres of the stuff!'

Somehow she didn't mind discussing her size with Isabel. 'Which is weird,' Dee said out loud, utterly relaxed thanks to the second bottle of wine they were sharing, 'because I hated you at first for being so slim and sexy.'

'Me, sexy!' gasped Isabel. 'Nobody has ever called me sexy before. *You're* the sexy one, Dee. Haven't you noticed the way every man in the office watches you when you sashay across the newsroom? Poor Tony Winston's going to have a heart attack some day watching you, especially when you wear that little black velvet mini. His eyes are out on stalks looking at you.'

Dee giggled. 'He looks like a rabbit with myxomatosis every time *any* woman walks past. He's a walking hormone, that man. But you *are* sexy, Isabel. You're classy and elegant. You could have any man you wanted.'

Isabel thought of Jack. She wanted only him.

'I'm falling in love with a married man,' she said dreamily and sipped her wine, her eyes dark, briefly wondering why she was telling Dee all this. To hell with it, she needed to tell *someone* and it was very easy to confide in Dee. 'I suppose, when you're wearing your agony aunt hat, you'd advise me against it?'

Dee gave an ironic little laugh. 'Being an agony aunt, and having the right answers to questions about life, the universe and everything, are two vastly different things,' she said. 'I spend hours telling other people what to do in succinct, pithy answers that make it sound as if I'm some sort of bloody oracle, while my own life is a complete mess.'

'Your answers are always excellent, you give great advice,' Isabel interrupted. 'Everybody thinks so. You'd have made a great psychologist, Dee.'

'Yeah, but I'm a disaster when it comes to my own problems. "Physician, heal thyself." So I'd be the last person to tell you what to do, Isabel. How serious is it?'

The other woman shrugged. 'Well, we haven't done anything yet, if you know what I mean. We've only just met, to be honest. But I'm crazy about him, I can't help it. After breaking up with David, I can honestly say I didn't think I'd give a hoot for any man ever again.'

Dee nodded in understanding.

'But this is different,' Isabel added. 'He's special.'

'Be careful you don't get hurt,' warned Dee. 'It's easy to rush into things and forget about the future.'

'I think about the future all the time,' Isabel said softly.

CHAPTER SEVENTEEN

Isabel sat in the lobby of Moran's Red Cow hotel and tried not to stare too fixedly at the car park visible through the wall-to-wall glass front. Jack had said he'd be there by nine-fifty a.m. He was always on time, and it was now a minute past ten. Where was he?

She couldn't concentrate on either her cooling cup of coffee or the magazine in front of her, and felt as if she had 'secret assignation' written in giant letters all over her forehead.

The man opposite, who was pretending to leaf through the *Star*, was certainly eyeing her up speculatively. Maybe he'd been able to see through her disguise and knew that she wasn't a businesswoman meeting a contact for an important commercial discussion, but was instead a nervous thirty-nine-year-old separated mother-of-two about to meet a married man so they could escape for a mid-week break.

It was too difficult to get away for the weekend, as Robin, not to mention her mother, would be bound to ask lots of questions.

Isabel could imagine it: 'A newspaper conference in a country hotel *at the weekend*? Sounds ridiculous to me,' all said in Pamela's ringing, imperious tones. A Tuesday-till-Thursday conference on the future of the *Sentinel* sounded much better, although it had been difficult packing her suitcase the night before for a supposed three-day business convention with Naomi and Robin marching in and out of the room at inappropriate moments.

'What do you want this for, Mum?' asked Naomi innocently, extracting a cinnamon-coloured push-up bikini from the case, moments after Isabel had hurriedly jammed it into one of the side pockets.

'Did I put that in there? I must be totally losing my marbles,' Isabel said, grabbing it. 'Naomi, could you get me my . . . er . . . tweezers, please, and the big nail file? They're both in the bathroom.'

The second Naomi swung out of the door, Isabel folded the bikini, wrapped it up in the middle of a T-shirt and shoved it back into the case.

Robin sauntered in, eating a very messy peach and wearing the silky kimono dressing gown Isabel had carefully washed, ironed and stored in the airing cup-board, especially for the trip.

Determined not to lose her temper, she said mildly: 'Robin, I'm actually taking that dressing gown with me.'

'Whatever for? Who's going to see you?' she said truculently.

Isabel counted to ten. 'Nobody, but I'll need a dress-ing gown and that's the lightest one I've got so it'll take up less room in the case.'

Robin shrugged it off, stomped into her own room and returned, wearing her own pink towelling dressing gown, to supervise the packing with an eagle eye.

'Do you want your tampons, Mum?' asked Naomi helpfully, dropping the tweezers and the nail file on the bed.

Hopefully, no, prayed Isabel. Although it would be

just her luck that she'd get the curse on this, her first night away with Jack. Bad luck or God seeking retribution for the crime of going away with another woman's husband. No, there was being prepared and there was asking for trouble and bringing tampons would be like asking for trouble.

She folded up a voluminous cotton nightie she had no intention of wearing with Jack around. Pink-striped and with a colourful teddy on the front, it had been a long ago Mother's Day present and would kill any lustful longings stone dead. Mindful of her audience, she ostentatiously placed it on top of the pile of packed clothes.

Now, from her vantage point in the hotel, Isabel scanned the car park anxiously and again thought of all the items she'd *planned* to bring with her – a suitcase full of frou-frou bits of lingerie, lacy push-up bras to emphasise what cleavage she had, sexy little wisps of knickers and even a long-forgotten suspender belt, if only she could remember to buy stockings to go with it.

Naturally, in the last-minute panic involved in taking three days off work and organising everything so that the girls went to stay with their grandparents complete with a wardrobe-full of clean, ironed clothes, and plenty of frozen meals so nobody could complain about eating food they didn't like, there hadn't been time for shopping for stockings.

Which was just as well, she thought ironically, as with two sharp pairs of eyes watching her every move, there was no way she'd have been able to pack anything in the sexy underwear department.

In the end, she'd given up and packed a suitcase of her usual elegant work clothes, with one evening outfit:

'Just in case the editor decides to finish off the conference with a posh dinner,' she'd lied to the girls. Which was why she had a *second* bag – this one an enormous Marks and Spencer's plastic carrier – sitting in her car beside the suitcase, stuffed with bras, knickers and the silvery spaghetti-strap evening dress she only wore on very special occasions. Lord knew how squashed it would be by the time they reached Ashford Castle.

She hated lying to Robin and Naomi. Guilt pierced her intestines and caught them in an iron grip every time she thought about it. What sort of mother did that make her? A lying, horrible one who was joyously excited at the prospect of practically three whole days with Jack. *Three whole days* . . .

Isabel poured herself some more coffee, sat back in the armchair and sipped it, staring out into the car park for his car.

He'd never been late before. He was always early, in fact. *She* was the one who'd been late last week when she'd got stuck in traffic behind a broken down bus on her way to Cooke's for lunch. Jack had been white-faced when she got there, twenty minutes late.

'Thank God,' he'd said fervently, catching her hand in a vice-like grip. 'You're so utterly reliable, I was sure you'd had an accident when you didn't turn up on time.'

He hadn't let go of her hand for ten minutes, crushing it tightly in his until the colour came back into his face.

That was it, Isabel thought in horror now. He'd had an accident.

Visions of car wrecks flickered on and off in her head. Jack sitting in a pool of blood in his crumpled up car, desperately hurt and terrified, with no way to contact her . . .

'Phone call for Isabel Farrell at reception,' announced a cheerful voice over the hotel tannoy.

Isabel practically ran to the reception desk, grabbed the courtesy phone and gasped into it: 'Yes?'

'Isabel. I'm sorry I'm late . . .'

'But you're OK, aren't you? Has something happened . . . you haven't had an accident?' she said, the words coming out garbled.

'I'm fine, darling. I'm so sorry you were worried,' Jack said apologetically. 'I was on a long-distance conference call and couldn't get away. Listen . . .' A voice interrupted him, a female voice saying the conference call to Australia was set up. How could Jack manage to take several international conference calls when he was supposed to be miles away from his office, driving her into the depths of County Mayo to stay in a glorious thirteenth-century castle set amid acres of woodland and the calm shoreline of Lough Corrib?

He was going to cancel, Isabel realised. The wonderful trip she'd longed for wasn't going to happen. Her heart sank down to her cream and navy leather sling backs. Misery washed over her as she wondered why she'd let herself become so utterly involved with a married man when it would inevitably mean trouble.

'Isabel,' he was back on the line. 'Sorry about that. This is one of those days. I'm very sorry but I'm going to be delayed here for at least another hour.'

She knew what was coming next. *Can't go, we'll do it again soon, I promise.*

'So I had a brainwave,' he was saying. 'Let's go down by helicopter. We can fly directly to Ashford Castle and arrange to have a hire car waiting for us if we want to drive around. The only thing is, you'll have to drive to the airport to meet me, is that OK?'

'Fantastic!' said Isabel, her eyes dancing. 'That's wonderful. I thought you were going to say you couldn't go at all?'

'I haven't thought of anything else for the past week,' said Jack, in a low, husky voice that made Isabel feel as if she was dive-bombing naked into a huge feather bed.

'Me neither,' she answered, aware that the hotel receptionist was staring at her curiously.

Isabel drove too fast along the M-50, hurtling towards the airport as if afraid the helicopter would leave without her. It was ridiculous to feel this girlishly excited about the trip; ridiculous how often she'd played the whole scene over and over in her head, imagining what a wonderful time they'd have. It had been Jack's idea. They'd planned it after their fifth lunch, this one a picnic in the Dublin mountains for which they'd both taken the afternoon off work.

After consuming an horrendous quantity of pâté, crackers, French bread and Cheddar, watched by around a hundred interested ants, they'd hoisted themselves up on a huge rock halfway along the pony track and gazed out at the city spread below them. It had felt like the most natural thing in the world to be sitting there together, Jack's sweater-clad arm around her shoulders, her hand resting on his thigh.

Something flashed in front of Isabel, a dart of grey plumage with a hint of the darkest pink.

'That was a bullfinch, I'm sure of it!' she cried, twisting her body round to see if she could see the rare bird. She'd leant on Jack, both hands on him as she peered over his shoulder at the trees behind the rock.

'I don't know how much longer I'm going to be able

to take this birdwatching,' he said in a strangely high voice.

Isabel stared at his watering eyes then glanced down. In her attempts to track the progress of the bird, she'd leant on Jack so that one hand was on his upper thigh, the other jammed into his groin, flattening him in what had to be a particularly painful place.

'Sorry!' she yelped, moving her hands.

'That's better. I don't mind being this close to you,' he said in a low voice, 'but I sort of hoped it would be in a more comfortable setting than this.'

Isabel could feel a brick red colour flood rapidly up her chest to cover her face. She knew exactly how it looked – ugly and hot, as if she'd been hanging over the cooker for half an hour making hollandaise sauce.

'I've put my size ten feet in it again,' he said immediately. 'I'm so sorry, Isabel. Making jokes when you're nervous is one thing, but that was unforgivable.'

Isabel said nothing, praying her colour would tone down. She never flushed like this normally, except when she was very hot. But Jack had such an extraordinary effect on her.

'Sorry,' he repeated tensely. 'I'm pushing you too fast – I didn't mean to. I don't know what to do or what to say, I'm so useless at this.' He raked back his hair again, eyebrows pulled into a dark line.

'No, you didn't do anything wrong.' Isabel was amazed at how firm she sounded. She could feel her skin cool down and was immediately calmer and in control. 'Honestly.' She squeezed his arm affectionately. 'I don't usually go puce all the time either, but when I'm with you, nothing is normal.' She laughed.

'Is that good or bad?' he asked, his face lighting up.

'Good. Very good,' she replied.

Jack shifted into a better position on the granite rock so that he was almost facing Isabel, eyes boring into hers. He'd taken both of her slender hands in his larger ones, caressing them almost unconsciously. 'Tell me, how do I make things not normal? How do I make you feel, Isabel? I want to know.'

She studied him closely. 'I thought I'd never want another man,' she said, speaking softly as if they were sitting somewhere with people close enough to hear, instead of on a deserted hillside surrounded by birds, trees and without another human being in sight. 'After David, I though there'd never be another man in my life. I know that sounds drastic,' she admitted, 'but it made sense to me. Our marriage was unravelling for years though I tried to ignore it. I loved David and hated him at the same time. Do you know what I mean?'

Jack nodded and she felt his fingers increase their pressure on her hands; strong fingers kneading the soft fleshy part at the base of her thumbs. They got so sore and tired from constant typing and he seemed to know that, without her even telling him. Isabel closed her eyes briefly, loving the sensation of the massage, luxuriating in how it relieved the ache in her hands.

'Go on,' he urged her.

'I remember commissioning an article once about marriages that were too bad for you to stay in them and not bad enough for you to leave. At the time, I thought that's what my marriage was.'

Isabel allowed her gaze to move, focussing idly on the hillside behind him. It was rampant with gorse, the spiny branches clustered with a profusion of acid yellow flowers, but she didn't see any of it. She was seeing herself a year ago, lonelier within her marriage than she'd ever been out of it but afraid to take that first giant step.

'When I left, I was so tied up with worrying about the practical side of things at first, the girls and money, that I didn't really think about what I'd done,' she continued. 'I'd left my husband.'

'I'm so very glad you did,' Jack said suddenly. 'Or I'd never have met you. And I can't imagine anything worse than not having met you.'

'It wouldn't have done you much good to have met me in the beginning,' she said wryly. 'I was a mess. When I eventually realised what I'd done, I went to pieces.'

'And nobody ever knew because you kept all the pain and fear locked inside,' he said softly. 'Everyone thinks you're the epitome of calm, the sort of woman who can handle anything, but that's merely the façade you show the world. What's inside is very vulnerable.'

He knew her so well, Isabel thought, not really surprised. Everyone *did* think she was firm, unshakable, dependable. When on the inside she felt like she was on an emotional rollercoaster half the time. Jack knew this when so few other people in her life did. David, her mother, her father, even Robin, all thought Isabel could cope with the sinking of the *Titanic* without ever losing her quiet confidence.

'And then I met you,' she continued, 'and you turned my carefully ordered world upside down. I couldn't stop thinking about you. I still can't,' she admitted quietly.

Jack took her face in his hands and looked at her lovingly. He traced the curve of her cheekbone, and touched the full rosebud mouth.

Isabel stared back, deep into his eyes. He put his arms around her and they clung together tightly.

'I didn't mean to be crass earlier,' he murmured, his face buried in her soft, blonde hair.

'You weren't,' she said. 'Not at all.'

Jack moved so that his face was right beside hers, so close she could feel his breath against her skin. His eyes sought hers, warm dark eyes looking for the answer to a question he wasn't going to ask outright. Isabel reached up and rested one palm against his cheek, feeling the warmth of his skin, tracing the strong-planed face with gentle fingers.

She loved Jack's face.

'Despite the fact that I blushed like a schoolgirl earlier, I *am* ready, you know,' she said carefully. 'If you want me . . .'

'Want you?' he said fervently. 'You have no idea how much I want you, Isabel. But I want it to be right – the right time. I don't want to rush you. I feel that I keep saying the wrong thing, I'm so eager to say the *right* one . . .'

Isabel moistened lips dry with nerves. Jack was looking at her with a passionate yet anxious expression. She smiled, letting him see the warmth in her eyes. Then he kissed her and she felt herself melt. It was a strong, urgent kiss, their mouths eager. Isabel closed her eyes and gave herself up to the sensations coursing through her. She felt his body hard and tense against hers, the taut wall of his stomach muscles.

'I want you too, Jack,' she whispered into his ear.

'Will you come away with me for a few days?' he asked, his voice low and throaty. 'Next week. I want to take you somewhere beautiful. We could go to Ashford Castle, do you know it?'

Of course she knew it. One of Europe's most exclusive five-star hotels, a castle that probably had four-poster beds, vaulted rooms hung with medieval tapestries and roaring great fires to lounge in front of, wrapped in fluffy white bathrobes, until it was time to make love . . .

'Will you?' he asked again, anxiously this time, as if he'd taken her silence for hesitation. It was funny to hear him sound unsure, this man used to ordering other people around for a living.

For reply, Isabel wound her fingers round his neck and kissed him open-mouthed, letting her tongue gently explore his mouth. Jack groaned and kissed her in return, arms circling her to hold her in a crushing embrace.

'I'd love to,' said Isabel finally, when she'd caught her breath after the ferocity of their embrace.

Now she threw the toll-bridge money into the machine's gaping mouth and put her foot to the floor when the green light appeared on the traffic lights. Jack probably wouldn't even have left his city-centre office yet, but she wanted to be at the airport before him. She turned the car radio up loud and sang tunelessly along to the Bee Gees, doing her best falsetto as she shrieked out the words to 'Tragedy'.

She opened her window to enjoy the August sunshine and the wind blew her hair back in a rippling blonde mane. A van driven by a long-haired youth overtook her and the driver beeped his horn loudly as he whizzed past, an admiring grin on his face. Isabel smiled back delightedly, for once not caring that she'd been eyed up by a kid young enough to be her son. It was a glorious day and she felt just thrilled with life in general. If a twenty-year-old kid liked the look of her with her hair rippling free and wearing a very grown-up cream double-breasted trouser suit, then Jack had to love it!

CATHY KELLY

He was waiting for her beside the helipad, face creased up into a smile as she hurried to meet him.

Isabel wondered if he'd shake hands with her, anxious to maintain the pretence that this was a business meeting and they were flying to Mayo on Roark International business, especially in front of a row of helicopter company employees who probably knew his itinerary better than she did.

Instead, he grabbed her suitcase and set it down on the ground before sweeping her into a hug that crushed the breath from her body.

'Wow!' she gasped.

'Wow is right,' Jack said. 'You look wonderful.' He stood back to admire her, taking in the colour in the high cheekbones and the sparkle in her huge blue eyes. Isabel was glad she'd worn her elegant Mondi trouser suit and the multi-stranded pearl necklace that emphasised her slender neck.

She just wished she had a fortune to spend on clothes to make herself beautiful for Jack, and didn't have to rely on a wardrobe of things that were either several years old or second-hand designer stuff she'd cleverly altered and updated to make them look new.

'You look pretty good yourself,' she replied.

Jack's mouth curved into an even broader smile. 'Nobody's ever told me that *I* look good.'

She patted his pinstriped arm consolingly. 'Poor Jack. Well, you *do*.'

He did. With his wolf's hair brushed sleekly back from his forehead, the tanned face relaxed and the narrow, pewter eyes warm and tender, he looked nothing like the corporate giant who ran his company with an iron hand. Apart from the well-cut grey suit that sat beautifully on his big frame.

When they climbed into the helicopter, Isabel squeezed his arm excitedly. 'I've never been in one of these before,' she said. 'This is an adventure.'

Jack put his big hand over her slender one. 'The first of many, I hope.'

As the helicopter dipped down on the approach to Ashford Castle, Isabel leant forward eagerly in her seat to get a first glimpse of the legendary hotel.

The trip had been so quick she still hadn't tired of staring out through the giant glass bubble at the lush greenness below. Miles of sun-drenched Irish country-side had sped by underneath the helicopter's rotors; winding country roads snaking through patchwork fields, swelling into villages, towns and sprawling cities. She'd adored the trip and Jack had seemed happy to share her enthusiasm, pointing out landmarks and admiring pretty farmyards.

'I could get used to this,' said Isabel when they'd soared above a snaking queue of cars backed up in the heat.

'So could I,' he answered, with feeling.

'That's Cong,' Jack said as they passed the tiny village that nestled on the outskirts of the castle's demesne.

'They filmed *The Quiet Man* here. You know, the John Wayne, Maureen O'Hara movie?'

'I love that film,' said Isabel. 'My grandmother adored John Wayne and I remember seeing it with her one Christmas on TV . . .'

Then Ashford Castle filled the horizon, cutting Isabel off in mid-flow. It wasn't listed as one of the most notable hotels in numerous travel guides for nothing. The castle rose majestically from the distance, a sprawl-ing, craggy edifice, battlements thrusting into the sky as they had done for the past three hundred years.

Lough Corrib glittered in the midday sun. The stately oaks, beech trees and undulating private golf course splayed out in front of them, creating the perfect setting for the castle. If it hadn't been for the scattering of luxury cars parked in the castle forecourt, and the sound of the helicopter humming in their ears, they could have been stepping back in time by at least a hundred years.

Nothing much had changed since then, Isabel was sure, looking at the weathered grey stone of the castle and the elegant, neatly clipped shrubberies surrounding it.

The helicopter hovered over the moat and the pilot brought it down expertly on the helipad, blades whirring slowly as the giant bird settled on to the ground.

'Welcome to Ashford Castle,' murmured Jack.

It was like stepping back into another era, Isabel thought as she admired the exquisitely panelled entrance hall with its rich old furnishings, suits of armour and gigantic oil paintings.

Everything seemed bathed in a warm, golden light, as if candles still burned in the wall sconces. Even reception was nothing like your average hotel's, being a low desk without a 'Have a Nice Day' sign in sight.

Every inch of the hotel screamed taste, opulence and olde worlde charm. Isabel was enchanted simply walking around.

Their suite was furnished with lovingly polished antiques, an enormous carved bed and a giant brocade-covered couch so comfortable you could curl up and sleep on it. The stone-edged arched windows looked out past the ornamental gardens on to the lake at the back, where a small boat sat among the reeds, slowly making its way over the gleaming, smooth surface.

Isabel sank on to the couch, closed her eyes and leant back.

'I love this place,' she said, breathing in the scent of the flowers on the table. 'I feel like a Victorian lady who's arrived by chaise from the station and is about to command her maid to unpack her tea gowns.'

'If you were a Victorian lady,' said Jack, 'my valet would be doing the same for me, *in a separate room*. So I'm thrilled you're not Victorian. Tea, however, is a great idea. I'm starving. Come on, Milady.' He hauled her to her feet.

They sat on a vintage leather couch in a richly decorated ante-room off the very grand dining room, ate the most delicious chicken and salad sandwiches and drank fragrant coffee. Isabel hadn't realised she was so hungry until she'd taken the first bite. When they'd devoured one platter of sandwiches, they had to order more.

They talked eagerly and smiled at one another as they ate, laughing at each other's jokes and trying to figure out where their fellow diners came from. The three elegantly dressed women at the next table were tanned, well-heeled, determinedly ash blonde and could have come anywhere from Arizona to Australia, but they spoke so quietly it was impossible to tell.

The large group of men in bold checked trousers at the far end of the room had to be golfers.

'American,' guessed Jack, hearing a Boston Brahmin accent and discussions about the golf course in Augusta.

Next they did the quick version of the crossword in the paper, amazed to finish it in seven minutes.

'I've never done the cryptic one,' Jack said, sitting back on the couch once they'd figured out that blue dye had to be 'anil' because nothing else would fit.

'Me neither. Although Phil in the office does it in about fifteen minutes every morning when she's eating her breakfast.'

'Clever woman,' he remarked. 'Isn't she the one with loads of children and horses?'

'You left out loads of dogs and a rabbit,' Isabel pointed out. 'Phil is the ultimate earth mother. She adores minding small creatures. I always feel as if I could talk to her about anything and she'd look after me.'

'Is she good at her job?' Jack asked in a matter-of-fact tone.

Isabel took a sharp intake of breath. She didn't want to discuss her friends and colleagues with Jack. This had to be out-of-bounds. It would be wrong to talk about the people she worked with. Not because she'd colour his view of the ones she loved, but because she'd undoubtedly change his impression of the ones she didn't like. Tanya, for example.

'Yes, Phil is wonderful at her job,' she replied quickly. 'Let's go for a walk,' she added, finishing her last sandwich. 'I feel so full of energy and this place is so beautiful, it would be a pity to waste a lovely day.'

Back in their suite, Isabel grabbed some clothes and, in a moment of shyness, retreated to the bathroom to change. What are you like, you fool? she asked her reflection in the mirror. Some laid-back woman away with her lover you are! You can't even take off your clothes in the same room as him – how are you going to cope when it's time to go to bed? Because there's only one bed in this room, no matter how inviting the couch looks. What's he going to think of you now, running away like a scared kid to change clothes?

She splashed water on her flushed face, took a deep breath and pushed open the bathroom door.

'Isabel, look.' Jack was standing beside the window in the sitting-room, stripped to the waist. He wore only a pair of jeans, his bare tanned back tapering down from strong shoulders to lean haunches. Isabel stared at the strong muscled back and the rich dark hairs growing coarsely from his arms.

'Swans.'

She stood beside him, only mildly diverted by the sight of two snow white birds skimming across the water. She could smell the lemony scent of his bare skin beside hers. She'd known him for a month now, yet this was the closest they'd ever been. More than anything else, she wanted to touch him, to feel that warm skin next to hers, nipple to nipple in the big, old bed, with no mobile phones, conference calls or the day-to-day traumas of life to interrupt them. Just clean, fresh-smelling sheets wrapped around them and nothing between them.

'I can't wait to walk around the grounds,' Jack said eagerly. 'There's bound to be loads of wildlife out there.' He pulled on a grey sweatshirt. 'Ready?'

They walked companionably past the turrets that guarded the moat and down the rolling drive, keeping an eye out for wild creatures all the time. But apart from a surfeit of birds and a bedraggled sheepdog making his muddy way across a marshy bit of bog behind the hotel, they didn't see anything.

'Not even a rabbit,' Jack said in disappointment, putting an arm around Isabel as they trudged back up the drive.

'It's this new perfume,' she said, wiping her hot brow. 'Eau de Sweat. Animals run a mile when they smell it.'

'It's lovely.' He buried his nose in her neck, sniffing like a bunged-up person inhaling Friars Balsam. 'Lovely.

But I can't smell it properly outside. We need some shelter.'

Laughing, she let him drag her into one of the turrets, up the stone stairs and on to the top of the small battlement.

'I thought you needed shelter?' she laughed.

Eyes glittering, he pulled her close and kissed her long and hard. Isabel pressed herself against him, not caring that any member of staff could look out and wonder at the people who'd flown down in such style and were now embracing on top of the turret. It was bliss; sheer, unadulterated bliss. She could feel Jack hard against her, feel how turned on he was. Her insides turned to mush the way they always did when he held her closely.

'Let's go back,' he murmured. 'I want to lay you down on that glorious bed and make the most wonderful, exciting love to you.'

Isabel could feel her stomach fluttering with nerves as they walked back to their suite. This was it. The moment he saw her saggy thirty-nine-year-old body. The moment when only the second man in eighteen years saw it. And it wasn't even dark, so she couldn't hide her stretch marks or the cellulite that dimpled her bum by making him turn the lights off.

'I've got to go to the loo,' she said suddenly and bolted for the bathroom. Inside, she sat on the edge of the bath and took a deep breath. God, she was nervous. It was ridiculous, she knew.

After all, she was crazy about him, desperately in love with him. She wanted to be there, he'd hardly twisted her arm to make her come along. But she felt so insecure, so unsure of her own attractiveness. Even though Jack knew she was much softer emotionally than she let people realise, he still thought she was poised, calm and confident. How could he know that she'd lost all of those things and that she was surviving on just a wing and a prayer?

'Isabel, are you all right?' he asked from outside the door, his voice anxious. For a moment, she thought of all the things she *could* say – it had all been a terrible mistake, she felt too guilty about Elizabeth. But she didn't want to say any of them.

She was crazy about him. Had lain in her lonely bed at night, imagining what it would be like to have Jack beside her, his arms around her. Since she'd met him, she hadn't been able to keep him out of her head or her heart, Elizabeth or no Elizabeth. She couldn't just back out now because of an attack of nerves.

Isabel opened the door. 'Sorry. I just felt . . .'

'It's all right,' he supplied gently. 'It's scary, isn't it?'

She nodded.

'Come here,' he said tenderly, enveloping her in his arms. 'I *do* want to make love to you, desperately, if I'm honest. I want to make love to you and make everything right in your life . . . But only if that's what you want too, my love?'

Isabel half-laughed, half-gulped at his words.

'You're beautiful, gorgeous and I adore you,' he said softly, stroking her hair. 'I wouldn't want to be here with anyone else but you.'

Isabel hugged him then and as they began to kiss, all her worries about cellulite and how long it had been since she'd made love vanished. They stood like that for a few moments, enjoying the closeness and the warmth of their embrace.

'I think you need a few distractions to help you relax,' announced Jack as he pulled away reluctantly. 'Let's explore this place.'

They spent the afternoon wandering around the castle, admiring mementoes of the heads of state and long-dead European royalty who'd visited in style at the turn of the century. With the help of a guide book, they tried to figure out which bits were genuine thirteenth-century and which bits had been restored a hundred years ago.

At seven, they went to dinner in the Connaught Room restaurant. Isabel wore her silvery spaghetti-strapped dress with her hair piled on top of her head so that her elegant neck and shoulders were bare.

'You look beautiful,' Jack said slowly when she emerged from the bathroom in her finery.

After a wonderful dinner, they walked slowly around the gardens, breathing in the scent of the woods and enjoying the night air.

And when Jack carefully shut the door to their suite, Isabel was more than ready. They stood wordlessly at the end of the bed, her arms encircling his neck, his hands clasped around the base of her spine. Jack bent his head and their lips touched, slowly, like two people unsure of each other.

As their kiss deepened, their bodies responded with passion and the uncertainty melted away. Isabel felt herself bend towards Jack, her body arched sensuously into his. His strong hands caressed the small of her back through the silky dress.

'Oh, Isabel,' he murmured hoarsely. 'I've waited so long for this, it's like I've waited all my life.'

'I know,' she replied simply. 'I feel exactly the same.'

And she did. Safe in the circle of his arms, with his lips nuzzling her, she was content. Perfectly and utterly content.

She let her fingers stroke his neck lovingly, one hand

massaging the muscles of his shoulders. She loved the feel of his body close to hers. Used to being the tallest woman in any room, Isabel loved feeling so petite beside Jack. He towered over her, could clasp both her hands in one of his. He made her feel what no other man had ever made her feel: dainty and adored. It was a new and wonderful sensation.

Jack feathered kisses over her face before softly tapering down towards her neck. Tenderly, he left a trail of kisses along her collar bones, his lips hot against her skin, burning her with restrained passion.

Finally, Isabel moved so she could loosen his tie and open his shirt to rain her own tiny kisses on his neck and throat. But still he held back. It was as if he didn't want to let himself go fully, Isabel thought. As if he thought he'd scare her away.

Didn't he realise that nothing could scare her away? Not now. Slowly, and with great deliberation, she unbuttoned his shirt.

She quickly undid his gold knot cufflinks and he helped her slide the shirt over his shoulders. Then, she wrapped her arms around him, and pressed her body against his, loving the feel of his skin against her bare shoulders.

'Isabel, Isabel,' he moaned, 'you're incredible, so sensual. I'm afraid to . . .'

'Don't be,' she replied, breath warm against his satiny skin. 'I won't run away, Jack, my darling. Make love to me.'

He gently unzipped the long, silvery dress. Isabel stepped out of it, no longer nervous at the thought of Jack seeing her in her white silk panties and nothing else.

When they clung to each other, bare skin to bare skin,

she knew she'd finally come home. Jack's lovemaking erased all thoughts of everything but the moment itself. She loved him back with just as much passion and vigour until finally they slept in each other's arms.

It was a magical couple of days. When they weren't making love, they walked miles around the estate, visited the tiny, picturesque town of Cong or simply sat and talked. They talked about their childhoods, their families, and all the funny things two people in love want to hear about each other. Like favourite colours, favourite foods, first record, first kiss, first love. Jack delighted in painting Isabel's toenails, while she giggled at his attempts and made him smudge the pearly pink.

She spent an hour massaging his shoulders, kneading away the knots under his shoulder blades while he groaned appreciatively under her expert touch. Then he insisted on returning the favour, leaving Isabel limp after his hands had worked their gentle magic on her.

'Have you ever thought of taking it up professionally?' she murmured, face down on the bed, too exhausted even to move.

'Only if you're my sole client,' said Jack, starting on her feet.

On their last morning, they had breakfast in bed and, propped up against the pillows as they finished their coffee, Jack finally talked to Isabel about his wife and her drug addiction.

'I didn't even know Elizabeth was taking drugs for a long time,' he said sadly. 'That sounds stupid, I know, but I just didn't realise. Her sister was the one who mentioned it to me. She phoned me one day and said that Elizabeth was in hospital because she'd crashed the car. Then she said it was a miracle nobody else was hurt

376

because Elizabeth had been so stoned, she could have killed someone. I was shocked.'

Isabel squeezed his bare arm. He still looked a little shocked, even at the memory.

'I had no idea, can you believe that? She'd been using drugs for at least two years and I had no idea.'

'When did the accident happen?' Isabel asked quietly.

'Eleven years ago. We'd been married for four years at the time. She gave up then, got one hell of a fright. She was brilliant about giving up. Elizabeth is very strong-willed when she wants to be,' he explained.

'But about seven years ago she started again and she hasn't stopped since. She's quite careful now, doesn't do it every night. But I can read the signs these days. The way her eyes glitter. The way she tries not to look at me in case I notice.'

'Why don't you send her for treatment?' asked Isabel.

Jack raised one eyebrow. 'She's been to half the treatment centres in the US and UK, and simply books herself out when the going gets tough. You can't make someone give up drugs if they don't want to.'

'What about the money – surely you can stop her having the money to pay for the drugs?'

'Elizabeth has her own money, her father was wealthy. I can't control her allowance.'

They sat quietly for a moment, both lost in thought about a woman with the funds to feed her drug habit and not the slightest inclination to give it up. Isabel knew it was very difficult for Jack to talk about his wife's problem. It was a measure of his feelings for her that he could open up about the subject at all.

'Do you know how she started or why?' Isabel asked.

'It was not being able to have children. I'm not guessing here, I know it for a fact. She told me one night

– screamed it at me,' Jack said wearily. 'Like it was my fault. In the beginning, we kept trying for a baby and nothing happened. I thought of having tests done when nearly two years had gone by and Elizabeth wasn't getting pregnant, but she wouldn't hear of it. All her side have large families and she was convinced it was just a matter of time. She said she was only thirty-two, it was early days. Finally, she gave up and we had the tests.'

He sighed. 'I'd almost hoped it was my fault because no matter how difficult it would have been for me to think I was to blame, I knew it was going to be worse if it was her fault. She was so *convinced* she was well able to conceive. She adores kids.'

'What happened?'

'The doctors discovered she has an abnormally shaped uterus, which meant it would be very difficult for her to carry a child to full term. And she has blocked fallopian tubes, which was why she'd never conceived in the first place. "A freak" was what she called herself when she found out. "I'm just a freak of nature, Jack." ' He massaged his temples tiredly. 'She said it over and over again.'

Isabel was shocked. 'How awful for her. She must have been devastated.' She remembered how the loss of her beloved baby had nearly destroyed her, and she'd already had two precious children. How much more unbearable would it be to be told you'd *never* have any children at all?

'She was more than devastated,' he recalled. 'She was destroyed mentally. For about a month after we found out, she went on a complete bender. She was never sober. And then, she seemed to get over it. Of course,' Jack reached over to the tray and poured them both more coffee, 'I now know that she *didn't* get better. She just switched from booze to drugs.'

'It must have been very difficult for both of you,' Isabel said gently.

'It was. But it doesn't matter so much any more, not since we've drifted so far apart. You grow harder when you live with an addict. Eventually you care less and less until there's no love left at all. I love her in my own way,' he admitted. 'We've been together a long time. But it's hard to love a drug addict, Isabel. They take all you can give, twist it and throw it right back in your face. You get tired of it eventually.'

She moved the tray and the coffee so she wouldn't upset them, and hugged him tightly. She didn't want to ask any more questions because it was obviously so painful for Jack, but as she held him in her arms, she felt a tremor of fear about what the future might hold.

Dee threw the property supplement down on the kitchen table in disgust. There was nothing there she'd like to buy – or could afford to, for that matter. House prices had gone berserk. Wearily, she got up from the table and boiled the kettle. Unfortunately, she wasn't making another coffee so she could lounge around reading the papers. She was boiling more water to clean the woodwork in the sitting-room. She'd scrubbed every part of the kitchen until her fingers were raw and resembled prawns a few hours out of the freezer. Now, after an enjoyable ten minutes' rest, she had to tackle the sitting-room and hall. What a way to spend a Friday morning off!

But there was no way she could let an estate agent put one Gucci-tasselled loafer past the front door unless she did a spot of spring cleaning first. And as Gary would undoubtedly send more notes threatening Mafia-style retribution if she didn't get the house on the market very soon, she had to get down to some serious house scrubbing.

If temper made a person clean and polish faster, Dee would have been finished much sooner because vitriolic thoughts of Gary filled her head to the exclusion of all else.

Bloody, bloody Gary! she raged, rubbing away at a bit of candle grease on the skirting board in the sitting-room. It was blue candle grease at that. Only stupid Gary would buy bright blue candles when the room was painted in warm amber colours, the settee was brown and the carpet beige. The moron never could co-ordinate anything. He only managed to wear the correct ties with each shirt because he bought every-thing matched up at Next, although he would have died before admitting it. Dee would have loved to have told everyone this. Not to mention all his other little peca-dilloes.

For a few happy moments, she envisioned a vengeful ex-files newspaper, one written by disgruntled, dumped partners where they got to spill the beans on the dumper.

'My boyfriend never put the loo seat down, picked at his toenails every evening in front of the news, and the only culture he ever consumed came from yoghurt.'

'Really? *Mine* worshipped the ground his mother walked on, believed that the sheets only needed to be changed when there was a full moon, and thought that the clitoris was one of a group of islands under French colonial rule in the eighteen hundreds.'

Dee grinned to herself and carried on scrubbing. By twelve, her leggings and T-shirt were grubby, she was hot, exhausted and hungry, and wanted to take the rest of the day off. At least she didn't have to be in until after lunch. She took a deep draught of Diet Coke and decided she'd have a long bath and a toasted cheese sandwich before ambling into the office. She was taking things out of the fridge when the phone rang loudly.

'Dee.' Jackie sounded flustered on the phone, as she always did when Tanya Vernon was prowling round the office like a leopard looking for a baby antelope that had strayed from the herd. 'Tanya's having an editorial meeting at half-twelve and she wants you there.'

'Half-twelve!' squawked Dee, thinking of her greasy hair, empty stomach and the pile of unironed clothes on the bed. 'Why didn't you phone me earlier?'

'Sorry,' Jackie said apologetically. 'It's just that Tanya only called it now. Sorry.'

'It's not your fault,' sighed Dee, sorry for snapping. 'Tell Isabel I'm on my way in but that I may be ten minutes late, OK?'

There was no point in telling Tanya she might be late – the other woman would be at the door with a stopwatch and a smirk on her face that said, 'You're fired.'

What a manipulative cow she was, Dee thought as she ripped off her clothes and clambered into the shower. There had been no mention of an editorial meeting the previous evening; everyone had been too busy concentrating on getting stuff ready for the extended Saturday edition of the paper. Tanya just liked throwing her weight around by calling an extra meeting, hoping to upset Dee – because she knew Dee had the morning off and wouldn't be in till half-two – and Isabel – because she had taken a few days' holiday and might possibly be in late. With Isabel absent, Tanya could really boss everyone around. But Isabel was sitting serenely at her desk when Dee rushed into the news-room at twelve-thirty-five, damp ringlets flying.

'I thought Jackie said you weren't due in until after lunch?' said Isabel, smiling when she spotted her deputy.

'I'm not supposed to be,' snarled Dee, 'but the Bitch From Hell called a half-twelve editorial meeting and got Jackie to ring up and summon me to it.'

Isabel's mouth formed a perfect oval. She winced. 'Oh. You're not going to believe this, Dee, but Tanya's cancelled the meeting. She and Eugene Flynn have gone out to lunch instead.'

'The cow!' shrieked Dee at the top of her voice. 'I've just raced in here at ninety miles an hour and she's *cancelled the meeting*? I'll kill her!'

'Join the queue,' said Phil Walsh, arriving at her desk carrying a pile of stationery with a cup of tea balanced dangerously on top. 'Apparently, Chris Schriber is out for her blood and rumour has it she's only gone out to lunch with Slasher Flynn to try and charm him into taking her side if there's a war between the two departments.'

'Really?' Both Isabel and Dee were fascinated.

'Go away for three days and you miss everything,' Isabel remarked.

'Tell you what,' said Emily, the pretty freelance who now worked almost exclusively for Isabel and Dee in the women's section, 'now that we've been reprieved, why don't we all go out to Magee's for a spot of early lunch and you can fill us in on the gossip, Phil?'

'Brilliant idea,' she said. 'I didn't feel like drinking that tea anyway.'

Dee was the last into the pub as she'd taken a call on

her mobile phone and had stood outside to finish it. She hated walking into pubs and restaurants talking on her mobile, it always felt so stupid and pretentious. Narrowing her eyes to get used to the dark atmosphere of Magee's, she stuck her phone into her handbag and walked straight into a tall man who'd just got up from a bar stool.

'Sorry,' she muttered, jerking backwards.

'My fault, Dee,' said a familiar voice. She peered up, eyes still not accustomed to the light in the pub. Whoever he was, he was at least six foot tall and he knew her.

'It's Kevin Mills, the photographer,' he said sardonically, black eyes crinkling up with amusement. 'I know we haven't worked together for a few months, but I didn't think you'd forget me that easily.'

'Sorry, Kevin, I couldn't see you in this light. Hi,' she said, conscious that her hair was flapping wetly around her face like rats' tails. She hadn't seen him since they'd joined forces on the story about Chazz, the singer who'd trashed his hotel room in the Conrad.

Kevin was dressed in his customary casual clothes: a tan suede shirt, jeans and Timberlands. He'd had his dark hair cut very short so it clung to his perfectly shaped skull. It suited him, highlighting the gypsyish good looks and broad shoulders that got worked out by constantly dragging an enormous camera bag around with him.

'Haven't seen you for ages,' he said, his shrewd photographer's eyes travelling slowly over her face and body.

Dee silently cursed Tanya Vernon again. If that horrible woman hadn't dragged her out of the house at top speed, she might have ironed something nice to wear instead of being caught in a crumpled indigo silk wrap shirt and a matching skirt she only wore when she was desperate.

'I'm working in the women's section now,' she explained. 'I've been promoted.'

'To deputy women's editor,' he said. 'I know. Congratulations.'

Dee couldn't believe it. How did he know she'd been promoted? Paparazzi photographers rarely got too involved with what went on in individual newspapers. They worked for themselves and preferred to keep to themselves, so the hirings and firings in the *Sentinel* wouldn't be of much interest to him, she'd assumed.

'Now that you're in management, I guess we won't be doing any more jobs together,' he said with a hint of regret.

'No,' said Dee. He had a lovely voice, pitched real low and sort of growly. She wondered who he was seeing these days? Probably some catwalk cutie.

Photographers often ended up dating models, and with a photographer as ruggedly handsome as Kevin, the models would be queuing up to date him, instead of the other way round.

He turned to go then looked back at Dee abruptly. 'We never had that drink,' he said. 'Remember, the day we did the story on Chazz?'

Dee remembered all right. She'd been flattered when Kevin had asked her if she wanted to join him for a drink in the Conrad bar. She'd nearly gone with him but hadn't, stopping herself because she was cross with Gary and didn't want to put herself in temptation's way by spending time with a man who looked like Kevin Mills.

They'd never have that drink now, not unless they

ended up on a story together, which seemed unlikely.

'Give me a ring sometime when you're free and we'll get together,' Kevin said.

Dee blinked at him. *He* was asking her out for a drink?

'Yeah, I'd love that,' she said, brown eyes as wide as saucers.

He gave her a heart-stopping grin. 'See ya round, kid.' And he was gone.

Maeve was loading up her tray with lasagne, chips and a pint glass of milk.

'I saw you talking to the delectable Kevin Mills,' she said, taking her change from the barman.

'You're not going to believe this, but he asked me out for a drink!'

'Why wouldn't I believe it?' demanded her friend. 'The way you go on sometimes, O'Reilly, you'd swear you were the Hunchback of Notre Dame's uglier sister. You look great, you silly eejit! You're the only one who can't see it. Well,' Maeve said darkly, 'you and that prat of an ex-fiancé of yours. I wish Kevin Mills would ask *me* out for a drink.'

'He didn't mean it *that* way,' Dee protested. 'It's just that we were supposed to go for one before and we didn't.'

'God, give me strength,' muttered Maeve. 'Get yourself some lunch and we'll talk about this later. I swear you need therapy, Dee. If only we could remove some of Tanya's excess superiority cells and inject them into your head, then maybe you'd both be normal. She wouldn't be so big-headed and you might start appreciating yourself.'

'I do, it's just that . . .'

'Just nothing!' interrupted Maeve. 'You're always running yourself down, Dee, and it's not good for you. If you keep saying all sorts of negative things about yourself, other people will eventually believe them, even though they're not true. Lecture over. So when are you going out with Kev?'

Dee chewed her full bottom lip. 'He said to give him a ring sometime.'

Maeve raised her eyes to heaven. 'If Kevin Mills asked me out for a drink, I'd demand to know when, where, and watch him write it down in his diary. Run after him this second and pin him down.'

'Have you got your lasso handy?' asked Dee, with a smirk.

Maeve stuck out her tongue at her.

'You're an awful nag, Maeve, do you know that?' she said good-humouredly, nicking a couple of chips from her friend's plate. 'If you weren't my best friend, I think I'd have to kill you.'

'You couldn't,' Maeve replied. 'I'm too valuable to society. Who else would lay out Carol-Anne's dreadful articles in the paper or zip you into your man-pulling black corset if it wasn't me, huh?'

'Point taken.' Dee stole some more chips. 'I'm just going to get a sandwich. Don't start gossiping without me.'

Over soup, sandwiches and lasagne, Isabel, Dee, Phil, Maeve, Emily and Jackie chatted, bitched and gossiped to their heart's content, concentrating on Tanya Vernon whom they all loathed.

Everyone had something to say, apart from Isabel who sat quietly listening, barely touching her bread roll or her mushroom soup.

Dee couldn't help staring at her. Isabel's face simply glowed with some inner joy and the corners of her rosebud mouth were permanently upturned, as if she was remembering a glorious private joke.

Dee wondered if Isabel's few days off had included time spent with the mysterious married lover. It must have, she decided, watching the way Isabel's eyes misted over dreamily during even the juiciest bits of the conversation. She really was miles away.

'Apparently, Tanya has gone so completely over the departmental budget with her spending on freelances and photographers, she's going to have to eat into the news freelance budget, which is why Chris Schriber is going mad,' Phil explained, spreading mustard liberally on her ham sandwich.

'Before Tanya left, I saw her in the loo plastering on the Estée Lauder and that horrible Moschino perfume she wears,' Emily revealed. 'She brushed her teeth *and* flossed. I can imagine what she's planning and it's not lunch.'

Maeve's eyes narrowed. She loathed Tanya. 'Obviously planning to seduce Slasher in the hope he'll give her more cash to spend,' she pronounced.

'I don't know though.' Emily's cat-like eyes glowed wickedly. 'If you saw the way she canoodles with our glorious leader, Jack Carter, I'd put money on it that she hopes *he'll* turn into her sugar daddy.'

If she hadn't been reaching over for the milk, Dee wouldn't have noticed Isabel stiffen imperceptibly and blanch at the mention of Jack Carter.

So *that* was it, Dee thought, shocked, surreptitiously studying Isabel's white, stunned face. Her married man had to be Jack Carter. But he couldn't be, could he? They'd only just met and Jack was the boss, after all, *the* big boss.

Dee went through the whole thing in her head but still came up with the same answer. Isabel had looked as if somebody close to her had died when Emily mentioned Jack and Tanya in the same breath. What else in the conversation could have produced such an extreme response? Hardly Tanya being over budget.

Dee pretended to eat her lunch but kept an eye on Isabel. The other woman's hand shook ever so slightly as she raised her soup spoon to her mouth. The colour had drained away from her face and the rosy glow had gone. She *had* to be having an affair with Carter, why else would she react so violently to the conversation?

Poor thing, Dee mused. Jack Carter probably eats decent, hard-working women like Isabel for breakfast.

Emily was getting into her stride now. 'You should have seen the way Tanya was all over him last month when he came to give us the speech,' she continued, revelling in the story. 'She was practically sitting on his lap afterwards, according to my spies. There's a big company hooley next week in the K Club where they're all going to be patting themselves on the back over the smooth takeover and the rise in circulation. I bet you a tenner Tanya gets to first base with Big Jack that night.'

'Who do we know who's going to the K Club?' demanded Maeve, eyes alight with glee. 'We need a source to tell us exactly what happens. That's one story I really want the inside track on. Do you think we could get pictures?'

'We want the negatives,' joked Phil. 'You could barter a great job for yourself with the opposition if you brought them a scoop like that. The rival chairman – married chairman, I should point out – canoodling with a jumped up, beautiful though tarty member of staff at a corporate do, while his lady wife does her bit for charity . . . The *Globe* would love that story.'

Isabel was so pale she was almost white now, the veins on her neck a milky blue. Dee felt a surge of protectiveness towards her. She couldn't begin to imagine what it must be like to hear this sort of thing about a man you were secretly involved with. It must be hell.

Dee moved to let the waiter refill her coffee cup. Whatever Isabel saw in Jack Carter, it had to be serious because she wasn't the sort of woman to jump headlong into a relationship with a married man.

Isabel had to be crazy about him. She'd said so the night she'd had Dee over for dinner. She'd fallen hook, line and sinker, she'd said. Which wasn't that surprising, Dee thought, because Jack Carter was very attractive, charismatic, and had an aura of quiet strength that would make any woman fall for him. Dee could understand how Isabel felt, all right.

But she was pretty sure that Isabel hadn't bargained on hearing her married lover discussed cold-bloodedly at the office as if he was some cheating rock star with the morals of an alley cat. Nor had she thought about the implications of having an affair with a man who ran a newspaper. It was a cut-throat business. Rival papers would indeed kill for a story like that – a thought which obviously hadn't even occurred to Isabel.

If Dee had been having an affair with Jack Carter, she'd have been scared to look crossways at him in public in case some rival snapper was there with his long lens, snapping a magical Kodak moment of infidelity for the next day's front page.

She only hoped Isabel and Jack were being cautious when it came to dates and weren't forgetting that high-profile, wealthy business magnates like Carter made great story material.

'I'd love to see the sort of dress Tanya will wear to

that party,' Emily was saying. 'Liz Hurley's ultra-revealing Versaces will look like a couple of demure sacks beside it, I shouldn't wonder.'

Everyone laughed.

Dee glanced at Isabel's taut expression and knew she had to say something to get the conversation on to safer ground before Isabel's increasingly shocked demeanour made it obvious to everyone what was wrong.

'Get real, girls,' she said briskly. 'Jack Carter isn't the slightest bit interested in Tanya. He's got taste, for God's sake. She's just a complete slapper who'd sleep with her grandad and his German Shepherd if she thought it would get her somewhere. Put her in the same room as any powerful man and she'll be oozing compliments all over him like cheap musk oil.'

'That's true,' muttered Maeve.

'If Tanya was all over Jack Carter like a cheap suit at any gathering, I'm sure it was only because he was too decent to push her away,' added Dee.

'I can't imagine where she thinks she's going to get by going out to lunch with Slasher all dolled up,' Phil said. 'I think the only thing that turns him on is filthy lucre.'

'Funnily enough, that's the only thing that turns Tanya on too,' Dee couldn't resist saying.

But Emily was not to be deflected from Jack Carter. She must fancy him, Dee thought briefly.

'I hear Elizabeth Carter has a serious drug problem,' she said.

Phil glanced at Isabel.

'Mrs Carter doesn't have a drug problem,' Maeve quipped. 'She can afford it.'

'This might not be the wisest subject to talk about in the pub across the road from the *Sentinel*,' Phil reminded them in a low voice as the guffaws died down.

Gossiping in Magee's was a dicey business as you never knew which member of staff was sitting unnoticed behind a banquette, ears wiggling like Bugs Bunny's for any stray comments that could have nuclear repercussions if repeated in the wrong company.

'It's OK, I looked around when we came in, there's nobody within earshot,' said Jackie eagerly.

'I've heard she takes cocaine by the bucketload,' Emily whispered. 'They say the cops caught her once but Carter had it sorted out so she was never even charged with possession.'

'Why doesn't he book her into detox?' demanded Maeve. 'It's not as if they haven't got the cash.'

'Maybe he prefers her stoned out of her mind,' said Emily with a shrug. 'Then he can have it off with the Tanya Vernons of the world.'

Isabel's hand jerked and she spilled coffee all over the table. Everyone shoved back their chairs so they wouldn't get dripped on.

'I've got to get back to work,' announced Dee, standing up. 'You have too, haven't you, Isabel?' she asked blandly.

'Yes.' Unable to look at anyone, she got unsteadily to her feet and banged into the table clumsily. They all stared at her. Isabel Farrell was the least clumsy person they knew. She usually glided through the newsroom as elegantly as if she moved on rails.

'Isabel, are you getting one of your migraines?' asked Dee loudly. 'You shouldn't have come in if you thought you were getting one. Maybe you should go home to bed.'

Isabel glanced up, looking horrified as she realised what Dee was doing. She squeezed Isabel's hand silently.

'You poor thing. You should take the rest of the day off if you're getting a migraine,' said Phil in a concerned voice. 'I was wondering why you were so quiet during lunch. You've been doing too much. You should have taken a longer break. Three days off isn't enough.'

'I'm fine, really. Just a bit headachey,' lied Isabel, recovering her composure somewhat. 'I'll take the long route back to the office, it might clear my head.'

She walked off with Dee close behind her. As soon as they were a few feet away from the girls, she turned, her face a mass of questions.

'How did you know?'

Dee put a finger over her mouth.

'Not in here,' she murmured. 'The place is probably bugged.'

Outside, Isabel leant against the pub wall tiredly.

'I had to say something to put them off the scent,' Dee said quietly. 'Emily would be on to you like a shot otherwise. Not that she'd rush off and tell people, because Emily adores you for all the work you've given her and how nice you've been to her. But the more people know, the more chance your secret has of getting out. And believe me, Isabel, this would be the office gossip of the century.'

'How did *you* know?' asked Isabel, ashen-faced.

'I saw your face when Emily started talking about Jack and Tanya and I thought of what you told me that night at your house. I reckoned either you'd suddenly remembered you'd left the gas on at home this morning, or you were upset by what she'd said. I didn't need to be Einstein to figure out why. Actually,' Dee said, 'I *still* don't know for definite. You're having an affair with Jack Carter, aren't you? Or am I totally off beam?'

'I am.' Isabel sighed. 'I'm not very good at this,' she

said weakly. 'I'm too transparent.'

'Not a good poker player,' agreed Dee. 'But you'd better learn how to be from now on. People are always going to be talking about Jack Carter and if you look as if you're going to faint every time it happens, someone will cop on. I'm not going to tell anyone, you know that,' she added reassuringly. 'But you've got to be careful.'

Isabel still looked drained. Dee took her by the arm. 'We should walk back to the office. Do you want a bar of chocolate? It always helps me when I've had a shock.'

Isabel shuddered. 'No, I couldn't eat a thing.'

Dee grimaced. 'That's the difference between you and me,' she said. 'When I'm upset, I head straight for the fridge or the sweet shop, one or the other. You can't eat. That,' she patted Isabel's arm kindly, 'is why you're reed thin and I'm on the cardboard diet.'

'The cardboard diet?' asked Isabel, fascinated in spite of the knot in her stomach.

'Yeah. Cardboard. Whenever you feel hungry late at night, you get a bowl of whatever fibre-rich breakfast cereal reminds you most of cardboard and you eat a huge bowl of it, soaked in hot water. It's horrible but filling.'

Isabel burst out laughing.

'You're a tonic, Dee,' she said. 'And a real friend. Thanks.'

'It was nothing. You'd do the same for me,' she said firmly. 'If you want to talk about it at any time, you know where I am. But please be careful.'

They reached the *Sentinel*.

Tanya's silver Mazda was back, Dee noticed with a shiver. Obviously the planned long, liquid lunch with Slasher Flynn had backfired and become a short, sharp meeting and now she'd be like a bear with a sore head for the rest of the afternoon.

As they climbed the stairs to the newsroom, Dee considered saying something to Isabel about not being up to Ms Vernon's customary tantrums that afternoon. But Isabel was back in her dreamworld, going into the ladies' loo with her mind a million miles away.

Dee engaged in a little daydreaming herself. Kevin Mills had asked her out for a drink. That was the second time. What did he mean by it? Did he mean it in a friendly, platonic way? Did he know that she and Gary had split up?

Or, she thought morosely, there could be a third reason. Kevin himself might be planning a career away from the front line of paparazzidom and he might think that the recently promoted Dee was in a position to give him other work, like fashion shoots or cushy portraits. She sighed. Perhaps that was it. He wanted to bend Dee's ear about his plans and thought that a couple of Jack Daniel's and Cokes would have her eating out of his hand.

It didn't take long for Tanya to appear, breathing fire and brimstone. Dee had only just arrived back at her desk when she heard Tanya's steel-tipped stilettos tapping out an angry beat as she marched down to the features end of the newsroom.

'I want to talk to you,' Tanya snapped.

The unnerving thing about Tanya, Dee thought, looking up at the editorial director apprehensively, was that she was breathtakingly beautiful even when she was mad. But because she was such a fiercely confrontational person, you stopped noticing her beauty within two minutes of meeting her.

Today, the hard little face was even more spiteful

than usual. Tanya's almond-shaped eyes glittered with temper but didn't detract from the symmetry of the perfectly shaped glossy pink mouth and Slavic cheekbones set off by a flawless complexion.

She stood beside Dee – Tanya never sat when she could tower over someone and intimidate them with her height – and started an angry tirade.

'I want to know why you've been hiring freelances for jobs you could perfectly well do yourself?' she snapped. 'It's sheer laziness. We're way over budget and we've got to cut back. I don't want to see any more expenditure on unnecessary items. That article on the TV soap star from *Coronation Street*, for example. You could have done that yourself instead of getting Emily to write it.'

'I couldn't,' Dee defended herself nervously. 'Isabel was away, I was busy with the fashion pages *and* the interview piece. There was no way I could fit another interview in. The actress was only in Ireland for one day. It was take it or leave it.'

'You should have left it then,' said Tanya. 'I'm trying to run these departments efficiently and cost-effectively and you're ruining my good work. I want you to consult me in future before you hire anyone to do any job.'

Dee goggled at her. If that was the case, she'd be in and out to see Tanya every five minutes because the women's department was incredibly understaffed. She and Isabel relied totally on a panel of freelance journalists, which meant they hired people on the spur of the moment every single day.

Dee was about to point this out but Tanya had swooped on to another subject, like a hawk spotting a well-fed rabbit. 'And as for spending money on that beauty salon spy thing, that's a waste of time!' she snorted derisively.

'Now that the government has tightened up regula-
tions surrounding hygiene in beauty salons, I thought it
would be a good idea to see if the salons are actually
putting the new rules into practice,' explained Dee, eyes
darting towards the newsroom door to see if Isabel was
on her way back from the loo. Tanya would certainly
shut up when she appeared. Isabel, where are you? she
prayed.

'Oh, please,' Tanya drawled snidely. 'I suppose you
only came up with that idea so you could get free
treatments yourself?'

Dee was stunned. 'Of course not,' she said, horrified.
'I wouldn't dream of it!'

'Gimme a break,' Tanya snarled. 'You think you've got
it all sorted out, don't you, Dee? You don't want to do
any work. You simply want to sit on your big fat
backside and get the freelances to do what you should
be doing, while you swan off and get your blackheads
squeezed. You think you've walked into a cushy number
with this job, don't you?' She jabbed one manicured
finger in the direction of Dee's chest.

Unable to speak, she sat there bewildered. She
couldn't believe all the appalling things the other
woman was saying to her. She felt as if she'd been
suddenly transported back eighteen years to Saint
Veronica's Secondary School, with a gang of kids cruelly
taunting her about her weight. Dee had always frozen
up then too, unable to speak from shock and misery.

'All you lot who've been here for years think the
Sentinel is a cushy number, a retirement home for crap
journos who couldn't get a job anywhere else. But it's
not.' Tanya leant forward until her face was inches away
from Dee's, so that she could smell the sickly acidic
smell of her breath. 'People like me are going to drag

this paper kicking and screaming into the future, with a circulation you wouldn't even dream of. And you and your lazy ways aren't going to stop me.'

'I don't want to,' mouthed Dee ineffectually.

'You better not!'

With that, Tanya straightened up and marched off in the direction of the editor's office. Feeling like she'd just gone ten rounds with Lennox Lewis, Dee sat in her chair, utterly dazed.

Why does she hate me so much? she asked herself tearfully. What have I done to make her so vile, malicious and horrible to me? Dee couldn't come up with a reasonable answer. There was no point in remembering Maeve's opinion that Tanya hated everyone and picked on people because she was a bully and could get away with it. That didn't make Dee feel any better.

Because Tanya didn't pick on Maeve, she picked on Dee. And on Jackie, when Isabel and Phil weren't around. She picked on the people who wouldn't answer back, and she got away with it. Now she'd done it again. And Dee had sat there, like a mute and let Tanya slander her senseless. Dee had said nothing. Not one word.

Hot tears of humiliation burned beneath her eyelids. Once again she'd been used and abused, and she'd let the bully do it. Practically given her permission for it. Coward, coward, coward!

Isabel hurried into the office, looking a little more relaxed than she had ten minutes earlier. Dee longed to tell her everything, all the appalling things Tanya had said, about how she was sitting there on her 'fat behind' and how lazy she was.

But she couldn't. Tanya had always been snide and attacked Dee by subtle means up to now. This full-frontal assault was something new. Isabel would be utterly shocked to learn that Dee had taken all those remarks without answering back.

Isabel was brave, she had self-confidence and self-respect. Dee didn't want to be diminished in her eyes by revealing just how lacking in those qualities she was.

'Tanya was here, giving out yards about us hiring freelances,' she said in a small voice. 'She says we should be doing the work ourselves.'

'Nonsense,' Isabel said briskly. 'We're so understaffed that we wouldn't have a paper at all if it wasn't for the freelance contributors. That woman is a menace. She wants us to suffer when she blithely spends the budget elsewhere. Where is she?' Isabel looked around inquiringly.

'She went into Malley's office,' Dee said.

'Right.' Isabel marched off to do battle.

Dee watched her silently.

Five minutes later, Isabel was back, her mission successful. 'Tanya is all talk,' she sighed. 'She caves in like a shot if you push her. Don't let her bully you about her problems, Dee,' she advised. 'If she hadn't overspent, she wouldn't be hassling us now.'

'You're right,' Dee said in a quiet voice. She sat at her desk and tried to write, but she kept typing dyslexically, all the words coming out backwards because her concentration was shot and her hands were shaking. She worked quietly all afternoon, not wanting to leave the safety of her desk in case she bumped into Tanya again. But eventually she had to go to the bathroom.

There was no sign of Tanya as Dee walked past the conference room where the other woman routinely held court when she wasn't at her desk in the newsroom. In the ladies', Dee put on some lipstick to bring back some colour into her face. She was nearly out of her favourite colour, a rich coffee shade. She'd go shopping later. Buying cosmetics always cheered her up. Some of that new waterproof mascara would be nice too, and maybe bubble bath. Passion fruit aromatherapy stuff. Feeling somewhat happier, Dee went back to the newsroom and nearly collided with Tanya, who was coming out of the editor's office.

When Tanya walked by, she smirked knowingly at Dee, a smirk that said, 'You didn't tell anyone that I called you a fat, lazy lump, did you?'

Dee felt sick to the pit of her stomach. She'd failed again. Somehow she'd let Tanya get the upper hand and unless she did something about it, Tanya would ruthlessly exploit that power for all it was worth. What was the point of vowing she'd never let someone like Gary walk all over her again when she let someone do it every day in the office?

Why didn't Tanya pick on Maeve? Dee knew the answer. It was because her friend wouldn't take it. One moment of speaking to Maeve like that and Tanya Vernon would be flat out on her Prada-clad back with Maeve's fist imprinted in her face. Well, she'd get a verbal lashing anyway.

Tanya respected people like Isabel, Phil and Maeve. She didn't respect Dee one little bit. Why would she, Dee thought bitterly, when Dee wouldn't even stand up for herself? You're a spineless coward, O'Reilly, she told herself.

Isabel barely noticed how quiet her deputy was all afternoon. Her mind was full of Jack Carter, the discussions about him and Tanya, and the fact that Dee had so easily cottoned on to the identity of Isabel's married man.

She didn't know whether to be relieved or not about the latter. She knew that Dee wouldn't tell a soul but the whole incident had given her a scare, let her see what she was really taking on.

Everyone had spoken so coldly about Jack, as if he was bound to be having flings with every woman who threw herself at him. Isabel didn't know what to think. Did they all know something she didn't? And how could she ask without attracting raised eyebrows and knowing stares?

Isabel looked out of the window blankly. She was stunned to find that she still felt unsure about Jack. The wonderful warm feeling in her belly after their glorious holiday in Mayo had disappeared totally, to be replaced by the gnawing emptiness to which she was used. The emptiness of being with a man who was as faithful as a cat in a tuna fish factory.

CHAPTER EIGHTEEN

Robin looked at her watch ostentatiously and sighed, the sort of sigh a mother was supposed to hear from about twenty feet away.

Isabel, sitting a mere foot away with a much-needed cup of tea in front of her, ignored it. Her feet ached from traipsing around Dublin's city centre looking for new clothes for Robin and she wasn't about to be blackmailed into getting up from the coffee shop seat a mere five minutes after she'd sat down.

With another great sigh, Robin shoved her half-empty glass of Coke away from her. Isabel went on sipping her tea, while Naomi delicately bit into her cream bun. Isabel hadn't bought her half the clothes she'd got for her demanding elder daughter, but Naomi still sat there happily, nose buried in a teen magazine. *She* hadn't moaned and complained for the entire day, sulking when she couldn't find the exact type of black PVC schoolbag she wanted. It was Naomi's turn next, Isabel decided firmly. The next hour would be dedicated to buying clothes for *her*. Isabel wasn't going to make a distinction between her two daughters.

'Susie will be waiting for me outside Oasis!' said Robin in exasperation after another minute's silence.

Isabel gave her a grim stare. 'She won't be. It's at least another ten minutes until we have to leave. I'm not budging until then. Thanks to you, we've spent my Friday off walking miles looking for exactly the right clothes that won't disgrace you before your pals. Now I'm going to enjoy this chance to sit down.'

'I can meet her on my own,' Robin said crossly. 'It's only a bit up the street from here. I'm hardly likely to get mugged between the Jervis Centre and Oasis . . .'

'You won't,' Isabel interrupted. 'I want to meet Susie to find out who's picking you up from the disco tonight – her mother or me,' she added, enunciating each word crisply and dangerously.

'Suit yourself.' Robin, recognising that tone of voice, turned her attention to the numerous carrier bags strewn on the floor around their table. Her face lit up as she examined the two tiny strappy tops and the fake leather jacket she'd bought in Miss Selfridge's, courtesy of a generous gift cheque from her father.

Isabel would murder David when she saw him. It was a ridiculous sum of money to send to a teenager, especially when he'd insisted Robin spend it on 'fun stuff' for herself, instead of boring old school clothes being the implied message.

Isabel had just bankrupted herself buying boring old school clothes for both girls as the autumn term started in ten days.

Not that something so mundane would ever occur to David. Oh, no. He probably thought school uniforms came free instead of being so ridiculously expensive you'd assume John Galliano had designed them. Isabel simmered as she thought of all the things she had to say to him. The only good point was that she wouldn't have to wait very long as he was arriving in Dublin first thing the following morning, to spend the weekend with Robin and Naomi.

Apart from its providing her with the opportunity to tell him some home truths, Isabel dreaded it. The few times David had visited the girls previously, he'd only been able to stay in Dublin overnight, which meant he'd spent a day with them and she hadn't set eyes on him. On this occasion, he wasn't flying back until Monday evening, so he'd be dropping in and out of the house all weekend, picking up the girls and dropping them off whenever it suited him. He'd even had the temerity to ask could he stay in Eagle Terrace, which Isabel had flatly refused. Her mother had raged at the idea when Isabel had inadvertently told her.

'That wastrel deserves to be shot, and now he wants to stay with you?' Pamela had shrieked down the phone. 'The nerve of the man! The sooner you get divorced from him the better.'

Isabel couldn't agree more. Unfortunately, whenever she thought about divorce these days, she thought about Jack Carter and how desperately she longed for him to get divorced from Elizabeth. She thought of nothing else. They'd never even discussed it, of course. How could they? Jack was crazy about her, she was sure of it, but he'd never mentioned the word 'love'. And Isabel loved him. Madly and desperately. But all she could do was wait.

'Mum, it's nearly time!' said Robin impatiently. Isabel finished her tea. In this mood, Robin would drive both her and Naomi insane.

Susie stood outside Oasis, hopping from one foot to the next and shivering like a whippet in a skimpy T-shirt that wasn't suitable for a chilly late-August day. She had goosebumps on her arms and had her enormous fake suede handbag clasped to her chest as if it was a hot water bottle. Isabel idly wondered when her daughter and her friends would realise it was more sensible to arrange to meet *inside* a shop than outside it.

'Hiya, Susie!' cried Robin, magically transformed from sulky teenager to smiling, merry one. She pushed her dark blonde hair back off her face as she delved into the carrier bags to show off her bounty.

'Fake leather!' squealed Susie in delight, the cold forgotten. 'Rob, you babe!'

They giggled in unison as Robin ripped the tags off the jacket and put it on to be admired.

'Susie, what's the story about the disco tonight?' asked Isabel, who didn't want to stand outside all day.

'My mom can't pick us up, she's got a dinner party. She says she knows it's her turn but she's sorry,' Susie said, without taking her head out of Robin's Miss Selfridge bag.

Great, thought Isabel glumly. Another person with a social life. That means Dogsbody Farrell will have to stay awake till half-one in the morning to ferry home four hot, sweaty, excited teenagers even though it isn't her turn for the disco car pool. Marvellous.

'Well, I'll see you all at half-one outside the gate,' she said firmly. 'Don't be late.'

'We won't. Thanks, Mum,' said Robin, eyes shining as if she hadn't just spent the past two hours in a vicious sulk.

'And lend Susie your new jacket, she's freezing. Come on, Naomi,' Isabel said, putting on a bright, forced smile for her younger daughter. 'What are we going to buy *you*?'

As she drove home two hours later, shattered and broke, Isabel thought about Friday nights in the lives of women in love with married men. Tonight, Jack was at one of his wife's charity fundraisers, the sort of party where the only people who didn't arrive in limos were the waiters, and where only the finest wines, champagnes and hors d'oeuvres were served.

She, on the other hand, would be sitting at home in leggings and a sweatshirt as she flicked through the channels and contemplated doing the ironing. Thanks to Susie's mom and her dinner party, Isabel couldn't have a couple of G & Ts and go to bed early either. She'd have loved to be going to a dinner party, to get dressed up and talk to new people instead of watching TV on her own. But going anywhere without Jack would be horrible – so horrible that it was easier to stay at home and think about him instead of go out and look sadly at the other happy couples who could afford to be seen together.

This affair thing wasn't all it was cracked up to be. If she wasn't so in love with Jack Carter, there was no way she'd have been able for it.

At home, she rustled up a speedy dinner of stuffed chicken breasts for herself and Naomi and wondered what people had done before Marks and Spencer made ready-cooked meals.

'This is lovely, Mum,' Naomi said, eating twice as fast as she normally did. 'Can I go out to the park? We're playing rounders tonight.'

'Sure. But be in by half-seven,' Isabel said, kissing her on the cheek. 'The evenings are getting darker and colder.'

With Naomi gone, the house seemed very empty. Isabel washed the dishes and wondered if Jack would phone her. He'd said he would. Then again, with a glamorous party to go to, he might forget.

He *could* have phoned while she was shopping, although Isabel had told him she'd be gone most of the day.

What if the only chance he'd had to phone had been while she was out? She imagined the phone ringing plaintively in the empty house, while she, who longed for it to ring now, had been stuck in rush-hour traffic day-dreaming about Jack.

Depressed, Isabel decided the only solution was to clean the place. She'd been letting the housework slide and with David destined to drop in and out all week-end, she didn't want him to think they were living in squalor. Not that it mattered to him, she thought testily.

So far, he hadn't contributed one penny to the girls' upkeep and she hadn't heard a word about The Gables or whether he'd managed to sell it or not. She could have had a red bulb outside the door for all he seemed to care.

Forget David, she told herself sternly. You're on your own now. Being broke is just part of separated mother-dom.

Just then, a picture of Elizabeth Carter slipped into her mind. Elizabeth in a seductive red dress that had probably cost more than Isabel's salary, pre-tax. How could she compete with that? Jack wouldn't ring. Why would he?

Isabel fought the impulse to run upstairs and take one of her anti-depressants. She'd managed to cut down the number she used by over half and planned to stop taking them altogether within the next couple of months. Falling in love with Jack had given her the boost she needed to give them up. And falling in love with Jack sometimes made her need them more than ever . . .

Isabel took a deep breath and started on the kitchen, methodically cleaning the worktops, hob and sink. Then she washed the kitchen window until it sparkled and mopped the floor. The back garden was still a disaster zone but the pretty china pots of pink and white geraniums she had arranged on the windowsill meant your eye was distracted from the weeds. Or so she hoped.

It would be just like David to peer outside and make some fatuous remark about getting a man in to do the back garden, when she didn't have the spare cash to do any such thing.

When the kitchen gleamed, she attacked the hall and stairs. Would she hear the phone over the roar of the vacuum cleaner? she wondered anxiously.

An hour and a half later, the small house shone and Isabel was dog tired. There was nothing like house-work to take your mind off emotional problems, she thought with satisfaction. Five minutes of encounter-ing balls of dust under the furniture and in the corners soon had you cleaning manically – along with idly wondering how much those overhaul cleaning firms charged for a day-long, reclaim-your-home-from-the-dust session.

Glancing at her watch, Isabel saw it was nearly time for the start of a new TV mini-series set in the forties. She loved programmes set in the past and felt like getting immersed in somebody's fictional life. It might make her forget her own.

Upstairs, she washed the dust from her face and carefully reapplied her moisturiser. You're getting old, Isabel, she told her reflection. You'll be forty next month. Forty!

She gazed at her face morosely, not seeing the fine

CATHY KELLY

bone structure that gave her an elegant, classical air. She didn't notice the clear, ocean blue eyes but saw only the fine lines around them and the dark shadows that only a vat of Touche Éclat would camouflage.

When the phone rang, she thought it might be Robin, ringing to say they were all going to a different disco and could Isabel pick them up there? It wasn't. It was Jack.

'Hello, Isabel.'

Her heart leapt at the sound of his voice.

'Jack.' She said his name with pleasure. 'I hoped you'd ring.'

'I phoned several times but nobody answered. I had to talk to you.'

'I was hoovering,' she explained. 'I thought I'd be able to hear the phone but obviously . . .'

'I miss you,' he said, voice low and deep. 'I wanted to talk to you so badly all day. I knew you were out this afternoon but I kept phoning, hoping you'd be back early.'

'Darling.' Isabel sat on her bed and smiled. 'I spent the whole day thinking about you, too.'

'I wish I could see you tomorrow.'

'But you've got to go to the K Club,' she said miserably. The executive conference in the plush Kildare hotel, where Emily, Phil and Maeve had joked that Tanya Vernon would put the moves on Jack.

What was it Emily had said?

I bet you a tenner that Tanya gets to first base with Big Jack that night.

She didn't believe it but the little bud of jealousy had already sprouted in Isabel's heart, sending spiteful shoots into her subconscious. Tanya and Jack, it said. Jack and Tanya . . .

'I'm leaving very early in the morning but I'll be back on Sunday by lunch,' he said. 'Could I see you then?'

Isabel wanted to curse. 'I'm having lunch with my mother,' she wailed. 'She invited me because the girls will be with David. What about later?'

He groaned. 'I've got to fly to London at half-three.'

Neither of them said anything for a moment. Adultery was worse than co-ordinating Middle Eastern peace talks, Isabel thought bitterly. When one side could manage a date, the other one couldn't. Perhaps he didn't really want to see her. Perhaps it was more convenient this way.

'I'm back in the office on Monday,' she said, her voice cooler. 'You can phone me there.'

'You mean, I can't phone you at home?' he asked, suddenly anxious.

'It's difficult,' she said slowly. Two could play at that game. 'Robin is so very curious and if she answers the phone, she's going to wonder who the hell this strange man is who's suddenly phoning her mother up.'

'Isabel, my darling.' Jack's voice was like a caress, touching her over the phone line. 'I want to see you so badly, you must believe that, but this weekend is impossible what with the conference. I'd come over early tomorrow but I'm flying down with Malley McDonnell, Eugene Flynn and Tanya Vernon.'

Isabel took a sharp intake of breath, sick with envy.

'Can I see you on Tuesday?' he was saying.

'I don't know. I might be busy. You know, parties to go to, conferences to attend,' she said off-handedly to hide her hurt. He was flying down with Tanya! How could he? Had the girls in the office been right?

'Don't be like that, Isabel,' he pleaded. 'I know this is difficult for you. Christ, it's impossible for me . . .'

She could imagine him running a hand through his hair impatiently and for a brief second she weakened. Poor, darling Jack. She loved running her fingers through his hair.

Then she imagined Tanya Vernon sitting limpet-like beside him in the helicopter, where Isabel had sat on their trip to Ashford Castle.

She envisaged Tanya's hot little hand snaking along Jack's thigh at dinner; her giving him a half-lidded, tempting look from those cold, calculating eyes. A come-and-get-me look. Men were all the same. They never could resist temptation. David had never even tried to.

Thinking of him, her heart hardened. He had made a fool of her for years; it wasn't going to happen again.

'Phone me at work, Jack,' she said in the brusque tone she used with Robin when she was playing up. 'And remember to enjoy yourself, won't you? I'm sure you'll find Tanya great company.'

She hung up and immediately regretted sounding so bitter, so much like a spoilt child.

Damn! But she couldn't help it. She felt so jealous, so scared and hurt. Had Jack any idea what it was like to sit at home and long to be with him with all her heart? Did he know how it felt to think of a man morning, noon and night, and know that he was with someone else? No, was the answer. And he never would.

The phone rang again, shrill and insistent. Isabel stared at it but refused to pick up the receiver. Inside, she wanted to. Desperately. She wanted to hear Jack's voice telling her he was crazy about her and that he understood how difficult it was for her.

The phone stopped ringing. A minute later, it started again, the shrill sound drilling into her skull. Isabel wanted to lie down on the bed and sob her eyes out.

'Mum, I'm back. Sorry I'm late. I was batting.' Naomi was home.

'Hi love, I'll be down in a minute,' Isabel called downstairs. 'I'm just answering the phone.'

She picked it up hesitantly.

'Isabel, what's wrong?' Jack asked. 'You're not worried about Tanya, are you? That's ridiculous.'

'Why is it ridiculous?' she asked hotly. 'It's common knowledge that Tanya Vernon is madly keen to get you into bed . . .'

'Common knowledge?' yelled Jack in astonishment. 'It's the first I've heard of it, Isabel. Tanya's an ambitious junior executive I've barely spoken to before this and I'm only giving her a lift in the helicopter because I want to talk to Eugene Flynn who said he was driving her down to the conference.'

'Oh.' Isabel felt incredibly foolish.

'And if Ms Vernon fancies the idea of sleeping her way to the top, then she's in the wrong company. Eugene Flynn has no interest in women unless they have a bank balance bigger than his, and I'm not interested in hustlers like her. Why would I want to look twice at Tanya when I've got you, Isabel? Don't you understand that? Don't you trust me?'

'Yes,' she said slowly, feeling awful. She'd let her own insecurities mess things up dreadfully.

'Shit!' Jack cursed. 'I wish I could see you tomorrow, Isabel. I hate leaving you like this. I know it's impossible for you. But I want you to understand that I've always been totally truthful with you, about how I feel for you and . . .' He hesitated briefly.

'We can't talk about this over the phone. I must see you, soon.'

There was no mistaking the urgency in his voice or the emotion.

Isabel felt very emotional herself. She hadn't meant to say she didn't trust him. It was just so difficult. Where did she stand? Why had she fallen for him so hard when there didn't appear to be any future for them?

'If you don't want me to phone you at home over the weekend, Isabel, please phone me on my mobile?' he begged.

She grinned for the first time. 'You *can* phone me at home,' she relented. 'I was just being stupid, saying you couldn't.'

His voice relaxed too, changing from slightly strained into the rich, warm tone she loved.

'I'll get you back for that, you brat,' he warned. 'Which is the worst place for tickles – your sixth rib or your feet?'

'You tickle my feet and you're dead!' she joked back. 'Jack, I'd better go. Naomi has just come in and she'll be upstairs in a moment. I'm sorry about earlier . . .'

He cut her off. 'Don't say sorry, Isabel. You've absolutely nothing to be sorry for. I know it's horrible seeing me waltz off to this party without you. I'd hate it if it were me waiting at home, thinking about you with lots of strange men ogling you. So I can understand perfectly. But you've no reason to be jealous, honestly.'

'I'm glad, really glad. I'll talk to you tomorrow, then. 'Bye, Jack.'

'Goodbye, my darling.'

Isabel stared at the phone for a long time before she left the bedroom. She'd nearly done it when she'd said goodbye. Nearly said, 'I love you.' She did love him but she couldn't say it, not when he'd never said it, not when it would have meant so much to her if he had.

412

If he didn't love her, where was their relationship going? She laughed mirthlessly. Even if he *did* love her, where was their relationship going?

Further along the road of a double life that would include long illicit lunches and stolen nights in five-star hotels?

All she wanted were cosy evenings in, waking up in the same bed in the morning, eating breakfast in companionable silence, sharing their lives, normal lives.

But he belonged to another woman and after the things she'd been through, Isabel knew how much it hurt when the man you loved strayed . . . Or did she really mean that any more? She realised with a jolt that she'd stopped thinking of Elizabeth in quite the same charitable way. Elizabeth was like a spoilt child, a creature who lived entirely for pleasure and put more money up her nose than would feed a small African village for a month. Isabel wasn't sorry for her. In a way, she despised her for wasting her life. And she hated Elizabeth for being married to Jack.

Isabel loved him, adored him: it was every woman for herself.

'Did you have a nice time, Naomi?' she asked, taking a few deep breaths to calm herself as she went downstairs.

After a sleepless night where she wondered over and over again if Jack loved her or not, Isabel finally drifted off to sleep as dawn was creeping in at the bedroom window. She awoke to the sound of Robin's yells.

'Dad's here! He's here!'

Isabel groaned and massaged her head, feeling a headache of Krakatoan proportions rumbling at the base of her skull.

'Let him in and make him a cup of tea,' she croaked, peering round her bedroom door. 'I'll be down in a few minutes.'

She stumbled into the bathroom. A hollow-eyed face stared back at her from the mirror over the sink. This hadn't been part of her plan.

She'd intended to be at the door to greet David, beautifully dressed, perfumed and carefully made up, with her handbag and car keys in her hand so he'd realise she was on her way out and that he wasn't being invited into 12 Eagle Terrace.

Her night of anxiety over Jack had completely screwed up that plan. Now she looked like she'd been in bed with the 'flu for a month and it was going to take more than ten minutes to salvage her sleep-ravaged face. Which would give David plenty of time to snoop around downstairs, letting his overexcited daughters entertain him while he idly riffled through electricity bills, her briefcase and anything else personal he could lay his hands on. Blast!

'Naomi, take your dad into the sitting-room,' Isabel yelled with a flash of inspiration. She'd barely finished decorating it and there was nothing even vaguely private there apart from swatches of curtain fabric.

'He says he's fine here, Mum,' replied Naomi.

Double blast!

Isabel jammed her shower cap on – she couldn't meet David for the first time in months with her hair plastered to her head – and had the quickest shower of her life. Ten minutes later, she went downstairs as calmly as she could, dressed in a cream trouser suit David had never seen before. She'd quickly applied all her war paint and a generous spray of Ô de Lancôme. She didn't care that it looked odd to be so formally dressed at half-nine on a Saturday morning. She wanted to look businesslike so that David didn't even attempt to mess her around. For, as she admitted to herself with that final shaky breath before she pushed open the kitchen door, she *was* nervous. Seeing your husband for the first time after such an acrimonious split wasn't going to be easy.

'David, hello,' she said to the back of his head.

He turned from looking out of the kitchen window and smiled broadly at her. Naomi and Robin flanked him, Robin clinging to his arm while Naomi made coffee.

Isabel had forgotten how tall and lean he was, how graceful he looked in casual clothes like the pale chinos and rich green polo shirt he was wearing now. The light coming in at the window burnished his dark hair to a rich shade of chestnut.

His hair was shorter and his face thinner but otherwise he was still the same old David: totally relaxed despite the tension of the whole situation. Isabel had often felt that he'd have made a master criminal. Now she was sure of it. His face was as untroubled as if he'd been away for a few days on business and had just returned home to an ecstatic welcome. He didn't look like a man who was seeing his estranged wife for the first time in her new home, a home where he wasn't particularly welcome.

'You look wonderful, Izzy,' he said warmly.

Isabel steeled herself to remain self-possessed. She threw him a calm, poised look and ignored the comment.

'What are your plans for today?' she asked.

David ruffled Robin's hair playfully, not noticing that she'd braided it into intricate little rows and that ruffling messed it up.

'Dad!' She ducked and immediately started smoothing it with her hands.

'Sorry, Robin,' he said contritely. 'For that, you get to pick what we do today. What do you say – bowling and burgers?'

She shot him a scathing look and Isabel smothered an impulse to laugh. It was about time that David discovered that his precious little kitten had grown into a teenage lioness during the summer holidays, a lioness always ready to unsheath her claws.

The Robin who'd have been happy to spend Saturday bowling and eating burgers was nothing but a memory. The new Robin wanted to be taken shopping or into elegant restaurants for her lunch so she could pose up a storm.

'I'd love to go bowling, Dad,' said Naomi eagerly.

Ever the peacemaker, Isabel thought fondly.

'For God's sake, bowling is for kids,' snapped Robin.

'Come on.' David put an arm around both of them and drew them together. 'I don't want my two beautiful girls fighting.'

Robin was mildly pacified at being described as beautiful.

'We can go bowling if you like, Naomi,' she conceded, 'if we can go to the Clarence for lunch. U2 own it and all the movie stars stay there. A girl from school went there for dinner and said she saw Leonardo DiCaprio in the bar. Please, Dad?'

'Of course, Robin. Anywhere you want.'

'Well, that's settled,' Isabel said briskly. She glanced at her watch and started picking up her briefcase and papers. 'I've got to head into the office for a meeting and then I've a lunch to go to. What time will you bring the girls back this evening?' she asked David.

'I don't know . . . nine, ten?'

'Be more specific,' she said, trying to keep the hostility out of her voice but failing.

'Are you going out tonight?' he inquired silkily.

'That's none of your business,' she snapped. 'I expect the girls back by eight.'

''Bye, Mum.' Naomi came over for a hug but Robin walked out with a blithe, 'See ya.'

David waited until the girls had left the kitchen before he spoke. 'I'd hoped we could have a drink sometime this weekend, Izzy. We've got things to talk about.' He looked at her with big, hangdog eyes.

Isabel would have loved to have told him to take a running jump, that she had no plans to talk to a man who hadn't even mentioned maintenance for his daughters. But she couldn't do that. He was the girls' father and he was right – for once. They *did* have things to discuss.

'Tomorrow evening when you bring the girls back. We can go out for an hour,' she said firmly. By Sunday night, she might be able to cope with him on a one-to-one basis.

'Great. I'll look forward to it,' David said breezily. He walked past and kissed her on the cheek before she'd had time to step back. Furious with herself for not seeing it coming, Isabel wiped her cheek angrily as he sauntered out of the room, calling to the girls. The front door slammed and she was alone, wondering whether she was far too overdressed to do her supermarket shopping.

The leg of lamb was, naturally, perfectly cooked. Pamela Mulhearn was an excellent cook. Floury potatoes, minted peas, broccoli spears and carrots just the right side of *al dente* all tasted beautiful and were a testimony to Isabel's mother's habit of getting up before eight on Sunday mornings to put lunch on before she went to Mass.

'I don't hold with staying in bed late at the weekend,' she always said.

But Isabel simply wasn't hungry. Not wanting to hurt her mother's feelings, she pushed everything round her plate and tried to hide the uneaten lamb under a couple of bits of potato. She'd had another miserable night thinking about Jack and couldn't face food.

Breakfast had been a cup of coffee and half a slice of brown toast on her own because David had picked the girls up at eight to take them to Wexford for the day.

Isabel felt weary and lonely without them. A proper Sunday lunch was her idea of hell at that moment.

'More peas, Isabel?'

'No, thanks, Mother,' she said, hoping her mother wouldn't notice her largely uneaten meal. But for once, Pamela didn't seem interested in making her daughter eat up every morsel of food. She was animatedly talking about her new project, a charity clothes shop nearby where she'd started working.

'They simply don't know how to run that place. As I said to your father, they've organised it all wrong. There's no proper book keeping system, they never know how much stock they have in at any time and they don't even have an iron in the back to run over items that come in crumpled!'

'I didn't know you knew much about stock control and book keeping, Mother?' Isabel said with interest.

'I did some book keeping in the doctor's office where I worked before I married your father,' Pamela answered. 'And you only have to watch one of those real-life television shows about shops and businesses to see that stock control is vitally important. I don't know how that shop keeps going.'

Seeing that her mother wasn't interested in her lamb consumption, Isabel gave up pretending to eat and sat back holding her glass of white wine.

'Who's running the shop?' she asked.

'Mrs Jewison used to run it and she was very good apparently but she broke her hip so Mrs Flaherty took over. And, believe me, that woman shouldn't be in charge of a supermarket trolley.'

Pamela's face was animated and happy, eyes glittering behind her bi-focals as she explained her plans to turn the tiny one-time dry cleaner's into the most successful charity shop on the east coast. Her enthusiasm was infectious. The normally gloomy Sunday lunchtime atmosphere was replaced by something approaching gaiety.

Isabel's father wasn't chewing his lamb with a wary expression on his face in case he made the wrong sort of noise and had Pamela demanding to know what was wrong with her cooking. She was transformed, Isabel thought with amazement.

There were no disparaging remarks about the stringi-ness of the meat or the deterioration of the butcher's shop now that 'nice Mr Hill has gone and left it to that untalented, gormless son of his.'

Pamela ate heartily and even drank some of the white wine Isabel had brought, though she rarely drank any-thing other than sherry.

'I think we need to be more choosy about the clothes we accept,' she was saying. 'Otherwise shoppers with money will give us a wide berth because they'll think we stock nothing but junk. And we'll get better quality clothes if we get a better quality of customer. The richer ones will give their old clothes to us, so we'll get all the good labels.'

'You're really enjoying it,' Isabel said encouragingly, pleased to see the positive change in Pamela. 'You should have done something like this years ago.'

Her mother looked slightly shamefaced. 'I know. I regret not getting more involved. People were always asking me to help with the Vincent De Paul and the local charities. But I wanted a proper job, do you understand?'

Isabel shook her head. 'Not really.'

Pamela sighed. 'I was proud, you see. I always thought I was so clever and that a job where they'd take *anybody*, like in a charity, would be beneath me. That I was better than that. So I wouldn't help out. After all those years, I now find it's fun and I'm good at it. And,' she smiled ruefully, 'that charities need clever people just as much as proper businesses do.'

For the first time in years, Isabel leant over and gave her mother a spontaneous hug. Her mother wasn't a huggy person, she wasn't keen on affectionate kisses and tactile people. Even now, she held on to Isabel woodenly, not quite sure what to do with her arms. But it was still a hug.

'Well done, Mother,' Isabel said warmly. 'I'm so proud of you. If anyone can make that charity shop work, you will. I know it.'

Pamela beamed, the smile lighting up her normally stern face. She patted her perfectly coiffed frosted curls. 'I hope so. Now why didn't you eat your lunch?'

The day passed with painful slowness. Isabel felt lost without Naomi and Robin. She tried to occupy herself by sorting out the garden but it was such a hopeless task, and pulling up weeds simply gave her more time to think about Jack and their relationship. A relationship that was going nowhere fast.

As she stuck her trowel into the hard, compacted soil, determined to uproot a particularly resilient dandelion, Isabel kept seeing Elizabeth Carter's face smirking at her. Elizabeth . . . rich, privileged, idle – well, not that idle, Isabel conceded. She did a lot of charity work. Although she couldn't somehow see Elizabeth standing in a small charity shop sorting through second-hand clothes with Pamela telling her what to do in the background.

Elizabeth's sort of charity involved big parties, designer dresses, people telling her she was 'Wonderful, darling!' and the odd line of coke in the bathroom afterwards. And Jack by her side, handsome in his dinner jacket, eyes crinkling up when somebody made a joke.

Isabel stabbed the trowel into the heart of the dandelion. Bloody weeds!

David arrived back with the girls at half-eight. Isabel forced herself to say nothing about their being home an hour later than he'd promised. Instead, she calmly got her jacket, told Robin there was a pizza in the freezer if she or Naomi was hungry, and told David he could follow her in his car to the Harbour Bar. That way he could drive back to his hotel afterwards without going back to Eagle Terrace.

In the Harbour Bar, Isabel found them a seat in a corner and let David go off to buy her a white wine spritzer.

The pub was bustling, jammed with locals who'd been going there for years, and with tourists who liked the cosy atmosphere of a genuine Irish bar. A pretty girl with lustrous black hair and a pair of trousers practically sprayed on to curvy hips eyed David as he stood at the bar ordering the drinks. Isabel watched her watching him and knew that David, even though his back was turned to the girl, was aware he was being watched. He'd always had a sixth sense for things like that.

The girl nudged her female companion, whispered something and they laughed – high girlish laughs. David turned his head a fraction so that he could see where the laughter was coming from. The girl smiled shyly at him and he smiled back.

Isabel looked away, not wanting to be caught watching. God, it was like a French farce. She was watching her husband flirting with another woman on an occasion when he'd brought her out for a drink to try and reconcile their differences. Because she was sure that's what it was all about. David thought he could wangle his way back into her life, even if on a part-time basis.

Why else had he pumped Naomi for information about Isabel's social life the last time he'd visited, and why else had he been so very pleased to find out that 'Mummy doesn't go out much' as Naomi had innocently put it?

He placed the drinks on the table and took a deep draught of his Guinness.

'I needed that,' he said, wiping his mouth with his hand. 'It's been a hectic weekend.'

'What did you want to talk about?' Isabel said abruptly.

'Us, the girls, the house.'

'There is no "us", David. You know that. As for the girls, I'd like to know when you're going to start paying maintenance for them? It's been over six months and you haven't paid a penny. I'd also like to know what the position is with The Gables? Do we still own it, and, if so, when are you selling it? I need the money.'

He reacted to her bluntness in his usual way. 'Hold on, Izzy. You're always in such a rush. Let's not talk about selling The Gables yet . . .'

'Why not?' she said.

'Listen, Izzy.' He put down his glass and moved closer to her so that his knees were almost touching hers under the small table. 'The new agency is doing well. Freddie reckons we'll be in the black in a few months and then we'll be in the money. I'm still holding out for that villa in Portugal. You know, the one we talked about? Down the coast from Lisbon so we're near the city but still in the countryside . . .'

'David, you still don't get it, do you?' Isabel asked in exasperation. 'This isn't about a second home in Portugal or about how well your ad agency is doing. Frankly, I don't give a damn about that so long as you agree to pay maintenance for your daughters.

'This is about *us*. You want us to be a couple again and it just isn't going to happen. Understand?'

She'd raised her voice as she was speaking and the couple sitting at the next table glanced in their direction curiously. Isabel flushed; she hated being watched.

'You're certainly not beating around the bush,' David said flatly.

'No. There's no point.'

'Listen . . .' He tried to take her hand in his but Isabel pulled it back rapidly. She knew his tricks.

'Isabel,' he said, his voice wheedling.

She knew he was serious when he started calling her 'Isabel'.

'Listen to me,' he repeated, without any attempt to touch her. 'Don't cut me off, please. I've been thinking about you so often recently, wishing I could turn back the clock. We had some great times, didn't we? Remember this time last year, when we all went to Scotland for a week?'

Isabel remembered the utter peace of the cottage they'd taken for five days, and the glorious two days they'd spent in Edinburgh. They'd been – on the outside, at least – like any other family, two parents and two daughters. Not one struggling parent with one sweet daughter and one difficult one.

David reached for her hand and this time Isabel didn't jerk it away.

For a fleeting moment, she thought how nice it was to sit in a pub with a man and not have to worry about who saw them. David didn't have to rush home to his wife; *she* was his wife. Then she remembered what it had been like being his wife. The arguments over bills; the crazy, money-making schemes; his ability to shut out reality and live in fantasy land; her inability to live like that.

And she thought of Jack, darling Jack whom she loved so much. It was time she told him, she decided. The next time she saw him, she'd do it. He could make his decision then about their future, but at least she'd have been honest with him. And if he couldn't cope with hearing that she loved him, that was his problem. Isabel would walk away, agonising though it would be, knowing she'd done the right thing.

'We've been through so much together,' David was saying softly. 'I can't believe you can simply throw all that away, Isabel. Can you?'

His eyes were beseeching, almost irresistible in his boyish face.

Isabel gazed at him, wondering how she could have

even momentarily listened to a word of his nonsense, and resisted. 'I'm not throwing it all away, David, it's already gone. We're separated and I want to get divorced.'

This time he snatched his hand away. 'You can't be serious?' he said shortly.

'I'm perfectly serious. I'd like us to be grown-up about this, for our sakes and for the girls'. They don't need their parents at each other's throats.'

David sat and scowled into his pint.

'We should try and sort out issues like visiting rights before we see our solicitors. It'll make things easier,' Isabel said, matter-of-factly. 'They could visit you for half term, it's a long weekend in October. Or,' she paused, hating the very idea, 'if that doesn't work out, perhaps you'd like to see them for Christmas. I *do* have them all the time, I suppose. Although I'd miss them so much . . .'

'I don't think Christmas would work out,' he said quickly. 'I've . . . er . . . already fixed something up.'

Isabel lost her temper again.

'I can't believe you came here, begging me to come back to you, when you've already made arrangements for Christmas,' she said angrily. 'How did you plan to tell me? Were you going to announce it after we'd got back together? "Sorry, Izzy. Sorry, Robin. Sorry, Naomi – I'll be away for Christmas. Your presents are under the . . . oops! Forgot to buy presents. Still, there's always next year." '

'Don't be so vicious, Isabel,' spat David. 'It doesn't suit you. The Christmas trip is business, and it'll probably be as boring as hell. How else are we supposed to build our client list if we don't keep them happy and give them what other agencies give them? That's what the Jamaican trip is all about. I don't know why you've never understood that. Why you've never been able to support me when it comes to business trips.'

'You're right, David,' she said coolly. 'I never could support you. Not when I knew that the trips were eating up the company's profits – profits our family could have benefited from if they weren't being frittered away on expense account lunches for clients who grow obese on five-star cuisine.'

'You're so short-sighted, Isabel,' he said scathingly. 'You don't understand at all.'

'On the contrary,' she replied, pushing her unfinished drink away from her, 'I'm being far-sighted. Our marriage is over, David. If we can't have a civilised discussion after fifteen minutes in each other's company, it's hardly likely we'll manage a few more years of blissful togetherness, is it? Now, let's talk about The Gables. I want to sell up.'

On Monday morning, Jack was on the phone at half-nine. Isabel had only just arrived in the office and Jackie stood beside her waving a sheaf of phone messages.

'I've missed you so much,' he said.

'Really?' Isabel said in a bright tone, conscious that Jackie stood about six inches away, writing another message on her notepad.

'Morning,' muttered Phil, dumping her briefcase on to her desk beside Isabel's. 'Malley wants us in an editorial meeting in five minutes, I met her on the way in.'

Isabel nodded. 'I'm afraid I can't really talk right now, er . . . Susan,' she said into the receiver.

'*Susan?*' laughed Jack. 'Couldn't you have pretended I was a man, at least? Juan, Philippe, Dirk . . . something masculine, something to make them all wonder who your exotic lover is?'

Isabel bit her lip to stop herself giggling. 'That would be inappropriate under the circumstances, *Susan*, but if you want, I'll take out an advert in the paper – we get a staff discount – and mention your name over and over again!'

'Great idea,' Jack said suddenly. 'That's exactly what we should do. I'm sick of this clandestine assignation stuff. Anyway, as you obviously can't talk right now, I'll ring you at home tonight. 'Bye, darling. Have a good day.'

Isabel was still too stunned by thinking about the implications of what he'd said to pay very much attention at the editorial meeting.

The rest of the day turned out to be so hectic that she had no time to sit quietly and wonder what Jack had really meant earlier. It was only as she drove home to Bray that evening, exhausted after a ten-hour day where *everything* had gone wrong, that she went over the conversation in her head again.

I'm sick of this clandestine assignation stuff.

So was she. But what had he meant by that? Was he going to leave Elizabeth? Or was he merely being flip, fed up with the bizarrely one-sided conversations they were forced to have when other people were present?

At home, Robin had defrosted and started re-heating a home-made aubergine lasagne, while Naomi had laid the breakfast bar for dinner. Wonderful smells emanated from the oven and Isabel, who hadn't had time for anything more than a yoghurt for lunch, realised she was hungry.

'Sit down and I'll make you tea,' offered Robin solicitously.

Isabel suspected that her elder daughter's weekend with her father had not been a huge success. But she knew better than to probe her about this. When Robin felt like talking, she would.

After dinner, she disappeared up to her room and Naomi and Isabel watched TV. When the phone rang, Isabel was too tired to move from the chair and let Naomi run into the hall to answer it.

'It's for you, Mum,' she said a moment later.

Isabel sank on to the bottom step and picked up the phone.

'You sound tired,' Jack said. 'Bad day?'

'Exhausting. Well, it wasn't just today,' she admitted. 'It was the whole weekend. It was such a strain. David and I went out for a drink,' she said tiredly, pulling the pins out of her chignon. She ran her fingers through her hair to settle it.

'You did?' Jack asked tautly.

'Yes. He said he wanted to talk about the girls but he got on to some long-winded story about the business and a villa in Portugal he wants to buy for us.'

'A villa in Portugal?' Jack's voice was raised now. 'I hope he was joking? I thought he was bankrupt?'

'Not according to him,' Isabel remarked. 'I don't understand it. But talking about a villa in Portugal when he doesn't have a bean is pure David.' She raised her eyes to heaven. 'He's talked about buying a place there for years. He loves it and we went there for holidays a lot. The idea was pie in the sky, naturally. He always spent every penny so there was never enough even for necessities, never mind second homes.'

'What do you think about all this – the villa?' Isabel recognised more than a hint of jealousy in his voice and she smiled to herself.

'I'm not sure,' she said playfully. 'I've always fancied the idea of a holiday home somewhere hot, somewhere you could wear nothing but a bikini all day long. And I love Portugal.'

'Oh, I see.' Jack sounded crestfallen.

'David can buy all the villas in Portugal he wants,' she said, relenting, 'I won't be visiting him there. He was looking for a reconciliation, actually. That's why he asked me out. But I told him I wanted a divorce.'

'Thank God,' said Jack with relief. 'For a moment, I thought you were trying to tell me you were going back to him?'

'I know, I'm sorry. I thought you knew there was no chance of that, Jack?'

'I do,' he muttered. 'But . . . hell, I don't know, Isabel. I suddenly felt so terrified that's what you were saying: that you'd had enough of me, enough of the secrecy and lies.'

'Don't be silly,' she said softly. 'I wouldn't look at another man, don't you understand that?'

'I know, thank you.'

'I'll tell you what,' she said, wanting to cheer him up, 'let's go out tomorrow night, to dinner? We can go somewhere discreet . . .'

'Mum, aren't you off the phone yet?' shouted Robin, thundering down the stairs. 'I want to ring Susie.'

Isabel sat bolt upright on the bottom step. 'Er . . . just a minute, Robin, I'm talking to Phil. I've got to go,' she said apologetically to Jack. 'I'll see you in work tomorrow. We can talk about it then. 'Bye,' she added in a falsely bright tone.

There was no point in continuing the conversation with Robin hanging on her every word, but as Isabel hung up, she felt utterly miserable. She hated all the subterfuge, hated lying to Robin and pretending to be talking to someone else on the phone. Why couldn't she and Jack have a normal, out in the open relationship like other people? Was that too much to ask?

CHAPTER NINETEEN

'You'll enjoy yourself, you know you will.' Maeve reached around the back of her computer and switched it off. 'Fiona would love you to come and you know she always gives amazing parties. What were you planning to do tonight?'

'Go to the gym,' said Dee, leaning against her friend's desk. 'I've got to go to three aerobics classes a week and I missed Wednesday's.'

'There's no point in being incredibly fit and thin and living till you're a hundred if you have such a boring life you never go outside the front door,' Maeve pointed out.

'After one week of aerobics, I'm hardly incredibly fit and thin,' Dee answered. 'But I've lost five pounds.' She ran a hand over her hips, wondering if she looked noticeably slimmer or if she was the only person who was aware of the difference.

'You look great,' Maeve said encouragingly. 'A veritable man trap. Which is all the more reason to come out tonight and flirt with all the hunky single men at Fiona's birthday party.'

They left the office and walked out to the car park together, Dee weighed down by the armloads of papers, supplements and freelance articles she planned to read as she had the weekend off.

'Is Karl going?' she asked. 'I don't want to play gooseberry.'

She didn't say that she couldn't face an evening as the only single girl at a party chock-a-block with besotted couples, all talking softly to each other and sharing couplesy jokes and Eskimo kisses. She couldn't bear an evening like that.

Maeve unlocked the door of the classic Triumph Herald that cost her a fortune in garage bills. 'He's going to be late because he's working until half-nine tonight, so I need moral support. Please come with me?' she pleaded. 'It'll be fun. You know what'll happen if you don't, Dee. You'll come back from the gym and be bored rigid sitting in front of the box all night.'

That was true, Dee realised. A low-cal fish meal with a green salad, two glasses of Californian Grenache and, as a special Friday night treat, a ninety-five-per-cent-less-fat chocolate mousse awaited her, along with the TV guide and a mediocre detective film she wouldn't have dreamed of watching if Gary had been around. Another thrilling Friday evening in the life of Dee O'Reilly, glamorous journalist incarnate. If she really felt healthy, she might slop on a bit of that sauna face mask, pluck her eyebrows and paint her toenails. Whoopee!

'I'll go,' she said suddenly. 'Will we drive or get a taxi?'

Dee noticed him long before he saw her. She and Maeve had just arrived at the party and Dee had followed her friend down the stone steps into the vast kitchen when she spotted him. Dressed in head-to-toe faded denim, he lounged against a giant fridge, eating ice cream and looking at the only two other people in the room, who were kissing each other with the passion of teenagers on a first date.

He was blond, with a boyish, finely sculpted face, sea blue eyes and a full-lipped mouth more suited to a girl than a twenty-something man. But his athletic, lean-hipped figure looked anything but feminine. Maybe it was the after-effects of the bottle of Frascati she and Maeve had shared when they'd met up at Maeve's house earlier. Or maybe it was because she'd lost five pounds and felt pretty fabulous in her black silk skirt and dainty, caramel-coloured crochet cardigan, but Dee felt like behaving recklessly.

And as she watched the young man's laughing mouth curve around the ice cream, for a moment Dee wished she were that chocolate-covered ice lolly.

'Dee, Maeve! You made it at last!' shrieked their hostess, appearing from the door into the garden with bits of twig in her hair and a handsome black guy in tow.

He was at least a foot taller than Fiona who, dressed in black leather jeans and a spray-on purple rubber T-shirt, with auburn hair extensions rippling down her back, looked more like an MTV heavy metal show presenter than a thirty-year-old advertising agency executive.

'Hi, Fiona. Sorry we're so late. We got held up. But we brought booze. And . . .' Maeve held up a parcel wrapped in flowery paper, tied with a big pink bow '. . . your birthday pressie!'

'You darlings!' Fiona squealed with delight. 'Thank you. I hope it's sexy undies! Everyone else has given me crystal fruit bowls and house stuff, or perfume I don't like. Now, I must introduce you to Fabio. He's the best birthday present a girl could have. For once, my hopeless brother got me something I really needed – a man!'

She dragged him out from behind her and wrapped both arms around his jeans-clad waist happily.

'Fabio, meet Dee and Maeve. Maeve and I were at college together, Dee works with Maeve and they shouldn't be allowed out together!' she trilled, obviously tipsy.

'Hi.' Fabio grinned. 'Pleased to meet you,' he said in a soft accent.

'You're American?' said Dee in surprise. She'd assumed that with a name like Fabio, he had to be Italian.

'My mom loved Italy,' he explained patiently as he picked bits of twig out of Fiona's bird's nest hair. Dee wondered what they'd been doing in the back garden.

'My dad was overseas when I was born, so she got to name me before he got home. Otherwise, I'd be Luther.'

'I much prefer Fabio,' growled Fiona, sliding one hand into his jeans pocket. 'My brother Conor's back from South America,' she explained to the girls. 'He was on a college expedition in Ecuador, Chile . . . well, *everywhere*. He arrived home yesterday with four of the guys from the expedition, including Fabio. Joey's upstairs trying to sleep in my room because he's jet-lagged, and keeps screaming at us to turn off the music. I think Che is in the conservatory rolling joints as big as carrots. And Daryl . . .' She peered over Dee's head towards the fridge where Mr Ice Cream was licking his fingers lasciviously. 'Daryl is eating us out of house and home. I keep trying to get him to go upstairs and join the party, but he says he likes hanging out in the kitchen. I think he's shy.'

'Where's Daryl from?' asked Dee, trying to sound as

nonchalant as possible as she eyed up the handsome, golden-haired guy.

'Texas,' Fabio said. 'We called him Cowboy on the trip.'

Perfect name, Dee thought, taking another quick peek in Daryl's direction. All he needed was the Stetson – he had everything else, from the big buckle on his leather belt down to the dusty brown cowboy boots.

'Fiona, I think I'll put this in the fridge,' Maeve said, holding up a bottle of white wine.

Fiona wasn't listening. She was staring raptly at Fabio. 'And what was *your* nickname?' she purred.

'Come on, Dee,' urged Maeve. 'You've got the beer.'

She pushed Dee in the direction of Daryl, who had finished his ice cream and had his head in the fridge trawling for more food.

'He's a bit of all right, isn't he?' Maeve whispered in Dee's ear as they admired Daryl's muscular figure.

'You can say that again,' she murmured, unable to take her eyes off him. She loved the way his narrow hips gave way to broad, strong shoulders, the way the denim shirt stretched over his muscles.

'He's gorgeous.'

'Go for it, then,' Maeve hissed. 'There's only one way to get over a man, and that's to get another one, pronto. A quick fling with Daryl is just what you need, my girl.'

'Don't be daft, he wouldn't look at me . . .' began Dee.

Suddenly, Maeve pushed the bottle of wine into her arms and rushed off. 'Must go to the loo,' she said quickly before disappearing upstairs.

Dee stared blankly at Daryl's rear end for a moment until he extricated himself – and a large tub of potato salad – from the fridge.

'Well, hell-o,' he said in a soft, Southern drawl as he straightened up, turned round and looked at Dee appreciatively. 'What would your name be, honey?'

Dee went weak inside. The way he said *honey* sounded like he'd just suggested they strip off and do something wild and sexy on the floor. Something that was illegal in the Bible Belt. Something that involved strawberries, ice cubes . . .

'My name's Dee,' she gulped, unable to think of anything else to say.

He held out both golden-skinned hands towards her. 'I'm Daryl.'

Was he looking for a hug? Dee thought, bewildered.

'Let me take some of those cans and put them in the refrigerator,' he said instead.

'Of course.' Flustered, she looked down and realised she was still holding Maeve's six-packs and a bottle of wine.

When the beer was safely stowed, Daryl cracked open a bottle of Budweiser and offered it to Dee. 'Thanks,' she said, even though she rarely drank beer.

He opened a second one, took the potato salad and a fork and sat down at the table.

'You want some?' He gestured with his fork.

Dee shook her head.

'Why don't ya'll sit down and keep me company while I eat?' he said. 'I don't know anyone at this party, and I feel kinda lonely.'

Dee dropped on to the chair beside him, making the kissing couple look up briefly from their session. Upstairs the party was obviously in full swing. She could just hear Hot Chocolate's 'You Sexy Thing' being played. It was probably being belted out at full blast but the old stone walls of Fiona's Georgian cottage meant you were insulated from upstairs noise when you sat in the basement kitchen.

Maeve and all her college buddies were upstairs, chattering, drinking and dancing, while she was downstairs with a complete stranger and a couple of youngsters who were obviously stoned out of their minds and in danger of getting lip lock. Was she mad? Dee decided that she must be.

She sipped her beer and watched Daryl. He was all sun-toned colours – the blunt-cut hair that fell over one eye, the hairs gleaming on his slim, finely muscled arms, and the skin visible through the open-necked denim shirt. Like a honey-skinned child who'd played outdoors in the sweltering Pan Handle sun from birth, and probably thought sun cream was for sissies.

Daryl plunged a forkful of potato salad into his mouth, displaying ultra-white teeth and a pink tongue. Dee had never seen anyone eat the way he did. He didn't just eat – he devoured the food, making the entire procedure look like the most sensuous experience she'd ever witnessed.

God, he was sexy! An utterly laid-back, effortlessly gorgeous cowboy, who could – and probably did – have anything he wanted in life. She was very attracted to him. It was intense, exciting and utterly mad. It felt strange to be openly flirting with a man. She still felt so *attached*. At the back of her mind, she half-expected Gary to appear from upstairs, take one look at Daryl, and drag Dee out of the party, lecturing her all the way home on the dangers of talking to strange men.

Dee, really! How many times have I told you? You're too friendly for your own good. You're as undiscriminating as a Labrador puppy. Who knows what that man must have thought? He could have believed you were chatting him up, do you realise that? I can't leave you alone for a second . . .

Daryl regarded her from sleepy blue eyes.

'You don't talk much, Dee, do ya? I like that in a woman, I gotta admit.'

She quivered inside.

'Sure you don't want some food?' He proffered the fork in her direction, a soft pulp of salad glistening on it.

Dee, who was on the sort of murderous diet which meant she could only eat Lean Cuisines, low-fat cheese, rice cakes and fruit, drooled. And not only for what was at the end of Daryl's fork.

She leant over towards him, opened her mouth slowly and ate the potato salad. Her eyes never left his.

'My kind of girl, all right,' said Daryl, letting his face slide into a big, sunny grin.

Dee gave him her hottest come-hither look and was gratified to see it was having the desired effect. He held out another forkful of food and she ate it, even more slowly this time.

Then she panicked. What the hell was she doing? She was supposed to be moping at home, thinking about her ex-fiancé and sobbing whenever she heard a sad song on the radio. Which was what she'd done for the past two and a half weeks. Instead, she was flirting with a stranger at a party, licking his fork like she was auditioning for a part in a Thai sex show.

And he could be doing this for fun, teasing the big fat girl and making her think he fancied her until – *kapow!* he left with some willowy eight-stone goddess who'd been in the bathroom for most of the party putting on more eyeliner.

Daryl grinned at her and winked.

'I love your outfit, honey. It sorta moulds you. Whaddya call that stuff?'

Dee beamed back at him. 'Crochet.'

Oh, what the hell? She could sit here all evening, nervous as a turkey at Christmas, wondering if he *really* fancied her or if he was only *pretending* to fancy her for some nefarious reason – and totally miss out on having any fun.

All she ever did was over-analyse things and where did it get her? Nowhere. So stop analysing. Maybe this sex-on-legs cowboy actually fancied the knickers off her and she'd waste her opportunity wondering why.

After all, they could be keen on bigger women in Texas. And Gary wasn't here. He was in London, probably propped up on a barstool in Wardour Street, ogling girls and telling everyone that leaving Ireland was the best thing that had ever happened to him.

'So . . . what do you do, Daryl?' Dee asked brightly.

'Ah'm studying South American Culture in college in New Mexico,' he said, taking a slug of beer. He wiped a trace off his mouth with the back of his hand and Dee gazed, transfixed. He might as well have said he was studying cows on Pluto.

'What about you?' he asked.

'I'm a journalist.'

He looked interested. 'That's cool. Whaddya write about?'

'I work in the women's section of a daily newspaper, so I write about everything and anything. I do features, health reports, interviews . . .'

'Bet you're real good at it,' Daryl said, giving her his lazy smile once more. 'Bet you're real good at every-thing.'

There was no mistaking what he meant, 'specially as he'd taken one of Dee's hands in his and was paddling the inside of her palm with calloused fingers.

'Did you get those in South America? she asked nervously, staring at his work-roughened hands. 'Tell me about it?'

Daryl needed another beer for the story. While he opened the fridge, Dee fretted. She should have asked him about his college degree but was too uptight to ask him anything about South American culture. She didn't know the first thing about South America and didn't want to appear stupid. Then again, he hadn't asked her anything particularly rocket-scientist-clever about her job.

Daryl lounged back into his chair, one denim-clad knee nudging Dee's thirty-denier-covered one companionably.

'A college professor I know in San Antonio was working with this film maker and they wanted to make a film on religious ceremonies in South America. It was all low-budget stuff so they needed volunteers. Hell, it was the chance of a lifetime, so I signed up,' he said in his drawling voice. 'It wasn't a paid vacation or anything like that, but it was pretty exciting all the same.'

An influx of partygoers arrived in the kitchen, noisily demanding booze and crisps.

'Fiona said she had Hula Hoops stashed away somewhere,' said one girl, pulling open cupboards frantically. 'I'm ravenous.'

'Daryl, you eaten everything on the premises yet, huh?' said a voice and Dee looked up to see a cigarette-slim dark-eyed man sink into the chair beside Daryl.

'Dee, honey, meet Che, one of our expedition leaders, a man who knows South America like the back of his hand. Che, meet Dee.'

He stretched across the table, took Dee's hand and kissed it, Spanish-style.

'Pleezed to meet you, *cara*,' he said, flashing black eyes giving Dee the once-over.

She glowed with delight. 'Lovely to meet you, Che.'

She was enjoying this evening. It sure made a change from the ones she'd spent with Gary's cronies where the only terms of endearment used were when someone – usually Dee – was required to hit the shops for more beer and Pringles.

'You got the munchies, Che?'

'Yeah. Real bad.'

Daryl handed him the potato salad container and the fork. He took Dee's hand in his and stood up.

'Whaddya say we have a dance, Dee? I was tired earlier but I'm gettin' my energy back now. I musta been hungry.'

Thanks to her newfound enthusiasm for exercise, Dee was able to run up the stairs with Daryl without disgracing herself by panting *too* heavily at the top.

Upstairs, it was noisy, crowded, and the air was scented with the dual party smells of booze and smoke. People sat on the stairs or on the floor, chattering loudly and drinking out of bottles, mugs and the odd glass. Dee peered into the gloom of the sitting-room looking for Maeve but couldn't see her friend anywhere.

'Come on.' Daryl pulled her into a large room which had been turned into a make-shift disco, complete with flashing lights near the sound system and a big mirrored ball on the ceiling. Nina Simone was on the CD player; fragrant non-cigarette smoke filled the air and couples mooched slowly around the centre of the room, locked together as they danced to the slow, melancholy music.

Dee was determined not to notice that most of the dancers, Daryl included, were about eight years younger than she was. It was Fiona's party after all, and if she, just two years younger than Dee, liked having twenty-something-style parties, complete with dope heads and snogging couples now that she was in her third decade, then Dee wasn't going to get upset about it. What was that saying? You're as old as the man you feel.

Daryl was around twenty-four so Dee would have to be twenty-four for the night too. She wasn't going to tell him she was thirty-two and had just become disengaged.

'I love this kinda music,' he said, sliding his arms around Dee and gently pulling her close to him. He wasn't as tall as Gary. In fact, he was the perfect height for Dee. Even wearing high heels, her head was on a level with his biceps, so she snuggled close to his chest while he buried his head in her hair and inhaled deeply.

'You sure smell nice. You feel pretty nice, too,' he drawled.

Dee forgot about feeling fat and frumpy. She forgot about Gary and how she still sobbed every time she thought about how cruelly he'd destroyed her self-confidence and their relationship. She forgot everything except the sensation of being held tightly in a man's arms. A man who clearly fancied her rotten. After nearly three male-free weeks, it was a wonderful feeling. Daryl's shirt felt soft against her cheek and she closed her eyes contentedly as she leant closer to him. He smelled of apple shampoo, fresh male sweat and some sort of cologne she didn't recognise.

They swayed gently together, not really dancing, just trundling around slowly to the music. Daryl's arms held her close, one hand under her crochet cardigan, stroking the small of her back through her silky camisole. Nina Simone gave way to Billie Holliday huskily asking where her lover boy was.

Dee grinned silently. An hour ago, she'd have wanted to cry into her Budweiser on hearing that song. Now, locked in an embrace with a handsome, albeit young, Texan demigod, she didn't give a damn about her ex-lover boy. She merely hoped he fell off his London barstool and sprained something.

'Dee!' hissed a familiar voice.

She opened her eyes to see Maeve, circling the dance floor slowly with Karl, giving her an energetic thumbs up sign.

'Way to go, babe,' she mouthed encouragingly.

Dee grinned back, feeling like a teenager at her first dance. Karl swivelled his head round and winked bawdily.

After an hour of dancing, drinking copious beers and holding CD covers up to the light to see what track to play next, Dee was feeling very tipsy and needed to sit down. Daryl agreed.

He looked down at her with sleepy, blue eyes.

'Shall we sit this one out?'

The couple on the bench in the crowded conservatory hooched up so Dee and Daryl could squeeze into the last space available. 'Squeeze' being the operative word. Their thighs were jammed together like cellophaned packets of chicken breasts in the supermarket and neither of them could move their arms.

'Hold on,' Daryl said. He wriggled around, grabbed Dee by the waist and lifted her effortlessly off the seat before plonking her on his lap. She was stunned. He'd actually lifted her up and hadn't given himself a hernia!

And he wasn't gasping as though he'd been flattened by a steam roller, the way Gary always had when space had been tight and she'd ended up sitting on his lap.

'I'm not squashing you, am I?' she asked anxiously,

convinced that once Daryl knew how heavy she really was, he'd go off her like a shot. She vainly tried to lever herself off him so he wouldn't feel her full weight. 'We can always go back to the kitchen. There's sure to be loads of room there.' She got one foot on to the floor and with a hand on the back of the bench, could just about hoist herself off Daryl . . .

'Relax, honey. This is perfect. Cosy, dontcha think?'

He swept her arm from the bench and held her body so her entire weight was on him and her feet could no longer reach the floor. He settled her on to his lap and enveloped her in strong arms.

When his lips closed on hers, Dee thought her heart would explode, it was beating so fast. Surely he could hear it, beating furiously because she was so hopelessly excited?

But Daryl didn't appear to have heard any such thing. Instead, he kissed her leisurely, the pool-drain lips melting against hers as though they'd been made for each other. Dee kissed him hungrily in return, letting her tongue play with his while his mouth devoured her the way he'd devoured his ice cream earlier. His lips scorched hers, burning every place they touched.

He tasted slightly salty with a hint of peppermint mingled with beer. Dee tried to remember if she'd brushed her teeth before going to the party, but soon gave up all rational thought as Daryl kept kissing her, his mouth insistent.

One hand cradled her head, pulling her closer to him, while the other explored the contours of her breasts through her cardigan. She couldn't feel the callouses on his hands, just the touch of his fingers brushing her bare skin.

'I love your body,' he murmured huskily, moving

away from her mouth for a brief moment.

Dee felt her loins melt with a mixture of lust and gratitude as his hand made it inside her cardigan, navigated the cream camisole and burrowed inside her underwired bra. His fingers tweaked a nipple gently, making it rise like a pressure-cooker trivet on 'cooked'. He liked her, fancied her and hadn't passed out at the weight of her on his lap. What a guy!

She kissed him even more passionately and let her own hand sneak furtively inside his shirt to caress his smooth, tanned chest. His skin was warm and satiny. In the dim recesses of her brain, Dee was aware of being glad that it was almost dark in the conservatory and that most of the other couples in the candle-lit greenery were doing exactly what they were doing, apart from the ones concentrating on smoking joints.

But, amazingly, she wasn't too worried about being spotted snogging a strange man at a party. It felt good. Damn' good. Maeve was right: she deserved some fun.

Daryl was languorously licking her earlobe. He sucked it, sending rockets of excitement cruising through Dee's body straight to her groin. Little explosions went off inside her with every caress.

'Oh, Dee,' he murmured. The hand that wasn't stroking her gently was moulding her closer to him. Daryl moved his mouth from her ear to her neck and slowly along her throat, trailing hot, passionate kisses as he went.

She couldn't take it any more. She wanted him so badly, she thought she'd spontaneously combust. He was just as excited as she was, that was obvious.

But not like this, Dee thought suddenly. Not at a party with loads of other people. She couldn't believe she was doing this at all, groping a strange guy thanks to a few compliments and several beers, even if he was the most gorgeous one she'd seen in years and even though she was feeling pretty abandoned right now.

No, she couldn't see herself having a one-night stand with Daryl in someone else's bedroom on top of all the coats while the party raged on around them.

If they didn't stop, that was exactly what was going to happen. Not that the other partygoers would mind as nobody was paying them the slightest bit of attention.

Gently disentangling Daryl from her, Dee sat up straight on his lap, raked her hair out of her eyes and gasped for breath.

'Wow! That was something else,' she breathed.

'Yeah, you can say that again.' Daryl regarded her hazily through pupils black with desire.

'I just don't know . . .' She paused, at a loss to know how to say this. After all, *she'd* been wriggling around on his lap like a sex-starved trollop simply gagging for some lurve action. Daryl would hardly be too impressed when she said she wanted to call a halt to the proceedings even though they were both saturated with lust.

'I . . . I . . . just don't know if I want us to have a quick bonk here,' she stammered, face pink from a mixture of desire and embarrassment. 'I'm not used to that sort of thing. I know it's old-fashioned but I've been involved . . . sorry, I *was* involved with someone for a long time and I'd feel a little uncomfortable just . . . you know.'

'I know.' Daryl ruffled her hair affectionately. 'You're one hell of a sexy lady, Dee, d'ya know that? I thought we were both a gonner there, I thought I'd have to drag you into the flower garden and rip this knitted thing off.' He fingered her cardigan.

Dee's breath quickened at the thought.

'But, hey,' he continued, 'we can arrange a date so we get to know each other a bit better. I'd like that.'

'You would?' she asked, utterly astonished. 'You mean that?'

'Sure. I've only been here two days. You can show me around Dublin. Whaddya doin' tomorrow night?'

'It's like being a teenager again!' Dee told Maeve delightedly. 'Actually, I never did anything like that when I *was* a teenager, because I was fat, self-conscious and . . . yeuch, I don't even want to *talk* about then. But tonight, it was like being a teenager for the *first time*!'

She pirouetted around Maeve's tiny sitting-room gaily, hugging herself with delight. 'So *that's* what it felt like to be groped at a dance by someone you'd never met before?' she crowed. 'When I was in college, the girls used to talk about it and I'd pretend to know what they were talking about, but I hadn't a clue, really. I used to nod and look like I'd done it too. I even invented a guy who snogged me senseless at one party after I did my Leaving Cert exams. But,' she looked up at Maeve, her face momentarily sad, 'it never actually happened to me.'

'Well, it has now, you floozie,' said Maeve, giving her a poke in the ribs. 'I thought we were going to have to have him surgically removed from your body like the face-hugger in *Alien*. He was glued to you.'

'Oh, yes,' murmured Dee, remembering. 'Daryl can be glued to me any time. He has the most amazing body. He's all muscle, as hard as nails . . .'

'Hard?' asked Maeve. 'I should hope so, Ms O'Reilly, after all you were doing to him. If he *wasn't* hard after an hour of you sitting on his lap doing the Dance Of The Seven Veils And One Cardigan, I'd be worried.'

Dee grinned. 'I don't mean *that*,' she said. 'I didn't want to feel him up too much on our first date. I'll wait for the second.' Her eyes sparkled with glee. 'He's taking me to the movies tomorrow night and then we're going for a meal!'

'If you manage to get a seat in the back row in the cinema, you'd better book a take away for dinner,' advised Maeve, 'because if tonight's performance was anything to go by, the pair of you'll never make it to the restaurant. It'll be home. Wham, bam, thank you, mam. And, "Have you got anything to eat, honey? I'm ravenous." ' She mimicked Daryl's Texan drawl.

'I don't know if I could bring another man home to bed yet, not in mine and Gary's,' Dee said, sounding uncertain.

'Damn Gary. He swanned off and left you,' said Maeve belligerently. 'You could have it off with an entire army band in that bed and it's none of his bloody business. You should have brought Daryl home with you tonight and had mad, passionate sex in the bedroom, in the hall, in the front garden and on the kitchen table. That would have exorcised bloody Gary's po-faced ghost.'

'If I'd had any more to drink at Fiona's party, Daryl and I would've certainly ended up on the kitchen table,' joked Dee, 'but I'm glad we didn't. He's so lovely,' she added with a dreamy look in her eyes. 'I'd love to go out with him.'

'Don't book the church just yet,' warned Maeve. 'He may be one of those men who peak at two dates, you know. And don't forget, he's only here on his holidays. He might have a girl in every port and a few at home in Texas for spares.'

'I'm perfectly aware of all that and I don't care,' Dee

448

said happily. 'He's absolutely stunning and he wants me.' She had a flash of wicked inspiration. 'Do you think I should bring him to one of the pubs Gary's mates go to?'

Maeve cackled with delight. 'Brilliant idea! Please do. Can I come along and watch? I'd love it. Wear something utterly sexy and spend the evening wrapped around delectable Daryl, sticking your tongue in his ear. I bet you a tenner Gary will hear all about it before you've slammed the door on the taxi outside the pub.

'I've just had a better idea,' Dee breathed. 'Millie's dinner party . . . I'll bring him to that.'

CHAPTER TWENTY

Dee threw the tenth outfit on to the bed and despaired of ever finding anything utterly sexy for her date with Daryl. Everything looked horrible, especially the black jeans she'd bought at horrendous expense that morning. She abandoned the search for the perfect, irresistible outfit and looked in the mirror for what felt like the ninetieth time. The pale coral lace teddy – another credit card splurge earlier – was surely one of the most flattering pieces of underwear she'd ever worn. It'd need to be, she mused, it had certainly cost enough. Delicately laced under-wired cups were finished off with satin ribbon fashioned into tiny rosebuds, while the control panel that held in her tummy was covered in the same rose-patterned lace. Seriously high-cut legs completed the sexy but classy effect.

Even Dee, who'd been known to cry at the sight of herself in bra and knickers, was impressed. She hoped Daryl would be too. And for once, she'd managed to apply the fake tan evenly so that she wasn't mottled white in places and the colour of an elderly Jaffa orange in others.

Maeve had phoned that morning, strongly recommending a post-horrible-fiancé bonk.

'It'll do you good. There's nothing to beat the love of

a good, hunky Brad Pitt lookalike to make you feel better about life in general,' she urged. 'And stop panicking about AIDS. You've got your Dutch cap, you've got condoms. Just don't let him try anything with handcuffs.'

Dee had laughed uproariously but hadn't mentioned her fuck-me undies or her ruinously expensive new jeans. She still hadn't quite decided if she was up to having sex with another man after so many years with Gary. She wanted to make that decision herself, at the last minute.

The jarring ring of the doorbell interrupted her mental debate.

'Yes?' She peered out of the front bedroom window.

'Taxi, love,' roared up a middle-aged taxi driver. 'You going out in that?' he added with a salacious wink.

Dee wrenched her dressing gown off the bed and wrapped it around herself.

'You're early,' she yelled down at him, and glanced at her watch. 'Fifteen minutes early.'

'There's a concert on in the Point tonight, love,' the taxi driver retorted. 'I've got a booking for that and you won't get a taxi for love nor money then. So it's now or never.'

'All right. Give me five minutes,' Dee grumbled. She slammed the window shut and stared at the mess on the bed in horror. What the hell would she wear? Damn, damn, damn! It'd have to be the jeans. She'd already found everything to go with that outfit and if she decided on anything else, who knew how long it would take her rummaging around in drawers for the perfect tights to go with that perfect skirt or whatever?

Cursing, she dragged on the jeans, a slinky white low-cut T-shirt and her black leather jacket. She found her mercilessly high ankle boots – the only ones that looked good with jeans because they gave her some much-needed extra height – and pulled them on. Pausing only to fluff up her hair and give herself another squirt of Obsession, she ran down the stairs and was in the taxi a mere six minutes after it had arrived.

The taxi driver, a grizzled man who wore a tweed cap pulled disreputably down over one eye, grinned at her. 'I preferred the first outfit, love.'

Dee sniffed and looked out of the window. That was all she needed – a lecherous driver chatting nineteen to the dozen for the entire journey. But he didn't attempt any more conversation and drove at breakneck speed into the city centre, getting her to the Savoy cinema twenty-five minutes before she was due to meet Daryl. She couldn't hang around O'Connell Street that long, Dee realised. She'd be arrested for loitering with intent.

So she bought an evening paper, went into Madigan's and ordered a mug of coffee, resolutely ignoring the lure of the cheese and onion crisps that everyone else in the pub seemed to be eating. When she arrived at the Savoy again, Daryl was waiting for her, wearing his jeans, a white cotton T-shirt and a huge fisherman's sweater that looked like it had been knitted from Shredded Wheat. His blond, freshly washed hair flopped engagingly over his eyes and he kept having to flick it back with one hand.

'Hi, Dee.' He enveloped her in a huge bear hug, the sweater arms swamping both of them. He must have borrowed it. 'How're ya doing?'

'Fine.' She beamed up at him. 'Looking forward to this.'

'Me too.'

Arm in arm, they walked into the cinema, bought

their tickets, a vat of buttered popcorn and sat in the darkness waiting for the movie to start. Dee barely concentrated on the film, she was so conscious of Daryl sitting beside her in one of the cinema's few double seats.

She tried to sit as thinly as possible, holding her stomach in and keeping her crossed leg lifted off the one underneath, so it wouldn't look as if she had fat thighs.

Daryl didn't appear to notice all this effort on his behalf. At first, he merely held her hand, but when the scary bits started and Dee involuntarily shrank into the seat, he put one arm around her shoulders and held her close. She cuddled up to him and, even if she was going to have a crick in her neck from sitting at a slightly awkward angle, she wouldn't have moved for anything. Eventually, she abandoned her thin-thigh exercise and let her stomach flop out naturally. It *was* dark after all. He wouldn't be able to tell anyway.

Afterwards, Daryl was all praise for the director, a horror flick *wunderkind* he loved.

'Nobody does violence the way he does, he's so cool,' he enthused, as they strolled down O'Connell Street for Temple Bar.

Dee nodded, determined not to let on that she couldn't stand horror movies. She hadn't really cared what they'd gone to see. If he wanted to see a scarefest where everyone and their granny ended up as dog meat, then she wasn't going to argue. This was a *date*. You had to suffer for love, she thought happily.

Why else had she spent hours watching Gary's team play football on freezing Saturdays or endured hour after hour of European football when she really wanted to watch the romantic comedy on the other channel?

Temple Bar, Dublin's trendy Left Bank, was buzzing by the time they got there, Daryl's long left arm draped around Dee's shoulder, her arm around his waist.

Music poured from the open doors of the bars and pubs, and revellers spilled out on to the pavements, drinking their pints and eyeing up the talent that walked by. As on so many Saturday nights, the cobbled streets were jammed with half-plastered hen and stag parties from other countries, all giggling as they lurched from atmospheric pub to pub, intent on drinking too much Irish booze, grabbing a quick bite, and finally clubbing until the wee small hours.

As a result, the myriad restaurants that lined the streets were all full and by the time Dee and Daryl had made their way from the Elephant And Castle down as far as Bad Bob's via Fat Freddy's, Dee was beginning to wonder if she should have booked somewhere.

If all else failed, she decided, they'd squash their way into the madly popular Oliver St John Gogarty and order Guinness and lots of crisps to keep them going until the stag parties staggered off to Club M to dance the night away and the restaurant tables freed up.

'What about this place?' asked Daryl, spying a small Italian place down a laneway.

The tiny Italian restaurant had one empty table left and Dee sank into her seat gratefully. Her feet were killing her in the stiletto boots, she was ravenous, and the scent of garlic bread drifting out from the kitchen was doing unmentionable things to her taste buds.

They shared a basket of bread, drank a carafe of house wine and both had the special: clam linguine, which came with ciabatta and roasted peppers into the bargain.

Looking at his clean, faded denims, the cotton T-shirt

that had obviously been washed to within an inch of its life, and his plain old Timex with the worn leather strap, Dee reckoned that Daryl didn't have much money. She didn't want to embarrass him by ordering anything expensive.

He was determined to pay for the meal.

'You got the movie and the popcorn, dinner is my treat,' he'd insisted earlier.

She loved watching him eat and he certainly loved Italian food, twirling the coiled strands of pasta like an expert.

'Back home, my momma and grandmomma are into local American food so we don't go in for much foreign cooking. My brothers and I love this sort of food,' he said, forking pasta into his mouth with gusto.

'How many brothers do you have?' she asked. 'And what do they do? I don't know anything about you, do you realise that?' By the second hour of their second date, Dee had known everything imaginable about Gary, from the size of his family to how good he was at soccer and the highest break he'd ever had playing snooker.

Daryl was different. He wasn't a talker, had no real interest in telling her about his life. And she wasn't sure he was that curious about hers. To someone as incorrigibly inquisitive as Dee, that was strange indeed.

In fact, the more they sat there, drinking their spicy red wine and mopping up the tasty pasta sauce with the extra bread, the more Dee realised that she and Daryl had practically nothing in common. She was a reporter, permanently on the lookout for a fresh piece of gossip and eager to know everything about the handsome guy sitting across the table from her. He was happy to spend the entire evening with her without once asking her a personal question. She was a worker bee, constantly thinking about the next thing she should be doing and worrying if she wasn't achieving it. He'd drifted his way through college, had finally gone back to finish his degree at the age of twenty-five – he was, she was amazed to discover, twenty-seven – and wanted to travel the world for the rest of his life.

The South American trip was his third adventure. Before that, he'd spent six months in Alaska on an environmental protest – 'It sure was cold and there wasn't much to do where we were staying' – and several months in a commune in Mexico. His next trip was a year-long one to Nepal.

Dee felt her life story was horrendously boring by comparison.

'Going to work directly after college and staying in the same job for six years sounds like vegetating when I look at what you've done,' she said ruefully. 'I never wanted to leave Ireland. For good, I mean. I love travel and I'd love to be able to go all over the world but I don't know if I have the guts to do what you do, to work anywhere. I sound like a coward.'

'Hey, different strokes for different folks,' Daryl remarked, pushing his empty plate away from him. 'My two older brothers are married with kids, one in Austin, one in San Francisco. There's nothing wrong with it, I just don't want that sort of life.

'But,' he leant forward and wiped a smudge of sauce from her mouth, 'don't run yourself down for what you do. You've got a great job, a home, a life. Who knows? I may end up with nothing more than a worn-out back pack and some tropical disease that's eatin' me up from the inside out when you're a happily married woman with kids.'

Dee smiled wryly, thinking of how she'd screwed up

her most recent chance of being married with 2.5 kids. Spending four years with her had sent her last boyfriend hotfooting it to London. Perhaps she should hire herself out as some sort of incentive scheme for reluctant emigrants: Date Dee And Get The Courage To Leave Home And See The World.

'Fiona was tellin' me about this guy you were going to marry?' Daryl said.

Dee stared at him in surprise. She couldn't believe he'd asked Fiona about her, that didn't sound his style. No, Fiona must have brought it up when she heard he was going out on a date with Dee. She wasn't sure she wanted him to know about Gary. It was all too recent, too painful.

'You mentioned it last night,' he added, 'about how you'd been with this guy for years, so I wanted to know about him. He sounds like a complete asshole, that's for sure.'

Dee grinned. 'You said it.'

'Thing is,' Daryl looked faintly uncomfortable for the first time all evening, 'I don't wanna be moving in on you if you're still cut up about this guy. I don't wanna be an asshole too. You might need some time without another guy in there.'

Dee was incredibly touched. This handsome Texan drifter she fancied like mad, and with whom she'd practically had sex the previous night in someone else's conservatory, was behaving like the perfect gentleman.

He might only be in the country for a few weeks, but he didn't want to rush in, break her heart and then dump her. Her boyfriend of four years hadn't been that considerate.

'You're the least asshole-like guy I've met for a very long time,' she said softly.

Their eyes met over the flickering red candle that had melted halfway down during the meal. Dee knew how it felt. She'd been wondering what to do all evening and now sweet, thoughtful Daryl had shown her the way.

'If you like, we could skip coffee here and have it in my place?'

His eyes lit up wickedly and the handsome, golden face creased into one huge grin.

'I'd sure like that.'

By the time they got to Dee's house, she felt the taxi driver should have been paying *them* for the in-cab entertainment they'd provided on the trip home. Daryl had taken up where they'd left off the previous night, kissing Dee passionately as soon as they got into the taxi. When he'd slid his hand up inside her T-shirt, she could see the taxi driver's eyes drinking in the scene from his rear-view mirror.

'Nice place,' Daryl said, taking his mouth from hers briefly while she unlocked the front door and let them in. Then he was kissing her again, tongue probing hers, hands pushing off her leather jacket.

They practically fell on to the stairs, limbs everywhere as they grabbed at each other. By the third step, his Shredded Wheat jumper was off and Dee's T-shirt was around her armpits as Daryl kissed her body from her belly button up.

Halfway up the stairs, he unzipped her boots and wriggled her out of the skin-tight jeans.

He was so enthusiastic and so passionate that she didn't stop to worry about the red marks on her skin from wearing tight jeans. She was concentrating on pulling his T-shirt over his lean, muscled torso. Sitting up straight to pull it over his head, Dee had a chance to admire the flat, six-pack stomach tanned the colour of peanut butter, before he was pressed against her again, hungrily kissing her. His mouth was wide and desperate, his tongue thrusting against hers frantically.

The wool of the stair carpet was wiry and harsh against Dee's back. She moved uncomfortably, trying to settle herself into a decent position but it was impossible. With Daryl lying on top of her, she was being squashed into the stairs. It was a nice way to be squashed, but it was still uncomfortable.

'Let's go to bed,' she murmured into his ear.

Without saying a word, Daryl helped her up and followed her up the remaining stairs and into the bedroom, holding her hand tightly with one hand. The other was travelling over her coral-lace-covered bum.

Dee grimaced as she saw the bed covered in all her earlier discarded outfits – skirts, trousers and skimpy tops flung around haphazardly. She hadn't had time to put it all away. The place looked like a tornado had passed over.

But Daryl didn't appear to notice. He was engrossed in nuzzling her neck and sliding the straps of the teddy over her shoulders. Dee picked up a bundle of clothes, dropped them messily on the bedroom chair and turned back to him.

'Where were we?' he growled, pulling her to him and sliding the teddy down with one hand.

'You're beautiful,' he said, gazing at her full breasts, uncovered for the first time. He sat on the bed, pulled Dee towards him so that she was standing between his knees and buried his face between her breasts.

As he kissed, licked and sucked, Dee wrapped her hands around his head and let the desire flow through her. She felt wanton and earthy, a sexual and desirable woman.

Daryl touched her greedily, anxiously, as if she was a fantasy woman who was going to disappear if he didn't make love to her as if his life depended on it. Dee felt wanted and beautiful: an aphrodisiac cocktail that no amount of oysters, strawberries or champagne could equal.

Lovemaking with Daryl was a revelation. She was used to Gary's tried and tested methods which consisted of passionate snogging for five minutes followed by a further ten of foreplay and then another ten of energetic sex. A swift and exciting session, like a quarter of an opera, starting with slow song and moving up to a triumphant finale.

But if Gary's technique was one brisk, expertly executed movement where the conductor had one eye on the clock to avoid paying overtime, Daryl's was the entire opera with an award-winning symphony orchestra playing their hearts out as they recorded an album with Pavarotti.

He started gently, and after two hours reached a bed-shaking crescendo. By the time he finally slid inside her, Dee was damp inside and out, had already enjoyed two shattering orgasms and couldn't wait to feel him plunge into her quivering body. Moving in and out of her with long, precise strokes, Daryl waited until she'd come an unbelievable third time before he let himself go, his lean body shuddering with pleasure as he came.

'You're beautiful, Dee, so sexy,' he groaned, sinking on to the pillow beside her. 'That was somethin' else.'

'You're telling me,' she purred. Her body felt exquisitely tired, muscles warm and relaxed. She nuzzled into his shoulder, loving the feeling of his long arm draped comfortably over her waist.

She closed her eyes happily and waited for the

inevitable snores. Gary always fell asleep immediately after sex. It was better than Mogadon, he joked. But Daryl didn't drift off, leaving Dee on her own on one side of the bed as he settled on to the other with his back towards her. Instead, he moved until his mouth was beside hers and he could kiss her softly. His lips brushed her mouth, then her forehead and eyelids. His hands stroked her hot, damp skin tenderly. Cuddled up beside him like two spoons in a drawer, Dee was utterly content.

Sated and exhausted, they fell asleep a little after one a.m., limbs wrapped around each other, totally comfortable in the other's presence.

Dee awoke at three, hot, sweaty and thirsty. Moving in the bed to untangle herself from the mess of sheets and duvet, she woke Daryl up.

'Where are you goin', honey?' he murmured, stretching for her as she climbed out of bed.

'To get some orange juice, I'm so thirsty. Do you want some?'

'Yeah. Don't be long now.'

He welcomed her back to bed with the ardour of a round-the-world yachtsman who hadn't seen a woman for a year.

Dee found that half a litre of orange juice and a passionate lovemaking session put the kibosh on a burgeoning hangover far better than a pint of water and two paracetamol before going to bed ever had. And waking up with a warm, aroused body beside hers was infinitely more fun than being woken up by the blistering ring of the alarm clock.

Millie and Dan lived in a large semi in Malahide in the sort of housing estate that was perfect for kids. A large green dominated the centre of the estate, complete with adventure playground. As Dee and Daryl drove slowly into The Maples the following Saturday, gangs of kids playing football on the road stepped back to let their car pass. It was nearly eight on a balmy August evening and there was at least another hour of decent light left. The game restarted once they'd driven by, loud yells and squeals puncturing the calm.

Dee remembered watching the kids on her street playing five-a-side when she was young. She'd never joined in. Instead, she'd hung out of her bedroom window, stared at all the skinny kids racing up and down after the ball and wished she could play sports. Her brother Shane had been admitted to the football-on-the street club when he was old enough. He was always getting into trouble with their mother for using clean jumpers for goalposts and getting tar on them when the road surface melted in the sun. The only stains Dee ever got on her jumpers were from ice cream.

'Dan's a good cook, right?' Daryl asked when they stopped outside a neat, well-maintained house with a gleaming brass number 20 on the door. 'I'm starvin'.'

Dee laughed. 'You're always starving, Daryl. I don't know where you put it.'

He gave her a lopsided grin. 'My momma says she thinks I have a tapeworm inside me, that's the only reason I can eat so much!'

'Gross!' shrieked Dee as she pushed open the small white gate. 'I won't be able to eat a thing thinking about that.'

'Great.' He pinched her bum. 'We can go home then.'

'No, we can't.' She wheeled round and slapped his wrist.

Dan had obviously been busy in the garden, Dee realised guiltily as she and Daryl walked up the path past a tiny, beautifully manicured lawn and weedless flowerbeds. Dee's own garden was looking more like a butterfly sanctuary than ever. Not that it had been any better when Gary still lived with her.

Why was it that Millie had got one of the keen on gardening, keen on tidying-up and utterly responsible Redmond brothers, while she had ended up with the housework/gardening-phobic one?

Millie met them at the front door, her round face wreathed in a welcoming smile. 'Dee! I'm so pleased you could make it,' she said, giving Dee a sideways hug so as to avoid squashing her bump. At six months pregnant, Millie was the shape of a round-the-world balloon and nearly as big, as she joked herself. Tonight, she was dressed in a black silky cardigan that was stretched across her stomach revealing a pale blue T-shirt dress underneath. She'd put on loads of weight and looked as if she was ready to pop at any moment. Her strawberry blonde hair shimmered lustrously, her skin glowed and her freckles were more pronounced than usual thanks to hours spent in the back garden soaking up the summer heat.

Dee pulled Daryl into the Laura Ashley-papered hall. 'This is Daryl,' she said, a shade nervously.

'Hello, Daryl, welcome,' said Millie, and gave him a friendly peck on the cheek. 'I hope you like lamb *tagine*? Dan has been cooking for hours and he'll have a fit if you don't all love Moroccan food.'

'I love Moroccan food,' Daryl assured her.

Millie pushed open the dining-room door and led them in. Two other couples were seated around the glass-topped wrought-iron table. Dee's heart sank when she realised she didn't recognise anyone. She said a little prayer that nobody tactlessly asked how she'd met their hosts.

'Did you tell Dan I was bringing someone?' she asked Millie out of the corner of her mouth.

'Yes,' Millie whispered back. 'I think he got a bit of a shock.'

'Not half so much of a shock as I got when his beloved brother dumped me,' muttered Dee, rattled by the idea of introducing her new lover to her ex-fiancé's elder brother. This entire evening was a big mistake. Why had she ever thought she could pull it off? Dan would probably try to strangle Daryl between the lamb *tagine* and the Sambucca.

'Relax,' Millie said. 'You're entitled to bring anyone you want, Dee. Gary left you and that's what I told Dan. He's fine, don't worry.'

Dee felt so apprehensive she was almost nauseous but it was a bit late to back out at this point, so she said nothing. The last time she'd been in this house, Gary had been with her and they'd been celebrating Millie's birthday. It was only a few months ago but it felt like years. The memory was crystal clear. Gary had got plastered on illegal poteen from Millie's Donegal home-town and they'd ended up staying the night in the spare room on an ancient double bed that squeaked every time you moved an inch.

The next day, Dee, Dan and Millie had had a whale of a time teasing Gary about how much he'd drunk, asking him if he wanted a 'hair of the dog that bit him' hangover remedy purely for the fun of watching him turn forty shades of green at the very thought of touching alcohol . . .

Millie guided Dee to a seat beside the head of the

table and Daryl, ignoring the dinner-party etiquette which would have placed him opposite, sank into the seat beside her.

'You okay, honey?' he asked, knowing how uptight she was.

'Fine.' She gave his arm a grateful squeeze.

Millie made the introductions, instructed Daryl to pour the wine and made for the kitchen, from where the most amazing scents were drifting, along with the odd curse and the sound of saucepans clashing. Whatever Dan was cooking, it required lots of attention and he remained in the kitchen for ages.

After two gulped back glasses of red wine and the arrival of the last guests, Dee had almost forgotten how nervous she'd been about turning up on Millie and Dan's doorstep with a new boyfriend in tow.

Chrissie and Pat, newly married and unable to keep their eyes off each other, worked in the bank alongside Millie and kept finishing each other's sentences as they told how Chrissie could barely make toast and Pat had to do all the cooking.

'She's ruined one kettle already,' he said fondly, gazing across the table at his new wife with adoring eyes.

'Clever move,' remarked Jane, an attractive blonde woman who owned a dressmaking business. 'I wish I'd done that when we moved in together.' She shot Clive, a partner in Dan's firm, a meaningful look. 'Clive thinks housework is one of the great feminine mysteries, like waxing your legs and dyeing your eyelashes.'

Dee giggled into her wineglass. 'I used to go out with someone just like that. Thanks to an adoring mother, he thought housework was beneath him,' she said, before she realised where she was and who she was talking about.

At that instant, Dan appeared at the dining-room door, wearing an apron, a rather silly chef's hat and a frazzled expression.

'Hi, all,' he said. 'Sorry I haven't been talking to you but something went a bit wrong in the kitchen and I've been trying to sort it out. A man's work is never done.'

Dee blanched and hoped to hell he hadn't heard what she'd just said. But Dan wasn't looking at her. His eyes were on Daryl who was lounging back in his wrought-iron chair, heavy glass goblet in one hand and a proprietorial arm around Dee's shoulders.

Dan's eyes narrowed. In another sloppy jumper – this time, an enormous moss green one – black jeans faded to a shade of grey and with several thin leather bracelets wound around one wrist, Daryl looked like a street musician, a million miles away from Gary, the king of Next chic.

'Hello, Dan, lovely to see you,' said Dee gamely. 'This is Daryl.'

Dan said nothing for a moment.

Millie, watching everything over her glass of mineral water, prodded her husband with one finger.

'Hi, Dee. Hi, Daryl,' he said evenly, and loped around the table to give Dee a rather strained hug. For a dreadful moment, she thought he was going to say something about being sorry she and Gary had split up. But he didn't. He straightened up and held out a hand to Daryl.

Dee could see that Dan's mouth was set in a tight line. Not unlike his mother's, she thought absently. Gary had looked like that sometimes, generally when he was doing something he resented. The two men shook hands. Dan then sat down at the head of the table and poured himself a glass of wine.

'Cheers,' said Chrissie, who was sitting on his right.

'Cheers.' Everyone raised their glasses and the uncomfortable moment passed.

'What are you cooking?' Jane asked. 'And whatever it is, could you take Clive into the kitchen and show him how to make it?'

'He should show *you*,' snapped back Clive.

Dee winced and wondered if she and Gary had often brought their quarrels out with them, carrying the private war into other people's homes.

Probably.

The dinner party was anything but plain sailing. Clive and Jane bickered throughout the meal, and even though everyone else appeared to be used to their constant sniping, it unnerved Dee who felt more wound up than a clockwork toy.

It had been a mistake bringing Daryl here, she decided anxiously. It didn't matter that Gary had dumped her – Dan was still his brother and, as such, was watching Dee and Daryl with the disapproving countenance of the head nun at the second years' first mixed disco.

But eventually, lubricated with plenty of red wine, he loosened up and began to play the part of the genial host. He was helped along by Millie, the peacemaker, who kept refilling his glass with wine. The first course – lots of unusual dips with crudités, pitta bread and tortilla chips – was wonderful and spicy enough so that everyone but Millie and Dee, who was driving, drank far too much.

The lamb *tagine* melted in Dee's mouth, in much the same way as Daryl's right hand melted on to her flesh as it made its way under her mini skirt and headed north to the tender skin revealed by her stockings. It was a bit over the top to wear a charcoal suede mini skirt and sheer black hold-ups to an ordinary dinner party, but she hadn't been able to stop herself. Daryl made her feel so sexy that she loved dressing up for him and seductive lingerie drove him wild.

From the moment he had discovered what she was wearing under the suede mini, he'd been unable to keep his hands to himself. His fingers were like a mole on a timer, burrowing under her skirt every ten minutes.

When he was doing it, he didn't look at her, merely forked up his succulent lamb and appeared to listen intently to what was being said. Dee didn't know how she stopped herself from gasping while Dan recounted some long-winded story about a motorbike he'd once owned, because Daryl's long fingers were wickedly twanging the elastic on her knickers. He never stopped, she thought a little wearily. He had sex on the brain.

'Gosh!' she said, bright-eyed with interest as she pushed Daryl's hand away. He pushed right back. Dee could feel herself going pink in the face. She had to stop this. It was like sitting beside a horny octopus and the other guests were bound to notice soon. Hanky-panky in the bedroom was one thing, but Daryl didn't seem to realise that there was a time for everything. And this wasn't it.

She slid her fingers down to his knee and caught it in a vice-like grip, hoping he was ticklish. She squeezed expertly, fingers tightening on the sensitive hollows. He jumped, hit the table with both knees and all the glasses and the wine bottles vibrated noisily from the impact.

'Are you all right, Daryl?' inquired Millie.

'He's fine,' smiled Dee, thumping him hard on the back. 'A bit went down the wrong way, didn't it, darling?'

She gave him another thump for good measure.

'Sure.' He grinned back at her.

By dessert, Dan was nicely drunk and Daryl had wisely given up groping Dee's thighs in favour of running his fingers up and down the arm closest to him, occasionally sneaking in a quick stroke of her boob.

More relaxed because she figured Dan was too merry to care what Daryl got up to, Dee stopped minding and sat with one hand resting on his thigh.

When he and Jane weren't bitching at each other, Clive was a wonderful raconteur and had them all in stitches with a selection of stories and jokes. Dan's eyes were glazed by the time he served dessert, a summer pudding that was laced with *crème de cassis* and was truly lethal. Dee took one look at her heaped plate, covered with an over-generous dollop of cream, and vowed to eat nothing but grapefruit the next day.

'This is beautiful, Dan,' said Pat, licking his spoon appreciatively. 'I wish I could cook like this.'

'Darling, you can,' cooed Chrissie across the table.

Jane caught Dee's gaze and raised disbelieving eyes to heaven.

When they all retired to the sitting-room to drink coffee and liqueurs, Dee decided that she and Daryl would make their excuses after ten minutes.

'Fine by me, honey,' he whispered. 'I just wanna get you home and take a good look at those stockings.'

'Shush!' hissed Dee, conscious that Dan was right beside them, unsteadily placing bottles of Bailey's and Drambuie on the coffee table.

'D'ya want some help?' asked Daryl.

Dan gave him a hard look. 'I think you've got your hands full already,' he slurred.

Dee felt her heart skip a beat. Oh, no, there wasn't

going to be an argument, was there? She hated arguments. They shouldn't have come. It was a bad idea.

Spending time with Millie and Dan was one thing when she and Gary had been dating, but spending time with them now was a recipe for disaster. She and Millie had things in common and genuinely liked each other. But Dan, while he liked Dee, loved his brother and would probably never be able to look at her without thinking 'if only'.

'Dan,' interrupted Millie judiciously, 'boil the kettle, love. We need another cafetière of coffee. There are eight of us, you know.'

Dan left and Millie sank on to the settee beside Daryl and Dee. 'Poor dear, he's not taking it too well,' she said, watching her husband's lanky form shuffle into the kitchen.

'Dee didn't leave Gary, he left her,' pointed out Daryl helpfully.

'I know, but don't say that to Dan,' warned Millie. 'He'll go ballistic. He's very easy going normally but he's lost his sense of humour over this. He was convinced you two were meant for each other,' she added to Dee.

She sighed wearily. 'We'd better go,' she said. 'I don't want a fight and I reckon that's the way things are heading.'

'Don't go yet,' begged Millie, pale blue eyes filling up. 'I wanted us to have a lovely evening together. I don't want to lose touch with you simply because you're not going out with Gary any more . . .'

Dee put her arms around her. 'We won't,' she said, more hopefully than she felt, and handed Daryl the car keys. 'Do you want to go out and wait in the car while I say goodbye to Dan?'

'Sure.' He kissed Millie, said his goodbyes and left.

Dee made her way reluctantly to the kitchen. She didn't know what to say to Dan and wasn't in the mood for a drunken lecture on how she and Gary should get back together. Hell will freeze over first, she thought.

But Dan seemed to have got over his fit of pique. He was staring drunkenly out of the kitchen window into the moonlit garden, ignoring the steaming kettle beside him.

Dee cleared her throat. 'We're going, Dan,' she said awkwardly.

'Dee,' he muttered and flung his arms around her.

She felt a lump in her throat. Damn it, she didn't want to cry. Why was she even thinking about crying?

'I love you, you know,' he mumbled into her shoulder. 'You're like the little sister I never had.'

That did it. Dee felt a fat tear roll down her face.

'I love you too, Dan,' she said brokenly. 'Gotta go.' She tore herself away from him and marched into the hall, wiping away tears savagely.

''Bye, Millie. I'll phone you,' she called into the sitting-room before she banged the front door behind her.

'Why do they all behave as if *I'm* the one who broke up the bloody relationship?' she raged to Daryl as she climbed angrily into the car. 'Gary's the one they should be giving the guilt trip to, not me.'

'Hey, they're never gonna change the way they think,' he said pragmatically. 'You should keep out of their way. It's over and that's it.'

'You're right.' She crunched the car into first gear. 'I've had it up to my tonsils with the Redmonds.'

Morning was streaming in through a gap in the curtains when the phone rang beside her head. Dee opened one eye groggily, reached for her bedside table and dragged the receiver from the phone.

'Hello,' she croaked, barely able to talk from exhaustion. She and Daryl had made love for hours when they'd returned home. It had been at least two in the morning before Dee had turned out the light.

'Dee.' His voice made her sit bolt upright in the bed.

'Gary!' What was he phoning her for at . . . she glanced at the clock radio . . . ten-thirty on a Sunday morning? The answer was blindingly obvious – Dan had rung to tell him all about the previous night's dinner party, and, no doubt, the handsome young American who'd been all over Dee like a rash.

'I rang you in the office but they said you weren't in. I hope I didn't interrupt anything?' Gary said in a bitingly sarcastic voice, obviously having no clue as to what he *was* interrupting. 'You're not hungover *again*, are you?'

'I took today off,' she said.

Suddenly, Dee shot up in the bed again as she felt Daryl's hot, naked body stretch up from the bottom of the bed to press seductively against hers. His long arms reached up to caress her breasts, while his tongue jammed itself into her belly button, flickering kisses against the tender skin.

'Aaah!' she gasped in pleasure as his head went lower.

'Dee, what's going on?' Gary demanded.

She stifled a giggle. Maeve would adore this scenario – one man making love to her while her ex threw a tantrum over the phone, demanding to know what was going on. Gary would never in a million years think she was in bed with Daryl: it simply wasn't the sort of thing Dee did. Well, the *old* Dee wouldn't have. The new Dee was relishing the experience.

473

Daryl's tousled blond head appeared beside her and he kissed her deeply before turning his attention to her breasts. He attacked one nipple voraciously, sucking it into a little hard peak.

Dee moaned again and started stroking the back of his neck with one hand. The other hand, the one holding the phone, slipped down absently on to the pillow.

'Dee!' Gary sounded utterly outraged now, his voice was at that, 'What have you boil washed my football jersey for, you stupid cow!' tone. It was all she could do not to burst out laughing and tell him exactly what she *was* doing. How hilariously ironic.

A week ago she'd have been on the edge of her seat with nerves if Gary had rung, desperate for him to say he was coming back and that he still loved her. But four dates with a charming, polite, admiring and devastatingly sexy man had given her a whole new perspective on things. Gary had dumped her unceremoniously and now Daryl, lovely, sexy Daryl who was stroking her intimately with his clever, probing fingers, had given her back her confidence and made her feel like a desirable woman again, instead of a lump of lard who wore too much eye-shadow.

Tough bananas, Gary, she thought triumphantly. Yes, I *am* in our bed with another man and it's wonderful.

She sat up, kissed the top of Daryl's head gently before motioning him to be quiet and jammed the phone to her ear again.

'What do you want, Gary?' she asked, thrilled to have the upper hand for once.

'I want to know what's going on?' he demanded.

Dee's eyebrows lifted in amusement. 'What do you mean, "you want to know what's going on?" ' she said.

474

'I'm in bed, right? I was out late last night and now I'm tired. I've got the day off so I can spend all day in bed if I want to.'

Daryl's mouth turned up at the corners at this and he went back to kissing her nipple. Dee just stopped herself from moaning with pleasure.

'Anyway,' she continued, 'it's none of your business what I'm doing.'

'Who were you out with?' Gary asked.

Dee grinned to herself. He was playing games. He knew perfectly well. 'A guy.'

'A guy! What guy?' Gary demanded.

Daryl's white teeth gently nibbled her nipple, making her squirm excitedly. God, but he was good at that.

'You don't know him. He's American, a friend of Fiona's brother.'

'*American!*' Gary's voice was at screeching point now.

'Texan, actually,' Dee said. She was enjoying this.

'From Austin,' supplied Daryl loudly.

Dee sniggered.

'He's there now, isn't he?' Gary's voice was a howl of outrage. 'He's in bed with you, in *our* bed. I don't believe it. How could you?'

Dee lost her temper. 'What the hell do you mean, how could I?' she raged. 'You complete bastard! You left me nearly a month ago and I haven't heard from you since, apart from a bitchy note telling me to sell the house. You have no rights over me any more. We've split up.'

'Well, *I* haven't been out screwing around,' howled Gary angrily.

'And I haven't been screwing around either,' yelled Dee into the receiver. She felt Daryl place a calming hand on her shoulder and he kissed her softly on the cheek.

'Don't let him get to you, honey,' he whispered into her ear.

She nodded and took a deep breath. Why was she wasting her time even having this conversation with Gary? He had no right to ask her what she was doing now or who she was seeing. How dare he?

'I'm only screwing one person,' she announced calmly. 'We're sleeping late because we're exhausted. We were at it like rabbits all night. Satisfied, Gary?'

She listened to his outraged splutter for a couple of seconds.

'Anyway, I don't know why you're pretending you don't know about Daryl,' she emphasised his name, 'because I'm pretty sure Dan was on the phone to you at first light, filling you in on all the details of his dinner party.

'I just wish you'd tell your family that *you* left *me*, not the other way round, so they'd stop feeling responsible for getting us back together,' she hissed. 'It's about time I told Dan and Millie what a complete shit you've been. Maybe then they'd get the message.'

She slammed down the phone.

'Well done.' Daryl grinned at her. 'You told him.'

Dee grinned back, feeling like a naughty schoolgirl who'd just been caught round the back of the bike shed with a strange boy. She'd told Gary about Daryl and now he was insane with jealousy and rage. Ha bloody ha! Wait till she told Maeve.

Millie levered herself on to the armchair in Dee's sitting-room carefully and Dee put a cup of tea and a plate of biscuits on the small table beside the chair. Smudge appeared from nowhere and sniffed Millie's ankles with interest.

'Gary isn't impressed,' she said, trying to settle herself comfortably. 'He rang Dan almost immediately this morning, demanding to know everything about this Daryl you were seeing.'

Dee giggled into her coffee mug.

'Dan told him he'd only met Daryl for the first time last night,' Millie added, 'and said it was Gary's own fault if you were going out with some American. He left you after all.'

Dee blinked with surprise. Dan taking Gary to task for dumping her? She'd love to have heard that.

'When you went last night, I gave out stink to Dan and told him he had no right to give you or Daryl such a hard time,' Millie admitted. 'It really wasn't right. So, what happened with Gary?' she asked eagerly.

'It was priceless, Millie,' Dee smiled at the memory. 'He was outraged. I still can't believe I told him Daryl was there in bed with me!'

'That gave Dan a bit of a shock, too, I can tell you,' Millie said. 'He's furious with Gary for breaking up with you but was still hoping you two would get back together and this rather knocked him sideways.'

Dee shrugged. 'I understand, but I can't stop living and wait for Gary to get his act together and decide he really loves me after all. I need a life and I needed Daryl.'

'I agree completely,' Millie pointed out. 'He really is sex on legs. Hearing about him was just what your spoiled ex-fiancé needed. Realising he's got a serious rival might make Gary see sense.'

'I don't know if I want him to see sense,' Dee said blankly. 'I'm having fun, finally. It wasn't fun when Gary left, I can tell you. But Daryl is good for me. I'm not so sure Gary ever was.'

Millie sighed. 'I know what you're saying,' she admitted. 'It's just that Dan would love to see you two back together, it's his little dream.'

Dee didn't look at her for a few moments. She was thinking what a naive man Dan Redmond was.

'I don't know if I want Gary back. You know what he said to me.'

'You told me some of it,' Millie said, 'about your weight . . .'

'That wasn't the half of it,' Dee exclaimed. 'He said I hid behind a ton of make-up and that my clothes were loud, vulgar and not the sort of thing a deputy editor wore. I don't know if he really meant it or not but it was incredibly hurtful. And not very good for the old self-confidence.'

'He's a bastard, isn't he?' Millie said with a sigh. 'I mean, how could he say those things?'

'You tell me. Anyway,' Dee sat back in her chair, 'tell Dan that his precious brother really messed up this time.'

'I will.' Millie sat back with her mug in her hand and stared at Dee. 'I blame their mother, you know. She really got her claws into Gary when their father died. At least the others had some sort of normal home life, but he was Margaret's little pet. She spoiled him rotten.'

'She's welcome to him now,' Dee said flatly. 'More tea?'

When Millie left, Dee pottered around the house, tidying up and thinking about the past few days. When Gary had first left, his comments about her being a fat, ugly, over-made-up slob had cut her to the bone and made her think that everyone else would judge her in the same way. Now Dee was beginning to think that

Gary's viciousness showed just that – that *he* was vicious, not that she was guilty of all the things he'd accused her of.

She really was better off without him.

CHAPTER TWENTY-ONE

Isabel gazed blankly at the carpet. She couldn't concentrate on what the speaker was saying. The subject was Women In The Media and, as she was the next person on the podium to deliver an address to the several hundred delegates in the Burlington Hotel conference room, she *should* have been paying attention to everything the female TV producer was talking about.

Instead, she was thinking about that morning's trio of financial disasters. The bank manager had rung about her overdraft, which was now turning into an Atlantic Ocean-sized trough.

'Mrs Farrell, you should come into the bank so we can discuss things,' he'd said gravely. 'There are a few options I can recommend but we've got to sit down and talk about it.'

Isabel quailed at the thought of discussing her overdraft, particularly as it was December, Christmas was just around the corner, and Robin had put in an order for a computer.

Even worse, the gas boiler had just broken down and would cost hundreds to replace. Hundreds Isabel didn't have and which the bank clearly wouldn't be keen to lend her.

They'd woken up that morning to a freezing house

and no hot water. When Isabel went to investigate the only thing the boiler produced was a worrying belch.

To add insult to injury, she'd brought Naomi on a routine trip to the dentist before lunch to be told that train-track braces were definitely on the cards. Naomi had groaned at the thought of getting braces, particularly as she'd thought she'd managed to escape them while most of her class at school boasted metal mouths. Isabel had groaned even louder at the thought of the bill.

You were always so ready to criticise David's mishandling of finances but you've made just as big a mess of them yourself, she thought morosely as she gave up all pretence of listening to the speaker.

At least she hadn't wasted oodles of cash on any mad get-rich-quick schemes, but buying a Ralph Lauren blazer with matching chinos the previous Saturday – albeit at a designer second-hand shop – wasn't the wisest financial decision she'd ever made, either. The outfit was very classy and would have cost four times the amount Isabel had paid for it if it had been new. But given the crimson colour of her bank balance, it was an impulse buy she now regretted.

And all subconsciously to compete with Jack's wife, a woman who wouldn't put on a nightie unless it had Janet Reger written on it. Elizabeth Carter's make-up bag was probably Prada and Isabel was sure *she* didn't stock up on moisturiser while she was doing the weekly shop in the supermarket, throwing Oil of Ulay into the trolley along with the loo roll and a raft of yoghurts.

Isabel wished she didn't feel the constant need to compete with Elizabeth. It was so ridiculous, childish and unlike her. But she couldn't help herself. Simply hearing that Elizabeth had attended some glamorous party clad in head-to-toe designer clothes was enough to send Isabel into a fit of insecurity where she tore through her wardrobe, looking for something, *anything*, expensive and beautiful to wear the next time she saw Jack.

Not that he ever really talked about his wife, apart from saying whether she was in the country, out of the country, or busy organising some charity event or other. He certainly never discussed what she'd been wearing or how much she spent when she went on her regular shopping trips to Harrods and Harvey Nichols. In fact, his voice was always neutral while speaking of her, as if she was some distant relative whose movements were of little interest to him.

Isabel, however, found that she couldn't avoid hearing or reading about her lover's wife – and about her social butterfly existence and wardrobe to rival Nicole Kidman's.

Never a huge fan of the gossip columns, she was now drawn helplessly to them every day. Elizabeth's name constantly leapt out of the pages of newspapers and glossy magazines.

'Elegant as always in Gucci jersey and Manolo Blahniks to die for, Elizabeth Carter attended the opening of . . .'

'While most racegoers froze in their flimsy dresses and got heels stuck in the muddied grass of the owners' enclosure, Mrs Carter was both warm and effortlessly stylish in a cashmere Jasper Conran coat worn with a rakish Phillip Treacy hat . . .'

The articles were always accompanied by pictures of the fabulously dressed Elizabeth, looking as if a team of stylists had just spent a month working on her. She was so glamorous she made Isabel feel dowdy and dull.

Isabel, who'd never hated anyone in her entire life, found that she almost hated Elizabeth. If she was honest with herself, it wasn't because Elizabeth could afford to spend thousands of pounds on one outfit, while Isabel was worried sick about spending a fraction of that on a second-hand jacket. It was more than that.

Elizabeth had the things Isabel didn't – *she'd* never needed to start over again with no money because she'd had a feckless husband who'd ruined them. She'd been born with a silver spoon in her mouth and a private allowance which meant she had never needed to hold down a job. And she had a wonderful husband whom she didn't appear to appreciate.

That was it in a nutshell: Isabel hated Elizabeth for having Jack and not even appreciating him. Then again, Isabel admitted to herself, she only knew one side of the story. Perhaps Elizabeth adored Jack and was devastated when they'd drifted apart. And now she, Isabel, had practically taken him away from Elizabeth. So she didn't have everything, after all. She didn't have children, either. The poor woman had been denied that. Isabel couldn't imagine life without Robin and Naomi.

The familiar guilt crept into her head and she thought of how horrific it would be if Elizabeth found out about her husband's infidelity. Despite her otherwise charmed life, Elizabeth had had her share of sorrow.

To discover her husband was seeing someone else, was serious about someone else, could destroy a woman as emotionally fragile as her . . .

The sound of applause startled Isabel back to reality and she jerked her head around to the podium where the TV producer was wrapping up her speech with a few comments about how women had to do everything *twice* as well as men to advance their careers.

Isabel closed her eyes, took a few deep breaths and reminded herself never to agree to speak at one of these conferences ever again. She'd said yes on impulse and had been regretting it ever since.

Tanya Vernon had also been asked but had refused. 'Presumably,' Phil Walsh had remarked caustically, because there'd be nobody there she could sleep with to further her meteoric career.'

There was always the TV producer, Isabel thought wryly, as the very masculine-looking woman left the podium, stage lights glinting off glossy black hair that was barely an inch long.

Isabel rose, smiled a professional smile at the delegates and began her speech. As she stared at the interested faces below her, all women who'd battled their way up the career ladder in a male-dominated world, she felt a surge of pride at having won the women's editor's job in the *Sentinel*. She loved her job, loved the work and even the pressure that came with it. Her speech wasn't going to be one of those doom and gloom ones about how hard it was to be a working woman.

Twenty minutes later, after a standing ovation for Isabel's positive woman power speech, there was a break before dinner and the evening session. Now that she'd done her bit, Isabel had absolutely no intention of hanging around any longer. But before she'd managed to sidle out of the door, she was button-holed by one of the organisers, Alva.

'Isabel, you must have a glass of wine,' she announced. Alva was a formidable grey-haired woman dressed in a grey suit. 'I want to introduce you to some of our other panellists.'

Saying no to her was impossible, so Isabel graciously

allowed herself to be propelled towards a group of women in the centre of the room.

She sipped a glass of mineral water and chatted amiably, wondering how soon she could leave without being rude. The discussion wasn't anything to do with women in the media. Everyone was eagerly talking about a hatchet job of a biography that had been written about one newspaper proprietor and was about to be serialised in another paper.

'You can't get your hands on a copy for love nor money,' Alva said. 'There are no review copies available and the author has wisely left the country.'

'I'm sure I could get a copy if I wanted to,' remarked one woman coolly.

Isabel recognised Sophie Walker, a statuesque redhead who wrote a scurrilous diary page for one of the women's magazines. In her early-thirties, she would have been quite attractive had it not been for an over-large, upturned nose and the slightly surly expression on her heavily foundationed face. She was dressed entirely in pale blue, from her knitted jacket and long skirt right down to her glass bead necklace. Isabel suspected that a colour consultant had once told Sophie that pale blue was her 'best' colour. They'd been wrong. Only doe-eyed supermodels could get away with iridescent blue eyeshadow dusted over their eyelids.

'From what I hear from my contacts, the book blows the lid on everything from the way he runs that paper like his own private army, to stories about his many female friends,' Sophie said with heavy emphasis on the word 'friends'. 'They say he makes a big deal about the lack of morality in modern Irish society – and then made one of his girlfriends leave the country in case his wife found out they were having an affair. Are you planning to write anything about the book?' Sophie said, turning sharp eyes on Isabel. 'It'd be just up the *Sentinel's* street,' she added snidely.

Isabel felt a prickle of unease. There was something about the way Sophie had made that comment, which made Isabel think it wasn't just a throwaway remark from one journalist to another. Definitely not.

She shrugged. 'I don't know,' she said airily. 'That sort of article would hardly be my type of thing.'

'Really?' Sophie's face was disbelieving. 'I thought executive flings in rival papers would be grist to any tabloid's mill? Everybody loves a good gossip and stories about married newspaper bosses having it off with other women will have the whole country spellbound over its Cornflakes.'

Isabel's prickle of unease turned into full-blown, stomach-clenching fear. She was sure the other woman was talking about more than just one newspaper boss. What exactly had she heard about Sophie Walker? That she was a tough cookie with a nose like a bloodhound for gossip. And that an officeful of lawyers went through her articles with a fine toothcomb to make sure she didn't libel anyone – and that she could print as scandalous a story as was legally possible. The words *Sophie Walker* and *dangerous* ran through her head in a jarring refrain.

Unless Isabel was very much mistaken, Sophie knew something about her and Jack. After all, they'd been seeing each other for over four months and it was entirely possible that somebody had noticed something. Did Sophie know the truth or was she only guessing? Isabel dreaded to think of the consequences if she knew the truth.

'We all love reading about affairs, don't we, girls?'

Sophie trilled in an insincere tone.

Feeling rattled, Isabel rapidly ran through her options. She could laugh it off and hope to put Sophie off the scent. Or she could dump her glass and run, letting the gossip columnist think what she wanted to.

Isabel knew which option she'd prefer but she stayed where she was and planted a big fake smile on her face.

Dee had once told her she was utterly transparent. Now Isabel needed an Academy Award-winning performance.

'I'm not sure readers are that interested in affairs these days,' she said in a bored tone. 'It's so sordid, so low-rent. Being fascinated by other people's sex lives always strikes me as rather pitiable. I thought this country had advanced too much in the past few years to be interested in who's doing what to whom.

'Anyway,' she added, staring Sophie Walker down, 'the people who write about that sort of stuff nearly always get it wrong. You have to be so careful of getting your facts right, don't you? Or you and your paper get taken to the cleaner's. The most recent libel case won record damages, so it's not worth publishing if you're going to be damned all the way to the bank.'

'Don't talk to me about libel suits,' groaned a magazine editor. 'They're the bane of my life.'

'Really?' said Isabel interested. She swapped her mineral water for a glass of white wine and watched Sophie out of the corner of her eye. Her ploy appeared to have worked. The other woman looked a little taken aback at the direction the conversation had taken. That cocky look was gone.

She began to tell a bitchy story about an acquaintance's married boyfriend. Isabel pretended to be interested in a long-winded tale of a legal battle. But if anybody had noticed the way she was clutching her glass, they'd have seen that her knuckles were white.

After twenty of the longest minutes of her life, Isabel figured she could leave without giving Sophie Walker pause for thought.

'It was lovely to meet you,' she said, shaking Sophie's hand warmly. 'I'm sure I'll see you again.'

Outside, Isabel breathed in the cool December air and felt her stomach heave. She wanted to retch from fear and anxiety. Every instinct told her that Sophie Walker knew what was going on between her and Jack.

What should she do? Pray that she'd put the gossip columnist off the scent with her blasé act – or she hoped it had been blasé, anyway. Tell Jack? Or say nothing and wait for the inevitable piece in Sophie's column? She could see it now: *Which newspaper magnate has been getting overly involved in his paper, taking one of the tabloid's attractive female management team out to lunch to discuss ways to increase circulation over the Puligny Montrachet and lobster?*

Jack answered his phone on the third ring. Nobody knew the private line number but her and only he ever answered it.

'Oh, Jack, you won't believe what happened,' Isabel gasped into her mobile phone.

'What, darling?' he asked anxiously. 'What's wrong? Have you had an accident? Are the girls all right?'

Relief at hearing his voice made her suddenly emotional. Afraid she would cry, Isabel took a few deep breaths and tried to compose herself before continuing.

'No, I'm fine, and the girls are too. It's nothing like that. I was at the Women In The Media conference and I met this woman, Sophie Walker, a gossip columnist with one of the magazines ... I think it's *Hype* ...

Anyway . . .' Isabel took another deep breath . . . 'I think she knows about us. In fact, I'm *sure* she does.'

She shuddered at the thought.

'Isabel, don't panic, please.' Jack's voice was calm. 'What makes you think this woman knows anything?'

Isabel told him the whole story.

'I've heard of Sophie Walker before,' Jack said grimly. 'She's written some pretty nasty things about friends of mine, although she was rapped over the knuckles last year when she made a not-so-veiled reference to a relationship between a trainer and one of his grooms. The magazine was stung for a couple of hundred grand, so she's got to be careful what she writes now. And you handled the situation perfectly,' he said encouragingly.

'I don't know,' fretted Isabel. 'She was so cocky, so sure of herself. What if she writes something?'

'She won't. She was simply prodding you for information. She didn't get any so she's not going to print anything.'

'Are you sure?' asked Isabel. 'I'm so afraid . . .'

'Don't be,' Jack said firmly. 'It'll be OK, I promise. Forget about Sophie Walker. What time can you meet me tomorrow?'

Isabel dried up the last plate and put the stack in the cupboard. She balled up the tea towel and stuck it in the washing machine then surveyed the kitchen. Everything was sparkling, ready for Jack's visit. Eagle Terrace wasn't a palace by any means, certainly not up to Temple Isis standards. But she was proud of it. She'd worked hard to make the small terraced house into a home and reckoned she'd done it more successfully than Elizabeth Carter had with her icy, antique-filled mausoleum.

Stop that, she told herself. She hated being so jealous, so competitive. But she couldn't help it. At the back of her mind there was always the thought that Elizabeth had to have something she didn't . . . Stop it, stop it, stop it! she raged.

Determined to keep her mind off Elizabeth, Isabel rearranged the settings on the breakfast bar for the fourth time. Jack always brought champagne when he came for lunch, so she had bought two pretty champagne flutes to drink it out of. She kept them right at the back of the saucepan cupboard so Robin or Naomi wouldn't find them.

Isabel wasn't sure if she could cope with questions about mysterious champagne glasses when they never had any. It was bad enough coming up with excuses for taking so many calls at night on her mobile phone. Robin was openly curious but apart from giving Isabel knowing looks when the phone rang, she'd said nothing, partly because she was receiving more than a few phone calls from a deep-voiced youth herself.

The doorbell rang and Isabel felt her heart race. He was here. Jack stood at the door, handsome in a grey open-necked shirt worn with a charcoal suit, pewter eyes glinting excitedly. His arms were full of flowers, a huge bouquet of the Stargazer lilies Isabel loved, and stuck awkwardly under his arm was a bottle of champagne.

'Hello, darling, I think I'm going to drop this,' he said. She ushered him in, took the champagne and the flowers and put both on the hall table. Jack grabbed her and threw his arms around her, hugging her to him fiercely as he kissed her.

'I missed you,' he murmured, as his lips sought hers.

'I missed you too, Jack,' she replied before they lost

themselves in an urgent kiss.

Isabel felt a surge of desire as she clung to him, arms entwined. No matter how often they saw each other, and they met up at least every second day, she still felt that rush of passion whenever he held her.

Jack left her mouth and buried his face in her neck, resting his head on her shoulder briefly. She stroked his hair, loving the way the tension seemed to leave his body when he was in her arms.

'You feel wonderful.' He held her at arm's length. 'And you look beautiful, as always. Is this new?' he asked, fingering her red crêpe blouse.

'Yes,' Isabel answered. Well, it was new to *her*. Not telling him about her second-hand clothes foraging was her only vanity.

'You have such beautiful taste, my darling,' he said. 'Mine isn't anywhere near as good, but I bought you a present. It's in the car.'

He went out and returned with a carrier bag and a large white box, carefully tied up with a white ribbon. 'I hope you like it,' he said, handing her the box.

Isabel delightedly opened it, unwrapped several layers of tissue paper and gasped.

There lay the most exquisitely finished ivory silk dress she'd ever seen. She held it up carefully, revealing a beautiful long bias-cut dress that rippled as she examined it. Two delicate straps held it up, crossing over in the most intricate back detail. With her practised eye, Isabel didn't need to look at the label to see that it was a Ben De Lisi, an original from one of her favourite designers.

She'd featured it in her fashion column a fortnight previously, an amusing piece about what a committed shopaholic could buy if money was no object. Jack must have read the article. She felt a lump rise in her throat. Nobody had ever given her such a thoughtful present before.

'It's beautiful,' she said. 'I love it. Thank you, Jack.'

He kissed her forehead tenderly. 'I thought you could wear it in Paris. If you'll agree to come with me, that is?'

'Paris?' she asked, in amazement.

'I thought we could go next month, three days on our own with no interruptions,' he said eagerly. 'As a belated birthday celebration for your fortieth.'

'But we went to Belfast for my birthday,' Isabel pointed out, remembering their three-day September break in the Culloden, the only hotel she'd ever visited where the grown-ups got a rubber duck in the bathroom.

'That doesn't count because we didn't have to fly anywhere,' Jack argued happily. 'And Paris in the springtime sounds so romantic. Please say you'll come?' he begged.

Isabel pretended to look confused. 'January isn't springtime, is it?' she asked. 'Maybe we should wait . . .' She beamed at him. 'I'm only teasing, darling. I'd love to go with you.' Paris in January. It sounded wonderful.

After a lunch of omelettes, crusty bread and champagne, they went upstairs to Isabel's bedroom and made slow, languorous love.

They then curled up together under the duvet and talked, perfectly content in each other's arms.

Isabel kept a wary eye on her alarm clock, nevertheless. The girls got out of school at four, went to her mother's for an hour, and were usually home by half-five. But every time she and Jack had spent the afternoon in her home, Isabel had been nervous that they'd arrive home early for some reason and every noise in the

street made her jump. Which was why she leapt frantically out of bed when the doorbell rang at half-three.

'Oh, no,' she shrieked. 'Who could that be?'

'It's not the girls, they've got keys,' Jack reminded her.

'You're right,' she gasped in relief.

'It's probably somebody selling something, Isabel.
Don't answer it, they'll go away.'

'You're right.'

But the bell rang again, this time a longer ring. Isabel
peered out of the window, trying to see who was below
but she was at the wrong angle.

The bell rang a third time.

'Damn!' She pulled on her dressing gown. 'I'd better
go down.'

She opened the front door, prepared to give out stink
to whatever salesman had rung three times. But the
words died in her mouth when she saw who stood on
the step.

'Isabel,' said a very smart, forty-something blonde
woman in an expensive-looking beige wool coat with a
matching hat jammed on her dead straight bobbed hair.
It was Robin's best friend, Susie's mother. 'I knew you
were here when I saw your car. Are you sick or
something?' she asked, staring at Isabel's hastily tied
dressing gown.

She felt herself flush. 'No, Amanda,' she lied. 'I . . .
er . . . took a couple of hours off to . . . do some
housework. The place gets so messy. I was having a bath
afterwards,' she said nervously, hoping she didn't look
like she'd just got out of bed after a glorious afternoon
in bed, glowing from Jack's lovemaking.

This was all she needed. Amanda was anything but
stupid and if she figured out exactly what Isabel was
doing at home at half-three on a Thursday afternoon,

494

she was bound to let it slip to Susie, who'd tell Robin . . .

'I thought you were hoovering or something and didn't hear the bell,' Amanda said.

'Come in,' Isabel said hurriedly. She was about to lead the way into the kitchen but remembered that the debris of a romantic lunch for two was still there, so pushed open the sitting-room door instead. Unfortunately, it was directly under her bedroom. The floorboards upstairs creaked suspiciously.

Amanda looked up in alarm. 'What was that?'

Isabel blinked. 'A mixture of ancient floorboards and next-door's cat,' she announced. 'Tiddles sneaks in through the kitchen window and goes up to lie on the beds.'

'How awful!'

'What did you want, Amanda?' Isabel asked as politely as she could. 'It's just that the bath will get cold.'

'Oh, I just wanted to check if you could pick up the girls tomorrow night for me? We're going out to dinner and I hate asking but . . .'

Isabel gritted her teeth. Amanda was always 'just asking'. But this wasn't the time to refuse.

'No problem,' she said cheerfully.

'Great.' Amanda went into the hall. 'I do love what you've done with this place,' she added, looking around. 'It's so elegant. My best friend lives five doors down and her place is nowhere near as nice as this.'

'Really?' said Isabel faintly.

It was getting even worse, Amanda had a friend who lived down the road – a friend who probably noticed a strange Jaguar parked outside Isabel's house at least once a week.

The upstairs floorboards creaked again.

'Bloody Tiddles,' said Isabel, wrenching open the front door. 'Don't worry about tomorrow night, Amanda,' she said brightly. 'I'll pick up the girls. Must fly, I hate cold baths. 'Byee.'

'Tiddles?' said a highly amused voice from the upstairs landing.

'Tiddles will be shot for making so much noise,' said Isabel, climbing the stairs wearily. 'You were like a roomful of cats, not just one.'

'I wanted to know who it was.'

'The mother of Robin's best friend,' she answered, 'who is, no doubt, already planning to ask my daughter what outsized breed of cat our neighbour has, the one that sleeps on the bed and weighs ten times as much as any normal cat?'

'She won't,' Jack said consolingly.

'You don't know Amanda,' brooded Isabel. 'And I don't really know the neighbours here. For all we know, there could be ten rival reporters living across the road, waiting for the day they catch a glimpse of us starkers in front of my window so they can have an interesting front-page splash.'

Jack cuddled her. 'Don't fret, Isabel,' he said softly.

Isabel felt a sense of foreboding from the moment she walked into the Clarence, clutching her coat closely around herself to ward off the freezing cold. A monument to modern design and elegance, the Clarence was all Art Deco, polished wooden floors and minimalist furniture. It was also, she knew, very fashionable and almost always busy.

Not really the ideal spot for a quiet lunch with your married lover, she thought, pushing open the door into the Tea Room restaurant and relinquishing her coat to a waiter.

Having their romantic lunch at home so rudely interrupted the day before had given her the jitters. She'd spent the evening half-expecting Amanda to phone up and say, 'Bath? Pah! You weren't having a bath, were you? My friend saw a man leave your house at half-four . . .'

'This way.' The waiter led her past the other diners to a table where Jack was waiting.

'Isabel,' he said with a smile, rising as she arrived.

'Jack,' she said warmly.

Seeing him relaxed her. What had she been worrying about? Plenty of people met for lunch every day. That didn't mean they were having affairs, did it? So what if the neighbours and nosy Amanda suspected that Isabel was involved with someone who arrived at the oddest hours? It was her business.

She slid gracefully into her seat – and gasped.

Sitting a few tables away, clad in her trademark blue, was Sophie Walker, the columnist who'd been making innuendoes at the Women In The Media conference earlier that week. She wasn't looking at Isabel or Jack but, from the position of her table, she wouldn't be able to miss them. Isabel felt her legs grow weak and sank back in her chair.

'You won't believe who's sitting about fifteen feet away,' she said from between clenched teeth.

'Who?'

'Sophie Walker.'

'You're not serious?' Jack asked.

'I really wish I wasn't,' Isabel said, attempting to keep a fixed smile on her face as she took the menu from the waiter. 'If she sees us – and there's no way she *can't* when she turns away from the man she's with – she'll definitely write about it.'

'Let's look like we're having a business lunch,' Jack suggested.

'Right.' Isabel dragged her chair as far away from his as she could. Then she pulled some papers from her handbag and laid them ostentatiously on the table between them.

'We can pretend we're talking business if she comes over,' she said anxiously, knowing in her heart of hearts that a few papers between the wineglasses wouldn't fool someone like Ms Walker for a nanosecond.

Lunch was hell. Isabel hardly noticed the delicious food, she was so busy concentrating on looking business-like and smiling brightly at Jack in what she hoped was an unlover-like way.

By the time Sophie and her party left, she hadn't looked in their direction once and Isabel crossed her fingers that the other woman simply hadn't noticed them.

'Maybe she didn't see us,' she whispered to Jack hopefully.

But as Sophie pushed in her chair, she turned in Isabel's direction and gave her a little wave, a malicious smile on her normally surly face.

Isabel felt her stomach sink but waved back, her own smile frozen in place.

'I should have known,' she said bleakly. 'We're fin-ished, Jack. That woman will have it on the six o'clock news.'

He walked her back to the car park, doing his best to comfort her. For some reason, he didn't appear to be too put out by the gossip columnist's appearance. He seemed calm and quite relaxed.

'We haven't been that lucky lately,' he said wryly, putting a strong arm around Isabel as they stood beside her car in the high-rise car park.

'No,' she said shakily.

He kissed her on the lips. 'Don't worry, Isabel, it'll be fine,' he promised. 'You'll see.'

She didn't see how it could be, but she said nothing. On the drive back to the office, she thought of their planned trip to Paris. If news of their affair was made public – as now seemed inevitable – she could forget that.

'Mum, can I borrow your crystal drop earrings for the disco?' Robin didn't bother to come downstairs, she simply leant over the banisters and yelled loud enough for Isabel to hear her in the kitchen.

'Sure,' Isabel replied wearily. She didn't give a damn. Robin could borrow her entire wardrobe for all she cared. She sat miserably in the armchair in the kitchen, staring blankly at the TV but not seeing anything. Naomi was upstairs with her friend, Emer, who was staying over for the weekend.

Robin was tarting herself up for the disco. She'd spent an hour in the bathroom and the overpowering scent of bubble bath, deodorant and Isabel's Ô de Lancôme wafted through the house.

Amanda was picking Robin up in half an hour to drive her and Susie to the disco. Isabel couldn't face her and had asked Robin to get the door when Susie arrived.

'I've got a headache. Susie's mother is sure to want to come in and chat and I'm not feeling well enough,' she'd told her daughter.

It was hard to imagine that just a day before she'd

been so frantic at the thought of Robin's meeting Amanda and discussing the exploits of the non-existent Tiddles, Isabel thought glumly. It didn't matter now, not in the slightest. Jack would soon be out of her life, she wouldn't have to cover up any more.

She wiped away the tear that slid down her cheek. It was as if Amanda's interruption had signalled the destruction of everything precious in her life. It had all seemed perfect until Amanda had turned up, and until lunch earlier today. Since then, Isabel's affair had turned from the most wonderful thing in her life to something doomed.

She felt so desperate, so utterly miserable. Seeing Sophie Walker had brought everything to a head. Sophie would spill the beans, Isabel knew it. The *Sentinel* women's editor having an affair with the paper's proprietor was too juicy a story to sit on. It would be plastered all over Sophie's magazine within days, and then all over Dublin.

Isabel couldn't bear to think what would happen when Elizabeth found out about it. She'd give Jack an ultimatum and Isabel was so very scared that he'd choose his wife. Well, of course he would. Which would leave her picking up the pieces of her life. Again.

When Robin left, Isabel heard Naomi and Emer belt into her bedroom, giggling madly. Naomi had suddenly become very interested in clothes and took every opportunity to try on her elder sister's things. Only when Robin was out, naturally, as she wasn't so keen on having her things borrowed as she was of borrowing Isabel's.

'What's yours is mine and what's mine's my own,' Isabel teased her occasionally.

She almost didn't get up when she heard the phone

ring loudly in the hall. It couldn't be for her, she thought morosely, before remembering that it *could* be because her mobile phone's battery needed recharging.

It was Jack.

'Hi,' she said in a monotone, and sank on to the bottom stair. 'How are you?'

'Great, but you certainly don't sound too good,' Jack replied, his voice concerned.

'I'm not,' Isabel said, and suddenly fat tears started to pour down her face. It was as if a dam had broken and all the misery, loneliness and worry came flooding out. 'I'm sorry,' she snuffled, 'so sorry.'

'What's wrong, Isabel?' he asked in desperation.

'Everything,' she sobbed. 'Everything. That woman seeing us today . . . it means it's all over, you know that. She'll write about us and then you'll leave me.' She hated sounding so clinging, so desperate, but she couldn't stop herself. 'I can't bear to think of not being with you, Jack,' she said. 'I love you, don't you understand that? I love you.'

There, she'd said it. It was out in the open. She loved him. There was silence at the other end of the line. Oh, God, what had she done? She'd scared him away. Isabel wiped her face roughly with her sleeve, waiting.

'Isabel,' he said abruptly. 'I need to see you. I don't want to say this over the phone, I want to see you.'

Suddenly, she felt scared. What was he going to say? What could be so portentous that he needed to be with her while he said it? That he'd decided to end their affair – especially as she'd declared her love for him and put him under pressure? She could imagine it: *It was just fun, Isabel, I thought you knew that? I thought you felt the same? I never meant you to fall in love with me . . .* Her heart fluttered painfully in her chest and she felt a fresh flood of tears rise inside her. Please, no . . .

'I love you, Isabel. I'm crazy about you too. And I don't want to spend any longer living this half-life with you. I want to be with you all the time. I want to live with you, if you'll have me?'

'Have you?' she whispered. 'I'd love to be with you, it's what I've dreamed of. I always hoped, I just could never be sure . . .'

'You can be sure now,' Jack said fervently. 'Being with you has made me see what a sham my marriage is. I can't stay with Elizabeth, I don't love her the way I love you. We've just stayed together because it was easier, simpler, to do that than to part. But I can't do it any more.'

Isabel listened joyously. Every word he said was music to her ears.

'I know that we haven't even known each other that long, but it feels like a lifetime,' he said.

'I know,' she replied. 'I can't imagine my life without you. I thought that's what you were going to say just then. I thought I'd scared you off by telling you I love you.'

He laughed, a deep throaty sound. 'I've wanted to say that for so long, but I was afraid of rushing you. I think I've loved you from the moment I saw you, even if that does sound as corny as hell.'

'I don't care,' she said happily. 'You can be as corny as you like when you say wonderful things to me. I feel just as corny – I love you so much.' Isabel searched her pockets for a tissue.

'I don't want us to have to hide how we feel any more. Lunch today made me realise that. I hated you pushing your chair away from me. I hated the fact I couldn't touch you or kiss you in case that woman saw us. So I want all that subterfuge to end.'

Isabel glowed with happiness.

'I need to do one more thing before I leave Elizabeth,' Jack was saying. 'I want to get her into a rehab programme so that she's off drugs. I owe her that much, Isabel. It'll take a little while, but you do understand, don't you?'

'Of course,' she said automatically. Anything was OK so long as she had Jack.

'Oh, Isabel, I love you, I love you, I love you. I'll never get tired of saying it,' he murmured.

'Don't stop then,' she replied.

'I've got to go, I'm afraid,' he added regretfully. 'I'm still in the office and I've got to meet one of the directors from the UK company for dinner.'

'You're still at work?' Isabel asked, shocked. 'It's half-eight, Jack! You'll kill yourself.'

'No, I won't,' he laughed, 'but it's lovely to have you worrying about me, although there's no need to.'

'Of course there's a need to when you work such ridiculous hours,' she fretted.

'I'm crazy about you, Isabel, do you know that?' he asked warmly.

'Yes,' she replied ecstatically.

When they'd hung up, Isabel sat on the step, hugged her knees to her chest and looked around the small hall with pure delight. Everything looked wonderful, even the dusty hall table with its bowl of wilting roses and the collection of trainers, umbrellas and tennis balls under it. Life was wonderful. Jack was wonderful. And he loved her, adored her, wanted to be with her.

He'd finally said it: he loved her. And not just that. He was going to leave Elizabeth. They had a future together, a glorious future. If only Jack could help Elizabeth to get over her drug addiction. He'd do anything to get her off drugs. Isabel felt a quiver of unease. What if he couldn't? What if Elizabeth got worse? Would he leave her then?

CHAPTER TWENTY-TWO

Dee signed the document with a flourish and handed back her solicitor's pen. She'd done it! The house finally belonged to her. Of course, she'd be utterly broke for Christmas, not to mention most of the following year, and had already warned her family and friends not to expect anything but the tiniest presents. But it was worth it.

Ever since Gary had left, he'd been harping on about selling the house they owned jointly so they could split the profits.

Dee had soon realised that she didn't want to leave the pretty little townhouse. She liked living there, she liked the area, she liked her neighbours and she liked being so near to the office. So she'd decided to buy Gary out.

'Signed, sealed and delivered,' she said happily to her solicitor.

'The building society has to amend the documents to show just your name, which may take a couple of weeks, but otherwise, yes, it's signed and sealed,' he answered.

Dee left his office on a high, the sort of high that would normally send her straight to Grafton Street on a shopping binge. Not for the moment, she told herself firmly. Shopping, even her favourite January sales blitz, would have to wait until she'd cleared all the stamp duty and solicitor's bills. Women of property had to be careful with their cash.

She hurried along Baggot Street in her short fake fur coat, a spring in her step. The sight of a pretty girl in glossy black fur, shapely legs emphasised by sheer tights and spindly suede court shoes, a swathe of chestnut curls swinging along behind her head, elicited a whistle from a passing motorbike courier.

Dee winked joyfully at him and then ducked into Searson's pub when she thought he was stopping the motorbike to talk to her. She had to stop being so bouncy and friendly with strangers. It was always getting her into trouble.

Peering around the pub door a minute later, she saw that the courier hadn't stopped after all and resumed her journey, resolving to keep her eyes firmly on the ground.

The house was hers. Yahoo! She need never worry about Gary Redmond again.

A silver Porsche growled to a stop beside her and the driver honked his horn loudly, giving her a shock. What had she done now? Dee wondered in astonishment. Was she giving out invisible Come-and-get-it-big-boy signals or something? It must be the coat. Fun fur seemed to attract all sorts of unwarranted attention. Men thought that 'fun fur' equalled 'fun girl'. It'd have to go.

She flicked back her hair, stuck her nose in the air and hurried on.

'Dee,' roared a low, husky voice she recognised. She stopped and stared at the Porsche's driver. It was Kevin Mills.

'Do you want a lift?' he asked, leaning over towards the passenger window.

Dee hurried towards him. 'No,' she said regretfully. 'I've got my car. It's parked around the corner.'

Trust her to have her car with her on the one occasion when the utterly gorgeous photographer offered her a lift. And he *was* looking gorgeous today. His short dark hair was sleeked back from his forehead, he had a few days' stubble on his square jaw and wore a black polo-neck jumper that made him look like the hero in some hip French movie.

'Where's your car?' Kevin asked.

'Parked beside the canal.'

'Hop in. I'll drive you round,' he said, black eyes glittering.

Suppressing a beatific smile, Dee opened the passenger door. She hadn't realised the seats were so low and practically fell on to the cream leather, ending up with her flirty little chiffon skirt halfway up her thighs, exposing a lot of leg.

Kevin's eyes flickered over her before he turned his attention to the wing mirror and nosed his car back into the traffic.

Dee sat back in her seat gleefully and tried to arrange herself elegantly, pulling down her skirt and adjusting her coat so he'd realise *it* was bulky and not her. Kevin was really going out of his way to drive her back to her car, she thought with pleasure as he pushed through the heavy traffic. It would take at least ten minutes to reach it this way. On foot, the journey would have taken her five.

She flashed him a radiant smile. 'You're very good for doing this,' she said, watching his handsome profile.

Kevin's mouth curved up at the corners.

'No problem. I haven't seen you for ages anyway. You can tell me what you're up to.'

Dee couldn't wait to. 'I've bought my ex-fiancé's half

of the house, so it's totally mine now. I've literally just signed the papers in my solicitor's.'

'Congratulations,' Kevin said. 'He didn't deserve you.'

Dee's smile widened. 'When he left, I realised I liked living there on my own. He wanted me to sell up so we could split the money. He's in London and wants to buy somewhere there, I suppose,' she said. 'This way, I never have to see him again.'

'You've no regrets, then?' Kevin asked, eyes on the road.

Dee briefly wondered why he was asking her that question. 'None at all,' she answered firmly. 'What have you been doing anyway? Any good assignments?'

'Mostly news and celebrity-hunting. I've been offered a skiing junket to Kitzbuhl next month and I'm still trying to work out whether I should take it or not.'

'Skiing,' said Dee dreamily. 'I've always wanted to go skiing. I have this little fantasy that skiing holidays are all adorable log cabins, with roaring fires, soft rugs and big glasses of *gluhwein* when you come in after a hard day on the slopes.'

Kevin stopped the car and ran his eyes over her again. 'That's a very nice fantasy,' he said softly, his voice like hot, dark honey. 'I can picture it right now. Is it a fantasy for one or for two?'

Dee flushed rosily. 'Two,' she muttered, suddenly not knowing where to look. The way Kevin was staring at her, his black eyes drinking her in, was too much.

'I'd better go,' he said ruefully, glancing at the diver's watch on his wrist. 'I'm late for a job.'

'Of course,' Dee said in confusion, and grabbed the door handle.

'Congratulations again, on sorting out your house,' he said. 'I'm happy for you.'

He bent over towards her. Dee expected him to peck her on the cheek but instead he kissed her deliberately on the mouth. Stunned at the feeling of his lips against hers, she did nothing for a moment. Just closed her eyes and breathed him in. He smelled and tasted wonderful, his mouth so warm, so soft.

Kevin moved away slowly, his face only a fraction away from hers.

'I've been inviting you for a drink for months now, do you think you might be free soon?' he asked, eyebrows raised quizzically.

'Yes! Tonight in fact.' Dee could have kicked herself as soon as she'd said it. *Tonight!* He'd think she was desperate. Why hadn't she ever been able to play it cool? But Kevin was nodding. He leant back in his seat and stretched out one long thigh easing the bunched-up muscles with his left hand. Dee tried not to stare.

'Tonight would be wonderful. Will I pick you up?'

'No,' said Dee abruptly, thinking of the mountain of dishes in the sink she'd have to do before inviting anyone in.

'I'll meet you somewhere then. How about eight in Magee's?'

'Perfect,' she breathed.

'I'm looking forward to it,' he said.

She climbed out of the car and waved as he roared off down the road. Wow!

Dee wasn't sure how she drove back to the office without crashing the car, she was on such a high. She had a date with Kevin Mills that evening. Wait till she told Maeve and Isabel.

It was odd that Kevin had never asked about Daryl, even though Dee was sure he knew about her Texan boyfriend. Well, ex-boyfriend. Daryl had gone home over a month ago and while Dee missed his exuberant lovemaking, 'specially when she was alone in her big double bed with nothing but the cuddly seal he'd bought her for company, she was quite content without him.

Daryl had been a lovely, deeply sensual interlude, like the sexy bit in a novel – thoroughly enjoyable for a while but not the sort of thing you wanted all the time. He'd been sweet, charming and lots of fun. But the only thing they'd had in common was sex and after two months of putting up with Daryl's non-stop sexual appetite, Dee was exhausted and, she had to admit, bored.

He was the genuine Martini man, she'd explained to Maeve one day: 'Anytime, anyplace, anywhere.' When Maeve had stopped giggling long enough to inquire what was wrong with that, Dee had pointed out that constant sex was like constant chocolate – eventually, you'd had enough.

'He never stops, Maeve,' Dee explained. 'He wants to make love at least three times a day, and if we go out anywhere, his hands are everywhere.'

'I've noticed,' Maeve said. She'd seen Daryl in action and knew that he liked to keep his hands busy, normally burrowing under Dee's clothes with scant disregard for who was watching or where they were.

'We never talk, all we do is go to bed, and there are times when I'd like to have a pizza in front of the telly and a conversation instead of a sexual marathon,' Dee complained.

Thankfully, there hadn't been any scenes or uncomfortable moments when the inevitable split had come. One day, Daryl had simply said he was going back to the States. After a night of tender lovemaking when they talked about how they'd enjoyed spending time with each other, Dee drove him to the airport and waved him goodbye.

She'd cried, naturally, as he ambled off past the security gates, rucksack in hand, and had spent that evening sniffing miserably and wondering if she'd been wrong to let him go, if she shouldn't have made him stay. Then her natural resilience came into play and she settled down to do the chores she'd ignored while he had been there.

Sorting through the laundry basket and realising that she hadn't worn a single piece of underwear for eight weeks that hadn't been either a G-string, all lace or designed for immediate removal, Dee grinned to herself. Daryl *had* been wonderful but a relationship based totally on sex couldn't work in the long term.

He'd done wonders for her self-confidence though. Thanks to him, Dee's long-absent belief in herself had reappeared. When he was around, she'd felt gorgeous, sexy and desirable. She was thrilled to discover that those feelings didn't vanish when he did.

Now she was going out with Kevin Mills. Tonight. Whatever would she wear?

'A thong and nothing else?' Maeve suggested. 'That's what I'd wear. You are one lucky girl! I know women who'd pay to go out with Kevin Mills.'

Dee pretended to consider this. 'I'm a bit broke right now, what with all the legal bills and paying the mortgage on my own. How much were you thinking of offering cash-wise?'

'I wasn't talking about me,' Maeve said, throwing a balled-up paper bag at Dee. 'I'm blissfully happy with Karl. But I have had my girlish daydreams about that delectable photographer . . .'

'There was nothing girlish about them, I'll bet,' Dee joked. 'Unless you mean "girlish" in a "Girlish Vixens In Leather Get Their Men" sort of way.'

'That's *exactly* what I meant,' Maeve agreed, with a salacious smirk. 'It's the idea of going out with a photographer, you see. Normally, you have the bother of wondering where you're going to get your sexy photos developed because Boots aren't going to do it. But with a photographer, he has his own darkroom . . .'

Dee threw the paper missile back at her friend. 'We're only going out for a drink, not re-enacting this month's colour spread in *Hustler*.'

'Shame.' Maeve grinned. 'So, what *are* you going to wear?'

Dee wore the russet velvet trouser suit she'd bought ages before and had never had the confidence to wear until now. She'd worn it around her bedroom, naturally, figuring out what would look nice underneath as she flounced about, gazing at herself critically in the mirror. But she'd always balked at wearing it outside in case the velvet fabric highlighted every lump and bump unmercifully. Until now.

Kevin had known her for years, he'd seen her at her fattest and her thinnest. Regular aerobics sessions meant she was more toned than she had been for years, but she wasn't thin by any means, as the bathroom scales testified. And he'd *still* asked her out.

He knew what she looked like and obviously liked what he saw, spare tyre or no spare tyre. So there was no point in desperately trying to gild the lily before their date. All of which made things much more relaxed, Dee thought cheerfully as she closed the top button of her black fitted shirt for the third time. It kept popping open.

She didn't really need any lipstick at all, she realised

as she pouted in front of the mirror. Her mouth had been permanently stretched into a grin since this morning. But she slicked on some glossy russet lipstick and, with a squirt of Obsession, was ready.

She was about to leave the house, when she made a quick detour into the kitchen. Just in case, she thought, as she filled the sink with suds and washed up three days' breakfast dishes.

Meeting Kevin in the pub right beside the office might not have been such a good idea, Dee reflected as she walked into Magee's at five past eight to find at least a quarter of the *Sentinel* staff propping up the bar inside the door. She waved weakly at a couple of reporters who'd spotted her. Yes, definitely a mistake. So much for having a quiet drink together.

With a fixed grin on her face, Dee wove her way through the throng, eyes peeled for Kevin's dark head. She couldn't miss him, he was so tall. Too tall for her, really. Still, having a crick in your neck would be a small price to pay for dating him. Then again, he mightn't be dating material. Just because he *looked* nice didn't mean diddly squat. He could be a lazy, possessive, bad-tempered pig with a mother from hell and the sensitivity of an armadillo who'd wait just until he got his feet under the table before he started criticising her clothes, her make-up . . .

'Dee! Over here.'

Kevin stood at the long bar at the back of the pub, surrounded by the remaining three-quarters of her colleagues from the newsroom. Talk about getting stuck in an embarrassing situation.

There was no way they'd be able to slip out of the pub together without everyone demanding to know if they were going on a date. Or, worse still, without

513

people laying bets as to how long it would take them to end up in bed together. The staff of the *Sentinel* weren't great on respecting other people's privacy, especially fellow hacks who might be having a fling.

Dee wasn't ready for the jokes to start, not just yet. Few things ruined a relationship quicker than having the chief news sub running a book on how long it would last and laying fifty to one that the guy would get bored before the girl did, which was what had happened to one ill-fated couple dumb enough to make their liaison obvious. Blast, blast, blast!

We can say we're doing an assignment together, she thought, improvising wildly as she approached the bar. She gave everyone what she hoped was a laid-back grin, determined not so much as to look in Kevin's direction in case she let the cat out of the bag.

He, however, didn't appear to have any plans to cover up their date. He pulled her into the small group of reporters, slid one long arm around her waist and bent down to whisper in her ear, his lips brushing against her skin as he did so.

'I *was* going to kiss you but I thought I'd better check first, in case you didn't want your colleagues to see you going out with me?'

Dee nearly choked.

'I was going to suggest saying we were going on an assignment together in case you didn't want people to know you'd asked me out,' she whispered back.

He gave her waist a squeeze. 'You think I don't want to let people know?' he said. 'I want to order drinks for the entire bar to let everyone know you've finally agreed to go out with me. It's taken you so long to say yes, I want to celebrate. Or would you prefer we kept it a secret?'

Dee's eyes sparkled up at him. Not only was he pleased to see her, he wanted to tell everyone about it into the bargain. 'No.'

Slowly and deliberately, Kevin Mills kissed her full on the mouth, leaving nobody in any doubt as to why they were meeting that evening.

'Whoa!' howled Gerry Deegan. 'Barman, get the hose out – we've got another pair who need to be cooled down!'

Once the good-humoured ribbing had died down, Dee didn't know when she'd enjoyed an evening so much.

She and Kevin stayed in Magee's for another hour, chatting to the other journalists and gossiping about the stories they were working on. Eventually, she found herself leaning against Kevin, her back touching his stomach and his arms loosely around her waist as he propped himself against the bar. It felt comfortable and right, somehow. Every few minutes, he bent down and spoke to her, in a low voice not meant to be heard by anyone else. Dee couldn't resist a small, self-satisfied smile when she saw one of the barmaids staring at her with undisguised envy. Tough bananas, Dee thought triumphantly, he's mine.

It was after nine when they decided to go.

'Are you hungry?' Kevin asked, stifling a yawn.

'Starving,' Dee said. She took in the dark circles under his eyes and the way his face was pale under the five o'clock shadow. 'You're exhausted, aren't you?'

He nodded wearily. 'I was up till three last night on a stake out. If I hadn't been meeting you tonight, I'd have been in bed an hour ago.'

She put her arms around his waist, marvelling at how she felt able to do something so intimate so easily. 'Why don't you come back to my place? We'll have a quick pizza in front of the telly and then you can go home to bed.'

Kevin's relieved grin lit up his face. 'That sounds marvellous. Sitting in front of the TV is all I'm capable of tonight,' he admitted. 'I know I should be bringing you to an exotic restaurant or a club for our first date, especially when you're wearing such a wonderful outfit and look so good.' He fingered the lapel of her velvet jacket. 'But I'm bushed.'

'We can do the exotic restaurant thing another time,' Dee said.

'Tomorrow,' he promised.

Nobody whooped embarassingly as they left, although Dee wouldn't have minded if anyone had. She felt confident now, happy to be with Kevin and, amazingly, sure that he was equally happy with her.

After they'd eaten the takeaway pizza, they curled up together on Dee's settee and watched half of a science fiction movie before she noticed that Kevin had fallen asleep.

She smiled as she watched him, amazed at the almost girlishly long black lashes that fanned his cheeks. They were the only feminine thing about him. Without being even the slightest bit macho or aggressive, Kevin Mills was very male.

It was funny, she thought, gently stroking his short dark hair. If she'd been here with Daryl, they wouldn't have got past the movie's credits before he'd have had her underwear off. Which had been fun once, of course, but ultimately boring.

Spending the evening with Kevin had been very enjoyable and entertaining, yet he hadn't even attempted to grope her. Nor had he taken her invitation to eat a pizza in her house as carte blanche to go to bed with her. The most sensual thing he'd done all evening was wipe some mozzarella cheese from her lips. Yet that tender gesture had, strangely, been more erotic than a million French kisses from Daryl.

Just the way Kevin's long fingers had touched her lips had sent little quivers of excitement rippling through her body. Dee knew that when she did end up making love with Kevin, it would be an experience she'd never forget.

She didn't want to rush into it, though. This was special; *he* was special. She had no intention of jumping into bed with him at the first opportunity and ruining their chance of a future.

'Sleepyhead,' she whispered softly in his ear. 'I think you should go home.' She kissed him on the cheek and then untangled herself so she could go into the kitchen and boil the kettle to make coffee.

'Sorry,' Kevin said, wandering in after her and rubbing his eyes. 'I'm a great guest. Feed me and I pass out.'

Smudge, who had already decided that she loved and adored Kevin and had rubbed herself against him with blissful abandon earlier, followed him besottedly.

Dee went back to making extra strong coffee. 'Don't worry. You can't expect to stay up half the night working and then be the life and soul of the party the following day. Sugar?'

'Yes, honey,' he joked. 'Two. Can I bring you out to dinner tomorrow night to make up for passing out on you?'

Dee pretended to think about it. 'I'll have to check my diary. I think the Sheik is bringing me to Paris for the night. Or was it Cannes . . . Yes, I'd love to go to dinner with you tomorrow night,' she said with a smile and handed him a mug of very strong instant coffee.

When he'd left, she tidied up the kitchen, stuffed the giant pizza box in the bin and headed upstairs, unable to wipe the smile off her face. Smudge had got there before her and was, unusually, curled up on the bed.

Dee threw herself down on the duvet and rubbed her cat's ears until Smudge purred orgasmically.

'Isn't he wonderful?' she said.

Smudge purred louder.

'We can share him,' Dee offered.

Curled up in bed, she thought of Kevin. The way he'd wrapped his arms around her in the pub, laughed at her jokes and chatted companionably. He was lovely, she thought. Handsome, kind, fun. And sexy, that was for sure. Suddenly she remembered what Maeve had said about photographers and sexy photographs and laughed out loud, dislodging Smudge from her position at the end of the bed. Now *there* was a thought.

The newsroom was practically empty when Dee waltzed in early the following morning, determined to catch up on all her work before going out to dinner with Kevin.

She had to write up an interview with a rather eccentric fashion designer, finish her *Dear Annie* column and make dozens of phone calls, all before half-six when Kevin was picking her up from work. She couldn't wait!

'Where have you been?' screeched Tanya Vernon, appearing like the Wicked Witch of the West as soon as Dee dumped her briefcase on her desk.

She shrank back at the ferocious look in Tanya's eyes. Dressed in head-to-toe black with a large jet crucifix dangling at her slender throat, Tanya looked positively malevolent and was clearly very angry with someone. Dee gulped, aware that she was going to be the stunt double for that someone and take the brunt of Tanya's anger. 'I was ringing your mobile phone for *hours* last night!' Tanya hissed. 'Where were you? Don't you ever turn it on, you stupid fat cow? You don't give a damn about this paper or this department, do you?'

For a moment, the only thing Dee was aware of was the pulsing of her own heart, a frantic, rabbit-caught-in-the-headlights sensation. Then, as Tanya started yelling about a hot story they'd missed because she hadn't been able to send anyone to do the interview, Dee realised that the few occupants of the newsroom had stopped what they were doing and were staring.

All eyes were upon them, nobody saying a word, like people on a jeep safari watching a carnivorous lioness rip the throat out of a bewildered animal she'd managed to scare out of the herd.

'Chantal *never* gives interviews! She was here on a flying visit and we had an exclusive last night if only I could have reached you, but I couldn't!' raged the other woman, eyes black pinpoints.

Helplessly, Dee glanced around, desperate for someone to come to her aid, looking for someone to save her.

Suddenly it hit her: nobody was going to save her from Tanya. Oh, Isabel would have done or Maeve. They'd stand up to Ms Vernon all right. They wouldn't let her ride roughshod all over Dee. They knew she couldn't bear confrontation and could never strike back when someone was screaming at her. Especially an irate editorial director.

But they weren't here. Dee was on her own now.

'I'm . . . I'm sorry,' she stammered. 'I was out . . . off duty,' she said feebly.

'That's not good enough,' shrieked Tanya, going in for the kill. 'You either work here or you don't, Dee, and from the way you're behaving, you soon won't. There are plenty of hard-working people who'd be perfect for your job. People with the hunger to do it properly.'

Dee felt her bottom lip wobble. She couldn't be going to cry, not now. It'd look so weak, so cowardly, like an admission of guilt. She *had* been off duty the night before. She was entitled to have her mobile phone turned off. It wasn't as if she worked in news any more where you needed to be permanently available for work. The women's department was hardly a hotbed of breaking news stories.

It did occur to Dee to wonder why, if Tanya was that desperate to get the interview, she hadn't asked someone else? But one look at the editorial director's furious face told Dee it would be a mistake to say anything. Except sorry.

'I'm sorry,' she said again.

Tanya looked down her nose at Dee, grey eyes glacial. 'Sorry's not good enough,' she snarled, before turning on her heel and marching off.

'Jesus,' breathed Anna, one of the freelance reporters who'd seen everything. 'What a bitch. Are you OK, Dee?'

Dee couldn't trust herself to speak. She nodded blindly, hoping she wouldn't cry until everyone had stopped looking at her, and quickly went into Isabel's partitioned office, sank on to the chair and stared at her hands. They were shaking like leaves in a force-ten gale.

She was shaking. That had been one of the most horrific moments of her life. Being publicly screamed at by someone as razor-tongued as Tanya was a terrible experience.

'Morning, Anna.' Dee heard Isabel's warm, friendly tones ring out across the office and felt panic-stricken. She couldn't face her. Just one kind word, one mention that an enraged Isabel planned to confront Tanya and make her apologise for screaming at the staff, and Dee would cry for sure. She had to get out of here.

She bolted out of Isabel's office, cannoning into the women's editor as she did so.

'Dee, what's wrong?' asked Isabel after one look at her deputy's stricken face.

'Can't talk,' she said hoarsely, scooping her handbag off her own desk and running for the door.

She ran out of the office, out of the car park and found herself standing on the street, traffic zooming past her. Dee looked around blindly, wondering why she'd left, why she hadn't hidden in the ladies' and told Isabel the whole horrible story? But she'd had to get away from the office and, if she was honest with herself, Dee knew she couldn't bear to tell Isabel what had happened. She looked up to Isabel, respected her. How could Isabel respect *her* after this?

Dee walked up the street to a small café, ordered a cappuccino with a double helping of sprinkled chocolate and drank it slowly, her mind turning over the morning's events. How she hated Tanya Vernon! No, hated wasn't bad enough on its own: loathed, detested, despised *and* hated. If only she knew why Tanya despised her so much. That was the baffling thing.

Tanya had so much: incredible beauty, a size ten body and long, long legs that made Dee look like one of the seven dwarves by comparison. So why did she hate short, overweight Dee O'Reilly so much? It was a mystery.

After a comfortingly chocolatey second cappuccino,

she phoned Kevin and told him what had happened.

'That bitch!' he spat, venom in every syllable. 'I'll fucking kill her.'

Despite her misery, Dee was thrilled by his reaction. Gary would have told her she was over-reacting. Daryl would have dragged her off to bed to cheer her up. Kevin Mills, on the other hand, knew exactly what to say. And he knew what Dee should do as well.

'I've been working with your news team a lot recently and I keep hearing people say that Vernon is hiding something,' he said thoughtfully, once he'd raged against Tanya for a few moments. 'Nobody had even heard of her until earlier this year and then she appears, saying she's worked in newspapers all over the world.'

'She has?' asked Dee, astonished. 'That's more than I've ever heard about her.'

'Australia, apparently. According to Chris Schriber, she was something in a Sydney newspaper group. The question is: *what*? Hardly a reporter. She's too much of a bimbo to be one and as her management skills are zero, she's obviously only just been given an executive position.'

Dee grinned inanely. It was nice when your boyfriend described a woman you envied as a 'bimbo'. Tanya's endless legs and supermodel cheekbones obviously didn't cut any ice with him. She eyed the café's chocolate éclairs speculatively.

'Don't get upset by her, Dee,' Kevin was saying. 'Get even. You were an investigative reporter for years. Investigate her. Find out where she came from, what she did, and then you might figure out what her problem is. It'll also give you ammunition for the next time she decides to tear you apart in public.' His voice became softer. 'I'd love to go in and tell her that if she says one word to you ever again, she'll have me to contend with. But I can't.'

'I know. I've got to do it myself,' Dee said, without much conviction.

'You do,' Kevin pointed out gently. 'But not today. You're too vulnerable, too upset. I'll cheer you up tonight, I promise. I'll buy you the best dinner in Dublin and then you'll be able for that bitch tomorrow. Oh, hold on for a minute, will you, Dee?'

She could hear another, muffled voice speaking to Kevin.

'I've got to go,' he said rapidly. 'I'll phone you before lunch, OK?'

'OK. 'Bye.'

Pushing thoughts of her unfinished column out of her mind, Dee wandered aimlessly up the street, peering into shop windows. In a tiny boutique, she tried on a slinky silk sweater, a caramel V-neck style that was very slimming. Even though she knew she shouldn't even *think* of buying it as she had enough bills as it was, Dee dug out her credit card and bought the sweater. Then she saw a fake amber necklace that would look lovely with it, so she bought that too. Who needed therapy, she thought, when they could shop?

In the boutique next door, she was riffling through a rack of discount blouses when her mobile phone rang. It was Isabel wondering if she had written her agony column yet. She obviously hadn't heard about the row because she asked if Dee was feeling all right.

'You looked so pale, I wasn't sure if you were sick or something,' she said, sounding concerned.

'I'm not sick,' Dee said reluctantly. Just sick in the head. 'I had to go out for half an hour. I'll be back in a few minutes and I'll finish the column then.'

She had to go back. There was no point hiding any more. Unless she gave in her notice over the phone, she was going to have to face Tanya Vernon again and again, every single day. That was the reality of the situation. And she couldn't resign, although perhaps that was what Tanya wanted.

There are plenty of people who'd be perfect for your job . . . she had said. And Dee had a pretty good idea who she was talking about: her own friends. Tanya wanted to create a mini-empire around herself, made up of sycophantic pals who were undoubtedly as talentless as she was.

Women who had degrees in bossing people around and savaging their self-confidence, but were completely incapable of actually *writing* an article.

Then it hit her: if Tanya had been so desperate for the scoop with Chantal, why hadn't she done it herself?

After all, in an emergency, any newspaper editor worth their salt should be able to do a reporter's job. Dee knew that plenty of editors had started as sub-editors and therefore designed pages, wrote headlines but rarely wrote articles. But Tanya wasn't a sub-editor; she'd said so one day when one of the subs was sick and the head of production needed a stand-in. So her background – if she had any journalistic background at all – had to be in reporting. Which made it doubly strange that she hadn't interviewed the actress herself. Unless she wasn't a reporter, either?

There were three categories of journalist in the newspaper business: sub, reporter or photographer. If Tanya wasn't any of the above, what was she? Apart from a monumental pain.

Kevin was right. Tanya Vernon had to be hiding something. And Dee was determined to find out what.

Dear Annie,

I've had my ups and downs recently but I truly thought things were working out for me at last. I've got a lovely new man in my life who seems to be everything a girl could want and my job is going pretty well, but one of my bosses keeps picking on me.

I know I'm not imagining it. She really seems to hate me. No matter what I do, it's not right. She gives me all the horrible assignments to do, criticises my work and makes me re-do things I've worked really hard on. The last straw came today when she humiliated me in front of my colleagues over something that wasn't my fault at all. What was worse, I let her do it. I didn't say anything and actually apologised, even though I wasn't in the wrong. Please help.

Desperate

Dear Desperate,

You know what I'm going to say, don't you? This woman is a bully and she'll never stop bullying you unless you do something about it. Not somebody else – you. There are occasions in life when you have to ask for help but from what you've told me, this isn't one of them. This woman will continue to bully you because you let her do so. She'll only stop if you stand up to her . . .

Dee sighed. It was true. Unless she took action, Tanya would *never* stop. Even her own alter ego could see it: it was now or never.

She walked back to the *Sentinel* office, dumped her shopping in her car and marched up the stairs to the newsroom. Tanya wasn't in the conference room, which suited Dee perfectly. What she had to say she wanted to say in front of an audience. Dee took a deep breath and pushed open the newsroom door.

The editorial director wasn't difficult to spot. Tall and striking in her black outfit, Tanya was bent over one of the subs' desks, arguing about something if her body language was anything to go by.

Dee walked up to her and spoke loudly, not caring if she was interrupting. 'Tanya, I want to talk to you. Now.'

Disdain on her perfect features, Tanya looked up briefly. 'I'm busy.' She bent back to the screen.

'I said, I want to talk to you now,' Dee said in a firmer voice.

This time, Tanya stood up straight. 'How dare you interrupt me . . .'

Calmly, Dee pulled herself up to her full five foot three and stared coldly at the other woman.

'Shut up, you stupid bitch,' she said, her voice icy. 'Don't *ever* talk to me like that again. This is a newsroom, not the fishmarket.'

Tanya stared back, amazed. 'Listen . . .'

'No,' said Dee loudly, so that everyone could hear. '*You* listen. You are a talentless, bullying bitch and if you were that desperate to do the story, you should have gone and interviewed Chantal yourself. But you couldn't because,' she paused, aware that you could have heard a pin drop in the deathly quiet of the newsroom, '*you* couldn't write an article to save your life and you're too stupid to do an interview. You haven't written a single piece since you came here, and that's because you *don't know how to.*'

Tanya's face was a picture of outrage but Dee didn't hesitate, afraid that if she did the editorial director would shout and it would turn into a screaming match.

'We all know that your only skill is kissing ass,' Dee added coldly. 'That and desperately hoping that some executive will become so besotted with you he promotes you above your abilities – which wouldn't be much of a promotion. But that hasn't worked here, has it? Because there's nobody desperate enough to want to sleep with you, so all you're left with is screaming at people who have some writing ability. If you're going to screw your way to the top, Tanya, it helps to have some shred of talent to fall back on when your knees give in!'

Somebody sniggered loudly but Dee didn't stop. She was beginning to enjoy this. Tanya was open-mouthed with anger and shock, her eyes startled.

Dee looked down her nose at the other woman like she was a piece of dog dirt on her shoe. 'Nobody in this office will take your crap any longer, Tanya, especially not me. If you try any more of your bullying, I'll get the union behind me so you're blacklisted and not one single journalist will work for you again. Got it?'

Dee didn't even know if that was possible or not but it sounded good and was having the desired effect on Tanya who was now white-faced with temper, her Slavic cheekbones practically vibrating with temper.

'Who do you think you are?' she shrieked.

Dee summoned every reserve to give Tanya such a look of disdain that the other woman actually recoiled. 'Somebody you'd better have respect for or you'll be sorry. Very sorry,' Dee said in a voice low with menace.

She flicked back a curl, turned away and went to her desk, a grin the size of the Golden Gate Bridge appearing on her face. She'd done it, she'd actually done it!

Behind her, Tanya spluttered. 'D-did you hear that?'

'I think that's game, set and match to Ms O'Reilly,'

said a cool, amused voice which Dee recognised as Chris Schriber's. 'Or don't you like it when the tables are turned, Tanya?'

It was as if the spell was broken and the awe-struck audience breathed again.

'Well done!' said Maeve, rushing up and giving Dee a huge hug.

The subsequent round of applause sent Tanya rushing from the room.

People crowded around Dee, several colleagues clapped her on the back, Jackie kissed her and the subs queued up to shake her hand.

'Tanya deserved that,' said Anna, who'd witnessed the earlier performance. 'I couldn't believe all the things she said to you this morning.'

'What happened earlier?' demanded Isabel. 'Dee, did she attack you?'

'Attack?' cried Anna in disbelief. 'Attack wasn't the word for it. She almost fired Dee because there was nobody to interview some bloody actress last night. She screamed the office down.'

'Is that true?' asked Maeve. 'Oh, Dee, how awful . . .'

'Not so awful after all,' Isabel pointed out proudly, as she grabbed Dee's hand and squeezed it tightly. 'Whatever she said forced you to deal with Tanya, once and for all. I know saying that every cloud has a silver lining is a bit of a cliché, but in this case it's true.'

Dee grinned infectiously. 'I agree.'

'You do realise that Tanya will *really* have it in for you now, Dee?' Maeve cautioned.

'Yes, but I'm working on it.'

When everyone had gone back to their desks, Isabel made tea and brought it back into her cubbyhole for Dee and herself.

'This has been going on for some time, I suppose,' she said. 'I wish you'd told me Tanya was being so vile to you and so hurtful, Dee. I'd have stopped her.'

'I know.' Dee patted Isabel's hand gratefully. 'I know you would have. But I couldn't tell you,' she admitted. 'It was so embarrassing not being able to stand up to her, like being the fat girl in the schoolyard all over again. I felt powerless, useless. And,' she stirred her tea, 'Tanya seemed to sense that. She always commented on my figure, constantly said I was fat.'

Isabel's huge blue eyes were as fierce as Dee had ever seen them.

'Don't listen to a word that woman says. You're one of the sexiest, most vibrant women I know. You can light up a room with your presence. Something Tanya hasn't a hope in hell of doing.'

'Unless she wears a dress made out of Christmas tree lights,' quipped Dee happily. 'It's funny, I can joke about it now. Confronting the lion in its den really is the only way to deal with something like this,' she added thoughtfully. 'I should have done it ages ago.'

'You've done it now, that's all that matters. And I'm so proud of you. I know you hate confrontations or fights.'

'I *used to*,' Dee said. 'I almost enjoyed that. Towards the end, anyway. Because I was winning, I suppose. In the beginning, I was terrified.'

'What I don't understand,' Isabel said, 'is why Tanya's so venomous towards you. I just hope you didn't listen to a word she said earlier, Dee. You work so hard at your job and I certainly appreciate you. I'm going to talk to Malley about this. The editor should be aware of what's going on.'

'She's probably listening to Tanya's sob story right now,' Dee said cynically.

'Probably,' agreed Isabel. 'But she's going to hear my version too. Maeve's right. Tanya will have it in for you now.'

Dee gave a secret little smile. 'Don't worry, Isabel. I'm not finished with Tanya yet, not by a long shot. If she thinks she can mess up my career, one I've fought hard for, she's got another think coming, I promise.'

None of the big Sydney papers had ever heard of Tanya Vernon. Neither had the TV news stations. By the time she'd contacted every news organisation in the city, Dee was no longer surprised. It had taken her three days to cover them all, what with the time difference and the difficulty of locating the correct person to talk to in each organisation.

Kevin had helped, of course. An old friend who worked as a photographer in Melbourne had been making his own discreet enquiries.

'Tom spent two years in Sydney freelancing before he got this job,' Kevin explained. 'He still knows a few journos there.'

Whoever Tom knew, they came up trumps. On day four, Dee opened her e-mail to find a message from him.

Discovered your pal worked as a weather girl about four years ago in one of the small New South Wales stations for a couple of months. A paper ran pictures of her from a soft-porn mag, something she did when she first arrived in Australia. It caused quite a scandal because she'd made a big deal about being this holy, Catholic Irish girl. That was part of her trademark, the cute but holy thing.

Dee was stunned at the notion of the hard-nosed, malicious Tanya managing to pull off any combination of cute and holy.

It really worked. She was quite good at it. My friend says she could have made it in the big stations. But she left after that and nobody's heard of her since. She never worked in any of the papers here. This might be useful to you.

The paper that printed the pics said her real name was Concepta Gorman and she was from a village near Athlone, which they said was a few miles outside Dublin.

When you're in a country as big as Australia, Athlone does seem like it's only a few miles outside Dublin! I've got a bad photocopy of the article. Will I fax or snail-mail it? Only it's such bad quality it might not fax very well. The pictures are hot!

Dee felt a faint glimmer of pity for Tanya. Or Concepta. It must have been dreadful to find something you were good at – and Dee could imagine Tanya being very good at TV, she had just the right looks for a faintly insincere, sexy smile – and then have it all ripped away from you because of something you'd done in the past. None of us is perfect, Dee thought. Everybody has a skeleton in the cupboard. What a pity Tanya's had turned out to be soft porn pictures.

Then she realised what she was doing – feeling sorry for the woman who'd systematically made her life a misery for the past six months.

'Snail-mail it,' she typed on to the computer.

'Thanks a million, Tom, I owe you.'

A couple of phone calls later, and with the help of an Athlone-based reporter she knew from her time as a news reporter, Dee had tracked Concepta Gorman down to a small secondary school in the Midlands. Three school yearbooks from around about the period Tanya would have been there were being posted up to her. If the pictures of Concepta Gorman were obviously

531

of a young Tanya Vernon, then Dee had hit paydirt and could find out for sure whether Tanya had any journalistic experience or not.

'You wanted me?' asked Dee sweetly, standing outside the conference room where her nemesis sat at one end of the massive table, surrounded by newspapers, A-4 pads and pens.

It was a week after their confrontation and so far, Tanya had studiously avoided Dee, not even speaking to her at editorial conferences.

Today Dee had arrived back after lunch with Kevin to find a note from Tanya stuck to her computer screen: 'See me in the conference room when you get in'.

No 'please' or 'thank you', she noticed without surprise. Tanya had never been much of a one for the simple courtesies.

'Yes.' Tanya spoke with barely disguised dislike.

'Come in.'

Dee went in and sat down, purely because Tanya hadn't asked her to. Sitting back in a leisurely manner, she put her notebook on the table, crossed her legs calmly and adjusted her suede wraparound skirt carefully, to hide the fact that she was actually as nervous as hell.

Confronting Tanya in front of the entire office when her adrenaline was as high as an Olympic athlete's had been one thing; confronting her on a wet Tuesday afternoon with nobody around to back Dee up if things got nasty, was another scenario entirely.

'I've an assignment for you,' Tanya said.

Dee raised her eyebrows questioningly but said nothing.

'There's a new fish canning factory ship just about to be launched in Donegal. The biggest in the world. We want you to join it for twenty-four hours of the maiden voyage.'

'*We?*' asked Dee sceptically.

'The editor suggested it. She asked me to tell you,' Tanya replied, making it perfectly plain that she detested having to pass on as much as the time of day to Dee O'Reilly.

'Why me?' Dee asked. 'It's hardly women's pages stuff.'

'Malley thought you'd be able to write a good colour piece, something atmospheric.'

'Oh.' Dee sat up straight and widened her eyes innocently. 'You mean, the editor likes the way I write and thinks I'd make a good job of this?' she asked pointedly.

'Yes,' snarled Tanya. 'You go tomorrow.'

'Tomorrow!' said Dee in shock.

Tanya gave an evil little smile, having finally scored a point in the battle of wits. 'Tomorrow. At seven. Several other journalists are going.'

'Bitch!' hissed Dee to Maeve a few minutes later as they stood in the kitchen making coffee. 'She must have known about this for days but only told me now. How am I expected to finish all my work and still be ready for seven in the morning?'

'I told you she'd be out for your blood,' Maeve said. 'You're lucky she mentioned the trip to you at all. If she was as clever as she thinks she is, she'd have pretended you knew all about it and couldn't be bothered, which would go down like a ton of bricks with Malley.'

'True,' Dee muttered. 'Anything for me?' she called, seeing the post girl walk by with a trolley of afternoon post.

'Just one.' She handed Dee a parcel with an Athlone postmark.

'If this is what I think it is, I'm in a better mood already,' crowed Dee, ripping open the envelope.

'The year books,' said Maeve, who knew the whole story.

They found Tanya in the earliest year book – 'Making her at least three years older than she pretends to be,' Maeve said.

Dee couldn't say anything at all. She was speechless. The pictures were generally all pretty unflattering, the way year-book pictures are. Most of the people pictured probably wouldn't recognise themselves twelve years on. But Tanya Vernon, or rather Concepta Gorman, was even more unrecognisable than most.

Her eyes were half hidden by a deeply unflattering shaggy perm and the heavy rock 'n' roll moll eyeliner didn't do her any favours. But what was most startling was Tanya's size.

She was huge, a vast moon face staring at the camera, fat cheeks obscuring the cheekbones everyone now admired, and several chins hiding the modern Tanya's delicately pointed chin. The photo stopped at shoulder level but it was enough to show off enormous shoulders squeezed into a brown jumper, a colour that did nothing for her sallow skin.

'It can't be the same woman,' said Maeve, peering at the picture close up.

'It is,' Dee said in amazement. She'd recognise Tanya anywhere: those hard, cold eyes and that slightly surly expression on the full lips. Several extra stones couldn't hide Tanya from Dee. She was used to looking at a heavy woman in the mirror and wondering what she'd look like about three stone lighter.

'She must have lost a hell of a lot of weight,' Maeve commented. 'Maybe that's why she hates you so much,

Dee? Because you're gorgeous and voluptuous and she wasn't.'

'That's too much analysis to waste on bloody Tanya Vernon,' Dee said briskly. 'You could spend half your salary trying to work out why she's such a bitch and it'd still be a waste of time and money. There are some people for whom in-depth personal analysis is wasted – people like her. She's a cow. End of story.'

Maeve laughed. 'So who wants to be the one to cover the psychoanalytical convention in Galway next month, then? You sound caring and interested enough.'

'I *am* interested in therapy,' protested Dee. 'But there comes a time when it's pointless trying to work out what motivates someone to do something horrible. It's far better to stop thinking about the other person at all and work on developing your own coping mechanisms to deal with them.'

'Sorry, Dr O'Reilly, my mistake. I think you should *join in* the psychoanalysts' convention.'

'I might need a few days intense psychoanalysis after the weekend,' Dee pointed out. 'Millie and Dan are having their baby christened on Saturday. And guess who'll be there?'

'Lovable Gary?' Maeve said sourly.

'Yeah. I'm not looking forward to it,' she admitted. 'I haven't seen him for so long, it's going to be very strange . . .'

'It won't be strange at all. Just garotte the pig if he comes near you. Is Kevin going with you?'

'I haven't asked him,' Dee confessed. 'It's not really fair to bring him along as a "look, I've-got-a-boyfriend" prop. I tried that with Daryl at Millie's dinner party and it was nearly a disaster. No,' she added thoughtfully, 'I've got to do this on my own.'

'I'll go with you,' offered Maeve. 'I'm not working on Saturday.'

Dee grinned. 'Knowing how you feel about my ex-fiancé, we'd spend the night in a cell somewhere while I tried to convince the police you didn't really mean to stab him with a pastry fork!'

Isabel touched the velvety petals of the pale pink roses and smiled. They brightened up her desk, and her face, she admitted happily. Trust Jack to know that she'd be utterly miserable that morning, faced with four days without him. She read the card again, written in Jack's elegant scrawl.

Darling Isabel, just a note to tell you I love you and that I'll be home on Sunday night. I miss you so much even though it's only been a few hours since I saw you. All my love . . .

Brussels felt like a million miles away. But he'd phone several times a day, he'd promised.

'I want to hear your voice all the time,' he'd said the night before.

And she wanted to hear his.

Isabel glanced at her watch. Nearly half-twelve. He'd be there now, on his way to a meeting probably.

'What a trip! I thought it'd never end.' She looked up abruptly to see Dee appear beside her, looking decidedly the worse for wear. Her curls were tied back severely in a scrunchie, the only make-up she wore was the smudged remainder of the previous day's mascara and her eyes were red-rimmed.

'How was the canning ship?' Isabel asked, not expecting a thrilled response from the exhausted look on Dee's face.

'Not my finest hour,' she said, stifling a yawn. 'You'll

never believe what happened. Tanya told me to be there at seven for the flight to Donegal and when I got there, they'd gone! The woman who'd organised the whole thing told me they'd faxed Tanya yesterday evening to say the trip was starting an hour earlier. The cow never told me!'

'Ouch,' said Isabel. 'What did you do?'

'Panicked for about ten minutes,' Dee admitted. 'Then,' she grinned mischievously, 'I hired a helicopter to fly me there! I had to. They wanted the story and there was no other way I'd be in Donegal for the maiden voyage otherwise. And it was one of the editor's ideas, after all.'

'You did what?' Isabel gasped. 'Tanya will go out of her mind.'

The thought of Tanya Vernon's apoplectic expression when she discovered what had happened struck both of them at the same time and they burst out laughing.

'She'll have a spasm!' roared Dee.

'So long as I can be here to see it,' chuckled Isabel, wiping her eyes. 'Are you sure you'll be able for her when she gets angry?' she asked in a more serious tone.

Dee nodded confidently.

'Come on then, I'll buy you lunch,' Isabel said fondly. 'You look like you need some pampering and building up before you face Ms Vernon.'

'Thanks, that sounds wonderful,' said Dee. 'I'm starved.' She glanced at the huge bouquet on Isabel's desk and smiled.

'Jack?' she mouthed.

Isabel beamed at her.

'Tell me all about it over lunch,' Dee said, collecting her handbag.

Isabel didn't quite tell her everything – she didn't

want to blab that he was leaving Elizabeth; not until he'd actually done it. Then, she promised herself, Dee would be the first to know. Dee had been so kind to her since she'd found out about Jack. She'd covered for Isabel so she could go for long leisurely lunches with him and had been a shoulder to lean on when Isabel needed to talk to someone about how hard it was loving someone who was married. So she told Dee about the proposed trip to Paris and her new Ben De Lisi dress, but not about their plans for the future.

'*New* designer clothes instead of second-hand ones,' Isabel joked. 'Imagine it. I'll be turning into Elizabeth Carter soon, right down to a Gucci G-string to go with my Ben De Lisi dress.'

Dee, who'd been quite animated during the meal, suddenly became subdued. She didn't finish her ricotta cake, pushing the half-empty plate away from her.

'Isabel, there's something I have to tell you,' she said hesitantly.

'What?' She sat up, startled. 'What is it? Has someone at work said something to you about Jack and me?'

Dee shook her head slowly. 'No. I don't know whether this is good or bad news . . .'

'Tell me?' urged Isabel.

'Kevin's best friend is a photographer too. This morning he told Kevin about this great scoop he'd got last night in a nightclub in the city. Pictures of Elizabeth Carter with this young bloke. She was wrapped around him all night, apparently.'

Isabel was stunned. Elizabeth with another man? It was unbelievable.

Dee wasn't finished. 'This snapper followed them back to a hotel nearby. They booked a room, went in and left together this morning, still in the same clothes.

Kevin says they're great photographs, apparently. She was obviously strung out on something in the nightclub. This photographer has seen her with scores of other guys before, but he's never bothered to take photos until now.' Dee paused.

'He took snaps this time because the guy she was with is that TV presenter from the young people's programme. His name is Mannix Delaney,' she continued. 'You know, the good-looking, squeaky clean guy? I didn't know whether to tell you or not. I thought maybe Elizabeth knew about you and Jack and this was her way of getting back at him. And . . .' Dee grabbed Isabel's arm and squeezed it comfortingly. 'Well, you know the way guys go back to their wives when they think *they*'re being cheated on,' she said gently. 'I was afraid this would ruin things for you both. I know you love him so much. I'm sorry, Isabel.'

She sat silently for a moment, digesting the information. Elizabeth with another man. Elizabeth with lots of other men. Elizabeth with a twenty-something youth TV presenter who'd made a career out of being a favourite with both teens and their mothers. Robin adored him, never missed his programme. He was very good-looking after all, in a floppy-haired, arty way.

'Isabel, are you feeling all right?' Dee asked anxiously. 'I didn't mean to upset you but I thought I'd better let you know.'

Suddenly, Isabel laughed, a joyous sound that cut through Magee's like an alarm. She threw back her head and laughed, with Dee clutching her arm, shocked.

'Are you all right?' she demanded, frantically.

Isabel stopped laughing. 'I am absolutely wonderful! Happy. Delirious. That's the best news I've had in years.'

'It is?' Dee asked.

'It is. You see,' she leaned forward conspiratorially, 'I didn't tell you that Jack is planning to leave Elizabeth but he's worried about her. How upset she could be by the news . . .'

'But if you're being given lots of lurve by the hunky Mannix Delaney, who could be worried?' supplied Dee, immediately getting the point.

'Exactly!'

'This calls for a celebration!'

'I've been celebrating ever since Jack told me he wanted to be with me,' Isabel said, eyes shining. 'This puts the icing on the cake. Elizabeth has her problems,' she explained delicately, 'but he felt responsible for her and hated the idea of hurting her. If she's been having affairs herself, she can hardly complain, can she? She'll probably jump at the idea of a divorce. It'll leave her free to pursue Mannix.'

'My only fear was that Jack would get a shock, hearing about her relationship,' Dee said. 'I don't know which paper the photographer will sell the pictures to but they're bound to run it soon, and I kept thinking the scandal could push the Carters back together.'

Isabel shook her head confidently. 'Their marriage is over. Jack would never go back to her, I know that for a fact.'

Still high from the bottle of champagne – 'cheapie stuff, I'm too broke to buy good champagne' – Dee had insisted on buying to celebrate, they finally wandered back towards the office at half-three, giggling and whispering happily.

'No, we're not hiring a helicopter to go back,' Isabel teased. 'I know you only travel in style, Dee, but really, you must be prepared to walk occasionally.'

'Please, please, let me have a helicopter?' begged Dee, before dissolving into giggles. 'Just because you fly all over the country with our dear and glorious boss in one, doesn't mean the rest of us can't . . .'

Tanya Vernon, who met them at the door to the newsroom, wasn't giggling. Far from it. Her face was furious, the perfectly arched eyebrows drawn down in an angry line.

'I want to talk to you,' she hissed at Dee.

Before Dee could say a word, Isabel drew herself up haughtily and stared at Tanya. 'Don't speak to my deputy like that,' she said in a clipped voice.

You'd never think she'd finished half a bottle of champagne just minutes before, Dee thought, full of admiration for Isabel's instant poise and calm.

'You've been attempting to bully Dee for months now, Tanya, and I've had enough of it.'

Isabel swept into the newsroom with Dee and Tanya following her.

'You have no idea what's happened,' snapped Tanya, taken aback by Isabel's attack.

Dee decided it was time to speak up for herself. Isabel was so good and so loyal, but the only thing Tanya understood was being stood up to in person.

'She knows exactly what happened,' Dee said loudly.

Tanya whirled around, gimlet eyes fixed angrily on her.

'Does she?' she snarled.

'Yes. So does the editor, in fact. You see, Tanya, when I discovered that you'd purposely misled me about the time the trip to Donegal started, I decided to get some evidence to back me up.' Dee was pleased to see Tanya's eyes widen in astonishment. 'So I got a copy of the fax sent to you on Tuesday, confirming the earlier departure time, and I've given that, a report of exactly what happened, and a copy of the helicopter bill to Malley. She can decide whether I made the right decision in hiring a helicopter. But as she was keen to get the story done, and as she'll see that you deliberately tried to mislead me into missing the trip, she's unlikely to take your side in this.'

'How dare you try and go behind my back?' Tanya blustered.

'I dared because I won't take any more of your bullying, Tanya. You should have remembered that,' Dee said, her voice strong and confident. 'And if that makes you wonder if you want to continue working here,' she whispered in a voice only the other woman could hear, 'I believe they're looking for a weather girl in a TV station in New South Wales, although they want one without glamour photography credentials, I believe – *Concepta*.'

Seeing the look of sheer horror on Tanya's face made the hours spent checking into her background well worthwhile.

'What did you say to her at the end?' asked Isabel, watching in amazement as Tanya ran from the room.

'I'll tell you the whole story later,' Dee replied quietly.

CHAPTER TWENTY-THREE

The phone line from Brussels was very poor. 'I'm in a bad signal area,' Jack said, his voice crackly with interference. 'Can you hear me?'

'Just about,' Isabel replied, pressing her mobile phone even closer to her ear so she could hear better. 'Can you speak up?'

'I'm already shouting. We're in heavy traffic, maybe that's the problem.'

Isabel grinned. She was in very heavy traffic herself. Usually, driving home in rush hour sent her insane, stuck behind a line of cars, all moving at three miles an hour. But tonight she didn't care. Tonight she was blissfully happy.

Elizabeth Carter was having an affair, a madly passionate fling with a handsome youngster, which would surely make it much easier for Jack to walk away from the marriage without too much guilt. Of course, the scandal of seeing his wife's face plastered all over the papers would be dreadful, but Isabel was convinced that Jack had enough influence to kill the story stone dead. There was always a trade-off to be made in the world of media moguls.

She wondered if he knew yet? She'd tell him, but couldn't over their mobiles, especially if Jack was in the back of a chauffeur-driven car in Brussels yelling his head off because they had a bad connection.

'I miss you,' Isabel roared cheerfully. 'Did you hear that?'

'Yes, I miss you too. But, Isabel, something's happened . . .' He stopped for a moment. His voice sounded funny, she thought, and not just because there was interference on the line.

'Are you all right, Jack?' she asked, not minding that a woman with a walking stick was moving faster than her line of traffic.

'No. No, I'm not,' he said slowly. 'I've had some terrible news. Terrible. I'm devastated.'

Isabel practically hit the car in front in shock. She slammed on the brakes and wondered if she'd heard him correctly. He was devastated, he felt terrible.

'Isabel, I can't talk about it over the phone . . .' He hesitated. 'I know we were to go out on Monday night but I won't be able to. I can't explain now, I'll need to see you in person, to explain properly,' he added ominously.

Isabel listened mutely, her brain processing what Jack had said. Then it struck her: he'd heard about Elizabeth's affair and was devastated by the news. He hadn't said he was shocked or angry at the thought that his wife's affair would soon be breakfast-time reading for the nation.

No, he was devastated. Which meant he loved Elizabeth and couldn't bear to think of her with another man. *He loved Elizabeth.* Why else would he be so shocked by the news? And he wanted to see Isabel in person to explain that he was going back to his wife.

'Isabel, I'd better go,' he said. 'This line is hopeless. I can't hear anything so I hope you can hear me. I'll phone later when I get to my hotel.'

She drove shakily into a pub car park at the side of the road, unable to think about driving further. Her whole body was quivering. She was a wreck.

Isabel leant her head against the steering wheel and closed her eyes. Pain washed over her, a grief so bad she felt as if she'd die from it, yet she couldn't cry. This wasn't misery – it was like death. She loved Jack, and he loved his wife. Those were the simple facts. Dee, wise, clever Dee, had been right. What was it she'd said earlier? Men went back to their wives when they realised *they*'d been cheated upon. How right she was. And how stupid, naive and gullible Isabel had been.

She slammed her hand against the wheel in sudden anger. How stupid could she be? Another bloody man had made a fool out of her. Only this time she loved him desperately. And in vain. Or so it seemed.

Dee felt elated as she drove out to Millie and Dan's house. She'd done it! She'd finally told bloody Tanya Vernon that she wasn't taking any more bullying. Judging from the horrified look on her face as she'd backed out of the newsroom at the speed of light, Dee would never have any trouble with her again.

It *was* a bit mean, she conceded, to have snooped around in Tanya's past for ammunition to defeat her. But it had been worth it, she thought gleefully.

When Millie opened the door, Dee was glad she'd gone to the bother of bringing a giant bottle of perfumed body lotion for her along with a big box of chocolates. Millie looked exhausted, her eyes red-rimmed with tiredness. But she was in great spirits, hugging Dee delightedly.

'Thank you for my presents!' she whispered. 'We're

keeping quiet because Tara's asleep.'

'When I visited you in hospital, I realised you had enough baby clothes to keep sextuplets in babygrows for a year, and nothing nice at all for the poor woman who'd done all the work,' Dee said, hugging her warmly. 'Tara has enough presents. You deserve some.'

Over mugs of tea, Millie was remarkably keen to discuss things other than her adorable but sleepless three-week-old baby girl.

'I have been eating, breathing, sleeping – well, not sleeping, actually – nothing but babies ever since I got pregnant and it's nice to talk about something else,' Millie said, adjusting the strap of her maternity bra. 'I love her to pieces but there *is* more to life than Tara.'

'She's so lovely, though,' Dee said, cooing into the crib at the dozing baby. She stroked one tiny hand and admired Tara's pink, round face and downy red hair.

'When she's asleep, she's wonderful. When she's awake, you wonder why Oasis haven't been on the phone asking her to do a backing track on one of their albums,' Millie said. 'She has the most amazing lungs and comes alive at around three in the morning, unfortunately. I swear I'm giving up breast feeding soon. She is so demanding.'

'Can't Dan feed her with a bottle you've made up earlier?' Dee asked.

'He could, but she refuses to have any truck with anything except real boobs,' Millie groaned. 'Unless it's attached to me, Tara won't suck it. She's like her father in that respect,' she said as an afterthought.

Dee laughed as quietly as she could.

They talked in low voices for an hour before Millie got round to Gary.

'I knew we'd end up talking about him,' Dee remarked.

'Well, he *is* going to be Tara's godfather and you're her godmother,' Millie pointed out. 'So you'll be seeing quite a lot of each other on Saturday.'

'I know. I promise I won't bare my fangs across the church at him.'

Millie snorted. 'It's not *you* I'm worried about, Dee. You know how to behave. It's him. I can tell you,' she said, lowering her voice even more, 'if Dan hadn't been so terribly keen to have Gary as Tara's godfather, there's no way I'd want him to be. After the way he treated you, he's hardly the right role model for my child.'

Dee smiled at her affectionately. 'Thank you,' she said. 'Does this mean I am a good one?'

'Absolutely. The thing is, I'm not afraid Gary will act his usual arrogant self on Saturday, I'm afraid he'll be the opposite.'

Surprised, Dee asked why.

Millie rolled her eyes. 'He spent at least two hours on the phone to me the other night, quizzing me about what you were up to and who you were seeing. He's a changed man: in his own mind, anyway.'

'What do you mean, changed?' Dee asked curiously.

'Deconstructed. Or is it reconstructed?' Millie asked. 'I can't remember. Anyway, he misses you like mad, he's lonely in London and wants to come home. And he's even realised that there is no such thing as a Laundry Fairy.'

'I see,' Dee muttered without rancour. 'He's coming home, he's sick of doing his own washing and he hopes that dopey Dee will let him back into her life with access to her Hotpoint.'

'I don't think it's that simple,' Millie said thoughtfully. 'I know he spent three months living with Adrian and Natasha, who is, as you know, a minimalist freak with a tidiness phobia. I think Gary finally discovered what a wonderfully carefree life he had with you.'

'That's hardly flattering, now is it?' Dee asked. 'A few months with a sister-in-law who insists he pick up his dirty laundry and now he's longing to come home to me?'

'But he also says he misses you like crazy and that he was a fool to leave you,' Millie added quietly. 'That he'd be back like a shot if you'd have him.'

Dee stared at her for a moment, listening to the sound of Tara's breathing. 'Dan put you up to this, didn't he?' she said finally.

Millie looked shamefaced. 'Sort of. I did feel a teeny bit sorry for Gary when he rang. I think he really regrets how he treated you and the things he said about your size. And I hate to think of you on your own . . .'

'I'm *not* on my own,' Dee said proudly.

'Is Daryl back?'

'No, I couldn't cope with any more Daryl. The bed would disintegrate. There's a new man in my life. He's a photographer.'

'Why didn't you tell me before this?' demanded Millie so loudly that Tara whimpered in her sleep.

'I haven't seen you since you'd just had the baby,' Dee whispered.

'Are you bringing him to the christening so we can meet him?'

Dee laughed. 'A minute ago you were trying to set me up with my ex-fiancé. Now you want to meet my new boyfriend.'

Millie grinned. 'I've done my bit,' she said. 'Gary's on his own. So, is this photographer coming with you on Saturday?'

'No, I'm not bringing Kevin . . .'

'Kevin! What a lovely name!' cooed Millie.

'. . . to the christening. Tell me,' Dee said, changing the subject, 'has Mumsy Redmond been round once a day and twice on Sundays to see if you're treating the first grandchild properly?'

Millie groaned. 'Don't talk to me about her. That woman is a menace! I thought Dr Spock was someone from *Star Trek* until she started bombarding me with books on the right way to raise a baby.'

'I bet she's none too thrilled that I'm going to be Tara's godmother?'

'Livid doesn't describe it,' Millie said with a smile. 'So I do hope you're going to wear something spectacularly sexy and unconventional just to irritate her? Who knows? Maybe she might go home in a sulk if you do.'

Dee's eyes glinted wickedly. 'I have the perfect outfit in mind. A gownless evening strap . . .'

Millie laughed quietly and Dee pretended to look astonished. 'I meant it,' she joked. 'I suppose I'd better make more tea?'

Although she never did it as a rule, as soon as she got home Isabel went straight to the cupboard where she kept the drinks and poured herself a stiff gin and tonic. She downed it quickly and poured another to drink while she made dinner.

Both girls were upstairs studying for their Christmas exams, Robin with a lot less application than her sister, Isabel knew.

Naomi had now settled into her school brilliantly and worked very hard at her homework. Robin, on the other hand, spent more time drawing up prettily coloured study timetables than she actually spent studying.

But, Isabel thought, hating herself for such an

unmotherly feeling, she was glad they were in their bedrooms this evening and couldn't witness her standing hollow-eyed in front of the cooker, staring into space as she stirred milk into the dried pasta mix.

She'd forced herself to think about the future of her relationship with Jack as she'd driven home. He'd want to keep on seeing her, of course, she'd suffer without him permanently in her life, and he'd always go home to Elizabeth. The eternal triangle. Isabel couldn't face a lifetime of that.

The affair had to end, she decided, feeling a heaviness in her heart that she knew wouldn't go away for a very long time. The affair was over. She wouldn't see him again. Couldn't. She must have been mad having an affair with a married man, and her boss into the bargain. So she was destined to see him for years and years. They couldn't even melt discreetly out of each other's lives. He'd be the boss of the *Sentinel* for a long time.

A tear dropped on to the cooker. Isabel felt as if her heart would truly break. She took a slug of her drink and tried, desperately, to feel strong. She could do it, she knew. She had to get angry with Jack. If she stayed sad and thought of how much she loved him, she'd crumble. Taking deep breaths, she remembered all the things he'd said to her, the loving things he'd said when, all along, he'd really loved Elizabeth. That was it; that would make her angry.

How could he, *how could he*? The bastard, she hated him.

Well, she thought, defiance and pain battling for supremacy inside her, she wasn't giving up her job for anyone. Women who had affairs at work were nearly always the ones who left the office when the relationship soured. Isabel couldn't take that risk. She certainly wouldn't get another job as good as this one and she had fought too hard for it to merely pack her bags and leave.

Her daughters needed a stable environment and a mother with a bank account in the black. She'd put up with seeing Jack Carter snub her for the rest of her life for their sakes.

Isabel blinked back the tears and finished her drink, before mixing a third one. The shrill ringing of the phone made her jump. For once, she got to it before Robin.

'Yes,' she said hoarsely.

'Isabel.' Jack sounded better this time, not so upset. The bastard. 'Hello.'

'Hello,' she said, her voice breaking.

It was his turn to ask, 'Are you OK?'

'No,' she said, 'not since you told me you were devastated about the news.' She dragged the phone into the kitchen so the girls wouldn't hear her. 'You see, Jack, I thought you really loved me, so when I find out that you're "devastated" because Elizabeth is having an affair, then I can finally see the truth. You don't love me after all, I'm just your bit on the side, your piece of fluff. At least you have some vestiges of decency left – you want to see me in person to explain why you're leaving me. Well, don't bother.' Her voice rose hysterically.

'Isabel,' he said, 'you don't understand . . .'

'No. *You* don't understand: we're over. Our fling, our cheap, tawdry affair, is over. Call it what you will, it's finished, Jack. So don't ring me again. I don't want to talk to you. I hate you for making me love you and then doing this to me. I hate you for that. Goodbye. I hope I never see you again!'

She slammed down the phone, dumped it on the kitchen floor and burst into tears.

It rang again, shrill and insistent. Isabel stared at it but refused to pick up the receiver.

Inside, she wanted to. Desperately. She wanted to hear Jack's voice telling her he was crazy about her and that it had all been a big misunderstanding, that he loved her, not Elizabeth.

But she couldn't allow herself to do that. Picking up the phone would be another huge mistake. She'd made her choice – now she had to live with it. To live her life without Jack.

She'd only known him such a short time, four months, but already he was a vital part of her life. She'd felt as if she'd found that perfect person, the one she wanted to spend the rest of her days with. And now it was over. The phone stopped ringing. A minute later it started again, the shrill sound drilling into her skull.

Isabel picked up the phone and pressed the button to cut Jack off. Then she laid the receiver on the ground. If she left it off the hook for a few hours, he'd get the message. Better still, she'd disconnect it. In the hall, she pulled the connection out, stuck the phone on the hall table and went back into the kitchen.

She roughly dried her tears with a piece of kitchen roll, poured herself another drink and returned to the cooker, where the pasta mix was now a congealed mess. Like her life, she thought bleakly.

Saturday morning dawned bright and sunny for late-December. Perfect, thought Dee, who'd planned to wear a clinging V-necked black body under her velvet trouser suit if it wasn't pouring from the heavens. Rain ruined velvet, so her other option had been a navy pinstripe coatdress Isabel had insisted she buy. Classy and elegant though it was – a lot like Isabel, Dee thought – the coatdress didn't have the immediate 'wow' impact of the richly coloured velvet. And Dee wanted people at the christening to say 'wow' when they saw her. Especially Gary and his insufferable mother.

Not that Mrs Margaret Redmond would say 'wow' exactly, Dee thought with an evil little grin as she sprayed a blast of Contradiction perfume into the heaving valley of her cleavage revealed by the daring black top. Her one-time future mother-in-law would more than likely mutter, 'Thank God my Gary didn't marry that trollop!' But he couldn't fail to be impressed by her rig-out, she thought.

With the tortoiseshell sunglasses that went so well with her rippling curls and subtle make-up that had taken ages to apply, Dee looked a million dollars.

'Hello, Gary,' she practised in front of the bathroom mirror, pitching her voice low and sexy, and making sure she bent forward, to give him a tantalising glimpse of fake-tanned bosom.

An hour later, she got the chance to do it for real. She was standing just inside the church door talking to Millie's mum when Gary appeared beside her. For someone reputedly pining away with misery, he looked pretty good. He wore a Prince of Wales check suit she'd never seen before with his favourite yellow tie. His wavy hair was collar-length and neatly brushed back, and he radiated health and good spirits. He was obviously still playing soccer, Dee thought, noticing that he was as lean as ever.

He briefly kissed Millie's mother in greeting and turned to Dee.

'Hello, Dee,' he said softly. For a moment it looked as

if he was going to kiss her too, but he apparently thought better of it.

'Hello, Gary,' she said coolly.

Millie's mother, who knew the whole, sordid story thanks to regular bulletins from her daughter, drifted discreetly away.

Gary's expressive eyes roamed over Dee's figure, taking in the more toned curves and the glamorous outfit she wore with such verve and confidence.

'You look great, really great,' he said admiringly.

'I know,' she replied, tossing back her hair. 'You look pretty good yourself,' she added. 'Still playing soccer?'

'Yeah.'

'I've got your old sports bag in my house.' She emphasised the word 'my'. 'You left it behind.'

He shrugged. 'It's ancient, throw it out.'

Dee was about to ask if that was what he did with everything that had passed its sell-by date: throw it out. But she restrained herself. She didn't want to start a battle over the font. Baptismal candles weren't there to be hurled at your ex.

Millie arrived with Tara, who was wearing yards of antique lace and screaming at the top of her voice.

'I hope you've got earplugs with you,' Millie groaned. 'You look fabulous, Dee. As *always*,' she added, with a glare at Gary.

'Hello, Millie,' he said, without rising to the bait.

She ignored him. 'We're about to begin,' she addressed Dee. 'Are you ready?'

Grafton Street was packed. What seemed like the entire population of Dublin thronged the pedestrianised street, pushing and shoving as they did their Christmas shopping.

Isabel stopped counting the number of times she'd been elbowed in the ribs and tried to feel grateful for the fact that it wasn't raining, so at least there was no chance of being poked in the eye by an army of umbrellas.

Robin was leading the way, shoving through the crowd expertly. Naomi and Isabel followed her black, PVC-clad back into Next, where another million women congregated, grabbing at hangers and cute bits of jewellery like there was no tomorrow.

'I'm tired, Mum,' said Naomi, leaning against the stairs as Robin disappeared in search of the perfect present for Susie, with the enthusiasm of Indiana Jones looking for the Lost Ark.

'Me too.' Isabel put an arm around Naomi and leant wearily next to her. 'An hour and a half of this is enough for anybody. I just want to sit down.'

She didn't add that she wanted to sit down on her own in a darkened room and sob her eyes out, because she felt more alone than ever before in her entire life. Life without Jack stretched out in front of her like a barren expanse, with nothing to see, nothing to believe in, nothing to love.

She'd got through Friday on autopilot, barely functioning. She'd hung up on Jack twice when he rang the office. He couldn't get through to her at home as the phone was still disconnected – a fact which hadn't pleased phone-a-holic Robin.

'Nuisance calls,' Isabel had said blandly when her daughter demanded to know why the phone jack had been pulled from the socket. 'Use my mobile if you must make a call but turn it off immediately afterwards.'

She couldn't bear the thought of having to talk to

Jack. She was so afraid she'd weaken and tell him she loved him, that she didn't care if he stayed with Elizabeth, so long as she could still see him sometimes. Which would be emotional suicide, she knew.

She might as well go back to David if she wanted that much pain in her life, Isabel thought in one of her rare, clear-headed moments.

Now she was spending Saturday trawling through the shops on a shopping trip she'd been promising the girls for ages. Isabel had planned to keep an eye out for a Christmas present for Jack, something special. She was always useless at keeping surprises and just days before he'd joked that he wouldn't be home from Brussels five minutes before she'd have spilled the beans on his present. What a difference a few days can make, she thought sadly.

On Thursday at lunchtime she'd been the happiest woman in the world: now, she was the most miserable. Although, naturally, she was pretending to be jolly for the girls' sake. It wasn't fair that they should have a bad day simply because she'd messed up her love life so spectacularly. They were her first priority, not her broken heart.

Naomi wilted beside her, her small frame resting tiredly against her mother's.

Isabel gave her a hug.

'C'mon, let's find Robin and get a cup of hot chocolate somewhere,' she said brightly. 'We'll need our energy for one last batch of shopping when I buy your Christmas present. And then you've got to decide which film you want to see!'

Dee had always loved buffets. That way, you could pick the most delicious dishes and leave all the boring stuff like celery and curried rice. Yeuch! Who'd want to eat curried rice?

She sailed past bowls of lettuce, celery, cucumber and tomato before stopping at the egg mayonnaise and fat, glistening spirals of pasta drenched in olive oil. That was more like it.

She had just lifted a generous ladle of egg from its bowl when Gary materialised beside her with an empty plate. Immediately determined not to look like she was still a big eater, Dee capsized the ladle until only two puny slices of mayonnaise-covered egg remained on it. Then, she delicately transferred them to her plate. Five pasta spirals joined the egg before Dee dumped a forestful of iceberg lettuce on top, with a few lumps of celery for good measure.

Bypassing the bread rolls steadfastly – she was *so hungry* – Dee finally turned round.

'Hello again,' she said, smiling icily at Gary. 'Are you following me?'

'No,' he said evenly. 'I wanted to talk to you and you left the church so quickly I didn't have a chance to.'

'What did you expect?' Dee asked tartly. 'That we'd drive to the hotel together, holding hands and giggling about how wonderful the old days were? I don't think so.' She wheeled around and headed for a table beside a picture window overlooking Dublin Bay.

Gary followed once he'd filled up his plate. *He'd* got a ton of pasta salad, Dee thought enviously, as she munched a bit of lettuce. It was very difficult playing Ms Sophisticate. Eating, drinking and enjoying yourself were out for a start.

Gary dug his fork into some coleslaw. Dee drooled. She'd eaten all her pasta and was still hungry. This was hell.

'Wine, madam?' asked a waiter.

'Lovely,' Dee said thankfully, grabbing a glass of white wine. She needed it, considering she wasn't eating.

'How've you been?' Gary asked.

'Wonderful,' she said brightly.

'I mean, *really*, how've you been?' he repeated.

Dee gave him a hard stare. 'I've had a relationship with an incredibly sexy Texan, whom you might remember.' She ignored the muscle flickering in Gary's jaw. 'And now I'm seeing someone else.'

'Anyone I know?' he asked tensely.

'No.' She beamed at him. 'How about you? Is London stuffed to the gills with skinny, classy women who dress correctly, don't drink and never wear too much make-up?'

At least he had the grace to look ashamed, she thought triumphantly.

'I wanted to apologise, Dee,' Gary said, his expressive eyes sombre. 'I said some terrible things to you, I shouldn't have. I had no right to . . .'

'No, you bloody didn't,' she snapped.

'I'm apologising now,' he pointed out.

'How nice for you,' she said pointedly. 'But it's a bit late and I wouldn't bother getting Dan and Millie involved any more. It's a waste of time.'

As if on some secret cue, Dan appeared, cradling his daughter in his arms, a photographer in tow. 'We're doing spur-of-the-moment pictures,' he said, crouching down between Dee and Gary and holding Tara at an angle for the photographer.

Dee posed. The flash went off and Dan straightened up.

'How are you two getting on?' he asked tentatively.

'Great,' said Gary, tickling Tara's tummy and making her giggle.

Dee kissed her goddaughter tenderly before Dan loped off to the next table.

'I love kids,' Gary said, surprising her. 'We'd have had wonderful kids, you know.'

Dee stared at him, imagining how voluptuous she'd look if she were pregnant. She remembered all the awful things he'd said to her about being fat, about how he'd have loved to have bought her sexy little dresses but hadn't been able to because of her size.

Kevin Mills didn't mind her size: he loved the way she looked, fancied her rotten – both for her body and her mind. And she didn't feel the need to sink six vodkas when she was with him, simply so she didn't feel like heap of the week when they went out. He gave her confidence, didn't take it away.

'Don't you want kids?' Gary said longingly.

'Of course. But can you imagine the trauma of being seen in public with me while I was pregnant, Gary?' Dee demanded. 'You found it hard enough to be seen with me normally. If I was pregnant, you'd have to have a special trailer made to tow behind the car so I'd fit in it. Imagine the shame.'

'That's not fair,' he protested. 'I only said you could lose a few pounds and that you were hung up about your weight. You look stunning *now*.'

'That,' said Dee calmly, 'is because I feel happy, confident, and have nobody telling me I'm a big, fat lump, day in, day out. It took me a while to get my confidence back, Gary, after you'd knocked me down like a rag doll. But,' she leant forward and poked him firmly in the chest as she enunciated each word, 'I did it. And if you think you can rewrite history and forget all that, then you're wrong.'

'Dee, come on . . .'

Dee wasn't listening. She was thinking of Kevin. They were going skiing in January and she couldn't wait. He was so wonderful, so funny, kind and . . . well, he liked *her*. Not who he wanted her to be, but *her*.

That was what she wanted, a man who liked her for who and what she was. Not one who couldn't say two words to her without reminding her why she was well shot of him.

'Hello, Mother,' said Gary.

Dee's eyes widened. Margaret Redmond stood in front of her, sturdy in a floral two-piece with a rather mad purple hat jammed on to the tight perm that had, unless Dee was imagining it, been treated to a faintly blonde rinse.

'Deirdre. Long time no see. How are you? Still working for that newspaper?' Margaret said primly.

'Yes,' Dee answered shortly. 'And you?'

'I'm doing very well since I have lovely Tara, my first grandchild,' Margaret said happily, her face alight with pride.

'Tara's beautiful,' Dee said fondly.

'I was surprised to see you were her godmother,' Margaret said, the shrewish expression returning to her face.

'Why?' Dee asked, resisting the impulse to say something very rude. It would be fun but Margaret simply wasn't worth upsetting herself over, Dee realised with stunning clarity.

'Well, it's not as if you're going out with Gary now, you're not one of the family . . .'

Margaret looked down her nose at Dee, gaze directed at her cleavage.

'*Mother!*' hissed Gary.

'It's all right,' Dee said, watching Margaret's shocked

expression with delight. Gary had never, ever spoken to his mother like that before. No wonder she was shocked. 'Your mother can say what she wants. She always did anyway.'

Margaret's mean eyes grew smaller.

'I never did like you, Deirdre,' she hissed.

'*Mother, stop that!*' shouted Gary, so loudly that everyone in the room turned to look at them. 'How dare you speak to Dee like that?'

'Gary, how *could* you?' shrieked Margaret, stomping off in high dudgeon.

Dee watched her go with amusement. Once, Gary's mother had had the power to drive her to despair. But not any more.

'I'm sorry about that,' he apologised.

Dee looked at him thoughtfully. Even that, even telling his horrible mother to shut up, hadn't made any difference. Gary was history. She still cared for him: she always would, she supposed. You couldn't spend four years of your life with someone and then consign them to limbo because they weren't around any more. But as for being *in love* with him . . .

'That was sweet, Gary,' she said. 'Very, very satisfying and sweet. But it was also about six months too late. Six months and four years.' She leant forward and kissed him on the cheek, a sisterly kiss, which seemed appropriate.

She looked into his earnest face and sighed. Poor Gary. He really had thought that he'd trundle up to her at the christening, apologise, tell her she looked beautiful, and then everything would be forgotten. They'd be back to square one again: Gary 'n' Dee, like egg 'n' chips. Only even more boring and predictable.

'Dee . . .' he began anxiously.

561

She didn't let him finish. That was the last thing she wanted: to humiliate him when he was doing his best, poor love.

'Gary, it was nice of you to try again,' she said, her voice sympathetic, 'but you must realise it's over between us. I'm happy now.' She patted his shoulder. 'I do hope you find somebody special, I'm sure you will. Take care.'

With that, she rose elegantly from the table and walked across the room, conscious that more eyes than Gary's were focused upon her. Tough, she thought happily. She had a date tonight, a date with a handsome photographer who was cooking her dinner: mussels, despite all the scrubbing they entailed, and chicken Kiev. She wouldn't have to lift a finger. Except, perhaps to unbutton Kevin's shirt . . .

Being in love made you promise ludicrous things, Isabel thought, as she laid the dining-room table for dinner. Why else would she invite her parents for dinner on a Saturday night when she *knew* she was going to be spending the entire day in town with the girls and would, therefore, be exhausted? But then, the dinner invitation had been pre-break up, when she'd felt invigorated and full of zest. It wasn't her parents' fault that she now had all the vigour of a dead halibut.

'Mum, Granny and Grandad are here!' yelled Naomi from the hall.

'Mum, the pork steaks are burning!' yelled Robin from the kitchen.

Isabel ran to the pork steaks. In the few minutes it had taken her to organise the table, the pork had turned from soft and succulent into the sort of things art students could quite possibly draw with. Robin, mashing potatoes industriously and watching TV at the same time, hadn't noticed until it was nearly too late.

Isabel gazed at the smouldering mess. She didn't care. Everything she'd eaten for the past two days had tasted like charcoal anyway.

'Mum?' Naomi stood beside her, hopping from foot to foot in a way she hadn't since she was at least nine.

'What is it, love?' Isabel asked tiredly, trying to remember what she had in the freezer that her mother would actually eat.

'A man came in with Granny and Grandad. He says his name's Jack and he wants to see you.'

Isabel gasped. Jack was here! At the same time as her mother?

She rushed to the hall. Standing in a formal little threesome were her parents and Jack. Making even her stately mother appear small by comparison, Jack looked wonderful in an elegant Italian suit.

'Isabel,' he said, his strong face lighting up at the sight of her.

'Isabel?' said her mother reprovingly, clad in her lavender twinset and tweeds. 'Aren't you going to introduce us?'

'Er . . . yes,' she stuttered. 'Mother and Father, this is Jack Carter. Jack, these are my parents, Pamela and Harry Mulhearn.'

All three shook hands formally, as if they were at a royal garden party instead of standing awkwardly in Isabel's tiny hall.

'Nice to meet you,' Pamela said warmly.

Isabel's eyes locked with Jack's. He looked exhausted, she realised with a sense of shock. Very pale and tired. He was overdoing it, she thought worriedly. As usual.

'We'll go on in,' Pamela announced.

Isabel followed her mother into the kitchen.

'I know it's strange, Mother, I'll explain later. Jack is . . .'

'Your lover?' Pamela supplied helpfully.

Isabel stared.

'You think I didn't know?' her mother asked, raising one eyebrow. 'Goodness, Isabel, what sort of fool do you take me for? I knew there was a man in your life and assumed that when you'd sorted it all out, you'd tell me. He seems very charming,' she added. 'So sort it out.' She fluttered her hands, as if shooing chickens. 'Robin tells me you've been like a zombie for the past two days. I presume he's the reason.'

'Robin said what?' asked Isabel anxiously. She was sure she'd managed to hide her misery from the girls, or at least had thought she had . . .

Her mother's eyebrow lifted another couple of milli-metres. 'Robin isn't stupid, either, Isabel. She knew something was wrong and came to the same conclusion as I did – man trouble.'

Isabel's jaw dropped. 'Robin knew?'

'Since the day he dropped you home in his car. A Jaguar, I believe. She's nearly sixteen, Isabel, not six. Of course she knew.' Pamela paused. 'A Jaguar suits him, actually. Such a nice car.' She sniffed the charcoal-scented air with distaste. 'I hope he likes omelettes – assuming you have eggs?'

Isabel grinned, hugged her mother, and returned to the hall.

Jack stood there silently.

'You're home a day early,' she said, immediately wondering why she'd said something so obvious. 'I thought you had an important meeting?'

'I did. This was more important,' he said quietly.

'You're more important than any meeting.' He moved towards her.

Isabel took a step back towards the kitchen. What did he want? she asked herself. If he came any closer, she wouldn't be able to control herself. She'd let all her good intentions fly out of the window and then she'd cling to him and never let him go. And she couldn't do that. She'd promised herself she'd never see him like this again. He was gone from her life forever. She closed her eyes at the thought.

'Isabel.' His voice was like a silken caress. 'I had to come home, to make everything right. When you wouldn't answer my calls, I couldn't understand it at first. I was so upset on Thursday, I couldn't see what had happened.'

Isabel, who'd been staring at his broad shoulders longingly, stood up ramrod straight. 'Upset, were you?' she asked, feeling the pain in her heart like a JCB crushing through every tender part. 'I wonder why? No, don't tell me. I know.'

'But you don't.' He stood so close to her she could smell his aftershave and the scent of his skin. The scent she'd dreamed of for the past two nights, imagining his body wrapped protectively around hers, holding her close and telling her he'd never let her go.

'Isabel, did you believe I loved you? Did you believe I would leave Elizabeth for you?'

'Yes.' Her words were just a whisper. She wanted to scream at him to leave her, to go away. But she couldn't. She wanted to be with him just a few moments longer, even if then he left forever.

'How could you think I'd lie to you about anything?' he asked softly. 'When I spoke to you on the phone on Thursday, I'd just heard that the man who started me

off in business had died. William James . . . I owe him so
much. He had a stroke. It was very sudden. We hadn't
spoken for months because we'd both been so busy, and
then he was gone.' There was a catch in Jack's voice. 'I
was devastated. Life can be so cruel.'

Isabel gazed up at him, suddenly comprehending
what he was saying, why he'd sounded so upset when
she'd spoken to him on the phone that terrible evening.

'You thought I was upset about Elizabeth?' He
laughed hoarsely. 'I didn't even know about that at the
time. It was only the next day, after I'd spent the night
trying to phone you here and on your mobile, that I
found out about her. It was a shock, I'll admit it, and it
meant I had to spend an hour on the phone getting the
story quashed, but it was hardly devastating news. Did
you think I could just abandon you?' he asked seriously.
'Did you think I was lying when I told you I loved you
and wanted to be with you?'

'Oh, Jack.' She fell into his arms, clinging to him with
all her strength. He held her tightly to him, arms
clutching her body hard against his. 'Isabel, I've never
experienced anything like these past couple of days. I
couldn't understand what had happened, why you
wouldn't talk to me. You hung up on me twice and I
went crazy when your phone just rang and rang. I
thought something awful had happened, until I found
out about Elizabeth and it all fell into place.'

Her face buried in his shoulder, Isabel explained: 'I
thought you'd heard about her and Mannix Delaney
and that's why you were so upset.' She was almost
unable to believe how wonderful it felt to be in his arms
again. 'I love you! And was so upset. I thought you loved
Elizabeth, I thought . . .'

'I understand.' He held her away from him so he